Wavebreaker

Book II of the Stone War Chronicles - Trickle

A.J. Norfield

Cover art © 2018 A.J. Norfield
Photo by Zach Dischner
Edited by Laura M. Hughes

ISBN: 978-90-824945-5-6 (kindle)
ISBN: 978-90-824945-4-9 (epub)
ISBN: 978-90-824945-3-2 (sc)

To those who shape us, for better or for worse.

*Mom, Dad, thank you for a great childhood
and for allowing me to grow up chasing my dreams.*

BY A.J. NORFIELD

Stone War Chronicles
Windcatcher
Wavebreaker Part 1 – Trickle
Wavebreaker Part 2 – Flood

Other
Revolt of Blood and Stone
(A Stone War Chronicles Novella, Sebastian #1)

Sign up for the **Stone War Readers Group** to receive
a FREE copy of 'Revolt of Blood and Stone'.

Check out the website url at the end of the book.

ACKNOWLEDGEMENTS

Many thanks to my friends and family for their support. Especially Elisabeth and my wife Desirée, for digging through the early stages of writing and providing feedback.

I want to thank my editor, Laura M. Hughes, for her professional work, wit and guidance to get my story in the best shape possible.

And—as always—thank you, the reader, for walking this road with me and taking the time to see how the story unfolds.

WHITE NORTH
FOREST OF DAHALAES
Forsiquar
AETERRA
GREAT WESTERN DIVIDE
Shid'el
CRESCENT MOON MASSIF
Eore
Azurna
GREAT EASTERN DIVIDE
DRAGON'S TOOTH CONTINENT
DROWNED MAN'S FORK
Baratta
HIGHER LANDS
AROSH'AD ISLANDS
RED PLAINS
Tal'Ostar
ENDLESS SANDS
Tal'Kabur
N
W E
S
SOUTHERN CITIES
The full World map is available on www.ajnorfield.com

PROLOGUE

Decan inched forward. He carefully placed his toe to the ground and eased his weight onto it. The sand crunched beneath his bare foot.

Movement!

He froze, his legs trembling from the tension in his muscles. Sweat dripped from his face in concentration.

He had planned this for days; covered all possible scenarios; gone over all the different escape routes. If he did not make his move now, who knew when he would have another opportunity?

He pushed all doubt from his mind and leaped through the air. He stretched his arms forward, spreading his fingers as wide as he could. As his shadow flew across the sand, the small bearded lizard jerked its head around and shot off toward the shrubbery.

Barely missing his pet-to-be, Decan's hands caught nothing but sand. He scrambled after the little reptile as it dashed across the dune behind their house. The wooden planks he had put in its path narrowed toward the end, leading the critter straight to the bucket.

Just a little bit further!

The small lizard hit the plank and continued running along it. Decan kicked up a wave of sand, urging the frightened animal to stay on course.

It's going to work! thought Decan, his excitement peaking in the heat of the chase.

The lizard's small, beady eyes saw the bucket's dark hole looming ahead. Its head jerked sideways as it spotted a sparkle of light. Its tiny claws pushed off as if its life depended on it. The lizard jammed its head between the side of the bucket and a plank, and frantically wriggled through the loose sand.

"No!" shouted Decan.

It was too late. His prey was gone. Or was it?

Arriving at the bucket, Decan saw the lizard run along the back of the plank toward the tall, dry grass. Fully intending to jump over the obstacles in front of him, Decan pushed off, only to feel the loose sand give way. His foot caught on the edge of the bucket and he tumbled forward, flat on his face. His mouth—open in surprise at the bucket's devious betrayal—took a big bite of crunchy sand.

Jumping back to his feet, Decan spat out the sand and dusted off his clothes. He looked around. The lizard was nowhere to be seen. His plan had failed.

He picked up the bucket and stomped back toward the house, going over the details of what happened and the flaws he had discovered. He kicked a small, innocent stone out of the way, then narrowed his eyes as he watched it skid along the ground.

Perhaps if I add some rocks…

When he reached the house, his mother was cleaning the day's catch under their extended roof.

"Did you catch it?" asked his mother as he walked into the kitchen area.

A strong gust of wind made their wooden home creak. It was not much to look at from the outside, but inside was cozy, and it was enough to shield them from the elements. This far south, keeping warm was never really a problem, but the ocean winds could blow a mean blast of sand on certain days.

"No… it got away right at the end."

He wiped his mouth with his sleeve in an attempt to get the last of the sand out.

"Well, I'm sure you'll catch one next time," she said with a soft smile. "Now, why don't you come over here and wash that sand away… then you can help me prepare supper."

Decan let out a groan.

"Do I have to?" he asked. "I still need to find some rocks near the cliffs for tomorrow…"

"In that case, you can look for your sister while you're at it."

Decan's father exited the house. From the smell of it, he had been prepping the central stove for dinner. "I haven't seen her all day after she stormed out this morning, and it's getting late."

Decan's mother rested her hands on the wooden counter. Fish guts dangled from the thin knife in her hand. Her stern expression softened as she looked at both men, and she let out a sigh.

"Fine. You can't sit still for long, anyway."

"Must be all that ancestral nomadic blood running through our veins," said his father with a wink at Decan.

"Well, I blame you for that," teased his mother. "My family has always been more than content with working the land. Oh, how my mother warned me not to fall in love with a fisher."

His father laughed.

"Can't be helped… my charm is great."

Decan's father gave his mother a quick hug.

"Just be thankful we're not moving from island to island or along the coast anymore, following the migrating fish and sea mammals like our ancestors did. Nowadays, the only thing that truly makes us waterclan is the fact that we're ocean born."

"Oh, I remember. Trust me," said his mother.

She walked over to her son and took the bucket from his hands.

"The swell of the waves was nearly seven feet when you were born," she said. She smiled at Decan, tapping the tip of his nose with her finger. "I can still see the restlessness of that day in you."

She walked back, rinsed the bucket and shoved all the guts and scales into it.

"As true as the ocean's blue. I thanked the goddess that night for keeping you both safe," said his father. "Now, enough chatting. Go and find your sister."

"Yes, father!"

Decan turned around and ran off—anything was better than cleaning fish.

Since their father was one of the clan that still fished, their house lay on the outskirts of town, close to the ocean and their father's fishing boat. What they caught and did not use, they traded with others from the clan who instead specialized in working the land.

Decan loved it. He spent days roaming the beach and island. He was still too young to actively help with the more serious labor during the day. Besides, their father was usually out on the water way before dawn and done with most of his fishing by the time Decan and his sister woke up.

That would all soon change. When he turned fourteen, his father expected Decan to join him on the boat and start his training as a fisherman. He looked forward to spending more time with his father, but he was still not sure if fishing was what he wanted to do for the rest of his life. He would rather visit the mainland, get off the island, and see the world. Perhaps live as a hunter—or a merchant, even.

Decan circled the house and took off toward the sea. His sister would surely be somewhere down at the cliffs; she always went there to blow off steam. He had followed her a couple of times, whenever she had stomped out of the house. Their family was tight, but father and daughter did not always see eye to eye.

Their relationship had improved over the last few years as Trista moved out of her teens, but this morning they'd had a huge falling-out. Decan did not really know what happened, but he had heard his sister shout something about a stupid boy. Their mother had tried to calm things down, but in the end his sister ran out of the house and disappeared for the rest of the day.

Decan turned to his right before he reached the beach and headed up the path that led to the cliffs. If she was on the beach, he could spot her from the top. If not, he would continue south along the cliffs to check her usual spot.

People always thought his sister was a bit strange. Decan never thought so; she was just his big sister. She was almost eight years older, but that never stopped them from being close friends. She loved nature. As a natural hunter, his sister excelled in spearfishing, and had since she was young. Decan once asked how she was able to catch fish so well, but the only answer he had gotten was that she *felt* the water.

The reason most waterclan found her strange was because she did not look like any of them. Most of the clan had darker eyes and hair—black, brown, dark blond—but his sister was different. Her hair was a deep red, which looked almost like fire when the sunlight hit it just right. Her green eyes were a fierce contrast with her hair and made her stand out in any crowd on the island. Mother and Father always said they had no idea how it happened, but some people told stories. The most common rumor was that Trista was a child of the sun god.

The waterclans worshipped the goddess of the sea. The goddess kept them safe and provided the people with plentiful food from the ocean—but only those who lived in balance with her oceans. She would not hesitate to claim the lives of those out to ruin the balance of her domain.

Their stories told that the sun god was in love with the water goddess. He traveled the skies to follow the goddess of the sea, whispering sweet promises of his love. At the end of each day he would seduce her, try to lure her to leave her lively oceans and follow him up into the sky, but each night the sun god failed, for the water goddess was far too wise to fall for any of his tricks.

Decan had never heard it directly, but he once overheard his mother and father arguing about it. People claimed his mother had been visited by the sun god at night. The sun god, angry at the water goddess' unwillingness to follow him, had bed a member of the waterclan out of spite. His sister was the result of that night.

His father had never doubted their mother, but that night they argued because his father had apparently punched a man in the face after hearing remarks about the sun god throughout the evening. His mother told his father to just ignore it. It did not matter what everyone else thought. The only thing that mattered was their family. How they loved each other and took care of each other—and that's what they did.

Decan never believed any of those stories, but agreed his sister was not like anyone else. The boys had always flocked around her. She might not be the prettiest girl on the island, but had certainly received enough of their mother's looks to turn some heads. But when Decan saw his sister and a boy together, it was like she was never really interested in any of them. Or, at least, not for long.

Some of his friends had overheard the grown-ups talk about her; how, within the waterclan, where the women were plenty accustomed to hard work, his sister was so very tough for a woman. But while it was true that she was quite lean and muscled from her days of spear hunting and swimming, Decan never really saw her as unusual. She was what she was.

When they explored the island together, she would show him the many secrets it held. Hidden warm water pools, how to catch crabs during the low tide, where to find nests with freshly-hatched furry birds chirping for food. She always managed to show him something new, and Decan had learned a lot from her. One of the more important lessons he observed was that despite their dependence on the animal kingdom for food, his sister always handled any creature with care and respect—even the fish she caught and ate. She took the lessons of the goddess to heart… even if she did not always listen to their parents.

He smirked. Then again, neither did he.

Decan panted as he made his way up the path. He had just halted to catch his breath when a tremor shook the earth. It started as a low, rumbling vibration, but soon swelled into a heavy shaking of the ground. He quickly lay flat on his stomach like his sister had taught him, and kept an eye out for falling rocks. When these quakes had started last summer, they had frightened him, but now they came so often that his reaction was instinctive. The most important thing was to stay away from the precarious rocks and steep cliff sides; apart from that, you just had to wait for it to stop.

When the tremor passed, he got back to his feet and ran across the last part of the path onto the cliff. He reached the top, expecting to see the eternal movement of waves rolling calmly onto the sand while the clouds drifted peacefully by in the sky. He hoped he could spot his sister trailing the coastline, like he had seen her do many times before. But as he arrived at the top of the cliff, his jaw dropped at the scene in front of him. He rubbed his eyes and pinched himself to make sure he was not dreaming.

With the setting sun on his back, the endless ocean indeed stretched out in front of him, but he did not see the calm waves of a summer's day. Instead, Decan saw rough water, with a storm brewing on the horizon… and dozens of ships from the north on a direct course to the island. As far as his eyes could see, the unfamiliar ships were spread out across the ocean. Their hulls and sails were colored black. They rode the strong winds with sails fully raised, approaching the island's beaches at high speed. Shapes walked the deck of the closest ship, but they were still too far for Decan to see much detail.

The sheer number of ships was overwhelming, but that was not the reason Decan stopped dead in his tracks in disbelief. It was the fact that, above those sailing ships, a dozen other vessels were floating in the sky. Each one had sails on the side and a strange contraption above the deck. It looked like a giant inflated *shar'ac*—the ferocious flesh-eating fish. The ships slid through the air, just passing the outer reefs; it would not be long before the first ones reached land.

Decan stared at the scene. Those ships were not right. Whatever it was that came toward him sent fear creeping over him. Forgetting all about his sister, he turned around and sprinted down the path as fast as his legs could carry him.

"Father! Father!" shouted Decan, out of breath as he came running back around the corner of their house.

"What is it? Is something wrong with your sister?"

The sound of panic in Decan's voice made his father hurry out of the house.

"Ships, father. The dead are rising from the deep. There's so many of them and—and some are flying! In the air! They're flying, father!" rambled Decan, so fast that his father could barely understand him.

"Hold on. Slow down! What do you mean, 'flying'? What ships?" the man questioned his son. "Wait… did your sister put you up to this?"

"No, really, father! Go see for yourself! They're at the beach… coming right at us."

Decan's father saw the mix of disbelief and fear in his son's eyes. The man grabbed his harpoon spear just as a shadow passed over the house. Son and father looked up; the ship creaked and groaned as it passed overhead and moved in the direction of their little town's center. Another one to the left crossed the cliffs and dunes, as a third and fourth came in from the right.

Shouts of alarm sounded from the people in the town. Decan's mother came outside to see what all the commotion was about, and stopped on the veranda, clutching the door.

"What do you think they want, father?" said Decan.

"Stay with your mother, Decan," was the only reply his father gave before he ran down the path to keep the flying ships in view.

In the distance, round bags were dropped from the ships' sides. Decan's father was halfway to the town's center when one of the ships threw out a small, flaming barrel. As soon as it hit the ground, a pillar of flames erupted and instantly set fire to three fishermen who had the misfortune of being near the explosion. The two nearest houses on the street also caught fire as people screamed out in terror. Men and women shot away in all directions. Panic and chaos swept through the streets as crossbow bolts rained down from above.

Holding on to his mother, Decan saw his father rush back toward them.

"Merryl! We need to go! *Now*! Leave everything and head for the caves! Go! *Go*!"

Decan's eyes filled with tears. What was going on? Why was this happening?

"Triss! I haven't found Triss yet!" he screamed as his mother dragged him, spurring him to run as fast as he could.

His father caught up with them as they plowed through the soft sand behind their house. But as they turned the corner, they saw a group of soldiers already coming up the path in front of them. Turning back, they ran the other way. This time, they did not even make it three steps before they saw another group of men coming at them from the other side, crossbows and swords at the ready. It was too late.

As the arrows flew through the air, both mother and father did the only thing they could. Decan felt their protective embrace surround him. The outside world seemed to disappear. He remembered such hugs, often given to him throughout his life. The kind of hug where you squeeze someone tightly and refuse to let go, just to enjoy it a little while longer. The hug that says, *I am there for you. You can count on me.*

Decan squeezed back as hard as he could. His parents' love poured through him. The smell of his father's sweat mixed with the sweet scent of his mother's hair. He wished for nothing more, even if somewhere in the mix was the rude interruption of the smell of fish.

He did not mind staying like this, hidden far away from the outside world. From what was about to happen.

But reality has no patience. It waits for no one... and there was no escape. Decan flinched as the sounds from the world forced their way into his protective shell. The thuds that reached his ears were like death knocking on his door.

CHAPTER ONE

Storm

S TUPID FATHER!"

Trista threw a rock from the cliff. A second one was already in the air before the first splashed into the ocean below. Both were swallowed by the waves. She watched the restless water. Large, foaming waves crashed against the cliff, so strongly that each erupted in a spray of water toward the sky. The salty water wet her face in a soft mist.

"What are you so angry about?" she yelled at the ocean. "Who has offended you so, that the oceans swell and waves slam against the land? Or do you have a father, too?"

Trista observed the goddess' fury. She could relate. Frustration gnawed at her insides. The morning's conversation crept back into her mind again and the low simmer of her anger flared up once more.

She threw another rock. *How could they do this to me?*

She knew she had her moments, but they were a close family and they always looked out for each other. Which was precisely why it all felt like such a betrayal.

Earlier that day, her father had started up *that* conversation again. Though, actually, it had started two years ago, when her mother carefully inquired whether she 'liked' anybody in the village. When Trista had told her no, the conversation had quickly flowed to the unpleasant topic of a waterbond. They were worried about her staying alone; she should find a boyfriend, a husband—think about having a future with someone.

Back then, she had been able to brush it off quite easily, but as the months progressed, her mother and father brought up the topic more often in the hope that she would begin taking their advice.

Trista never really knew why she resented it. Most girls in the waterclans were bonded when they turned seventeen or eighteen, choosing their husband during the yearly springwater festival, which was held in celebration of the returning fish migrations. It was a time of abundance in food and joy as the ocean waters warmed up and the whales came to the island waters to have their calves. As the official guardians of the water goddess, these gentle, giant creatures were considered a very good omen for anyone who wished to build a future together.

Often the bonded couples had been courting for quite some time. But sometimes a girl would bond with a man she had met only that day. Trista's friends talked about how you instantly knew when you saw the person meant for you, but she had never experienced it herself, and highly doubted if there was such a thing as *the feeling*.

She pushed her red hair back behind her ear as the wind tried to take hold of it. She turned around to escape the rain of another colliding wave and noticed a small, fuzzy ball of feathers fluttering back and forth at the foot of the higher cliff wall behind her. She moved from rock to rock until she reached the chick. Its feathers were brownish-white with darker spots.

"Did you want to get out of the house, too?" she said as she carefully used her scarf to pick up the chick. She took a step back and looked up in search of a nest.

"You know, it's not that I've not gotten enough attention from the boys here," she said to the young bird. "I mean, I went on plenty of dates, but they always seemed to want something from me."

The chick let out a squawk.

"Or as soon as I had beaten them at their own game, like catching the biggest fish with a spear, or seeing who runs across the cliff's boulders the fastest, they lose interest. I guess they preferred the pretty house girls from the town... not that it bothered me, or anything," said Trista, adding a small lie at the end.

"If only mother would leave it alone. But no, she needs to bring it up time and again."

And the talks had become more unsettling every time, not only for her, but also for her mother.

"She thinks I can only be happy if I find a man, but I don't see how that works. I'm perfectly happy as I am."

The spotted chick stared at her, its head tilted as though listening intensely.

"One time, mother got so upset. She yelled at me, 'Do you want to end up alone in this world?'"

Trista flashed an apologetic smile at the chick, recollecting that particular day.

"I nearly exploded," she confessed. "'Alone would be better than putting up with your constant nagging every day'—or so I would have screamed if I had not bitten my tongue, for there wouldn't have been a point in saying it."

And she would not have meant it. She loved her mother and father; had a great deal of respect for them, too. So she was glad that she had stopped herself from uttering such hurtful words. She knew the stories that went round the island about her. She never let it bother her, but she did see the strain it had on her parents' relationship at times.

"See, I really don't mind being alone. Besides," Trista continued, "most of the men from the clans are perfectly happy on the islands, ready to follow in their father's footsteps with no sense of adventure. That's not me. I love the islands, the ocean, but I want to see what's out there beyond the horizon. Sail the world, like the clans did in the old days. That must have been amazing."

It was like a flow inside her; a trickle that constantly drove her mind beyond the edge of her vision. And she was certainly not the only one in their family. She had seen it in her little brother, too.

She had hoped her parents would support her desire to explore, but this morning her father had made it abundantly clear this was not the case. Apparently, others were starting to wonder if something was wrong with her, so he and her mother had discussed things and chosen to make arrangements for a locked waterbond. The words had hit her like a twenty-foot wave.

Locked waterbonds were not unheard of, but usually took place between a girl and a boy from different islands who would never have a chance to meet by themselves. It kept the bloodlines from the waterclans from crossing themselves too much. And everyone knew that refusing a locked waterbond brought the anger of the water goddess upon your family. It was unthinkable.

It had been too much. After throwing out her frustration, Trista had stormed from the house, her mother calling after her to tell her that she had been locked with Landon—one of the more handsome men on the island.

Trista's eyes filled with tears again as she spoke to the young bird. "Landon is a dumb ox! Handsome, yes, but with the intelligence of a drunken seal. He could not offer a decent conversation if his life depended on it. Sure, he's always been kind to me and Decan, but I could never see myself with him. How can they do this to me?"

She let out a frustrated sigh and let her gaze slide along the cliff wall again.

There. She spied a small recess.

She let out another sigh to calm herself for the climb, and carefully put the chick in her shirt. It was not very difficult to get up there. The cliff had plenty of places to grab, or put her feet on. Bracing herself, she carefully put the young bird back in the empty nest.

"Best wait here for your parents to come back. I'm sure they haven't forgotten about you."

She made her way back down, but with ten feet still to go, the wall she clung to began to shake. It started softly, but quickly picked up strength. Unable to hold on, she dropped the last few feet, bending her legs as she hit the ground. She immediately moved away from the wall and threw herself flat on the ground. Small pieces of rock rained down from the cliff behind her. At the same time, she heard the earth grunt as the tremor moved through it. Somewhere on her right, the cracking of rock broke through the air like a lightning strike. A cloud of dirt, mixed with shards of rock and a spray of water, shot up into the sky less than a hundred yards from where she lay. The rocky terrain split open as a crack rushed along the ground all the way to the second level of cliffs, where the birds' nests were. Those able to fly flocked to the air with loud protests.

As the tremor subsided, Trista carefully got back to her feet.

The shaking has never been this bad...

She looked at the bottom of the cliff and then at the recess, happy to see the small chick was still in its nest. Exploring the area, she made her way toward the chasm in the ground, checking her footing on the different-sized boulders to make sure they would not give way.

The chasm was not very big. She could easily jump across it if needed, but why take the risk? She lay flat on the ground and peered over the edge. White foam rushed in below. Even an experienced swimmer like herself would not make it out of there alive if she fell in.

The crack ran all the way to the entrance of a cave system she knew all too well. She smiled at the memory of taking Decan there for the first time. He had been so scared, but she had been exploring the grotto for days, trying to find out how many chambers it had and how deep they went.

One day, her little brother snuck after her into the cave and got lost. She had heard him crying out in the dark. It had not taken her long to find him, and after she had calmed him down a bit, she offered to take him deeper into the caves.

How tightly he held my hand.

Standing at the mouth of the cave, Trista saw the crack disappear into the darkness.

She wanted to go in and check the damage, but without a torch it would be dangerous to go any further. Even if she knew the caves well enough to find her way in the dark, the danger of making a mistake without anyone knowing she was there was just too big. The underground system was huge and had several smaller caves at different heights—not to mention some very slippery tunnels. She looked up. The ceiling also showed a crack that had not been there before. Trista wondered if it had been caused by the tremor just now, or if it was older.

With the sun setting, the daylight was quickly fading. She lingered a while longer, checking the cracks in the ceiling, before deciding reluctantly to return home. The tremor had shaken off most of her anger, and knowing her parents, they were probably worried about her. She just hoped that the subject would not come up again… at least for today.

As she followed the cliffs home, she thought of her special cave. A few of the more distant rooms had large holes in the ceiling that let in the daylight. But the nights were when the cave was at its best. She had occasionally snuck out to visit the cave when the moon and stars were very bright. She would lie in the soft moss of one of the open caverns, staring at the stars and moon, fantasizing that the sky was an ocean and each star an island to explore. This particular part of the cave had a special kind of plant growing on the walls. She had seen it many times during the day, but when in bloom, the plant was simply breathtaking at night. The wall-plant's tiny white flowers were like stars poured into the cavern, decorating the walls. Trista had never seen anything like it before and guarded it as one of her most precious secrets.

Her stomach growled. She had stormed out just after breakfast, and in her anger and stubbornness had completely forgotten to eat anything for the rest of the day. She looked out across the sea. The dark clouds on the horizon were rolling in fast, painting the sky in an ominous mixture of red and black as the setting sun sank in the west. Soon, the sun god would start his seduction again, offering a sky full of sparkling gems to win the hand of the water goddess.

Perhaps I'll sneak out tonight if these storm clouds break. Trista smiled.

The eastern shore came into view as she rounded the cliff. The village lay just beyond. But as she scanned the distance for the silhouettes of familiar buildings, she saw instead dozens of ships anchored off the coast. She stopped, spotting others that were still sailing on their way to the west side of the island. Their sails were as black as the gathering storm clouds above them. Thick, black smoke rose from the village, illuminated by an orange glow much too bright for a house lantern or a bonfire.

Fire!

Mother! Father! Decan!

The last of Trista's anger evaporated. The hole it left behind immediately filled with a dreadful, gnawing fear. By the time her head had caught up, her feet were already running. She flew across the boulders, moving faster than she had ever done before on the tricky terrain. When she raced the island boys, she had always been careful not to lose her balance on the wet spots, or get her foot stuck in one of the many holes between the boulders, but now her cautiousness was pushed to the back of her head by the panic that overtook her.

She felt light-headed, sucking in breaths in short bursts. Her legs began to wobble, losing their strength. Then a rumbling suddenly roared up. It was not her legs; instead, the ground had begun to shake once more.

But where the previous tremor had started softly, this one exploded out of nowhere. Trista did not even have time to stop. As the earth shook and the boulders vibrated from the sheer force of the quake, her moving foot missed its step. She threw her arms forward in a futile attempt to soften the fall, but she could not prevent her head from hitting the boulder that had seemingly moved heaven and earth in an effort to meet her. The world disappeared into nothingness as the wet stone introduced itself to her with firm self-assurance.

"Are you sure you're fit enough to do this?" yelled Raylan, grabbing a rope to keep himself upright. "It looks awfully dangerous."

His voice was lost in the blasts of wind, but Galirras got the gist of it.

"*Do not worry; my wounds are fine,*" said the dragon's voice in his head. "*The storm is much worse than we hoped. If I do not get clear of the ship, I might bring the entire thing down.*"

Galirras' claws dug into the wooden deck to keep himself in place. Around them, dark clouds raced past as curtains of rain swept along the ship. Raylan did not have a dry piece of clothing on him anymore.

"*We should have gone further around,*" replied Raylan in private, shaking his head.

"*That would have taken days,*" spoke Galirras. He had scouted the storm front; it went on for miles.

They had intended to go around, but a sudden shift in atmospheric pressure had changed the winds. Down below, they had tried their best to stay ahead of the storm by using the bladed fan that propelled them forward in addition to the sails, but the dark clouds had soon swallowed them up as they tried to stay on course. From there, it had only gotten worse.

Thunder rolled in the distance. Frowning, Raylan watched a faint glow lighting up the clouds.

"Can't you divert the wind from the ship with your power?"

Raylan shouted the words. He had gotten used to sharing his mind with the dragon; after all, they were linked. Galirras had said so himself when he hatched from his egg. "*You are mine, and I am yours.*" But sometimes it just felt better to say his words out loud and, in this case, challenge the wind with them.

It had been a bit of an adjustment, sharing his head. These past few months it had rarely been quiet in there. The dragon had an enthusiastic, innocent interest in getting to know the world, so they spoke about all kind of matters: animals, people, cities, forests, fishing—everything. Luckily, Galirras' enthusiasm was infectious, though Raylan found it tiring at times.

"*The wind is too strong, the ship too big. My power would have no effect,*" answered Galirras.

Behind them, Marek called out to them. The boy was making his way across the deck when a gust of wind shifted the ship without warning. Marek lost his footing and half-slid, half-stumbled dangerously close to the railing. Raylan made a grab for him, but the fabric of Marek's shirt slipped between his fingers. Galirras' tail, however, was long enough to cover the distance. It shot in front of their comrade, allowing Marek to cling onto it.

"Thanks," shouted Marek with a grin at the dragon.

"Be careful," yelled Raylan. "We're still a long way above the ocean."

"I know, but I need to check the balloon for tears. The boiler is using way too many stones."

Without another word, the agile lad shot up the ropes toward the large balloon above their deck. On the side of the ship, several of the sails had been reeled in to prevent them from ripping. Only a few of them were still being used to control the flying boat.

A bucket dangled around Marek's neck as he clambered upward. Over its edge spilled drops of a sticky goo. On his other side was a bag that held different sizes of leather patches and a few security lines with clasps.

Raylan was glad to see their youngest tagalong had recovered from the beatings he received during the night of their getaway. A bit of greenish-blue below still showed below Marek's left eye where the brand of a closed fist displayed his previous status as a slave of the Stone King. Thankfully, the swelling had gone down quickly.

There was another tagalong in their group with the slave brand on his cheek; Sebastian. He and Raylan became friends when the group had come across a settlement of escaped slaves in a giant forest on the Dark Continent. Together they rescued Marek the night of their escape, as Marek and Sebastian were long-lost friends. They were originally captured together by the Stone King's forces when they were just children. They had not only survived years of brutalities, but had also been a vital part of their daring exit from the Dark Continent—especially Marek. The teen had offered the needed knowledge and ingenuity to prepare and launch the small scouting airship they had stolen from their enemies.

Raylan smiled at the thought of how perfectly comfortable the adolescent now was around the dragon. It was a strong contrast to the first time they met, less than fifteen days ago during their escape from the enemy harbor. Marek had been below deck, working on the vapor oven to get the ship in the air. He had been unaware of most of the fighting, along with the fact that a dragon had traveled with the group for weeks.

When everything was over, Marek finally came up from the lower decks for some air. There, he had stumbled upon the sleeping dragon, who had taken enemy fire during their escape and was exhausted from his efforts. Marek had let out a scream as he tripped over Galirras' tail, startling the dragon awake. In turn, Galirras had let out a roar of surprise at his rude awakening, jumping to his feet and spreading his wings so wide they hit the ropes on both sides.

The youngster had instantly wet himself—though this was heavily denied afterward—and fled back below decks. It took some convincing before the two would officially meet again, but eventually apologies were made and the two had hit it off.

Raylan looked back at Galirras as Marek disappeared behind the curve of the balloon. Looking at his size, it was hard to imagine the dragon had not even seen six full moons yet, but from his behavior anyone could see the world was still new to him.

"*Here is my chance,*" said Galirras in his head. The dragon shot forward and dove off the deck, his long tail whipping after him.

Galirras' ability to see the wind, and control it if needed, had saved their hides many a time. Now, Raylan only hoped it was enough to prevent his friend from being ripped apart by the gale force winds. He tightened his grip around the rope, feeling the tension on it as the balloon was pushed back and forth. The storm threw their little ship around like a ball tossed by a child.

Most of their squad was below, working the bladed fan at the back of the ship; if they wanted any control over the ship, they had to keep moving forward. Raylan had taken the deck. It allowed him to manage the sails—whenever possible—but also kept him near his winged friend, as the deck was the only spot on the ship large enough to house the dragon. Galen, their heavy hitter, assisted them in case they needed more muscle—which, with these winds, was not an unnecessary luxury.

Raylan watched as Galirras struggled, back and forth, up and down. Even with the ability to shield himself by diverting some of the wind around him, Galirras needed all his concentration to prevent him from slamming back into the side of the ship.

Raylan blinked. He had only taken his eyes off him for a moment, but now Galirras was nowhere to be seen.

"Galirras!" shouted Raylan, with voice and mind. But his only answer was the roar of the wind.

Raylan waited for another swing of the ship and then pushed off to the other side, where Galen hung on for dear life.

"Galen! Did you see where Galirras went?"

The big guy shook his head. Raylan grabbed the ropes and hung over the railing to look down. Saying visibility was poor would be an understatement. They were surrounded by clouds, with no way of knowing if they were a mile or a foot above sea level. Raylan peered into the different shades of darkness.

A lightning flash deep within the clouds illuminated everything for the briefest of moments. Galen grabbed Raylan by the shoulder and pointed. Another flash showed the silhouette of a dragon on the port side of their ship.

"Galirras, can you hear me?"

Still no reply. He was about to shout again when, out of nowhere, Galirras sheared past them, narrowly missing the ship.

"Sorry, I cannot talk. Winds… are very strong."

Raylan felt the strain on the dragon's thoughts. Galirras needed all his concentration to stay in the air. The dragon disappeared again, swallowed up by the clouds, this time for longer. When he re-emerged, Galirras positioned himself in front of the ship and tried to keep his place. Immediately, Raylan felt a jolt, as though a force pulled them forward. The vibration of the ship decreased.

"*What are you doing?*" he reached out to Galirras. "*You said the ship was too big to protect.*"

"*A bow wave… to smooth out the ride. But I cannot keep it up for long,*" said the dragon. Raylan saw him struggle to move his wings in powerful enough strokes. "*I do not think we can climb. Marek is almost done, but it will take time to refill the vapors. So, down we must go. There is a way; sharp right turn. It is close.*"

Raylan relayed the message to Galen and ran to the other side, reaching for the sails. Several of them could be swiveled horizontally, acting as diving rudders.

A long, high-pitched howl reached Raylan on the edge of his hearing.

"*Was that Marek?*"

"*He is done. Securely fastened… and apparently enjoying himself, howling like a wolf against the wind.*"

"*He reminds me of a certain captain,*" remarked Raylan, absentmindedly touching the whirlwind scar that snaked along his arm.

"*What?*"

"*Nothing. Just tell me how far we need to dive.*"

Close by, Galen was shouting orders down the voice tubes to the rest of the squad.

"Come on, put your backs into it!"

A jolt ran through the vessel as the team below increased their efforts to turn the bladed fan, propelling the ship forward. Raylan kept a close eye on Galirras, who kept pushing forward, using his wind power as much as possible to pull the ship in his wake. The clouds around them turned darker.

"*Are you certain this is the way out?*" asked Raylan.

"*Fairly certain. Though things can change swi—*"

Galirras retracted his wings and rolled into a straight dive. A moment later, a lightning flash shot through the air. It barely missed the dragon, but struck one of the side sails' metal rings. Its mast ripped apart. Wood splinters flew everywhere. Raylan ducked and covered his ears, ringing from the deafening thunder that accompanied the lightning strike. Part of the sail caught fire.

Raylan smacked the side of his head a few times to counter the pain inside before rushing toward the sail to cut it loose.

"*Galirras, are you alright?*" screamed Raylan, while he hacked at the sail's rope.

"*Keep going. We are almost there.*"

A final slash from his blade sent the burning sail flying; it disappeared in the blink of an eye, sucked up by the storm. Raylan tightened another rope and hoped the strain would not rip off what was left of the side mast. He ran to the stern again.

The darkness lifted. He looked over his shoulder and was greeted by a few tiny rays of sun. The clouds ahead of them split apart, forming a gray cotton tunnel for them to pass through. The ship shifted as a tailwind pushed them past the storm's border and into clear air. Relieved, Raylan let out the breath he had been holding.

"It seems we live another day to tell the tale. Thank you, Galirras. Make sure you come on back when you need a rest."

CHAPTER TWO

Caves

THE RUMBLING OF thunder brought Trista back into the world. Wet drops fell on her face; first a few, then a lot as the clouds released their cold ocean rain.

She blinked and groaned; it took a few tries for her eyelids to clear the double vision, though the pain in her head seemed less inclined to abandon her. She sat up carefully when a lightning flash crawled across the clouds in the distance. Another rumble followed.

A shiver ran through her. Despite the warm night, the rain cooled her down quickly. The hairs on her arms stood up. She rubbed her damp skin and noticed the stars that filled the sky to the east, where the storm clouds had not yet covered them up.

How long was I out?

She got to her feet, needing a moment to find her balance. She touched her forehead where she had struck the boulder. A big lump, and… wet. Rain? Or blood? She looked at her fingers. Blood.

The village!

The thought shook her. She spun around and squinted. The orange glow was less, but still present. Without it, Trista doubted she would have seen the houses at all against the dark skies. She looked up once more, but could not see the moon.

Is it midnight already?

She started moving again, slower this time, her head pounding with every step. The blood trickled down her cheek and washed away with the rain.

Following the cliffs, she saw campfires on the beach, each one encircled by shadows. Small boats were pulled up onto the sand. As she got closer to the village she heard screams and laughter carry through the night. The sounds terrified her, but she forced herself forward. She wanted to go home—to find her parents and brother.

Staying on the village's outer edges, she saw no one. Some of the houses were destroyed. Burned down. One or two were still on fire. Crawling through the low island shrubbery, she struggled to put some distance between her and those awful sounds, moving away from the laughter mixed with screams and closer to her family's house near the beach.

Maybe it has been spared…

It was a wishful thought against her better judgment, but she thought it nonetheless. As she moved on, still crouching, her hand bumped into something cold. The lifeless eyes of Moran—one of the elderly fishermen— stared at her from the darkness. Trista pulled back her shaking hand, swallowing tears of fear. A large gash split the man's neck and his mouth hung strangely crooked to one side, pulling his lips into a thin line. Suppressing a sob, she closed her eyes and moved around the body.

Just keep going, Trista. You're nearly there.

When it finally came into view, Trista saw part of the structure had collapsed. Flames and glowing wood lingered in small piles of rubble. Her heart raced in her chest. She had trouble breathing, as though a heavy stone rested on her throat.

Standing up, she stepped through a hole where the wall had once been and entered the house. All their possessions, their furniture, her bed, her clothes—nothing was left. New tears stung her eyes.

Outside, two male voices intruded on the silence. Trista ducked against the wall and listened to the strange words as footsteps strolled lazily by the house. She wished she knew what they were saying, but few on the island ever learned the more exotic tongues of the Southern Cities… and she was not even entirely sure this was one of those.

When the conversation moved away again, she risked a brief glance through one of the remaining windows. Two soldiers in thick, dark armor were on their way toward the village. Trista leaned closer to get a better look.

Her elbow knocked against the stone bowl resting on the windowsill. It teetered, then clattered to the floor, shattering in a dozen pieces. She ducked back down as both men stopped their conversation and looked back in her direction. Her heart jumped in her throat when she heard the crunch of footsteps near the house again. Metal scraped slowly against leather as one of the men drew a sword. Close by, a masculine voice called out a question.

Trista clamped both hands over her mouth, trying to stifle the sound of herself hyperventilating. Just in front of the house, a plank creaked as the soldier put his weight on the first step up to the veranda. Trista desperately looked around for anything that could serve as a hiding spot, knowing full well any movement would immediately give away her presence. She was trapped. Her eyes widened as another plank creaked just outside the door, which hung crooked on its hinges. A large hand with hairy fingers grabbed it, ready to pull it open.

A loud clang rang out from the side of the veranda. The soldier turned, and with two quick strides brought down his sword. Trista peeked over the windowsill just as he grabbed something from the sand and held it up, evoking a laugh from his fellow soldier. In his hands dangled the severed bottom half of a lizard.

The soldier cleared his throat and spat on the floor. He tossed the slain lizard aside, then wiped his sword on the side of the house and sheathed it. He jumped down the stairs and commented on something that received another loud and hearty laugh.

Inside, Trista released her nose and mouth. Tears streamed down her cheeks as the soldiers' voices disappeared once again toward the village. She waited another thirty counts before she dared another brief look.

They were gone. She let out a sigh, resting her hurting head on the windowsill. When she finally looked up again, a strange shape on the ground in front of the house drew her attention. It was difficult to see in the low, dancing light of the flames, but the gnawing feeling in her stomach already knew what it was.

"No, no, no…" she whispered. Nausea overwhelmed her, and she stumbled outside.

She approached the remains of her mother and father and fell to her knees beside them. She cried uncontrollably; the strange mixture of salt, rain and iron from the blood invaded the corners of her mouth. She clawed at the bodies, trying to pull them in, to hug them as close as possible. All the while she wailed at their loss, burying her face in their clothes and smothering her own sounds with the cold, lifeless shells that were once her parents.

"I'm sorry, father! I'm so sorry. I didn't mean to yell," she cried, "Oh, mother…"

All of a sudden, her anger of the day felt like the most regrettable thing in the world. Storming out. Screaming at her parents. She would never be able to apologize for it.

She never could recall how long she sat there that night. She remembered that she was afraid of someone finding her, but her hands were unwilling to let go. In her head, though, reason gradually gained ground against the raw emotion of loss. Eventually, with great effort, she forced her fingers to release their grip. Her parents were here, but there was no sign of Decan. Trista stood, weak kneed, and looked around in the remains of the house, scared of what she might find. But there was no sign of her brother anywhere.

Perhaps he really did get away...

Another high-pitched scream. She looked toward the village.

Or perhaps not.

She did not want to go to the village center. Turning into the wind, she heard men laughing and shouting; people wailing. But she had to know if her little brother was still alive.

"Mother, father... I'll go look for Decan now. I hope he's okay. If he's alive... I'll do everything I can to save him, I promise. So please watch over us. I love you both so much," she whispered.

She started moving toward the village, but halted after a few steps. Turning around, she quickly ran back into the destroyed house and started digging in the rubble. A moment later she emerged with two of her small fishing spears and a knife. She had hoped to find more, but most of her gear had not survived the collapse of their roof.

It's not much, but it's better than nothing.

Taking a deep breath, Trista dried her tears and headed in the direction of the dreadful sounds. She made sure to keep low and moved through the high grass for as long as possible. She used the houses, or what was left from them, as cover to get as close to the village center as she dared.

Hidden behind a couple of fish-filled barrels with a mass of nets and other fishing gear piled on top, Trista was finally able to lay eyes on the village square. She barely recognized their clan's gathering place. Two large bonfires burned on either side of the square—in their light she saw the dark color of blood tainting the stones on the ground. Crude cages had been constructed by tying pointed branches together. She could see women and children sobbing within them; at least, that was what she assumed the little trembling piles of clothes and flesh were.

This late in the night, few soldiers were still awake. It seemed they had located the village's liquor stores and helped themselves to the edge of fall-flat-on-your-face drunk.

Some of the more resilient types were laughing loudly at their own self-made entertainment. Trista saw one of the soldiers pull a woman out of a cage, dragging her to one of the burned-out houses as she kicked and screamed, trying to get away.

To the side, several men with ripped clothes were on their knees, hands tied behind their backs with rope that also encircled their throats. Trista counted seven of them.

In the center of the square, two more men—bare-chested—faced each other with their fists up, but seemed to lack the spirit to fight. The soldiers were cheering and bawling at the two unwilling combatants, shoving them in the back if they lingered too long around the edge of the makeshift circle. Trista suddenly recognized one of them.

Landon!

Her mother's voice from this morning echoed in her mind.

"We chose Landon for you! He's kind and handsome!"

Her fiancé-to-be was breathing heavily, his skin covered in black smears of dirt and blood, his dark blond hair filthy and full of knots. His knuckles were bleeding, probably from the fight. His opponent looked no better, but seemed to be the better fighter as he landed two blows on Landon's ribs and another on his nose. As they went at each other again, the soldiers cheered, throwing their drinks over the duo and kicking up dirt if either one of them ended up on the ground near their feet.

Trista recognized the exhaustion in their movements; they must have been at it for a while now. As they clung together in a momentary embrace, Trista finally got a good look at the second man's face.

Wait, Sterak? That's Landon's best friend!

Landon let out a roar of frustration as he put his remaining energy into a final flurry of punches. Sterak, unable to withstand the force of the blows, slammed backward onto the ground, unable to get up. A number of soldiers cheered loudly; it seemed they had bet on the winner. Landon fell to his knees, looking at his blood-covered hands. His defeated friend lay on the floor, motionless but for the heaving of his chest.

One of the soldiers approached Landon and threw a short sword in front of him. Landon looked up with hazy eyes. The soldier pointed to Sterak on the ground. When Landon did not move, the soldier kicked him in the back. Dragging him up again by his hair, the soldier pushed the sword into Landon's hands and shoved him toward Sterak, shouting something incomprehensible.

Trembling, Landon looked at his friend's face. The soldier made a stabbing motion and imitated a death cry while the others laughed. The row of kneeling prisoners cursed or turned their heads away, eyes tightly shut. They already knew what was coming.

Slowly, Landon lifted the sword up in the air, the tip pointed downward. Trista, her eyes wide with horror, could see the blade shaking.

Don't! Don't do it!

Perhaps her unspoken words reached Landon's mind; he abruptly threw the sword to the side, cursing the soldiers with all the terrors from the ocean's depths. The first soldier jumped forward and struck Landon with a closed fist.

For the second time, Landon ended up with his face in the dirt. The soldier picked up the sword, dragged Landon to his knees and then kneeled behind him. Locking his own hands around Landon's, he touched the sword to Sterak's chest. The soldier pushed Landon's hands downward, forcing the blade into his dazed friend's chest. Another cheer rose from the spectators as Landon let out a wail, struggling to escape the soldier's cruel grip.

Trista remained motionless, unable to process the atrocities happening in front of her. Her heart raced painfully when the soldier pulled the sword from Sterak's chest and, in one motion, stabbed Landon straight through the neck.

Trista once again put her hands over her mouth to muffle her shocked scream.

They mustn't hear me. They mustn't hear me…

Luckily, no one took notice. The soldiers laughed as the young man whom Trista's mother had intended her to marry slumped forward across the corpse of his best friend. Trista felt ashamed of her outburst that afternoon. She had called him a dumb ox, unworthy of being her partner. But not even the worst townsfolk deserved a fate like this.

A voice suddenly filled the air.

"Landon! No! You monsters! Why did you do that?! He won!"

It was a voice Trista knew all too well. It had called her home for dinner on sunny late afternoons; had teased her when she returned home from her dates, and annoyed her immensely when she was not in the mood for any silliness. But now… now the sound of her little brother's voice was like a songbird's call at dawn, full of promise.

Her eyes frantically sought for the source of the sound.

There!

There he was—across the square, beside the shrubbery. Trista saw her little brother rage against his captors from inside one of the primitive cages. The soldiers only laughed at the boy's outbursts, eventually throwing a burning piece of wood toward him to make him shut up.

He's still alive! He's really *still alive!*

A storm of emotion flowed through her. Relief and excitement about her brother being alive battled the fear of having to push further and closer to the danger in front of her.

"Just keep quiet, Decan. I'm coming," she whispered to give herself the strength and courage to continue.

Wiping tears of sorrow and happiness from her face, Trista slowly backed up and retreated to the edge of the village. She would have to take the long way round to get to her brother unseen.

Moving only when she was absolutely certain none of the soldiers were looking, Trista made her way toward Decan. Above her, the clouds scattered, showing that the moon had gone way beyond the highest point. Luckily, it also meant more of the soldiers were now passed out.

As she skirted the square, she passed the remains of two more captives. These men had been used for target practice; arrows, throwing knives, even an axe had all introduced their own form of suffering to the victims. Trista was glad their screaming had ended along with their torture.

Trista had just double-checked to see if she was moving toward the right cage when a soldier's shout startled her. Stopping dead in her tracks, she quickly looked around to see if they had spotted her. But the soldier was moving toward the seven remaining men to pick out two more contestants. Both captives struggled to get away, giving Trista the opportunity to cover the distance to her little brother's cage. She hated that others were suffering, but her brother was everything now. She needed to save him. There was no past, no future—only the danger, and her task to get him out of there.

"Decan," she whispered as loud as she dared.

He didn't respond.

"Decan… it's me, Triss."

Still her brother remained motionless. Perhaps he had passed out from exhaustion. She looked closer, but barely recognized him. His face was swollen on the left side, his cheek and eye covered in dark bruises.

Trista felt as if she was being watched. She turned her head; two large eyes looked right back at her. Trista stared back in silence at the girl in the cage next to her brother, afraid that she might scream. The girl looked like she had been through hell. Her clothes were ripped, part of her hair was scorched and someone had taken the liberty of bursting her lips with a punch or two. It took a moment before she recognized her as Hali.

Hali and her friends had never liked her, although Trista never really knew why. Over the years, they had developed numerous ways to make Trista's life as unpleasant as possible, from name-calling when they were little to gossiping and false accusations as they got older. They even tried to corner her after one of the summer dances; Trista had given two of them bloody noses, and the girls had never resorted to physical harassment again.

Now, on this dark night, eyes which had always looked at Trista with disgust and rejection were begging her for help.

"Trista? Is that you?" the girl asked shakily.

Quickly, Trista put her finger against her lips to urge the girl to be quiet. She eased her hand into her brother's cage and rested it on his leg.

Decan twitched and looked over his shoulder. He seemed exhausted from his earlier outburst, but when he recognized her face Trista saw a sparkle of light in his one open eye. The smudges on his face showed lines of dried-up tears.

In the meantime, the soldiers had chained the two chosen captives' hands together, as well as their feet. The chain between them was only a few feet long, keeping both men close together. Each was ordered to sit down while the soldiers started a small fire in the spot between them. Their limbs and chains formed a circle around the fire.

While the soldiers were distracted by this new form of entertainment, Trista quickly took her knife and started on the ropes that tied the thick branches of her brother's cage.

"Trista!" hissed Hali. "You're not going to leave me here, are you?"

Again, Trista put her finger to her lips, urging Hali to keep quiet. The soldiers were bawling loudly in that unfamiliar language, but if any of them were to hear or see them, Trista doubted that she could get away.

But Hali had no intention to keep quiet and risk losing her only chance of escape. She grabbed Trista's wrist

"Help me. Please! You don't understand what they do to the girls," she whispered, tears running down her face. "Please…"

There had been moments over the years when Trista had hoped an accident would happen to Hali; maybe a broken leg, or a stingray jabbing her. The girl had not been a pleasant part of her life. But here in the dark, with the horrors forming in front of them, she just wanted to get her little brother to safety. So she tore her arm loose and kept working on the ropes of the cage.

As she cut the third rope and started on a fourth, the branches of the cage became loose enough to move. Her brother watched her progress intensely with his one good eye.

The soldiers were feeding the fire between the two captives. As they threw on fresh wood, the fire increased in size, and the flames crawled closer to each shackled man. The iron of the chains was slowly heating up; it would not be long before it would start to burn their flesh.

With a soft snap, the fourth rope sprang loose, giving Trista and her brother enough room to push the branches apart and let Decan wriggle out of the cage.

Meanwhile, the fire had grown so big that the heat was getting too much for the captives to bear. Both men feared the flames, trying to get away from the fire as the soldiers kept throwing on more wood. If they side-stepped too far, the onlookers jabbed them with their swords. But if one man pulled away from the fire, the chains pulled the other one toward it. It had become a tug of war to the death.

Hali seemed hypnotized by the flames, perhaps wishing they would free her of things to come. But as Decan finally slipped from his cage, she suddenly turned and clung to Trista's leg.

"Wait! Help me get out of here, or… or I'll scream, and the soldiers will get you," Hali whispered with a sudden viciousness in her voice.

Trista shot fire from her eyes. Part of her wanted to let Hali rot in there, but she had already seen so much suffering this dark night. Her mind played out all the terrible possibilities of what the soldiers might do to a young girl. She would not wish that on anyone—not even Hali—but she had no intention of keeping herself or her brother in danger any longer.

Grinding her teeth at Hali's rude, arrogant ways, Trista slowly twisted her knife around in her hand. Just for a moment, she thought of stabbing it in the girl's arm, but instead she stuck the blade in the ground beside the cage.

"Here. Do it yourself."

Hali snatched up the knife and started working on the ropes, completely forgetting about her savior. As Trista and Decan snuck away, screams rose up behind them. The sizzling of flesh announced the end of the tug of war as one of the men lost the struggle and was pulled into the flames.

Afraid to look back, Trista pushed her little brother forward. They had to put as much distance between them and the soldiers as possible.

They rounded a corner and the village square dropped out of sight. Unexpectedly, Decan half-fell, half-jumped toward Trista, throwing his arms around her neck and hugging her with all his strength.

"Sis…" he sobbed.

"Shh, it's okay. It's okay. Just be quiet. We're not safe yet. There's soldiers everywhere," she whispered.

"But they shot Mother and Father. They killed them."

Trista fought back her own tears. She needed to be strong for Decan.

"I know, I know. But we can't mourn them yet. We must survive first. We've got to get out of here."

"But where do we go? We're on an island!" the boy whispered with a panicked voice.

"A big island. And it doesn't matter where. Anywhere but here."

Her day at the cliff slid back into her mind.

"The caves. Let's go to the caves. We can hide there."

Decan gave a quick nod, relief in his eyes. He turned to face the direction that would take them the shortest route to the caves.

"Not that way," said Trista. "I want to stay as far away from the square as possible."

"Shouldn't we help them?" asked Decan softly. Trista remembered his earlier protests at Landon's unfair demise.

"I wish we could, but we can't. There are so many of them. The entire beach is crawling with them, too. I made a promise to Mother and Father when I found them that I would do everything to keep you safe, and that's what I'm going to do."

Their hushed conversation was cut short by shouting from the village square. It was not the soldiers' usual sadistic laughter. It sounded like something had unexpectedly gone wrong.

Trista snuck to the corner of a house and briefly peeked around it.

"It's Hali! They spotted her trying to sneak away."

The girl was running as fast as her legs could carry her away from the village center, with several soldiers shouting after her. Some of the soldiers stayed behind, laughing at the escape attempt, but their fellow bullies closed in on her quickly. Hali would not be able to outrun them for long.

Trista swallowed hard, every fiber in her body wanting to jump out of hiding and help her former nemesis, but her fear was too great. She knew there was nothing she could do. The only upside—if one could call it that—was that the distraction would at least allow them to escape more easily. Trista instantly felt guilt at the thought.

"Trista!"

The panic in her brother's voice made her jerk around. Decan backed away from a swaying soldier who looked too drunk to fully understand what was going on. He appeared to have stumbled upon them by accident while looking for a place to take a piss and seemed unsure as to whether he was dreaming.

Tripping over his own feet, Decan landed ass-first in the sand. The soldier made a grab for him as he squirmed away, then lunged forward again to grasp the boy's feet.

Trista's mind raced looking for a weapon. With her spears out of reach, tugged behind her back, her hand found something hard and solid in the sand. The rock's weight was just right, light enough to swing at speed but heavy enough to make a real impact. Somehow, it had a familiar feel to it. It was like the entire island was in her hand. It felt like... home. She had been here all her life, walked on these grounds, and now it was like the island recognized her—wanted to help her.

For the drunk soldier, Trista came out of nowhere like a ghost. The rock slammed into the soldier's temple, cracking it open as the force of the swing slammed the other side of his face into the wall.

Trista did not look at the result. She jumped up, dragging Decan to his feet and started running.

Shouts from behind told her the soldier might have been taken by surprise, but he surely was not dead yet. As they raced through the narrow streets, the shouting increased as more soldiers joined the search. Trista dove into a burned-down house; climbing out the window on the opposite side they quickly closed in on the border of the village.

They ran like the wind, Trista pulling her brother along so fast his feet barely had time to touch the ground. Her head started to pound again as her breathing intensified. Dizziness lingered in the corners of her mind, ready to intrude as soon as Trista let it. Her earlier fall had certainly given her a concussion.

They left the last buildings behind as they ran across a sandy plain dotted with dry grass toward the cliffs. If they had been running any faster, Trista would have sworn they were flying.

The rain had stopped. The clouds split as the land gave off the day's collected warmth and drove the gray blanket high above them apart. Stars and the moon sent down their light, which made it easier for Trista and Decan to see where they were going. Unfortunately, it also allowed a group of soldiers to spot them. Each came from a different direction, the light of three torches clearly headed across the plain toward them.

The ground, which changed from hard to loose sand and back again, was not easy to run on if you were not used to it. One of the soldiers had already gone down once, and it was obvious that they were all still heavily under the influence of liquor. However, what they lacked in speed and coordination they made up in sheer determination and perseverance.

"We just have to make it to the caves. We can lose them there," said Trista to her brother between heavy breaths. "We'll take the high path that goes down just before the caves."

The ground became firmer when they reached the cliffs. Trista tried to keep up the pace, but her—and Decan's—exhaustion was gaining even more quickly than the pursuing soldiers.

Suddenly, a shape loomed up ahead. A soldier walking the cliffs had spotted them coming toward him—no doubt alerted by the shouting men giving chase.

"Decan, whatever happens, stay behind me and *keep going*! Do *not* stop! Get to the caves, go in as far as you dare. Remember your way. It will be dark." Trista let go of her brother's hand.

The soldier looked like he was ready for them. Sword in hand, he was focusing on Trista as his main target.

This one is not drunk like the others. He's much too alert. He's dangerous, she thought in a panic. *I'll only have one chance.*

Closing in on her foe, she grabbed one of the two small hunting spears in her throwing hand. Hopefully he would not expect her to be armed.

She pushed her hesitation out of her mind.

It's just like hunting fish...

She counted her steps as she closed the gap between them. As she felt the ground change under her feet, she chose her moment.

Now!

Twisting her heel into a groove in the rocky ground, she launched her short spear with a quick movement of her arm. The thin spear was barely visible in the darkness. If it had not been for Trista's sudden shift in movement and the glimmer of moonlight on oiled wood, the soldier would never have seen it coming. Instead, he dove out of the way, but the weapon's speed was too great and the distance too short.

The spear hit the soldier's arm just below the metal plate protecting his shoulder. It barely even pierced his leather armor. Trista screamed and continued her charge without slowing down.

The soldier recovered quickly and swung his sword in a vicious arc. But his timing was off, as Trista—anticipating his attack—slightly adjusted her speed. The slash left the soldier completely open to Trista's desperate lunge. Knees forward, she hit the man in the chest with her full weight. His armor caught the blow without much trouble, but he toppled backward from the force of the impact and slammed to the ground.

Gripping her last hunting spear near the head, she stuck the point in the only vulnerable place she could spot. As the spear burrowed into the soldier's neck his surprised roar was replaced by a deep gurgle rising from his throat. Warm blood poured over her hand. Her stomach turned.

Decan shot past them as Trista tumbled forward from her own momentum. Miraculously still holding the spear, she scrambled to her feet and ran after her little brother, ignoring the heavy protests from her legs.

As they took the path down to Boulder Beach, Trista saw Decan trip over a rock and land in the dirt. She tried to pick him up, but he could no longer stand. His breath came in short, husky bursts, and he clutched his ribs with both hands.

"Get up," urged Trista, but her brother only lay in front of her, dry heaving from exhaustion.

Her brother was not a large boy. He had never had much meat on his bones and was quite short in comparison to other boys his age. Trista had also been a late bloomer, as thin as a rake until she hit fifteen and grew into her curves. Since that time, the daily work routine and constant outdoor activities had given her a body that she was proud of—and provided her with plenty of strength.

She crouched in front of Decan.

"Get on my back. Quickly!"

Gasping for breath, Decan put his arms around her neck and wrapped his legs weakly around her waist. As Trista stood up, the shouting from the three pursuing soldiers came closer. They still refused to give up.

Her legs felt as heavy as the stones she ran across. Their progress was slower then she wished, but at least the drunk soldiers behind her did not go much faster. The sand had been difficult for them to run on; the boulders were downright treacherous. Wet from the rain and waves that crashed upon them, the stones were unforgiving of any mistakes. Trista was deliberately taking it slowly, even if it meant that their hunters were closing in.

She turned at a shout from one of the men chasing them. A wrong move had made him lose his footing and he tumbled forward between two boulders. Unable to break his fall with anything but his head, the soldier's neck snapped sideways. He would not be getting up again.

Finally, Trista reached the flat stretch leading to the entrance of the cavern complex. As they reached the dark mouth of the main cave, she swiftly put her brother down. She coughed as the choking pressure around her neck was released.

"Can you walk again?" asked Trista. Decan nodded meekly.

For a moment, they both stared at the gaping black hole. The cavern looked like a sea monster waiting to swallow them whole.

"We need to move now," said Trista. She pulled her brother along into the darkness. "We need to stay ahead of them. They have torches."

By the time the soldiers arrived at the entrance, the siblings had made it a fair distance into the cave. But they were moving slowly, sliding their hands along the wall, searching for a way to escape their pursuers. Small patches of light trickled in through cracks in the ceiling. It was enough to let Trista know where they were. She heard the soldiers' voices as they entered the caves in search of them both.

Their hunters had no problems moving around. They simply held their torches high and entered the underground complex. But the caves were a maze and both Trista and her brother had already taken several turns, moving deeper into the tunnels.

It was a deadly game of hide and seek. If she and her brother could get deep enough into the cave system, the soldiers would be unlikely to find them. They would be safe, for now. But if they were found, Trista had no doubt they would never see a new day.

"I'm scared."

It was the first thing Decan had said since the village. Trista heard the tremble in his voice.

"I know. Just keep going. We know these caves, remember? We can do this. We just need to go deeper, where they won't find us."

When they turned a corner, the infinite darkness gave way to a bluer luminescent light. It was her sanctuary, the cavern where Trista had spent many nights lying in the moss staring at the stars as they poured into the chamber. Even Decan stopped whimpering for the briefest of moments as the cave's full glory came into view.

As brother and sister stepped into the naturally formed room, Trista noticed a huge sheet of rock had fallen from the ceiling and squashed her favorite stargazing spot.

It must have happened during the tremors.

Her eye caught something else that had not been there before. On one of the walls, where the flowers normally flowed as a river of lights, was a large crevice.

A soldier's voice carried through the tunnels, taunting them in that unknown language and making them both flinch. Trista had hoped their pursuers would get turned around inside the caves, making it harder for the soldiers to run into them, at least until they could find a good enough hiding spot. But the voices were closing in on them fast. She already saw the glow of a torch in the tunnel they had just exited.

She pulled Decan toward the split-open wall. She was not entirely sure why; there were other tunnels out of this cave, all of them leading deeper underground. But there was something about this unfamiliar crack that drew her in.

She poked her head in to check it out. It was big enough for them both to squeeze through, but she could not see where it led.

"I think we can fit through," she said to Decan. Her brother opened his mouth as if to protest, but the approaching soldiers' voices made him swallow his words.

She ushered her little brother into the crevice. As he disappeared into the darkness, he let out a soft whimper. He had never liked the dark, especially after getting lost so long ago. Trista was a bit surprised he had not objected sooner.

He must be terrified out of his mind.

She reached out just in time to grab his hand.

"I'm right here. Keep going," she murmured.

The soldiers chose that moment to storm into the chamber. They spotted Trista right away—she was still sticking half out of the wall. They burst toward her.

Slipping further into the tear, the rough stone wall closed in around her. Panic clutched her stomach. Had she misjudged the space? But her brother was still moving forward, inching away from her. She tried lowering herself and found enough space to continue.

She screamed when an arm plunged into the crevice, grabbing at her shoulders and hair. She bent her knees, half-falling, half-stumbling forward, tearing both clothing and hair as the soldier refused to let go. Behind her, a sword introduced itself with a clang of metal. It was thrust through the crack as the soldier extended his arm as far as possible, but he was too large to enter the thin fissure completely. Unable to move away in time, the blade cut into her arm. She grit her teeth against the pain.

"It's opening up here," she heard Decan say anxiously, but before she could take another step the walls of stone started to shake violently.

Not now!

The stone wall moved beneath the pressure of moving earth. Behind her, the shouting was cut off by a loud crash and sounds of falling rocks. The ceiling in the moss chamber had given way completely, burying both remaining soldiers under its crushing weight.

The shifting walls tightened around her. The harder she tried to move forward the more the mountain pressed down on her.

"Decan! Help!" she screamed in panic. *I'm going to be crushed!*

Her little brother pulled on her arm.

"Lower! You need to go lower, Trista!"

"Lower."

"I can't!" screamed Trista.

"You must!" The voice in her head did not entirely sound like her own.

Her head was pounding again, her chest heaving rapidly. *Chest... hurts. Can't... breathe.*

"Ignore it."

Need to breathe. Help!

"We are helping. Now breathe out."

"Breathe out, Triss! You need to breathe out!" yelled Decan.

But I need air!

"IGNORE IT."

Fighting her body's natural instincts, Trista forced herself to breathe out, decreasing the size of her chest. She could finally move again. She lowered herself further. Decan pulled with all his might while Trista kicked herself forward out of the closing space.

And just like that, the shaking stopped. One of her feet still rested in the crawlspace she had just escaped; the passage was now no larger than a rabbit hole. Trista stared at it, gulping in air as if she had spent ten minutes under water.

"Are you alright?" asked her brother, staring at her foot. She still needed a moment to catch her breath, but pulled out her foot and nodded at Decan.

"We're not going back that way, that's for sure."

She sat on the ground, panting, and Decan threw himself into her arms. He cried as all the horrors of the night came out. Trista could do nothing but hold her little brother. She hugged him tightly, making shushing sounds as she let her own tears flow as well.

As Decan's sobbing subsided, she looked up to take in their surroundings. That was when she saw it for the first time. A weak light flowed in from the ceiling. Multiple cracks ran across it, providing a spectacle of illumination as the moon's rays fell like a net into the cavern. There, toward the wall, was an egg.

Decan relaxed in her arms. Now that the danger had passed, exhaustion grabbed them both. Her little brother was already half-asleep, but Trista pushed her own tiredness away, mesmerized by the egg in front of her. It was huge. Much bigger than any egg Trista had ever seen. It had a bluish-green color in the moonlight, almost as if it was covered in moss.

Carefully, she lay her softly snoring brother down on the ground and crept over to the egg. It had a strange mystique to it, as if it was very old. She briefly put her hand on it, but the egg was almost too hot to touch. Trails of steam came out of the ground near the base of the egg. The air in the entire room was like a warm blanket. When Trista put her hand on the ground, she found it too was unusually warm.

The heat made Trista drowsy, and suddenly she wanted nothing other than to sleep for a week. She sat down close to the egg, pulling her brother a little closer. She put her arms around him, hoping it would make him feel safer. The warm ground relaxed her body with its heat and made it impossible to fight off sleep any longer. She let it take her. Somehow, she felt safe here. Her eyelids grew heavy, and the world slipped away into darkness.

"Rest now."

There it was again, so very soothing to hear; a voice not quite her own.

CHAPTER THREE

Flee

FLAMES CLOSED IN on Trista from all sides. She looked around desperately for her little brother.

"Decan? Decan! Where are you?"

She could hear nothing over the roar of the fire. She coughed into her arm; the smoke was suffocating.

There—an opening!

But as soon as she stepped toward it the flames closed ranks again, creeping slowly toward her. Behind the flames rose the screams of men, while the stench of burning flesh penetrated her nose.

"No! Stay away!" she screamed at the orange tongues licking at her feet. "Leave me alone! Decan!"

"*Calm down.*"

"Who's there?"

Trista looked around, but it was too dark. She could not even see the stars through all the smoke.

"Where's my brother? What have you done with him?"

"*Your brother is fine. He is sleeping still.*"

"The fire is coming closer. Help me!"

"*It is alright. It will not reach you. Look for the water.*"

"Water? What water? There's no water, just fire! Someone help me. Decan, help me!"

"*Above...*"

The smoke stung her eyes and the hot air burned her lungs as she tried to breathe, but each attempt led to more coughing. She fell to her knees, clasping her throat with her hands as she tried to clear the smoke inside. It was no use.

There was barely any air to breathe. Panicked, she rolled onto her back and pulled up her knees, unable to move away from the approaching danger.

"Above…"

As she stared toward the unseen sky behind the thick black clouds of smoke, the thought kept repeating in her head.

"Above…"

Something hit her face. It was small, cold, and wet. Another drop followed, then another.

What's happening?

The roaring of flames was pushed back by the thundering sound of rushing water. A wave burst from the smoke and crashed down toward her, straight from the sky, extinguishing the flames in a combination of loud hissing and steam. Trista's lungs filled with the hot, moist air, making it only a tiny bit less difficult to breathe.

Drenched, Trista uncurled herself and looked around. The flames were gone. Everything was wrapped in a thick blanket of steam, but she caught movement from the corner of her eye. A shadow moved toward her slowly, deliberately. But the fog was too thick; she could not make out who or what it was, even when the shadow was right on top of her. Then the dark shape spoke, brushing her forehead with the lightest of touches.

"You are mine and I am yours. My name is Dalkeira."

A rush of warmth flowed through Trista. She opened her eyes, awakening from her dream. The shaded surroundings of the cave came into view. But as her eyes adjusted, the shadows somehow seemed less dark—and not just because of the sun's rays falling in through the ceiling. Shades of gray and brown colored the cave. Water drops on the dark stone walls glittered in the light like little stars. Even the sunlight itself seemed more vibrant.

As Trista sat up, a creature came into view. It was unlike anything she had ever seen, yet it seemed very familiar. The size of a large dog, its skin was a combination of lizard and fish. Small scales of a deep blue color ran the entire length of its body, overlaid with a darker green glow. The animal was magnificent, and rivaled the deep colors of the ocean itself. It appeared to be waiting patiently for Trista to take it all in.

As she stared at the creature, it shook its entire body, spreading out two large, beautiful wings before tucking them back in again.

"Would you mind not staring? It is quite rude. It is as though you have never seen a dragon before," said Dalkeira.

"That's because I haven't," said Trista, hesitantly and without much thought. "Hold on! You can talk?"

"*Of course I can talk.*"

The dragon leaned closer. Instinctively, Trista moved back a few inches. The dragon backed off again immediately.

"*I mean you no harm.*"

"But you're not moving your muzzle… jaw… I mean, mouth." Trista stumbled over her words as she tried to process one thing at a time.

"*One does not always need a mouth to speak. Nor do you have to use yours to let me hear you. We would not want to wake up the smaller version of you, would we?*" said the dragon.

Trista looked at Decan, still sleeping beside her. The cave was pleasantly warm, and although it was a bit damp Trista imagined it definitely beat sleeping in the cold air in one of those awful cages. Flashes from the night before rushed into her head.

I hope he's okay.

"*He is just sleeping, albeit restlessly. Much like you were yourself, I might add,*" answered the dragon in response to Trista's thought.

"*You can hear me?*"

"*Like I just said, no need to talk out loud if you do not want to.*"

The dragon tilted her head as Trista's thoughts raced. It all seemed so strange, yet now that the drowsiness of sleep had worn off, she felt absolutely no fear. The dragon's eyes looked at her with expectation. They were beautiful eyes, layered with deep colors. In each, three pupils floated in a blue iris which contained tiny swirls of intense yellow and patches of dark green. Each pupil was a swirling, sparkling vortex, and out of each leaked a small line to the side of the iris—like a tiny river. Mesmerized, Trista stared into those ocean blue eyes.

The dragon stared back.

"*Where did you come from?*" Trista said finally, as if coming out of a trance.

"*I believe you already know,*" answered Dalkeira.

Trista looked at the large egg that she had spotted before falling asleep. The top was cracked open and parts of the side had been pushed outward. Hot steam was still escaping from the floor around the empty eggshell. A puddle of clear liquid ran from the egg, down the stones to the spot where the newly hatched dragon was now sitting. She saw the dragon's scaled skin still gleamed from it.

Small fins lined Dalkeira's head: three rows running over the top toward her neck, and two vertically on the back of her jaw. Each jawline also had a similar fin running along its length, although it was barely visible. Two small barbel whiskers ran from her chin. From nose to tail, the slender lines of the dragon's neck and body shone and weaved like the ocean.

"Are you the goddess?" she asked, surprising herself with the thought.

"*Goddess? I am not familiar with the word. I am a dragon, as I already told you,*" said Dalkeira. "*Did you perhaps hit your head yesterday?*"

"And it was you who I heard last night, wasn't it?" Trista continued out loud.

"*It sounded like you needed some encouragement,*" said Dalkeira.

"I suppose I did."

Trista heard a grunt beside her as Decan stirred.

"Oh… it hurts," the boy groaned, holding his head.

As he sat up, blinking, Dalkeira watched him expectantly. Trista saw her brother's eyes stretch wide.

"Aah! Get away!"

Decan scrambled backward, perhaps afraid that the king of lizards had come out to take revenge for all the times he had tried to catch one of the small island reptiles. His hand found a small rock which he lifted right away to throw at the unknown creature.

"It's okay, Decan, it's okay!" said Trista, quickly catching him by the arm.

"This is Dalkeira. She won't hurt you… *us*, just as I won't let anything hurt her."

Trista was a bit surprised by that last part, especially given the determined tone in which she had said it. She barely knew this enchanting creature, yet she knew she would do anything to keep her safe.

Dalkeira enforced the statement by making a gracious bow to the young boy, who still had a look of disbelief on his face.

"She says she is pleased to meet you, and thanks you for saving me from the crushing walls," said Trista, translating the soft growls and peeping sounds coming from the dragon's throat.

"So… you aren't here to eat me? Or punish me for hunting lizards?" said Decan, still sounding unsure of the whole situation.

"*I would not eat either of you, but perhaps he can help me catch some of those small lizards he talks about. I am so very hungry,*" said Dalkeira's voice inside Trista's head.

Trista's stomach rumbled. Yet below her own hunger was a second, powerful urge, and suddenly she realized she *felt* that Dalkeira was famished.

Having grown up on the island, Trista had always felt in tune with nature. With the animals, and especially the ocean; reading the water, learning to enjoy its power without losing sight of the dangers. She enjoyed the excitement of the hunt, but could just as easily find joy in observing the animals by blending into the surroundings and letting things go by undisturbed. Over the years, she had learned to trust her sense for nature; her gut feeling on what she could take and give back.

Now this feeling—this sudden urge—was clearly steering her one way. *Feed the dragon.* She knew in her core it was very important, as if it was needed to secure their bond.

A bond. I can't describe it any other way.

"That's because you are mine and I am yours," said Dalkeira simply.

Trista smiled. The warmth she felt looking at her newfound companion was complex and yet so simple. As if it had always been there. Or at least a place for it had always been there; one which had now been filled.

"She says she's hungry, and would like to know if you can show her where and how to catch the lizards," said Trista to her little brother. "I could use something to eat myself."

She looked around.

"Which means that we have to get out of here."

"But what of the soldiers? What if they're still out there?" said Decan, tears welling up in his eyes. "I don't want to get caught again."

"I know, but we can't stay here forever. We need to eat."

Examining their surroundings more carefully, Trista noticed that there were no tunnels connected to their room. The space they were in went around a few corners, but they were all dead ends. The way in had been blocked when the walls closed, which only left one way out.

Trista looked up at the sky and the light that fell in. The ceiling of the cave had several cracks in it. Most were too hard to reach or too small to fit through, but one looked like it might just work.

"There, that one," she said, pointing. "It's big enough for us to climb through, and there's no overhang. Just the wall going straight up."

She saw her brother look doubtfully at the wall. She lowered herself onto one knee and put a hand on his shoulder.

"Don't worry, we'll take our time. Look for the right route. And once we've found it, you can go first. I'll spot you while you climb."

It took the rest of the morning to find a suitable route. Twice Trista fell off the wall, welcomed only by the rocky ground to break her unintended descent. But each time she got back up without any serious injuries. They had to make haste, for without food, they would eventually grow too weak to make such a climb.

Dalkeira paced around, unable to sit still with hunger driving her. Impatiently, she waited for Trista to find a route, only to give up shortly after and look for one herself. She was surprisingly quick in climbing the walls. Her claws gave her excellent grip on the otherwise slippery stone surface. Before they knew it, the dragon disappeared through the crack and encouraged them from above.

But it was much more difficult for Trista and Decan to find large enough handholds and foot rests. Decan had never really climbed like this before, while Trista had only learned through the challenges the island youngsters had given each other over the years. She now had to use all that experience to coach Decan to the top.

"That's it! Now put your left foot a little further up… more… more… there!"

"I don't like this, Triss! I'm scared!"

"It's okay to be scared, but I know you can do it, Decan! It's just a little further. You're almost there! The next step is moving your weight on your left leg and putting your right hand in that crack just above you."

"Which crack?"

"It's just above you, a little to your left."

"I don't see it! My hands are getting tired, Triss! I'm going to fall!"

"*Come on. I'm hungry,*" Dalkeira's voice said in her head impatiently.

"No, you're not. Put your weight on your legs. Relax your arms," Trista called out to Decan, ignoring the dragon's plea. "It's just above you; you'll have to feel for it."

"*Can't you help? Can you climb down and point him at the next grip?*" asked Trista privately to Dalkeira.

"*What about food?*" asked the dragon.

Trista saw Dalkeira hop around impatiently.

"*The sooner we are out of here, the faster we can find food,*" Trista sent across to the distracted dragon.

"Help!" called Decan, his arms shaking from the effort of holding on.

Trista thanked the goddess as she saw the small dragon start to descend the wall. Trista quickly positioned herself directly under them, ready to catch them if needed.

"There, Decan! Right where Dalkeira's claw is. Just reach around that piece of rock."

Finally, Decan's fingers found their grip, allowing him to pull himself upward. From there, it was two simple steps before he was able to grab the edge of the crack and push himself through the tear in the ceiling and out of the cave. Dalkeira immediately disappeared after him.

Trista made a small jump of joy and let out a deep breath. Decan stuck his head back into the cave.

"I made it, Triss! Now it's your turn."

She had little trouble following her brother up the wall. Reaching the top, she pulled herself out of the cave and let herself fall on her back, enjoying their small victory for a moment by soaking up the rays of sunlight with her eyes closed.

It was not long after that she felt a soft nudge to the side of her head. She opened an eye and saw the dark silhouette of Dalkeira's head hovering above her.

Just like in my dream, thought Trista.

"*Hungry*," was all Dalkeira said.

Trista and Dalkeira walked toward the ocean with Decan trailing close behind them. After exiting the cave system, they carefully moved back toward the edge of the cliffs to ensure they would not fall into any of the tremor-created crevices.

Playing it safe, they spent some time on the high ground, checking for soldiers. But Dalkeira quickly grew impatient, assuring both siblings there were no other people in sight.

Looking back, Trista saw the smoke from her village still creeping slowly into the sky.

It's not as thick anymore. Most of the fires must have gone out.

As she approached one of her favorite fishing spots, she held tight to her last fishing spear. She was glad she had only jabbed the soldier with it, or she would have had to fish with her bare hands. They had looked for lizards on their way down from the cliff, but it was too late in the day already; most of the little reptiles had soaked up enough sun and had gone into hiding from the heat. It would not be until the end of the day that they would leave their shelters again.

While Trista waited for her chance to spear a fish, Decan went looking for small crabs and cockles, his makeshift bag at the ready.

Dalkeira was watching Trista intensely.

"*What is taking so long?*" Dalkeira complained. "*You have been standing there doing nothing for quite some time now.*"

Trista was positioned over a shallow inlet of ocean water. Each foot firmly set on a rock, she patiently watched the water below her. Small fish swam by, but she held her spear firmly, waiting for the right moment.

"Patience, please. I don't want to waste time on any of the small ones," Trista replied privately so as not to not disturb the fish. She was getting the hang of these unspoken conversations.

"But there is one there… and there… and another one there! Why do you not get them?" Dalkeira paced back and forth.

"The timing has to be right, else we'll just scare them off and fish behind the net."

"But you are not using a net."

"No, it's a figure of speech. It means that we'll lose the opportunity to catch the fish if we scare them off first. Now please, try not to move. Your pacing is frightening our meal," said Trista softly so as not to hurt the dragon's feelings.

Dalkeira held her pacing, but Trista noticed her skin twitch nervously. The dragon did not want to wait; she wanted to eat. The hunger was almost unbearable as she watched the fish slide by while Trista waited for the opportune moment.

Dalkeira's hunger overflowed into Trista. It was driving her to distraction. She could only imagine how ravenous the beautiful creature truly felt; it took all her willpower not to give in, and to instead wait for the right moment to spear a good-sized fish.

* * *

A ways off, a glimmer moved below the surface. Dalkeira spotted the large fish as it swam by, unaware of any danger. Unable to control herself any longer, the dragon leaped into the air, beating her wings wildly. Startled by the shadow, several fish shot away in different directions, and Dalkeira's intended prey darted toward the deeper water between the rocks near Trista.

Dalkeira folded her wings tightly around her sleek body and dove head-first into the water, neck stretched forward, mouth wide open to reveal rows of sharp teeth. She hit the water right on top of the large fish. Two of the dragon's eye membranes closed in response, to protect her eyes, but she could still see just fine.

As she crashed into the water, Dalkeira expected to feel the fish firmly between her jaws, but her target easily dodged her attack with a quick flip of its tail. The fish moved with such force that it broke through the surface of the water and leaped straight up into the air.

As Dalkeira came back up in a turmoil of water, she looked wildly around for her missed prey. Lightning-fast Trista had thrust her spear, impaling the fish just behind its head. She moved onto the rock as the fish thrashed futilely, trying to free itself.

Before Trista could speak, the dragon spotted another fish and dove back under to chase it.

* * *

Trista kept a firm grip on the one she had speared, watching as Dalkeira moved around. Waving her body left and right, the small dragon used her tail to propel herself through the water, sometimes using her claws to quickly move direction as she tried to catch up with the fish.

After two or three attempts, Trista decided it was enough for now. There might not be soldiers here now, but that did not mean they could not appear at any time and hear the splashes the dragon was making.

"I've got your fish right here, little hunter. Why not come and eat it while I focus on catching more?" said Trista after the small dragon finally surfaced for air.

Dalkeira quickly swam over and launched herself out of the water. As she reached the fish, she sank her front claws into it so Trista could pull out her spear. Looking at the dragon's claws, Trista noticed they were webbed.

No wonder she can move so swiftly through the water! thought Trista, impressed.

Dripping wet, Dalkeira did not waste another moment. Sinking her teeth into its head, she pinned the half-dead fish down with her claws and pulled, twisting her neck back and forth. After several attempts, the head tore free, after which Dalkeira threw it up in the air and swallowed it whole.

Seeing the speed with which Dalkeira was eating, Trista quickly returned to the water. She got lucky; another fat fish was passing by and she was able to spear it quickly. Just as Dalkeira finished her first meal ever, Trista offered her the second fish. It was still thrashing wildly. The small dragon, overjoyed at having another thing to sink her teeth into, went straight in for the kill.

After the second fish, the worst of Dalkeira's hunger was stilled, allowing Trista a little more time to spear the next. Without hunger dominating her behavior, Dalkeira returned to Trista's side to observe the woman's fishing techniques, this time remaining perfectly still so as not to scare away their prey.

"How do you know where the fish are in the water?" Dalkeira asked after Trista successfully speared several smaller ones. *"From here, it looks like you should miss every time, but still the fish end up on your spear. Do you look at the sparkles as well?"*

"*Sparkles? You mean the sunlight hitting the water's surface?*" said Trista as she raised her spear again.

"*No, the light from the sky just makes the sparkles move faster. They are deeper. Moving back and forth with the waves. The sparkles flow around the fish as they swim. They are very small, but there are a lot of them. You should be able to see them easily.*"

Dalkeira looked up at the sky.

"*They are in the air too, although far less.*"

"I'm sorry. I don't understand what you mean," said Trista out loud, shaking her head. "I know the light bends when it hits the water. The fish is actually at a slightly different spot than it looks from up here. So I compensate for that when I aim my spear, but I don't see any sparkles. Sorry."

"*Strange,*" declared Dalkeira. "*They are clearly there. I would have expected you to see them as well.*"

Trista's let her gaze glide across the water, scanning for any sign of ships. She thought she saw a few of them on the horizon, but it was hard to tell. It made her uncomfortable not knowing where the soldiers were. Were they still on the island or had they sailed on? Would more of them come?

"*This is taking too long. We're too much in the open like this,*" she expressed her concerns. "*It would go a lot faster if we had a net; every time I catch a fish, it scares away the others and I have to wait for them to come back. If we can catch a couple more we should have enough for our dinner as well.*"

She checked over her shoulder to see where Decan was. Her heart skipped a beat when he was nowhere to be seen. She was about to yell his name when she saw something move behind one of the more crooked stone slabs. As Decan got back to his feet again, Trista saw him put another small crab in his improvised bag.

"Decan, don't go out too far. We'll be heading for higher ground soon," she called as loud as she dared.

In the meantime, Dalkeira was studying the ground intensely. She followed the small coves of water and seemed to have an interest in the flow of the waves coming and going.

"*I have an idea,*" she spoke inside Trista's head. Trista watched Dalkeira walk along the shoreline and dive straight into the water. As the small dragon moved further away from them, into open water, Trista's stomach gave a nervous tingle.

"*What are you doing?*"

The ocean could be a very dangerous place for those too inexperienced to recognize the signs. But Dalkeira did not answer straight away; she simply stopped and turned toward Trista again.

"Get ready."

The dragon swam in a curved line parallel to the shore. Every time a little bit closer toward the entrance of the water inlet. Sometimes she shot forward; other times she deliberately slowed herself down.

Trista had no idea what she was doing at first, but as Dalkeira closed in on the shore, it quickly became clear. The sleek silver fish were shooting back and forth below the surface of the water; Dalkeira was doing her best to cut off their escape route, herding them toward the shallower part near the shore. A large group of fish was headed straight toward Trista, too many to count.

"Decan! Get over here, I need your help!" she called out quickly.

By the time Decan made his way over, the fish were directly below her.

"I catch, you kill," she said quickly. "Just knock their heads on a rock, as hard as you can."

With that, she thrust her spear into the water. She hardly needed to aim; every strike hit its mark. After a few fish, Trista abandoned her spear and simply used both her hands to flip the fish out of the water.

As she threw the fish to her little brother, the boy did his best to knock each of them dead to end their suffering. It quickly became clear that he could not keep up with his sister. Within moments, several fish were flopping on the rocks. Some were even lucky enough to make their way back into the water—only to be met by Dalkeira's waiting jaws. The newly hatched dragon took great pleasure in using the opportunity to eat her fill.

The abundance of food was attracting seagulls, and although they were careful not to come too close to Dalkeira, the insolent birds had no trouble trying to steal the fish away from Decan.

Looking up, Trista decided to call it quits. The sudden increase of birds in the air would draw too much attention to them—especially birds as loud as these.

"That's it. We're done," said Trista, as Dalkeira surfaced. "That was a wonderful idea, my dear. Thank you. We've got plenty to eat for now. Taking more would be wasteful, and the water goddess teaches us to never take more than we need."

Dalkeira pulled herself from the water with a satisfied look in her eye. Out of instinct, she snapped her jaws around a fish just about to fall back in the ocean and swallowed it. She looked too full to fly. Her round stomach swiveled from left to right as she plodded over to Decan. She flapped her wings, scaring off the seagulls long enough to allow Trista and Decan to gather the remaining fish.

Trista used her knife to cut off a few pieces of fresh fish. Decan eagerly took them from his sister, trying to ease his own hunger as fast as possible.

"Let's get going. I think there are ships coming, and I don't want to be surprised by soldiers who are alerted by all the birds," said Trista with her mouth still full of fish.

She slung the sack—heavy with fish, cockles and crabs—over her shoulder.

"But where do we go?" Decan asked. "The village is gone. Our house is gone. Mother and Father… gone."

"We'll figure it out. Let's find high ground first; we'll need to keep watch through the night, and our fire should stay out of sight if we want to prepare our dinner."

Dalkeira dove back into the water then jumped back out again.

"And afterward, perhaps you can help me clean some of these fish guts from my skin? I feel unclean. After all, I did do all the work," said Dalkeira, with what Trista expected was meant to be an innocent look on her face.

Later that night, Trista looked at her little brother. Decan lay curled up beside the fire in the inland cove they had travelled to that afternoon. He had cried softly while falling asleep, but she was glad to see the swelling in his face had gone down a bit.

They kept the fire deliberately small, but had at least been able to grill the fish they had caught. Dalkeira had eaten another bellyful, while Trista and Decan had supplemented the fish with the cockles and crabs.

The previous night's rain had left a small puddle of water in the corner of the cove. It tasted like mud, but at least looked free from any insect larvae. Trista had used some of the water to wash Dalkeira from head to tail. Pleased with the fact she was properly clean again, the dragon now also lay curled up near the fire. She slept a little closer to the fire than Trista would have thought comfortable, but Dalkeira did not seem to mind the heat of the flames at all.

Trista looked around and listened to the sounds carried by the wind. They were a good half-day's walk from the village, but she had seen multiple signs of the soldiers' forces roaming about the island. Fortunately, they had not run into any patrols yet, but it was clear they could not stay here lest they run the risk of being found by the invading force.

A few quick steps took Trista up the rock formation they had taken shelter near. Her legs objected slightly, still recovering from all the running and climbing. It was a very clear night, with the full moon providing plenty of light to look around.

At least we don't have to worry about rain.

Standing atop the rock formation, she had a clear view of the north-east side of the island. The smoke was barely visible now, but lights on the horizon showed her that the soldiers were still camped nearby on the plains outside their village. She wondered if Hali had managed to escape.

She turned around and surveyed the rest of the island. Of the five settlements, their village was one of the smaller ones. It was not hard to pinpoint where the others were from her viewing point; in each direction was a lingering column of smoke. It looked as though the soldiers had invaded every settlement at once.

They're probably plundering the fields to get the early summer crops… I wonder if any other villagers got away.

In the distance, Trista saw a small herd of animals grazing on the low vegetation as though nothing out of the ordinary had happened.

Wild donkeys, she guessed.

The animals strolled lazily from one patch of grass to another, occasionally nibbling on a low bush, eating the fresh leaves from between the long, spiky thorns. In the midst of all the nerve-racking events of the past two days, the scene of casually strolling donkeys left Trista feeling oddly serene, as if everything that had happened was just a bad dream.

But then she saw the flying ships gliding through the air. Most were far beyond the island's reef, but one was passing directly above the village and the soldiers' encampment. The dark shape slid across the sky, heading toward the east. This was no dream, but a nightmare.

She was startled by the sound of scraping rock behind her. Instantly, she spun around on the balls of her feet, fists clenched ready to hit whatever was sneaking up on her.

Two rectangular pupils stared directly at her.

"Behhh."

The goat stood some feet away on one of the rock boulders. It looked somehow happy to see her.

"Where did you come from?" asked Trista, slowly approaching the animal. The rope around its neck suggested it had been someone's property. "Did you escape from the soldiers, too?"

With an open hand, Trista reached for the goat's head. She carefully scratched it behind the ear.

"It's alright, I'm not going to hurt you."

Slowly, she took the rope. Then she patiently encouraged the goat to follow her. The animal was actually better than Trista at traversing the rocks; Trista's feet slipped multiple times, while the goat followed her down almost casually.

As they turned into the small rock cove, the goat pulled back on the rope. The fire, along with the scent of an unknown creature, made it too nervous to continue.

"It's alright. Nothing is going to hurt you."

Keeping the fire between the goat and Dalkeira, Trista tied the rope to some small, dried-up trees at the base of the rocks. Trista sat down for a moment, fully intending to go back up on the rocks once she had had a moment to rest. But her head felt heavy from the long, intensive day, and before she realized it, sleep had invaded her. Trista nodded off into a restless dream.

CHAPTER FOUR

Flight

Land ahoy!"

Marek dropped down from the balloon at a dangerous speed, both feet landing on the deck with a solid *thump*. Excited, he pointed toward the bow of their unusual transportation.

"Land! I can see land!"

Galirras, snoozing in the afternoon sun, lifted his head.

"*What is it?*" the dragon asked Raylan, not yet fully awake.

Raylan looked past the bow. Dark lines shaped the horizon.

"*Aeterra. We're almost home.*"

That got Galirras' attention. Raylan knew the dragon had wondered about Aeterra since first hearing Raylan and the others speak of it. The cities, fields, forests, and of course the people—he was dying to see everything for himself.

Raylan did not entirely share his enthusiasm. It was great to be back home, but they had bad news in tow. They needed to inform the king and council of their mission, the expected invasion… and Raylan would have to face his father and tell him about the loss of his brother.

"*It was not your fault,*" spoke Galirras' voice in Raylan's head, sensing his sadness.

Raylan put a hand on his friend's scaled neck.

"*I know,*" said Raylan without much conviction.

Galirras' large, scaled head drooped. The tasks at hand would often keep Raylan busy and, for the most part, Galirras and the others saw a normal, happy person walking around the ship. But then a sound or remark would remind Raylan of his brother and immediately his spirit would dampen. Galirras let out a rumbling sigh, but did not press Raylan any further about the guilt he felt. Raylan was grateful; another discussion would not go any differently from the previous twenty.

As Marek ran up to them, the dragon directed his attention once more toward the far horizon.

"Can you see it, Galirras?" asked Marek breathlessly.

"I think I see a village," said Galirras.

"Really? Where?" Marek held a hand above his eyes against the setting sun. "I can't see a thing. How can you see that far with the sun in your eyes?"

Galirras' three vortex pupils swirled to the center of his eye and narrowed, focusing on the distance.

"Yes, definitely buildings, and some smaller boats," said the dragon.

"Don't bother, Marek. Galirras has exceptional eyesight. We won't see anything that specific for a while. Not until we get closer, at least," said Raylan, absently stroking Galirras' neck.

"Raylan, is that Azurna? The city you were telling me about?" asked the dragon.

"Not likely. If it's anything like the harbors I've seen, Azurna is much bigger than a simple village. If we're lucky, we won't have to follow the coast for long before we get there. It should be a little further to the north according to Seb and Richard."

"We'll be reaching land somewhere tonight. Should make it to Azurna before morning," said Richard, summoned to the front deck by Marek's shout. He had Xi'Lao in tow.

"Do you think we'll make it with what's left in the balloon?" asked Raylan, looking over the handrail down to the water.

"We should, as long as we don't come across any trouble," said Richard. "We're still taking shifts with the bladed wheel to get as much speed out of her as possible. But we took a real beating with that storm, and since we're out of vaporstones, we'll be cutting it close."

After the storm, they used the last remaining vaporstones to regain as much altitude as possible. Since then, the airship had gradually been descending. Without the stones to burn, they had no way to stop their decline. They would eventually hit water if they were unable to reach the Aeterran coastline in time. Which was probably alright, except none of them knew if the airship had been too badly damaged by the battle to still be seaworthy.

"Well, I plugged all the holes I could find, but the cold sea nights will still make us lose altitude as the vapors in the balloon cool. There's nothing more I can do," Marek said with a hint of frustration.

"Don't worry. You've done more than enough," assured Richard. "You kept us in the air during the storm. We wouldn't have gotten this far if it weren't for you and Galirras here. I'm glad the ship held together, but I doubt that these smaller airships were meant for such long solo journeys."

"Has transportation been arranged for when we reach the mainland? We need to get to the capital as soon as possible," said Xi'Lao.

Xi'Lao, official representative of the Tiankong Empire, was the reason their squad had been sent out to retrieve an ancient relic stolen by unknown forces. It had been a complete surprise to all of them when that relic turned out to be a dragon egg. Her nation had always thought that the egg was completely fossilized; the fact that Galirras was now amongst them proved otherwise.

"Horses should be available in Azurna, as well as a place to rest up while we send messenger birds to inform the king and council of events," Richard answered her. "We'll likely have a few days to catch our breath while we wait for their reply."

Xi'Lao looked about to object. But as she looked around at the hollow eyes and cheeks of those around her, she seemed to decide that perhaps rest was not such a bad idea after all.

"If that's the case, I would like to send a number of messages myself once we arrive," said Xi'Lao. "The birds I left at your king's court can relay my messages to the Empire."

"That shouldn't be a problem," replied Richard.

"How's the prisoner doing?" asked Raylan.

"Kept under close watch, though he's been pretty quiet lately. Ca'lek should be on duty at the moment," said Richard.

"No more attempts?"

"No, not after last week, but he has not eaten for a number of days. I think he's trying to starve himself."

The night they stole the airship, they had also taken prisoner three enemy Doskovian soldiers. It took Raylan and the others almost a full week to completely lose the pursuing ships, but when they finally did, Richard ordered the prisoners brought on deck to see if they could learn anything more about the Doskovian invasion force. Up until then, the three soldiers had barely spoken a word and Richard doubted they spoke any Terran at all.

However, Sebastian spoke the Kovian language well enough to act as interrogator, even though he was still recovering from his wounds. Galirras knew the Kovian language as well, but Raylan had chosen not to remind anyone of it. He would rather the dragon not be included in the interrogations. Those conversations were likely to turn gritty. It was a dark side of humans, one Raylan preferred to keep away from the dragon if possible.

Raylan shook his head, remembering what had happened.

"I still can't fathom how easily they forfeited their lives. Anything to prevent the extraction of information, I guess," said Raylan.

"It was a rookie mistake. I should have known better," Richard berated himself.

"You couldn't have known. It all happened in the blink of an eye," said Raylan. "No one in their right mind would expect they'd charge to the side and jump to their deaths."

"Well, if not for Harwin, it would have been a complete disaster," said Richard.

The veteran of their group, Harwin had thrown the shield he was cleaning into the legs of the last enemy soldier. The man had stumbled and slammed into the deck, where the archers Kevhin and Rohan immediately jumped him and held him down.

With everyone in shock after their leap toward certain doom, the third Doskovian soldier was taken below deck and properly secured. He had not seen the sky since. Twice more the soldier had tried to take his own life, once by hanging himself with his hammock and another time by trying to open an artery with a rusty nail he had picked from the wall. As a result, the man's hands and feet were now continuously tied, restricting his movement as much as possible.

As soon as Sebastian recovered enough from his shoulder wound to move around, they started their questioning. But days of interrogation had led to nothing. They had only received one answer after Sebastian had repeated a single question over and over for an entire day: where were they planning to invade?

"All of it."

They were the only words of importance that the soldier had uttered, the rest only serving to expand the company's Doskovian curse vocabulary tenfold.

Those days had drained Sebastian as much as they had the soldier. Eventually, Richard ordered them to wait until they were back at the capital, Shid'el, where people with more experience could try and extract the information. Except now the prisoner refused to eat, Raylan had his doubts if the enemy soldier would make it all the way there.

"Will they have meat in Azurna? I am getting hungry," said Galirras, completely off-topic.

"You're always hungry," laughed Marek.

Raylan was surprised Marek remained so cheerful given the little amount of food they had. Then again, it was probably plenty compared to the mines he and Sebastian were held captive in. Raylan's own hunger was strengthened by the dragon's rumbling stomach.

"They will have meat, I promise," he answered Galirras. "But for now, why not go and catch some fish? It will be a while before we reach Azurna, and we could use some dinner."

Galirras did not look happy about that.

"Fish again? I am not fond of the taste… or the water they swim in, for that matter. You know, I could fly ahead and see what I can find behind those cliffs on the horizon," said Galirras, hopeful.

"Not a chance, but nice try," said Raylan with a small smile. "I can already see the chaos and mayhem if someone were to spot you without the proper introduction. But tell you what, maybe you can spot a seal sunbathing on one of the rocks down there."

It had been almost three weeks since they made off with the small scouting airship. There had been plenty of provisions on board when they left. But the enemy, who had been preparing for an invasion, did not take into account a dragon—one that was still growing, at that—as part of the crew.

All the dried meat had been gone in a matter of days as Galirras built up his energy and recovered from his injuries. After that, the dragon was forced to look for his own food if he wanted anything else to eat besides hard biscuits and a small amount of dried fruit that he did not like the taste of.

Feeling guilty about his appetite, Galirras took it on himself to find food for everyone. And given the fact he had fully enjoyed catching the beautifully colored fish in the lake near the hot springs during their hasty travels across the Dark Continent, he had set out to catch some fish. But the ocean was completely different from the calm waters of the lake. His near-drowning experience on the Doskovian coast a few weeks before had scared the hell out of Raylan and made Galirras very wary of the deep, black ocean water.

Being a bit too careful, he had spent his entire first day looking for fish in the dark water, only to be disappointed time and time again. Whenever he thought he had finally located some, it turned out to be a branch or seaweed floating on the surface. Later, when he returned to the airship, both Raylan and Sebastian had told him all they knew about spotting schools of fish in the great wide ocean; from noticing birds and whales to looking around the area where the water changed colors because the changing depth.

The next day, Galirras had set out again, using his newly acquired knowledge to try and catch a meal. The information paid off as the dragon successfully located a school of strange fish which actually jumped out of the water toward him as he made his dive. They were not all that tasty, he thought, but he was able to eat his fill over the course of the morning. Late that afternoon he went out again and caught a fine meal for the squad.

Much like Galirras' first days of hunting on land, his methods improved every time he went out. Raylan had watched him try out different tactics, even using his windblast to try and stun some of the larger fish. Yet it remained difficult to catch enough to satisfy everyone's hunger, and it was not long until the salty taste of the water and his not-so-daily meal began to sit ill with him.

One day, they were lucky enough to spot a colony of seals, which was unusual given that they were so far out to sea. Unfortunately, they had no way to preserve the food, so Galirras only caught enough for them to eat lest the meat rot away unused.

"Even if we're hungry, it would be wasteful to take more than we can use," Raylan had said.

At the time, having just stuffed himself with numerous seals, Galirras could not have agreed more. Now, though, he wondered if he might not prefer the decaying flesh of a seal above that of the salty taste of fish. Contrary to what Raylan told him, he was fairly convinced he would not get sick from it… much.

As Galirras consumed more and more saltwater fish, his scales turned dull with the excess salt secreted by his skin. Raylan had noticed it first, feeling grains of salt roll beneath his hand when he ran it along the dragon's skin. It made the skin less flexible and dry. As a result, Galirras was plagued by tiny itches all over his body, often in places he could not reach himself. Raylan often saw the dragon's skin twitch, but Galirras assured him it did not bother him much.

Now, after two and a half weeks of eating fish or almost nothing at all, Galirras could not wait to sink his teeth into a nice, warm, bloody deer. He walked to the edge of the deck and looked down to the ocean. There did not seem to be any seal colonies here in the vicinity. He let out a rumbling sigh.

"I will see what I can do, but it does not look promising." He pushed off and let himself fall forward over the handrail. After dropping a good distance to get clear of the airship, he snapped open his wings and pushed himself up with a combination of his wings and wind power. He circled back around the airship once—a custom he had taught himself after the storm to check all was in order with the ship—before he stooped forward and took a nosedive toward the water.

Raylan followed his flight and saw him level off above the water, starting his first attempt to catch a few fish. Having no immediate chores, he observed the dragon's movements for a while.

As the others got back to their duties, Xi'Lao lingered too, silently studying Galirras' movements for herself. As the last remaining keeper of the dragon archive, she took every opportunity to study or question Galirras, hoping to collect information that had been lost over the centuries. Normally, she was quite enthusiastic about it. Now she was as quiet as Raylan as they stood side by side. He watched her from the corner of his eye, uncertain what to say. Her gaze frequently moved toward the distant horizon, her thoughts a thousand miles away. Perhaps she thought of home, but Raylan suspected she mourned the loss of Gavin, his brother.

Raylan stepped back from the edge and turned toward her. Words were racing in his head, but all of them got stuck in his throat. Xi'Lao and his brother had gotten very close during their escape from the Doskovian army. Raylan's mouth curled briefly into a sad smile, remembering how he had teased Gavin the night he stumbled across them in one of the hot springs. But his brother was gone now, and he was not the only one who felt that emptiness.

Gavin had been their commander from the beginning, leading them across continents on a long shot to locate the stolen relic and retrieve it for the Empire. His leadership and decisions had prevented capture time and time again. And perhaps if Gavin had not listened to Raylan on the night of their escape, he might still have been with them now. Instead, Raylan and the others had witnessed the enemy High General Corza Setra plunge a dagger into Gavin's chest. Both Raylan and Galirras had been powerless to stop it from happening.

As the official second-in-command, Richard had been forced to step up and take over the leadership position. He was doing a competent job, but Raylan felt the group's solidarity wavering without his brother keeping them together.

Only because of Gavin had Xi'Lao slowly opened up to the group and truly become one of them. Now, after that regretful night, she had grown cold and distant again. It was like she had become an empty shell, completely closed off and drained of emotion. Raylan knew how that was; he too had a hard time feeling anything. If not for Galirras, he would probably have given in to despair that night. It made him wonder who Xi'Lao had to turn to.

Raylan noticed Xi'Lao's knuckles whiten on the handrail as the ship swayed gently in the wind. The airship's movements were not sitting well with her. Raylan had seen her reach for a bucket or hang over the rail numerous times already. She was probably glad to soon be setting foot on solid ground again.

Xi'Lao stared straight ahead, ignoring him as he sought the words to speak. At first, Raylan had been certain she blamed him for the loss of her lover, as he blamed himself. But she was painfully honest that night about how she felt.

Gavin had always made his own decisions and it was his own actions that led to disaster. And Raylan was dead wrong if he thought that she would allow his self-blame and despair to tarnish Gavin's memory and sacrifice.

They had not spoken much since, and as more days passed, the more awkward he felt about the silence between them. So there he stood, trying to form a sentence that would leave his throat unhindered by shame and guilt.

But Xi'Lao pushed away from the rail and abruptly turned her back on him. She walked to the lower deck and picked up a quill to resume her notes, leaving Raylan pondering on how to fix things between them.

Preoccupied, he wandered around the ship, where he came across Sebastian in the cargo hold. The bearded former slave was crouching next to the toppled ghol'm. They tried to push two of them out of the hold the night of their escape. The first had fallen out as intended; this one, however, had slammed into the woodwork and landed face down on the floor. Too heavy to roll it over in the heat of battle, they had let it be.

"We're getting close to Azurna," announced Raylan.

Sebastian did not react.

"It's hard to believe they can actually move when you see them like this," said Raylan, looking at the fallen statue.

"Harder to forget once you do," replied Sebastian.

"What are you doing down here?"

"Nothing much. Reminiscing. It's been a while since I last saw one of them… before the harbor, I mean."

"The night you all escaped from the mines?" said Raylan.

Sebastian gave a short nod.

"I saw soldiers and slaves torn in half that night. Some were beaten to death, or simply walked over. It wasn't pretty."

"What happened to the ghol'ms that helped you escape?" asked Raylan.

The riots had succeeded because a small group of slaves had managed to take control of a few stone warrior ghol'ms. Sebastian had been amongst them. The complete chaos that followed allowed many slaves to escape the mines, which had been their prison for a long time.

"We used them as a distraction. To delay the Doskovian forces while we tried to get away through the forest. We kept one close for a number of nights, but in the end ordered it to walk off and create a fake trail to throw off the last of our pursuers." Sebastian idly ran his fingers along the roughly-shaped stone man.

"Isn't it strange?"

"What?" said Sebastian.

"To owe your life to something so dark, so… evil."

"The ghol'ms aren't evil. The ones who created them for power, those bastards who command these unnatural things, they're the real evil! For us, it could just as well have been an angel in white that night… if only no one had to die for it."

A knot formed in Raylan's stomach. Each and every one of the ghol'ms was activated by a sacrificial scroll. While staying in the treetop village, which Sebastian and the other escaped slaves had painstakingly built over multiple years, Raylan and the others had learned this horrible truth: the truth that for every walking ghol'm, a person—a child—an infant had been sacrificed, their life force stored in one of those unholy scrolls, ready to be used to awaken the ghol'm when needed. Raylan had seen hundreds of ghol'ms that night in the harbor, but according to Sebastian the number produced in the mines was actually in the thousands.

"Was Marek still with you at the time?" asked Raylan.

Sebastian looked up at him.

"You said he was with you in the mines, right?" said Raylan.

"Yes, you're right. I don't know precisely when we lost track of each other. During those days, he was never far from my side… but there was so much chaos that day."

"I was surprised how young he actually is. I think he's even younger than Peadar."

Peadar had been the youngest of their group. His addition to the squad was not so much for additional fighting power but because of his knowledge of animals. The boy's interest in birds had surfaced while practicing under the royal animal healer at the royal court, after which he had been assigned to take care of the messenger birds their group carried. Peadar's interest in Galirras had been apparent from the moment the dragon came into the world, and whenever Galirras sustained any injuries the eager lad had stepped forward to assist in their healing.

Raylan was well aware that Galirras would not be flying today if not for Peadar. The young bird keeper had helped readjust the dragon's dislocated wing on the day of his hatching. Even Xi'Lao had complimented Peadar on his skill and quick ability to learn.

"He probably is younger. Marek was just a water rat back then," said Sebastian.

Raylan knew the term well. He had seen his share of water rats during his years sailing. Orphaned boys with nowhere else to go. Stowaways on the ship searching for a better place, or adventure. Some of the boys were allowed to stay on board, if they worked hard enough and did not get in the way. After all, they did not eat much.

"It must have been his second or third voyage on board our ship. At the time my father said Marek was probably around eight, although even Marek himself was never sure. I think my father kept him around so I'd have company."

Sebastian's face broke out in a nostalgic grin.

"He loved to do all kinds of theatrics to make the crew laugh. He climbed the ropes with a fearlessness you've never seen, messing about, hanging upside down.

"One time, he even had my father scramble for the railing. He'd warned Marek multiple times already that day not to play hopscotch on the rail." Sebastian let out a laugh. "'It will be your own fault if you fall over. And you'd better not expect me to turn this ship around to come pick your sorry ass out of the water again, you hear me?'" Sebastian said in a deep voice, imitating that of his old man. "But when my father saw him go over the side, he rushed to the rail in earnest—only to find the boy dangling there, grinning up at him. We all had a good laugh about it, but my father was so furious he gave Marek three weeks of latrine duty."

"Sounds like he didn't take his work very seriously," said Raylan.

"Not at all! He worked like the best of us, else my father would never have let him stay on board. But even down in the mines he seemed to be able to keep going and going. What he lacked in strength, being a kid and all, he made up for in stamina. Which is probably what saved him from being dragged off by the guards. He never lost that fun streak, even if the guards beat him for it. I think it was his way of dealing with all the misery around him, to keep himself going."

"And so he became your best friend?"

"We were certainly close. I helped him out at times, took the heat off him when the guards were bullying him. It helped having each other around. It reminded us of better times, before those dark days. His enthusiasm and curiosity got him in trouble a lot, though. The guards had it in for him the more he made people laugh. Eventually, he ended up under Old Tom's wing as an assistant of sorts. But that was near the very end. Old Tom once said they were ordered to make strange things of metal, leather and wood."

"Old Tom? The tinkerer?"

"Yeah. You know the assistant I mentioned back at the treetop village? That was Marek. Come to think of it, that's probably why he was able to figure out this airship so easily. He's used to putting strange pieces together and making things from scratch. Old Tom spoke often of how Marek was a natural at those things. When something really fascinates him, Marek gets this intense look, and will stop at nothing to understand how it all fits together," said Sebastian, rubbing his shoulder.

"How's it healing?" asked Raylan, nodding at his friend's shoulder.

"It's fine. A bit stiff." Sebastian waved off Raylan's concern. "Xi'Lao says the wound is healing nicely."

The bearded man fell quiet for a moment, as if to gather his thoughts.

"I'm sorry your brother had to pay for my stupidity. If I had just dodged that damn hook... I know there's nothing I can do about it now, but I owe you my life for jumping after me. I—I just want you to know how sorry I am about Gavin."

The apology took Raylan by surprise. He had been glad to get his mind distracted for a moment. Now his sense of loss came rushing back.

"You're not to blame," he said in a soft voice.

"I know that. But neither are you. You shouldn't carry all that guilt by yourself. I can see how heavy it weighs on your shoulders. We all see it. But it wasn't you, *or* me. It just happened. And it hurts... a lot. But we have to accept it. And after a while it will hurt a little less and you'll be able to move past it a little easier."

The remark did not sit well with Raylan; Sebastian saw it in his friend's face.

"I'm not saying to forget him. I mean, I would punch anyone who told me to forget my father, no matter how much it hurts to think of him. All I'm saying is—is that if you'd like to talk, I'm here for you."

"No... no, I understand. Thanks," was all Raylan could bring himself to say before turning around and heading back up to the deck.

Later, Raylan found himself back in the company of his friend. He was staring across the ocean below, thinking about Sebastian's words when the former slave joined him. Sebastian did not mention their afternoon conversation. He simply stood beside Raylan, taking in the view. It was somewhat comforting to not be alone, yet not have to talk, even though his friend's offer was still there.

Together, they watched the stars come out. The ship was closing in on the mainland's cliffs, but Richard had ordered them to veer north to avoid stirring panic in the small fishing village that Galirras spotted earlier. It would still take them most of the night to reach Azurna.

"Looking forward to having both legs back on the ground again?" Richard joined them at the handrail.

"I don't mind being in the air. It's not so different from being at sea," said Raylan.

"*Apart from the fact that if you fall overboard from here, you will not be able to swim back to the ship,*" remarked Galirras, who was semi-napping behind them on the deck.

"*I don't think there would be much swimming at all. The fall would likely kill a person. Maybe even a dragon,*" replied Raylan in his head.

"*Good thing I can fly, then,*" rumbled Galirras, pleased with himself.

"Well, I for one can't wait until my feet are on Aeterran soil again," said Sebastian, unaware of the silent conversation between Raylan and Galirras.

"Don't worry, we'll be there soon," assured Richard. "But before we arrive, I want to talk to both of you."

"About what?" said Sebastian.

"A matter of sensitivity," said Richard. "I've already informed the others, but I think it best if we don't mention the invasion force when we arrive in Azurna."

Raylan and Sebastian looked at him in disbelief.

"What? Why not?" they said simultaneously.

"We haven't seen a Doskovian ship for over a week and a half. We've got no idea where their army will land. Telling anyone about it without first informing the king and High Council in Shid'el will only create panic. We need to follow the chain of command," said Richard.

"But if they do end up following us, the people in Azurna won't stand a chance! They need to get ready now! Even if they're fully prepared it will be a near impossible battle against the ghol'ms and airships!" said Sebastian.

"If we're not going to warn them, why not keep going and ignore Azurna completely?" said Raylan. The conversation made him uneasy, like he was being pushed along a road that he was not certain about wanting to follow. The danger they had seen was very real, even if they did not know precisely where the Stone King's army were planning to invade, and Raylan had decided for himself to follow his brother's last request and tell the people at home about the oncoming danger. But now they were forbidden to say anything about it?

Raylan had planned to deliver news of the invasion as soon as possible, giving the people of Azurna at least a chance against the dark tidal wave planning to swallow them all. After that he could focus on his other main priority: keeping Galirras safe. If possible, Raylan and Galirras would stay far away from the fighting, so in that aspect he would not mind going straight to Shid'el. Still, it did not feel right to withhold such important information.

"I've thought about that too, but we need to resupply," said Richard. "This ship isn't going to take us much further, which is why we need horses. We can get them in Azurna, which was Gavin's plan from the start."

"And while we take their food and use their horses, you'd rather keep your mouth shut than tell anyone about the danger approaching? You're gambling with all their lives," said Sebastian bluntly. "They deserve a chance to defend themselves."

"Look, I can see you don't agree with it, but our priority is to tell the High Council back in Shid'el about the danger that's coming," said Richard. "There's no way a single city can stop this invasion force. We're going to need the entire kingdom, and even that may not be enough. Who knows; perhaps the High Council would rather abandon the city to prevent the unnecessary loss of its soldiers."

"What if they don't believe us?" said Sebastian. "Do we just abandon these people?"

"Why wouldn't they believe us?" Raylan asked his friend, confused. "We've got a dragon, a ghol'm, even a flying ship."

"No, Sebastian has a valid point, one that I've also considered. We might have a dragon with us, but the ghol'm is just a statue without a scroll, and we'll never be able to drag the ship to Shid'el to show it. Living statues? Flying ships that drop fireballs? It's hard enough to believe it ourselves and we saw it with our own eyes," said Richard. "But I follow the chain of command. We wait for orders from the capital."

"But by then it might be too late!" said Sebastian. Raylan saw his friend's burn mark flush with anger. "You do what you like," the former slave continued. "I'm not part of your squad. You can't tell me what or what not to do. People have a right to know as soon as we land."

"You're right. I can't order you not to say anything, but I could let them detain you in Azurna. I'd rather not, as I believe we wouldn't have escaped that continent without your help, but if you leave me no choice, then I will," said Richard.

Raylan stared at his squad leader. "You can't mean that."

"Look, please… just keep it to yourselves until we hear back from the High Council. It should only take a few days using the fastest birds," said Richard.

Sebastian did not say anything more and stormed off to the mid deck. Raylan looked at Richard blankly. His commander waited for Raylan to say something, but when no reply came, he let out a sigh.

"Fine. Just know I expect you to follow orders, even if you don't agree with them," said Richard, and with that he too left Raylan to ponder by himself.

"You do not agree?" Galirras stretched lazily as he woke from his nap on the deck.

"You were listening?"

"It is hard not to listen when someone is yelling next to you."

Raylan put his hand on Galirras' head, scratching the dragon above his eye.

"I can't seem to decide if Richard is unfit to lead our group, or if I resist him because he's not Gavin. Don't get me wrong; he's a good man, and I would gladly have him by my side in a battle, but it looks like he doesn't want to make any decisions by himself. Perhaps it's just me, but I feel we're being pushed forward down a road that we can't step off."

The dragon thought about it for a while.

"The wind has a nice feel to it tonight," said Galirras.

The smooth flow of air passed Raylan's cheeks.

"It's the warmth of summer," he thought absentmindedly.

"Maybe… but it feels like more. It feels promising. Inviting. Playful. Perhaps the road is not the problem. Perhaps you just need a change of perspective." The dragon's eye twirled around to regard Raylan. *"Come and fly with me!"*

Raylan stared at Galirras.

"Fly with you?" he said out loud.

"Yes! It feels amazing to fly! It might clear your head. Allow you to see things differently."

Galirras swung his head close to Raylan's face, his three pupils shifting expectantly back and forth, glittering with golden sparkles.

"What about your injuries?"

"My injuries are fine. Most have completely healed already, and none bother me when flying," said Galirras, demonstrating by stretching his wings.

While Raylan had originally been curious about the possibility of flying with Galirras, the thought had not occurred to him once in the last few weeks on the airship. When Galirras plucked him from the sky after he jumped from a cliff to escape his pursuers, it had felt like a one-time act of necessity to save his life. Raylan was used to being on the ground, or in this case on deck, whenever Galirras took to the air and sheared through the sky.

But Galirras had kept on growing during their ocean crossing, and Raylan figured he would have no problem carrying him through the air.

"But how? You don't want to carry me again, do you? Your claws aren't the softest, you know."

Galirras took a moment to think.

"No, I suppose not. Why not climb on my back, below my neck? That will be the most stable, and you will not be in the way of my wings, either."

Raylan looked back at the others on the lower deck. Most were still enjoying the huge fish Galirras had managed to bring aboard. This new prey almost had a meat flavor, enough so that Galirras had taken part of his kill to still his immediate hunger. The rest was then prepared as a tasty fish stew.

The scent of the stew was carried over by the wind, the crew sat gathered around the hot pot that Galen had brought up on deck. Raylan saw Sebastian separate himself from the group, probably because he did not want to talk to Richard any more. None were taking any notice of Raylan and Galirras. Raylan looked at the dragon and made up his mind.

"Let's do it," said Raylan.

Galirras' eyes swirled with excitement as he quickly lowered himself to allow Raylan to climb on his back. One step on Galirras' front leg, another on the shoulder, and then Raylan sat at the base of the dragon's neck. As he tried to get a feel for the unfamiliar seat, Galirras rose and leaned over the handrail.

Raylan's stomach lurched as the deck of the airship disappeared, replaced by the drop toward the ocean waters below.

"Wait, where am I supposed to hold on—"

The words got stuck in his throat as his stomach flew upward, pushing all the air out of his lungs. Galirras had pushed off and was now headed straight for the dark water. Reflexively, Raylan threw his arms around Galirras' neck, feeling the muscles move beneath the rough hide. The dragon's scales scratched his skin, but the warmth of Galirras' natural high temperature pleasantly warmed Raylan's arms and legs.

Without warning, Galirras snapped open his wings. The forced change in direction made Raylan's already displaced stomach rush to his toes. His chin bashed painfully against Galirras' scaled neck as the powerful beats of the dragon's wings pushed them upward again.

"Easy! Easy, *please*," said Raylan, half out loud, half in his head.

Realizing the impact of his takeoff on Raylan, Galirras quickly adjusted his powerful strokes to a more relaxed movement.

"Sorry, I was not thinking."

They leveled off as Galirras steered them into the wind. Feeling the breeze blow through his hair, Raylan forced himself to relax. As he unclamped his arms from the dragon's neck, he slowly sat up, rubbing his chin.

"That was... unexpected," said Raylan, forcing a grin.

Adrenaline rushed through his body. Now he had a moment to take it all in, the entire experience surged into him. The slow beating of Galirras' wings; the small adjustments as his winged friend used his head and body to steer; the cool night air penetrating the cloth shirt below his leather armor; and Galirras' excitement rose up from the place where Raylan's stomach was settling back in.

Slowly, a more genuine smile formed on Raylan's face. The first time Galirras had took him through the air, it had felt like limbo. The place between life and death, a place where time stood still. But this was different. He felt lighter. He let his arms hang loosely as he tilted his head back and took a deep breath. He felt... free.

Raylan let out a sigh and breathed in deeply again. He shifted his legs slightly to make it easier to clamp down with them.

"Okay, let's try this again. *Gently*," he said.

Keeping himself in place with his legs, Raylan grabbed two spikes along Galirras' neck and tried to follow Galirras' movements with his body. As the dragon tilted from left to right, Raylan took note of the specific muscles working below him. Being so close to the wings, he felt them move together or separately, changing the pressure and influence on the wind.

"*Now up.*"

Galirras responded immediately. He beat his wings strongly and his body waved from head to tail, adjusting his bearing. Raylan's stomach still rose and fell, but he was able to compensate for the movement more easily now that it was not unexpected.

With his hands on Galirras' spikes, Raylan kept pressure on them for extra support. All those weeks on horseback were slowly flowing back into his posture. And although the flying movements felt much more abrupt and powerful, some similarities surfaced between steering a horse and maneuvering together with the dragon. He straightened his back and loosened his hips to move in sync with the beating of his friend's wings.

In no time, Raylan was unthinkingly repositioning his weight as Galirras steered toward the right, hanging into the turn, only to shift it to the other side as Galirras swapped directly back into a left turn. Slightly pressing his heel into Galirras' shoulder seemed to signal the dragon to make the turn tighter. They made turn after turn, sometimes climbing slowly, sometimes diving slightly.

After a while, Raylan bent forward, tapping on Galirras' neck.

"You were right. This feels amazing," said Raylan loudly as the wind rushed past them.

"*I am glad I can let you experience this,*" replied Galirras with a satisfied rumble. "*Now, how about this? Hold on tight.*"

Galirras' back arched just before he dove forward. This time, Raylan did not fight the movement, but let himself be led by the dragon. The pressure build again as Galirras pulled upward into a steep climb. As Galirras kept going, the force of the turn pushed Raylan's body into the dragon, and suddenly, for a brief moment, he was completely weightless. Stretching his back, Raylan tilted his head and looked upward. He did not see the stars any more; instead, he was staring at the dark ocean waters, as Galirras followed through on his loop.

Raylan let out a whoop. "This is incredible!" he shouted.

"*Better than sailing, right?*" teased Galirras.

"Much better!"

By now, Raylan's legs were beginning to cramp. He shuddered involuntarily; the night wind had cooled him down significantly.

"Let's head back, my friend," said Raylan. "I think I will have some of that hot fish stew to warm up again."

As Galirras steered back toward the airship, Raylan saw every member of their squad looking at them. They looked as though they had a million and one questions to ask.

"*On second thought, maybe just one more round?*" suggested Raylan.

In some ways, a weight had been lifted from Raylan's shoulders. When he and Galirras finally returned to the airship, everyone had been waiting for them, asking all kinds of questions. Even Xi'Lao had seemed genuinely interested again, asking several questions about the link and how it felt to fly together. The unusual performance seemed to have boosted morale after their gloomy crossing of the great eastern divide.

By the time they neared Azurna, the first rays of sunlight were lighting the sky again. They had stayed clear of the coast, though the ships they had inevitably encountered so close to the harbor often held baffled crowds on deck if any were awake.

On their own ship, some were on deck looking for a suitable place to land while most of the squad was busy strapping everything down below decks. After all, they had no idea how smooth the landing would be. Raylan was in the process of tying up sails while he kept an eye on Galirras. Ca'lek was on the bow as lookout and Marek had gone back to the vapor oven, readying it for what he hoped was going to be a controlled landing.

As they rounded one of the final cliffs before the harbor city, the full details of Azurna came into view, illuminated by the rising sun. Galirras, who had been gliding next to the ship, trumpeted excitedly. A dozen ships came and went while more lay anchored off the coast. The city itself was surrounded by high walls with a few large gates that—even this early in the morning—let through a constant stream of people. Fishermen, merchants, soldier patrols, beggars trying to appeal to anyone's generosity; the city was already buzzing with activity.

"I guess it's true what they say," said Raylan to Ca'lek as they regarded the harbor.

"What's that?"

"Azurna never truly sleeps."

Located between the great eastern divide and one of the largest rivers in Aeterra, Azurna was the most important trade harbor on the eastern coast. The large inner harbor could hold twenty ships with ease, while the entrance had deliberately been kept narrow. From the ocean, one saw that parts of Azurna had been rebuilt over the centuries. Originally the main capital of the eastern kingdom that was ruled by the Thyraulos royal family, the harbor had endured numerous attacks during its existence, some more devastating than others. But the peace and prosperity Aeterra had established a hundred years ago had clearly done the harbor city well, as large areas of housing had been built outside of the original city walls. These neighborhoods stretched along the coast and toward the river, formed along the main roads that led to the city gates. From the air, the white buildings and red roof tiles made the city bright as a painting as the sun rolled its warming rays over them. Small colored flags could be seen everywhere, hanging between the buildings. They made the city look alive.

The sight of the welcoming city had Raylan considering the extent of the damage an unexpected attack would have, but before long his attention was drawn by the start of their landing attempt.

"There!" Ca'lek called out as he pointed at one of the beaches a little farther away from the city. "We can set her down there. Plenty of room, and there aren't many people or boats around."

As Ca'lek signaled their destination to Richard, Raylan ran back to his post to help adjust the sails. Richard shouted commands down the pipe leading to the vapor oven room, telling Marek to start releasing the vapor from the balloon.

Another pipe, leading directly below the stern, was used to order Galen and Kevhin down below to reverse the direction of the bladed wheel. Marek—who had the best understanding of the ship, even if he was the youngest—had figured that would at least slow them down somewhat.

Headed straight for the beach, their transportation was drawing a crowd, with people seeming to pop up out of nowhere to look at them.

"Not good!" called Ca'lek, "We're going to hit some of them if they're not careful."

Raylan thrust his head over the side to see a small group of people gathering precisely where they were aiming to hit the sand.

"Galirras! Can you try and clear our landing spot?"

He could almost feel the dragon smile.

"No problem!"

With a few powerful beats of his wings, Galirras moved himself in front of the ship, accelerating further by pushing himself forward with his wind power. It had already become second nature for Galirras to constantly manipulate the airflow around him as he flew through the sky. Literally splitting the air in front of him, he minimized his drag and, if needed, could thrust short bursts of air toward himself to either push himself to higher speed, or greatly slow himself to make a quick turn.

Now, the dragon went for speed, darting toward the beach. Coming in low, he let out a roar over the heads of the spectators, who instantly scrambled to get away from the roaring monster.

Raylan had been right; people were terrified of him, perhaps even thinking he was set on eating them. The dragon still found it strange, but Raylan had explained that people simply could not know he was an intelligent creature and not a mere beast. In this case, though, Galirras was clearly enjoying showing off to Raylan how well he was able to clear the beach for them. To top it off, he added a windblast for the fun of it. The blast sent up a spray of loose sand as the wave of air rushed over the beach.

It had the desired effect. As the airship came in low, the beach was completely cleared of any curious bystanders.

"Call it out!" yelled Ca'lek from the bow.

All pipes were opened at once as Richard shouted down them as loudly as he could.

"Brace yourselves!"

Raylan grabbed the nearest rail as the ground suddenly rushed toward them for the last few feet. With a loud crack and heavy thump, the ship touched land for the first time in weeks. A fountain of sand was flung upward as the ship's bow dug into the beach. The sudden decrease in speed threw everyone forward, including Raylan, who twisted around the point he had securely grabbed, slamming his back into the rail.

A loud crash came from the cargo deck as the dormant ghol'm rammed through the hinges of the wooden cargo door and ground to a halt, half buried in the deep, loose sand. The airship shook and rattled as it tore across the ground, leaving a deep groove behind it. But the sand was acting too much like water, moving away from the hull as the airship easily cut through the sea of loose sand.

"We're still going too fast!" yelled Raylan.

Richard had steered the ship as parallel to the line of trees as possible, but it had not been enough, and the forest was rapidly coming closer.

Galirras swooped in front of the airship, hovering above the trees. Furiously beating his wings, he used his power to push the moving air toward the ship in an attempt to slow it down.

Raylan's eyes, tearing from the force of the dragon's wind, were locked on the trees in their path. The airship's speed was decreasing, but its mass did not easily surrender to the forces that were trying to stop it from moving. As the ship slid through the sand, the upward-sloping ground slowed it further. The crew flinched at the loud cracks of saplings snapping like twigs as the airship burrowed itself into the first line of trees. With this added resistance, it finally admitted defeat and ground to a halt. Slumping slightly to one side, the airship lay half buried in the forest with the stern still sticking out onto the beach.

Raylan pushed himself to his feet. Sweeping small branches from his face, he checked himself for injuries.

Seems like everything is still intact.

He saw Galirras' shadow move above the trees as the dragon circled their landing site nervously.

"Raylan, are you okay?" his winged friend asked.

"No worries. I'm still in one piece."

"Next time, you are not staying on the ship. You are much safer on my back," said the dragon, clearly worried about the rough landing.

"I appreciate your concern, little one, but we talked about this. I had to help with the sails, being one of the few real sailors on board. We can't just abandon our friends when they need our help," Raylan explained. *"But don't worry about next time. I don't expect us to fly in another airship any time soon."*

On deck, Richard and Ca'lek were back on their feet as well. As Raylan moved to the lower deck stairs, he noticed dark green smoke coming from below. The three of them rushed over to the stairs, shouting the names of their squad mates. The smoke stung Raylan's eyes.

Heavy steps followed by coughing and Peadar, Kevhin and Rohan were the first to emerge. They were followed by Xi'Lao, who was supported by Sebastian, and finally Galen, who was half dragging, half lifting a black-faced Marek up the stairs.

Marek let out a heavy cough as the others filled their lungs with fresh air.

"What happened?" asked Richard. "Is there a fire?"

"Not yet," coughed Marek, "but one of the pipes broke when I got knocked into it during the landing, and I think the vapor oven also ruptured. But I didn't see a fire yet."

"Well, let's not stay here to find out," said Richard.

"Hold on. Where's Harwin?" asked Raylan, looking around.

"He was guarding the prisoner before we touched down," said Kevhin. "He must still be down there."

Raylan pulled his shirt in front of his mouth and nose and rushed down the stairs. The dark green smoke stung his eyes and he moved as low as possible in an attempt to stay underneath it. At the bottom of the stairs, he turned toward the room where they had been holding the enemy soldier captive.

Raylan lowered himself even further to try and see below the smoke. Thankfully, with the cargo doors now completely missing, the smoke had a second way out of the lower deck.

A soft moan caught his attention. Turning the corner, Raylan stumbled over Harwin's feet.

"Harwin! Are you alright?"

The warrior sat with his back against the wall. His hands were pressed against his stomach, blood dripping through his fingers. Harwin let out a cough.

"That bastard got me good," said Harwin.

Raylan looked around. The prisoner was nowhere to be seen.

"Come—you need to get out of here," said Raylan.

Putting Harwin's arm around his neck, he pulled the warrior to his feet. Harwin grunted in pain.

"Come on. We'll go out the side doors," said Raylan.

The others were already on the ground, waiting for them near the ripped-open cargo hold. Galen and Ca'lek helped lower Harwin from the ship. Moving him a safe distance from the slumped airship, they carefully laid him down.

Xi'Lao and Peadar immediately began examining Harwin's wound.

"It's deep, but it looks like nothing vital was hit. We need to stop the bleeding as soon as possible," said Xi'Lao.

"The soldier," said Harwin, then clenched his teeth from the sharp pain Xi'Lao's checking fingers gave him.

"Save your energy; he's long gone. I found a single track of footprints going up into the forest, but they disappeared as soon as they passed the tree line," said Ca'lek.

As the group gathered around Harwin on the beach, the onlookers Galirras had scared away hovered around the edges of the forest, curious to see these people and their flying ship, but ready to flee at any time should things go awry.

"I'll get some wood for a fire. We'll need to close the wound if we are to stop the bleeding," said Peadar.

But before he could take a step, the thunder of hooves erupted from the forest. Soldiers on horseback came pouring out of the woods and along the beach. Within moments, Raylan and the others were surrounded by thirty horses and their riders. Looking at the crossbows and spears pointed at them, Raylan's hand automatically checked for his sword, only to find no such thing. Apart from Xi'Lao, who was rarely seen without one or more of her knives, no one on board the ship was carrying weapons. They had no way to defend themselves.

A dark-haired rider ordered his horse forward and slowly approached them, sword in hand. The emblem of a ship was clearly visible on his light gray chest armor. His cape was light blue with a yellow line on the border. On it, the same emblem was embroidered.

"By order of the royal seal of Shid'el and the Council of Azurna, city under the protective seal of the Thyraulos family, state your intent, or prepare to speak with our spears!"

CHAPTER FIVE

Goat

FLAMES ROSE UP around her in the dark night. The sound of swords clashing rang through the air. Trista looked around, but could not see beyond the fire.

"Decan!" she yelled above the roar of the flames. *Where is he?*

She tried to walk, but her legs felt heavy. Something grabbed her ankle, cold and boney. The corpse of Moran clung to her leg, moaning incomprehensible words. Trista pulled her leg away, but tripped backward on the scorched ground.

The decaying man pulled himself toward her, stretching his slumping mouth wide open. Raspy, choking sounds rose from his throat. Trista tried to crawl away, but the corpse lay heavy on her legs, making it almost impossible for her to move.

The corpse pulled itself closer and closer. Its rotten face pushed into Trista's clothes, then it went still. Trista dared not move, but nothing happened. She stretched out a trembling arm. Perhaps she could push it off now. But then its hollow-eyed face rose from her lap and stared straight at her. It opened its mouth a final time and screamed.

"Behhh!"

The image of Moran distorted further with every bleat that came from his mouth. Trista groaned, opening her eyes. The sight of the decomposing fisherman dissolved back into the far corners of her mind. Yet the bleating somehow persisted, much to the dismay of Trista's thumping head.

"*Is this my breakfast?*" said a voice in Trista's head.

It took her a moment to properly place the voice and assign it to her new companion. The goat let out another nervous bleat. Dalkeira slowly walked around it, observing the peculiar animal.

Trista abruptly sat up, now wide awake.

"What's going on?" said Decan, also woken by the ruckus.

"I'm so sorry. I fell asleep while keeping watch," said Trista quickly.

"Don't worry, Triss," said Decan, looking around. "We're all still here."

She looked at her brother, wondering if his words were wisdom or naivety.

"Can I eat this... goat, now?" said Dalkeira, who had searched the right word from an image in Trista's mind and was ready to pounce the animal.

"No, don't! She's not food," said Trista hastily.

"But it's leaking. I think it's broken. It would be wasteful not to eat it, right?"

"Leaking? Where?" said Trista, trying to understand what Dalkeira meant.

"There. On her belly," Dalkeira said. She nudged the goat's udder with her nose, almost giving the poor animal a heart attack.

"She's giving milk? She must have had a kid recently," said Trista, surprised. "I wonder what happened to it. Can you give her some space, please, Dalkeira? You're frightening her. You can't eat her, but there's some leftover fish from last night if you're hungry."

Dalkeira looked at Trista, apparently deciding if she would do as she was told. In the end, she reluctantly walked over to the leftover fish and sniffed it. With flies swarming around it, it did not look very appealing anymore. But she seemed too proud to complain. After all, she had caught most of the fish herself. She quickly gulped up the last few pieces and went straight to the water puddle to wash her muzzle.

In the meantime, Trista approached the goat, reassuring the animal she had no ill intent.

"Here, Decan, I'll show you what to do," said Trista over her shoulder. Spitting in her hand, she quickly washed the dirt off a teat. Milk already dripped out of it.

"The udder is rock-hard. She must not have been milked for days, poor girl. No wonder she was happy to see us," said Trista, "Hold your hands like this, little brother."

Trista squeezed the teat, moving from top to bottom. The goat let out a relieved bleat as the pressure in her udder slowly eased. Dalkeira returned from washing her mouth and sat down a ways from the animal, trying to see what was happening.

Decan thankfully drank the warm milk puddling in his hands. Trista sipped a few handfuls herself before moving to the next teat.

"You have to drain the udder equally or you risk creating an infection in the teat," she explained to Decan.

"How do you know this? We didn't have any goats back home."

"Granny Lulak showed me once when I helped them with the fields."

Dalkeira's head poked around Trista's shoulder.

"Do you want to try some, Dalkeira?" said Trista, holding a hand full of goat milk toward her.

Dalkeira sniffed the white liquid, but then backed away quickly, letting out a disapproving rumble.

"No, thank you. I will stick to water, if you do not mind."

"Guess she doesn't like the smell of it," laughed Decan, resulting in a somewhat offended-looking dragon. Dalkeira turned around and jumped up the rocks with a few beats of her wings. Scrambling to the top, she surveyed their surroundings, no doubt looking for something to eat.

Decan fell quiet, looking at the goat.

"Trista, what are we going to do?" he asked softly.

Trista stroked her little brother's hair. "I think we need to leave the island," she said carefully.

"But everything we know is here," said her brother. The insecurity in his voice made her ache.

"I know, but let's think of it as a big adventure. You've always wanted to get away from here, haven't you? Be a merchant, or a hunter, perhaps go to one of those big cities father used to tell stories about?"

"I want to go there," Dalkeira suddenly declared.

Trista looked confused. *"Where?"* she replied privately in her head.

"There. You call it… west."

The dragon looked to the western horizon, and although she struggled for the right words, Dalkeira sounded strangely determined.

"Why do you want to go there, Dalkeira? Do you see something?" said Trista out loud, standing up and looking at the dragon on top of the rocks.

"No. I just have a feeling that is where we need to go. Where I need to go. Something is there, far beyond what we can see. I would like you to take me there," said Dalkeira in a way that would not accept no for an answer. The dragon spread her wings and glided down toward them.

"What is it?" asked Decan, who could not hear what Dalkeira was saying to his sister.

"Dalkeira wants us to go west. Toward the mid-continent," said Trista. "And I think perhaps we should."

Trista gathered a few rocks, arranging them in a pattern before drawing lines in the sand with a twig.

"Father explained to me that east of us is the large island of Tal'Kabur. You know that name, right, Decan?"

Her little brother nodded quickly.

"The big ships that the villages trade with come from there, right?" said Decan.

Those trade ships came twice per year with all kinds of goods. Smaller ships would take fish and crops to Tal'Kabur more often, but the big trade ships were always special. People would save for many months to buy one of the many colored fabrics or metal tools that were created on the island, or came from the mid-continent through the main port of Tal'Kabur.

"Right. Father once said that Tal'Kabur is known for two things: wood and iron. Most of the island is covered in thick forests with trees that grow nowhere else in the world. They're known for their hardness and endurance, and easily reach hundreds of years of age—yet they grow fast in their younger years," Trista explained, accustomed to telling her brother interesting little facts.

Decan listened intently. The island on which they had spent their entire lives was a stark contrast to such forests. It only had low vegetation with the occasional thin, twigged tree. Neither brother nor sister had even seen a proper-sized forest.

"For the iron, they mine the purest ore in the world. They may mine less than the great kingdom of Aeterra, but it's not for nothing that throughout history, the ruler of Tal'Kabur has been deemed the King of Iron."

The combination of wood and iron had led to generations of carpenters and smiths within the island kingdom. Family secrets were passed on from generation to generation about how to craft the best steel in the world. Be it swords, arrowheads, or—in smaller quantities—farm tools, having Talkarian steel at your side meant you could not do any better in the world in that particular respect.

Decan knew some of the older boys went to work on Tal'Kabur, either loading and offloading cargo in the main harbor, Tal'Ostar, or getting jobs as lumberjacks or miners. He had always wanted to go there as a first step on his worldly travels.

"The ships that we've seen, flying or not, all come from the east and are headed toward the west," continued Trista.

Decan quickly caught on.

"They're coming from Tal'Kabur?"

"Maybe," she said. "But I don't think the port of Tal'Ostar could house that many ships, or soldiers. Father said that at any time, only fifteen ships would be anchored there... and these soldiers don't look Talkarian."

"*How do you know?*" asked Dalkeira, interrupting her thought process.

"Talkarian soldiers are known for fighting with two swords. One of the boys from the village worked a few seasons in the harbor. He told me stories about how King Baltor's great-grandfather held a tournament to determine the best fighter, many years ago. The winner, one of the local lumberjacks, had come up with this unusual style of fighting with two swords—although some say it was actually two axes," said Trista. "Anyway, after the tournament it was announced that from that day on the style would be known as the official Talkarian double style. There are still shield-bearers and archers, but the majority, and certainly the highest rank, of soldiers are all double sword style fighters."

"I haven't seen any soldiers fighting with double swords," said Decan, swallowing the memories of that night away.

"Me neither. They had lots of weapons on them, but none had two swords, which makes me think they attacked Tal'Kabur as well. There's no way to be certain, but either way it seems unwise to go there. Besides, it will take at least three days by boat to get there, longer if we can't find one of the small sailing boats instead of a normal rowing boat."

Trista continued drawing the crude dirt map.

"So, we're west of Tal'Kabur, the side where the sun god approaches the goddess. Further west is the mid-continent with the Southern Cities, and way north, the kingdom of Aeterra."

As Trista recalled all the things her father had taught her, she was glad that her parents had insisted on teaching her the ways of the world. Her father might have been set in his ways as a fisherman, as was the traditional waterclan way, but he was by no means limited in his understanding of the world and that which happened in it—even though much of his information and knowledge was confined to what came through the trade ships or what he heard in Tal'Ostar.

"Between us and the Southern Cities on the main continent are dozens of islands. Some have people living on them, others are nothing more than rock and sand. If we can find a boat, we can move from island to island until we get to the mainland."

"But the black ships are out there too, aren't they?" asked Decan.

"Yes. That's why we should leave under cover of darkness, preferably tonight. Hopefully, that will allow us to get away without being spotted. Old man Moran's son used to store his sailing boat in one of the coves on the south west end of the island. If we're lucky, it might still be there."

"And the goat goes with us? I cannot eat her?"

"The goat goes with us."

The unusual quartet spent the entire day moving toward the western coast, further moving away from their own village. Judging from the column of smoke, every step brought them closer to another burned settlement, but also closer to possible escape. Twice they had to detour as Dalkeira spotted a small group of soldiers on patrol. It seemed dragons had exceptional eyesight, because neither Trista nor Decan had spotted the soldiers until much later.

Dalkeira was quick to get up in the air and fly short distances, but her flight muscles were not fully developed yet. To prevent herself from getting too tired, the dragon was alternating between walking and flying.

She was quick to adapt her flying into hunting—surprising one of the island hares during a flight. It was her first official land prey, which she proudly declared. She immediately tore it apart as Trista and Decan took a moment to rest.

"The main problem will be water," said Trista, "The ocean is too salty to drink, so we need to find some water to take with us on the boat. Most of the islands are pretty close together. It shouldn't take more than a few days to get from one to another, but the boat will offer us little protection from the sun. The exposure is sure to dehydrate us quickly if we don't drink enough."

Dalkeira swallowed the last of the hare.

"Can you not drink the milk from the goat?"

"What about Rudley?" asked Decan at the same time.

The boy had named the goat after one of the old men from the village. Trista had mentioned the goat was a female, but he had not cared; the beard reminded him of Rudley, the village storyteller.

Trista smiled at his use of the name.

"Dalkeira just said the same thing, and yes, that's why I want to take her with us. But she will need to drink water to be able to make milk. Not to mention it will be a challenge to find food for her if she does not eat fish."

The goat looked at them and simply commented with a bleat.

"That's really not helpful at all, Rudley," chuckled Decan as they got up to begin the final stretch to the coast.

"When we've found the boat, I will circle back to the village—what's left of it—and see if I can find some water bags," said Trista.

She did not like the idea of getting close to the village, as the soldiers were likely still there, but she could think of no other place to find the much-needed drinking water, and she did not want to go out to sea unprepared.

By the time the sun touched the water, they were overlooking the ocean toward the west. They had taken the long way around the burned settlement and moved further south along the coast. There, they saw several ships still lying anchored near the destroyed village.

Trista looked around doubtfully. She had been convinced that she would know where to go when they got closer, but as she surveyed the shore, nothing seemed familiar.

"It's been years since I was here," she said apologetically. "I think it was past that rock point in the distance."

They moved slowly, deliberately staying close to large boulders on the rocky shore in case anyone was watching. As they turned the point, things started to look more familiar.

"Yes, this is it. It should be just around this corner."

She held her breath as they turned the corner. There was no guarantee the sailing boat would still be in the same place after all these years. Perhaps someone had taken it already to flee; or maybe the soldiers had found it and destroyed it, or Moran's son might have simply moved it somewhere else during the years.

Scenarios flashed through Trista's head, but as they went on, it became clear the water goddess was watching over them. The sailing boat lay, slightly tilted, on the beach. A rope secured it to a rock and the back of the boat was just getting wet from the rising tide.

The boat was well-hidden from sight in case any ships came by. A natural bridge at the entrance of the bay shielded the beach from prying eyes. They would be safe here for now.

As they approached the boat, Trista saw two barrels tied to the bottom of the small mast. She jumped on board, checking inventory. Ropes, some hooks and a net, with two long oars tied along the sides.

Next, she approached the barrels to see what was inside. The first barrel did not look promising; flies covered it and Trista could smell the stench of fish. She opened the lid and saw scraps of fish still on the bottom. The flies buzzed around it and maggots crawled inside. This was clearly the bait barrel.

Still hopeful, Trista opened the second barrel on the other side of the mast, her heart making a small jump of joy. The barrel was half-filled with water. A spoon roughly constructed from a piece of leather and a twig hung from the side. She quickly took a sip.

"It's stale, but freshwater," she said excitedly.

"That means you won't have to go to the village, right?" said Decan, hopeful.

The boy did not like the idea of splitting up from his sister again, even if it was only for a little while.

"It would be easier if we had some water bags, or a bucket, too, but I'm not going to ignore the water goddess' gifts and push our luck," said Trista.

"*I found some stuff over here, too,*" said Dalkeira, who had been wandering around the cove looking for things to eat.

Trista hurried over. A small wooden chest was hidden under one of the rocks. She pulled it out and opened it.

Thank you, Goddess.

One by one she pulled out a bucket, a set of flints and a knife. There was also a bunch of dried wood in there, as well as a metal pot for cooking. It seems that Moran's son had made sure he could make a campfire and cook in case he ever needed to spend the night near the boat.

"Good eye, Dalkeira! Now we just have to stay hidden and wait for the tide to come up and the sun to go down," said Trista.

"*If we are to wait, I would appreciate it if you could assist me in finding some food. I am still so very hungry...*"

Dalkeira had spent the entire day—walking or flying—looking for her next meal, but it had not been enough. Trista did her best to provide for the blue dragon, but it was becoming clear that she might not be able to give Dalkeira enough to still the growing dragon's hunger. She felt bad about it, but they were all hungry now. Besides, she had to take care of her brother, too.

It left her torn. The bond pressured her to focus toward the dragon, but no matter how strong the link was, the promise to her mother and father to keep Decan safe was constantly reminding her that another needed her help.

* * *

She did not know that Dalkeira was in turn growing more annoyed by the fact that Trista was not providing her with ample amounts of food. It was one of the main reasons the dragon had chosen to link with her. The boy had not been an option; he was still much too young as far as the dragon was concerned, barely capable of catching his own food, let alone food enough for a dragon. Trista clearly had the skill, but now it seemed that Dalkeira had to share the red-haired woman's attention with the boy.

"You did do a decent job of cleaning me yesterday. That, at least, is something," said Dalkeira as she checked her scales and wings and rubbed her nose on a spot that had developed an itch.

"What was that?"

But Dalkeira did not repeat the remark.

As they walked around the bay, the dragon noticed that Decan was busy offering Rudley some moss and seaweed to eat. It meant she had Trista to herself for a few moments, which immediately lightened her mood. She darted past Trista, halted as she reconsidered her hunting chances and then stalked the last few feet to the shoreline to see if there were any fish to catch. As she noticed her own reflection in the water, she pondered about how little she actually knew about the world.

"Have you ever seen another dragon?" she asked Trista.

"No, I can't say that I have."

"But there are bound to be some to the west, yes?"

"Honestly, I don't know. I've never heard anyone speak of a dragon before. Not my father, nor the sailors of the trade ships. But the mainland is a large place. It could very well be that there are others like you."

Trista thought about it for a moment. "Is that why you want to go west?" she asked the dragon.

"Perhaps. I do not know precisely. It is like someone… something is calling, but the sound is just out of hearing range."

"Well, at least you have us," said Trista, trying to make the dragon feel better.

The dragon's deep blue, sparkling eyes briefly looked toward Decan and the goat before lingering on Trista herself. Without a word, Dalkeira turned her head away and jumped into the water after a fish, leaving Trista to wonder if she had said something wrong.

* * *

Trista shivered. The storm from two nights before had brought the colder winds from the north. The drop in temperature was increasingly noticeable as the sun went down, enhanced by the fact that the nights had gone by without a single cloud. But they could not have asked for a better night to make their escape. The constant spray of the warm ocean waters created small floating water drops in the cooler air above it, and a thick sea mist had formed across the water. Flurries of fog were floating up onto the island, wrapping everything in a white haze. Somewhere within, the sound of rocks clattering to the ground could be heard. Startled, Trista looked up, listening intensely.

It was not uncommon during the summer season to have these foggy nights, but with enemy soldiers stalking the island, it gave the damp silence of the mist a very eerie feel.

"Probably nothing," whispered Trista when no other sounds followed. "Ready to go?"

She and Decan were pushing the boat toward the water. Dalkeira and Rudley watched together from inside the boat, doing their best to keep their balance as the boat rocked back and forth. Nervously, Rudley gave a bleat in protest at being stuck in the same place as the winged predator.

"Shhh," Trista soothed.

"But how do we know where to go?" asked Decan softly. "We can't even see the moon and stars."

"*I can see the moon and stars just fine,*" commented Dalkeira inside Trista's mind.

"Dalkeira can guide us. She can still see the moon and will make sure we stay on course. The mist will give us cover from any soldiers on watch. If we don't go now, who knows when we'll have the chance to get away unseen?"

Trista saw the doubt in her little brother's eyes. Decan was eager to make their escape, but he had never been off the island before. The unknown world out there was as scary as staying.

"Look, I know there's a lot we don't know, but we can't stay here. Our home is gone. You saw what they did to Landon, Sterak and the other villagers. They enjoy making people suffer. If we're caught, they'll toy with us first, just for fun, before killing us. I promised Mother and Father I would keep you safe, and that means getting out of here right now," said Trista, almost reading Decan's mind like only a dragon could.

The boy gave a hesitant nod and jumped in the boat as it started floating freely in the water. Trista took the oars in hand and began rowing toward the natural bridge and open ocean.

"A little more toward the right... no, my right," said Dalkeira, steering them clear of the overhanging rocky bridge.

Trista heard the splashing of waves against the boat change ever so slightly. *Open water.*

Sweat mixed with the mist on her skin. The boat was of reasonable size, sturdy enough for the open sea, but it also meant that rowing took a fair amount of energy, especially this first part as she moved against the waves.

Ignored, Rudley had given up her protest and now lay in the bottom of the boat. Dalkeira sat behind Trista, keeping an eye on the moon and correcting their course when necessary while Decan sat at the rudder, steering the boat so that Trista could focus on rowing. Trista's muscles were already beginning to burn, but with no wind she had no choice but to make use of the oars and get as far away from the island as possible.

The coast was quickly swallowed up by the mist and it was not long before Trista completely lost all sense of direction. Everything was wrapped in a silent, white blanket. Checking behind her, she noticed Dalkeira staring at the heavens. She followed the dragon's gaze, trying to see if she could spot the moon god traveling the sky.

"Stop!" hissed Decan suddenly.

Dalkeira spun around to see what had made Decan react.

"*Oh, hold on!*" said Dalkeira as the hull of a large sailing ship loomed.

On reflex, Trista pulled in her oars to prevent them from getting stuck between the two boats. Their own little ship slammed into the side of the larger hull, sending a loud thump to carry across the water. Startled, Rudley let out a bleat.

Shouts emerged from the larger ship's deck, but the mist was too thick to actually see the handrail above them. Trista quickly put her finger to her lips, softly shushing the goat. But it was no use; Rudley moved nervously from side to side, as if just deciding she no longer wanted to tag along with them.

The goat bleated again. Trista saw the faint light of oil lamps moving above them, as if the soldiers were trying to see what was out there. The sound of the goat echoed across the water, where it was drowned in the constant sloshing of the sea and then muffled by the mist. Trista hoped that meant the soldiers would be unable to pinpoint where the sound came from.

"Keep her quiet," she whispered to Decan.

The boy quickly moved over to the goat. He started scratching her chin and ears to calm her down while whispering soothing words to the frightened animal, but the constant movement of the boat upset the goat more with every sway. She let out another shrill bleat, resulting in more shouts from above and feet stomping around on the deck.

Their own mast did not even reach two-thirds of the height of the ship, but Trista did not want to find out if the soldiers on deck would be able to see it. She quickly moved to the side of their boat and started pushing them forward along the large ship's hull.

THUMP.

"Behhh!"

Another shock ran through their boat as it bumped into the black ship again. Decan was trying his best, but the goat was beyond calming. She started thrashing around, trying to get away from Decan's grip and drawing in the lights on deck with the resulting racket.

"*I knew I should have eaten it earlier,*" said Dalkeira.

Before Trista could react, Dalkeira leaped nimbly across the boat and sank her teeth into Rudley's neck. Blood sprayed across Decan's face as Dalkeira tore out the panicking animal's throat. Immediately, the bleating stopped.

The boy's eyes were wide as he fell backward into the boat. Trista knew the scene in front of him was triggering all the memories of the last few days at once: the killings, the torture, the savageness. She saw him open his mouth to scream, but Dalkeira locked eyes with him before any sound came out. Decan froze, breathing heavily, the terror from the last few nights no doubt rushing through him.

Dalkeira's eyes swirled back and forth as she took a step toward him, only for Decan to quickly back away from her in shock.

Tears streamed from Decan's eyes. Dalkeira turned around and leaped back toward the front of the boat, where Trista was once again struggling to pull them forward without bumping into the other ship's hull.

Decan lay down on his side and pulled up his legs toward him, crying softly as the shouting from the deck approached the handrail above them.

"*We need to get out of here or we are sure to be discovered,*" said Dalkeira to Trista. The dragon swiftly took one of the heavier ropes tied to the boat between her jaws and silently slipped into the water.

Swimming in front of the boat, the dragon pulled them forward while Trista kept them from bumping into the hull again. As they moved away, Trista saw an oil lamp on a rope being lowered from the deck, but by the time it was at water level, they had already moved from the immediate vicinity of the enemy ship. As the incomprehensible shouting of the soldiers on deck dissipated behind them, their little boat quietly slipped away into the thick blanket of mist.

"Let's try not to do that again," whispered Trista, taking the oars back in hand. She started rowing with all her might. "Keep going, Dalkeira. Time to put some water between us and this place."

A pleasant tingle shot through Trista's body as the boat jolted forward. The dragon seemed happy that they were doing this together.

CHAPTER SIX

Tal'Kabur

THE CLANG OF metal rang out as High General Corza Setra looked out of the window. The castle offered an excellent view over Tal'Ostar, the capital port of Tal'Kabur. Its main street ran in a spine-straight line from the front gates all the way down to the harbor. Beyond the city, lush forests covered most of the island, with a handful of settlements and larger cities spread out along the coast.

The large street was used as the main vein for cargo transportation. Iron rails ran in the center of it, allowing mine carts to move along them. Coal, ore, iron, merchandise, anything that could be transported. Going uphill was done with the help of huge muscular oxen that equaled the finest of their Doskovian warhorses in strength.

At the top, a large plaza allowed the carts to be turned around while cargo was loaded on or off. Several iron rails branched off the main track to allow carts to pass each other. The way down was simply powered by gravity. A clever brake system on the carts made sure none of them could run rampant, even if the person guiding the cart lost control over it.

I wonder how many people were killed before they got that one right, Corza thought with morbid fascination.

Tal'Ostar had never been a clean city. With a third of the working population being blacksmiths and another quarter manning the iron smelters, the city was buried under a constant layer of grime. But the clouds of black smoke Corza now saw everywhere were not from the ovens; part of the city had caught fire during the fighting.

When they had tried to go up the main street, Talkarian forces had pushed carts down the iron rails on both sides. Some were filled with soldiers with crossbows, others with liquid iron. By rigging the carts to crash on purpose, the Talkarians had ensured numerous Doskovian soldiers were maimed and killed by the hot liquid metal. The Talkarian troops had even managed to take down one of the ghol'ms.

But the biggest blunder had been committed by one of Corza's captains, who had sailed his ship close to shore to quickly offload their troops. Small ramps were present near the edge of the water, complete with the iron rails that ran up the main street. Neither the captain nor the troops had thought much of it, but as the fighting broke out, a cart full of hot liquid iron had raced down the street. As soldiers jumped out of the way, the cart ran its intended course and flew off a ramp, launching into the air. It had crashed into the waterline of the anchored ship, where the rapid cooling of the iron caused a giant explosion, ripping open the ship's hull. The ship had quickly sunk to the bottom of the harbor, taking a platoon of soldiers and the fifteen ghol'ms still on board with it.

Corza silently berated those responsible as he watched the mast of the sunken ship sticking up out of the harbor water. They would have to figure out a way to get the ghol'ms above water again. His informants were going to pay dearly for providing such incomplete information on the fighting tactics of the Talkarian forces. And if the captain of the ship had still been alive, Corza would have executed him on the spot as an example of where carelessness could get you.

"Honestly, I don't know why you all keep fighting, King Baltor," he said out loud.

He looked next to him, where the king of Tal'Kabur stood with a tense look on his face, watching the general's every move.

"Your men fought valiantly, soldiers and commoners alike. But your alleyways are littered with corpses. Our ghol'ms have smashed their way through your defenses and filled your gutters with blood. I would not be surprised if half the harbor water has turned red by now."

Leaving a path of destruction in their wake, the Doskovian forces had flanked the plaza at the top of the main street. There, together with the fireballs dropped from their windships, they had cleared the area of enemy forces. As the Talkarians recognized their imminent defeat, they hastily retreated into the castle, taking position on the walls to rain down arrows upon any who dared come close.

The man beside Corza said nothing.

"Oh, come on. Not a word?" Corza continued to torment the man. "Your castle was barely a challenge for our windships' bombardments. The doors were easily ripped out of their hinges by our ghol'ms' hands. Even now your men are dying down there in the barracks, and you do nothing? Say nothing?"

The Talkarians had made small victories, like the two windships that had been unable to avoid the arrows coming from the higher towers. Both vessels were forced to retreat, but the ships would not be out of commission long; they were currently being fixed down in the harbor.

Corza let his gaze slide over the dead enemy soldiers on the main plaza in front of the castle. He had to admit the two-sword fighting style made for fierce opponents, but with skin of stone and the strength of at least five men, there was little that swords could do against the ghol'ms.

There were still pockets of resistance in parts of the castle and city, but most of the Talkarian armed forces had been decimated whenever the Doskovian army had encountered them.

Soldiers rushed across the plaza, spreading out further into the city. At the waterfront, a group of men was being organized to haul water into the city, as per Corza's order. If they were going to make use of the ovens and smelters, the Stone King required the city to be intact as much as possible. A large group of ghol'ms had been put to the task of tearing down any burning buildings until the fires were under control. Thankfully, the Talkarians had been wise enough to erect their houses from stone, a necessary precaution when working with hot, melted metal, so Corza expected it would not take too long before things were under control again.

The Stone King. Even the name gave Corza a bad taste in his mouth. For years, he had been working himself up in the ranks of the Doskovian army to get close to Lord Rictor—the Stone King's real name. Only after becoming one of his supposedly trusted advisers did Corza learn that the Stone King did not really trust anyone.

In his dark hours, Corza sometimes suspected the king was fully aware of his attempts and conspiracies to overthrow the man. That he only kept Corza around to show him how futile it all was and how insignificant his existence; that it was never spoken about, never mentioned out loud, just to torment him.

Then logic and anger would push away such insecure thoughts. There was no way that Lord Rictor knew of his plans. He had always been careful, making certain that not even the smallest connection could be traced back to him. Lord Rictor might not find him pleasant company to have around, but Corza's skill in long-term military planning was indispensable. He could thank his miserable family for that skill at least, he thought bitterly.

No, he was certain the Stone King would never permit any such schemes. He would surely have put Corza to death as an example. The man was not exactly stable.

Corza thought back on his appointment to the position of High General. It was no wonder Lord Rictor distrusted all those around him. At the time, many years ago, treason had run deep in the highest ranks of those surrounding the Stone King. In one night, the entire high council of generals had been massacred after an attempt on the Stone King's life. Not even the servants had been able to escape the horrors of the bloodbath; not a single one of the staff had seen the next day's sunrise. The only known survivor was the Stone King himself, who was said to be a creature of the underworld when they found him, rambling incomprehensibly and waving his sword around, his face and clothes completely covered in blood.

Still, Corza could not deny that the Stone King was more easily agitated these last few months than during a decade of preparations. Where before Corza's methods to get things done were ignored or, at the most, met with a sneer or icy silence, now he had to be careful not to get his brains smashed in by his lordship's right arm.

Perhaps it's the stress of the invasion, Corza tried to convince himself.

After the Bloodnight, as people had named the massacre, the Stone King had not shown himself for several months while selections were made to replace those lost—a process that put Corza in his current position of power. But Lord Rictor was nothing like Corza expected; rumor even said he was a completely different man when he finally emerged after his months of solitude. It was after his reappearance that Lord Rictor brought his Darkened—his very own murderous king's guard—to life.

Corza figured the stress of the situation had really done a number on the old fool, as any man who spoke to phantoms could hardly be deemed sane. Still, the Stone King's cold, calculating way of ruling the Dark Continent always prevailed over the unsettling nature of those abrupt, private discussions.

Far below, in front of the harbor, lay the Stone King's ship. The *Behemoth* was an immense vessel, larger than any other ship in their flotilla and big enough to hold hundreds of men. It was currently packed with Darkened and ghol'ms. The Silent Shadows—as the tongueless Darkened were sometimes referred to by the common folk—had a crude gesture system, supported by a variety of hisses and grunts. In combination with their training, it was enough to run a smooth ship without the need for any dedicated sailors.

The *Behemoth* had arrived shortly after Corza and his men began their assault on the anchored ships. It was an unexpected visit; Corza had figured the Stone King would not involve himself in the early stages of the invasion. Throughout the entire battle, at sea and on land, Corza had felt those calm, calculating eyes judging his every decision.

His lordship had not once left the deck of the *Behemoth* during the fighting, nor sent any of his men to assist. But now that most of the city was in their hands, the Stone King had apparently decided it was time to visit the occupied castle. Corza watched the man make his way up the main street, accompanied by a full squad of Darkened.

What's he up to now? thought Corza, narrowing his eyes at the silhouette with the red and black cloak coming up the hill.

The Stone King took his time reaching the castle. It was as if he was taking an afternoon stroll, only instead of admiring the flowers, Lord Rictor was surveying those captured during the fighting. Men, women and children were brought to the main street and forced to kneel in the gutters that still ran red with the blood of the fallen. Anyone who resisted was put to the blade, their blood added to the streams running downhill.

Corza saw a woman spit at Lord Rictor's feet. At once a Darkened moved in and slammed the pommel of his sword in her face. She was pulled to her feet screaming and dragged away toward the harbor. Probably to be kept on the ships for entertainment during the upcoming voyages, figured Corza.

He briefly wondered if he should send some men to push a few minecarts down the main street unseen. Maybe he would get lucky and take out his lordship.

No. It would be too risky with this many eyes watching, and he's already nearing the top of the hill.

Behind Corza, the shouting and grunting continued. The swishing of metal through air mixed with the sound of heavy panting. Every now and then, Corza heard a gasp or a sob from behind the island king. He looked to the side and saw King Baltor, eyes still fixed on him as he shielded his wife and daughter from harm. The king's hand was on one of his swords, but he had not drawn it yet.

Corza looked at the queen and princess, who were more focused on the scene in the middle of the room than he was. Looking at them, he licked lips gone dry from anticipation. His hand unconsciously moved to his Roc'turr, the sacrificial dagger on his belt.

Such fine lines, both of them. The same gracious figure. When this is all over, perhaps I'll pay them both a visit. I can keep the mother within earshot while I work on her daughter.

When they forced their way into the throne room, Corza's crossbowmen had quickly taken out most of the Talkarian soldiers present. But one enemy soldier had been just as quick to strike down any man who held a crossbow. The Talkarian fighter wielded the largest sword Corza had ever seen. It had been a surprise to see such an unusual weapon, especially as the majority of the resisting soldiers had fought with two shorter swords.

King Baltor, his wife and one of his daughters had been at the far end of the throne room when Corza and his men barged in. There was nowhere for them to go. All the exits were covered, and the king was smart enough not to try and make a run for it with his wife and daughter in tow. Had they fled, they surely would have been struck down by one of the waiting Doskovian soldiers.

However, Corza's men found that the Talkarian soldier with the large sword was a force to be reckoned with. Helmet and steel chainmail offered the man some protection, while small steel shoulder pads made certain the soldier could make full use of his arms. His legs and one of his hands were armored so they could be used to stop any incoming attack, even if made by a sword or spear.

The man had single-handedly halted the Doskovian forces from reaching his king, and was now the only soldier left to guard the royal family.

Since the ghol'ms were busy with the fires and clearing the enemy barracks at the other end of the castle, Corza had ordered his men to kill the soldier without much thought. But within moments ten more had lain dead on the floor, the white marble floor slowly coloring bright red as their blood and guts poured from their bodies.

The blade of the large sword looked thick and heavy, but the Talkarian wielded it like it weighed nothing. It cut through Corza's own soldiers with a sharpness that seemed unlikely for something so thick. The brute had cleaved an unlucky soldier in two with his first strike, completely separating torso from legs. Several other Doskovian soldiers who had attacked at the same time met an equally definite end. Some missed arms or legs, and all lay heavily bleeding on the floor. It seemed the weight and speed of the large sword gave it a momentum that could not be stopped. The last two Doskovian crossbowmen had fired at the lone Talkarian soldier, only to hit air or blade as the fighter dodged and deflected the bolts before striking down those that had taken the shot.

Corza looked back now in time to see a Doskovian soldier venture too close and receive the full force of a downward slash. The blade cut through the side of his neck all the way to the opposite hip in one clean movement.

Most of the time, the Talkarian soldier used both hands to guide his blade. The extended grip provided plenty of space for it, but Corza now saw that the man also used his armored glove to support the blade itself during a swing, giving it additional force should it meet any strong resistance. The man made circular motions with the sword, keeping himself out of reach of his enemies. But he did not merely swing the blade; at times, he let it rest on his shoulder while spinning himself around. He even moved the blade around his neck to the other side, quickly changing directions with the large weapon.

Corza's men chose that moment to launch a new assault. The Talkarian soldier reacted by ramming his blade straight down onto the floor and using it as a vertical wall to deflect the first attack. He grabbed one man's incoming sword with his armored hand, ripped it from the soldier's grip and struck down the attacker with his own weapon. Right away, he threw the sword straight through the neck of a third and kicked the point of his own massive sword to bring it up into full swing again.

Hesitation surged through the group of attackers. Blood had made the floor treacherously slippery, yet the large man's stance remained as rooted as that of an ancient tree. They circled around the Talkarian fighter like wolves trying to take down a large, dangerous quarry.

The king and his family were being ignored by everyone but the general. None of Corza's men dared look away from the dangerously long reach of the brute's sword.

There were too many opponents for the Talkarian soldier to win, but it seemed pride refused to let him surrender to the Doskovian forces. *And for every man that falls, there's another five waiting to take their place.*

Corza turned back toward the window again. The fight bored him; the outcome would not change. His own men would keep attacking the lonesome fighter with his monstrous sword to the point of exhaustion. Eventually, they would land a hit, however small, and another, and another, till the Talkarian soldier was losing too much blood and energy to keep on fighting. At that point, one of his soldiers would simply go in for the kill.

Below him, the Stone King entered the castle. Each Doskovian soldier he encountered made certain to properly salute the ruler with a closed fist to the chest. As the party crossed the drawbridge, Corza let out a sigh. He did not look forward to the Stone King's unpleasant company.

The general had not spoken directly with Lord Rictor for some time; not since he was sent out from the Dark Palace on his assignment to recapture the Tiankong Empire's dragon egg and punish the traitors who had stolen it.

At the time, Corza had needed all his expertise in groveling to prevent the Stone King from throwing him off the palace balcony. The egg had been his responsibility, and Lord Rictor had not taken his failure lightly. Little did the man know that Corza had always intended for the egg to be stolen—but by his own men, not some sorry excuse for an Aeterran squad.

At least Corza was able to use the opportunity to rid himself of High General Wayler. Being the high general in charge of their homeland security, Koltar Wayler had been one of the bigger obstacles standing in Corza's way of getting rid of Lord Rictor and taking his place on the throne.

In the official reports that Corza had sent, he deeply regretted that his esteemed fellow high general had fallen victim to enemy forces during the attempt to retrieve the dragon egg. Naturally, he did not fail to report that, however unfortunate, High General Wayler's incompetence had tipped the battle in the enemy's favor, resulting in the death of the two Darkened that had accompanied them and the enemy squad being able to flee—with Corza in hot pursuit.

Corza gritted his teeth. He would never admit it, but he had greatly underestimated the small Aeterran squad, and the rapidly-grown dragon had been a very dangerous wildcard in the whole situation. His intent had been to hatch the dragon and keep it for himself; then, once fully grown, to use the beast to rid himself of the Stone King and take over as ruler of the entire Dark Continent. That future seemed less and less likely with each day that passed.

He wondered if the windships he ordered to follow the Aeterran squad had caught up with them yet. If not, he would have to make new arrangements— and quickly, or he would lose the chance to secure that winged menace for himself. But there was no choice but to wait for their report before he could decide his next step.

A shout from the princess snapped Corza out of his thoughts.

"Turak, look out!" she screamed as the Talkarian fighter took a blow to the back.

The big man spun around as his sword flew through the air, barely missing the Doskovian soldier who had heroically tried to stab him in the back. Curiosity getting the better of him, Corza turned around fully, but he was disappointed; the Talkarian's armor had taken most of the damage, though he did see that blood now ran down the man's arm from a cut on his shoulder.

So, the princess cares for this man. I bet I can use that to my advantage.

Unable to look away from her protector, the princess had a frantic look in her eyes. She clung to her mother as tears ran down her cheeks.

Yes; they might even be lovers. She would be the right age for that.

The door at the other end of the throne room swung open. Corza pushed his thoughts aside and forced himself back to the situation at hand.

Silence fell over the room as the Stone King strode in and looked around. In his wake, several Darkened quickly moved along the walls, all with swords and axes already in hand. Their tattooed faces looked like demons, always watching from the shadows.

"Lord Rictor, what a pleasant surprise," exclaimed Corza.

"What is going on here? Why is this man still allowed to fight?" said Lord Rictor.

The Doskovian soldiers halted their attack and opened their ranks as the Stone King approached the circle. Fists hit armor in salute. A few soldiers nudged those next to them, whispering words of excitement that the Stone King would grace them with his presence. One or two held their heads down in shame for not finishing the fight sooner.

"That is a fine weapon you have, sir. What is your name?" asked the Stone King in the Terran language.

"Turak," answered the Talkarian fighter. He was clearly not feeling chatty.

"Well, Turak," Lord Rictor carefully pronounced, "my name is Lord Leonard Rictor, but you can call me 'my king,' or 'my liege' if you prefer. Turak, why not lay down that heavy-looking sword of yours and admit defeat? I am sure it feels as heavy as a mountain after all that waving it around."

The Stone King looked silently at the fighter, who seemed to be taking his time to come up with an answer.

"You are not going to win this, Turak, and you know it. Look at yourself. You are sweaty, bleeding and exhausted. Please allow me to make it easier for you. If you lay your weapon down now, I will permit you to work in the iron mines. We can always use strong men like you."

Turak looked over his shoulder, locking eyes with the princess. They held a conversation without words, her eyes pleading for him to do as he was told, his trying to make her understand this was never going to end well.

The Talkarian fighter turned back to the pale man in front of him. A fine black cape, a thin black ring around his head, white hair hanging down to the shoulders. The man who had introduced himself as Lord Leonard Rictor was apparently not an image that impressed the fighter.

"Not gonna happen, you bastard!" Turak suddenly shouted.

The Talkarian fighter launched himself forward, using the momentum to bring up his sword and let it fall like heaven's judgment on the invader of Tal'Kabur.

As the blade fell down, Lord Rictor stepped forward, bringing up his right fist. The solid stone arm to which the Stone King owed his title forcefully knocked the incoming sword to the side. The blade landed heavily on the white marble floor, missing its intended target.

Lord Rictor swiftly moved in, his stone fingers sliding over the sword, pressing it down. Sparks flew from the edge as stone challenged steel. At monstrous speed, the inhuman hand reached up to clasp around the Talkarian fighter's face and helmet. The princess shrieked as her lover was lifted off his feet and slammed backward onto the marble floor. The Talkarian clawed at the stone arm pinning him to the ground.

"You should have lain down your weapon," the Stone King said softly, kneeling beside the pinned soldier. The sounds of crumpling metal and cracking bones echoed through the room as Lord Rictor clenched his stone fist and crushed the fighter's head and helmet.

"No!" screamed the princess.

The queen dragged her daughter to the ground to prevent her from running into Corza's soldiers. She held her close, comforting her even as tears ran down her own cheeks. King Baltor's knuckles whitened as his hand tightened around his sword grip.

Lord Rictor stood, took out a napkin to wipe the blood off his stone hand and walked toward Corza.

"Milord, to what do we owe this honor? I hadn't expected you to involve yourself so early in the plan," said Corza with his most flattering smile.

"High General Setra, so *nice* to see you again. It seems like you have made it through the day alright. As to why I am here… well, your ability to bring your given assignments to a successful close has not been that great lately, so I wanted to make sure things went as planned here. Speaking of which… was there not another assignment that required your attention?"

It was said in the most casual manner, but Corza felt the weight of the question in the air.

"My lord, perhaps this is not the best time to discuss these matters." Corza spoke softly, trying to move away from the dangerous topic. Lord Rictor's face tightened as the man's stone-cold eyes locked onto his.

"Tell me, High General Setra, when have I ever given you the impression that you can dictate what I should or should not do?"

"Apologies, my lord. I merely meant that the information is not intended for outsider's ears," pleaded Corza, motioning toward King Baltor and his family. "Perhaps my lord might choose that there are more important matters to attend to at this time?"

Lord Rictor looked over his shoulder to the king and his family. The cautious king had not moved, guarding his wife and daughter from this new threat.

"Of course! How rude of me. Where are my manners? Let's meet the famous *King of Iron*," said Lord Rictor.

The Stone King turned around and walked toward them. King Baltor carefully pulled out his two swords, ready to engage.

"There is no further need for unpleasantness, Your Highness," said Lord Rictor, smiling as he stopped a few steps short of the king of Tal'Kabur. "I can see you value your family's lives, as well as those of your subjects. Let me offer you a chance to keep them all safe."

But before Lord Rictor had finished his sentence, the princess pushed her mother away and launched herself forward, snatching at one of her father's swords.

"You killed him!" she screamed. "You monster, you killed him!"

"Kayla, no!"

Dropping one of his swords, King Baltor grabbed his daughter's wrists and held them in an iron grip. He pulled her close as she fought to get out of his embrace, clawing the air to try and reach the face of the Stone King.

"Olivia, take her," bellowed the King of Iron to his wife as he pushed their daughter toward her.

As he turned back to face Lord Rictor, King Baltor slowly picked up his fallen swords and sheathed them both again. If the man in front of him had worn an expression that even came close to resembling smugness, no doubt the King of Iron would have launched himself at the Stone King, consequences be damned. But the face of Lord Rictor betrayed no emotion, no inclination he was startled, angry or mocking the sorrow of King Baltor's daughter. He calmly waited to see what the King of Iron would do next. The King of Iron fought visibly to keep his rage inside.

"My apologies for my daughter's outburst. You should understand it is her betrothed lying on the floor there with his head crushed. They were supposed to be wed in a few weeks."

Lord Rictor looked at the Talkarian fighter, lying in a pool of blood on the white marble floor.

"An unfortunate turn of events. To be fair, though, I did give him the chance to surrender," said Lord Rictor calmly. "I admire the fire in your daughter. How old is she? Seventeen? Eighteen summers?"

The King of Iron swallowed hard.

"Nineteen."

"Most interesting. But perhaps mother and daughter would feel more comfortable retreating to their private chamber while we discuss the terms of your surrender."

The King of Iron looked to his wife. The queen seemed uncertain at first, then gave a small nod in agreement.

"Excellent! High General Setra, would you please take a few of your men and escort the royal family to their private chambers?" said Lord Rictor. "They will remain there until called upon."

Corza saluted and beckoned a few of his men.

"Oh, and Setra? Make sure they are not harmed in *any* way."

* * *

As mother and daughter were taken to the royal chambers, Lord Rictor turned his attention back to the King of Iron.

"She must be a handful with that temper. Honestly, I have no idea how people with children do it," said Lord Rictor with a smile as warming as that of a corpse. "I am told you have another daughter, and even two sons. Your youngest daughter is currently visiting the southern trade cities as part of her education, if I am not mistaken. What about the boys? Where might they be?"

"Far away from here. You will never get to them," said the King of Iron, shocked by the fact the intruder knew so much.

"See, that right there is your first mistake, King Baltor: you underestimate the extent of my reach. Your second is thinking I care whether I can get to them or not. I am merely trying to prevent any more harm from coming to your family. I recommend you choose your words carefully from now on."

The Stone King turned to look out the window, letting an icy atmosphere settle around him.

"What are you here for, then?" asked King Baltor, breaking the silence.

"A means to an end. You have something I need, and we are here to take it."

"You're here for iron and steel," said King Baltor solemnly.

"The best in the world," Lord Rictor said with a grand hand gesture. "I always appreciate it when they put a person with intelligence in charge of a kingdom. It makes negotiations much more civilized," added the Stone King.

"Is that what we're doing? Negotiating? Why not just raid the harbor warehouses and take off with the iron in storage there? Why slaughter all these people only to stop and talk now?"

"You are right. Just taking the iron and steel would have been easier. But you see, I do not merely need the materials. Our plans are what you might call a bit longer term. I fully intend to keep the fires hot and the ovens burning. Tal'Kabur will be at the heart of our efforts and provide us with a constant stream of much needed equipment."

* * *

Bogoris Baltor looked around his throne room. The white marble had always been a strong contrast to the gray city outside, but the King of Iron learned long ago not to argue with his queen's taste. Doskovian soldiers were busy clearing out the corpses, but dark blood still colored much of the stone. His house was tainted, his kingdom invaded. Gradually, reality set in; the Doskovian forces were here to stay.

He looked down at his hands. They were shaking. Anger demanded action. He still had his hands free; they had not even bothered to tie them, nor take his swords.

A deadly thought crossed his mind. But as his gaze swept the room he saw how futile the idea was. They would harm his wife and daughter before he could fight his way through—if he could fight at all with so many soldiers nearby, not to mention the Darkened positioned along the walls. He was glad his other three children were not here now.

He looked at the special forces of Lord Rictor. The skeleton-faced men looked even more incongruous in the bright throne room than the blood. None wore a helmet, in contrast to the normal soldiers. Their armor was of a higher quality, but looked messy with so many weapons hanging from different straps around their chests and waists.

They would take me out before I could even come close. I need to buy time. Maybe we can find a way for our people to escape into the forest. This is our *land, and I'll be damned if I let some outsider take it from us without a fight.*

"You have had your fight, and lost," said Lord Rictor, as if the king had spoken his thoughts out loud. Bogoris looked at the invader in horror, but the white-haired ruler simply stared out of the window and observed the turmoil in the city.

"It will take some time before things quieten down," said the Stone King.

King Baltor wondered if the man had spoken to him at all. The intruder seemed so lost in thought, it was as if Lord Rictor had forgotten that he was still in the room.

"You mentioned a way to keep our people safe?" said the King of Iron after a while.

"What? Oh, yes," said Lord Rictor. "Once things have been tidied up a little, you will announce your allegiance to me. You will tell the good people of Tal'Kabur to lay down their weapons and cooperate. Tal'Kabur will officially fall under the rule of the Stone King. We will send out messengers to the other cities along the coast and inland. They will be ordered to lay down their weapons and wait for my forces to take over their cities."

Lord Rictor studied his reaction with a watchful eye, but the King of Iron was a seasoned diplomat, too skilled to let anything show that he wanted to keep to himself.

"Those who behave," continued Lord Rictor, "will be allowed to work in the mines and forest. If they listen well and obey, they can return to their loved ones each night. What remains of your armed forces will be disbanded and put into labor camps. Armorers and swordsmiths will work day and night to provide the highest grade of weapons and armor they can make."

"And once you have your weapons? How can I be sure you'll not burn the city to the ground when you are done here?" asked King Baltor.

"Done? Whatever gave you the idea that we will ever be done? As king, it is your duty to protect and lead your people, is it not? You can keep your kingdom in name, but from now on, stone will rule iron in these lands. Please do not expect to regain your kingdom from me, *Bogoris*. Ever. Either you make sure your people obey, or this entire kingdom will be cleansed."

The King of Iron looked at Lord Rictor with growing anger and disgust. The man's complete indifference to the existence of an entire people was appalling.

The inhabitants of Tal'Kabur were renowned as a strong and proud people. Life in the kingdom was tough, and the labor often physically demanding, but its citizens were proud to say workmanship was as important as bloodlines. The various guilds, like those of the armorers and sword makers, had their own hierarchy. It did not matter whether you came from the gutter or the castle—if you had the skill, you got the recognition. And here this man was, thinking himself high and mighty, treating them all like vermin.

A loud bang echoed through the room as a door was thrown open. A young man with bound hands walked in, escorted by Corza.

"Father!"

"Bronson! What are you doing here?" called out the King of Iron.

His son had clearly been part of the battles outside. His armor was dented, scratched and smudged, while dried blood had created brown knots in his blond hair. As Bronson hurried through the room toward his father, Lord Rictor held up his hand to halt the Darkened, who had started to move to intervene.

"Father, are you alright? Where's mother? Kayla? Are they safe?"

The young man had his back to Lord Rictor as he grasped his father's hands. Baltor saw the look in his son's eyes as Bronson took in the swords still at his father's side. He forced his son to raise his head and looked him in the eyes. The King of Iron shook his head very slightly. He had no need for a second outburst from one of his children to make matters worse. Somehow, the King of Iron was certain the Stone King would not tolerate a second attack on his life.

*　*　*

"Young Bronson…"

Lord Rictor let the words hang in the air as if he was tasting them. Bronson turned to face the man.

"So good of you to join us. I was led to believe you were not on the island at all, so you can imagine my surprise to see you here," said Lord Rictor pleasantly.

"And who are you?" said Bronson, his voice thick with disdain.

Corza grabbed the king's son by the shoulder and gave him a sharp kick to the back of his leg. The young man landed heavily on his knees.

"You will know your place. You may address Lord Rictor with 'my liege', 'my king' or 'my lordship' if needed. But you'll speak *only* when spoken to, and you'd best watch your tongue," snarled Corza. He did not particularly care if Lord Rictor was being insulted; on the contrary, he had plenty to add himself. However, it never hurt to show loyalty in front of the Stone King, and he would play that game for as long as it was needed.

He leaned closer and whispered in the young prince's ear.

"You know, you remind me of a certain dark-haired Aeterran soldier," he hissed, twisting the collar of Bronson's shirt so it tightened around his neck. The prince looked at Corza in confusion as he struggled for air.

Corza noticed King Baltor's hands trembling. He smirked and pushed the prince away, allowing him to breathe again but making sure the insolent boy stayed on his knees.

"They just brought him up from the harbor, my lord," said Corza to Lord Rictor. "Their ships came into range this morning after we landed in the city.

They were trying to take over one of the isolated ships anchored outside the harbor. Apparently, after they boarded, this one took out eighteen of our men before he was knocked out in the fight. My men said he demanded to be brought up to the castle to speak with whoever was in charge."

The Stone King still stared at the young man's face.

"Normally they'd put such a nuisance to the blade immediately, but he was wearing the royal seal of Tal'Kabur on his armor and ring so the men thought it best to see if he was telling the truth," added Corza, to fill the silence.

"The resemblance is remarkable," said Lord Rictor, completely ignoring Corza. "You must be dear Kayla's twin, correct?"

"Kayla? What have you done with my sister? If you've hurt her in any way, I'll—"

Corza hit the prince on the back of his head with the handle of his Roc'turr, knocking him to the floor and cutting his threat short.

It was the final straw for the King of Iron. Before Corza had straightened himself fully, King Baltor's armored fist rammed into his jaw. Corza fell to one knee beside the young prince. Blood sprayed from his mouth and onto the floor.

Recovering immediately, Corza jumped back to his feet, slashing his Roc'turr directly at King Baltor's throat.

"Setra!"

The Stone King's voice thundered through the hall. The general's dagger froze mid-slash, blade pressing against King Baltor's throat and drawing the tiniest drop of blood.

Corza turned his head to look over his shoulder, grimacing in anger and bewilderment.

"I need him alive—for now."

Corza looked back at the King of Iron, clenching his teeth to hold back his words.

"Corza... do not make me repeat myself."

Composing himself, Corza reluctantly lowered his dagger.

"Bogoris, you would do well to refrain from attacking my subordinates. I understand this is an emotional day for you, but next time I may not feel obliged to stop the consequences of your actions."

The King of Iron give a short nod and knelt to help up his son.

"Hold your tongue, son," Corza heard him whisper as he dragged the boy back to his knees.

"So... twins?" asked Lord Rictor again, as if nothing had happened.

Still on one knee, the King of Iron turned toward Lord Rictor.

"They are indeed."

"Oh, so you confirm that this is your son Bronson? Correct?" said Lord Rictor in light surprise.

"Correct."

"If that is the case, then you have lied to me about his whereabouts—and after I just warned you not to make a third mistake."

"I can assure you that I was speaking the truth. Bronson here is—was not supposed to be back for another week," said Bogoris with conviction, looking sternly at his son as he got back to his feet.

"Is that true, young man? Why did you return home earlier than expected?"

The boy looked up at Lord Rictor, but this time he kept his mouth tightly shut.

"It is a shame you have not inherited more of your father's manners. Guards, take King Baltor here away. We will put his head on a pike tomorrow morning for obstructing our plans."

"No, wait," exclaimed Bronson. "Wait. It's true. My father speaks the truth. I was out delivering goods to the Southern Cities. The negotiations ended earlier than expected and we had a fair wind guiding us back."

"Now, that was not so hard, was it?" said Lord Rictor. "A strong leader should speak his mind and stand by his words. What about your older brother?"

"Brent? What about him?"

"Where is he?"

"He sailed north. I doubt he's reached his destination already," answered Bronson.

"And what destination is that?" Lord Rictor asked patiently.

"That's enough," interrupted the King of Iron.

Before Lord Rictor could say anything else, a fierce rumble shook the castle. Shouts could be heard from the inner courtyard where it seemed part of the wall had collapsed, presumably as a result of the ongoing fires.

"Milord, perhaps we can continue this conversation at a later stage? After we have the fires and the city under control?" Corza dared to suggest.

Lord Rictor looked out of the window; a new column of smoke rose from a distant part of the city. He stretched his stone fingers. The movement drew Corza's eye. It looked like one of the fingers had difficulty moving. A few small pieces of stone crumbled to the floor. Lord Rictor looked down and then moved his hand below his cape.

"Yes, perhaps this would be a good time to take a break. Escort these two gentlemen to their separate chambers. I will take my leave for the *Behemoth*; we can continue this later."

Corza dragged Bronson back to his feet and shoved him and his father toward the large doors.

"Oh, and Setra?"
"Yes, my lord?"
"I expect a full report from you soon about your other assignment."
"Certainly, my lord."
Corza swore under his breath.

CHAPTER SEVEN

Order

*A*ND *YOU ARE certain the riders did not have any of those flopping animals nearby? I am certain I heard them shout something about seals,"* said Galirras, his stomach requesting his next meal.

"Different kind of seal, little one," Raylan answered sleepily.

Both lay enjoying the warm morning sun. The slow rise and fall of Galirras' chest made Raylan feel as if he was back out at sea. Every now and then he would wake enough from his slumber to open his eyes and see what was going on around them. City guards surrounded their encampment in the meadow, to keep people at a distance as much as to prevent Raylan and the others from leaving while their credentials were being checked. As morning stretched into midday, they were beginning to draw quite a crowd.

The guards had not been as welcoming as they had hoped—but who could blame them? Their arrival from the forest completely startled Galirras, who was preoccupied by the foul-smelling smoke coming from the ship. Seeing weapons at the ready, Galirras had panicked as they surrounded his friends on the beach. Not waiting to see if they truly meant harm, Galirras immediately went into a dive.

Just before the dragon released a wind blast, Raylan reached out to his winged friend's mind to call off the attack. Galirras was just able to use his wind power to push himself up in time, the guards below calling out in alarm as the dragon soared right over their heads. Two of the horses had bolted, their riders feverishly trying to regain control, while the other mounts trampled around nervously trying to keep an eye at the entire sky at once.

It had taken a few tense moments for Richard to calm the guards and properly introduce the group. After explaining the circumstances of their arrival, he managed to convince the guards they were returning from a special assignment and needed to contact the capital as soon as possible. Galirras was presented as a member of the squad, which went as well as could be expected considering they had introduced a talking mythical creature to a skeptical and cautious people.

But it was the request to provide Harwin with a healer's attention that eventually pushed everything into motion. They were escorted to a meadow outside of the residential area, where the group was ordered to stay while Harwin, Richard and Xi'Lao were escorted away.

Raylan looked at the sky.

Almost midday, he thought before continuing his nap.

A stirring amongst the gathered people made him open his eyes again. The crowd split apart as a convoy of guards entered the meadow, accompanied by Richard and Xi'Lao. Behind them, several servants followed with a wagon of supplies.

"Comfortable?" said Richard.

"I figured if we're waiting, we might as well get some sleep," said Raylan with a grin. "Not to mention it makes us look less threatening."

After his adventurous flight the night before, Raylan found it a little easier to laugh again. He looked at Xi'Lao, who gave him a brief smile back.

Raylan tapped Galirras on the neck to rouse him.

"Come on. I expect you'll want to hear this," said Raylan in the dragon's head, giving him a mental nudge.

While the servants started setting up tents, their squad gathered round to get the update they had been waiting for. The dark-haired guard from the beach spoke first.

"Gentlemen. M'lady," said the guard, with a small nod to Xi'Lao. "The city of Azurna extends its apologies for making you wait, but as you might imagine, there was a lot to discuss. My name is Kenneth Whitflow, captain of the city guard. You'll be pleased to know the council of Azurna has arranged for your accommodations, as well as providing your meals during your stay, compliments of the Thyraulos family."

That seemed to get everyone's attention.

"Finally, we get to eat," said Rohan, as if he had been starving for days.

"Is there any ale?" Kevhin asked hopefully.

"Shut it, both of you," ordered Richard.

Raylan watched the two archers laugh off the warning.

"I wonder if they would have been so bold with Gavin still around," remarked Raylan to Galirras.

Captain Whitflow gave Richard a disapproving stare. "Doesn't look like you run a very tight ship."

"We've been on the road for a very long time," apologized Richard.

"Well, you're free to enter the city, but stay out of trouble," said the captain. "The annual summer festival is about to begin, and my guards have their hands full with the festivities."

Raylan noticed a twinkle in the eyes of Kevhin and Rohan. Beside them, Marek's smile instantly grew wider at the mention of a festival. The young lad slapped Peadar on the back and whispered something in his ear. Raylan saw the young dragon healer's cheeks flush.

A low "moo" drew everyone's attention. Two fat cows were led onto the meadow from the road. Galirras' stomach instinctively reacted to the presence of fresh meat with a loud rumble.

"Those are for your winged companion there, and feel free to ask for more," said Captain Whitflow. The dragon's joy, mixed with his hunger, rushed through Raylan. "However, since the city is already chaotic enough, please make sure the—the dragon remains within this meadow at all times. I don't want to spread panic throughout the city during the busiest week of the year. He's drawing enough attention as it is."

The man directed himself to Richard again.

"I'll leave you with that. You would probably do well to expect a visit from the council, or a member of the Thyraulos family. I'll let you know as soon as we hear anything of your man Harwin; the healers should bring a report soon. Same goes for any message from the capital." With a short nod to Richard and Xi'Lao, the captain headed back to the city gates, his guards following closely behind him.

"It seems news of Galirras is going around like wildfire," said Xi'Lao.

It was the truth. A steady stream of onlookers poured out from the city as people heard about this never-before-seen creature lying just outside the gates. If things were to continue, they would have to post more guards to keep everyone at a distance.

Galirras did not seem bothered by any of it. His attention was drawn by the walking meat that was being paraded past them.

"*What kind of animals are they?*" Galirras asked Raylan, swinging his head low.

"*Cows. People keep them for food and milk. There are probably tens of thousands throughout the kingdom,*" said Raylan.

"*Do you ride on them, too? Like the horses?*"

"Hmm. Kids might if they're fooling around, and some are used to pull carts for farmers, but they tend to walk much slower than horses. Stronger, but slower."

"That means they are easier to catch, as well," Galirras deduced. *"I wonder what they taste like."*

"You'll know soon enough." Raylan added a small scratch above the dragon's eye.

"A little attention never hurt anyone," he said out loud in reaction to Xi'Lao's remark.

"That might be true, and I am not worried about the curiosity of the common people, but how do we know who is watching? I am worried about the double language document that we found before, when we reacquired Galirras' egg. It is clear that someone in the Tiankong Empire is providing information to the Stone King's army; who is to say there are no spies in Aeterra as well?"

"She has a point," said Richard.

"I can take care of myself. I grow stronger and bigger every day. It would be a foolish person indeed who thought that they could hurt me. I can simply blow them away with my wind blast," boasted Galirras.

"But they would not necessarily attack you directly, would they?" said Xi'Lao. "They would try to weaken you first. Perhaps sneak up on you while you are sleeping—or poison your food."

Both Galirras and Raylan looked at the two cows tied to a small fence at the edge of the meadow.

"That is a very dark way to look at the world," Raylan said, absentmindedly regarding the cows.

"But that doesn't mean she's wrong," said Ca'lek, who had listened to the captain and their conversation. "My father used to tell stories of a lizard that could take down prey many times its own size. These predators did not fight them directly, but merely snuck up to them and bit them once. The prey would slowly lose its health and the lizard would lazily wait for it to collapse, too weak to get up anymore. Then the lizard would eat it alive…"

"We must not make the mistake of thinking lightly of recent events. The way the Stone King's army invaded our empire through the north; the invasion force in the harbor. Someone has been planning this for a very long time. They would need to have eyes and ears everywhere to make such a thing work," said Xi'Lao.

"And from what we've seen and heard of Corza, I wouldn't think it beneath him to use any means necessary," said Richard.

For a brief moment, the image of Corza stabbing his brother flashed through Raylan's mind. The knot in his stomach tightened. He swallowed the thought away.

"Corza Setra has made it clear through his actions that he wants Galirras under his control. From the start, he was hunting for Galirras' egg; every time we encountered him, he tried to capture Galirras alive," said Richard.

"True. It would explain a few other things, too. Like the fight at the stone arch. That has always bothered me, in a way," said Raylan. "Why would he attack his own forces? But when I look back at it now, I believe he never intended for the egg to reach the Stone King. That other leader must have been loyal to their ruler. To get the egg for himself, he had to take him out first."

"Which means that he will not stop there. As soon as he finds out that Raylan and Galirras are linked, he will come for them both," concluded Xi'Lao.

"Can't we leave tonight? Keep going until we reach the capital? We'll be safe there, right?" suggested Peadar.

"What? D'you know how long I've been waiting to get some time to relax?" said Kevhin.

"And what about Harwin?" said Ca'lek.

"Alright, alright. Quieten down, all of you," said Richard. "Ca'lek is right. We can't leave until we know more about Harwin. Besides that, I think it's best to wait for orders. Birds have been sent out to Shid'el. With a little luck, we should have a reply before the week's turn, enough time to unwind, for those who feel the need. I'll send someone to get us an advance on our pay; we'll need some coin if we're to spend time in the city."

"What about me?" said Galirras.

"He's right. If the food offered can't be trusted, he'll need to hunt," said Raylan.

"Good point. Little chance to do him harm if one can't predict what he'll eat," said Richard. "I'll talk to Captain Whitflow, arrange for Galirras to catch his own food. As long as you both stay away from any human settlements, I'm sure he'll agree. He seemed like a reasonable man."

"I suggest we all play it safe as well," said Xi'Lao. "If we go into the city, make sure someone accompanies you. We might not be a target, but anyone close to Galirras should be aware of any possible ill intent."

"Agreed. You heard the lady; keep your eyes and ears open and pair up," Richard ordered.

The group split up, each getting back to business. Peadar, Kevhin and Rohan approached the servants laying the cooking fires. After some objections, the trio were able to convince them that the squad had no trouble preparing their own food, and quickly sent them on their way.

Marek tailed behind Richard, asking all kinds of questions about the city and other things that had been on his mind since they left the Dark Continent. Raylan saw their commander sigh as he tried to answer all the random questions from their team's latest addition.

Raylan looked at Xi'Lao.

"Thanks," said Raylan.

"For what?" asked Xi'Lao, returning to the present from her own thoughts.

"For keeping an eye out for us all this time."

"It is my duty, and an honor."

"I know it's more than that. I just wanted to say thank you. Galirras and I look forward to clearing your family's name when we reach the Tiankong Empire."

Xi'Lao gave a hesitant smile, giving Raylan the sense that he had said something inappropriate.

"Were you able to send your messages?" asked Raylan.

"Yes. They should reach Shid'el tomorrow, after which I expect them to be forwarded to the emperor's court."

"I wonder what kind of man the emperor is," said Galirras. "I am sure he will be impressed with you when you introduce me to him."

"I am sure he will be," said Xi'Lao.

"You don't seem very enthusiastic about it. Is something wrong?" asked Raylan.

"Wrong? No, of course not. It is just that there are still many dangers between here and the emperor's court," said Xi'Lao, before adding, "I made a promise to your brother to keep you both safe. I am just trying to figure out the best way to do so."

As Xi'Lao walked away, Raylan had a gnawing feeling that he was not being told the entire story. It reminded him of their conversations before they had located the dragon's egg.

"*Raylan, may we hunt?*" said Galirras.

Raylan looked at Galirras. The small vortexes in the dragon's eyes were calmly spinning, changing colors.

"Do you have the feeling there's something she's not telling us?" said Raylan.

"*If there is, I am sure she has a good reason for it,*" Galirras said simply.

The dragon had never doubted Xi'Lao's intentions. Raylan let out a sigh.

"I suppose you're right. Alright. Let's hunt."

"*Finally.*" Galirras lowered himself. "*Get on.*"

A smile broke out across Raylan's face again. He used Galirras' front leg to quickly climb on to the dragon's shoulders.

"Here we go."

Galirras leaped into the air, a push of wind assisting the jump. The dragon's wings unfolded and began to beat. Raylan watched the meadow and people shrink rapidly; he could not imagine ever growing tired of this. He noticed some of the guards started to shout and run around. Onlookers scattered in all directions, and somewhere in the middle of it all a child started to cry.

On the ground, Richard moved to intercept the guards, explaining their intentions with large gestures. Galirras circled until Richard gave the *all clear* sign.

"We're good," announced Raylan.

Instantly, Galirras launched them forward with a wind push, heading inland to find something to eat. As the sun's warm rays warmed Raylan's back, Galirras trumpeted with the joy of being in the air together again.

"Let's find you some food," Raylan added.

It was well after midday meal by the time Raylan and Galirras returned to the meadow. The field was completely transformed: the tents were now fully erected, and the meadow had been prepared for their squad's basic needs. Screens had also been placed to give Galirras a place to escape the public's gaze.

Galirras descended to a spot deliberately left open for him. Raylan noticed a small group of people moving their way; their clothes were official looking, with slight differences in color and decorative patterns between them. A few had put up their hoods against the sun, but most looked like they were enjoying the open air. Richard and Xi'Lao accompanied them.

"Milord, please allow me to introduce Raylan Stryk'ard and Galirras," said Richard as soon as Galirras had folded his wings. "Raylan, Galirras—meet the council of Azuria, as well as the chair—and head of the Thyraulos bloodline—Lord Algirio Thyraulos."

"You can even fly the beast. Wonderful!" exclaimed Lord Algirio.

Raylan wanted to correct the man for calling Galirras a beast, but before he could say a word, the lord disappeared behind the dragon. In contrast to the other members of the council, Lord Algirio was dressed in eccentric, colorful clothes. Galirras swung his head around to follow the lord's movements. The other members of the council closely followed the man and politely listened to the comments his lordship was making.

"Such marvelous color. Could you open your wing? Oh, my. The wingspan is amazing. And who would have dreamed such eyes existed in the world!"

It went on and on.

While most of the council members seemed to share the lord's enthusiasm—or at least pretended to share it—one man kept a fearful eye on Galirras. The balding man's council clothes were more faded than the others'.

Galirras' tail twitched under the unusual inspection. Raylan had seen the different reactions people had to his presence. Sometimes they ran away screaming—which he had to admit was justified on some occasions—while others gawked at him. However, none had yet dared approach him to get acquainted—unless Raylan was present, of course. But this was an entirely new level of enthusiasm than he had previously encountered.

Galirras looked perplexed as he continued to observe his exuberant examiner. It was quite a comical sight to see; a dragon, who had surpassed the size of a man many weeks ago, looking so intensely at a human, who had no idea he was being observed in turn. Raylan remembered the first time that he realized he could no longer wrap his arms around Galirras' head anymore, so it came as no surprise to him that several of the council members were visibly startled when Galirras suddenly leaned in very close.

But Lord Algirio remained unmoved by the curious creature, even when he noticed the large mouth and rows of sharp teeth. The man stood his ground, showing a calm smile as Galirras moved his head around him and his council members.

Galirras sniffed at the strange clothes, no doubt intrigued by the bright colors; they were completely different from the armor sets and practical working clothes that he had encountered up till now.

"Galirras, what are you doing?" whispered Richard, obviously afraid of offending Lord Algirio. The lord was one of the most powerful men in the city, and although none of them had expected the man to come with such an extravagant personality, Richard clearly did not want to risk ending up on Lord Algirio's bad side.

Galirras swung his head around to look at Richard.

"Well, they were studying me up close with such intensity, it only seemed polite to return the favor," said the dragon.

Everyone seemed to hold their breath for a moment. Then Lord Algirio's mouth broke out into a smile and he started to laugh. The rest of the council joined in, except for the balding man, who still seemed too nervous.

"Wonderful deduction," exclaimed Lord Algirio, clapping his hands once before resting his index fingers together against his lips. "It seems you have brought back quite the unique and intelligent creature from the Dark Continent, Mister Stryk'ard."

"Thank you, milord. We're indeed fortunate to have him in our midst. Without him, I don't think we would be standing here."

A messenger walked up and whispered something in Lord Algirio's ear before quickly departing again toward the city gates.

"Wonderful! It seems preparations are almost complete, so allow me to officially extend the invitation. All of you are invited to attend our festivity dinner at the castle, where your squad's braveries will be honored and celebrated during the summer festival opening feast. I have arranged an exquisite meal for Galirras here as well, of course," said Lord Algirio. "I wish your friend could join us at the castle, Mister Stryk'ard, but Captain Whitflow urged me to keep the dragon out here to prevent mass panic amongst the people of our fine harbor city. He says it is already bad enough having it flying around the countryside; as I understand, Galirras prefers to hunt for himself?"

Before Richard could react, Raylan spoke up.

"Your offer is much appreciated, milord. However, I prefer to stay close to Galirras after such a weary journey, and make sure he has everything he needs while we rest up for our travels to Shid'el."

"I'm convinced that Galirras will be fine," said Lord Algirio. "He will be under the protection of my city guards and will have servants to bring him anything he needs. I'm certain you understand that people will want to ask you lots of questions about your trip and what you saw—"

"Few of which we'll be able to answer until we've delivered the official report to Shid'el, Lord Algirio," Richard interrupted politely.

"Naturally, but I will not take no for an answer from Mister Stryk'ard. Nor you, Lieutenant Brand," said Lord Algirio to Richard.

Xi'Lao shifted closer to Raylan, putting her hand lightly on his shoulder. She kept her voice down while facing away from the others.

"It is fine, Raylan. You go. I am not feeling too well, so I will stay with Galirras and keep him company. I will make sure nothing happens to him."

"Still not feeling well? Are you alright?" whispered Raylan.

"It is fine. I just need some sleep," said Xi'Lao.

"*You alright with that, Galirras?*" asked Raylan privately in his head.

"*It is fine. We had a great hunt. I am so full I just want to sleep anyways. Just be careful,*" answered the dragon.

"*I'll ask Sebastian to come with us to the castle, and Richard will be there as well. Perhaps others, too. I'll see if Galen wants to stay behind for extra security. He said he isn't very fond of royalty anyway. Don't get too comfortable with people you don't know yet… and can you do me a favor? Keep an eye on Xi'Lao. I think she may be coming down with something."*

"I thought you said she just needed to get the sea out of her legs?" said Galirras.

"I don't know. Maybe it's more than that. We've not always had the best of meals. She's might be coming down with something."

"So I can assume you will be joining us tonight, Mister Stryk'ard?" Lord Algirio interrupted the silent conversation.

"I believe you can," confirmed Raylan, sighing internally.

"Wonderful! I will see you and Lieutenant Brand, together with any others willing to join us at the castle tonight. Please take the remainder of the afternoon to acquire a more appropriate outfit. I will send one of the servants to arrange everything for you downtown."

Raylan looked down at his clothes. What was wrong with them? But it was as if the presence of Lord Algirio's clothes had suddenly made his own look worse for wear. The cloth shirt beneath his armor was dirty and torn in multiple places; his armor was scratched, smudged and missing a chunk here and there where it had saved his flesh from a sword. And now he thought of it, his fur coat had seen better days too.

"Thank you for that gesture, Lord Algirio," said Richard. "We look forward to attending tonight."

Satisfied with their visit, Lord Algirio turned to lead the council back to their coaches.

"Come along now, people. Plenty more to do before the festivities," said Lord Algirio, setting a firm pace for the others to keep up with.

Raylan stood silently beside Richard as they watched the council party return to the city. When the coaches were gone, Richard again brought up the topic that had led to their heated discussion the night before.

"Raylan, I want you to stay close to Sebastian tonight. Make sure he joins you at the festivities so we can keep an eye on him. He's not allowed to talk about our mission, especially not the invasion," said Richard. "Not to anyone."

Raylan's face must have shown his disagreement; Richard's own face settled in firm determination.

"He'll be your responsibility, understood? He needs to keep his mouth shut. Restrain him, if necessary," said Richard clearly.

Raylan's own discontent festered below the surface, but he did not trust his mouth to keep him out of trouble. He pressed his lips into a thin line. The lack of response did not go unnoticed.

"That's an order," Richard added stringently, after which he turned and walked off.

Raylan held up his arms and tried not to move. A sharp needle slid dangerously close to his skin as the tailor took his measurements. His old clothes lay in a pile on the floor. As he looked at the scars on his arms and legs, Raylan saw they were healing nicely.

Sebastian, who was standing to the side, had a grin on his face. The former slave already had his new outfit on. Dark green and bright orange colored him from head to toe in the form of wide sleeves and tight pants with leather boots. A white puffy collar was sticking out of the top of his shirt. He had shaved off his beard, revealing a strong jawline and wide mouth.

"What are you grinning about?" asked Raylan.

"I think you look more uncomfortable now than when you were wearing Doskovian armor and surrounded by hundreds of enemies," laughed Sebastian.

It was no lie. Raylan had watched in horror as every single person going to the festivities that night had been measured and dressed in the most hideous looking clothes he had ever seen. Everyone else had already left for the castle or city, and Raylan was the last in line to receive his new clothes. He was glad that his friend's mood had improved somewhat, but would have been happier had it not been at his own expense.

"Well, I don't care what they say about latest nobleman fashion. I can't imagine it's comfortable to wear, and I wouldn't want to be found dead in such a fabrication," Raylan said grumpily. "It looks nothing like what the people are wearing in Shid'el. There even the noblemen tend to wear very practical clothes."

"Actually, it doesn't feel that bad," grinned Sebastian. "A bit breezy, perhaps."

A servant girl, who stood quietly in the corner of the shop, suppressed a chuckle.

"Sally, was it?" said Sebastian to the girl.

"Yes, milord," said the girl, instantly turning red.

"Oh no, I'm no lord! Just call me Seb. Sally, since when has this been the latest fashion in Azurna?"

"For some time now, sir."

"Please, I know I look the part, but I am barely a sir. A few weeks ago, I was still living in trees trying to make sure we had enough to eat," said Sebastian. He twirled around in his outfit, bowing formally to imitate the noblemen he remembered from his childhood years.

The girl stifled another laugh.

"Whose bright idea was it to introduce such *fabulous* clothes?"

"My friend said a number of merchants from the southern cities visited the castle with strange clothes like this. She was serving drinks for Lord Algirio and his guests when she overheard our lord say how wonderful the colors looked and how he enjoyed this fresh, new look," said the girl softly.

"Please hold your breath, sir."

The tailor held his tapeline around Raylan's chest.

"Remind me again why we have to go?" said Raylan.

"Because you do not turn down an invitation from one of the three noble houses in Aeterra. An insult now will cause trouble later, I'm sure of it," said Sebastian in his Richard-imitating voice.

"I suppose you're right—or he's right, I mean. It's just that I've never felt comfortable at formal parties. I'd prefer to be outside the city, with Galirras," Raylan said with a sigh.

"Please hold still, sir," came the comment from below.

It was not just formal parties; tight, crowded streets always pressed down on his shoulders and chest as well. He wondered when he had first started feeling that way. He had disliked small spaces for as long as he could remember, but it had never caused any problems in his day-to-day life, not even when he was below decks on a ship.

Raylan thought back to the moment under the deflated balloon in the Doskovian harbor, how suffocating it had felt as they were climbing aboard under the cover of the heavy fabric. His body had suddenly stopped, frozen, his head spinning and his lungs screaming for air. Someone from their group had reached out to him, snapping him out of it, but he could not remember who it had been.

"I'm sure Galirras is fine. I believe Xi'Lao wanted to teach him some kind of game."

Sebastian looked back to the girl, still patiently waiting until they were done. She was not the definition of pretty, but she had a sweet face and deep, dark eyes.

"So, Sally, has Lord Algirio always been so… curious about new things?" asked Sebastian.

The girl looked around uncomfortably.

"It's alright. I won't tell anyone. I just want to know what we're getting ourselves into. Am I expected to come up with a dance routine?" joked Sebastian, jumping lightly in the air.

This time the girl had to bite her lip so as not to laugh.

"He's known for collecting all kinds of novelties from all corners of the world," she half-whispered. "They say people who bring him something new are generously rewarded. His main collection is focused on statues, many of them exquisite and one of a kind, but some of his other interests are said to be quite… strange. There's a room filled with bones, apparently, and the girls in the castle even whisper of a room filled with objects, small and large, with very strange shapes. Milord gives *very* private parties there for his guests; not even the servants are allowed in when…"

A look from the tailor made the girl swallow the rest of her story.

"I—I'm awfully sorry, sir. I really should get back to attend to the preparations for the festivities. I leave you in capable hands," she said quickly, then hurried out the door.

The tailor shook his head and walked to his back room for a moment.

"I wonder where that story would have ended up," said Sebastian with a wink. "Lord Algirio seems like a man to keep your eye on. I for one am happy to get new clothes, even if they are a bit elaborate. I haven't been able to really own anything for… I can't remember how long. Most of the things in the village were shared with everyone, since we had little to work with—especially in the beginning."

Raylan was about to say something when the tailor returned, holding up his clothes. Fringes, loops and stripes danced in front of Raylan's eyes.

"No. There's no way I'm wearing that. I want something simpler, more practical. Please," pleaded Raylan.

The tailor simply smiled and turned around. After a few moments spent in a cold sweat, Raylan let out a sigh of relief. In front of him the tailor held up a dark blue shirt, ornamented with fine yellow thread here and there. The pants were dark, sturdy fabric with leather patches on the inner thighs for horse riding. They looked wide enough to be comfortable, yet tailored enough to look formal. A sturdy sleeveless jacket and flexible leather boots finished the outfit.

Raylan gladly put everything on. It was a near perfect fit.

"Hold on—that was possible? We could have said no?" Sebastian started to protest, but the tailor was silently focused on fitting Raylan's clothes and pretended not to hear him.

"Sir, can I please change my order as well?" attempted Sebastian one last time.

"No time, my good sir, I'm sorry." The man finished the last adjustments of Raylan's outfit. "I really need to get back to finalizing the rest of the clothes for my other customers."

One final thread was put in before the tailor stepped back.

"You are all set, sir. Have a good day."

The man disappeared into the shop's back room, instantly making lots of working noises to indicate he had no intention of coming out again any time soon.

"What's the matter, Seb? I thought you said you were happy with your new clothes?" countered Raylan as they waved their goodbyes to the shopkeeper and walked back out onto the street. "I'm sure you'll be a hit with the ladies… and perhaps some of the men."

"I can't wait…"

Sebastian's mood did not stay down for long.

"It's definitely not the worst I've worn in my life," Sebastian concluded. This seemed to close the issue, and after a few streets he was busily talking again about the festival activities they saw, Kevhin and Rohan's drinking plans and how nice it was to have some basic washing facilities back at the meadow, not to mention the bath house, which lay just a few streets from where they were based.

"Why did you decide to shave your beard?" asked Raylan as they discussed the facilities.

"I don't know. It just felt… good. New beginnings, perhaps? I don't have to hide my face anymore."

Raylan thought perhaps there was more to it, but decided not to push the issue. When they rounded the corner of the street, Sebastian grew quiet again. For some time, he was deep in thought. He looked around, often stopping momentarily before continuing on his way again.

"What is it?" said Raylan after Sebastian looked behind them for the third time.

His friend turned toward him, trying to decide what to do.

"I know we're supposed to attend a royal dinner, but do you think we could make a small detour?" said Sebastian.

"I don't care if we're late, but Richard will probably tell us off. Why? What do you have in mind?"

"I want to visit my old house," Sebastian said quietly.

Raylan looked at Sebastian, stumped. He blinked once, then twice.

"Your house? You grew up here? In Azurna? Why didn't you say something before? Like this morning, when we set foot on solid ground? Or even before, during the weeks on the airship?"

"Because—because—I don't know. So many things! I don't know how much has changed. I've been trying to pluck up the courage to go to the house. Everything feels so familiar, but it's all different. It's been ten years,

Raylan. Ten years! My mother, my family, the house—they might not even be there anymore."

Raylan was speechless. Come to think of it, he had never thought to ask where Sebastian was from. He felt like an idiot. He had assumed it was one of the harbor cities on Aeterra, but he never actually asked, nor had Sebastian mentioned it himself. Then a thought floated to the surface of his mind.

"Wait. The argument yesterday with Richard. No wonder you were so angry about not telling people here about the invasion! It's your home. And your family might still be here."

Sebastian stood still.

"I wanted to go first thing this morning, but we weren't allowed to leave the meadow. And then I started thinking about how long I've been away. How different I must look. How much must have happened here. I barely recognize the city streets. And then to bring such unbelievable tales about a dangerous invasion…"

The waterfall of words made Raylan take a step back and regain his composure. It was clear his friend was nervous being so close to his old home, a place he had not expected to see again in this lifetime.

"Seb, it's alright. I understand. Let's go. To your house, I mean. I'm sure your mother will be beyond words to see her son again."

"If she recognizes me at all," said Sebastian with a nervous laugh.

"I don't think a mother will ever forget her child. And the news of the invasion—let's wait till after tonight's festivities. I've asked Galirras to take to the air a few times tonight and fly along the coast. If he spots anything from the Doskovian army, he'll come straight to the castle and let us know."

That seemed to calm Sebastian somewhat.

"What about Richard?"

"Well, he did tell me to keep a close eye on you. If you insist we go to find your house, there's nothing much I can do except follow," said Raylan, giving his friend a firm slap on the shoulder. Sebastian flinched at the pain in his healing wound.

"Sorry! I'd forgotten about that," Raylan exclaimed before making a polite bow and adding, "Shall we, good sir?"

The former slave shook his head, a smile creeping onto his face. Now that the cat was out of the bag, Sebastian was quick to follow up on his choice to visit his parents' house. In fact, he seemed in such a hurry to get there, it was like every moment that passed had the potential to be the difference between failure and success.

With long strides, Sebastian navigated the streets with Raylan in tow. They sped through alleys, then crossed a large street busy with carts and market stalls selling everything from baskets to jewelry. But Sebastian did not stop to look at any of the activities. He dove into another small alley at the other end, one that twisted and turned. Twice, the escaped slave held still before turning back to go the other way, but after passing what felt like half the city, Sebastian suddenly slowed and then halted in front of a large house.

The house stood two stories tall, lying directly on one of the main streets. The brown wooden beam structure was a strong contrast to its white plastered walls. Large windows and a double door dominated the front view of the house. Sebastian looked at it.

"They have painted it," said Sebastian hesitantly. "I'm not so sure I want to do this."

"The house looks very nice," said Raylan, trying to take Sebastian's mind off his nervousness. "Your father must have been a great merchant."

"My father loved taking risks. He was quite good at it. Big risks meant big rewards, if you succeeded. But it also meant that there were times we had almost nothing to eat for weeks, as all our money was in some cargo being hauled off to some distant city we had never seen. But the house… the house always looked fabulous. We always had to keep up the pretense that everything was going great, even when it wasn't, or else the customers would lose their confidence in him as a successful trader."

"Did he work from home often?"

"When he was in the city he did. He had a small office here, at the front of the house," said Sebastian, pointing to the lower windows. "But more often he was out at sea for months on end. Sailing for the southern cities, bringing back tales of exotic food, performers who spit fire and swallowed swords. My mother was the one who was there for us."

"Don't you want to see her again?"

"I do. But how do I explain where I've been for the last ten years? How do I tell her that my father—her husband—is gone?"

"I don't know, but don't you think it's better to know than to spend your entire life guessing? Even if it's hard to hear, it will probably give her some closure, don't you think? And she'll be happy to see you, without a doubt!"

His friend looked at him before finally giving a small, silent nod. Sebastian walked up the stairs to the large wooden doors, his stride skipping every other step. It was the movement of someone who had climbed those steps hundreds of times before. He may not have been here for many years, but his feet had not forgotten what it was like to come home.

Raylan saw Sebastian hesitate. Then he pushed his uncertainty to the side and gave a firm knock with the large iron ring that hung on the door.

CHAPTER EIGHT

Maim

THE KNOCK ECHOED through the hallway beyond, and for a moment nothing happened. Raylan saw tension on Sebastian's face before they heard sounds of someone moving around inside; shuffling feet, the sound of a lock being pulled back. With a deep clunk in the hinges, one of the doors opened. An elderly woman stood in the doorway. She looked at Sebastian and briefly glanced at Raylan behind him.

"Yes? May I help you?"

"Mrs. Wrinkle? Is that you?"

"Wrinkle? My name is Wiggle. I've not been called Wrinkle since… well, since the young master Halloar disappeared, I suppose."

"Mrs. Wiggle, it's me. Don't you recognize me? I'm Sebastian."

"Sebastian… Sebastian?" said the elderly woman, leaning in closer to compensate for her bad eyes. "Dear lord! Sebastian! Could it really be? I didn't recognize you! You've grown so much—and what are you wearing? Where in King's name have you been?"

Tears ran down the old woman's face as she pulled Sebastian close and hugged him.

"Please… please come in," she said, as she held the door open.

Sebastian stepped inside, and Raylan followed him in. The door closed behind them as old Mrs. Wiggle, or Wrinkle—Raylan could not decide which was the more appropriate name—showed them into the front study.

"Please, sit. Sit," offered the old lady. "Would you both like some wine or ale? I'm sure the master won't mind."

Raylan was thirsty after spending the entire afternoon in the tailor's shop, but Sebastian declined.

"No, thank you Mrs. Wrin… Wiggle. While I hate to say so, unfortunately we have other obligations tonight which we must attend. I was hoping to speak to my mother and explain what has happened. Is she nearby, or coming home soon?" Sebastian said hopefully from the edge of his seat.

The elderly woman fell silent. She walked to the empty chair across from them and slowly sank into it. Fresh tears formed in her eyes.

"Oh, I'm so sorry, dear. I thought you knew. I thought you were here just to visit little old me," said Mrs. Wiggle. "Your mother passed away years ago. I work for a new master in this house now."

Heavy silence filled the room. Sebastian sat motionless, processing the news he had known to be a possibility but which hope had pushed to the back of his mind.

The old woman stood up and took Sebastian's head in her arms, pulling him close. Raylan saw his friend's eyes shining wetly and felt the sting of his own tears welling up. His thoughts were with his own sorrows. His mother and Gavin. Soon, he would have to deliver similar news to his father. The knot in his stomach twisted further.

From the darkness of his mind, Corza's face floated forward, laughing at his hurt, and for the first time since his brother's loss Raylan felt something other than guilt, loss and numb regret. Anger seeped into him and quickly swelled. It screamed at him to give Corza what he deserved.

But as quickly as the anger flared, shame followed not far behind. Here he was, getting angry at someone thousands of miles away while his friend had just been confronted with the loss of one of the most important people in his world. At least Raylan had someone to blame for his sadness; something to focus on besides his sorrow. Sebastian had no choice but to go through it.

"I'm sorry, Sebastian," said Raylan softly.

Sebastian broke away from the old woman and straightened up. He cleared his throat and dried his eyes.

"Perhaps I'll have that drink after all. If you don't mind?"

Mrs. Wiggle offered him a glass of red wine, which Sebastian emptied in one gulp. He stayed quiet for a while, clearly trying to come to terms with things as best he could.

"What about my sister? Is she gone, too?" he asked carefully.

"No, she's still alive," said Mrs. Wiggle with a smile, happy to be able to bring some good news as well. "She lives near the Sailor's Gate. Small house on the corner with round windows in a narrow street to the left of the gate. You can't miss it."

"Is she... doing well?" said Sebastian.

"I think so. I don't see her very often, but I did run into her the other day. I believe she's happily married and has two little rascals of her own. They remind me very much of you both when you were small. Why don't you go and see for yourself if you have the time?" said Mrs. Wiggle. "She'll probably be back from the afternoon market by now."

Sebastian looked at his friend. Raylan shrugged.

"I'm game," he said in answer to the unasked question.

As they headed out the door, Mrs. Wiggle hesitated.

"I understand you have to go, but before you do... can I ask you to please tell me what happened to Master Halloar?"

Sebastian's hand froze on the door handle. He was so preoccupied with finding his family that he never actually explained to the old woman what had happened. He turned around.

"He... didn't make it. I'm sorry that I don't have the time to tell you all the details, Mrs. Wiggle, and we're likely to continue our travels soon. But if I can, I would like to drop by and tell you all about it," said Sebastian.

"I understand, Sebastian. And you're *always* welcome, dear. Now go. Go and let your sister know you're alive. Quickly!"

With that, both Sebastian and Raylan again set out onto the streets. The sun had started the final part of its descent, coloring the clouds red and purple.

"Mrs. Wiggle helped my mother around the house. With my father so often away and my mother busy with running the household *and* local business in his absence, Mrs. Wiggle was like a second mother to me," Sebastian explained as he and Raylan moved through the streets.

Raylan gave a polite smile, but could not help feeling an involuntary sting. Two mothers? Growing up, he did not even have one. It was an unexpected, childish, hurtful feeling, especially given the fact that Sebastian had just heard that his mother was gone. Raylan quickly pushed it to the side.

"We don't have a lot of time left if we're to make it to the festivities," said Raylan after they rounded another corner.

"I know. We should hurry. Luckily, the Sailor's Gate is on our way to the castle from here, so it's not much of a detour," Sebastian called back as he sped up his pace.

The harbor city of Azurna buzzed with activity. The inns and markets were rarely empty, as the main trade routes from the southern cities that ran over the Great Eastern Divide all came together at the city's port. Large seafaring ships unloaded their cargo, which was then transferred to the smaller ships traveling further inland via different rivers. Merchants, information brokers, bargain seekers and thieves; all kinds of people constantly came and went. The city blossomed under the constant stream of people and their never-ending need for rest, food and entertainment.

But if Raylan and Sebastian had thought the streets crowded during the day, it was nothing compared to the sheer mass of people that flowed along them now. The festival's first night was about to begin and it seemed every able body had dragged itself into the street to kick off the festivities. Raylan took deep breaths as he followed Sebastian through the crowd. He wondered how Galirras was doing.

Thankfully, the back alleys were a little easier to move through, but not by much. Children were playing soldiers with sticks, men were drinking ale, and women gossiped about what would happen in the next few days.

A door slammed open in front of Raylan just after Sebastian passed it. Tumbling out of it, assisted by a large pair of hands, was a man who landed heavily against the wall on the other side of the alleyway. The impact did not seem to have much effect; he simply got up and staggered off, jabbering about going to look for his next drink.

Raylan noticed several people's heads turn to follow Sebastian in his brightly colored outfit. In comparison to the ordinary folks of the city, he stood out like a jester amongst monks. Raylan did not think his friend noticed, or at the very least did not seem to mind. He was too focused on his family reunion.

After a few more streets, they turned a corner and looked straight at a large gate built within high city walls. Behind it lay a stone bridge, large enough for two wagons to pass each other, crossing the wide river toward the castle. The large gate contained two iron portcullises, one on the city side and one at the waterfront.

"That's the Sailor's Gate," said Sebastian. "We're almost there."

Behind the gate, Raylan saw the castle of Azurna. The structure rose directly from the river, as if built on the back of a giant turtle. Its large stone walls had been built to resist constant wear and tear from the moving water, which was forced to split in two by the castle island before being allowed to rejoin at the other end of it.

"It's massive," remarked Raylan.

"Come on. I think it's this way," said Sebastian, heading for a smaller street to the left.

Before long, a small house with round windows came into view. This time Sebastian did not hesitate at all. He knocked on the door and waited, but there came no sound from within to indicate someone was on their way. He knocked again. Still no answer.

"Maybe she got held up by the crowds," suggested Raylan.

His friend walked around to the back of the house. Raylan was surprised to see a small garden, fenced off by a low stone wall. Most cities were too crammed to offer space for a garden—a privilege held only by those wielding religious power, or the very rich. A thick tangle of grapevines grew upward supported by a wooden frame; it was too high for Sebastian or Raylan to see the other side. Sebastian peered through the leaves of the vines to check if anyone was in the garden.

"Hello."

Startled, both men looked down.

"Hello to you too," said Sebastian to the young girl beside him.

The girl's hair was full of tangles. A few smears on her face were evidence of her outside activities. Her clothes were basic, with a few patches here and there covering everyday wear and tear. She could not have been more than five years old.

"What yah doing, mister? Mommy says it's bad to peek into people's houses."

"She has a point," said Sebastian.

"So, why'd you do it then?"

The girl had a smirk on her face that clearly showed she enjoyed being on this side of the interrogation for once. Raylan suppressed a chuckle when he saw the look on Sebastian's face. With his friend lost for words at the child's logic, Raylan jumped in.

"My friend here is looking for someone he hasn't seen for a very long time. We were told she lives in this corner house with her children," said Raylan.

"Why did it take so long?" asked the girl, tilting her head to look at them.

"He was very far away," said Raylan.

"Do they all wear those silly clothes there?"

The girl stepped forward to touch the green fabric of Sebastian's new clothes. Raylan saw Sebastian roll his eyes at the remark.

"Not so much. But listen… I was wondering if perhaps you know who lives in this house?"

Before the girl could answer, a small metal clank sounded. The creaking of wood announced the opening of a small door in the garden fence around which a woman stuck her head.

"There you are. Emily, stop bothering those men and get back in here. It's almost supper time," said the woman, who threw an apologetic look at Raylan and Sebastian as she went back into the garden.

"But Mother," said the girl as she ran to the gate. "The man in the strange clothes says he is looking for you."

"What are you talking about?" said the woman as she came back out.

Raylan had already seen Sebastian's face change when he saw the girl's mother for the first time. Had he not, the resemblance between the two would still be enough for Raylan to know Sebastian had found the family he was looking for.

Sebastian slowly walked over to where the girl held her mother's skirt. The woman looked at them questioningly, keeping a protective hand in front of her daughter.

"Hey, Sis."

The woman looked at Sebastian. Her eyes went down to his boots and back up again, stopping at his face. Raylan saw a mixture of confusion and wonder cross her face. Then her eyes grew wide as she recognized who stood in front of her.

"Seb? Is that you? It *is* you, isn't it?"

The woman jumped forward to hug her brother, pulling young Emily, who still held onto her mother's dress, with her.

"How? Where did you come from? You look so different, and I don't mean the clothes. What happened to your cheek?"

Tears rolled down Sebastian's cheeks, ten years of pain, hardship and survival released in a single moment. The embrace broke the wall Raylan's friend had built around himself to survive the mines and cope with the losses and horrors of those dark years.

"What's wrong?" asked Sebastian's sister.

"Nothing. There were just so many times I thought this would never happen. I—I'm just glad to be here," said Sebastian.

His sister took a step back.

"But what happened? And who's your friend?"

Sebastian smiled.

"This is Raylan. Without him I wouldn't have made it here. Raylan, this is my sister, Elena."

Raylan was about to say "Hello" when the cry of a second child came from inside the garden.

"Excuse me."

Elena disappeared through the tiny gate. The little girl was hot on her tail. Sebastian and Raylan quickly followed to see what was wrong, but by the time they entered the garden, the small baby boy who had been the source of the sound had already quieted down in his mother's arms.

"He fell over, with his little clumsy baby feet. Right, Tobias?" said Elena in a soft, loving voice. "Tobias, I would like you to meet your uncle, Sebastian. Seb, this is my youngest, Tobias. And you already met Emily, of course."

She put Tobias down. He could not have been older than a year and a half. Right away, the baby boy started wobbling around again, his tiny legs trying to keep up with where he wanted to go. With a large smile, he wrapped his two little hands around Sebastian's leg and bent backward to look at his newly-introduced uncle's face.

"He likes you," said Elena with a smile.

Sebastian picked up the smiling boy and handed him over to his sister again.

"It's great to see you're doing so well, Sis."

"How did you find me?"

"Mrs. Wiggle. We just came from the old house."

"Ah. So you know about mother?" asked his sister.

Sebastian nodded.

"And father? Is he here with you as well?

Sebastian shook his head.

"How? What happened? I need to know," said his sister quietly. "No, wait. First, come inside. Have a seat."

"We were boarded off the coast of the Dark Continent. Father fell defending the ship," said Sebastian, deliberately sparing his sister the details as they followed Elena inside.

Sebastian turned his head away as he spoke, as if it was his fault.

"I was captured, forced to work for them until we were able to escape. I've been looking for a way home all these years, but it wasn't until Raylan came along that we were able to cross the Divide and get back here."

As her brother fell silent, Elena grabbed his hand. Her eyes shone with tears.

"I'm ashamed to say I gave up on you both years ago," she confessed. "Mother never did, though. She always hoped for you both to return. But I—I moved on."

She gave a sad smile, even as a tear fell for the loss of their father.

"And I don't blame you," added Sebastian with a meek smile of his own.

Tobias pulled on Elena's arm, and her daughter gave her a hug.

"Are you sad, Mommy?" asked Emily.

"Just a little," Elena said as she gave both children a firm hug. "And a whole lot of happy."

She picked up her food basket.

"Perhaps it's best to keep the details for another day," she said. "You and your friend are welcome to stay for supper." To Raylan, she said, "The summer festival started today. In this house, we traditionally celebrate with a large supper. Lucas, my husband, will be home soon. I'm sure he'll be very glad to meet the both of you."

"I'm sorry, Elena," said Raylan. "I know Sebastian would love to stay here tonight, more than anything. However, we're required to attend Lord Algirio's festivities… which are about to start, so we need to leave."

"At the castle? But you just got here," protested Elena.

"I know. I'm sorry. When I decided to join Raylan's group, I signed up for a few things I have to see through," apologized Sebastian. "But I'll come back tomorrow, I promise. They're keeping us all camped just outside the city walls in one of the meadows toward the beach. You can come and visit us there if you wish."

"Outside the city? You're with the group everyone is talking about? They're saying there's a monster, larger than any man, sleeping in those fields," said Elena, worried.

"News travels fast, as always," Raylan said with a smile.

"It's true. Well, I mean, not a monster. A dragon," said Sebastian. "He's called Galirras and he's very friendly. He's a very good friend of Raylan here—and myself. If you bring the children tomorrow, I'm sure Raylan will introduce you all."

Elena looked mortified.

"You must be mad! Bring the children? Surely a dragon would eat them for a morning snack!" she exclaimed so loudly that Tobias pouted, deciding if he should cry or not.

"I can promise you Galirras won't do anything of the sort," said Raylan, reassuring. "He's quite fond of children—in a non-food way—and I'm sure Galirras will be delighted to meet members of Seb's family."

Elena successfully delayed their departure with her questions until her husband returned from work. As predicted, he was happy for the chance to meet them both, and so the first stars showed bright in the sky by the time Raylan and Sebastian walked back onto the main street toward the Sailor's gate.

"I can't believe how late it already is," said Sebastian. "I hope the lord is not easily angered."

"Or Richard. He's been trying very hard to fill my brother's boots," said Raylan. "But I wonder if he's up for the task. I think he has his own doubts as well."

They presented themselves at the Sailor's Gate, where they were escorted to the castle.

"Wow," murmured Raylan in amazement.

Up close, the complex was even bigger than he originally thought. On each of the three levels, a ring of pillars held up the wide balustrade of the level above. The majestic construction created a large, open hallway between the pillars and the wall on which the next level rested. On the balustrades were the next level's double wall and battlements, their floor acting as the lower level hallway's ceiling. Raylan's trained eye immediately noticed the hundreds of trapdoors and murder holes, which allowed soldiers to attack any invader stupid enough to think the open hallway would keep them out of sight and out of harm. The pillars themselves were so thick they could not be moved or easily knocked down by human hands.

"There are three gates, each with its own stone bridge," said Sebastian as they walked. "Most of the city is at sea level, so the south and the east bridge are low above the water. They merge together just ahead and act as the main route to get to the castle from the harbor, while the Old Gate on the left leads into the oldest part of town."

Approaching the castle gate, a carriage passed them with rattling wheels. It turned left near the wall, where the water-level hallway held the stables. It was crawling with carriages, coachmen and horses dropping off guests for the feast.

At the end of the bridge was a large wooden drawbridge, complete with another set of portcullises. The heavy gates on the castle's lower levels would easily stop any approach by land, thought Raylan. An attempt from the river would be equally difficult; the slightly sloped walls that rose from the river water were coated with slippery algae, gray stone turning dark green near the water level. It was, as Sebastian said, a strategic layout that had proved its worth for centuries.

Twin stairways separated by a slope led to the next level; the stairs split where they entered the inner hall of the battlements on each side. From there Raylan saw more iron gates; more fortified doors. Each ramp coming into the battlement could be secured by a thick horizontal iron gate, with on top, a heavy, wooden door.

"There's no way to breach these gates. No battering ram can push up," Sebastian said proudly, as he pointed at the uncommon setup."

"But a few ghol'm might easily push through," said Raylan.

He remembered the night in the harbor, when they had wandered into a warehouse; it held hundreds of ghol'ms to be loaded on the ships in preparation for the invasion.

"Not only that; every single castle in Aeterra—perhaps the world—is designed to withstand an attack from land or sea, but all the Doskovian soldiers have to do is step into their airships and fly over these walls. It's going to be a slaughter no matter where they invade," added Raylan.

"The castle in Dahalaes lies under a roof of trees," started Sebastian.

"Yes, but trees won't stand a chance against their fireballs. They'll burn the entire forest down."

With night setting in, the torches on the castle walls were lit, while the bastions had slightly larger fires. Hundreds of lights, large and small, burning along its walls gave the castle a magical feel.

Entering the first plaza, they saw a night market was ongoing. Small stalls displayed wares for visitors to admire as merchants tried to convince those with money to buy their uniquely qualified products. Further along, people in masks performed acrobatic tricks, and near the far wall a street play brought a loud laugh from the spectating crowd.

"Lord Algirio indeed has some exotic tastes in new discoveries," remarked Sebastian. "There must be merchants from all around the world here to present their findings. Seems the weirder, the better."

As they continued up to the next level, Sebastian pointed to the side.

"There's the High Gate with its bridge connecting to the northern shore," said Sebastian. "My father took me to watch the ships pass under it when I was very young. Its arches run a hundred feet above the water, easily, so boats can sail under them."

Most of the city lay on the southern bank, yet a small part of the city was on the north side, like a stubborn child trying to go its own way. Historically, it had never grown much, as the steep incline of the terrain into the northern hills made it difficult to build, yet it was never abandoned. The cliffs ran for miles along the north side of the river, before the land finally lowered again to water level.

"He also said they used to hang criminals there, to act as a warning to those people traveling over and under it. But Lord Algirio's father put a stop to that, thinking it was an unappealing sight for the city."

"Don't want to scare away your customers," said Raylan, half joking. "Better to trade and make profit."

"And the profit can be spent in the city right away. I never knew my hometown had so much gambling, whoring and drinking," added Sebastian, sounding uncertain if he preferred this newfound adult view or his child's image of the city. "For those seeking to lose their money, Azurna sure has plenty to offer."

They passed the official public auditorium and made their way to the third level, reserved for Lord Algirio's keep and council chambers. It was there that

Lord Algirio held tonight's festivities, for invited guests only. By the look of things, Lord Algirio had invited half of Azurna.

Raylan and Sebastian followed the sounds of laughter and music to the great hall; the space literally crawled with people. Long tables stood throughout the hall. A small group of musicians were playing songs in the corner, where a few of the guests had gathered to laugh and dance. But most people sat to enjoy the plentiful food offered on overloaded tables. Potatoes, roasted pig, steak of deer, grapes and other fruit; the abundance of food was overwhelming after months of hunting their own dinner and getting by on minimal rations each day.

Quite a few people wore the same clothing style Sebastian had received that afternoon; the women in particular appeared to be in competition to see who could wear the most extravagant dress to the feast. But Raylan was glad to see other guests dressed in simpler clothes, although it did little to suppress the urge to turn around and run back out again.

They took in the festive scene in the hall, Sebastian in awe, Raylan wondering why he had not stayed with Galirras. He was just about to turn around when Richard appeared from the crowd.

"You're late! Where have you been?" said Richard. "Lord Algirio has been asking for you constantly. Come and join us at the table."

Reluctantly, Raylan followed Richard to the table at the end of the room. Sebastian refused to look at Richard, showing a hardness which Raylan had not seen before in his friend.

Lord Algirio's private table stood slightly higher than the rest of the room. Raylan recognized several of the council members present. The Lord of Azurna himself sat next to a charming, dark-haired woman in a long, light blue dress.

"Ah, there's my good man," bellowed Lord Algirio as Raylan and the others approached. "I was beginning to wonder if you had gotten lost in the city. Swallowed up by the crowds, perhaps."

"Our apologies, milord. It seems we lost track of time during an important errand," Raylan said formally after Richard gave him a hard nudge in his side.

"Oh, is that so? I would be curious to know what was more important than my given invitation?" said Lord Algirio, with a small smile.

Raylan wondered if the man was genuinely interested, or if he was testing them to see how deep they would dig their own hole. The lord did not seem like the kind of man who was bothered much by the actions of other men—very few rich people were. On the other hand, there was the common phrase a *rich man's temper*. All too often people with an abundance of possessions began to think of themselves as more important than others; better, smarter, more handsome, funnier, hungrier. When that happened, it was only natural that anyone who disrespected that self-touted importance—with words or actions—surely deserved the full force of their anger. Still, Raylan could not yet see if Lord Algirio fell in that category or not.

"It really was my fault, milord," said Sebastian. "Azurna is where I grew up. I wanted to visit my mother and let her know I was still alive after ten years away."

In Raylan's mind it seemed ridiculous to apologize for such an important reason, but before he could react, Richard cut in as if he had been completely aware of the unplanned detour.

"I'm sure milord can appreciate the importance of family ties—especially after your announcement earlier this evening," said Richard, giving a polite nod to the dark-haired woman beside Lord Algirio.

Raylan saw the woman put her hand on the lord's arm. Her other hand lay lovingly on her slightly rounded belly, which she rubbed softly.

The lord looked at his wife, who met his gaze with a warm, loving smile. The woman's green-brown eyes sparkled with love. Long, dark hair fell past her shoulders. Her face showed slightly rounded cheekbones, and fine lines around the eyes and mouth complemented her elegant appearance.

"This is true. Lady Leandra and myself met so late in our lives we did not know if we would even be able to have a family."

He gave a soft, supportive squeeze of his wife's arm.

"Please, good sir, join our table and tell us of the happy reunion with your mother," Lord Algirio said, gesturing to the empty chairs. "The food is for all to enjoy. It is the time of summer abundance, after all."

Raylan saw Sebastian swallow his newly discovered loss as they took their places. Then the escaped slave began his story.

It was not long until Lord Algirio voiced his regret for Sebastian's loss, as did his wife, but he also had many questions about the Dark Continent and the people who had taken Sebastian captive. Both Sebastian and Raylan, who was quickly pulled into the conversation, tried their best to answer them without specifying the details of their worrisome discovery. On the far side of Lady Leandra sat Richard, watching them like a hawk.

Raylan still did not support his brother's replacement's decision to keep silent about what they had seen. Here they were, celebrating the summer while the enemy could knock on their door at any moment. He had to bite his tongue multiple times. Eventually, he calmed himself with the decision that even if he wished to inform the lord of Azurna of this possible danger, the festivities—and company—were hardly the right place to discuss these matters.

He looked at Richard, wondering why he was bothering to follow the man's orders at all. It dawned on him that his loyalty had lain mostly with his brother, and not the army ranks.

Raylan was glad he had at least asked Galirras to keep an eye out when flying along the coast. He just hoped Captain Whitflow would not object to it. It would give them only a moment's notice to prepare in case they were attacked, but it was better than nothing. Apart from that, Raylan could only hope that word soon came back from the capital.

Later that evening, the conversation turned toward the flying airship. Such a unique vessel had not failed to pique Lord Algirio's curiosity. And as Marek and Peadar had both chosen to skip the royal invitation in favor of exploring the city, Raylan was asked to explain all the details he had learned from Marek during the weeks of crossing the Great Eastern Divide.

"Can you imagine?" Lord Algirio said excitedly after hearing Raylan's description. "A ship… flying! I wish I had been near the beach for a hunt this morning."

Raylan saw Lady Leandra smile. She seemed fully accustomed to her husband's excessive curiosity, although Raylan figured a flying ship would pretty much grab anyone's attention.

"We don't have to imagine, milord. We lived it," replied Raylan politely.

"I asked Lord Algirio to send a few men to the beach to dig out the statue and ship. We'll take the statue with us to Shid'el, and I've requested approval from the capital to let Azurna's shipbuilders examine the ship, under Lord Algirio's watchful eye," said Richard.

"Which I have absolutely no problem with," laughed Lord Algirio, clearly happy that he could indulge in his deep-driven search for novelties.

Raylan tore off another piece from a chicken's leg. He took his time to chew the food, not really feeling hungry. In the meantime, the wine flowed richly all around him. The people grew merrier; laughter filled the hall from wall to wall. But Raylan found it difficult to enjoy any of it. His mind lingered on the bad news about Sebastian's mother, and the realization that he had to confront his father soon while his brother's murderer was still out there. His somber mood only deepened as the evening progressed. It did not matter how he looked at things; it did not sit right with him that they were not allowed to speak of the invasion.

All the while, Richard's behavior was as pleasing and charming as could be. Their current leader even got on stage to perform a song or two on the flute when the topic of conversation flowed toward the musical skills that ran in the Brand family. Raylan only half paid attention, politely applauding at the end, but both the lord and his wife seemed genuinely pleased with the performance.

Eventually, their hosts excused themselves. Lord Algirio was to escort his wife to her chambers so she could rest. They bid everyone a good night and exited the hall, but not before Lord Algirio had made Raylan promise to invite Galirras to the castle so that his wife would have a chance to meet this unusual creature. Unable to decline under the social pressure, Raylan promised he would. Not that he felt much like showcasing Galirras everywhere they went, but he was certain Galirras would love to have a closer look at the castle. After all, the dragon had made several admiring comments about the river island and its buildings during their earlier flight.

"Would Captain Whitflow not object?" Richard cut in as soon as Raylan had agreed.

"Let me worry about the captain, Lieutenant Brand. It will not be the first time that a strange thing upsets the people of Azurna, and I promise you it will not be the last."

The lord let out a loud laugh.

"You and your men just enjoy the summer festival and Azurna's hospitality," he added. "There is plenty of fun to be had in our wonderful city!"

Lord Algirio boosted his voice as he spoke the last part, triggering a loud cheer from those enjoying the feast. After that, the lord and lady left, leaving their guests in the capable hands of their staff. To be polite, Raylan stayed for a while longer, until he and Sebastian finally convinced Richard that Lord Algirio had no intention of returning.

"Fine, you two can go. I'll see you back at the camp."

They did not need to hear that twice.

The sound of Corza's discontented strides thumped on the wooden deck of the *Behemoth*.

He had been in the middle of discussing tactics with his commanders when the Stone King summoned him. Lord Rictor stood on the upper deck watching the city in the distance. Two of the Darkened carefully watched the shore and the ship, one on either side. It looked like a light guard, but Corza knew two Darkened were more than enough to hold off a sizable attack. Besides, the other skeleton-faced fighters were just below deck—ready to start a war, if the need presented itself.

"Ah, High General Setra, thank you for coming."

"Your wish is my command, my lord," said Corza as he greeted the Stone King with his fist on his heart.

"How is the day going? I trust most of the army will soon be able to move on from this island and make their way around the southern point?"

"They are no longer needed after the King of Iron's public surrender—unless the south part of the island decides to revolt."

"They will not if their king does not tell them to," stated Lord Rictor. "When the time is right, you will join up with High General Cale in the far western seas. Taimila and Calissa will assist me here until it is time for me to depart."

Corza cursed inside.

The twins? Are those bitches already here?

"A fine choice, milord."

Taimila and Calissa were two exquisite and dangerous women. Of all the females in the world, Corza probably distrusted them the most. In fact, he loathed them, second only to his mother. Not just because they had flawless looks, or the fact that they knew how to use them. But they had the annoying tendency to interfere with his plans whenever they felt like it. There was a viciousness in their approach—hidden just out of sight—that equaled, or perhaps even surpassed, his own.

That white-haired, stone-armed freak will let them do anything they please.

In an army that never actually accepted women as soldiers, the twins had been remarkably effective in securing a position and moving up the ladder—all the way to the point where they achieved the highest honor possible as part of the Stone King's inner circle. Everyone called them Mistresses of the Darkened, though they never officially received such a title. Lord Rictor's personal forces had no obligation to any of the official high generals like Corza; indeed, it was the high generals themselves who had to take care not to accidentally get in the way of any of the skeleton-faced forces.

It was a delicate power balance. Yet somehow these women had wiggled their way into the structure and earned the respect of the Stone King's most dangerous and ruthless killers. In Lord Rictor's absence, they gave the Darkened their assignments, which were followed without question. Both women were loyal to a fault and extremely protective of 'their' Lord Rictor. If the twins ever found out that Corza was plotting against the Stone King himself, he would certainly find himself waking up with two pair of cold eyes staring at him—if he woke up at all.

"How are preparations going?" asked the Stone King.

"All in order, my lord. The troops dispersed toward the forest and mountain settlements should have arrived by now. The royal degree King Baltor signed is expected to provide access to both strongholds and grant moderate cooperation to start with. Once the people see their armed forces being disbanded, it's expected the working population will pose little resistance. There should be an update on our progress before the morning."

"Very well. I am certain Baltor's announcement will quell any remaining will to fight back. Afterward, we can focus fully on the Talkarian steel production."

"You'll be pleased to hear that the first dedicated batch of swords has been produced and is being loaded on our ships this very evening, milord."

"I understand armor is also proceeding nicely, albeit a bit slower than expected?" said the Stone King.

Corza hesitated for a moment.

"I'll order them to go faster."

"Do not bother. As I am sure you are aware, High General, we're in this for the long haul. If we push too hard now, we will have exhausted our resources by the time we need them most. Besides, I will soon be giving the command for the production of swords and armor to stop. I will send over new schematics that are to be followed from that moment on."

Annoyed that Lord Rictor had apparently set him up to fail with his remark, Corza bit his tongue before speaking again.

"If not swords and armor, what will we be making here, milord?" asked Corza, puzzled.

"That is of no concern to you. I would rather have you focus on securing a new, constant supply of ore from the mines. The ovens in the city rely on it, and it has obviously not arrived for some days."

"Is there anything else, my lord?"

"There is the small matter of retrieving my weapon. That which you lost many moons ago."

Corza swallowed. A drop of sweat tickled the side of his head. Lord Rictor had a disturbing way of asking very innocent-sounding questions while expecting very important answers. In the past, Corza had quickly learned to recognize the tone that cost many other men their lives for answering too casually.

"Colonel Mercar said they lost sight of the stolen windship and thought it best to return to the main force, my lord. He instructed the other ships in his group to continue and travel to Azurna as per my order, which would be the enemy's most logical destination. Meanwhile, my spies—"

A quick glance from Lord Rictor made Corza reconsider his words.

"—*our* spies have indeed confirmed that the Aeterran squad has landed in Azurna, unharmed."

It had taken Corza years to set up a reliable network of bird messengers throughout the continents. Some doubled as official messenger servants, while others had hidden cots within the cities where the best breeds of pigeon provided a swift relay of information for the Stone King's plans.

"The group is currently camped outside the city, awaiting orders. The ships I sent will be able to catch up with them if they stay just a few more days. They should have no trouble taking over the city."

"And the dragon is with them?"

It was the first time Lord Rictor had mentioned the word 'dragon' instead of 'weapon'. It was an odd moment to drop the word, clearly intended to unnerve him. Corza wondered what else the Stone King knew about the animal.

"Not only is it with them, but our informants say it's communicating… with people."

Corza watched carefully for a reaction, but saw none.

"It seems to have a particularly strong connection with the young soldier it saved from the cliff during the harbor escape," added Corza.

"That would be *most* unfortunate," said Lord Rictor. "What else?"

"We know little about the soldier other than that his name is Raylan. It seems he befriended the creature and speaks with him often. He has even been seen on the dragon's back while it took to the air," said Corza, bitter.

The Stone King was silent for a moment. Corza saw his expression jerk slightly, as if the man was running different probabilities in his head that did not agree with each other, making his muscles twitch.

"I know, I know!" exclaimed the Stone King suddenly. "But it does not matter. They cannot stop us, even if they knew what we were doing."

"Know what, my lord?"

Lord Rictor turned around and looked Corza straight in the eye.

"I do grow tired of these mistakes, Setra. Perhaps I *should* have chosen High General Wayler to begin with," said Lord Rictor. "Alas, I am short on good men at the moment, so you will just have to do."

Corza scoffed internally.

"However, I believe a reminder is in order. You understand, do you not? See it as an incentive…"

The Stone King gestured to the two Darkened nearby. Before Corza knew it, they were flanking him on both sides. His reflexes jumped to high alert. He could have drawn his favorite dagger, but the odds did not look in his favor. The two Darkened stood silently, staring at him.

"Remind me again: which side is your sword arm?" said the Stone King.

Corza swallowed and straightened up.

"Right, my lord."

"Good, good," said the Stone King slowly, as if he had not yet decided what to do. "Then take out your Roc'turr and remove your left hand's little finger. That should not cause too much trouble, should it?"

Corza stared at Lord Rictor. The Stone King did not move a muscle; a content smile showed on his face. Anger roared inside Corza. It took all his discipline not to show it. He had no choice here. Failing to obey would mean instant death, and he had not worked and schemed for all these years to let it all be taken away from him now. Slowly, he pulled out his sacrificial dagger. The Darkened simultaneously drew their swords.

Corza knelt and put his hand flat on the ship's deck. He lined up the Roc'turr; pressed the blade against his skin. In silence, he looked up at Lord Rictor, who returned his look coolly. The silence filled with expectation.

Corza swallowed, looked at his hand—and pushed. The blade cut deep, quickly biting into bone. Pain sent shocks through his body. A scream was building deep within and Corza clenched his teeth to prevent it from escaping. Blood flowed onto the *Behemoth's* deck. Corza leaned forward and drove the Roc'turr down through the bone.

He sat back up and lifted his chin stubbornly, meeting the Stone King's condemning stare. Corza's own skin was probably just as white now as that of Lord Rictor, but he had not given his pale tormentor the satisfaction of screaming.

Lord Rictor observed the severed finger.

"It is a clean cut, but a bit on the small side, is it not? Barely half a finger," spoke the Stone King without emotion. "Perhaps I should not complain. After all, I never specified how much of your finger it should be. Very well. It should make the next part easier for you. I want you to pick it up, and swallow it."

Behind Corza, one of the Darkened grunted in amusement. Humiliation hit him like a hammer, but Corza had experienced worse. He forced himself to lower his eyes and kept his lips tightly shut. He reached out and picked up the chopped-off piece of finger, keeping his bleeding hand close to his chest to stop the flow as it throbbed in agony.

Corza looked at the piece of flesh between his fingers. A tiny part of the bone was visible, and in a moment of mental alienation, he noticed how incredible dirty the small finger's nail was.

"Go ahead, Setra."

Reluctantly, Corza brought the severed part of his body to his mouth and put it on his tongue. In hindsight, he should have thrown it to the back of his throat and swallowed it without breathing. The finger now rolled across his tongue and he had to adjust it twice to prevent it from getting stuck in his throat before he finally swallowed. The entire experience was nauseating—which came as a bit of a surprise; he never had any trouble when he worked on any of his toys, cutting them, poking them with holes. But it was not the wound that upset him, but rather the complete humiliation of being forced to swallow his own flesh. He would never have even entertained such an idea for his prisoners—there was too much chance of infection.

Corza got back to his feet, sheathed his dagger and firmly gripped his bleeding finger to staunch the flow of blood—gritting his teeth against the jolts of pain.

"Excellent. Now that you have a constant reminder of your failure, it is time to get back to business. Keep in mind that I expect you to really make an effort, or before you know it you will run out of fingers on your left hand."

Corza had to swallow again, fighting the feeling that his finger was stuck halfway down his esophagus.

"Once things are arranged here, you will head further west around the continent. Our masked friends there have made contact to let us know they are ready to deal. Since it was your idea to begin with, I am certain you would like to see it through successfully, am I right?"

The Stone King did not wait for an answer.

"High General Cale will continue the invasion of the southern trade cities and set up a supply line. Once we are done here, High General Nodak will be diverted to the north, to Azurna. Your force can hand over the city when they arrive."

Corza's mind raced. That meant there was not much time for those who were loyal to him and currently traveling north. Once they secured that pesky dragon, they would have to move it immediately—perhaps take it out to sea by ship, going the long way around to avoid High General Nodak's fleet.

"If any of our forces run into the dragon, they are expected to do everything in their power to capture and retrieve it. But if it becomes clear that the creature cannot be used for our cause, I want it gone. This has gone on long enough. Either capture it, or kill it and bring me its head. No excuses," said the Stone King.

The last words had just left Lord Rictor's lips when he bent forward and grabbed the side of his head.

"Are you alright, my lordship?" asked Corza.

"No. I mean, yes. I do not care," Lord Rictor growled through gritted teeth. "Our plans are what matters. We shall *not* be stopped."

Another grunt. Lord Rictor's stone hand gripped the railing, crushing the wood.

"Please remain calm, my lord. I am certain we can properly motivate the beast with the right incentives," said Corza, afraid that his intended prized possession would be snatched from under him by the greedy claws of death's reaper.

"Alright, alright!" said the Stone King, forcefully. "Alive, preferably alive."

Lord Rictor panted heavily, his pain seeming to subside. Corza watched the man straighten up, then methodically readjust his clothes. Once decent, Lord Rictor turned his gaze on Corza once more.

"What are you still doing here?" snarled the Stone King.

Corza looked down at his bleeding stump, swallowing an angry response.

"You can count on me, milord. I've got multiple plans in motion. You'll see; before you know it, I'll have returned to you with that dragon by my side."

And it will be the last damn thing you'll ever see.

Lord Rictor cleared his throat and turned back to stare at the lights of the city again.

"We will see. Now, take the rowboat back to the city and find a healer for that finger of yours. I do not want any more of your bloodstains spread out all over my ship."

CHAPTER NINE

Resistance

"Everything is ready, my king."

The voice whispered near the edge of silence. King Baltor had to strain his ears to catch the words.

A small smile formed on the king's face. He lay on a bed of straw on the floor, his back to the doorway where a Doskovian soldier kept an eye on him and the small servant who was allowed to bring Bogoris his food. The king knew the servant well; a thin, bony man, whose back was bent from walking the low dungeon tunnels for many years.

At first, the King of Iron had been comfortable in one of the larger guest rooms in the castle, but after a failed attempt to free him, the Stone King deemed it necessary to relocate him to the dungeons. The underground complex was harder to reach and, in all, not a very pleasant place to stay. The prison was constructed from old mining tunnels, on which the Castle of Tal'Kabur was built. It was cold and damp, with little light or fresh air, not to mention unsafe; the tremors that plagued the island had caused collapses in more than one of the tunnels over the past year. It was clear that Lord Rictor hoped to discourage further rescue attempts from the soldiers of Tal'Kabur.

"How many?" whispered King Baltor as softly as possible.

"Plenty. Sire." The man added the last word quickly, uncertain if he should keep up with formalities. The old servant crawled closer, pretending to clear out yesterday's wooden plate. "I'm told more forces will be waiting in the forest, just outside the city. White smoke will signal them to begin their attack. We'll be ready for your signal."

The King of Iron sat up and turned around, pretending to look at the food the man had brought.

"Thank you, Linus. This is much appreciated," said the imprisoned king in a normal voice. "Are they treating you well?"

"That's enough," bellowed the soldier.

Hastily, the man retreated from the cell. The Doskovian soldier slammed the door shut behind him.

King Baltor reached out to grab a piece of bread, but stopped when he saw his own dirty hand. Though it had only been a week, the filth of the dungeon had made quick work of King Baltor's clean clothes—or at least the clothes he had been allowed to keep, which basically amounted to a nightshirt. The thin fabric gave no comfort against the stale dungeon air or the cold, stone floor from which his straw bed provided little protection. The cold numbed his body, making it impossible to rest without waking up stiff and aching all over. The little food he received was barely enough to keep his strength up, let alone warm his body. If not for the knowledge of the resistance forming, the King of Iron would have felt utterly lost.

Those who remained with the resistance first made contact with a small, written note, hidden in his food, a few days after the king's transfer to the dungeons. Being cut off from the outside world, he welcomed any news about the status of his family and people. Linus had not been able to tell him much, but at least Bogoris knew his wife and daughter were doing well. Of Bronson there was no news, which made the king fear the worst. He suspected his son had been at the forefront of the first rescue attempt, which meant the Doskovians probably held him responsible.

The King of Iron looked at the bowl of gruel and piece of stale bread in front of him. Sometimes an apple or piece of cheese made its way to him, hidden in one of the many pockets Linus seemed to have in his clothes, but not today.

A pair of beady eyes twinkled in the darkest corner of the cell. It amazed King Baltor how some corners still looked much darker than others with the little light there was. While his thoughts wandered, there came the sound of little nails clicking across the stone floor. A rat carefully approached the plate of bread, sticking its nose in the air to check its surroundings. Satisfied, the rat sprang forward, quickly covering the last stretch to its intended meal.

The king's dirty hands shot through the air and snatched the bread from the wooden plate. Four tiny feet scurried back into the darkest corner and disappeared into a crack in the wall.

"Not today, my little friend. I will need my strength for the upcoming fight."

Bogoris Baltor ripped off a chunk and started vigorously chewing on it. It would take a while before the bread was moist enough to swallow, but he had an obligation to his people. He needed to stay strong. *Soon.* Soon, they would look to him to give the signal to start their fight for liberation.

* * *

Linus limped through the low tunnels. Torch in hand, he passed door after door until he reached the small stairway back up to the guardhouse. He glanced behind as he heard one of the prisoners scream. The stairs had a nostalgic feel to them. His eyes did not work as they used to, but his feet knew the way well. Every crack, every bump in the stone was an old friend—and sometimes an old nemesis.

The royal family had always been kind to him. Even now, when his malformed bones started to ache more every day. The princess had even thanked him for coming to her rescue with a broken mirror. She was such a gentle soul. He had seen her grow up and blossom in a wonderful young human being, full of life. Just like the other children of the king and queen. They were a proud family, keen to lift others up instead of bringing them down. Linus felt appreciated, which was a nice gift for him in his old age.

The princess, he thought fondly. It always brightened his day when she required his help.

He had many tasks in the castle, many more than people usually thought. That was no surprise; often, his tasks were done far from the everyday comings and goings of the castle. Someone had to make sure the lower levels kept their charm. Doors needed to be oiled, but not so much that they lost their characteristic squeak. Rats needed to be caught so that the castle was not overrun by them, but one or two certainly gave the lower levels a bit of… ambiance.

Ambiance. He liked that word. He had heard the queen mention it before the winter ball. It felt… weighty.

Linus carefully chose a key from the many on his keyring—he had an image to maintain, after all—and turned it. The metal lock produced a scraping sound. He turned the key back and reached into the satchel that hung on his back, producing a tiny jar of grease from it. He dipped his finger in the grease and pushed it in the keyhole. He wiggled his finger around, careful not to get stuck, until he was certain he had hit the right spot. The jar disappeared back in the satchel as quickly as it had been produced, before he gave the key another try. He jiggled it back and forth a few times to loosen the mechanism before turning it. With a characteristic clunk the iron door unlocked and swung open. Linus stepped out of the dampness of the lower tunnels and entered the warm, dry air of the guardhouse main hall.

Six similar doors led to this hall, which had a pleasant fire going in the central fireplace. Some of the doors led to the other cells, and one to the catacombs. The others merely worked their way toward the castle's upper levels. It was a crossroads, of sorts.

He looked back one more time down the dark stairwell to where his king was being kept in such an undignified manner.

The king has always treated me well.

"Why is it that you bottom feeders are always limping around instead of just walking properly?"

Startled, Linus closed the door, revealing Corza, who casually leaned behind it against the wall. The High General took a bite out of the apple that sat firmly staked on his Roc'turr.

"I don't dare guess, High General… sir," said Linus, his voice instantly beginning to shake.

* * *

Corza sneered at the elderly servant, unable to keep his face from betraying his loathing for the tiny man. It was like the world had combined all the worst aspects of his fellow human beings and then put them together inside this crippled waste of air. Even the large white hairs from the man's nostrils vibrated annoyingly with every pointless breath the man took.

"I trust you are taking good care of your king?" said Corza.

"Yes, sir, High General, sir," the old man quickly answered. "I do my best."

"Excellent. We wouldn't want him to miss his appointment with the proud people of Tal'Kabur."

"No, sir. Not at all, High General, sir."

The servant waited nervously, hopping from one foot to the other as though he needed to relieve himself. Corza observed him in silence for a moment, letting the man's discomfort drag on.

"Alright, you can go now," Corza said finally, waving the man out of his sight. "Off you go."

The man scurried away toward the kitchens. Corza watched him go before turning in the opposite direction.

Time to check on my other project, he thought as he started to climb the many stairs.

He was beginning to know the castle quite well. It was by no means as large as the Dark Palace, but Corza still managed to get himself turned around every now and then. He passed a few windows that looked out over the main plaza. All the signs of fighting had been removed, the bodies taken away, and a summer's rain the other day had washed away most of the blood. Still, not many people in the city dared set foot on the plaza nowadays; not without good reason.

Corza saw his soldiers practicing with the new steel nets they had constructed. They were lighter than the original nets fabricated back on the Dark Continent—one of the many perks of Talkarian steel—and twice as strong. Which meant his men had less trouble handling the dragon-catching tools.

He was pleased that one of his lieutenants had developed a new folding technique by observing the fishermen in the harbor. It allowed the men to throw their steel nets in a much more controlled manner, providing the maximum chance of hitting a target. Right away, Corza had ordered several groups of men from the windships to practice day and night until they could hit their target with their eyes closed.

Next to the group of men on the plaza, a large platform was being constructed. The scaffolding was high enough for all to see, even from the very edge of the large square. It was nearly finished; ready for the big day, two days from now. King Baltor would finally hold his official announcement.

It had taken longer than expected for them to restore order in the city. Who knew these Talkarians would be such poor listeners? But slowly, surely, the Doskovians weeded out every part of the opposition. Corza was certain there were still some pockets of resistance left—there always were—but none would be able to do any real damage. The Stone King was counting on the King of Iron's announcement to eradicate that last lingering will to fight, but frankly, Corza did not care. It was nothing they could not handle; besides, he was forming his own plans for that idiot king who had dared to strike him.

Corza passed a soldier standing guard. The man saluted him with fist on heart and opened the door to one of the higher tower chambers.

Inside, Corza was greeted by the sound of deep, erratic sniffing. Ignoring it, Corza walked over to the balcony and opened the thin, wooden doors, letting the last rays of sunlight fall into the room. He stared at the balcony across the way. The doors were closed tight, but he knew *they* were in there. After all, he had carefully chosen this very room because of it. The doors were not enough to block out the screams of pain. Corza could sometimes hear the sounds of their soft sobbing carried over on the slightest of wind movements. He took quite a bit of pleasure from it, especially the first time, and he was proud to say it had happened several more times since.

The Stone King had ordered him not to touch the queen and her daughter. He had said nothing about that disrespectful twin brother.

Corza took a deep breath, enjoying the cool evening air that filled his lungs, and turned around. Life was good.

"Now… where were we?"

Trista peered over the edge of a large rock at the three black ships. Her bare skin pressed against the rough stone surface. She glanced behind to where Dalkeira and her brother were both asleep; Decan made soft noises and moved his arms around in a restless dream. She was worried about him. During the day, he was quiet and withdrawn, while at night he would startle them awake with screaming. It was dangerous; a few nights ago, they were nearly caught when several soldiers had heard him from their camp nearby. Trista and the others had rushed back to their little boat and sailed off into the night to escape them.

She looked back at the ocean; the ships were barely specks on the horizon now. Just as she had expected, their little rocky island was of no interest to the soldiers. She slid down, ignoring the scrapes on her arms and legs. It was doubtful anyone would spot her from so far away, but she did not want to risk standing up.

Back on the ground, she turned her clothes over where they lay drying on a rock. She grabbed the spitted fish roasting over their smokeless fire and bit off a piece before proceeding to flip over Decan's clothes as well.

She startled as the boy let out a yelp in his sleep and kicked out wildly. Dalkeira stirred as one of his feet hit her tail. Sleepy, she raised her head.

"*Are you alright?*" asked Trista.

"*I am fine. But I could use a bite to eat. Is there still fish?*" rumbled the voice.

Trista tossed her a raw fish, which the dragon neatly caught between her teeth before tipping her head back to make it disappear down her throat.

Their current island was only a few hundred yards across and did not have freshwater. It was only a quick stop to get some rest—or if lucky, sleep—before the final stretch to the mainland. In the distance, the coastline was already visible on the horizon.

"Are your clothes dry yet?" asked Dalkeira.

"Almost. The sun is making quick work of it. We should be able to leave at dusk." Trista shivered as a breeze temporarily cut through the sun's warm rays.

"It will be another day or two before we reach the continent. Then we can leave these dangerous seas behind."

She sneezed.

"Are you certain your body is not badly influenced by the long swim?" Dalkeira said with some concern. *"Perhaps you two stayed too long in the water?"*

"Possibly, but it couldn't be helped. If we hadn't jumped overboard, the crew on those ships would surely have spotted us," said Trista, switching to a whisper.

Over the last week they had evaded half a dozen black ships thanks to Dalkeira's sharp eyesight. Thankfully, they had not seen any more of the flying ships, but one of the encounters with an ocean ship had been a very close call.

"I still cannot believe they were so easily fooled," said Dalkeira.

"When I heard the sounds from their deck, I thought we were goners," confessed Trista. "But it did the trick."

When the black ship had unexpectedly loomed up from one of the island bays, attempting to make their little boat look abandoned was the only thing that had popped into Trista's mind. It was also most likely the only reason they were alive right now. With lightning speed, she had pushed both dragon and brother overboard—much to their surprise. She had ripped down their sail, kicked a few things over and then thrown herself over the edge after them.

When the ship was finally distant enough for them to climb back into their boat, the current had dragged them far away from the island they had planned to stop at. But that was not the only problem; the summer water might be mild, but it was still quick to cool down anyone who stayed in it for too long. When the time came for them to climb back into the boat, both Trista and Decan were too cold and too tired to lift themselves out of the water. In the end, the siblings clung to the boat's side while Dalkeira dragged them toward this small, rocky island. After that, even Dalkeira, who had been swimming and pulling the boat every day, had been glad to get some solid ground under her claws and rest.

Trista looked at the dragon as she chewed on another piece of fish. The blue of Dalkeira's scales had deepened. It made it harder to see where she swam underwater. The green glow of her skin was still present, but not as strong as before. Most notably of all, the dragon had clearly grown several inches; Trista estimated Dalkeira's body mass had nearly doubled, and she could see that the blue dragon's constant exercise was resulting in a lean and muscled build. Dalkeira caught and ate fish whenever she could. Trista did not keep track of precisely how much the dragon ate, but she thought it was quite a lot more than she and Decan. And despite getting that excellent meal out of Rudley during their foggy escape, the dragon's hunger had only increased.

Dalkeira's swimming skills also continued to improve. She was an exceptionally fast swimmer, and could spend large parts of the day in the water so long as she could rest by floating on the surface. Her webbed claws let her maneuver swiftly, while her tail and hind legs provided most of the propulsion.

That day, Trista had discovered a new feature in the dragon's magnificent build; the dragon had two smaller wings of sorts. They were right at the base of the main wings, and often moved as one with the large membranes, which was likely the reason she had never taken note of them before. She had only spotted them earlier after seeing them fully stretched out in the water. They were sturdier than their larger counterparts, able to withstand the force of the water while her main wings were tightly folded against her body to minimize drag. Trista was certain they improved the dragon's maneuverability as she weaved through the water. Trista had already given the wings a name of their own: *rudder wings*.

"Which do you prefer? Flying or swimming?" asked Trista out of the blue.

Dalkeira looked out across the water.

"*Both. They are unique in their own ways, each providing joy and excitement. I would not feel complete if either one was not possible,*" said the dragon after some thought.

"You've been able to stay underwater for longer and longer," said Trista. "At least a hundred and fifty or sixty of my normal breaths."

If not for their mental link, Trista would have been worried sick whenever Dalkeira stayed underwater for so long. But they often chatted privately while the dragon swam, though Trista noticed that the distance between them needed to be smaller in the water than in the air to easily hear each other.

"*I am certain I can do much better with practice.*"

"Well, because of you we've made much better time than I expected. If not for you, we would still be drifting or rowing miles back thanks to those windless days—not to mention you saving the day this afternoon by bringing us ashore. Much longer and both Decan and I would have drowned, so thank you."

"*It bewilders me that your clan ever dared to venture out to sea in the old days, being so fragile before the elements of water.*"

152

"Our fear teaches us to be humble. It keeps us sharp and feeds our admiration of the ocean's might; thus grows our respect for the goddess' domain," answered Trista in her childhood teacher's voice. "It is one of the core values of the waterclans."

Dalkeira stood. *"I am going for a drink."*

"Alright. Our clothes should be dry by now. I'll wake Decan, and then we'll go."

Trista licked her dry lips. She was thirsty too, but would have to wait a while longer before she could drink. Food was not really a problem; Dalkeira provided plenty of fish meals for Trista and her brother. But their water had almost run out. A couple of days earlier, high waves and strong squalls had left the trio battered and broken from lack of sleep and their water barrel completely mixed with seawater.

Dalkeira was fine with drinking the salty water; she simply secreted the excess salt through her scales, making them slightly dull. But Trista and Decan required fresh water to get through the hot afternoons. They had gathered some rainwater the night before after emptying the barrel, but there was barely enough to last the day.

And we need to ration it for two more.

Trista swallowed the last piece of fish she had been chewing and licked her lips again, still wishing for a drink.

Think of something else. Like… we're almost there, and we won't get caught.

She had no idea what to expect on the mainland. The black ships were often headed in that direction. Trista and the others had already encountered multiple wrecked ships, and those islands big enough to hold a village or two showed large black columns of smoke rising skyward when they passed. It did not fill her with confidence.

Trista began to get dressed. The sun was just touching that distant, dark line of land on the horizon. It would be night soon. She walked over to one of the two most precious beings remaining to her in this world and softly shook his shoulder.

"Come on, little brother, we'd better get going. It'll be dark soon."

The click of the door made Bronson's eyes widen. His throat fought the short bursts of breath he tried to inhale. His mouth was dry. He thrashed around in his restraints, but none of them budged, and the straps burned his wrists and ankles.

Corza walked past him. Bronson's stare was drawn to that horrible dagger on the high general's hip. His flesh remembered every slice it had made—and every single time the wound was cauterized with a hot piece of metal.

The thought made him nauseous. Several times already, he had thrown up from the smell of his own sizzling flesh. And if he passed out, he often woke to the stinging sensation of someone cleansing his wounds.

Corza slowly crossed the room and opened the balcony doors. Bronson attempted to avert his face when the bright afternoon light stung his eyes, but there was little room to move with his head also strapped down to the thick wooden frame.

He tugged again at the leather straps holding his arms; a futile attempt. After days of imprisonment, he lacked the strength to fight. Stretched out as he was, his limbs, back and chest were all fully exposed, giving the high general—and that blasted dagger—all the access he needed. Bronson was entirely at the mercy of his captor, who in turn offered very little of it.

Occasionally, the merciless man rolled him out onto the balcony. There, the bastard would flip him upside down for the sheer joy of seeing the increased blood pressure to his head add to the pain of being cut and burned. Bronson's screams would echo between the city's smoking chimneys. His twin sister was near; so was his mother. He did not always see them, but he heard them every time they ran onto their balcony and begged Corza to stop, to show mercy. But the high general simply continued until the Prince of Iron fainted, at which point he was simply left in the sun in view of his family, who could only wonder if he had died or not. But Corza was careful—always careful—and while it seemed he had no intention of killing Bronson, neither was he merely toying with him.

"Now… where were we?" said Corza. "I always like to pick up where we left off the day before."

Bronson's voice screamed angrily through his gag. He shook wildly. Corza hit him across the face with his gauntlet.

"It's great to see you still have some fight left in you. There's still so much for you to learn."

Corza tilted the frame on which the prince was strung until it was horizontal, giving Bronson no choice but to stare at the floor. The high general circled his prisoner, letting his Roc'turr carefully slide across the prince's body.

Bronson's skin twitched at the sharp blade's touch. He clenched his teeth in expectation. What was left of his clothes hung in rags around his body.

Corza suddenly halted.

"It seems we have a problem," he said. "There are no places left to teach you anything else."

Bronson's entire body was covered with healing, burned and open cuts. Only his face had been spared, apart from the occasional punch.

"Perhaps you have a suggestion? Oh, wait. Never mind; I see I missed a spot here," said Corza as he walked behind the helpless prince. "Without your help, I might add. You know, it wouldn't hurt to occasionally participate more actively in the process."

Corza took the Roc'turr and cut deeply into the sole of each foot until a network of cuts ran from heel to toe. Bronson screamed, his voice turning hoarse as the pain dragged on.

"What have we learned?"

Bronson said nothing.

"*What* have we learned?"

Corza cut across both feet again. Bronson let out a cry.

"That—that my life is over."

"Excellent! Well done. I knew something would stick eventually," said Corza as he spun the wooden rack further, putting Bronson upside down. "But your life isn't over; not yet. It just doesn't belong to you anymore. From this day on, your life belongs to me, and only me. With every step you take, these scars you walk on will remind you that without me you would have no life."

Corza bent over to look at him upside down.

"Don't you agree?"

"Yes."

"Yes what?"

Corza dangled his Roc'turr in front of the prince's nose.

"Yes, my life belongs to you… sir."

"Excellent!" exclaimed the high general. "But I'm afraid there isn't much sincerity in your voice."

Corza spun the rack so hard Bronson went two full circles before finding himself upright again.

"Such balance," Corza said, pleased. "You can see it is real craftsmanship."

The high general walked over to a small chest in the corner, opened the lid and started searching through it. Bronson saw scrolls being shuffled around, a book or two and the occasional dried plant.

"Now, where was it? Ah, there it is!"

Corza pulled a large glass jar from the chest and walked back to Bronson. After carefully opening the lid, he took a pair of pliers and pulled something from the jar.

"Are you familiar at all with the animals on my continent, young prince?"

Bronson slowly shook his head, his eyes glued to the small creature squirming in front of him.

"There's this creature called a kzaktor. Nasty things. Burrowing through the earth, larger than two men put together. All twisted legs and jaws. They can rip a horse and rider to pieces in an instant."

Bronson looked at the armored worm-like thing in front of him, barely a finger long and about as thick. Its dozens of little legs were thrashing through the air as it tried to free itself from the tool held firmly in Corza's hand. It looked wet; white liquid oozed from between the tiny, hardened body segments.

"Now, few people know this, but amazingly enough kzaktors start their lives above ground—or more accurately, in the trunks of particular trees. They burrow through the hardest wood during their pre-adult life before eventually dropping to the ground, where they change their diet to flesh."

Tiny jaws opened and closed as the little creature continued its efforts to escape.

"Here; see this white moisture? They secrete some sort of acid, which stops the tree from *bleeding* as they burrow into the trunk. It's quite nasty stuff."

Corza tilted Bronson forward, exposing his back.

"I always wondered what would happen if I let one of them feast on flesh early." Corza spoke calmly. "Now, I must warn you, I'm quite new at this—but I believe I can keep it from doing any real damage. I got the idea when I ran into an unexpected guest a while back. He's quite a nuisance. In fact, you remind me of him."

Corza leaned in and moved the tiny kzaktor closer to Bronson's back. The Prince of Iron stretched his belly forward, contracting all his back muscles to try and arch his spine away. The hairs on his neck rose as he sensed the pliers—and the creature—inching closer until it slide across his back.

Cold and wet, the sensation gave him little more than goosebumps at first. Relieved, he let out a sigh.

Then came the pain. It burned worse than fire, as if his skin was being crushed between rocks and ripped apart at the same time.

"Stop! Aaah, stop, stop, stop!"

Corza paused, then ran a wet cloth across the acid trail. Immediately, the pain dissipated to a barely noticeable numbness.

"You're right," said Corza. "We wouldn't want it to burrow through your heart by accident. Let's start with the legs."

"No! Stop! Why are you doing this? Why? I told you: my life is yours. There's no need for this!"

"My dear friend, it is true that you said so. But there's a big difference between saying and believing. That look in your eye? It reeks of defiance."

Corza pressed the kzaktor hard against Bronson's leg. The creature started digging immediately. As it broke through the skin and crawled inside, Bronson's eyes widened until he was afraid they would pop out of his head. They blurred with tears as the pain took hold of him. His mouth stretched to scream, but the shock took his voice away. He jerked his arms and legs, thrashed harder against the frame than he had ever done before. The wood and leather cracked and creaked, but did not break.

His captor's hands applied pressure on his leg, steering the ferocious worm back and forth.

"Look at it go," Corza laughed. "And it stays just beneath the skin. Completely unexpected!"

When Bronson's voice found its way back from oblivion, his screams went on and on. The intense agony of the tiny jaws ripping through his flesh filled his entire world, then the burning acid trail took that world of pain and set it ablaze. He wanted everything to be over. He was losing himself, he could feel it. He just needed everything to stop.

"My life is yours! My life's yours! My life is yourgggrh—"

After that, his words morphed into unrecognizable screams and grunts. His own thoughts were driven from his mind, expelled by the pain.

* * *

"That's far enough," said Corza as the tiny creature started to work its way up Bronson's leg. "I don't want to lose you inside all those intestines."

Corza doubted Bronson felt the quick jab of his Roc'turr in the path of the kzaktor. The prince hung weak in his restraints, dry-heaving. His breathing rasped in and out; tears and saliva dripped down to the floor.

Using one hand for pressure to box it in and the other to work the pliers, Corza tried to get a hold of the squirming horror under the prince's skin.

"Slippery bugger," commented the high general as he pushed the pliers deeper inside Bronson's leg. "Almost… almost… got it! See? Nothing to worry about."

Corza stepped to the front and turned Bronson upright again. The high general proudly held the tiny kzaktor in front of Bronson's face, only to realize the young prince slumped in his restraints, unconscious.

CHAPTER TEN

Despair

W ATER SPLASHED AGAINST the side of the boat.

"*Dalkeira, where are you?*" Trista said privately in her head.

The dragon had been pulling them ashore when she suddenly darted off to chase after a "particularly juicy fish".

A couple of yards away, a big splash erupted from the water. Dalkeira broke the surface with a hard push of her tail, lifting herself clear of the water before opening her wings and beating them furiously to stay in the air. Having gained enough altitude, she leveled off her wings and glided over to their little boat. She came in a bit too fast and slammed down hard. Decan let out a startled cry and moved himself further away from the dragon. Dalkeira tried to conceal her clumsy landing by shaking off the water from her skin and presenting Trista with the large, thick and juicy-looking fish in her jaws.

"*Dinner,*" she announced proudly.

"You could've caught that after we reached the shore, you know," said Trista, looking at the waves rolling onto the beach a hundred yards from their boat.

"*But by then it would have been long gone. Besides, we should eat now. We might not have time when we set foot on that beach.*"

This was true. While they had carefully steered toward a part of the coast that seemed utterly abandoned, there was no guarantee they would not encounter armed soldiers once on land.

Dalkeira put the fish in Trista's hands, who quickly took a bite after clearing the scales off the skin.

"*I saw some dangerous-looking rocks beneath the surface; we had best make sure the boat does not tip over,*" said Dalkeira.

"*If that's so, you'd best stay in the boat as well. I don't want you to get cut up in the turmoil of the waves.*"

Trista ripped off another piece of fish as she regarded her quiet little brother.

"Decan, come here. Take a bite," said Trista.

But her brother simply looked at her, remaining seated in the other end of the boat.

"*What is wrong with him? He has been like this ever since the first night we left,*" said Dalkeira in Trista's head.

"*I don't know. Perhaps he misses the island.*"

She was worried about him. She did not think it was leaving the island that was the problem. He was staying out of Dalkeira's way as much as possible, avoiding looking directly at her whenever he could. Something had happened, and she expected Dalkeira killing Rudley had something to do with it.

"*Well, I certainly did not do anything to* him," said Dalkeira.

"*I never said you did… and what did I say about listening in on my thoughts?*" Trista admonished.

"*I cannot help it that you think so loudly,*" said Dalkeira.

Trista rolled her eyes, but said nothing.

"*And on the matter of the goat, it had to be done,*" continued Dalkeira, ignoring Trista's silent reproof. "*But I think it might have… broken something in your little brother?*"

It was more a question than a statement. The dragon's confused feelings flowed over into Trista. She knew Dalkeira had only acted on what she thought was best, but she wished it had not been necessary.

The boat began to tilt as they entered the foaming surf near the beach. The waves were bigger than she had expected. Trista grabbed the oars; it was hard work, but nothing she had not done before in her father's boat. As her muscles fought to keep control over the boat, she reached out to Dalkeira once more.

"*Maybe you should try and talk to him some time,*" said Trista.

"*Why? It is not my fault. I never told him to be scared of me. His fear is his own.*"

"*That doesn't mean you can't try to help him.*"

"*I suppose that is true. I tried before, but I do not think he can understand me.*"

"Hold on," Trista shouted at Decan as a large wave almost capsized the boat. She pulled like mad on her right oar to prevent the boat from spinning around and giving the rolling waves free rein over their flank. She strained to steer them toward the land that awaited their arrival.

"*Also, maybe now is not the time,*" she added to Dalkeira.

It was all she could say if she wanted to get the boat through the final stretch of waves—and onto the beach—in one piece.

The plaza was packed with people. Those who did not want to attend were forced into doing so by the dark soldiers going from house to house. By the end of the morning, only citizens too sick to leave the house or able to find a good enough hiding place remained scattered throughout the city.

High on the platform stood Corza, overseeing the crowd. In front of him, Lord Rictor wordlessly waited for the ceremony to begin. Below them, the Darkened formed a perimeter, assisted by two ghol'ms whose blue, smoking eyes quietly observed the masses while awaiting their orders.

Doskovian soldiers coerced everyone closer to be in earshot of the oncoming announcement. For once, the chimneys in the city stopped smoking. No hammers fell on their anvils. No steel hissed in cold water. The city was quiet apart from the murmur of the people on the plaza.

Next to Corza stood Bronson, hands hanging loosely at his sides. His face showed no expression as he observed the people below. He swayed softly, probably to give the soles of his feet as much relief as possible. Each step must be like walking on iron nails. He looked like he had been dragged back from the underworld.

The queen and princess were also present, dressed in their nicest clothes. Corza observed them carefully. The queen held her head high, refusing to show weakness. The princess had more difficulty keeping herself composed. She constantly threw glances toward her brother's bruised face. Bronson did not notice; from the numb expression on the tortured prince's face, Corza suspected the young man did not notice much at all. He grinned at the worried look on the princess' face, knowing there was nothing she could do about it.

The murmur of the crowd intensified. Something was happening. From the castle a small group of men approached. The Doskovian soldiers made a path through the unwilling spectators and escorted the King of Iron to the scaffold. For the sake of the announcement, King Baltor had been released from his shackles and provided with a fresh new outfit, though it did little to hide his hollow eyes and skinny face. The sleepless nights and lack of food had quickly worn down the once powerful-looking King of Iron. Cries of pity and support rose from the spectators.

Slowly, King Baltor climbed the stairs, visibly straining under the task. As he emerged on to the platform, Corza heard the queen's sharp intake of breath. A tear spilled from one eye. She silently mouthed a few words to her husband.

You make me proud, Corza read on her lips.

Despite his weakened appearance, King Baltor's eyes remained strong. He looked back at his wife before proceeding to the front of the platform.

Corza noticed the defeated king glance briefly up toward the forest, high on the mountain. A crooked smile flashed across his face.

Lord Rictor stepped forward and held out his left—human—hand. The murmurs from the crowd slowly died out, assisted by the soldiers who punched anyone not quick enough to fall silent. The entire city held its breath to see what came next.

The Stone King surveyed the crowd: men, women, children and the occasional stray dog. He turned around and gestured Corza to the front.

"Lend us your ears; your king addresses you," bellowed Corza. Behind him, the King of Iron awaited his signal to come forward. With a smile, Corza beckoned the man.

"Make it a good one, you old fool," whispered Corza, so softly the others did not hear it.

Corza saw anger flash across King Baltor's face. Satisfied, he took a step back and let the King of Iron have the stage.

* * *

"My dear, beloved people," started King Baltor, then broke out in cough.

His throat was so dry from lack of water that it took a while until the coughing subsided and the King of Iron was able to regain his voice.

"My dear and beloved people," he began again, his voice stronger than before. "I stand before you as a leader of proud people. Men and women who have learned to endure the challenges of hard labor. Who have grown and prospered by overcoming them, and take pride in what they have achieved."

Several voices rose up from the crowd to show their agreement. King Baltor took a moment to look back at his wife and children. His eyes froze when he noticed his son's face for the first time. Anger ignited inside him again. How dare they hurt his child? He looked again toward the forests. There it was! White smoke. His troops had begun their attack and would be on their way toward the plaza.

Just hold on a little longer, my son. Our friends will be here soon.

"And now we are at a crossroads. Now, there is a choice to be made. And that choice will determine how you will live your lives. For they have offered us a place to work. To live and provide for your family. To live *beneath* them. They expect us to use our hammers and feed our fires, only to give them all the fruits of our hard labor. They do *not* respect us! They do *not* value us! All we are is a means to an end… as *slaves*!"

The King of Iron stepped forward. Shouts from the crowd below grew in number. A few of the Doskovian soldiers shifted nervously, looking up at the platform to try and understand what was happening. King Baltor risked a glance at the Stone King; his face was hard.

This is the moment they have been waiting for, King Baltor told himself. Now his subjects would pull out their weapons, smuggled onto the plaza. His speech would rally them into one force, surprising the outnumbered Doskovian soldiers who surrounded them.

"But I choose *not* to live under their rule. I choose *not* to give in to their terror. For the iron pride is meant to be forged in the heart of fire. I say it is time we show these cowards, who let stone do their fighting for them, what such hearts of fire can do. Now pick up your weapons and regain our freedom! Show them that our iron pride and will may bend, but never break!"

The crowd let out a roar. There was a stir amongst the crowd, some movement of people charging toward the edge of the plaza while women and children drifted toward the center, away from the fighting. But something was wrong.

The numbers were completely off. According to Linus' information, the resistance should have consisted of hundreds of people, fully armed with hammers, knives and even swords. But the King of Iron saw no weapons. The men who engaged the enemy soldiers were fighting barehanded, and without armor. He watched in horror as the Doskovian soldiers formed a line and immediately pressed forward, slashing and stabbing anyone who came too close.

What have I done? Why are they not fighting?

His people were being slaughtered by the dozens. Panic broke out amongst those who did not want to fight. The cry of children filled the air as the Talkarian people were pushed closer and closer together.

Corza appeared beside him.

"Well done, milord! I didn't expect anyone to react, but your speech was very moving."

King Baltor stared, wide-eyed as the last remaining troublemakers were taken down with excessive force by one of the ghol'ms. Other soldiers poured onto the plaza, but they were not Talkarian. He turned his head toward the mountain road, wondering—hoping—for something he now dreaded would never come.

"There never was any resistance, was there? No armed forces in the forest," said the King of Iron.

"I'm afraid not."

"Linus…"

"It really wasn't that hard. He seemed like a man—and I use that term *very* loosely—who would be up for the task, with a little persuasion."

"No. Linus would not betray us," King Baltor spat at Corza. "I do not believe it. He is ironblood."

"Oh, he loves his king, that's for sure. But he values his own life, too. Yet it was the princess that sealed the deal for him. All I had to do was promise him he could have her after I was done with her—and he believed me. That man has some *serious* problems. Don't worry; I'll pay him a visit after this and make certain he doesn't lay a hand on her. He won't *have* hands for much longer. Or a head, for that matter."

The king stared at Corza in shock and horror. His mind jumped around, trying to make sense of it all, until it came across the nearest logical thought it could find.

"But the smoke—"

"Not that hard to light a fire, honestly. I just asked a few of our soldiers to be so accommodating," said Corza, icily calm.

King Baltor looked behind him to see his wife looking confused, their daughter grasping on to her as the sounds of people dying surrounded them. Finally, it sank in. The awful mistake he had made. The trust he had put in the wrong place.

It had cost them all their lives.

* * *

"No! I have to make it right!" the King of Iron yelled pitifully.

"You can't," said Corza with a smile. "He'll have no choice but to execute you."

"You bastard! It was you. You planned this all along!"

King Baltor made a futile attempt to wrap his hands around Corza's neck, but the high general quickly punched the weakened King of Iron to the ground and kicked him in the stomach and kidneys. Corza dragged the heaving ruler to his knees and held him there.

"And I'm pleased to see you followed the plan beautifully," hissed Corza in the weakened king's ear. "I bet you're sorry you hit me now. Old fool."

"Olivia, I am sorry. I did not know. You *must* make it right. You *must* fix my mistake, my love. Do not let them destroy our people!" cried the king hoarsely.

Corza looked at the Stone King. Lord Rictor's face was as dark and rigid as a ghol'm's. His small nod was all the high general needed.

In an instant, he drew his Roc'turr and cut King Baltor's throat. Behind him, the queen and princess screamed in agony. But the Prince of Iron seemed unaffected, still locked in his own world of horrors.

The Stone King approached the queen, who had dropped to her knees to comfort her daughter as they lost another man she loved.

"You are Queen of Iron now," his flat voice stated. "You have one chance to make this right. May I suggest you choose better than your husband?"

* * *

The queen looked up into the stone-cold face of Lord Rictor. The Stone King extended his right hand to help her to her feet. The queen looked at the stone hand in disgust, but Lord Rictor simply held it in place. In that moment of conflicted emotions, Olivia Baltor's will to survive and protect their people emerged.

Iron will bend, but never break.

The queen pushed her own fear, anger and grief to the side and thought of those who counted on her protection. With a trembling hand, she took hold of the dark, rough stone fingers before carefully rising to her feet.

The princess remained on the floor, sobbing and calling the names of her father and her betrothed. But the Queen of Iron could not afford to break down—at least, not right now. She forced herself to walk forward, her hand and lip trembling heavily as she neared the body of her late husband. The pool of blood crept slowly across the planks of the scaffold. It seeped between the cracks and dripped toward the plaza stones. She told herself not to look at it. To be strong. She kept her eyes on the rooftops, not daring to look at the massacre below either.

"People of Tal'Kabur, please listen to what I have to say!" she said.

Her voice was shaky at first, but grew stronger with every word. The people looked up at her, holding each other close, trying to seek comfort and shelter with one another. Lord Rictor raised his hand. The Doskovian soldiers quietly formed a line around the plaza, spears and swords at the ready. Citizens close to them cried in fear.

"I know you are all scared, and I know you are all proud. Proud of what we have accomplished. Proud of what we have built. Proud of what we *are*. But we need to make sure we do not lose sight of what is most precious: the lives of those we love!"

Tears welled up at the thought of her own loved one, lying dead mere feet away; killed for what he believed in.

"Our iron will, forged in the hearts of fire, will never break. About this your king was right. We will survive, even if that means living under an unknown ruler! So I ask you to stop and think. To stop and *live*, with me, as we accept our new position under the rule of the Stone King."

The queen took a deep breath.

"Lord Leonard Rictor has guaranteed that there will be no more trouble. If we work hard and obey, we can live our lives as normal. It is time to think of our wounded and ensure that those who depend on us are taken care of. From this day on, I, Olivia Baltor, Queen of Iron, pledge my allegiance to the Stone King and vow that the Talkarian people will do everything in their power to provide their army with all they need."

The queen felt sick to her stomach. Her head pounded as she tried not to choke on the words.

"Now, please; please stop this useless bloodshed before we are all slaughtered. Return to your homes and take time to mourn. Mourn those who were too blind to see that life is more important than sacrifice. And tomorrow we will return to what we do best: bend iron to our will and show that Talkarian steel is the best in the world!"

As the queen fell silent, the Doskovian soldiers started to direct everyone back to their houses. There were no shouts of anger anymore, no calls for justice. Just the silence of defeat and mourning as the people of Tal'Kabur tried to accept their new reality. A new existence, wherein they had sacrificed their iron pride to secure their future.

* * *

Bronson stood motionless on the scaffold. The wounds under his feet stung relentlessly no matter which way he leaned. His head buzzed. For the first time in days, he had slept in a bed again, but early that morning—after far too short a night—soldiers had dragged him out of it to bring him to the plaza. For what, he had not known, until they brought out his father.

He had tried to move when the high general pulled his dagger to slit his father's throat, but against his will his muscles' fear of being cut had immobilized him. In the back of his clouded mind he screamed at the world in front of him that felt as broken as he did himself. Fighting the memory of a kzaktor eating away at his legs, he watched through the windows that were his eyes and saw his mother hold her speech. Her surrender was as much a betrayal as his inability to save his father's life, but still his mouth did not move.

As the plaza was cleared and a grinning High General Setra approached him to take him back to the tower, a single tear ran down his cheek. A sight unseen by all, except for the man who could not care less.

CHAPTER ELEVEN

Drink

ＴHE STREETS WERE filled with people, even as the moon approached its highest point. The mid-summer feast was in full motion. Raylan had not been interested in the festivities, but Sebastian convinced him to walk through the old city, where he hoped to meet up with Kevhin and Rohan at the *Blackwater Tavern*. Apparently, one of the city guards had told them Blackwater ale was the finest in Azurna, and both archers had made it their night's mission to do some extensive sampling to determine if it was true.

As they entered the tavern, Rohan's loud laughter rose above the crowd's noise. Raylan and Sebastian pushed past the people at the bar and found Rohan and Kevhin in a far corner of the inn, talking to some locals. From the looks of it, both archers were well on their way with sampling the famed local drink.

"Raylan, Seb, come join us. This is T'maz and Gio. They were kind enough to introduce us to the local hospitality," called Rohan.

Rohan's face was flushed from the warmth and ale. His arm hung around Kevhin's neck as he chatted to their new drinking buddies. Raylan sat and listened to some of the stories being told as he drank from the tin mug someone had shoved in his hands. Both archers laughed heartily as the life of Azurna's harbor workers was described for them in colorful detail. The days were long and the work hard, but from the stories told it seemed something exciting happened at the docks almost every day. Especially with Lord Algirio's strange tastes drawing in all kinds of novelties.

Raylan was surprised to see Rohan so openly affectionate toward Kevhin. While they traveled the Dark Continent, the archer always held his fellow sharpshooter at a respectable distance. Raylan had only noticed small gestures of affection between the two, which made it clear to him that they were more than just friends. Perhaps the safe return from their mission had loosened

Rohan up, although Raylan suspected that the ale had also assisted in that. In any case, Kevhin showed no reservations about openly enjoying his partner's attention in return.

It was wonderful to see everyone in such a festive mood, but Raylan could not bring himself to be jolly. Sebastian, on the other hand, looked like he had decided it was time for some much-needed relaxation after all the heavy emotional reunions. Still dressed in his fancy outfit, he merrily caught up with the archers' level of drunkenness. But as his friend got swept up in the atmosphere of the festival, Raylan was stuck pondering recent events.

Once more, Corza Setra drifted into his mind. As that thin, long face emerged in his thoughts, the air in the tavern became too thick to breathe. His friends' laughter echoed in his ears as Raylan's vision started to spin. The scar on his right forearm throbbed intensely. The noise of the crowd became muffled, the sounds of his own breathing cutting through it all; quick, shallow breaths, sucked in through his teeth. The air was like syrup on his skin, and hundreds of sparkles flew in front of his eyes.

He slowly became aware of a hand pressing on his shoulder.

"Raylan? Hey, Raylan. You alright?" asked Sebastian. "You don't look so well."

He looked up. The world crawled back into its normal shape. The throbbing of his scar dissipated until only a gentle tingle remained. He looked at the others around the table.

"I'm fine. Just a bit warm. I think... I'll have a drink at the bar," said Raylan, seeing a spot open up. "Less people there. I'll be back."

His head spun as he stood, but he managed to stay on his feet. Arriving at the bar, he positioned himself next to a dark-haired man, who was taking his time enjoying his ale. Leaning both arms on the bar, Raylan ran his hands through his hair to pull himself together. Sweat on his back had soaked his shirt.

"Ale, please," said Raylan to the man behind the bar.

"Rough night?"

Raylan looked up to see the dark-haired man smile at him.

"Rough days," answered Raylan.

The bartender served him his ale, of which he immediately took a big gulp. The drink was cold enough for him to feel it flow down all the way to his stomach. The dizziness resided. He let out another sigh and regained his composure. It was not long before he found himself in conversation with the dark-haired man.

"Nice to meet you, Raylan. The name's Brenton, or Brent for short," said the man. "Are you local?"

"No, just passing through. We arrived yesterday, actually."

"Ship or land?" asked Brenton.

"Ship… of sorts," said Raylan.

"Same as me, then. I came in yesterday as well, from Tal'Kabur."

"Tal'Kabur? It's been a while since I met anyone from there. Our family line is originally from there," said Raylan, glad to put his thoughts on something light.

"Really? What's your family name? Your old man a caster or a smith?"

"Stryk'ard."

"Smiths, then?" said Brenton.

Raylan gave a small nod. "My grandfather moved to Shid'el when my father was still young," he said. "He took over his workshop in the city when his old man passed away."

"So you're here to sell the product you made?" said Brenton.

"No, no, I'm not involved in the family business. I decided a long time ago that a small, dark, hot smithy was not a place I wanted to be stuck in," said Raylan.

Brenton raised his eyebrows.

"It's hard, but honest work. Nothing wrong with that."

"Certainly," Raylan spoke fast, realizing he might have insulted the man. "And I'm proud to say my father is one of the better smiths in Shid'el. His work stands for quality. But it feels too confined within the workshop. I prefer the open sea… or air."

Raylan drank some more of the cool ale to stop the wrong words from flowing out of his mouth.

"Air?" said Brenton, puzzled.

"Never mind," said Raylan with a smile. "My old man sometimes told stories about Tal'Kabur, although he didn't remember much. I've never been there, though."

"You should. A man needs to know his roots," said Brenton, returning the smile.

Both men returned to their drinks in silence for a moment while the noise from the inn buzzed around them. From one corner came the high squeal of a woman as she was pulled onto a man's lap. Turning around, the woman slapped the man in the face and quickly walked off—something the man's friends apparently found utterly hilarious. The slapped man looked bewildered for a moment before he started laughing loudest of all.

"So, you want to tell me about your troubles?" said Brenton, who noticed Raylan's face turn gloomy again.

"I can't, really."

"It doesn't have to be specifics, you know, but what else is drinking ale with a total stranger for?"

This prompted a brief smile to break through Raylan's pondering.

"Let's just say I don't like the orders I'm given all that much," said Raylan.

"You are a soldiering man then, I take it?"

"That I am," confirmed Raylan solemnly.

A loud crash drew both men's attention. One of the serving women was on her knees, picking up the mugs that had clattered on the ground and yelling at the errand boy who had made her drop her tray. The boy quickly disappeared between the guests and out the back door to escape the woman's wrath.

"What about you? Are you here for business?" asked Raylan quickly, deciding it was best to steer away from the previous enquiry.

"Indeed. Two cargo holds filled with the finest Talkarian steel."

Raylan let out a whistle.

"That must be worth a pretty penny. You weren't bothered by pirates or anything?"

"No. We can take care of ourselves. Besides, we traveled with two other merchant ships to form a convoy, which made us a less easy target," said Brenton.

"Talkarian steel. I wish I could bring some of that back to my father in Shid'el. He would love to have a go at that in his forge, I expect."

"Sorry, can't help you there. The entire cargo has been spoken for. We'll meet our buyer in the next few days, after which we'll be heading back. But tell you what; if you ever do end up on Tal'Kabur, come find me in the port of Tal'Ostar. I'll give you a good deal."

Raylan was about to thank him for the offer when he heard heavy shouting behind him.

"Fucking cocksuckers!" yelled a man loudly.

"Sir, I apologized for my friend spilling your drink. There's no need to insult."

It was Kevhin's voice, trying to put the plastered man at ease. It was a bit of a surprise to see him speak up; usually Rohan was the more reserved of the two men. Today, though, it was Kevhin who kept a cool head, clearly wanting to prevent things from escalating and not spoil the evening's great mood.

Unfortunately, calming down was not what the large man had in mind. His hairy arms were thick as poles. He reeked of alcohol and sweat; his shirt was stained with food and drink and he wobbled on his feet. He stepped forward, out for blood. Within moments several of the man's friends gathered behind him, cornering Rohan and Kevhin.

"Yah damn pansies need a lesson!" said the big man.

"Get your own bar to wiggle your asses at each other!" said another of the group.

"Better yet, yer own city!"

"No—kingdom!"

These last two men laughed and slapped each other on the back. The leader slapped their heads.

"A kingdom? For *them?*" he growled.

As the two goons realized their insult had backfired, the leader turned his attention back to the archers and their new friends. Gesturing his own friends forward, the big man and his troublesome group circled their prey like a pack of jackals. The leader grabbed Rohan by his shirt and readied his other arm to strike.

"Sorry, I've got to go and help my friends," Raylan said hastily to Brenton.

"By all means."

Raylan pushed aside spectators, trying to make his way back to the group in time. But before he reached them, Sebastian stepped forward, still holding his own mug full of ale.

"You had to ruin the mood, didn't you?" said Sebastian to the man holding Rohan's shirt.

"Yah mind yer own business or yah'll get the same coming to yah," said the man, who now snorted like a bull.

Sebastian did not bother to respond with words. It was clear these men were not going to leave them alone, and if his life in the mines had thought him one thing, it was not to wait for the first punch.

Sebastian swung his tin mug around. The man's nose cracked loudly as the mug smashed right into his face. Instantly, the entire inn erupted into total chaos. Two of the men jumped Sebastian while the other went directly for Kevhin and Rohan. Despite Kevhin's docile and somewhat drunken exterior, the archer had no trouble reacting to the oncoming attacks. He dodged the first punch thrown at him, and quickly jabbed one of his own into his attacker's ribs.

Rohan had clearly drank a bit more than Kevhin; his face was the first to make its acquaintance with the hostile intentions of their attackers. The archer slammed backward into the wall, but bounced off and went right back into the fray, the adrenaline of the punch quick to sober him up. He threw himself onto his attacker, and both men crashed to the ground.

At this point, Raylan entered the chaos. He grabbed the arm of one of Sebastian's attackers as the man drew it back for a punch. A quick blow in his kidney and an elbow to the face slammed the man onto the floor.

A fist hit Raylan on the back of his head. He turned around just in time to see a wooden chair flying toward him. He dove out of the way, only to crash into Sebastian, who in turn tumbled over the man he had been fighting.

The brawl escalated into mayhem as others were accidentally pulled into the fight. Punches flew back and forth, with no clear winners. Tables were toppled; bottles and mugs flew through the air.

From the sidelines the man called Brenton calmly drank his ale, observing Raylan and his friends handling the group of attackers.

In the corner stood the squad's weapons, yet none of them tried to reach them. This fight was not on enemy grounds; there was no need to kill the competition. And although Raylan could not agree with the harassers' comments about his friends' sexuality, he merely sought to stop the fighting. Raylan had no illusions that they were teaching them a lesson; he doubted it would have made any sense in their attackers' drunken state.

Raylan punched his current opponent to the floor and turned to the next attacker.

* * *

Behind Raylan, the man who had started it all wiped the blood from his mouth and spat on the floor. His hand moved into his pocket and pulled something out that shimmered in the light of the inn's oil lamps.

The knife was small, but sharp. Raylan pulled back a lanky blond-haired man—who had been trying to put Kevhin's head in a lock under his arm—by the shoulders, unaware of the weapon that closed in behind him.

Just before the man thrust the knife forward, a stone plate smashed into pieces on the side of his head. The plate was not very thick, nor did it bring the man down.

The bloody-faced man turned around to face his unexpected attacker. Brenton leaned casually against the bar. The Talkarian merchant simply shrugged at him and smiled.

The man touched the side of his head and looked at the blood that stuck to his fingers. His face contorted in a turmoil of anger before he rushed forward, stabbing the knife toward Brenton's stomach. Brenton dodged the attack, grabbing the back of the man's head and slamming it forcefully onto the edge of the bar. The man slumped to the floor with a scream and grabbed his nose, now actively spurting blood. The knife fell to the floor. Brenton quickly picked it up and put it behind the bar.

"Thanks for that," called Raylan, seeing Brenton put the knife away and realizing what had happened.

"No problem," said Brenton. He leaned back and resumed his role as spectator.

Raylan turned to pull Sebastian up on his feet, but straight away they were both dragged back into the fight by two of the attacking group.

Suddenly, the door of the inn slammed open and two lightly armored men entered the poorly lit interior. Swords at their belts, they looked around the room and headed straight for Brenton when they spotted him, pushing others roughly to the side.

"Sir, city guards are on the way. Can I suggest we take our leave before they arrive?" said one.

Brenton nodded and downed the last of his ale just as Raylan slammed back-first into the bar next to the Talkarian merchant. Brenton stretched out a hand to help Raylan regain his footing and offered Raylan's own mug of ale to him.

"Better take another swig before it goes to waste," said Brenton, laughing. "I've got to go, and you probably should too."

Raylan looked back at his friends, who were starting to get the upper hand.

"Not without them," he replied with a grin. It felt good to blow off some steam. Nothing like a good honest fist fight to get the blood flowing—figuratively speaking.

"Fair enough. I hope you get things sorted. And about what you said earlier; back home, we always say, 'those who don't agree with orders either desert and die like cowards, or step up and lead themselves.' If I may be so frank, you don't seem like the cowering type to me."

Raylan wanted to reply, but was pulled into the fight once more. By the time he was free to look back at the Talkarian sailor, Brenton was gone.

A few more people had left the inn now, trying to stay out of harm's way. The added space gave them all room to think; the fight slowed down, and the jackals realized they had chewed off more than they could swallow. Rohan, Kevhin, Sebastian and Raylan were all still standing—albeit with a few bruises, and Rohan with a very large black eye. Half a dozen men lay spread across the floor. They were either out cold, or thought it wise not to bother getting back up.

With a bang, the inn's door burst open. This time a dozen city guards pushed into the room. A large, dark-bearded man stepped into the aftermath of the scuffle, which immediately ceased to exist.

"Alright, that's enough," bellowed the man. "Those who were fighting can come with us. I'm only going to ask nicely once."

For a moment, it looked like Kevhin was going to object that they were merely defending themselves. Thankfully, Raylan saw the archer swallow his words when he looked at the very large—and very serious-looking—city guard. The guard saw it as well.

"That's what I thought. Take them. They can spend the night in lockup to sober up."

Bronson lay in bed, staring at the ceiling. The image of blood gushing out of his father's neck was burned onto his retinas. His stomach turned. How could he have just stood there and done *nothing*? He did his best to recollect the events on the plaza, but so much from that day was hazy. He was better rested now, his mind slightly clearer, but his body still hurt. His legs and feet were the worst and he shuddered at the memory of the kzaktor beneath his skin. He had dreamed about it, too; sweaty, feverish nightmares in which that sadistic creep laughed at him as he screamed and screamed until his eyeballs bled.

He remembered the words he had repeated over and over. *My life is yours.* Even when his voice had broken, his mind continued to scream the words until it nearly broke as well. But he remembered his last thought, just before he passed out: he would choose death before his mind snapped. He would take back control over his own being, find his opportunity and deny the high general the satisfaction of breaking him.

Bronson grabbed a pillow and pressed it against his face. He screamed. His poor father. He had not deserved any of this. The King of Iron was not perfect, but he was a proud and just ruler.

Bronson screamed again. His mind crawled back from the edge of insanity every time he was allowed to rest, but it was a slow crawl. And every time the high general came in for a session, the road back to sanity was more difficult, a steeper hill to climb.

He cried into the pillow. He could only think of one thing; one thing to show that bastard he was still in control. He would have to await his moment, but when the time arrived, he would end his life. He would take back control and regain that which was taken from him.

The click of the door sent a shock through his body. Bronson froze, pillow still on his face.

Not again. Please, not again.

Bronson heard the metal hinges creak as the door opened and closed. Fear grasped his throat, his brave thoughts instantly forgotten. His breath rasped as he started to hyperventilate. Naively, he pulled the pillow closer to his face, like a shield protecting him from seeing anything bad. He remembered doing the same when he was a child; remembered thinking that if you did not see the bad, scary things, then perhaps they would not see you.

"Do you think he's hiding from us?"

"I don't know. If so, he's not doing a very good job. Perhaps he's trying to kill himself?"

"But you can't do that with a pillow yourself, remember? We've tried."

"I remember, but does he know that?"

"Perhaps we should ask him if he needs help?"

The strange conversation took Bronson's attention away from his fear. Both voices had a deep, warm, melodious timbre that reminded him of his mother's voice. His breathing slowed, and after some effort he was able to relax his hands.

The bed moved. Someone sat on the mattress near his feet.

"Are you okay?"

Cautiously, Bronson lifted the pillow and glanced at the unfamiliar visitors. He was welcomed with the warming smiles of not one but two beautiful women. He blushed, immediately feeling foolish for his cowardly, childish behavior. The women were obviously twins, but distinguished themselves with their looks; something Bronson and his sister obviously never had trouble with. Both women had lovely dark brown hair. The one closest to him, on his bed, wore hers down, while the other had it bound in a long braided tail. They were clearly his senior, but by no more than half a decade, Bronson guessed.

"Ehhh," he stammered, taken aback by the surprising company.

"He's adorable, isn't he, Lissa?" said the woman still standing. She put her boot on the foot of the bed and leaned toward him with her elbow on her knee. Bronson pushed himself upright against the head of the bed. The hairs on his arms rose as he looked at her. The warm voice did not match the look she gave at all—her copper eyes mocked him. She was dressed for battle. Heavy boots, tight pants, with greaves and tassets worn over them. Fine, low-cut chainmail and a pair of vambraces protected her upper body. Bronson was certain there would be a matching breastplate and pauldrons somewhere in the castle. A thin leather collar complemented the line of her neck; it held four tiny, black, diamond-shaped emblems.

Her sister wore the same emblem, but on her chest. Her attire was completely different, much more casual at first glance—but when Bronson looked closer, here too he could spot the different armored parts. Long tight pants with high leather boots. Tassets were hidden under the bottom part of a blue and brown leather dress that split down the front and held together tightly around the waist by a double belt. The top part looked like a leather armored corset, with a more flexible fabric running up her shoulders and largely covering her neck. Two large daggers hung from her belt.

"He's taking a good look, isn't he?" said the heavily armored woman.

"Don't they all?"

One of the women pulled back the blanket, revealing Bronson's fresh scars.

"Leave it to Corza to ruin a perfectly good body," said the woman closest to him. "Perhaps we should take him with us. Would you like that, young prince?"

"Come on, speak up," added the armored woman when Bronson did not make a sound. "Or did Corza already cut out your tongue?"

"Wh—who are you?" Bronson finally managed.

"Calissa," spoke the woman on his bed.

"Taimila," added the woman in armor.

"Do you work for him?"

"Him? Corza? Oh, honey, who would ever help someone as crude as that crawling weasel?" answered Calissa.

The woman bent forward and ran a warm hand over Bronson's chest.

"Did he hurt you much?"

Bronson felt like a hare talking to two foxes.

"We can take you away from it all, if you want," said the woman on his bed. "We just want to know why he's so interested in you. What does he want?"

The prince looked from one to the other, confused. His head pounded from lack of sleep. It was like an alarm, warning him that the road back to the top of the hill of sanity had just become a very slippery slope. Could it be true? Was there something he could do? To make Corza stop? The man never asked anything from him. Did he? Not information, at least.

"I—I don't understand. What do you mean?"

Calissa leaned closer, crawling along the bed toward him. The lines of her neck and breast swayed seductively with her movements. Bronson could not help but stare. He had his share of girls who were willing to present their appreciation to him, but none had ever moved like this. Her sweet scent reached his nose. Blood started to flow to lower parts of his body, making his headache worse. He dared not move. Calissa's face lingered a mere inch away. Bronson involuntarily licked his dry lips, but there was no kiss to receive—not just yet. Calissa's mouth passed his own. His heart raced at the sound of her whispered words.

"You can trust us, young prince. I'll take care of you. Corza would not dare touch you under my wing. Don't you want that? Don't you want to be close to me? Just tell us what the general wants."

And he really did. He really wanted to trust her; more so to *touch* her. To have the chance to feel the warmth of this woman's skin on his own, instead of the cold of a blade. To get a chance to heal, to wash away everything that had happened since his return to Tal'Kabur. Yet there was no answer present to satisfy the question. He looked past her at the woman in armor.

"Do not worry about Taimila. She doesn't always agree with my choice in men, but she *always* comes around eventually. She has her needs, too. You'll see. She can be quite… generous under that hard exterior."

Bronson swallowed at the mental image the words called forth. But the real appeal was not the sexual insinuation; it was the promise to be taken out of there. Out of this room of horrors. To be free from his captor's torments.

"I want to come with you. I *really* do, but I don't know what to tell you," he stammered. "He only cuts me and burns me. Does horrible things. But he never asks. Just does. Please, please take me away. Please don't leave me."

"Don't play dumb," Taimila broke in, but her sister sat up and quickly threw a glance over her shoulder.

"Dear, there has to be something," resumed Calissa in honeyed tones. "Corza always tosses aside his toys after a day or two. If you're still alive now—in this comfortable bed—it means he wants something from you. We just want to know what."

"I told you, he doesn't want anything—"

Taimila growled. She pushed Calissa aside, stepping forward as she drew her longsword and pointed it at Bronson's throat.

"This isn't working and we're running out of time. Listen, boy. You *will* tell us what you know, or you'll get a new breathing hole in that pretty little neck of yours."

Bronson fought back tears of desperation. He would do anything to know what they wanted to hear. He opened his mouth and closed it again. It was useless. His hands grasped the sheets of his bed and stared at the tip of the sword. Inside, he laughed at himself. Here was the opportunity he had waited for. A way to end his life… only now he was too afraid to take it. Had he not been ready? Had the tiny spark of hope they gave him ruined his resolve?

Bronson called forth his anger. Thought of everything they had done. His sister's betrothed, his father, their kingdom. It would be the push he needed. Not his desperation, not his fear, but his anger. The prince closed his eyes. He took a few deep breaths, tightened his grip on the sheets, and threw himself forward.

The door slammed open. With the speed of a fleeing deer, Taimila pulled back her sword and sheathed it, stepping away from the bed.

"What's going on here?" demanded Corza, hand on his Roc'turr.

Bronson, who sat upright—eyes still firmly closed, sheets clenched between his fists—looked up in surprise. His trembling hand moved to his throat, but there was no blood, no hole. No freedom. He had missed his chance.

Calissa casually stood up and adjusted her outfit.

"Corza, so nice to see you again. It's been far too long."

"Don't play nice with me, serpent. What are you doing in this room? With him?"

"This here? We're merely checking in to see how well you're treating your plaything. You know, in case there's something we can help with," responded Calissa.

"That's none of your business. And what did you do to the guards at the door?" sneered Corza. "Guards!"

"They were all too happy to let us through when we told them to stand aside. You always make them into such good listeners, you know, they listen to anyone that gives them an order. What you need to teach them is loyalty, like our own wordless shadows," countered Taimila, referring to the Darkened under their command. "Come on, dear sister. I think it's time we take our leave. Let's see if we can take some of our lovelies and make ourselves useful. I'm sure we can speed up dealing with the unpleasantness in the mining city if we assist the high general's forces there."

"That won't be necessary," said Corza through clenched teeth. "The town is already taken, and it's only a matter of time before those hiding in the mines are cleared out."

"Oh, don't mention it," said Calissa, running her hand along Corza's jawline. "It never hurts to help."

The two women strolled past a fuming Corza. Half a dozen guards stormed into the room, only to swiftly move aside to let both leaders of the Darkened pass without obstruction. As the twins walked away, their voices carried through the hallway, gossiping like girls in their teens.

"Perhaps we're not the only ones with a taste for young men," mocked Calissa.

"Stop it. The thought of him using that thing at all is enough to make me hurl," added her sister.

Behind them, Corza roared orders at the room. "You two, get him in his restraints! The rest of you, out!"

Bronson fought back as best he could, hitting, kicking, even biting. He kicked one of the men square in the jaw, but the impact was too soft to do any real damage. He wished he still had his energy and his swords. Things would be different then.

"Idiots! Don't make me come over there and do it myself," bellowed the high general.

A few well-placed punches knocked the air right out of Bronson's lungs. Corza panted from rage while the guards strapped Bronson to the rack, then shouted after them as they hurried away:

"From now on, no one is allowed into this room except myself. You hear me?"

He threw the door closed, changed his mind and reopened it.

"And find the two idiots on guard duty and execute them!"

The door slammed closed again. The entire room was swallowed by vengeful silence. Bronson heard Corza's breathing, heavy at first, then returning to normal. He strained his eyes to see where his captor was standing, but the rack prevented him from locating Corza. He startled when the high general's voice spoke so close to his ear that he felt the man's breath on his skin.

"You almost had me fooled."

Bronson jerked his head around—as far as that was possible. The high general stepped in front of him and moved the prince to eye level.

"You almost had me convinced that you had truly broken. Almost. And now I find you helping those serpents to get at me? What a fool I have been," said Corza, icily calm.

Corza pulled out the straight dagger on his belt and waved it a mere inch from Bronson's face; the instrument that had inflicted so much pain upon him already. Hate was too mild a word to describe how Bronson felt about it. The dagger was the embodiment of his complete and utter helplessness; of his fear in the face of his inevitable suffering. Bronson's chest started to hurt as his breathing turned shallow.

"I should ram this Roc'turr straight through your eye," screamed Corza with such intensity that his voice became a screech. Bronson flinched. He struggled to turn away in his restraints as Corza pointed the dagger toward his eye. The high general let out a sigh. "But that would help nothing. After all, the expectation is half the fun, as my mother used to say."

A silver bowl flew through the chamber as Corza swiped it violently from its table and roared, "That damned whore!"

Corza jammed his Roc'turr into the table.

"Oh, well. It just means I'll have to start back at the beginning. Let's get you to the balcony, shall we?"

"No, please, don't," begged Bronson. "I'll do anything you want. Please, no more. No more."

His words fell on deaf ears. Humming, Corza opened the balcony doors and, with some effort, pushed Bronson into the afternoon sun.

"Please, there's no reason to do this anymore. I told you, my life is yours. Really, it is."

"There are those words again, still lacking sincerity. There's no point in hiding it, young prince. I saw your reaction when I entered the room. You sought death. You expected it. That's not true devotion. That's deception. Deception of yourself; allowing yourself to believe there's going to be any other way. And when you deceive yourself, you deceive me."

Corza leaned on the balcony's balustrade.

"But that's nothing I can't fix. And with the way things are, we still have a bit of time before we set sail," spoke Corza pleasantly. "I'm sure you're dying to get out to sea again, yes? Perhaps we'll even take one of your ships. You're not using them for anything else, are you?"

Bronson threw a glance at the harbor at the bottom of the hill. It was still filled with black-sailed ships coming and going. Some of them were docked, and from the looks of it were being loaded. With what, he could not see. A deep hurt put a lump in his throat. How he loved this dirty city of his. How tainted it looked with the black army scurrying everywhere, like a plague of cockroaches impossible to eradicate. Extremely powerful cockroaches.

Corza approached him and turned the rack upside down. Blood immediately rushed to Bronson's head.

"There's still the little issue of that enticing double pair of... legs," said the high general. "Oh, everyone knows their story. That they lost their parents at the age of nine. Trying to make a living, the girls ended up in the wrong hands. Such heartache..."

Corza's voice trailed off as he walked inside. When he returned, he held a familiar glass jar in his hand.

"They were probably kept in the filthiest of holes for years. Starved, abused, raped and humiliated by their captors. Such a sad, sad story. It wasn't until their seventeenth year that they succeeded in escaping. Some careless drunk had taken his time with them, but the idiot passed out. It cost him his life. The girls slaughtered every single one of their rapists. Some say they're an example of finding the courage and strength to overcome the unbeatable. I just think they went insane. The human mind is fragile; women's especially so. And when they turn, they can be real demons."

The high general held the jar up in front of Bronson. Within it squirmed the tiny kzaktor.

"Lingers, too. Such darkness. You never really come back from something like that. They probably would have died out in the wilderness, or been killed by bandits, had our *glorious* leader not passed by the stronghold that very moment. So when both girls emerged from the dark tunnels—leaving a dozen men dead in their wake—they weren't greeted by their freedom, but by a group of twenty Darkened escorting Lord Leonard Rictor himself."

Corza used the long pliers to grab the kzaktor from its confinement. It let out a tiny shriek and thrashed around relentlessly.

"Anyone who encounters a Darkened would run the other way had they an ounce of self-preservation. But these girls—half feral, starved and fueled by adrenaline—they screamed a scream of nightmares and flung themselves toward the nearest skeleton face. But the Darkened, they're disciplined. Too disciplined, if you ask me. Skilled, too. Surely on a whole different level to those untrained drunks who held the twins captive."

Corza paused, poured himself a glass of wine with one hand and emptied the cup in one go. All the while, Bronson hung upside down, his face burning from his blood rushing to his head.

"And really, that should have been it. They should have died, right then and there. But when both girls lay groggy on the ground and one of the skeleton faces moved to slay them, Lord Rictor stopped him. The fool. It was a grand mistake; one which I now have to live with.

"But their time will come. I'll make sure of it. Biggest problem is, they're never far apart. Eating, sleeping, fighting—always together. It's even said they share their men," said Corza, bringing the tiny kzaktor close to Bronson's nose. The little creature snapped its tiny pincers at the prince. "But whispers say their lovers end up dead, most of them not even making it through the night. So I'm feeling a little protective here. I mean, they almost took you from me, my friend. Ruined all the glorious things I have in store for you. Question is, how do I keep them from trying to… upset you? Trying to tear you away from me?"

The high general walked toward the table again and poured himself some more wine one-handed.

"Wow, look at the little thing go," said Corza, admiring the kzaktor. "It must be really hungry."

He dangled it in front of Bronson's crotch.

"It really outdid my expectations last time. Perhaps I should use our little friend to make you a bit less interesting to the ladies. I've been told it's quite effective. What do you think?"

Bronson snorted a cough in reply, saliva spraying everywhere. It was hard to breathe and swallow normally upside down, let alone talk or object. Between his legs, his manhood shriveled in protest instead.

Corza put the tiny creature back in the jar and closed it.

"On second thought, that wouldn't be much of a challenge. There's much more satisfaction in the indirect way, and I'd rather prove to them that they can't stop me even if they try."

The general knelt and brought his face right in front of Bronson's.

"Shall I tell you a secret? Some say the Stone King treats them as daughters. Others say as lovers. But I think it's both. How sick is that?"

The high general disappeared back inside one more time. When he returned, the glass jar was no longer in his hand. Instead, the sunlight reflected off the crossed blades of the Roc'turr.

"Now, time to get reacquainted with an old friend of yours," said the high general.

Bronson's screams echoed from the top of the hill all the way down to the harbor. Corza bent down, smiling.

"Looks like it will be another lovely afternoon, don't you agree, Prince of Iron?"

CHAPTER TWELVE

Offer

RAYLAN WONDERED IF he had slept at all when the guards came to rouse them. His stiff back assured him he had, yet the fatigue in his head claimed he had skipped the entire night. Groans and curses rose from all around as a shouting guard woke the others from their slumber. Raylan figured his group should probably be thankful they were split from the troublemakers when the guards dropped them in here.

Raylan let out a groan of his own when he recognized the man who opened the steel-barred door to their cell. Captain Whitflow walked in, his face set in stern disapproval. Sebastian nudged Rohan and Kevhin—who still lay stubbornly on the floor in a corner—to get them to their feet.

"Didn't I tell you all to stay out of trouble?" said the captain to Raylan. "If it were up to me, you'd stay here for a few more days. A good soldier doesn't bring his battles home. Unfortunately, it's not up to me. Lord Algirio wants you released and returned to camp. Something about a meeting you're having."

"It wasn't our intention—" started Raylan.

"Save it for your commander," said Captain Whitflow formally. The man pointed behind him to where Richard waited, just outside the cell. The use of his official title left a bad taste in Raylan's mouth.

His brother's dutiful replacement kept his mouth tightly shut as they were all escorted from the building by the city guards, his steps those of an impatient man. The new morning's sunlight greeted them as they came outside. Raylan blinked to let his eyes adjust.

He flinched when Richard slammed the door behind them. Multiple voices started speaking, but before any of them could offer anything that resembled an excuse or explanation, Richard launched into his own tirade.

"What in the king's name is wrong with all of you?" he burst out. "First, Peadar and Marek are chucked from a brothel, then Raylan and Sebastian decide to show up late—which by itself is a great insult to our host—and *then* you all decide it must be a good time to get drunk? You know what? Fine. I can understand the need to blow off some steam. But you're still in the service of the king, *and* on a mission—most of you, anyway—so bloody act like it. Starting a brawl in a bar is *not* the way to do it."

Richard, who had been marching down the streets toward the outer gate near their encampment, suddenly stopped and turned around. A vein on his temple pulsed dangerously.

"And who waits for the city guards to show up, anyway? You should have been long gone. In and out."

Richard's face was red with anger, yet his eyes were hollow with bags under them, his knuckles white from clenching his fists. Raylan suspected they were not the only ones with a short night under their belt.

"It wasn't our f—" began Raylan.

"Who cares," shouted Richard. "We're guests of the Lord of Azurna; our actions reflect directly on our king and council. We finally have a moment's respite; we're able to rest and have plenty of food. Why would you disgrace our host like that? Not to mention that worrisome creature, which I could barely keep from tearing the city apart when you didn't return home last night. If Xi'Lao had not stepped in, I'm not sure I could have kept Galirras at the camp. Innocents could've been hurt. *You* could've been hurt. Your actions put you in a position where someone could easily have cornered you. Taken you. *Killed* you. We know they're out there; these people with their bad intentions. Who knows what they might be planning? But none of you thought about that, did you?"

Without waiting for an answer, Richard turned away and stormed off again, giving Raylan and the others no other option than to try and keep up. They sped through the city, still simmering from the previous night's festivities. They navigated between those who either considered themselves the most dedicated workers or simply could not afford to take it easy. But Raylan was certain that most of Azurna's citizens—those who could, in any case—were still fast asleep in their beds.

What I wouldn't give to join them.

He really did not see what the problem was. No permanent damage had befallen them. He admitted that things could have been handled better, but that hardly seemed to justify their new commander's level of anger.

"It was just a little bar fight. No harm done."

The comment slipped out before his tired mind had a chance to filter it. As soon as the words left his mouth, Raylan knew he would regret it.

"Gavin always said you had a tendency to ignore the proper way of things. I never really said anything, as it wasn't my place, but I see where his frustration came from," Richard snapped at him.

Raylan's own anger flared at the remark. Sebastian's hand touch his shoulder, offering restraint. Still, it took all the trained discipline of his exhausted mind to prevent a growled reply. They looked at each other, but with no words offered back to him, Richard turned again and stormed down the street.

"I've not seen Richard so angry since the 'proper versing in the *Ballads of Bravery*' debate," said Kevhin in a whisper.

The debate in question had occurred during their travels on the Dark Continent, when Richard was still Gavin's second-in-command. Their companion had unexpectedly burst into anger about the correct version of a hero song well known throughout the kingdom. Things had gotten quite heated, though the argument was mostly one-sided.

Later, Gavin had explained to Raylan that Richard's grandfather was forcefully dismissed from the guild of musicians. It had left the entire Brand family with a bad aftertaste that would carry on for generations.

Julian Brand, free-spirited man that he was, had challenged the guild's council on the proper origin of the Ballads of Bravery, and lost. His son—Richard's father—had been dragged down in the resulting fallout. The entire situation resulted in the ruling that no member of the Brand family would ever be accepted into the guild of musicians again. With their name put to shame and the guild pushing them out, Richard's father struggled to find work. It was a dark stain on their family's history, rich with many generations of musical talents. Since then, Richard's father had detested his own father for abandoning the rules of the guild.

To feed their family, Richard's father had to secure income somewhere else, and thus began their time as an army family. Young Richard had grown up alienated from his grandfather, but admiring of his father's perseverance in supporting his family.

"The rules are there for a reason, Richard," his father had always said. "They shape order in chaos; protect the honorable and proper citizens of this world. Those who cross or break them are a disgrace."

For Richard, they became words to live by.

As they followed Richard through the streets of Azurna, it dawned on Raylan that Richard's mindset was probably one of the reasons he and Gavin had gotten along so well, both as people and as a leadership team. Gavin always had a natural interest in other people's lives and cared about the rules that were set to live by.

In that way, Raylan was the complete opposite of Richard. He often tried to avoid rules and regulations, especially after he left Shid'el and headed out to sea. In fact, there had been very little he truly cared for during those days—except his carefreeness. It was not that he was afraid to work, but he had enjoyed his freedom too much to easily give it up. Getting drafted into the king's army had not sat well with him. During those first months, he frequently got into trouble, with all kinds of disciplinary consequences. In particular, he'd frequently clashed with their training commander.

Such talent in the hands of such a hothead. Those words had been thrown at him often.

Still, some of the army's teachings had rubbed off, such as the value of taking care of each other on and off the battlefield. Though thinking about it now, it was not until he went with his brother's squad that things truly fell into place.

In front of him, Richard's lecture went on and on, until at last they reached the encampment outside the city. Never before had Raylan been so glad to feel Galirras slip back into his mind, even though the dragon asked a million and one questions about what happened.

By now, the four of them had officially been forbidden to leave the camp until they departed for the capital, Shid'el. Yet as soon as Richard made the order, it was counteracted by events outside of his control; in his anger, Richard had completely forgotten about Lord Algirio's invitation during the feast.

"They want us to visit the castle this afternoon," said Raylan to Galirras after the official messenger left later that morning.

He sat with a bowl of hearty soup, leaning against Galirras' front leg. The dragon bent his neck. Galirras' nostrils flared wide as he drew in the soup's smell.

"What did you say was in there? Pirk?"

"Pork. It's corn soup with pork fat," Raylan answered calmly. "Did you hear what I said?" he added, fully aware that the dragon's appetite was the only thing that could overrule Galirras' natural curiosity.

"I did, and I will be happy to go, but can we hunt first? You were gone so long, and then immediately went to sleep when you got back. I did not get a chance to go out, and I hate fighting on an empty stomach."

Galirras sniffed again.

"This smells wonderful," he added.

A smile crept onto Raylan's face. He had been able to finish his tasks quickly that morning and catch up on some much-needed sleep after his long night, but that was not the reason he was grinning. He found that he often smiled during their private conversations. He got a lot of happiness from them, even the tiniest remarks or curiosities.

Galirras' hunger coursed through Raylan, intensifying his own. He quickly ate his remaining soup, with a slight twinge of guilt that Galirras had to wait a tad longer. The physical sensation of the warm soup mixed with the warm emotional feeling that was part of their unusual bond. Galirras moved his head closer to peer into the bowl.

"Almost done, insatiable little one," teased Raylan, using the nickname he had given Galirras when the dragon had just hatched. Since that time, Galirras had grown many times larger than any man. Being the only dragon in existence—as far as they knew—Raylan had no idea what to expect, but Galirras had grown tremendously fast. He constantly continued to mature into a lean-muscled, scaled and graceful creature—even more so after he finally took to the sky, despite his traumatic wing dislocation when he hatched.

Over time, his yellow color had deepened into a shining copper-bronze, and from the moment he took flight, his wing muscles had quickly developed, filling out the dragon's posture nicely. The scales and spikes that lay just below the skin had become more prominent. And as Galirras' body gathered more mass, his head developed characteristic scaled ridges that ran above his eyes, straight into the horned comb on the back of his head where his neck began. Overall, the dragon had grown into a magnificent and powerful creature.

The magnificent creature shot out his tongue into the wooden bowl and scooped up the last bit of Raylan's soup. The force of the movement knocked the deep dish out of Raylan's hands, where it landed upside down in the mud. Galirras' eyes glittered. The tiny, sparkling vortexes inside the three tear-shaped pupils playfully swirled back and forth.

"There. Now you are done," said Galirras, amused.

Raylan laughed.

"I guess I am. Alright, I'll just let the others know that we're leaving."

He picked up the bowl.

"I don't think we'll be fighting anyone at the castle, by the way," said Raylan to the dragon as he walked away.

"What do you mean?"

"You said you couldn't fight well on an empty stomach," explained Raylan. *"But we're not going to fight anyone in the castle."*

"And yet every time you decide to go somewhere by yourself, you end up getting hurt. Or have you forgotten what happened at the tree village?"

On the Dark Continent, Raylan had joined Sebastian and a few other escaped slaves from the tree village to steal food from a small storage facility. Though the mission ended up being a reasonable success, Raylan had run into Corza and almost ended up in the hands of the sadistic high general.

"I haven't, but I don't see how anyone could hurt us here. We'll be meeting with Lord Algirio and his wife; the place will be swarming with guards."

"Well, I will not take any chances. My stomach will be filled and my claws sharpened."

Raylan arrived at Richard's tent. He was about to enter when the same messenger from before exited the tent and bumped into Raylan.

"'Scuse me," said Raylan, moving out of the way.

The messenger nodded politely and went on his way. Raylan ducked into the shade of the tent to find Richard deep in thought behind his temporary desk.

"May I come in?" asked Raylan, who found himself acting distant toward Richard after the lecture that morning.

Richard looked up and waved him in.

"Galirras and I are about to leave for the castle. I just thought you ought to know."

No reaction came. Raylan took note of the worried look on his brother's replacement's face.

"Everything alright?" said Raylan. "Is something wrong with Harwin?"

"What? Oh, no, Harwin's fine. They have their best healers looking after him. I'm told he's resting very comfortably in the castle's mid-level wing. There's no sign of infection, and he should make a full recovery in a few weeks."

"That's a relief to hear. So why the troubled face? Did we hear back from Shid'el?"

"No, not yet. It's the ghol'm. It's gone," said Richard. "The guards at the beach last night were minimal because of the festivities, and since we didn't tell them anything about the danger it represented, there were few enough to begin with. This morning, the two men who remained were found passed out from several bottles of the hard stuff—and the ghol'm had disappeared."

"Bandits?" asked Raylan doubtfully, though he knew better.

"I don't think so. No value in a regular statue, I would think," said Richard, shaking his head.

"So, the escaped Doskovian soldier?"

"Most likely. Perhaps he had help."

Richard hesitated.

"You and the big guy searched the airship for those sacrificial scrolls, right?" he said, referring to their friend Galen.

It had been the three of them—Richard, Raylan and Galen—who destroyed the first ghol'm they encountered on the Dark Continent, but only after immense effort. It had been a fierce fight, one that had cost their friend Stephen his life. Richard and Raylan had finally been able to bring the ghol'm down, after which Galen and his large war hammer delivered the final blow. Or blows, rather, as the ghol'm's body possessed extraordinary durability.

"We did, multiple times," confirmed Raylan. "Do you think it's possible we missed something?"

"Who knows? It wasn't our ship, after all."

"Surely someone would have heard something if it was activated. That sound can't easily be missed, can it? Did they find any tracks?" said Raylan, as the possibility of a ghol'm waiting to attack sank in.

"I asked, but the messenger wasn't sure anyone bothered to check."

Raylan saw why Richard was so troubled. Even one ghol'm could do a massive amount of damage. Normal soldiers barely stood a chance against those stone abominations.

"We have to tell them," said Raylan. "They have to know the danger it represents."

"No, not yet."

Raylan looked at Richard, astounded.

"Still? What are you afraid of?" he exclaimed. "You can't seriously still wish to wait for official orders? By then, it could be too late. You have to start making your own decisions at some point."

"Don't belittle me. I'm fully aware of the danger," snapped Richard. "You have no idea of the sensitivity of the situation we're in. Do you think Aeterra is all one happy kingdom just because there's no war? Where there's power, there's people who wish to take it. We serve the king; who knows what kind of balance we'll upset if we tell one of the most powerful family lines in Aeterra everything we know? Can we even be certain? This is not for us to decide. There are rules in place for this kind of thing.

"Your brother was an expert in recognizing the power struggles, but he always stayed within the structure. Used it to his advantage. He was a brilliant strategist. I'm nowhere near his level, but I try. I play by the rules so that we don't find ourselves tangled up in them. So we wait, and keep our eyes open."

Richard kept his eyes locked on Raylan as if imprinting the order.

"After you visit the castle, I want you to cover the beach with Galirras. Find out everything you can about the missing ghol'm. Any tracks, cover-ups, leads.

Talk to those who might have seen anything. We need to find it before anything happens. Now, get out of here. I need to think."

Moments later, somewhat disgruntled by the brisk dismissal, the wind rushed through Raylan's hair. Galirras set a course northwest of the city.

The more Raylan joined Galirras on his flights, the more it felt like sailing on the wind. That same feeling of freedom that drove him to the ocean would wash over him whenever they took off. The world at their feet; four directions in which the wind could lead them. Yet this time, his mind was too preoccupied to enjoy the thrilling sensation. He did his best to let his worries slide away, but he found himself constantly surveying the ground below. Did he hope to catch a glimpse of a moving ghol'm?

Raylan reached out to Galirras. "*I hope you didn't jinx it, my friend.*"

"*Jinx what?*" asked the dragon, scanning the ground below for his own reasons.

"*We might find ourselves in battle sooner than I thought,*" said Raylan.

"*If that happens, let them come. I am not afraid of them. My wounds are healed and my wind is strong,*" Galirras said as he demonstrated a powerful windblast that nearly toppled a small oak.

"*Hold on,*" added the dragon as he spotted a group of wild pigs.

Raylan tightly gripped the leather belt they had put around Galirras' neck while the dragon dove toward the top of a grassy hill to let Raylan off. Flying together was amazing, but during the hunt Galirras sometimes had to make very sudden course adjustments if he did not wish his next meal to escape. Marek had helped to construct the leather belt so that Raylan had something to hold on to apart from the spikes on Galirras' back, but the simple handhold offered little additional safety. It was easier for Raylan to stay on the ground during the hunt.

Raylan sat down in the grass as Galirras launched back into the air and headed for his prey. A few miles to the east lay Azurna, with the shimmering ocean behind it. The water's distinct color was clearly the inspiration for the city's name. The layered castle on the river island rose watchful above the city. It was a magnificent view. It reminded Raylan of Shid'el, his home. That too was a place that called forth awe from those who traveled to it. Suddenly, it felt far too long since he had seen the city where he was born. Despite the meeting with his father that loomed over his return, it would be good to see his home once again.

Spread out across the southern mountain slope of the north point of the Crescent Moon Massif—a central mountainous area of the Aeterran kingdom—the capital of Aeterra was shaped differently from Azurna, but was certainly just as grand as the coastal city that lay before him. As he sat there, lost in his thoughts, Raylan wished he could paint—or at least draw—and capture the enchanting image of Azurna below.

In the back of Raylan's mind, Galirras' excitement spiked on the hunt, followed by the satisfaction of a kill well made. Raylan closed his eyes and breathed in deeply. If he did not think about everything else, this was a perfect moment. The warm, gentle breeze of a summer day's afternoon softly caressed his skin, like the lightest touch of a feather. For the briefest of moments, he was completely at peace. Relaxed. Like the entire world just dropped away.

When he opened his eyes and returned his gaze to the city, the ocean water was not the only thing that shimmered. The entire sky was filled with sparkles. Waves of them flowed through the air and gently moved with the wind. They shifted constantly, creating small vortexes here and there. Raylan's back and neck tingled and his head felt like it was floating on a cloud. The sparkles reminded him of Galirras' eyes. The already amazing view of the city intensified to something unworldly and Raylan wondered if he had ever seen anything so beautiful.

But the perfect moment did not last long. It was invaded by thoughts of the Stone King's forces, and of the missing ghol'm. The scar on his arm started to throb as his relaxation fell before his anger. Raylan could only imagine what horrors the invasion would bring. Azurna would be destroyed or occupied, its people captured or worse. He remembered Richard's words.

But is this not larger than the politics involved? thought Raylan. *What about all those people living in the city? Sebastian's family? They all deserve a chance to get away, don't they?*

Next to him, Galirras landed with a second kill locked in his jaws. The dragon put the carcass between his front legs, tore it in half and quickly threw back his head to swallow the entire piece in one go. The second half followed right after.

"I am ready. Are you?" asked Galirras.

Looking at the city below, Raylan made up his mind.

"Yes. Yes, I am."

By the time they descended toward the third level plaza behind the castle, Raylan could no longer see the sparkles. Thankfully, the throbbing in his arm had subsided as well.

Their destination was a private plateau, half of which was filled with plants and sculptures. If Raylan had to guess, these were probably the lord and lady's private gardens. The main square on the third level was in front of the highest-level buildings—he remembered it well from his walk to the festivities the previous day. But this back part was not accessible to the common people, it seemed.

From the air, Raylan saw the river and its northern cliff. Just outside the walls of the northern city quarter lay a lush forest following the river. A strip of land just outside the walls was cleared of trees, but other than that, the forest remained untouched; the trees did not grow very tall and their trunks were full of twists and turns, which made them unsuitable for planks. The wood also gave off a strong, unpleasant odor when burned: the 'beggar's stench,' so called because only those who had nothing to spend would resort to using the wood for fire. The animals in the forest were less lucky; it was a very active hunting ground for the royal family and poachers alike.

Further north, on the grassier fields beyond the forest, a herd of sheep made its way to the top of a hill. Galirras' interest sparked inside Raylan's mind as the dragon judged whether his hunger had dissipated enough with the meal just caught.

Sebastian had told Raylan that goat and sheep herding were the main professions of those who lived on the northern side. Small villages and settlements were found throughout the region there, while the south of the city was occupied mostly by farmers and fishermen. Together they provided a constant stream of food and drink, the most basic supplies to keep any city running.

Nearing the plaza, Raylan saw Lord Algirio and his wife waiting on their arrival. As a gesture of trust, only a moderate number of guards were present on the plateau. A bold move, thought Raylan, considering Galirras could easily attack and kill every single one of them if he wished.

Raylan and the others were so used to the dragon that it was sometimes easy to forget how impressive, scary and threatening his winged friend could be for those who did not know him. Captain Whitflow had been right in anticipating the people's reaction. During the flight, Galirras had informed Raylan that there were people shouting at the edge of the encampment that morning, before Raylan and the others returned. The dragon overheard them calling things like "the beast's got to go" and "keep our children safe" before the crowd was broken up by the city guards. It was clear that curiosity was not the only sentiment bringing the people of Azurna out to see the dragon.

Below them, a third person was present, patiently awaiting their arrival beside Lord Algirio and his wife.

"*It is Xi'Lao,*" said Galirras with surprise in response to Raylan's silent question.

Galirras' claws scraped briefly across the stones of the plateau before he came to a standstill and folded his wings. Raylan slid down the dragon's shoulder and landed neatly on his feet. He quickly ran a hand through his hair and dusted off his clothes. By habit, his hands slid along his belt to adjust his sword, only to find an empty space.

Raylan still had to figure out how to comfortably bring a sword along as on his flights with Galirras. He had attempted it once, but it had a tendency to poke Galirras painfully in his neck during certain turns. Perhaps a back holder for the sword would be the solution, but for now Raylan had decided to simply go without. Galirras' size made it unlikely they would run into any trouble.

"Lord Algirio; milady," said Raylan formally. He added a quick nod to Xi'Lao to greet her.

"Mister Stryk'ard, so glad you could join us once again within such a short time," said the lord of the castle, adding with a smile, "As you see, we have the lovely Miss Wén visiting us as well. I could not resist a chance to learn more about our mysterious trading partner. Unfortunately, I must admit she is well-taught in politely dodging my questions."

Beside him, Lady Leandra nervously held her lord's hand as Galirras shook out his wings once more and rearranged them neatly against his flank. Xi'Lao walked up to him and gave him a scratch on his nose to greet him.

"See, my dear, there is nothing to be afraid of. He is a perfectly wonderful creature. Not dangerous at all," said Lord Algirio to Lady Leandra. "Just look at his deep coloring, those wonderful eyes. Such a majestic creature."

Lord Algirio guided his wife a little closer.

"Miss Wén? Perhaps I might persuade you to introduce my wife to your friend over there? There are some matters that I would like to discuss with Mister Stryk'ard in the meantime."

"My pleasure," said Xi'Lao. She took Lady Leandra by the hand and guided her toward Galirras, who tried his best to look smaller and less intimidating than he was.

"Mister Stryk'ard, if you would be so kind as to follow me. I'm confident that Galirras will be adequately entertained by the two women."

"Actually, there's something I would like to discuss with you too, Lord Algirio. If you will permit me," said Raylan, imitating his host's formal tone.

"Wonderful. Let us be on our way, then."

Raylan followed the lord through a small part of the garden. A variety of plants and flowers ornamented their surroundings, most of which Raylan had never seen before in his life.

"Indeed, it seems that my curiosity of the new and unfamiliar has slightly rubbed off onto my wife. She has developed quite an interest in the exotic flowers our world has to offer," said Lord Algirio in response to Raylan's remark on the many different shapes and bright colors. "I myself am drawn more toward the wonderful stone creations you see among the flowers. I have collected quite a few from artists all around the continent. Just last year I was pleasantly surprised by a merchant, who brought a new addition for my collection as a present from one of the southern cities. It is always nice to see people who are thoughtful in their business relationships. But I always keep my eye out for the next grand discovery. In fact, I should have a new addition arriving very soon. One of my trusted collectors sent word this morning that he had found an extraordinary piece of unknown origin."

They entered the castle, but not before Raylan threw a glance over his shoulder to check on Galirras and his company. Both women seemed to discuss something as Galirras lifted one of his wings and turned around on the spot a few times. Raylan heard the women's laughter carry across the plateau just before the doors closed behind him.

Inside, Raylan followed his host through several hallways until they reached a more private chamber. The room was filled with books, most of which looked older than Raylan. A large desk littered with paper scrolls and several maps stood at the end of the room. Raylan walked closer to look at a map of the continent. It showed part of the Dark Continent's coastline, as well as the known trade routes to the Tiankong Empire.

A door opened and a servant came in with a tray that held two decorated cups and a metal carafe.

"Ah, can I offer you some wine, Mister Stryk'ard?" said Lord Algirio, pouring himself a cup.

"Thank you," said Raylan. "And would you please just call me Raylan? Mister Stryk'ard makes me feel like my father."

"If I'm not mistaken, your father is a well-respected smith in our kingdom's capital and nothing to be embarrassed about," replied Lord Algirio, to Raylan's surprise. He offered the cup. "However, if you wish, I will be happy to oblige… Raylan."

Raylan took a large gulp of the red, sweet wine. The drink slightly numbed his tongue, warming his throat and stomach on the way down. Why did he feel like he was being prodded into a corner right now? Did Lord Algirio already know more than he had led them to believe? Certainly a man of his position had his ways of gathering information. But this information was only known to their own tight group, so chances were slim it had leaked out.

"Do not worry," said Lord Algirio, observing how Raylan nervously shifted his stance. "I am not here to pressure valuable information from you. I respect the order of things, much like your leader—Lieutenant Brand—and I have no wish to upset the balance of our kingdom. It's not good for trade."

The man softly swirled his wine around, stuck his nose in the cup and inhaled deeply as he closed his eyes in clear delight. He put the cup to his lips and sucked in his first sip through his teeth.

"Though," he said thoughtfully, after swallowing. "It sometimes feels I am the only one trying. Just look at this mess happening up north with Forsiquar. First, all those rumors about tribes uniting brought the army north—which is fair, people are scared and need reassurance. But then nothing happens, apart from the region slowly draining its resources. With winter approaching, food becomes a scarcity and people are told to share everything. And things just worsen. But what does the capital do? Help them? No, they simply absolve the army and let those in Forsiquar fend for themselves."

Lord Algirio's gesture to reinforce his words nearly spilled his wine, but he skillfully prevented it by making a step back and quickly took another sip.

"It is no wonder public grievance rose... and with it, resentment for those that sit in Shid'el. Our city did its best to provide aid and bring relief, but then that whole mess with Lord Serlake's niece happened and everything just crumbled. Now, half of Azurna's soldiers are locked in a siege by order of the king and this entire region's commerce is under pressure."

Raylan wondered how many men the city had dispatched north but refrained himself from asking. He might learn more if he simply listened.

"No, I am a collector," continued Lord Algirio. "Peace and beneficial trade relationships make my life that much more interesting—and easy. So, I will not force you to tell me everything you know, *Raylan*. The crown and council can count on the full support of the Thyraulos bloodline... all I ask is that they keep Aeterra stable and prospering."

Lord Algirio emptied his cup and poured himself a new drink.

"But I digress, my apologies. For my proposal to you is of a much more personal note. Like I said, I am a collector. The world's novelties capture my interest, and it so happens that you possess one of the most novel things in existence," said Lord Algirio. "What I would like to discuss with you, is that you give Galirras to me."

CHAPTER THIRTEEN

Collection

Had Raylan not been mid-swallow, he would have sprayed his wine through the air like a blood fountain from a high-pressured wound. Instead, he went straight into a coughing fit when Lord Algirio made clear the intentions behind his invitation.

"You can't be serious," was all Raylan could manage as he tried to clear his throat. "How many times must I explain to people that Galirras is not a *thing*? I do not own him, and if I did, I wouldn't even think about giving him to some random person. No offense."

That last bit he added quickly in a failed attempt to stay polite, even as anger and frustration flared up inside. Raylan remembered Sebastian's and Richard's warnings that an insult might cause unforeseen and unnecessary troubles later.

"None taken, my dear man. I am quite accustomed to my wishes being met with bewilderment. But in addition, it seems I have insulted you, which was never my intent," Lord Algirio said politely. "I fear I may not have made myself entirely clear, so allow me to elaborate. Please follow me, if you will."

Lord Algirio walked over to a double door on the far side of the room. It was made of dark oak wood, held together by a wide banded steel frame. With some effort, the lord of the castle pushed the decorated door open and stepped inside. Reluctantly, Raylan followed him in.

The room Raylan entered was poorly illuminated until his host opened the heavy curtains. The air felt dry against his lips. It took a while for his eyes to adjust to the sudden light, but once they did, he had a hard time accepting what lay before him.

"You see, Raylan, I do not want Galirras from you now," said Lord Algirio. "I want him after he is dead."

Everywhere Raylan looked were bones and skeletons. The servant girl's words back in the tailor's shop echoed through his head. *There's a room filled with bones.* From the tiniest birds to larger mammals. A few were even larger than a horse. Skulls hung from the walls, while smaller skeletons were spread out on a small plate, like a complicated jigsaw puzzle. A few were articulated and standing in the room, bones tied together as if someone had just ripped off its skin and taken away all the flesh and muscles.

The sight made Raylan sick to his stomach. This man expected that he would give permission for Galirras' remains to end up in this morbid chamber, should the dragon be so unfortunate as to perish? Who would even suggest such a thing?

"I can see from your reaction that you are not so pleased with the chosen chamber decorations. Do not worry; I can tell you that few people are. However, I assure you it is not as distasteful as you imagine. I merely fulfill my curiosity of how things work in this world. With so many living creatures on these lands—and seas as well—I marvel in the differences that can be seen in their build."

The lord walked over to one of the larger skeletons in the corner.

"For example, notice here that this grazer—a cow-like animal from wet, warm lands—has wide-spread hooves, in order to easily move through the swamps' soft ground? Compare that to the claws of the more local mountain cats near Shid'el, how the foot is built to provide flexibility and power in their jumps. There is so much to learn from everything around us, even after they die."

Raylan frowned. He was not unfamiliar with the inner workings of living things. He had hunted, seen battle wounds, and anyone who stayed around Galirras for a prolonged amount of time would encounter bits and pieces of the dragon's meals. But not in a thousand years would he have thought to display it like some prized collection.

"You're insane," whispered Raylan under his breath.

"That's a common misconception by those who do not share my natural curiosity," said his host, overhearing. "But I assure you, the opposite is quite true."

Lord Algirio slowly walked over to a closet full of ancient books. He took one of the books from the shelf, its binding a deep blue. As his host carefully turned the pages, Raylan saw drawings of different animals in great detail. Some showed the coloring of feathers, while others were rough sketches of the skulls Raylan saw on the wall. All of them were alternated with drawings of flowers and plants.

"Raylan, as you might imagine, a man of my position has the ability and influence to make a person's life very easy—or difficult. I could offer that person more gold than most would probably see in a lifetime—or perhaps remind him that his friend is relying on my care to get back to full health."

Harwin, thought Raylan. The image of the old soldier from the ship flashed through his head.

"However, my father—may his soul rest in peace—made it a point to have integrity in his trade arrangements. Some said he was honest to a fault, straightforward and often rude. I tend to disagree; he was always very clear about what he wanted, but he always kept some knowledge up his sleeve, held back some piece of information in case the other party needed a little more incentive. He knew very well that there is *always* something that someone needs. If not now, then later. Find that need and they are bound to trade whatever it is you desire for it."

Lord Algirio closed the book with a cloud of dust. He carefully put it back on the shelf and strolled over to a stumped Raylan.

"I try my best to preserve that trade integrity of the Thyraulos family name. Besides, I dislike dabbling in other people's lives. It is messy, and frankly I detest those who dabble in mine. So I find other ways to occupy myself, lest I get bored. I do not judge other people's interests and expect to be treated in a similar way."

Silence followed those last few words as the lord looked at Raylan.

"What I offer here is not meant as an insult, nor a threat; just a simple trade suggestion to satisfy my curiosity, however long that will take. And in the end, my father had it right. There is always something a person needs. The question is, *Mister Stryk'ard,* what is it that *you* need?"

Raylan's thoughts raced around inside, but he could think of no polite way to decline the offer. He hated all this double talk, behind-the-back motives and wiggling power plays. It might be that Lord Algirio spoke the truth, or perhaps he only wished to bring doubt to his decisions. Raylan considered himself to be honest and straightforward. It did not always make him look smart—or subtle—but it was his own version of integrity. An integrity he did not so much choose, but more subconsciously followed. So he decided to speak his mind and not hold anything back.

"No."

"No?" said Lord Algirio, surprised.

"No. I don't wish to trade," Raylan spoke through clenched jaws. "I'm sure you have plenty to offer that could make my life very different, but I don't *want* it to be different."

In the back of his mind, a little voice spoke up. Did he really not want things to be different? Did he not miss his brother? Was Corza not still hunting them? Was his connection to Galirras all that mattered to him? Above anything else?

"Everyone believes they can own Galirras, like he's some kind of horse. Free to change hands when needed. Well, they're wrong," said Raylan. "He is his own. If anything, you should be asking him. But no matter what the world offers, or threatens me with, I will *never* allow him to be taken away from me against his will. And with any luck, he'll outlive us all."

Raylan's blood boiled. Why could these people not get it through their thick heads that Galirras was not to be owned, stolen or enslaved? First Corza and the Stone King; now a lord from the kingdom he called home, who "merely" wished to study him after he was dead. If he had not been so baffled, Raylan might have said something he would truly regret.

"Now, can we *please* drop the subject? There are more pressing matters to discuss. Matters that I feel you need to be aware of, so the citizens of Azurna have a better chance to—"

A polite cough interrupted Raylan.

"Milord, apologies for the interruption, but Lord Baltor from Tal'Kabur is here to discuss his shipment with you."

"Ah, of course. Please, join us," Lord Algirio said to the man standing calmly behind the servant. "You are a little early, but you know what they say; the early bird catches the worm."

"Brenton?" said Raylan in surprise as the man approached them.

"Oh, you gentlemen have met before?" asked Lord Algirio.

"We ran into each other at a local establishment during the festivities late last night," explained Brenton.

"Ah yes, indeed. I heard it was quite the party that was thrown there, chairs and all," said their host with a smile.

"Your family's name is Baltor? As in King Baltor—the Iron King?" said Raylan, perplexed.

He could not help but notice that lately his days were filled with meeting royalty.

"Prince Baltor here is the oldest son of the Iron King—and an experienced merchant, I might add. He has successfully made many a trade agreement between our two kingdoms."

"Many of which I'm sure benefited you greatly, Lord Algirio," laughed Brenton.

The two of them laughed heartily, until their host noticed that the servant still lingered on the edge of their conversation.

"Anything else?" asked Lord Algirio.

"Milord, I just wanted to let you know your delivery has arrived. It's awaiting your inspection in the Hall of Sculptures."

"Wonderful! It's about time. If you two gentlemen would allow me to indulge my curiosity right away, perhaps you can accompany me to the hall? Apparently, the statue in question is of a very unique design."

The Lord of Azurna took both men back through the corridors. Raylan let out a sigh when he spotted Galirras through one of the windows.

"It appears I've lost the opportunity to speak with Lord Algirio in private," he said to the dragon in his head. *"I'm going to be a while longer."*

"Take your time. I am in pleasant company," he heard back. *"I did a quick check when Lady Leandra asked me to show off my flying skills. Not a black sail in sight."*

That was a relief to hear. Perhaps Richard was right; maybe the Stone King had no intention of invading Aeterra after all. But that also meant that providing Lord Algirio with the details became even less easy to do. What if Lord Algirio made arrangements and panic broke out in the streets for nothing? What if people got hurt? Was that not precisely what he was trying to prevent here? Besides, it was one thing to inform one of the noblemen in their own kingdom, but he was hesitant to lay his cards bare in front of a different kingdom's representative. It was like ignoring Richard's direct order was more shameful with another person present—although it had been Brenton who told him that cowards run away while strong men take the lead.

Raylan found himself pondering the issue at hand all the way down to the Hall of Sculptures. He had not paid much attention to the pleasantries being exchanged between the Prince of Iron and their host. He caught the last part of it as Lord Algirio broke open a large wooden crate that waited in the center of the hall.

"…my collector says it is unlike anything he has ever seen. Very rough and powerful. And I'm told the stone is as black as the night."

With a loud bang the front of the crate fell to the floor. The sound shot right up Raylan's spine and into his brain, as if a warning shot had been fired within him. His eyes grew wide as he ran the last few steps and slid around the front of the box to look inside it.

Black as night…

Raylan saw two dim blue lights as the statue's eyes flared up and the ghol'm started to move.

"Move!" shouted Raylan, tackling both men with all his might.

A heavy, black stone fist slammed into the floor where the noblemen had stood a mere moment before. The stone cracked under the impact, leaving a small dent and some gravel as the ghol'm pulled back its fist. It let out a hollow scream that bounced around the hall.

All three men scrambled to their feet. The ghol'm—which stood slightly hunched over to fit in its container—put its hands on the sides of the crate and pushed it apart.

"How is this possible?" said Lord Algirio in wonder as the ghol'm drew itself up to full height.

"I can explain later," yelled Raylan. "Right now, we need to get out of here. There's no way we can fight this thing without weap—"

Brenton let out a war cry and swung a morning star he ripped from the wall into the stone giant's leg. One of the weapon's points stuck directly in the black stone. Raylan already knew it would not harm the ghol'm at all; Brenton found out a moment later. The ghol'm's punch sent the Prince of Iron sliding along the floor to smash into the far wall. Fortunately, his official Talkarian armor took at least some of the impact.

Raylan pulled the highly inconvenient, awestruck Lord Algirio with him on his way to the downed Prince of Iron. In the middle of the hall, the ghol'm removed the last pieces of the crate from itself and launched in pursuit.

On his knees, Brenton steadied himself by putting a hand on the wall, and coughed. He shook his head and was back on his feet just before the others reached him.

"Go! Run! It's too strong for us," called Raylan, pushing both Brenton and Lord Algirio forward.

All three men set a course for the large doors at the end of the hall. From behind them came the sound of scraping stone and a large crash. Raylan threw a brief glance over his shoulder to see the ghol'm had slammed into the wall, knocking over a decorative metal armor set.

In front of them, the doors to the hall flung open. Azurna guards rushed in, attracted by the ruckus of the fight. They immediately moved in to protect their lord, but found their swords and spears ineffective against the ghol'm's stone build.

They screamed as the ghol'm crushed their heads against the wall. It threw the men away like rag dolls. Raylan heard a man's flesh and tendons rip as the ghol'm grabbed the soldier's arm and swung him against the others until just the limb hung bloody in the black, stone hand. By the time Raylan, Brenton and Lord Algirio ran through the doors, none of the four guards were left alive.

Additional men rushed around the corner, but Lord Algirio had finally returned to his senses.

"Back! Everyone back. Do not engage it directly," he yelled.

Most of the guards pulled back, but a few of them ignored their master's order, hurrying to close the doors behind them. Raylan and the others ran down the hallway. As they rounded a corner, the sound of splintering wood made it clear that the guards' attempt to slow down their stone pursuer had been futile.

"We have to get back to the plateau. Galirras might be able to fight it," shouted Raylan as they ran through the corridors.

"Up here," said Lord Algirio as he shot up a small servants' stair. "It will not be able to fit through here."

Raylan, bringing up the rear of their retreat, was only eight steps up the stairs when the ghol'm smashed into the tiny opening behind him. Its arm swiped back and forth as it tried to wiggle its way into the stairwell, but their host had been right; their attacker did not fit.

Raylan heard shouts from guards further down the hall and groaned about the futility of fighting their enemy directly. Unless they could immobilize it and find something heavy enough to smash the head, none of them would be able to win. They needed Galirras, but they were still too far away for Raylan to feel his connection with the dragon.

At the top of the stairs, the men stopped to catch their breath.

"I wish I had my swords," said Brenton, panting heavily.

Raylan shook his head.

"It wouldn't do you any good. Only the heaviest weapons can damage it. The rest just bounce off harmlessly."

"What the hell is it, anyway?" wondered the Prince of Iron.

"We call it a ghol'm. Listen, we don't have time for this. It will find a different way up. We've got to keep moving and get outside so that Galirras can help us."

"Who's Galirras?"

Lord Algirio still hung forward, trying to catch his breath. Raylan gently shook his shoulder.

"Please, Lord Algirio," said Raylan. "I don't know where to go. Which way?"

The lord of the castle drew himself up and composed himself before he darted off again.

"This way, gentlemen."

"Wait, hold on. Who's Galirras?" yelled Brenton as he ran after them.

* * *

"I have to admit, Galirras, I'm pleasantly surprised to get acquainted with such a wonderful creature as yourself. My fears were completely ungrounded, and I would like to extend my gratitude to both you and Xi'Lao for taking the time to show me the error of my feelings toward you."

"I am pleased to meet you as well, Lady Leandra, and really, it was no trouble on my part. You have a lovely home here, and I appreciate the chance to have had a closer look at such an immense structure built by human hands," answered Galirras.

Galirras looked at the main castle complex. He wondered if Raylan would be much longer. The idea that Raylan was somewhere deep inside this stone-built construction worried him. If anything went wrong, there was no easy way to get to him, and the stone walls made it difficult to keep their minds connected.

During their first flights together in the area, Galirras had marveled at Azurna, the very first large city he ever encountered. It was completely different from the tree village they had seen on the Dark Continent, and much larger than the harbor they escaped from. It was hard to imagine human hands had dug up, cut and moved the many stones, trees and other material that were needed for such a place; to build each house, bridge and gate. The castle was large enough to hold dozens of dragons, if only the doors had been bigger.

Galirras was confused about why two people needed such a big house. Raylan's explanation that they had many servants and soldiers to protect the house from being taken from them did not make things any clearer. If everyone had the same house, none would see the need to try and take the larger house for themselves. In the end, Galirras had just attributed it to one of the peculiar things that humans did—perhaps even needed.

* * *

Next to Galirras, Xi'Lao suppressed a chuckle at the dragon's apparent imitation of Lady Leandra's way of speaking. The day before, when Raylan had gone into the city and she remained with Galirras in their camp, the dragon had expressed his concerns about how to approach the emperor. It was obvious this unexpected opportunity had him excited. He eagerly showed his flying skills above the castle's rooftops and had circled around the main complex a few times before gracefully returning to the two women.

Galirras had no idea how much Xi'Lao enjoyed watching him fly. As the last of the Dragon Archive Keepers, she admired how the dragon had refined his flight with the addition of his wind power. Galirras did not notice it himself, given the natural flow of the learning process, but he could land on a spot the size of a small wagon without much turmoil, or launch into the air with the force of a storm wind. He truly had become an expert flier.

"I do hope your tiny human is born healthy when the time comes," Galirras was saying to Lady Leandra. "As I also hope that the discomfort you are feeling will lighten before I—"

A rumble ran through the ground, cutting Galirras' sentence short. A loud bang manifested from inside the castle complex. Muffled shouts drifted out from deep within the building. Immediately, a few of the castle guards disappeared inside to check out the commotion. Galirras' tail twitched nervously. He shuddered his wings and tugged them anew against his flank.

"What was that noise?" Lady Leandra asked an approaching guard.

"We're not sure, milady. Please remain here while others check the center compound."

Five guards positioned themselves around the lady of the castle and her company. Those closest to Galirras nervously looked up at him. Even though they had just witnessed the friendly conversation between him and their lady, all they saw were claws and teeth that could easily rip a man apart. But Galirras did not notice, nor did he care. His attention was directed at the castle.

* * *

"Raylan is still in there," Galirras said to Xi'Lao. "He was almost done, but then he went back in again."

"I am sure he is fine."

A chilling scream rose from somewhere deep within the building.

"I have to go and look for him," said Galirras, crouching ready to launch himself upward.

But in that moment, the dragon felt his connection with Raylan slip inside his mind.

"*Galirras, are you there? We've got trouble,*" shouted Raylan's voice in his head.

"*I am here. What is happening?*"

"*Ghol'm. Right behind us!*"

Galirras now heard Raylan's actual voice shout something on the other side of the castle doors. It must have been directed at the guards in the hallway, as both doors swung outward and several guards scrambled outside.

Further down the corridor, Galirras spotted Raylan. The dragon momentarily let out a relieved rumble, until he noticed that his friend, Lord Algirio, and another man were running as fast as their feet could carry them. Behind them, screams sounded, but the ghol'm was nowhere to be seen yet.

The trio was halfway down the hall when a door shattered at the furthest end of the corridor. Pieces of wood were flung into the passage. What was left of the door was ripped off its hinges as the ghol'm skidded around the corner in full pursuit of Raylan and the others.

"Get the women to safety," Raylan called out privately as he spotted both Xi'Lao and Lady Leandra next to the dragon. *"Then hit it with everything you've got."*

Galirras jumped into action. Time was short; the ghol'm was running at high speed toward the plaza doors.

"You had both better stand back," said Galirras to Xi'Lao.

The dragon remembered this feeling. The slight panic at seeing Raylan in danger. The excitement of a fight made his blood rush through his body. His eyes shifted back and forth as he judged the situation and used a heartbeat's time to decide his course of action.

He braced himself, inhaled deeply, and bent his neck. In front of his muzzle he created the focus point. First, the spinning shell of wind; then he drew in the air around him and pushed it inside the stormball.

It had been Sebastian who had suggested the name. Galirras had practiced the offensive move ever since he used it in the harbor when they stole the airship, but it was no easy feat. It had taken him at least two dozen times to discover he did not actually have to roar to create it. It was all about his control over the wind; intent was key. That first storm ball had been born of pure desperation; natural instinct, an attempt to protect Gavin. It had been a sloppy attack. This one would be more calculated, deliberate.

But despite his focus, Galirras almost lost control of the fast-spinning outer shell as he remembered his failure to protect Raylan's brother in his moment of need. He quickly refocused on the ghol'm—on the blue, smoking light in its eyes and that dead, screaming mouth—as it neared the garden.

Raylan's small group burst from the castle and immediately turned the corner, avoiding the ghol'm's line of sight and giving Galirras the opportunity to attack.

"By the swords of Garkos. What's that?" called Raylan's new friend, seeing the dragon for the first time. He stumbled to stay on his feet, looking amazed and horrified at the sight of Galirras.

Unseen by Raylan, four guards stood pressed along the wall on the other side, ready to ambush the intruder. Each held the heaviest weapon they could find. Two large axes, a war hammer and a morning star twisted back and forth in their nervous hands.

Galirras had noticed them, but could not issue a warning without losing control of his attack. He just hoped they were smart enough to stay out of the way. He strengthened the encapsulating layer of spinning air a final time and quickly pushed a final stream of air inside.

He was more than confident that he could fit additional air into the ball and increase the destructive power of his attack, but time ran out as the ghol'm exited the building at full speed. Without any hesitation, the stone warrior turned the corner in pursuit of the three men. Galirras quickly adjusted the angle of his neck, amplified the air from his lungs into a concentrated burst with his wind power and took his shot. But just as he launched his attack, he saw to his horror that the four guards were running forward in an attempt to show their courage and ambush the intruder.

Galirras might not have needed to roar to launch the storm ball, but it was the only way to issue a warning that might reach the guards in time. The sound thundered across the plaza; everyone except for Raylan and Xi'Lao looked his way in shock. Raylan immediately noticed the reason for the warning and screamed at the guards.

"Get away, you fools!"

Two of the lord's protectors threw themselves flat on the ground, but the other two froze like deer surprised by an unseen predator. The dragon's projectile hurtled their way. With great effort, Galirras reached out and used his wind power to push the storm ball upward. It barely missed the closest of the two guards, who looked wide-eyed at the dragon, unsure if he was still alive. Dust and dead leaves from the ground got sucked into the traveling gust and spiraled after the orb.

Immediately, Galirras tried to push his attack down again in a desperate attempt to make it connect with the ghol'm as intended, but the storm ball was quickly traveling out of reach. And to make matters worse, the guards were not the only ones who had heard his warning roar.

The ghol'm dove to its knees and curled its arms protectively around its head. Harmlessly, the spinning ball of air overshot the stone warrior and hit the building behind it. Stone shards blasted from the wall. A few large chunks crashed down and battered the stationary ghol'm while smaller splinters shot all over the place and cut the guards' unprotected flesh. The two guards who did not lie flat were thrown several yards across the ground by the explosion.

But the ghol'm barely moved; it merely put an arm on the ground to steady itself.

Raylan and his two friends had stayed out of the damage zone and now made haste to circle the plaza, heading for Galirras.

"That… is Galirras," the dragon heard Raylan shout back to one of the men.

The ghol'm rose to its feet and picked up a large piece of stone, hurling it directly at Galirras.

The dragon launched himself up in the air, only to remember Xi'Lao and Lady Leandra behind him. The chunk of stone now headed straight at them.

"No!" trumpeted Galirras, shooting the most compact windblast he could muster down toward the ground.

* * *

"That… is Galirras."

Raylan's chest and throat hurt as he called back to Brenton. The ghol'm had chased them through the entire castle. *Perhaps even twice,* thought Raylan grimly. Black spots showed before his eyes and his lungs were about to burst. He saw the four guards get back to their feet, or at least try to.

Raylan's small group were nearly at Galirras' side. Behind the dragon, Xi'Lao and Lady Leandra tried their best to stay out of the way, but the lady of the castle could not easily run with the child that grew inside her. Raylan looked at Galirras. The dragon was their best chance to take the ghol'm down.

A high-pitched tone penetrated his head; the pain that accompanied it was like a dagger digging into the back of his skull. When he opened his eyes again, the world had burst into sparkles once more. The entire scene in front of him felt enhanced. A flow of unseen brush strokes showed the wind's presence and brightened the colors.

It was then that the ghol'm launched its projectile attack. The sparkle-filled air erupted in turmoil around the dragon as Galirras jumped up in an involuntary reaction of self-preservation. Raylan's thoughts mirrored Galirras' shocked realization when the dragon noticed his error; he had left both women behind him vulnerable.

"No!" Galirras' panicked call boomed across the plaza.

Shielded by Galirras' body until now, Xi'Lao did not notice the attack until it was too late. Even with no time to react, her trained mind and body sprang into action. She grabbed hold of Lady Leandra's dress and pushed off as hard as she could. But the rock was already upon them.

To the side, Raylan's own reaction was quicker, though very much unplanned. When Galirras trumpeted his frustration into the air, Raylan threw his arm forward in reflex as if he wished to grab the image of the two women and enclose it inside his fist to form a protective shield. But as his arm shot forward, a different feeling grew inside of him. It traveled up his spine, into his arm.

Images of Gavin popped in his head. That fatal moment when he had failed to protect his own brother. Raylan realized he was about to lose someone close again. It only added desperation to the storm that stirred inside him. It surged through his bones and muscles. Just before it reached his fingers, he realized he did not want to enclose the two women, to entrap them in a non-existing shield. On the contrary, this force wanted to be released. It needed to move, and all he had to do was let it.

The air in front of his hand bulged and erupted forward. A river of wind shot out in a spiraling vortex, as if the scars on his arm had twisted it in the last moment. To his own amazement, Raylan saw it speed across the plaza like a sparkling snake rushing in for the kill. It hit Xi'Lao in the back as her fingers curled around the fabric of Lady Leandra's dress. Both women launched through the air. Xi'Lao pulled the pregnant Leandra close, protecting her and the unborn child as they fell.

Galirras shot his own windblast down toward the ground, hoping to shatter the projectile that passed below him. But if it had any impact at all, Raylan couldn't see it. Thankfully, Raylan's unexpected move had been enough. The stone overshot Xi'Lao and Lady Leandra with barely a foot to spare.

The weight of Lady Leandra and her heavy belly knocked the wind out of Xi'Lao as they hit the ground. The thrown piece of wall scraped across the plaza tiles, tumbled and slammed into the stone railing that marked the plaza's edge. It obliterated the decoratively carved stone rail and both slab and rail disappeared from sight, plunging into the river hundreds of feet below.

"Are you alright, my dear?" said Lord Algirio as they helped Lady Leandra and Xi'Lao to their feet.

"Just scrapes and bruises, I think. Galirras pushed us out of the way just in time," said Xi'Lao in answer to Raylan's own worried look.

"That wasn't him," said Raylan, too stumped by what had happened to have any tact in the matter. He did not fully believe it himself.

"What? Then who? How?"

But there was no time to ponder on Raylan's unexpected new arsenal. Behind them, Galirras dove straight for the ghol'm, which in turn began to run at him head-on.

Galirras threw all four clawed feet forward to grab one of the ghol'm's arms and perhaps rip it off. It proved ineffective. Though Galirras had grown so much over the weeks and was now slightly bigger than the ghol'm, the high density and weight of the stone giant's body made it a difficult foe to tackle. Galirras' own build was slender and sleek. After all, a light body was easier to keep in the air—and that put him at a disadvantage.

The ghol'm caught Galirras' attack on its left side. One of his hind claws wrapped around the ghol'm's arm, the other scraping the stone warrior's leg. Small pieces of black rock chipped from the stone limbs, but there was no major damage.

Both of Galirras' front claws dug into his enemy's shoulders and the dragon's head shot forward, jaws spread wide. But the ghol'm did not topple over as Galirras had expected. Instead it braced itself, received the attack with barely a scratch of damage and promptly launched an attack of its own. Its right arm swung low, straight at the dragon's ribs.

Galirras quickly realized his mistake and how vulnerable he was. He wondered how he could have so completely underestimated the ghol'm's power. Hastily, he broke off his attack, twisting away from the ghol'm's incoming punch and using his wind power to push off with his wings.

The somewhat desperate attempt to escape the impact of the solid stone arm only partly succeeded. The ghol'm's closed fist rammed Galirras' lower back, instantly knocking the dragon off balance. His enemy used its other arm to throw Galirras across the plaza.

Just in time, Galirras tucked in his wings to prevent them from folding the wrong way.

"Galirras!" screamed Raylan.

In hindsight, Galirras was thankful for the time spent without proper use of his wings when he first hatched. Any other creature might have attempted to use its wings to regain its balance, possibly destroying them for good. Now, damage was minimal. He touched the spots where the ground had grazed the tender skin on his wing bones, but nothing else was hurt except his pride as he quickly scrambled back to his feet.

"*I am fine,*" Galirras assured Raylan privately.

Straight away the ghol'm turned back toward the lord of the castle and broke out into a run. Behind it, Galirras leaped into the air with a push of his wind power and shot forward to cut the ghol'm off.

* * *

"Here it comes again," warned Brenton, who had been busy directing the women and Lord Algirio to the far end of the plaza.

By now, dozens of guards had streamed into the area, attracted by the alarms and sounds of fighting. A group of archers rained arrows onto the ghol'm. Other individuals threw spears with impressive accuracy, and even though most bounced off harmlessly, some of the projectiles dug into its stone skin. A few arrows got stuck in the cracks between the arm and shoulder, or the knees, but Raylan knew they would not do much. His own squad had gone through the same motions when they faced their first ghol'm on the Dark Continent. They needed to destroy the head.

It was a strange scene unfolding before them. A black and monstrous stone hedgehog walked on two legs. Guards swarmed in from all sides to intercept the danger to their lord only to get knocked out of the way as though they were nothing but flies. Despite the casualties, they persisted until none remained able to fight. Raylan feared some of them would never get back up again. In the end, it did not buy them much time, and Raylan's anger rose at the sight of so many wasted lives.

"Brenton, you can fight. Come with me; we need to distract it. Give the others a chance to escape," called Raylan, pulling Brenton with him. He looked over his shoulder as they sprinted off.

"Xi'Lao, get them to safety."

"I can fight too," objected Xi'Lao.

"I know, but someone needs to protect them," Raylan shouted back as he ran off toward the ghol'm.

"Can your *friend* fire another one of those things?" said Brenton.

"I think so, but the ghol'm has to be immobilized. We need to destroy its head. That's the only way I know of that works."

Raylan scanned the plaza for something useful. He could really use a rope or a chain right about now.

Guards approached them and offered them each a sword and shield. Both refused the shield. Brenton preferred to fight with two swords, and Raylan had seen how little effect a shield had against a ghol'm's punches. Better to try and use his speed to evade.

Above the ghol'm, Galirras launched a new attack. He hovered in the air and maneuvered his wings into longer, turning strokes.

A rush of wind flowed across the plaza and Raylan noticed a change in the air. The sparkles moved swiftly, urgently; he had never seen anything like it.

The dragon used his wind power to reach into the turmoiled air. Sparkling vortexes stretched and turned into lines. It took a moment to get the timing right, but as soon as he figured it out Galirras brought his wings together and shot a wave of compressed air forward. Even those who couldn't see the air sparkles noticed the curved wave shoot toward the ghol'm.

Each powerful stroke of Galirras' wings drove forward another set of windblades. They rushed through the air and quickly caught up with the running ghol'm. The first ones hit just behind it, digging into the plaza's floor to leave two shallow cuts in the stone. As he ran, Raylan watched the continuous barrage rain down on the ghol'm, but it seemed Galirras was struggling to aim. Small chips of stone flew off the moving statue's body, the spears and arrows still stuck in its back splintering off with every attack that hit. The air filled with the sound of rushing wind, enhanced and compressed into a shape solid enough to leave an impact on stone. It was like a storm of invisible knives.

All around the ghol'm, scratches appeared on the ground, most of them several feet long. Raylan and Brenton skidded to a halt and quickly turned the other way.

"Go, go, go," urged Brenton, recognizing the danger at the same time as Raylan.

Raylan was convinced Galirras would never intentionally let them be caught in the attack, but if there was a chance it could take the ghol'm down, he did not want to ruin it. Not to mention it always took a while for Galirras to get a firm grasp on new techniques. Those windblades would probably have no trouble cutting through flesh, perhaps even bone. Raylan looked over his shoulder.

Maybe even trees. Smaller ones, at least. Yet their impact on stone was minimal.

"It's not enough," Raylan reached out internally. *"It's like a sword. It barely does any damage. I think your stormball is our only chance."*

The ghol'm was now hot on their trail. The ground shook as a fist thumped right behind Raylan's feet. He tried to speed up, but his pulse pounded in his head and his dry throat hurt from the rasping air. It was hard to swallow. Above him, Galirras broke off his attack; the ghol'm was too close to Raylan now.

"At least he took the bait," called Brenton as they approached the end of the plaza.

"Yeah, but we're running out of places to go," Raylan panted, pointing to the destroyed stone railing at the edge of the plaza.

Right before they reached the end, the Talkarian prince jumped sideways to dodge a swipe from the black giant. He circled around to divide its attention, slashing both his swords across the ghol'm's knee. The statue's feet scraped across the stones as it broke off its pursuit of Raylan and jumped back toward Brenton.

The two swords blurred through the air in a flurry of slashes. Brenton's feet moved in odd square stances as his arms alternated their attacks. This was not a fluent dance with weapons, more a firm set of steps to maximize stability and strength. Each slash was either a block or an attack. Brenton now knew—and respected—the strength of his opponent. The bruises he no doubt bore made sure of that. As Raylan watched, Brenton adjusted his timing so he did not block the ghol'ms punches head-on. Instead, he used the swords to deflect each incoming fist; to dive under, to sidestep, but it became harder with every breath. The ghol'm's speed seemed to increase with every blow, and the prince's swords only left sparks if they even connected at all.

"It's too dangerous to stay in too close," shouted Raylan, suddenly adding, "Stormball incoming!"

Brenton ducked out of the way. The hard stone plaza crunched beneath his armor as he rolled past the ghol'm. Raylan hit the floor flat.

Their stone enemy was just turning around to grasp its retreating attacker when the stormball hit. For the second time, an explosion boomed across the plaza. Raylan held his hands over his head. The shock wave hit him, but it did not seem as strong an impact as he expected.

"*Did you get him?*" Raylan asked Galirras.

He had expected the ghol'm to be nothing but dust, and was disappointed to see that the abomination was mostly intact. It was missing a large part of its right arm, but remained functional.

"*It blocked the attack?*" wondered Raylan inside Galirras' mind as he looked around for something to help.

"I know," roared the dragon out loud, frustrated. "*I held back, or you two would have been blown off the plaza.*"

Galirras swooped down.

"*I am coming in low.*"

Raylan spotted one of the guards' shields. He jumped to his feet.

"Brenton, get up," he shouted.

The shield was of a larger variety, not the small round version that Harwin liked to take onto the battlefield. No, this was a larger, oval-shaped version. Raylan had seen how city guards would form shield walls with them to push back attackers, or simply form a protective circle around their royalty. It weighed quite a bit.

Behind them, the ghol'm wasted no time reacting to Galirras' incoming attack. It took a few giant steps toward the stone railing and broke off a part with its remaining arm. It was a smaller stone than before; less dangerous, but it also meant it could be thrown faster. Stone after stone it shot at the dragon, each swishing through the air as fast as an arrow. Galirras broke off his dive to evade them from a distance; even then, it took all his concentration and wind power to turn, roll and dive out of the way.

In the distance below, large chunks of debris rained down chaos on Azurna's unsuspecting citizens. A market stand shattered; roofs broke apart; a wall crumbled. It did not take long before the people were screaming and running for cover.

Raylan had never seen Galirras fly like this. The dragon performed right-angled turns mid-dive, rolled onto his back, tucking his wings and spreading them back out at incredible speed. The air rumbled each time Galirras used his wind power to assist in a sudden turn.

Yet it was impossible to get close to the ghol'm and Raylan knew the dragon's fatigue grew with every turn.

"If Galirras is done for, we're all lost. We've got to help him. Grab hold; aim for the knee," said Raylan to Brenton, who had joined up with him again.

Raylan looked up at the dragon to time their attack.

"We'll distract it. Get ready," he informed Galirras. "Now!"

Together with the dual sword wielder, Raylan ran as fast as he could, shield firmly held between them. The ghol'm's focus remained on Galirras, who initiated a new low dive. Another piece of stone hurled through the air, but Galirras rose with a strong push of his wings and cleared it quickly. The giant warrior was already grabbing another piece of the railing, but Raylan and Brenton's sneak attack was quicker.

The shield slammed into the back of the ghol'm's knee. The unexpected impact did no damage, but that had not been Raylan's goal. The ghol'm's leg lost its stability. Their enemy's only choice was to use its remaining arm to keep itself from falling over. It was precisely the opening Galirras needed.

Raylan heard the heavy beat of Galirras' wings as the dragon increased his momentum. This time he caught the ghol'm off balance, and though it tried to brace itself for the impact, it was missing an arm. Galirras' claws shot forward as the ghol'm turned its shoulder toward its flying enemy. In response, Galirras adjusted his angle of approach at the very last moment. He grasped the ghol'm's arm and pushed off hard with his wings. This time his speed was great enough. The ghol'm stumbled back as its arm twisted around. Its second step found no resistance, as the ground beneath it was no longer there.

Raylan and Brenton watched as the ghol'm disappeared over the plaza's edge, dragging Galirras with it. The dragon quickly released his claws and moved straight into a steep climb. Those on the plaza raced toward the handrail to see what followed. Raylan stretched out his neck and peered down. His head spun at seeing how high they were. Somehow, standing on ground this high was worse than sitting on Galirras' back in the air. Here, the ground looked less forgiving.

Beneath them, the ghol'm first tumbled, then slid down the outer castle wall. Against all expectations, the ghol'm managed to stop its fall before hitting the water. Its hand scraped along the stone until it abruptly caught on a ridge in the stone. As soon as the ghol'm stopped its fall, it kicked its legs into the castle walls to create a foothold. Stone cracked and gave way, and slowly the ghol'm started its ascent.

"Is there no stopping this thing?" shouted one of the castle guards at the ledge.

"Find things to throw down," called another.

"No, wait," Raylan spoke with authority as he pointed at Galirras. "He'll finish this—I know he will."

* * *

The dragon circled high above the river. His wings beat calmly as he observed the slow and steady climb of the ghol'm.

"*Are you okay?*" asked Raylan privately.

"*I am… just tired from the fight. They truly are remarkable things. For all the destruction that they bring, I cannot help myself to wonder how such uncommon beings are created,*" said Galirras inside Raylan's head. "*One thing I do know; I have one shot left, and with that, I will claim my victory.*"

With those words the dragon shot forward. He tucked in his wings to gain speed without wasting his energy. As he dove below the castle walls, he pushed out his wings to level off and align himself with the climbing ghol'm. The timing had to be perfect. He could not afford to waste the energy it took to create another storm ball. His muscles already objected, his breath shortened. He needed to rest soon, or they might have to fish *him* out of the river instead of the ghol'm.

The vortexes in his eyes swirled nervously as he locked his gaze on the ghol'm's back. He prepared his focus for the stormball. A slight push with his wind power; an additional stroke of his wings. *Perfect.*

Galirras brought forth his claws and slammed into the ghol'm's unprotected back. The stone giant smashed against the castle wall. Unable to let go with its one remaining arm, the ghol'm struggled and shook itself to throw the dragon off.

But Galirras had no intention of lingering. As his claws dug into the black stone, he used his legs to catch and absorb the force of the impact. Without hesitation, Galirras opened his mouth and pulled the stormball together. He built it fast and strong, using what energy reserves he had left to strengthen the shell of wind and push more air inside.

The ghol'm regained its balance with both feet and wildly swung its arm around to get the winged attacker off him. But Galirras remained just out of reach. The stormball pulsed in front of him. It was filled to the brim, with only the slightest touch needed to set it off.

Galirras released all the stored tension in his legs and pushed off. The ghol'm slammed into the castle wall a second time, but this would be its last. Galirras shot his stormball forward as he increased his distance from the wall. The ghol'm had nowhere to go.

The attack hit it right on the back of its head. Galirras spread his wings and sailed the shock wave of the explosion. Small pieces of stone bounced off his skin and wings as the ghol'm's head completely shattered. A ring of the blue life energy which allowed the stone statue to move boomed through the air. The ghol'm collapsed and slid down along the castle walls, its stone just starting to crumble as it disappeared into the river with a loud splash.

The castle wall showed a neat, round impact crater from the attack. Together with the holes the ghol'm had made for its hand and feet, it almost resembled a giant flower growing from the river against the rising, fortified wall.

* * *

On top of the wall, everyone around Raylan broke out in cheers. Only Brenton, Lord Algirio, Lady Leandra and Xi'Lao kept their composure. The lord handed over care of his wife to the castle's healers and called for Captain Whitflow. The man emerged from the group of guards to attend his lord.

"I want the man who delivered the statue found. Now!" bellowed the lord.

The captain and a handful of other guards immediately marched off. Those soldiers lucky enough to be alive were treated for their wounds. Others began to clear away the dead.

"Best to clear them quickly, before diseases sweep in," said Brenton, who noticed Raylan's silent look at the activities.

216

"We could have prevented this," murmured Raylan.

"What was that?"

"Nothing."

Raylan looked down to where Galirras was making wide circles above the river. It was clear the dragon was tired and using the rising air of the warm summer's day to ascend back up to the castle's plaza. When he finally cleared the edge of the plateau, Galirras landed gently, immediately laying down his head to close his eyes.

"Wonderful. So wonderful," clamored Lord Algirio.

Now that his wife and unborn child were safe, the lord had regained his usual enthusiastic demeanor, as if there had never been a large stone statue trying to smash his brains in. Raylan started to doubt more and more whether the lord's enthusiasm was genuine, or if it was just an act.

"What an extraordinary creature," continued the lord. "Are you most convinced you will not reconsider my offer?"

"I'm certain, milord," said Raylan with a forced smile. "Now, if you don't mind, there are some things I think you should know."

CHAPTER FOURTEEN

Wave

I DO NOT REALLY see the problem. It is not like I will need any of it after I die," said Galirras.

"It's disrespectful, that's what it is," vented Raylan. "All these people who think you're an object to own. I bet he can't wait for you to die."

"Well, I agree there. Such an expectation is quite rude."

"To say the least."

Raylan had spent the remainder of the afternoon at the castle to discuss everything they had discovered. The Doskovian ships they had seen depart; the ghol'ms and the horrible truth about the scrolls that gave them life; the Stone King, ever a mystery; and Corza, who had nearly been the end of them all. It painted a convincing picture for Lord Algirio and his council of the Doskovian army's dark intent.

When one of the councilmen expressed doubt toward Raylan's incredible tales, Lord Algirio impatiently dismissed it. The Lord of Azurna assured the man he had not dreamed being chased through the castle by a giant stone statue, nor had those guards who lay dead. All in all, the question of the invasion's reality was not up for discussion; the question was how long they had before the ships arrived.

Eventually, Raylan went out to get some air and see how Galirras was doing. The discussions had gotten heated and those present in the room had all but forgotten him.

He leaned on the stone rampart of the castle's upper level, overlooking the city and harbor. The afternoon was pleasantly warm as the sun crawled low in the sky. It made the walls' shadows stretch far across the city's roofs. Around him, soldiers were surveying and clearing the damage done by the ghol'm's rampage. The few commoners called in to help fix everything made sure to stay far away from the dragon, even though Galirras did not really pay them much attention.

Below them, the river flowed slowly toward the harbor. There, dark river water collided with the lighter blue seawater, both dancing back and forth with the movements of the tide. A handful of ships lay anchored near the docks and numerous others lay in wait farther out to sea. Raylan observed a few of the smaller ones moored directly against the pier, their sails neatly stored and their landlines securely fastened.

It was a scene he thoroughly enjoyed. After months at sea, the buzzing of a busy harbor was always a nice change of pace. In this case, it was just nice to be back in friendly territory. During his years sailing, new harbors had piqued his curiosity, though it was never long before he was ready to get back out on the water again. As an eager and resourceful part of the crew, Raylan usually joined his captain in search of new merchandise. It led him to meet plenty of interesting characters. Yet as he touched the smooth scales of Galirras' skin next to him, he realized he did not miss it as much as he used to.

"I suppose you are right," said Galirras, laying the subject of his remains to rest. "I did, however, very much enjoy meeting Lady Leandra. Did you know she has a small human inside her? She gave off a very peculiar, sweet smell because of it, I think. She even showed the tight-stretched skin of her belly when the guards were not watching."

Galirras eyes swirled pleasantly at the memory.

"I could see the child's foot push against her skin," added Galirras.

Raylan smiled as the warm connection with Galirras tingled at the back of his head. He loved it when the dragon's curiosity made him see the world in a new light.

"Raylan," carried a voice across the square.

They looked up to see Sebastian jogging toward them.

"Hey, Seb. What are you doing here?" said Raylan.

"I was spending time at my sister's place when I heard Galirras' call. I came over right away to see what was going on, but they held everyone up at the gate," said Sebastian. "They didn't let me through until just now."

"Wait, were you not confined to camp?" Galirras asked, confused.

With a laugh, Sebastian rubbed the back of his head.

"Ha! I, uhm, snuck out."

"Richard is going to have your hide for that," said Raylan.

"Probably, but I'll deal with that later. I just want to make the most of my time with my sister and her family. Before we leave, you know."

"You could stay," said Raylan.

Sebastian opened his mouth and shut it again, uncertain.

"So, what the hell happened here?" he said, changing the subject as he gestured at a trashed wall where one of the ghol'm's blocks had landed.

"A ghol'm. It must have been the one from the beach. Richard mentioned it had disappeared this morning. Somehow, they got it into the castle."

"However did they manage that?" exclaimed Sebastian.

"Snuck it in as part of Lord Algirio's exotic statue collection. And that's not all he collects. The man is peculiar to say the least."

"But everyone's alright?"

Raylan shook his head.

"Several guards didn't make it, but Galirras managed to stop it before it could get to Lord Algirio and his wife. Xi'Lao was there, too. She's gone to give a full report back at camp," said Raylan.

"Did they catch the escaped prisoner?"

"No. The servant who dealt with those who offered the statue was found dead shortly after the attack. The Doskovian soldier is probably long gone," said Raylan. "You really heard Galirras all the way at your sister's place?"

"I wouldn't be surprised if the entire city heard him. People were quite nervous, especially when those stones came crashing down. One hit as far as the southern market square."

"I hope you assured them I was not actually the one breaking everything?" said Galirras.

"I might have mentioned that once or twice," assured Sebastian with a grin.

"Good," said Galirras simply. He returned his gaze to the ocean beyond the harbor.

"How's your sister doing?" asked Raylan.

"Fine. She still can't believe I'm alive," said Sebastian, still smiling. "We spoke for a long time today; went with the kids to the market, too. Did you know her husband works at the glassmakers' guild? He's considered among the best in the city."

Sebastian's expression changed briefly.

"I've missed out on so much."

"We've been over this, remember? You're here now, and that counts for something, right?" said Raylan, grabbing his friend's shoulder and shaking it briefly.

Suddenly, Galirras raised himself on his hind legs. Raylan looked up at him questioningly.

"What is it?"

"Black sails."

The dragon's eyes scanned the horizon.

"Blast! I knew we shouldn't have kept quiet," said Sebastian angrily.

"Four in the air; five at sea from the south-east. They are coming straight for us," Galirras counted.

"Only nine? That can't be right. Where's the main force?" said Raylan, confused.

"Maybe these are just the ones that followed us?" said Sebastian.

"No use wondering," said Raylan. "But against nine we might stand a chance."

He turned around and sprinted off, calling back over his shoulder, "Stay here and keep them in your sights. I need to warn the council."

The sound of metal ringing once again rose to the sky, but this time the signal did not originate from within the castle walls. A watchtower in the harbor had spotted the airships and called their forces to attention; with what had happened at the castle, the man in the tower knew better than to wait and see. Soon, the entire city followed suit.

By the time Raylan emerged from the castle again, the Doskovian ships had come dangerously close. A few sailing ships veered off toward the beach, while two others set a course for the harbor.

"Galirras, we need to take care of those in the air. No one else can get to them," Raylan called as he ran toward the dragon and Sebastian. "Sebastian, I told Lord Algirio you would tell his soldiers what we know of their forces and the ghol'ms. Even if their force is only nine ships strong, when the ghol'ms come into play it doesn't matter how many men we have; we're going to get slaughtered. Our only chance is to take out the ghol'ms before they're activated."

Raylan jumped on Galirras' back in one fluid motion.

"Tell them we need heavy hitters, like Galen. Men who know how to handle a war hammer. And they need chains, too, for the feet!"

Shouts and sounds of chaos rose from the city below as the leading airship moved over the harbor and dropped its first fireball. Flames shot up between the buildings. The two sea vessels in the harbor bay appeared to have small catapults on their decks. They too fired a salvo of fireballs into the city. The townspeople on shore shot in every direction. Women, children and men rushed through the streets to flee from danger. In the more distant parts of the city people hurried home to their houses, rushed along by the clanging alarm bells.

"We'll be back as soon as we can," called Raylan as Galirras launched into the air and took off with strong wing beats. "Good luck with the guards."

"Leave it to me," shouted Sebastian.

Raylan saw his friend run toward the gathering guards to meet up with Captain Whitflow, who started shouting orders immediately after hearing Sebastian's words.

"Let's take the closest one first. We have to stop those fire barrels," Raylan directed Galirras.

"I will come in from above. They have not seen us yet."

Galirras was right. The Doskovian crew on deck were so busy with what was happening below them it seemed none had seen Galirras take off and move into the higher—more dominant—position in the air. Without delay, Galirras dove toward the airship. With the sun at his back, the dragon sent off a windblast, throwing the first of two sentries from the balloon. The other sentry turned around just in time to see Galirras' claw come straight at him. The Doskovian soldier made a futile attempt to aim his crossbow, but the force from Galirras' attack snapped right through his safety lines and sent him tumbling toward the ground.

Cleared of obstacles, Raylan reached out with his mind and let Galirras turn sharply for another pass. His clenched knuckles turned white as he tried to hold on to the dragon and the leather strap. Other soldiers scrambled up the ropes, but Galirras was there quicker. He all but landed on the tightly-bound balloon. Four claws dug into the fabric and ripped it open as Galirras pushed himself up with wings and wind power.

The airship banked and immediately dropped away. Those on the ropes lost their balance and plummeted toward the city below.

Raylan did not have time to watch the ship crash. One of the other airships was on an intercept course and two rows of archers stood at the rail ready to shower them with arrows. Below them, the ship smashed into a building with a loud crash while Galirras pushed himself sideways to dodge the first salvo of shots. A large windblast helped to block the arrows he had not been able to get away from in time. The crashed ship broke out in flames, forming a thick black column of smoke.

Quickly, Galirras turned and sped off to put some distance between him and the pursuing ship, but it proved difficult to outfly the arrows.

"Another salvo," Raylan warned. He sat nearly backward, trying to keep the enemy in sight.

"Hold on."

The warning came as Galirras rolled over in the air. For a moment, Raylan hung upside down, doing his best to hook his legs around Galirras' neck to stay seated. The dragon's movement did not make it easy. Galirras fired another blast to intercept the arrows, but it was imperfect and insufficient to block them all. Two arrows pushed through his defense; one shot right past Raylan as Galirras' roll brought him back on top. The second struck Galirras in the side, just below his wing.

"Oh!" screeched Galirras at the unexpected pain.

"Are you alright?" shouted Raylan against the rushing wind.

"*It stings, but I will live.*"

Raylan noticed that Galirras was already more out of breath than usual. The ghol'm fight earlier had depleted much of his winged friend's energy. With the arrow in his side, the dragon's turns became wider and the beating of his wings more irregular.

Past their pursuer, the other sea vessels reached the beach closest to the harbor. Dozens of soldiers poured out, wading through the last yards of water to reach more solid ground. From the city, the first guards on horses raced to meet them. Charging along the beach, they were clearly convinced their mounts gave them a clear advantage over anyone who tried to come on land.

Then several deep thumps echoed through the air. Rings of blue light spread from the ships nearest to the coast.

Ghol'ms!

While the sea turned red from the first slain Doskovian soldiers, Raylan saw three ghol'ms emerge from the ships and make their way to shore. The stone trio reached dry sand and threw themselves into an oncoming charge of five riders. Two of the steeds buckled in fear as a third got its legs broken by a giant stone arm. The last two riders managed to avoid a head-on collision and now hastily retreated back toward the gate, where the first men on foot were coming out.

Near the harbor, buildings burned brightly from the barrage of fireballs. One of the airships slid slowly above the city's rooftops. Its cargo doors swung open and a familiar device was extended from the hold.

"*Look! Those are descenders, aren't they?*" said Raylan. Galirras made a turn in an attempt to lose a second ship closing in on them. "*What will th—No way!*"

A ghol'm was lowered from the airship directly onto the city streets with the help of two descenders. The ghol'm's feet scraped the rooftops and it crashed into a wall, but made it to the ground in one piece. It was clearly a practiced maneuver. As soon as the ghol'm hit the cobbles, it detached itself by breaking the steel chain wrapped around its torso. Right away, the descenders were retracted, after which another ghol'm was lowered to the ground.

"We need to take them out," shouted Raylan as another salvo of arrows flew their way. He quickly added in his mind, *"But we need to get rid of the archer ship first, or we'll never make it. Can you do that windblade attack you used on the ghol'm earlier?"*

"Let me try."

Galirras dove forward and pulled back up with his added speed. He twisted around and held himself stationary with his wind power. Through their connection, Raylan knew the arrow stung annoyingly in his side with every movement of his wings. The dragon growled as he increased the force behind the movement. His injury made it hard to move both wings in unison and create the necessary flow of air to manipulate.

On Galirras' back, Raylan's own adrenaline reactivated his wind vision, including the throbbing headache that seemed to come with it. He saw the airflow between Galirras' wings being pushed together, guided by the dragon's invisible influence on it. But it took five attempts to conjure the first curved wave of wind, and all the while their pursuers came straight at them.

Finally, a sharp-edged blade of wind shot through the air. But it was not as strong as the ones at the plaza; halfway toward the airship, it unraveled and vanished. Thankfully, two more succeeded immediately after, each more powerful than the last.

The second wind blade was stable enough to reach the ship. It cut a few of the ropes that tied the balloon to the ship's deck. The third blade struck a bit high, but managed to tear a hole in the balloon. The effect was not as immediate as the first airship they had taken down, but it was clear this ship would not be able to stay in the air. Its bow dipped low and before they knew it the keel scraped across the roof tiles and crashed into a church tower. Those few people left in the streets ran away screaming. And for good reason, for as soon as the crashed ship ground to a halt, the Doskovian soldiers streamed out of the hold and into the city.

Galirras was already on his way to the other low-hanging airship unloading its ghol'ms. Surveying the situation below, Raylan saw heavy fighting on the beach and in the streets. He recognized groups of city guards moving to intercept the invading force. In the harbor, small boats with soldiers—and fishermen brave enough to join the fighting—were on their way to board the two fireball ships. Azurna archers rained down arrows on the ships and men attacking the beach.

"Xi'Lao and the others have joined the fighting on the beach," said Galirras with a hint of concern as two more ghol'ms emerged from the Doskovian ships.

"They'll know to keep their distance," replied Raylan. *"Let's focus on the one in front o—Watch out!"*

Raylan did not know precisely why he had looked up. Perhaps some part of his mind sparked an alert that he had lost track of the fourth flying ship. But when he did, two ghol'ms were right on top of them. Their silhouettes plummeted toward them like two giant birds of prey. Between them hung an iron net.

Galirras' lightning-fast reactions were all that prevented a full-on disaster. Raylan's world disappeared into a blur as the dragon pushed himself into another roll and dropped toward the ground in an attempt to buy the slightest bit of extra time. It worked. The net and its stone handlers missed them by an arm's length. One ghol'm even made a grab for Galirras' tail in the brief moment they swished past, but got nothing but air. The two stone warriors slammed into the street and shattered into pieces. Two blue rings of energy burst outward, knocking over a few of the locals who were trying to put out a fire in a nearby building.

Throughout the twists and turns, Raylan had wrapped his arm through the leather strap around Galirras' neck a few times. The strap cut deep into his flesh with each sudden move, but he figured it beat falling to his death. He really missed having a weapon, but his sword would do no good on the back of a dragon. Perhaps he should consider a small, bow-like weapon if he wanted to contribute to the fighting. Though perhaps it was more important to function as an extra pair of eyes, with so many dangers from different sides.

Galirras had readjusted his course and now approached the highest airship. He dodged arrows, fireballs and spears left and right. Despite the arrow in his side, his wings now cracked like thunder with every stroke they made. He was about to pass the ship's rail when another iron net was thrown down. This time, all the speed in the world could not help the dragon dodge it; he practically flew straight into it, head first.

Fortunately, it was just the net, without any heavy weights—like ghol'ms—attached to it, but Galirras' head was completely tangled, making it hard to see as he dropped away from the ship again. The net's own weight pulled down on his head and neck as he tried to level out his flight, which meant his body automatically tried to follow.

"Hang on," Raylan yelled. He tried to grab the net while keeping an eye out for arrows at the same time, only to cry out a moment later, "I can't reach it!"

Raylan moved his feet under him and hooked his left arm through the leather strap. *Please don't break, please don't break...*

He pushed his legs out onto Galirras' shoulder and stretched his arm, but then another shape above them caught his eye.

"*Left!*"

The dragon banked left without question, even though his own eyes were obstructed by the net. A moment later, a fire barrel raced past them. They had nearly gone down in flames.

Raylan made another attempt. This time his fingers wrapped around the edge of the net. He flung it back over Galirras' head. It unraveled, finally allowing Galirras to shake himself free from the weighted confinement. He trumpeted triumphantly and approached the airship again, this time keeping directly under its keel, limiting the enemy's ability to attack him.

He grabbed the ship with his hind legs, using his front claws to tear out a large piece of the balloon. The airship keeled over and half glided, half fell toward the world below. As the ship dropped away, Galirras pushed off with his legs to give it extra momentum. He called upon his reserves and pushed the ship into a dive with his wind power.

The effort did not go to waste. The ship tumbled from the sky and crashed straight into the other airship hovering above the rooftops, still unloading its ghol'ms. A harbor warehouse, bar and house were completely obliterated as both ships slammed into the buildings. The whole mess erupted in flames and exploded in a ring of blue light as the activated ghol'ms inside the ship were shattered.

Galirras panted heavily. Even Raylan felt out of breath—which seemed silly, since Galirras did all the work. He watched the chaos beneath them. The dragon ruled the sky now, but down in the city and on the beach the fight was far from over.

"*Come on. We need to get back to the castle and have them send reinforcements to the beach. They're getting massacred down there.*"

Galirras dragged them both back to the castle, his movements heavy with exhaustion.

"Seb!" shouted Raylan as he dismounted.

His friend came running up.

"Great job with those airships, both of you," called Sebastian out.

"Never mind that. Can you find a healer who's not afraid to approach Galirras? He got struck by an arrow. And any food around for him? A cow or pig, perhaps?"

Sebastian ran off immediately.

"Are you sure you're okay?"

Galirras lifted his wing and sniffed the arrow.

226

"I am, but I would not mind it being taken out now. It stings when I move."

Shortly after, a nervous army healer went to work on the dragon's wound while Galirras distracted himself with a plump pig that he casually tore in half. Around them, fighters came and went. Those wounded returned to the fight if capable, and everywhere messengers ran back and forth with important orders.

Raylan was surprised the entire city was not one big war zone. Each time he had seen battle, he had always been in the middle of the action, but this attack was on a much different scale. By underestimating Galirras' presence, the Doskovian soldiers now found themselves forced into a ground battle instead of the intended chaos they had wished to unleash. It made it much more difficult for them to control a large part of the city.

Still, the number of ghol'ms on the shore was worrisome. And Raylan was certain there were still a few of the stone giants tramping along the city streets after surviving the airship crashes. Many more innocents would die before they could call themselves victors. *If* they could call themselves victors.

"Do you know where Captain Whitflow is? We need to send reinforcements to the beach. They're getting pummeled down there," said Raylan to Sebastian as the healer did his work.

"He left to do just that. The horseback units were sent first—being the quickest—but smaller squads are now on their way. To defend the streets and help down at the beach. They're supplied with metal chains and heavy war hammers—just like you said."

When the healer was done, Galirras hopped off toward a fountain to quench his thirst. He moved a bit better now the arrow was gone. He plunged his head in the water and started to drink.

But he had barely taken a sip when he raised his head again.

"Do you feel that?" said the dragon.

"Feel what?" asked Raylan.

Both men stared at Galirras with puzzled looks as the dragon stretched his long neck to scan their surroundings. Raylan looked around. In the distance, a large column of smoke rose toward the sky. On the plaza, soldiers were gearing up to go into the city, and a cart with supplies was being pulled by two large horses. But Galirras was not paying attention to any of them.

Then a slight vibration traveled through the ground. It grew stronger under Raylan's feet. It was as though the world briefly shuddered beneath them, but it was gone before he or Sebastian had time to fully become aware of it. On the other side of the river, a flock of birds took to the sky. Down in the furthest corners of the city—those parts still untouched by the fighting—stray dogs barked at nothing.

"What was that?" said Raylan.

Galirras, who stood on his hind legs to see even further, dropped back down. He swung his head around.

"I do not know. It seems to have gone now."

"Could it be the ghol'ms? Are they attacking the castle already?" asked Sebastian, worried.

"I certainly hope not," said Raylan, feeling the blood drain from his face at the thought of how many soldiers the ghol'ms would have plowed through if that were the case.

They saw others look around, uncertain, but everything seemed calm in the vicinity. The fighting was still confined to the outskirts of the city. Then something caught Galirras' eye down in the harbor.

"What is happening with the water?" rumbled the dragon.

Raylan pushed off the rampart with his arms and stretched his neck to get a better look.

"You mean the boarding parties trying to take over the fireball ship?" he asked.

He saw heavy fighting taking place on the first deck, while additional Azurna soldiers were still trying to board the second ship.

"No, there. Where the dark goes into light water."

Sebastian climbed on top of the rampart to see. Raylan quickly followed his example.

"What do you mean, Galirras? That white stuff?" asked Sebastian. "That's just the churning of the river water meeting the ocean."

"It was not there before."

Raylan surveyed the river and both shores. He had seen all kinds of different waters during his days of sailing—it could do incredible things. It was not uncommon for some of the more superstitious sailors to believe the water had a life of its own.

"I think Galirras is right. There's something off. The river's flowing faster— just look at the shores, and the water in the harbor. It—it's falling."

In the harbor, ships swayed back and forth in the rushing water. The sound of stretching landlines crackled through the air as the water level dropped even further at an ever-increasing rate. Already, a tiny fishing boat hung a few feet above the water, until one of its lines snapped and the boat crashed down on one side, cracking its hull against the stone dock.

"The ocean. It's retreating," said Sebastian, astounded.

"And the river water can't keep up," added Raylan. "What's going on? It's not even low tide yet."

The water was so low now that two of the larger merchant ships near the docks—one of them on fire—now rested with their hulls on the ground, leaning against the pier.

"Look, the fireball ships have also run aground," said Galirras.

The ship that had not yet been boarded hung dangerously to one side. It barely managed to stay upright as the keel sank deep into the harbor's silty ground.

"Are you sure this isn't the ghol'ms' doing?" wondered Sebastian.

Raylan shook his head.

"No, it wouldn't make sense. What would they do? Carry water with their bare hands? Something else must be going on—and I intend to find out what. Can you fly, Galirras?"

"I will manage," assured the dragon.

Raylan jumped from the highest part of the rampart onto Galirras' back. The dragon shifted back and forth to let Raylan settle down, but did not attempt to launch into the air just yet.

"What's wrong?" asked Sebastian, watching them linger.

Raylan stretched out his hand as Galirras turned his head. Raylan smiled. Sometimes they did not even need to share a mind to have the same thoughts.

"Are you coming or not?" said their two voices in unison.

"You've done all you can here, so let's stay together," added Raylan. "We can use an extra set of eyes up there."

Sebastian's puzzled look transitioned into a surprised grin. He jumped up the rampart, took a few steps and climbed up behind Raylan.

"Won't we be too heavy?" said Sebastian as an afterthought.

"Not like this. Just hold on to me," said Raylan. He firmly grasped the strap around Galirras' neck and clamped his legs together in anticipation of Galirras' next move.

"Go."

Galirras pushed off gently and dove off the rampart. Sebastian's grip tightened around Raylan's waist, but his friend did not scream. The castle wall was not very high here, but gave the dragon plenty of time to snap open his wings. The wind caught under them as their short fall transitioned into a glide.

The brief rest had done Galirras good. He beat his wings, applying his power to the wind to push them up. Within moments, they flew low over the rooftops.

Everywhere below, skirmishes took place in the streets. A ghol'm thrashed around and hit straight through a wall as it tried to squash its next victim.

Raylan knew Galirras wanted to help, but there was no way he would be able to muster up enough power for a storm ball. For now, the city's soldiers were on their own. The last of the houses dropped away behind them while the dragon made certain to stay clear of enemy archers.

They exited the harbor and stared down in disbelief. From Galirras' back, they saw right down to the ocean floor, both in the harbor and offshore. The river itself had decreased to a slightly smaller but fast-running stream. Raylan spotted soldiers marching through ankle-deep water to get to the two stranded fireball vessels. They kept slipping in the wet, silty ground.

On one of the merchant ships, the entire crew hung over the railing to keep an eye out for attackers. They all had knives, swords and bows at the ready.

A moment later the ship abruptly shifted. An angry scream rose from the captain on deck. The large, double-masted ship keeled over. Wood cracked and iron groaned as the ship landed on its side. Men screamed as crates, barrels and other cargo slid across the ship's deck and crashed into them. Some were knocked around quite severely, but Raylan was glad to see that none of the men had used up their sailor's luck just yet.

"What could do this?" Sebastian called out against the wind. The former slave had finally found his voice again now that he was accustomed to Galirras' movements.

"I don't know, but look how far it goes," Raylan replied.

The entire coastline of Aeterra—for as far as their eyes could see—lay dry. Pools of shallow water held schools of fish; crabs quickly dug into the silt to hide themselves, while thousands of shells sparkled in the lowering sun. Seagulls and other water birds flocked together to feast on all that remained visible on the dry ocean floor between the stranded boats.

Raylan saw three of the enemy ships had not even made it to shore yet. They were now stranded, just like all the others. Within the city, people simply stared at the strange event. Around them, the dark columns of smoke were a strong contrast against the mostly white and colored buildings.

"Look—those must be Brenton's ships," shouted Raylan, pointing down.

"The Talkarian merchant you met in the bar?" asked Sebastian.

"Talkarian prince actually, so it would seem. See? They carry Tal'Kabur's flag."

"Looks like they are about to have company, too," said Galirras.

Two of Brenton's ships leaned against one another on the dry ocean floor, their masts crossed like a pair of sword-fighting knights. A third lay with its belly wet in a pond of seawater barely big enough to surround the ship. Not far from them all were two Doskovian black sails, run aground.

Without the ability to get to shore easily, the Doskovian soldiers were now on their way to the closest action they could get. The Talkarian crews had pulled out their own weapons and nervously waited in anticipation of the fight. But who would make the first move? Raylan feared it was the ghol'm that was slowly but surely making its way across the slippery ocean floor.

Raylan tapped Galirras' neck.

"Let's keep going. I have a feeling we need to know what this is."

"Look at that," said Sebastian as they flew further from the coast.

Below them, the sandy ocean floor abruptly dropped off into the deep. Dark sea water churned and splashed against the exposed ocean wall. Raylan looked back at Azurna and the ships.

"We're about a mile out," he yelled back to Sebastian. "I think that's just the normal ocean drop-off; where the shallow coast meets the deeper ocean. See all those underwater plants on those rocks? Question is, where did all the water go?"

He had never seen anything like it. They banked left and flew parallel to the natural divide between sand and water.

"The water looks so calm out there," said Galirras.

"Well, not down here," remarked Sebastian, looking directly beneath them.

"He's right. Just look at how the water crashes into the reef wall," said Raylan.

The ocean below waved sluggishly, an unstoppable force that slammed into the exposed coral and water vegetation.

"Even the tiniest of waves just keeps pushing," spoke Galirras out loud. "They must have a lot of water behind them."

"You have no idea," called Raylan back. "Ships are nothing more than play toys if the ocean gets going."

"I don't think we're going to find anything out here," yelled Sebastian. "Shouldn't we get back to the fighting?"

Raylan looked out across the sea. The sky was clear; no storm was brewing. The wind was calm and there were barely any waves. It made the ocean floor cutoff look even more surreal.

"I don't know. Something doesn't feel right. Besides, we just got here. Let's do one more pass before we go back."

Raylan tapped Galirras on the neck again. The dragon immediately made a wide turn back toward where they came from.

"Little one, I know you don't really like to, but can you fly lower to the water? I want to have a closer look at that reef wall. Maybe we'll see something that explains all of this."

Without a word, Galirras slowly glided toward the water's surface, making sure he still had the strength to rise back up. Raylan knew he had not forgotten the terrifying moments where he nearly drowned off the Dark Continent's coast. Fortunately, the water looked calm enough, and he had enough room for his wings to keep moving.

Raylan was amazed to see they flew under the top edge of the reef wall. Water splashed upward with every wave, but it had receded so much he could barely see Azurna over the exposed ocean ledge. He watched the different colored corals and plants, but saw nothing that explained where the water had gone.

Sebastian suddenly yelled at the top of his lungs.

"Up! Up! Galirras, up!"

Raylan jerked around. A huge wave was right upon them. It was not a white foaming wave like one would see on the beach, but more a tower of water. Had they not been as low as they were, it might not even have looked dangerous. Yet now it was as if they flew between two walls that were about to collide. With great effort, Galirras pushed himself up. A gush of wind from Galirras' power launched them upward, followed not a heartbeat later by the full spray of water as the wave slammed into the ocean drop-off. It soaked them from head to toe. Galirras shuddered from the sudden cold, but continued to climb to safer heights.

Beneath them, the wave flowed over the silted sand. It looked like a melted, watery hand that tried to claw its way out of the dark depths. The water stopped for the briefest of moments before a new wave pushed forward, this one even higher than the first. It did not take anything else for Raylan to understand the danger.

"Go, Galirras, go! Back to shore as fast as you can. We must warn everyone. The water. It's coming back," he yelled.

With his gained altitude, Galirras stooped into a dive to gain as much speed as possible. The dragon's wings beat heavily, aided by his wind power on every push.

"Don't mind us. Go as fast as you can," pressed Raylan privately into the dragon's mind. He grabbed Sebastian's arms as tightly as he could as he held on for his own dear life. Galirras' breath rasped in and out of his throat.

Raylan's eyes watered from the wind that rushed past his face. He dared to watch over his shoulder and saw a swell of water blow past the drop-off.

They passed the Talkarian ships. The ghol'm had punched a hole in the side of the nearest ship, while the deck and ocean floor crawled with sailors and soldiers tied together in a fight to the death.

"The water's coming back," screamed Raylan at the top of his lungs, but he had no time to see if any of them heard it.

He pinched Sebastian's arm and yelled, "The coastal cliffs might slow it down a little, but not much. We need to warn the others to seek higher land, or they won't make it."

"What about the city?" Sebastian called out.

"Maybe the castle's upper level is high enough, but the harbor and Old Town…" Raylan dared not even think about it.

"Raylan, my sister… the kids," said Sebastian.

It was like someone stabbed a burning poker into Raylan's heart. He could only nod and press his thoughts to Galirras.

"Faster, Galirras. Like the wind."

CHAPTER FIFTEEN

Devastation

T HE SEA IS COMING! Seek higher ground!"

Galirras bellowed the words with such might they echoed in Raylan's head as the dragon trumpeted his call vocally and mentally. The people still near the harbor were all busy putting out fires. As Galirras flew past the harbor's first buildings, Raylan saw the confused looks they gave. Not all of them understood what had just happened; some did not even understand that the dragon's sounds were actually spoken words.

"Rogue wave!" Raylan called down in an attempt to help.

But all he saw were people looking up in fear of the large, winged shadow that shot through the sky. Their warning failed and only added to the confusion in the city streets, until those who had been watching the battle on the boats saw the water ram into the stranded ships. A collective realization settled in as Galirras' words sparked the fight-or-flight parts of people's brains. Shouts and screams reached the coast as sailors and soldiers alike were swallowed up by the water near the Talkarian merchant ships. The two entangled ships vanished under a blanket of water.

Galirras leaned forward and slid to a halt near their squad on the back end of the beach.

Raylan let out a sigh of relief when he counted the entire team present. Most were still on horseback; a few stood with reins in hand, trying to keep the horses calm. From the looks of it, they had been able to take down two ghol'ms, but at a heavy price. The beach lay littered with the dead and further along guards were still tied up in heavy battle.

Without delay, Raylan jumped to the ground as Galirras stood panting to catch his breath.

"Raylan, where have you been? We're getting slaughtered here," Ca'lek called out.

Next to the dark-skinned scout, Kevhin had his hands full with his mare, which was on the brink of blind panic.

"What's gotten into you?" the archer exclaimed, annoyed with the horse.

"Get on that horse and go. All of you. Right now," screamed Raylan. "Ride for higher ground. The sea is coming!"

Rohan look at him strangely. In his eyes, Raylan no doubt looked like a madman, completely soaked and dirty from the seawater, screaming and rambling insanely.

"What are you talking about?" asked Kevhin as he gritted his teeth and fought to keep hold of the reins.

Galirras snorted and stepped forward, spread his wings and roared his thoughts toward them. Sebastian screamed as he almost tumbled off.

"DO IT!" boomed the dragon.

Not a soul dared question the command. The sound awakened a primal fear buried deep in every human's core. Even the city's soldiers locked in combat turned around and fled.

No longer fighting to restrain their horses, Raylan's squad members jumped in the saddle and let them run. The frightened horses did not need to be told where to flee—they knew very well what was coming.

The dragon lowered his head to give Raylan better access. In a moment of enlightenment, Raylan grabbed a long piece of rope that lay nearby before jumping back on. Galirras launched himself back into the air, barely giving Raylan time to grab the rope around his friend's neck. Sebastian shouted in fright as he almost missed his grip around Raylan's waist.

In the distance, a thunderous rumble grew. From the air, Raylan saw the front of the wave roll into the city. People's screams were swallowed up in the mass of water. Both Doskovian fireball ships toppled. One of them exploded as it was swallowed up by the sea, a fountain of seawater shooting up from the blast.

Along the coast, the moving wall of water slammed into the cliffs and sprayed high above the land. The beaches were completely gone already, while trees near the coast were ripped from the ground, roots and all. In the distance, Raylan saw their group. Their horses were galloping madly, straight up the grassy hills, jumping over—or crashing through—any wooden fences they encountered along the way.

Raylan did not have any more time to look. Following Sebastian's directions, Galirras brought them straight to the little house with the round windows. The dragon crashed more than landed on the roof of a low building next to it.

"They might not even be here," said Raylan, hoping the opposite.

But it fell on deaf ears. Without a moment's hesitation, Sebastian jumped down, slid across the roof and fell into the tiny garden.

"Seb, there's no time," Raylan called after him.

The thunder of the ocean ravaging the land moved toward them from the harbor. The slush of water and debris pushed itself through the streets. Walls were swept away, roofs ripped open. There was no way Galirras could fight himself free of that rolling river of death.

Elena ran out with Tobias in hand, who, despite the alarms, had been calmly playing in the back kitchen.

"Seb? What's all that noise? The alarms rang, so I took the kids home, but Lucas isn't h—"

Galirras clawed his way forward and swung his head low. Elena let out a scream that sent Tobias straight into a wailing fit. Sebastian took her by the shoulders and shook her desperately.

"Elena, listen to me. Climb up now, or you and your son will die. Climb!"

Galirras slid down as far as he could into the garden, but it was impossible to fit in more than his chest. Sebastian grabbed Tobias from his sister's arms and half threw him up to Raylan. Elena's mothering instinct kicked into overdrive and she immediately scrambled after her taken son. Raylan held on with one hand and pulled as hard he could to get the woman on Galirras' back. The rush of water was so close now they could all feel the ground rumble.

"Where's Emi?" called Sebastian. Then Raylan noticed the girl standing in the back doorway.

"Mommy? What is th—"

The wave hit.

Galirras pushed off. Raylan knew full well he was abandoning Sebastian and the little girl, but there was nothing any of them could do. Raylan saw Sebastian dive for the girl. His friend's arms wrapped around her just before they both disappeared in a turmoil of brown, murky water that forced its way through the doors and windows.

"Sebastian," shouted Raylan.

His hands moved in a blur as he looped the rope into a loose bowline while Elena clung to her son and the dragon, screaming. Beneath them the seawater rushed between the buildings. Trees, carts and those unlucky enough to have drowned were all carried with the wave.

"Do you see them anywhere?" asked Raylan in Galirras' head. *"Do you?"*

The dragon landed on top of a higher building some ways down the street. Water already rushed past.

"*I cannot. I cannot see him,*" said Galirras, whose eyes shot back and forth, the small sparkling vortexes within them spinning crazily.

The dragon shot off a windblast, and another, but it had no effect on the massive amount of water.

Suddenly, a voice called from below, barely noticeable above the creaking debris and thundering river that had taken possession of the streets.

"Raaaaylan!"

* * *

It had not even crossed his mind to jump toward Raylan and the others. Instead, Sebastian closed his arms around the little girl, who had made him laugh more in these last few days then in all his years as a slave. When he felt the rush of wind from behind, he knew it was too late. Galirras had taken off. He did not blame him, nor Raylan—who likely had nothing to say in the matter. The dragon merely wanted to keep Raylan safe. It was as natural a reaction as it was for Sebastian to jump toward his niece. He had just found his family again, and they were worth protecting.

Emily's scream was swallowed up by the wall of water that smashed into the house in a spray of salty foam. The world disappeared in a dark, wet turmoil that crushed the air from Sebastian's lungs. The little girl panicked in his arms, struggled in his grip, but he dared not let go lest she disappear forever.

Something smashed into his back. He had no idea whether it hit him, or he hit it, but it knocked the remaining air stored in his lungs right out of him. A large gulp of water forced its way inside. He quickly swallowed to prevent it from going into his lungs. His teeth creaked from the sand between them. He moved his arm and legs around, trying to determine which way was up. Internally, he screamed Galirras' name, knowing full well they did not share the same bond as Raylan had with the dragon.

With rising panic, Sebastian suddenly noticed that his niece hung limp in his arms. He opened his eyes, but visibility was too low to make out anything. The water stung his eyes, like a hundred pins were jammed into them at the same time. He was forced to close them again as he continued to tumble with the strong flow of water and debris. His lungs burned for air. If he did not surface soon he would fail his sister miserably. He would fail his niece, not to mention himself.

Sebastian's mind turned his panic into anger. He did *not* escape the Stone King's slave mines to give up so easily. He did *not* forsake his friends back in the tree village only to die in his hometown. And he certainly was *not* going to let his niece slip away in his arms.

I will not stand for it!

Then his feet found solid ground. A strange wave pattern; under his soft boots, which could only mean one thing.

A roof. It's a roof!

He pushed off as hard as he could in the direction he hoped was up. He screamed an airless scream as he willed the water out of his way. It was still unexpected to see the blue sky pop up from the darkness. He quickly sucked in a breath before a wave overtook his head again. But he was at the surface now. He kicked his feet like a madman to keep his head above water, desperately trying to pull his niece higher in the process. Sebastian was able to grab the corner of a two-story building and coughed heavily. As soon as his throat allowed it, he screamed.

"Raaaaylan!"

His fingers began to slip. A tree trunk came out of nowhere and slammed into the wall, barely missing his hand. On it sat a frightened cat, claws dug deeply into the bark of the tree. Time slowed as Sebastian's eyes met those of the frightened animal. The tree slowly turned and slid off with the flow of water.

Above him, something smashed into the top roof. It thrashed around as it tried to regain its balance. Roof tiles fell, splashing all around Sebastian. Galirras' head swung over the edge of the roof.

"I cannot get to him," rumbled the dragon nervously. "Hold on, Seb. Just hold on."

Galirras scrambled off to find a better angle.

"I can't," Sebastian half coughed as another splash of water forced its way into his lungs.

The pull on his legs was too strong to fight. The water dragged his niece further away from his grasp. Only three fingers held on, but this was not a battle he could win. He heard his nephew cry and his sister's voice scream—not in fear for the dragon anymore, but in encouragement. For him, her brother, and her child.

Raylan's voice carried down. The words carved into Sebastian's mind, though he could barely understand his friend through the screams of his sister and nephew.

"Let go and grab the rope," shouted the voice from above.

Sebastian tried to look behind him, but the current was too strong to see anything. Water kept washing over his face. If he let go, that was it. He would not be quick enough to grab something else. They would be carried away. Sucked underwater again. His fingers were cold and cramped. They would not hold on much longer.

"Behind you," screamed Raylan again.

"I can't see it!"

The warning from above came at the same time Sebastian noticed the danger himself.

"A cart. Watch out," trumpeted Galirras.

A wagon headed straight for Sebastian, pushed forward by a wall of debris behind it. It was now or never.

Sebastian pushed away from the wall and spun around. For a frightful moment, he could not see anything but brown murky waves and floating rubble. Then he spotted the rope—just in time. He kicked his legs violently and threw his free arm and head through the loop that dangled just above the water's surface. He grabbed the limp body of his niece with both hands as the noose around him tightened. The rope cut sharply into his shoulder and neck, his healed wound complaining against the pressure.

His body felt heavy as the water dropped away below him. His clothes stuck to his skin, wet and cold. The shocks and jolts of Galirras' beating wings swung the rope dangerously back and forth. The dragon struggled under the added weight and his exhaustion.

Sebastian pulled the young girl in his hands closer and wrapped his legs around her. Her body hung limp in his arms, like a doll. His fingers tingled from the rope's pressure in his armpit, but he clenched his teeth against the pain and strengthened his resolve to keep a firm grip on Emily.

As they ascended and Galirras set a course for the castle's highest level, Sebastian witnessed the devastation that stretched beneath him. The lowest parts of the city were completely flooded. Around the harbor, most of the houses and buildings were completely gone. Fishing boats lay on rooftops, or had crashed through walls. The water still moved inland and up the river. But as it claimed more of the city's streets, the ocean's flow slowed down—as if the water had decided that simply flooding everything would be enough for now.

In the streets, drowned humans and livestock floated. Other people stood on the roofs of higher buildings, fearful looks in their eyes as they wondered whether the water would continue to rise. Beyond the city's borders, the freak wave had overtaken large parts of the lower land. Their encampment was not there anymore, just a dark tongue of water that licked the rolling hills miles from the coast. Sebastian saw people in the distance, some on horses, but it was too far to see who they were.

The city disappeared from sight as the castle walls rushed under him. Galirras did his best to land softly, but he could barely keep himself from smashing into the stone plaza. Raylan released the rope as Sebastian's back scraped along the ground, ripping his clothes. The momentum made him tumble sideways, unable to easily stop with his niece still in his arms.

Once the world stopped moving, Sebastian carefully opened his arms, which were cut and bruised from the stones, as were his legs. He looked down at the little girl. She was awfully white, with deep blue lips.

* * *

Raylan jumped from Galirras' back, helped Elena and her son down then rushed over to Sebastian.

"Seb, are you okay?"

But Sebastian did not hear him.

"She's not breathing. Help her," begged his friend. Raylan dropped to his knees and took the girl from Sebastian.

"She took too much water inside. The air can't get in," said Raylan, lying the girl flat on the ground. "We need to get the water out. Now."

Elena dropped to her knees, wailing.

"My girl. Save her. Please, save my girl. Please."

Raylan trailed his hands along her stomach and ribs, placed them on top of each other and pushed down as hard as he dared. He had seen it twice during his voyages out at sea; men brought back from the brink of death after they fell in the water. He knew what to do—pump the water from the chest—but had never actually done it before. And he certainly did not want to break the girl's ribs. But if he did not force the water out...

A gulp of water flowed from her mouth. *More. There's still more in there.*

Raylan pushed again, then turned the girl onto her side to let the water flow out.

"*She needs air,*" said Raylan inside Galirras' mind. "*The water is coming out, but no air is going in.*"

"Step aside," spoke the exhausted dragon. He dragged himself back to his feet and moved closer to the girl and Raylan. "Let me."

Raylan moved back a little to give Galirras space. The dragon towered above the girl's tiny, lifeless body.

"*Gently, now. We don't want to break anything inside her,*" added Raylan privately.

Galirras brought his head forward until it was mere inches away from the girl's face. Elena shot forward, but Sebastian caught her just in time.

"What's it doing? Stay away from my girl. Don't you eat her, you hear me? Don't you dare hurt her," she screamed.

"Elena, stop! He's trying to save her," shushed her brother.

Galirras carefully breathed out, guiding the air into the girl's nostrils with his wind manipulation. Raylan saw the child's chest slowly rise.

"Now press," spoke Galirras.

Raylan gave a light, short press, then pushed Emily's chest down again with a heavier second push.

"Again," urged Raylan. "We have to jolt the body awake. Remind it how to live."

Galirras breathed again, slightly longer this time, before Raylan repeated his own pattern. Behind them, Elena cried in Sebastian's arms. Tobias clung to his mother's leg, unable to make sense of everything that was going on. His crying had given way to intense staring at his older sister, who lay motionless on the ground.

"Again," growled Raylan.

Galirras blew in faster now that he had a sense of how much the small girl's chest could hold. Raylan applied pressure once more. Suddenly, the girl coughed, and water sprayed from her mouth.

Quickly, Raylan turned her on her side again. Elena shouted in relief and fell next to her daughter to help her. The girl coughed and vomited water once more before drawing a deep breath, then started to cry. She grabbed her mother's dress and tried to disappear into it. Raylan looked up to see tears running down Sebastian's smiling face.

"Thank you," said his emotional friend. "You too, Galirras. I thank you with all my heart."

Raylan looked around. The entire plaza was full of people who had sought higher ground to escape the oncoming water. A man suddenly pushed through the crowd gathered around them.

"Elena? Is that you? Elena!"

Elena's husband ran over and put his arms around her.

"You're safe. I can't belief you're safe. Come here, Tobias. Thank god you're all safe," cried the man.

Raylan was looking at the wall when Sebastian came over, obviously not wishing to intrude on his sister's reunion with her husband.

"What is it?" Sebastian asked.

"There are bound to be more people out there who need help," said Raylan.

Immediately, Galirras stepped forward and offered him his front leg.

"You had better climb on, then."

"No, you can't," said Raylan. "You're nearly collapsing as it is."

"I still have a few more flights left in me today," rumbled Galirras, though Raylan heard the fatigue in his winged friend's voice. "There may be others who can still be saved."

In the end, both Raylan and Galirras worked far into the night. They scouted from the air, looking for those in direst need of help. Galirras ripped open buildings to free those trapped inside. At other times, Raylan tied the long rope around Galirras' neck to lower himself down and pull people from the water. It was far past the moon's highest point before Sebastian eventually convinced them to rest lest their exhaustion lead to a fatal mistake.

Lord Algirio had ordered the city guards to bring any wounded to the highest square. It was one of the few places in the city the water had never reached. Some parts of the city on the northern river shore had been spared as well, protected slightly by the cliffs. The rest of the city was barely recognizable.

After the first, two more waves had forced their way inland, though neither as strongly as the original one. The Doskovian forces—ghol'ms and all—were swept away in the flood. Unfortunately, it seemed like many of their own forces had been taken by surprise as well.

When morning came and the water finally retreated, the full extent of the devastation became visible. The remains of those who had perished hung on broken walls and lay scattered throughout the streets. Others had drifted out to sea, following in the wake of the retreating water. Hundreds of lives lost, and many were still unaccounted for. Houses had crumbled; trees and wood stuck out of windows and doorways. And though the water had extinguished all the fires, the entire city was now covered in a thick layer of mud, seaweed and shells. In every corner, fish lay dead or dying, and on their second day of looking for survivors Galirras had even spotted a shar'ac as the large, swimming predator slowly made its way down one of the streets back to the ocean.

Constant patrols walked through the devastated streets. They did not find many enemies alive, and those who were fought to the death. A few ghol'ms were encountered, but most of them were broken or stuck, so disposing of them was not really a problem.

Now, on the fourth day, Raylan stood on the high-level ramparts and silently watched the ruins of the city below. It had been another long night.

Rescue efforts were still in full progress, with every able hand helping to clear the debris and rubble in the hope of finding people still alive.

Next to him stood Xi'Lao. Their group had made it out just in time, together with a good number of the city guards. They had pushed their horses to the limit as they tried to stay ahead of the wave. There were some close calls, but eventually they were able to stop on top of a large hill a few miles inland. When the water receded, they wasted no time in getting back to the city to see what was left.

When she found them, Xi'Lao had been so glad to see Raylan, Sebastian and Galirras alive she momentarily forgot the awkwardness between them and uncharacteristically hugged every single one of them. Raylan hoped it meant they could find themselves good friends again sometime soon and not let his brother's death leave a permanent fracture between them.

"All the dogs have returned," said Raylan, still shocked by the state of the city.

"Probably a good sign."

"It's like the world ended," added Raylan.

"For many, it did," said Xi'Lao solemnly. "We had better get moving. Richard is waiting."

"He's really going to leave all this behind without telling Lord Algirio—or the Azurna councilmen, or any of them—anything?"

Raylan still could not wrap his head around it, even if he had told Lord Algirio everything himself already. The official chain of command did nothing to help these people.

"Those were the king's orders," she said. "We're called to council to verify our 'unbelievable claims', as Richard said they called it."

"This is not some made-up thing," exclaimed Raylan.

"I know. Though it must seem pretty unbelievable to them."

"Surely Lord Algirio will confirm everything. And I mean, Galirras is right here. They can hardly deny his existence when I put him right in front of them in Shid'el. They need to get ready to fight, or Aeterra will be trampled."

Behind them, their squad was getting ready to depart. Only Harwin would follow later, when he was healed up. The rest of them would go immediately, to respond to the king's order that had arrived by carrier pigeon. It had not said much; just that they were to return to Shid'el without any further delay and keep their mouths shut.

"Do you think it was the Stone King? The wave, I mean," Raylan asked Xi'Lao.

"And sacrifice all his own men? I do not believe that."

"Why not? These men would rather throw themselves from an airship than talk. They're expendable."

Xi'Lao was silent for a moment, considering his reasoning.

"Still, it would be a stretch, would it not? That one man could do this."

"You tell me. You're the one who talks about everything having an energy, and masters who are able to perform acts far surpassing any normal human possibility."

He looked at his own arm, clenching his fist a few times. When he looked at Xi'Lao again, he saw a shiver run through her.

"It is a terrifying thought that a man could possess such power," she said. "But if it were him—whoever he is—why does he not make use of the fact that everything lies in ruins? Where is the rest of his army to finish the job? You would expect them to exploit the situation. Yet there are no other ships around for miles. Galirras said so himself; he flew out this morning to check."

"Yeah, he told me when I woke up," admitted Raylan. He suddenly let out a frustrated cry. "I don't know! Perhaps you're right. I just hate not knowing our enemy. Here we are, trying to warn everyone, and we're just grasping at straws. Who is the Stone King? What does he want?"

Raylan descended from the walls, unsatisfied. He did not like the fact he may never know what really happened—or how they could prevent it from happening ever again. He packed his belongings and said his goodbyes to their hosts, apologizing for the fact they could not stay to do more.

"You have done more than could have been expected from you, Mister Stryk'ard," assured Lord Algirio.

The lord smiled, his hand resting on the small of Lady Leandra's back. "And rest assured, I will look into the events of the past few days in great detail. You just make sure those big heads at the capital take you seriously."

Raylan gave an appreciative nod.

"I'll do my best," said Raylan before turning to Brenton. The Talkarian prince had joined the lord and lady of the city to see them off. "What about you?"

"We'll be stuck here a while longer. I'm sad to say most of our sailors didn't make it, so we need to replenish our crew. The *Hammer* and the *Forge* are beyond repair, shattered on the cliffs north of the city. But it looks like we can still save the *Twins* from an early demise, even if it will take time to make her seaworthy again. And though it does not make up for the loss of lives, I'm still glad the cargo was already offloaded. We've been finding crates all over town and a number were already at the castle, so all wasn't lost. It should be enough to pay for repairs and return to Tal'Kabur."

"Do not worry about the costs, Prince Baltor. We will see to it your ship is as good as new. It is the least we can do in thanks for your services."

"Thank you, Lord Algirio. A gesture most welcome," said Brenton with a polite bow.

The prince shook Raylan's hand.

"Be well on the road."

"And you at sea," answered Raylan.

"Thanks. For the time being, my men and I will continue to offer help and get the city back on its feet. At least until the ship is fixed. I've sent word back home about all that has happened. They need to be warned about recent events."

"Prince Baltor kindly offered to lend his organizational expertise to prepare for any other *unexpected* circumstances that may arise," added Lord Algirio.

"I can only hope none of it will be needed. But I fear this was just the beginning. Many more ships are out there," said Raylan. "Be safe."

He turned around, but turned back again.

"Brenton? Can I ask you a favor?" he said. "Can you check on Harwin every now and then? He will be bedridden for a few weeks, and I'm sure he'll enjoy the company."

"Of course."

Moments later, Galirras took off for a quick hunt while their group set out. Those who had seen the dragon in action during the last few days cheered their goodbyes. It was nice to see a different kind of reaction from the common folk, as well as the soldiers. Most of the people's fears had dropped away and the guards had willingly let go of their caution toward the dragon.

Riding out of the ruined city on horseback, Raylan found himself in the company of Sebastian. His friend had a strange look on his face.

"What?" asked Raylan.

"I told my sister to get out of the city," Sebastian said apologetically. "Apparently, there are some distant relatives living in a village miles up the river. They'll head there first thing tomorrow morning. I hope they'll be safe there."

"Safer than here," said Raylan gloomily. "Did you tell them about the Doskovian invasion force?"

Sebastian nodded.

"I couldn't help myself—"

"I know. I understand," Raylan broke in, holding up a hand. "I actually told Lord Algirio everything, right after the ghol'm attack."

Sebastian let out a whistle.

"Richard's not going to be happy about that."

"He doesn't know. He still thinks Lord Algirio is in the dark about why those ships showed up. Let him. If he so desperately wishes to follow the rules, that's his choice. But perhaps now they have a chance. When the next ships come. To get out, or defend the city. Their home."

Raylan saw his friend's face brighten as it dawned on Sebastian once more that he had truly made it home to his family, against all expectations. But his expression quickly grew dark when the former slave looked around.

"Too bad there's not much left to defend."

CHAPTER SIXTEEN

Sand

The SUN WAS HIGH. The air was dead calm, not even the lightest breeze to provide any form of comfort. Without the wind, the heat weighed thick in the air. Trista filled her water bag from a clouded pool they had run across at the bottom of a rock formation. Beside her, Decan dropped to his knees and put his entire head underwater to cool down. When Trista stepped back, Dalkeira went one step further than Decan and jumped in completely. She tried to catch a fish, but quickly gave up; they were barely bigger than crickets and not worth the energy.

Crickets. Those small, annoying animals Dalkeira had the displeasure of knowing. Trista said they were on the island, too, but Dalkeira had not heard them there. Now, with the constant noise they were making, the tiny jumpers quickly got on her nerves. Dalkeira had tried to get her revenge, but they did not taste very good. Now she mostly took joy from flying very low to the ground and making them all jump up at once before landing back in the grass again. It provided a moment's respite before the constant chirping began again.

"Why couldn't we just follow the coast?" complained Decan, pulling his head out of the water.

"You heard what the man said, right? Villages along the entire coast are being plundered and destroyed. They take no prisoners; they just kill everyone! Why would we want to stay there?" said Trista.

"But there's nothing out here. And I'm hungry! We searched for water for two days before we finally found this… puddle, and we haven't seen any remotely edible plants. And the lizards we catch are smaller than my hand! What do you suppose we eat next? Crickets?"

Tears mixed with the water on his face.

"Look, I know you're frustrated, and hungry, but there's little I can do. The hares we spot are so fast they even outrun Dalkeira, so we'll have to make do with what we can catch. There's no way we're going back toward the coast. You've seen the b—" Trista stopped herself mid-sentence. She did not want to unnecessarily remind Decan of the horrors they had seen. "You've seen the soldiers. Do you want to get caught again?"

She crossed her arms. The move reminded her of her mother.

"Besides, Dalkeira wants to go west, and I don't hear you coming up with anything better. Do you?" She frowned at him. "Have a better idea?"

"N-no," said Decan softly.

They were all hungry and it did not help the mood of their little group. They had been walking for days. At first, Trista had been glad no one had found them on the beach. They had taken their time getting organized before moving farther west. But before long, they had run into the first dead bodies on the mainland. Men, women and children all lay slain by the side of the road, their possessions either taken or set ablaze.

They had come across similar horrifying scenes at least three or four times. Every single time there were no survivors and the dead were left to rot under the scorching heat. Trista was accustomed to warm summers, but on their island the wind always provided some deliverance from the burning sun. Her pale skin had never liked direct sunlight much, so in summer she wore long sleeves to protect it. Here, it seemed the farther inland they went, the more the sun became the ruling element, and her clothes were worse for wear. These were clearly the sun god's lands, and her skin was not happy about it. The irony of being a so-called child of the sun god herself had not escaped her these last few days.

They had avoided every place that showed black columns of smoke and even successfully dodged two soldier patrols they had nearly run into. It became clear that this area was as dangerous as their own island the night they left. They had almost been safer at sea. Almost. At least here they had quite a few things to hide behind, although every day there was less vegetation as they moved further west.

A few days ago, they had come across their last piece of civilization. It had been a farm of some sorts. Dalkeira swore it was a goat farm, recognizing the smell, but there were no animals around anymore.

Part of the house had still been smoldering; they were lucky not to run into any soldiers. But as they got closer, Trista had seen a man slouched against one of the outside walls. As they approached him, the man nervously tried to get to his feet and run away, but the two arrows in his stomach prevented him from doing anything of the sort. After they assured him they meant no harm and Dalkeira had no intention of eating him, the man had spent his last breaths telling them about the soldiers. According to the farmer, stories from along the entire coast had mentioned the black ships arriving and their soldiers killing everyone in sight.

"I thought we were far enough from the coast. Away from the fishing villages. I hoped they wouldn't bother coming so far inland," the man had said, slipping in and out of consciousness.

"Oh, my poor babies. They killed my sweethearts…"

Tears flowed from his eyes. He mumbled other words, parts of which they could not fully understand. It seemed the man saw a world separate from theirs.

"*It won't be long now,*" Dalkeira had said after a while.

Trista had no idea how the dragon had known, but she was right. Once more the man had opened his eyes and looked at them.

"Oh, you're still here. You are… so kind… to keep a dying man company. But… you've got to get out of here. You hear me? Take anything that's left, you can have it all. Then get out of here, before they decide to come back. Others came by… villagers. They went west… toward the rolling hills. Cross them, and you might be safe."

It was the last thing he said. So they had searched the house, or at least the part that had been saved from the fire. They found clothes to replace their own, and Trista had taken two water bags she found in a corner. She also filled her own from the well behind the house.

After the farm, they had not encountered anyone else. No people, dead or alive, and luckily no soldiers either. The lack of food was becoming a problem, but not as much as the lack of water.

Dalkeira stuck her muzzle in the pool for the fifth time, drinking as much as she could. The dragon had shown that she could drink large amounts of water and then go without a drop to drink for days. It was like her body had its own internal water bags. But Trista and Decan had no choice but to rely on their external water bags, making sure to ration their water as much as possible.

Dalkeira wobbled over to the siblings, fully filled. Decan moved to the side, trying to avoid being close to Dalkeira as Trista handed him a small piece of dried meat. Dalkeira looked at the boy, her swirling pupils gazing calmly into his own deep brown eyes.

"What does she want from me? She's always staring at me," complained Decan in his child's voice.

Trista sighed. The situation between her little brother and Dalkeira had not improved at all. Dalkeira had tried to talk to him multiple times, but Decan only heard growls and rumbles.

"She just wants to know why you're always so afraid of her."

"I'm not afraid of her," countered Decan, upset.

"Well, it certainly looks that way."

"I'm not! And I'll prove it!"

Decan walked straight up to Dalkeira, his stride so unexpectedly bold that Dalkeira spread her wings and raised herself on her hind legs in response. The dragon was quite something to look at. Her wings had become a lighter blue on the inside. At first, it looked like the wings were turning green here and there. But now, after a few weeks, Trista spotted the first darker yellow patches coming through. The brown-yellow was a stark contrast to the deep blue of the rest of her body and the top side of her wings.

Standing on her hind legs, Dalkeira was now larger than Decan. Her long neck arched as she lowered her head to the same height as the boy's. The dragon's nervousness trickled into Trista; this was very uncommon for Decan. Dalkeira hissed at him.

But against all reason, Decan seemed unimpressed by the dragon's display of size and strength. His face moved closer to Dalkeira's, and he pointed a finger at her that reminded Trista of their father when he was about to lose his temper.

Guess we both have something of our parents in us.

"I'm not afraid of you. I just don't like you! Why do you have to meddle in everything we do? Why do we need to follow you? Do you have any idea what's out there? No. You're just a baby," Decan screamed. Tears were running down his face again. "You had no right to take Rudley away from me, like you have no right to come between me and my sister."

For a moment, Dalkeira looked like she wanted to pounce on the insolent boy. Instead, she turned around so that her tail knocked his legs from under him. Decan looked at the dragon with a child's anger on his face.

"*Suddenly he is all talk, and I am unable to say anything in return that he can hear,*" Dalkeira said inside Trista's head.

"Oh, stop it, you two," exclaimed Trista, throwing her hands up in the air. "You're both acting like spoiled children. Decan, I understand that Rudley meant something to you, perhaps a touch of home or a sense of normal, but this isn't normal. We're running for our lives, and Rudley would've led the soldiers right to us. I can understand you're angry, but Dalkeira only did what she deemed necessary to keep us alive."

She crouched in front of Decan and offered her hand. Reluctantly, he took it and got back to his feet.

"Listen, you're my little brother and I love you. I'd do anything to keep you safe—including killing your pet goat if I had to. We've been through a lot already and it's okay to be scared, but there's no reason to be afraid of Dalkeira."

"I'm not!"

"But even if you *were*, you don't have to be. She's one of us. You'd see that more if she could just talk to you. It's the three of us out here. It's all we have. We need to be able to count on each other. So, if you're not afraid, then please stop moping and let's work together to figure out how we can stay out of the soldiers' hands."

Decan stayed silent.

Well, at least he doesn't deny it anymore, thought Trista.

She turned toward Dalkeira, who had been listening from a distance.

"And you, my ocean beauty, how can such a magnificent creature feel jealous at having to share my attention?"

"*I am not!*" said Dalkeira as the remark hit home.

"It's fine, really. I'm yours and you're mine. I don't doubt that for a second, but you've got a package deal. Every day, I am grateful to feel your warmth— even if it is already scorching hot. But family's important, too. And you're part of that family now. Which means we'll look out for each other, even if we don't always see eye to eye."

Dalkeira's eyes darted briefly to Decan, who likewise pondered the words just spoken. The dragon adjusted her wings for a moment.

"*It is not like I wanted to fight with him. I know you would not like that,*" said Dalkeira.

"*I know, and I am grateful for that,*" replied Trista privately.

Trista looked at them both and decided not to stay on the topic any longer. She looked up at the sun, holding her hand above her eyes.

"I guess we'll have to decide if we're going to go through with this. That man said those other people were all headed west, but we've seen no one yet. Which means there must be something farther west for them, right?"

"*I do not care about other people,*" said Dalkeira in Trista's head. "*I just want to go west. Last night I had a dream. It was like someone was singing to me at the point where the sun touched the ground. Even now that I am awake I know it is still there, but it is like the sound is just out range of my hearing. I cannot hear it, but I can. It is hard to explain.*"

"Okay, you're right. And I'm with you, Triss. Whatever you decide," said Decan, dipping his head underwater one more time.

Trista climbed on the rock formation that sheltered the pool of water. She looked to the west. The low yellow hills looked hard and dry, with even less vegetation than those they had already crossed. Her heart beat loudly as she tried to decide if they should take the chance. She felt responsible for Dalkeira and her brother, but there were so many unknowns here she may as well have been flying blind.

Flying!

"Dalkeira, are you feeling better now that you've had a drink?"

The dragon had never said anything, but Trista noticed that she had trouble staying in the air after days without food or water. She figured that it still took a great deal of energy for the young dragon to fly, especially while she was still growing.

"I am fine."

Trista gave a small nod.

"Would you mind taking to the air and seeing if you can spot anything to the west?"

"Why not?" said Dalkeira as she took off.

* * *

As Dalkeira beat her wings to gain altitude. Trista and Decan sat down near a few boulders, staying hidden from anyone at ground level. While the dragon had been practicing her flying often, it was mostly horizontal. She was already higher than she had ever been, and her wings were starting to cramp. The days had been tiresome and although she was refreshed by her drink earlier, it had only filled her stomach with water where food was required.

"Are you okay?" asked Trista.

"I am fine."

"You're quite high up already. Can you see anything yet?"

"I can see plenty, but there are a few hills to the west that block my view still," said Dalkeira.

"Why don't you find a flow of hot air?"

"What do you mean? The air is hot everywhere here."

"No, I mean an upward flow. Back on the island I often looked at the seagulls soaring on the wind without beating their wings once. They used the winds hitting the cliffs to gain altitude. But even in the middle of the island they would circle and get higher and higher. Father explained that it was the warm air rising upward that carried them higher. Like a leaf that suddenly blows up into the sky above a campfire," explained Trista.

That seemed simple enough. Dalkeira leveled off her wings and locked them in place with her muscles. The flow of air passed underneath, but she noticed that she was slowly descending. She banked left, turning half a circle toward the west, and felt the different air pressures against her wings and skin.

She breathed in deeply, not only filling her normal lungs but also forcefully pushing air into her back lungs as well. During her time in the water, she had learned that she could take extra deep gulps of air. The additional oxygen helped her to stay underwater for long periods of time. She had not thought much of it, but figured now that it might help her more easily stay in the air, too. But the additional lungs were close to her main wing muscles, which constantly moved while in the air. This was not a problem in the water, as Dalkeira kept her wings tightly folded. But now, every time she used her muscles to beat her wings, puffs of air were being exhaled involuntarily.

She was contemplating this when she suddenly noticed an upward stream of air touch her left wing. Before she could react, she had passed it already.

"I think I have something," she said to Trista.

She steered right, circling back toward the spot where she had felt the rising air. She surveyed the landscape directly below her, and was just getting her bearings when she felt herself enter the upward stream of air again. She quickly rose several dozens of feet before she exited the stream again. Once more she circled, trying to get an estimate of the size of the updraft. As she entered the lift again, she adjusted her trajectory to stay in the rising airflow. It was a bit of a tight turn, but she was now quickly gaining altitude without beating her wings.

"You're climbing fast! Be careful!" said Trista.

Dalkeira looked down to see the land below her grow smaller by the heartbeat. The view was amazing; she approached nearly half a thousand feet already.

The constant tight turns put a strain on her wings. She let her eyes glide along the ground to see if she could spot another place where a lift might occur. She spotted a similar, larger layout of flat surface and rocky surroundings to her right. She exited the lift and veered off toward it. Surely enough, another air flow pushed her wings up as soon as she arrived above the clearing. She circled to determine the diameter of the stream and found it indeed larger than the other. The downside was that her rate of ascent slowed because of it.

She tried to reach out to Trista, but barely sensed her presence. Startled, she quickly looked down, where she easily spotted Trista and her brother watching her with hands held above their eyes. Dalkeira let out a nervous rumble. She did not understand why she had panicked there for a moment. It was not like she was dependent on them for her survival. If anything, she was helping them survive. Still, her mind was awfully quiet without Trista's thoughts seeping in from outside. It felt... unpleasant.

An abrupt gush of air forced Dalkeira to correct her course and abandon her thoughts. She was beginning to recognize a few patterns of airflows here, but it was more difficult than it had been before. During their time at sea the sparkles from the water had been abundant in the air as well, giving her guidance on how the wind was flowing. Dalkeira had never questioned the way she saw water. It differed from how she saw the rest of the world, but it had always been as normal as the grains of sand on a beach. However, the air here was so dry, she barely saw any water sparkles at all. Luckily, her instinct guided her, and she swiftly learned to recognize probable spots with lift or dangerous turbulence.

She peered down—she was well over a thousand feet now. It was time to do what she came up here to do. She turned and looked across the miles and miles of land between them and the coast. Beyond lay the shimmering ocean, which they had crossed. The land was brown, red and yellow, depending on the type of sand, along with the occasional patch of green where water was present, but what dominated the view were none of these colors. Columns of black smoke rose from the ground, as if they were pillars meant to keep the sky up. Most were fairly small, but as Dalkeira turned south she saw the walls of a large city, far off in the distance. The hot air made the image hazy, but from what Trista had told her about the southern cities, she was certain it *was* a city—a city with damaged walls and numerous fires that sent black smoke into the air.

Farther out, she noticed at least twenty ships in front of the large city, which lay directly on the coast. There were even a few ships circling the air above the city, which from a distance had the shape of an anthill. She also spotted at least three different groups of horsemen traversing the landscape, but none were on their way directly toward them.

Dalkeira turned her gaze toward the west. Her longing flared up as she peered into the distance. Several low, rocky hills lay directly ahead, but behind them was something Dalkeira could not have imagined herself. The ground looked like it had been scraped of any unevenness. It was flat and almost pure white for as far as she could see. The ground was difficult to look at because of the reflecting sun, but there was something that caught Dalkeira's eye; a dark spot that was blurry but relatively close to their current location.

As she turned another circle, she twisted her neck to keep her eyes focused on the place where she thought she had seen it. She reentered the lift to get above the sun's reflection. *There!*

The dragon trumpeted in excitement before she could stop herself. She quickly looked around to see if any of the horsemen had heard her.

Better not attract any unwanted attention.

She stooped into a full dive while getting her bearings back toward the two siblings. As the distance between them decreased, Trista flowed back into her mind again.

"…we… barely see… anymore!"

The dragon spread her wings out fully to slow her descent. She circled the rock formation once, before turning in sharply to land on the large boulder where Trista and Decan were waiting.

* * *

"You made me nervous there for a moment. We completely lost sight of you a few times with the sun in our eyes. I was afraid you wouldn't be able to find your way back to us," said Trista, her voice trembling.

"Never mind that. I found what we were looking for. I saw people, way off to the west."

"People? Not soldiers?" said Trista.

"No, regular people. I think. It was a wagon, of that I am sure. The soldiers were more to the east. The wagon was quite a distance off, but the terrain is very flat, and very white. I have no idea why that dying man spoke of rolling hills. I certainly saw none of those, but if we hurry we should be able to catch up with it in a day, or two if they are going very fast."

"How many?"

"I do not know; the distance made it difficult to see any humans. Even my eyesight has its limits. I guess we will see when we catch up to them. Come on. Let us go! We are wasting time, are we not?"

Trista had a feeling that it was not about the people at all for Dalkeira. The dragon had been drawn toward the west ever since she hatched from the egg. It was like their entire journey consisted of one long shot after another. But the water goddess had guided them well up till now, especially on the ocean waters. She had steered and provided; kept them safe. At night, when Trista kept watch, she often wondered what path the goddess had in mind for them. It made her uncomfortable to leave the waters—which provided so much life—behind and head out to follow the burning sun. If it was a good thing to follow the sun god, why did the water goddess not go with him herself?

"Maybe I was wrong; maybe we should go back to the boat and go south. Get around the southern tip and continue west by boat…"

"*We will never make it. The coast is crawling with ships, and those flying boats are moving down south,*" said Dalkeira.

"Are you sure?"

"Of what?" asked Decan, barely able to follow the conversation from Trista's questions.

"Sorry, I meant Dalkeira. She said the coast was infested with the black ships. But she saw a wagon to the west, which could mean people."

"And water. A wagon could be carrying much more water. Our water bags only have enough for a couple of days," said Decan.

"It just doesn't feel right," said Trista with a sigh. "But we can't stay here, and we can't go back."

"*Then let us stop wasting time and go,*" said Dalkeira, impatient.

"It seems we must," said Trista.

Both siblings slid down the rocks and fetched their equipment. They still had some daylight left. Decan was lucky; his skin was used to the long days of sun, and was merely turning a very deep brown. But the heat was something else. The nights here were strangely cold in comparison to the warm days. Had they not been in danger of running into soldier patrols all the time, Trista would have preferred to just travel at night and stay out of the sun during the day. Unfortunately, they needed to keep moving as much as possible, which meant only stopping to sleep or eat before continuing west both day and night.

It was late evening before Trista and her brother could see the white plains Dalkeira had spotted from the sky. They decided to use the shelter of the last hills to get some sleep before heading off onto the plains, which offered no protection from the elements for as far as the eye could see.

It was one of the shortest nights Trista had since they left the island. If they could get an early start, they could use the colder temperature of the night and morning to cover as much distance as possible. And so they did. But by the time the sun reached its zenith, Trista felt like she was walking in a frying pan.

"*It is not much further now,*" said Dalkeira as she returned from a quick lookout flight.

The dragon had searched for a water source, but it was futile; there was not a hole or well in sight, and Trista could tell flying took a lot of effort in this heat. Dalkeira returned to Trista and Decan, who had tied some of their clothes around their heads to provide protection from the sun. Her claws scratched the hard, white ground as she landed before she hopped between the two humans, trying to stay in their shadow as much as possible.

"*It seems they have stopped for a break.*"

Trista looked at her brother, who took a sip of water.

"Dalkeira says the wagon has stopped up ahead, but try to take small sips. We don't know how long we'll have to make it last."

Decan gave a small nod as he wiped his forehead with his sleeve. He was panting with every step he took, and all too often grabbing for his water to drink. It was understandable, thought Trista. His body was frailer than hers, in constant need of food and water to keep up with the growth rate of a thirteen-year-old boy. In some ways, he was very much like Dalkeira; however, it seemed a dragon's eating pattern allowed for more flexibility. Dalkeira could stuff herself and then not eat or drink for multiple days—though of course, she would never pass up an opportunity to feed.

Trista looked at the cracked earth beneath her constantly moving feet. The ground crackled under her toes. It did not look like any sand she knew. Besides, it was much too hard to be actual sand.

"*It smells like the sea,*" said Dalkeira.

The dragon lowered her head and flicked her tongue across the ground.

"*Tastes like it, too.*"

Trista picked up a small piece of white rock she accidentally kicked loose. With a slight hesitation, she put it to her tongue.

"It's salt. All of this is salt! No wonder it looked so familiar!"

She looked around. The hills were far behind them already. They were surrounded by nothing but flat, rock-hard salt. Soon they would have nothing but the path of the sun god across the sky to guide their way.

"This must have been a sea many, many years ago," said Trista.

"But how can all the water be gone?" asked Decan.

"I don't know. It must have been the sun, right? It has the power to make water disappear, like at home when we'd salt our fish."

She immediately regretted mentioning home. She saw the change on Decan's face right away. The remark had both siblings thinking about their parents as they silently continued their journey. In the meantime, with the sun moving in front of them, it became increasingly difficult to look toward the west. The glare in combination with the shimmering hot air was beginning to play tricks on their eyes. Multiple times Trista thought she saw people coming their way, and once she could have sworn she saw a house. But every time, as they walked further along, there had been nothing.

"*Did you see that?*" said Dalkeira.

"See what?"

The dragon had stopped for a moment to stretch out her wings.

"*I thought I saw something sparkle.*"

"That's just the sun. Let's keep going," said Trista.

"*No, behind us. That cannot be the sun. I thought I saw it earlier as well when I was flying, but it was on the hilltop then.*"

"Well, I don't see anything. What I *can* see is another figment of my imagination up ahead."

"You mean that large dark shape?" said Decan.

"Wait, you can see that too?" said Trista, surprised.

Dalkeira looked in the direction Trista was pointing.

"*It must be the wagon. Yes, I think it is!*"

All three picked up the pace as the wavering image took a more solid form. The promise of some shade and a chance to rest their legs made them forget the day's fatigue for a moment. But as they got closer, Trista noticed something was not right.

It was bigger than she expected, but the wagon tilted strangely to one side. She shouted a greeting, but got no answer in return. It did not seem like the wagon was moving, nor was there any sign of life around it.

"Something's wrong. They can't still be resting, can they?" said Trista out loud.

When they finally reached the wagon, it became clear they would not find any help here.

"No," whispered Trista. Dalkeira just stared at the wagon.

Decan let himself slide to the ground in the shade. He took a big gulp of his water and stared silently at the horizon where white and blue met.

"We're going to die, aren't we?" said Decan. "We have no idea what we're doing."

"Stop. We'll figure something out," said Trista, trying to keep a sparkle of hope.

"But—but we walked all this way. I don't think I can make it back again," said Decan.

Trista knew how he felt. Like hers, his head was no doubt spinning and pounding at the same time, his tongue feeling thick in his mouth. The shade was welcome and it looked like the wind was picking up a little—for which they were grateful—but even the escape from direct sunlight could not make up for the boy's disappointment.

"Look at it! It's broken! Your dragon brought us to a broken wagon in the middle of nowhere—"

"Decan!" Trista snapped before Dalkeira had a chance to react.

"Sorry," he said.

Trista approached the broken wheel and ran her hand along the shattered wood.

"There's scratches on the side of the wagon," said Trista.

The carcass of a dead ox, or what was left of it, lay in front of the wagon. One of its rear legs was broken.

"I think it got stuck in that large crack over there. See? There's still a piece of the wheel in the ground. The poor animal must have panicked and pulled the wagon over, snapping its leg and the wheel," said Trista.

Dalkeira sniffed the bones.

"There's no meat left at all," said the dragon, who had clearly hoped for a quick bite to eat.

"Vultures must have gotten to it. They can clean the meat off a carcass in half a day," said Trista.

Dalkeira joined Decan in the small strip of shade next to the wagon. Trista looked around. She did not see the hills behind them anymore. She looked in the direction the wagon had been traveling in. It was difficult to see, but it looked like there were hills or perhaps even mountains in that direction as well. She saw a vague, darker outline on the horizon, but there was no way to be certain. And mountains did not necessarily mean water, plants or food.

"I'm sorry, my dear, but I think we need to go back and try something else," said Trista to Dalkeira. The dragon lay down her head.

Decan took another gulp of his water.

"Small sips, Decan. You're going to need the rest of that water."

"But I'm so thirsty," said Decan. He suppressed a yawn. "And tired. I think I'll close my eyes. Just for a bit."

Her little brother lay down beside Dalkeira, for once not making a peep about how close she was.

"Can you keep an eye on him? I'll check out the inside of the wagon and see if there's anything left that we can use," Trista said privately to Dalkeira.

The dragon rumbled in return, almost sleeping herself. Trista looked at the little steps on the side of the wagon, then pushed the thin canvas of the canopy to the side and carefully stuck her head inside.

Her eyes slowly adjusted to the dimness, only to see the wagon was a complete mess. The wood creaked as she stepped into the gloomy interior. A few rays of sunlight came in through the holes of the canvas, making an intriguing spectacle of light. There were boxes and crates with clothes littered throughout the entire space. It was cooler than Trista expected. Often the back of a wagon was like an oven if it was directly in the hot sun.

But it seemed the holes in the canopy, and the fact that the canvas was not secured properly in some places, allowed the slightest of breezes to cool down the inside of it.

At the back, a large barrel lay on its side, its bottom all busted up.

Perhaps their water supply? If the wagon tipped over and broke a wheel, their water would have spilled, and they would have no choice but to continue on foot.

She turned the other way. A strange pile of clothes drew her attention. Tiptoeing through the mess, Trista carefully moved over and pinched a dark piece of cloth between her fingers to pull it back. The still face of a woman slowly revealed itself. Her skin, dark as night, had a slight white haze over it and looked rough from dehydration. The lips were white, with cracks running all over them. The dead woman sat uncomfortably slumped against one of the large crates, an empty wooden bowl in her hand.

Poor woman. Rest easy now, and may the goddess shower you with water to quench your thirst.

Trista had already turned around to go back outside when the faintest rustle reached her ears. She turned around, uncertain if she had actually heard it. For a moment, nothing but the sound of her own breath filled the air.

Then Trista heard a soft murmur and the movement of fabric. Something was in here with her. She saw the clothes of the woman move slightly.

She's still alive?

Trista dropped to her knees and softly shook the woman's shoulder.

"Can you hear me? Are you okay?"

But the woman did not reply. Instead, a soft mutter rose from her lap. Trista's hands trembled as she pulled the dark veil to the side. Two small, dark hands shot out from under it. Trista stared at the baby in surprise as the infant wrapped its little hands around her fingers, its lips showing the same signs of dehydration as the mother. Trista looked at the empty bowl.

She gave the last of her water to her child. Water... water! It needs water!

She grabbed the child as quickly and carefully as possible. As she exited the canopy, she nearly slammed into Dalkeira.

"*What's going on?*" said the dragon, who had felt Trista's astonishment. "*Did you feel it too?*"

"A baby. There was a baby inside the wagon! I need water. Where's my water bag?" was all Trista could stammer.

"What's going on?" Decan asked sleepily, stirring awake.

Trista rushed over to her water bag. It still felt heavy with her supply. She thanked the goddess she had been saving her water as much as possible. She held the baby's head up and wet its lips, then opened the blanket the baby was wrapped in to give it chance to cool down.

A little girl.

The water on the infant's lips seemed to spur the child's thirst. Carefully, Trista dripped more water into the baby's mouth, making sure the child had time to swallow it properly. She appeared to be well fed. The dark skin looked a bit dry, but she was a plump-looking child if Trista had ever seen one. The mother must have only just passed away.

Trista was familiar with the dangers of dehydration. Travels at sea could be unforgiving for those who did not watch their water intake. She had heard stories of infants found at sea, the nearest island days away, and how anyone wishing to help would probably provide plenty to drink to quench the child's thirst. But the biggest mistake one could make was to suddenly drink a large amount of water. Dehydrated sailors who did so got heavy stomach cramps, and some had been known to die.

Trista carefully let a few more drops trickle into the baby's mouth, who now held the water bag with both hands. Dalkeira's head came over Trista's shoulder to look at the small human she held.

"She is so tiny. And why is her skin so dark?" said Dalkeira.

Decan also came over to see what was happening. He stared at the baby in disbelief for a moment. Then he looked around.

"Is she—is she like us?"

"What do you mean?" said Trista, trying to concentrate on the child and water.

"I mean… did her mother die?" he asked.

Trista slowly nodded. The baby seemed to have exhausted her energy, and the child relaxed as she slipped into sleep. Trista gestured with her head at the wagon.

"Her mother's inside." *I hope we can keep her daughter alive.*

"How can a tiny person like that make the ground rumble so loud? Is she that hungry?" Dalkeira said in Trista's head.

"What are you talking about?" said Trista.

"Just before you came out, the ground began to rumble."

Trista frowned; that made no sense. Perhaps Dalkeira's sleepiness had made her confused.

"Decan? Dalkeira says she heard the ground rumble. Do you have any idea what she's talking about?"

"No. Sounds silly to me," said Decan, shrugging. Still, the boy dropped to his knees and laid his ear against the ground. Trista saw his expression change from faint mockery to confusion.

"That's weird. The ground *is* rumbling," said Decan.

"*I told you*," said Dalkeira in Trista's head.

"What?" said Trista.

She carefully laid the baby down and put her own ear to the ground. At first, she could not hear anything beside her own heartbeat, still racing from the adrenaline. But then her ears picked up a faint rumbling, like the swell of the sea. As the primal part of her brain recognized the strangely familiar sound, her eyes registered something completely different on the western horizon. It looked like the hills to the west had grown bigger—much bigger.

As her brain continued to work on this puzzling sight, the primal part of her that recognized the sound suddenly clicked.

Hooves!

The sound of horse hooves made the hard ground rumble like distant thunder. Trista jumped up and scanned the horizon. Were those shapes in the east coming toward them?

"Dalkeira! Tell me those aren't riders in the east!"

Right away, the dragon's hind legs launched Dalkeira upward. Something in Trista's voice had made it abundantly clear it was no time for discussions. She frantically beat her wings to gain altitude and checked out their surroundings.

"*Six—no, seven riders. They are headed straight for us!*" The words echoed inside Trista's head while Dalkeira trumpeted loudly.

As the dragon nervously circled in the air, Trista grabbed the child off the ground and looked around for anything that could provide them with a hiding place.

*　*　*

Dalkeira did not like this at all. Trista and her brother had nowhere to go, and now there was a baby, too. If she knew Trista even a little bit by now, she knew her linked human would never leave the child behind to perish. But what could Dalkeira do? She still lacked the strength and size to carry anyone, let alone two and a baby.

Dalkeira saw Decan scramble to his feet and run toward Trista, asking her what they should do. The dragon wondered if she should attack the riders herself—but no, that would be suicide. They surely had swords and spears; nearly all the soldiers they had spotted—and avoided—had them. Perhaps even bows and arrows, which meant she would not be much safer in the air.

A cloud of dust trailed the riders as the horses ran at full speed toward the tilted wagon. A lookout must have spotted the three of them while they journeyed across the flat plains. Her flying in the air like a great blue beacon had probably not helped, either. Dalkeira scolded herself for being so careless. For a moment, she thought of leaving the siblings to their fate, but immediately regretted the idea. She had chosen Trista for a reason, and although she did not know precisely why, she would not feel complete on her odyssey into the west without her. Which meant she was stuck with Decan as well.

Her journey to the west. The thought lingered in her mind for a moment, until she noticed an increased airflow pushing into her back. She banked around to face the direction she had longed to go toward ever since hatching from her egg.

"Trista, something is wrong," said Dalkeira.

*   *   *

"Don't you think I know that? Why don't you help us find a place to hide?" said Trista in her head, half panicked.

"No, I mean something else. In the west. Look."

Trista turned and looked beyond the wagon to the west. She could not believe what she saw. The dark shape on the western horizon had already increased in size dramatically.

"It is like a moving wall," observed Dalkeira.

"Not a wall—a sandstorm!" screamed Trista.

A massive sandstorm raced toward them. Trista had seen the autumn storms on the island reshape dunes in a matter of days, but this was something else. A cloud of dust rushed across the land for as far as her eyes could see. The wall of sand already reached higher than Dalkeira had ever flown. Without warning, daylight turned to dusk as the cloud of sand swallowed the western sun. Trista now heard the roar of wind rolling toward them. She felt like a cornered animal.

Her brain kicked into survival mode.

Run!

It was what they had done since day one, and she was not about to quit now. Soldiers would mean certain death, while the sandstorm announcing the end of the world at least gave them a chance. She pushed the baby girl into her brother's arms.

"Hold her, and don't you dare drop her," said Trista, locking eyes with Decan.

She did not wait for his nod but jumped back onto the wagon, pulling out her hunting knife. She stabbed the canvas and started to cut it as fast as possible. In the meantime, Dalkeira glided down.

"*What are you doing?*" asked the dragon.

"We're going to need something to protect us from the sand," said Trista.

She threw a large piece of canvas to Decan.

"Grab some clothes from the wagon and put them over your nose and mouth. Then put the canvas around your shoulders," yelled Trista.

"Then what?" said Decan, grabbing the first shirt he saw.

"Start running toward it!"

"Are you crazy?" yelled Decan. "We can't go in there."

The knife went in a second time, this time cutting out a much larger part of the thin but sturdy fabric.

"We have to! The sand will make it nearly impossible for them to find us. Now, go! You too, Dalkeira—and keep close to Decan!"

Hesitantly, her little brother and the dragon turned toward the closing cloud of dust and started moving toward it. Trista checked the distance of the riders. It would not take them much longer to reach the wagon; every yard they could put between themselves and the soldiers could be the difference between escape or capture—or worse.

As she cut the last corner, Trista jumped to the ground and ran without looking back. She bound a wide strip of canvas over her nose and mouth. The larger piece she used as an over-sized cape. It did not take long for her to catch up with the others. She urged them to pick up the pace.

Dalkeira took to the air to move more swiftly. Trista took back the baby, who was now crying her lungs out. Behind them, the riders spurred their horses, bringing them closer. The soldiers had noticed the sandstorm moving toward them, but had no intention of letting their quarry reach it and get away.

"Shh. Shh," Trista soothed the baby between her heavy panting.

While running, she tucked the baby inside her clothes as much as possible, to keep her safe and hopefully protect her from the oncoming onslaught of sand. The wind was getting stronger. The wall of sand was now so high above them she could not see the top anymore. It filled Trista's entire vision, like a mountain moving toward them. Having no sky as a reference made it hard to estimate the speed with which it was approaching.

Trista looked behind them. The riders were about to pass the wagon. She saw one of the men stop his horse and quickly duck under the canvas to see if anyone was hiding in there. The others continued their pursuit. It would not take the soldiers long to cover the few hundred yards Trista, Decan and Dalkeira had put between themselves and the wagon.

When she turned her head forward again, the roaring wall of sand was almost upon them. Startled, Trista looked up at Dalkeira.

"Get down here, now! Or you'll lose us in there!" she yelled.

The dragon had just come to the same conclusion, and plummeted toward them. Dalkeira was about to fold her wings and land when the wall hit. The force of the sandstorm instantly pushed Dalkeira's half-open wings back, like a sail. The dragon disappeared from Trista's sight as their world transformed into a raging whirlpool of sand. Trista stumbled, while Decan gasped and coughed beside her.

"*Dalkeira!*"

CHAPTER SEVENTEEN

Thirst

"DALKEIRA!"

There was no answer, just the thunderous roar of the sand blasting against them. Trista reached out once more with her mind.

"*Dalkeira, where are you?*"

"*Be calm. I am here. I am grounded, but I cannot see you anymore.*"

Trista sighed in relief. She grabbed her little brother, who was having trouble staying on his feet. Visibility was limited to only a few feet around them as the sand gushed past. She held the baby as close as possible and pulled Decan to her side. The horsemen could be upon them at any moment. They needed to move. Lose them in the storm.

"We've got to find shelter," she shouted to Decan.

The sand seeped in through the gaps in her clothes. The sensation on her skin was unpleasant to say the least. The sand scraped away layer by layer the longer they stayed exposed. Trista pushed her head down inside her shirt and listened to the baby underneath it. The child had gone strangely quiet when they were swallowed by the clouds of sand, but she was still moving at least.

"*We're veering off. Going south… I hope,*" said Trista.

"*I can still see the sun slightly. I should be able to move toward you.*"

Shielding her eyes, Trista tried to look around, but the sand made it hard to see anything at all.

* * *

A good distance away, Dalkeira's multiple eyelids allowed her to look around—she simply kept her innermost protective membranes closed—but there was nothing to see except a turmoil of sand. Once, the dragon thought she saw a shadow move, but before she could react, it had moved away again. She chose not to chase it; the shadow had been big, and was likely one of the horsemen.

"I'm sorry. We can't go on any further, Dalkeira. We'll have to wait this out and hope we're still around when it quiets down."

Dalkeira considered this for a moment. Her scales did not seem to have any trouble withstanding the constant spray of sand, but it would be difficult to find anything within the storm. Wandering around aimlessly would only waste her much-needed energy.

"I will stay put as well. We can hear one another without problems, so clearly you are close, but I agree it is best to stay put and wait this out." Dalkeira checked her surroundings a final time before she circled on the spot and lay down, tucking her head under her wing.

* * *

A small distance away, Trista and Decan took to the ground as well. The piece of canvas Trista had dragged with her was big enough to cover them completely. The color of the canvas faded into the stormy background, making them nearly invisible. Using their hands and feet to secure the fabric against the ground, the siblings created a shelter against the wind.

With hardly any sand forcing its way under the canvas, it was easier for them to breathe. Trista carefully moved the baby out of her shirt. Using her side to hold the canvas down, she fed the child some more water. She was happy to see—or rather hear and feel, as the lack of light in the storm made it difficult to see anything—the child responding again to the offered liquid.

I wish I had more to give to you, little one.

"What do we do now?" asked Decan quietly.

"We wait. Sooner or later, this storm will end. With a little luck, there will be no soldiers in sight when it does," said Trista.

"And Dalkeira?"

"She's nearby. I can still hear her, but it's no use trying to find her in this, so she's hunkering down as well."

"Are you doing alright?" Trista asked the dragon in her head.

"Do not worry about me. I am fine. I think I will try to get some sleep while we wait," replied the dragon, sounding weary after the day's travel.

Trista wondered how anyone could sleep at a time like this, but the more she thought about it, the more it made sense. They were not going anywhere.

They had traveled many days with only a few moments of real sleep each day. All three of them were near exhaustion and in much need of rest.

Beside her, the baby made some small sounds.

"I wish we had something to feed her with," said Trista to no one in particular.

"Would this help?" asked Decan, reaching around to grab something from one of his pockets. He pulled out a piece of dried meat and gave it to Trista.

"Thanks, little brother, but she's still much too young for solid food. She doesn't even have teeth yet. Besides, isn't that your last piece?"

"It's okay. I'm not that hungry," lied Decan. "And why don't we bird-feed it to her?"

"Bird-feed? What do you mean?"

"Yeah, like the birds on the island. Catch fish and spit it out again. Mother said it helps the young digest the solid food, even if they are still very small."

Trista looked at the piece of dried meat and suddenly had a flashback to her grandma chewing some herb leaves before putting them in the large pot of soup. Trista had been disgusted at the time, refusing to eat the soup, even after her nanna had explained it helped activate the flavor.

But as Trista looked down at the child, she moved past her initial objections. She bit off a piece and started chewing, taking a small sip of water to make it easier to bite down on the dry meat and mix her saliva into it. Trista's own hunger made it difficult not to simply swallow the piece for herself. Her stomach rumbled in protest as she spat it out and carefully put a small glob of it inside the baby's cheek.

The child instantly started clamping her jaws. As Trista's eyes adjusted to the low light, she saw from the tiny face that the little girl was not used to the taste. Trista spent the next few moments trying to figure out if the child was working the food to swallow it, or to spit it out. In the end, it was both. Part of it landed outside her tiny mouth, but part of the food found its way to the stomach as well. Once it was gone, the child opened her mouth, searching for more.

"Just like a bird," remarked Decan.

The baby tried her best to swallow a few more chewed-up pieces of food, but quickly tired. Afraid she would choke on the meat, Trista stopped and softly stroked the tiny belly to help the child fall asleep.

"I think we should try to get some sleep as well," said Trista, only to see Decan's head already lying on his arm with his eyes closed.

She did not blame him; the monotonous noise of the storm made it difficult to stay awake. Trista's own eyelids grew heavy. And while she was nervous about sleeping while the enemy soldiers searched for them so close by, it did not take long before she too was in the world of dreams.

Trista lay motionless, thinking how time often moved like an ocean. It could be hard to see how much of it passed. It could rush at you and surprise you, or seemingly stand still from where you stood. But time was always moving and it waited for none. She had no idea how much time they had spent under the canvas already. A night? A day? Two? Both she and Decan dozed on and off, having to readjust every time they woke to make sure they would not disappear under layers of sand as the sandstorm raged on around them.

The baby seemed happy to have people nearby. Trista fed her several times with the dried meat and tried her best to get rid of the waste she produced. Luckily, little came out because little was going in.

Trista had never thought about children before. What was the point if you had not found someone to be a parent with? Even if she had, she had no idea if she would want them any time soon.

If it had been her parents' choice she would already have given them several grandchildren. Most girls on the island seemed eager to start a family, but Trista had always been perfectly content with the family she had. She had to admit, though, that this small girl had a charming effect on her. Considering the circumstances, it was strange how the child's small giggles as it tried to grab locks of Trista's red hair brought a smile to their faces, but it happened nonetheless.

Trista was most worried about the water. Her bag was half empty, and Decan had finished his already. If the storm did not let up soon they would be forced to move through it in search of water.

"I like that sound," said Dalkeira in her head when the baby let out a giggle; Decan was making funny faces at her to pass the time.

"You can hear her? You must be closer than I thought."

The dragon had not spoken much during the storm. Trista had felt her touch her mind a couple of times, but mostly the dragon had slept, conserving her energy. Dalkeira had asked about the small girl, intrigued by how humans could start so helpless. But although the dragon never complained about hunger or thirst, Trista was worried. Dalkeira might be too proud to mention it, but the dragon would need to get some water soon.

"Just barely. I think the wind is lessening," said Dalkeira.

"Really?"

Trista concentrated on listening to the storm, but the sound of sand blasting against the canvas still seemed as loud as ever.

At some point, Trista must have dozed off again, because she opened her eyes to a world of silence. Moving carefully, she saw the baby and Decan were both still asleep. Their calm breathing was the only thing she could hear.

Cautiously, she moved the canvas, making sure none of the sand that had piled up on them fell on her brother or the baby. She was greeted by a cloudless sky filled with stars. Looking around, she saw the landscape around them had completely changed. The white plains had gone, covered by large dunes. It was like a sea of sand had pushed its way inland, its giant waves frozen in mid-swell.

The rustling of sand made her turn around. Dalkeira's head emerged from a small pile as she unfolded herself. Stretching her rigid wings and limbs, she shook herself from head to tail to get all the sand off.

"*I told you it was dying down,*" said Dalkeira.

The dragon looked up and marveled at the sight of the sky.

"*It is like the sparkling ocean waters took flight,*" she said.

Trista looked up and wondered if that was how the dragon saw water in their world all the time. It certainly reminded her of their nights out at sea. Without any light from the village, the stars were often magical at night. The dragon let out a sigh.

"*I am thirsty.*"

"I thought as much," Trista said. She walked over and poured some of her own water in Dalkeira's mouth.

"*What about you and Decan? And the child?*"

"We'll all have to share now, but there isn't much left."

"*Have you seen any soldiers?*"

"No, thankfully," she answered, looking around.

Both Decan and the child stirred, woken by the sound of Trista's voice.

"Is it over?" said Decan.

"Looks like it. Let's get moving while we can. I don't want to be surprised by any soldiers wandering around," said Trista.

Decan stood up and carefully picked up the baby.

"I'll carry her for a while. Can she have a bit of water?"

Trista was passing Decan the water bag when the sound of cascading sand made her look up to one of the dunes. The silhouette of a horse stood dark against the starry sky. The animal softly snorted and shook its head, shaking sand from its mane.

Immediately, Trista's hand shot to her knife.

"Does anyone see its rider?"

270

But none of them saw the owner of the horse. Dalkeira tried to move up the dune, but the horse nervously whinnied and disappeared out of sight.

"Wait, come back!" Trista called out as loudly as she dared. "Dalkeira, hold on. You'll scare it off. Let me see if I can gain its trust. It can carry us and the baby."

She moved up the dune as quietly as possible. Reaching the top, she spotted the horse down below on the other side. At its feet, a body lay half-buried in the sand. She pulled out her knife again and slowly slid down toward the nervous horse.

The man's head was buried in the sand, his body lying motionless, but Trista did not want to take any chances. As she inched forward, knife at the ready, the horse reluctantly moved away. Her hands shook as she stretched out her arm, reaching for the man's shoulder. She raised her knife, preparing to strike if needed. Grabbing the man's armored shoulder, she jerked him onto his back. The move exposed a small axe as his furthest hand was pulled out of the sand. Trista's heart skipped in panic, expecting it to swing at her face, but the expression on the soldier's face said enough. His mouth gaped and his clouded, half opened eyes were filled with sand.

A broken neck, Trista thought to herself.

She looked away. That image was certainly coming back to haunt her dreams.

Turning away from the head, she searched the body. It was her first opportunity to check out one of the soldiers up close without fighting for her life. The man's face was scarred, with strange patterns tattooed onto it. His muscular build made him look bigger than he actually was, lying still in front of her. The armor, a combination of leather and metal, was simple but supplemented the soldier's fierce look. A sword and two knives hung on his belt.

Carefully, as if a sudden movement would bring the man back from the dead, Trista took the weapons from the corpse. She did not know much about handling a sword, but figured it could always come in useful.

A snort right above her startled her. The horse had moved closer, seeing that Trista did not mean it any harm. The poor animal had dry crusts around its eyes and sand lining its nostrils. Its brown coat dull and still filled with sand. Slowly, Trista rose to her feet, holding her hand up to the horse's chin while she spoke soothingly.

"Shhh. Shhh. It's alright. I'm not going to hurt you."

The horse bobbed its head and Trista noticed for the first time its bulky saddle bags.

Although her only experience was with donkeys—there had not been many horses on their island—it felt natural to slide her hand across the jawline and down the animal's neck as she tried to ease the horse's nerves. Arriving at the saddle, she opened one of the bags hanging behind it. Her throat choked up as she saw the contents of it. Bread, dried meat, some dried fruit and some small, hard seeds she did not recognize—most of it untouched by the sand.

She quickly moved to the other side. Uncertain, the horse scraped the sand beneath it, but stood its ground. The other side had a bag filled with crabs and freshly caught lizards. The food would be enough to feed three people for a week, perhaps more if they rationed it properly. With a growing dragon, they probably would not make it that far, but Trista would try her best to spread it out as long as possible. The final bag brought even greater joy; inside, four large water bags filled to the brim greeted her.

She allowed herself to take a gulp of the stale water; it was one of the best drinks she had ever had. She carefully poured some in her hand, allowing the horse to quickly slobber it up. The animal seemed grateful for the gesture, visibly relaxing in her presence. She would have liked to give the horse more, but the water would better serve her other companions—however guilty she felt about it.

Trista took the reins and called out to Dalkeira in her mind to come and join her.

"It is not afraid anymore?"

"It's nervous, but if you don't approach it directly, I'm hoping it will tolerate your presence," said Trista in her thoughts. *"It's a large steed. I think it's just shaken from the storm. Its rider is dead."*

The introduction went better than expected. The horse was clearly trained, and as soon as it sensed Dalkeira was not a danger, the animal relaxed even more. Trista packed up the weapons as best she could, while Decan and the baby ate and drank some of the new provisions. Dalkeira allowed herself to eat two pieces of dried meat; not nearly enough to still her hunger, but with another gulp of water it resembled something close to a decent, albeit very small, meal for the dragon.

Trista helped Decan into the saddle and handed him the baby. The child now took more enthusiastically to the chewed meat than before, but mostly asked for water. Trista looked at the duo on top of the horse and could not help but feel utterly hopeless. Even with this unexpected gift, she had no idea what they were getting into. She was doing her best, but the running, and not knowing, was beginning to take its toll on her. She tried not to show it, fully aware that both little brother and growing dragon looked to her to make the decisions. But now they had such a small and delicate life added to their little group, all Trista could

272

think about was how many days the tiny child would have in this unforgiving landscape, and how quickly they would follow her into the afterlife.

The horse nudged her shoulder with its nose. It was as if the steed noticed her indecisiveness. She looked at the large, clear eyes surrounded by crusted sand, wondering what it wanted to say.

Keep moving, she told herself, filling in the words. *We have to keep moving. To give up is certain death. We must get somewhere safe.*

But in the back of her mind, a little voice quietly whispered, *What if there is nowhere safe?*

She pushed it away to the deepest parts of her brain, where she doubted even Dalkeira could hear it. For the second time, the horse gave her a push.

"I know, I know," said Trista. "We've got to get moving."

She grabbed the reins, after which she simply put one foot in front of the other. The horse meekly followed, Dalkeira joining them as well. West. The only direction that remotely made any sense. Trista just hoped it would lead to something better.

Raylan squirted water from his mouth in an arc then submerged his face, filling his mouth with the cool, fresh-tasting water once more. This time, he swallowed it with large gulps. He held his breath as long he could, looking at the shimmering sun that broke through the surface above him. He emerged to take a breath and shook his head, running his hands through his hair to get rid of the excess water.

Perhaps Xi will cut it tonight, he thought, feeling the length of it.

A loud yell warned Raylan to shield his face just as Marek launched himself from a rock and splashed right next to him.

The youngster resurfaced, exclaiming, "Aaaah, so refresh—"

Raylan drowned out the rest of it with a wave of water made by his own two hands.

"I'm glad we stopped a little early today," said Peadar, who sat atop a rock on the shore of the small basin. "We've been riding nearly nonstop since we left Azurna."

His feet dangled in the water. Meanwhile, Marek coughed and spluttered to recover from the surprise attack. Raylan could not help but laugh—until Marek returned the favor.

As the youngest official member of their squad, Peadar had been focused on keeping their message birds healthy as they escaped the Dark

Continent. Since the last bird had been sent off many weeks ago, the young man now made himself useful by doing small chores, like mending the holes in their clothes. His healing skills came in handy now as he applied needle and thread to the fabric in front of him.

"Why don't you join us?" called Marek.

"No, thanks. I like keeping the water out of my lungs."

"What about you, Galen?" said Raylan.

The large, heavy hitter of the team sat calmly dangling his feet in the water, much like Peadar did.

"I'm alright."

Galen had his shirt off to catch the sun. His chest and back showed many scars, some of which were the result of his fall from the stone arch on Doskova, including a particularly long and nasty one across his back. Raylan remembered how defeated they had felt after the large man went over the edge. But Galen had miraculously survived the long drop toward the water, only to be nearly ripped apart by the current and rocks.

"How much longer until we reach Shid'el?" asked Marek.

"We've been on the road for almost a week," said Raylan, making his way to the shore. "So at least another two weeks."

They had followed the river from Azurna ever since they left, but it trailed too far north in this area, so they were currently cutting through forests and low mountains before reconnecting with it as it came back south again. It would be a day or two, maybe three, before they would meet up with it again.

"We should probably get back now," said Raylan, adding with a laugh, "or else Sebastian will eat all the food again."

The four of them walked leisurely back toward their camp. The smell of hot stew drifted through the trees. Marek, who walked up front with Peadar, made a remark and gave Peadar a punch on the arm.

Despite the animal healer's more timid nature, Peadar and Marek were getting along uncommonly well. Ever since their escape, Marek had made it his business to pull the slightly older and shy Peadar out of his shell. And more often than not, the young one succeeded—even if that meant the duo resorted to some mischievous behavior. It was quite entertaining to see. The only one who had tried to discourage the growing friendship between the two had been Richard, who did his best to keep the group disciplined.

"I wonder if Marek will stay around—after we get to Shid'el, I mean," said Raylan to the big man walking next to him. "I hope for Peadar he does. But if he's a real water rat, he'll get restless after a while in one spot. Still, he must be strong to have survived so long in the clutches of the Stone King's army. So, maybe I'm reading it wrong."

In front of them, the two youngsters turned the final corner and disappeared for a moment.

Galen did not say a word, but Raylan was not too bothered by that. It had been more of a rhetorical question anyway. Their heavy hitter mostly conversed only with Richard, who was born in the same region of Aeterra.

When they turned the corner, the two boys came into view again. Both stood silently with their backs toward them. They blocked the small game trail that led back to the forest clearing where their camp was. Something in their posture struck Raylan as odd. As he approached them, their camp came into view. Kevhin, Rohan and Xi'Lao sat near the fire. Richard and Ca'lek stood silently behind them. Their faces had an urgent look about them. Raylan was about to ask why everyone was acting so strangely when the rest of camp became visible and an unfamiliar voice greeted them.

"Gentlemen, welcome. Why don't y'all take a seat?"

The stranger casually pointed his sword to a rock, assigning them each a place to sit. Marek and Peadar obediently obeyed. But both Raylan and Galen stood unmoved. Raylan scanned the camp as his hand checked for his sword, but found only his knife.

"Looking for these?" said the man, gesturing to the pile of weapons beside him. "Yah can throw those knives here as well."

Rustling leaves alerted Raylan to the two men who emerged behind him, both carrying swords, and that was not all; he saw at least half a dozen men and women scattered among the trees. Plenty of drawn bows pointed their way. Reluctantly, he and Galen both pulled out their knives, tossed them on the ground, and sat down.

"Well done. Now, is that everyone in your tiny group? I'd hate to be surprised again. I mean, I nearly shot y'all when you came walking up just now."

Raylan looked at him. The man had clearly not bathed in a very long time. A rugged beard that rivaled Harwin's hung from a strong chin. Raylan observed the others. Their clothes were mostly made of pelts.

Rabbits. Perhaps a badger or two.

"What do you want?" asked Raylan.

"Isn't it obvious, Raylan? They're bandits," put in Richard from behind the others.

"Bandits?" bellowed the leader, who burst out laughing. His entire group laughed with him. "Oh, dear lord, no. We're not bandits. We're businessmen. See, these forests have dangerous roads to travel, and we like to keep people safe. In return, we merely ask a voluntary contribution. After all, keeping y'all safe ain't cheap."

Raylan met Xi'Lao's eyes. The Tiankong woman briefly shot her gaze up to the sky and down again. Raylan shook his head slightly. Galirras had left right after they made camp to look for a suitable area to hunt. The dragon knew to stay away from any farms, so it usually took a while before he got back depending on their surroundings.

"We've got little to give," said Raylan.

The man laughed again.

"'Little to give', he says," called the man over his shoulder toward the others. "D'you really expect me to believe a man with such fine clothes doesn't have anything to share? Gilly, go check our friend, will you?"

Raylan looked down at his outfit. He had forgotten he was wearing the clothes made back in Azurna; they turned out to be comfortable *and* durable.

Two strong hands dragged him to his feet. The bandit woman in front of him smiled a gap-toothed smile. Her hands ran down his back, across his ass and thighs, all the way to his boots. Raylan looked down as the woman put her hands around his boots and squeezed. His shins protested from the pressure.

"Strong, isn't she?" Raylan heard the leader say.

The woman looked up at him with a grin.

"No other weapons, Jorak," she said to the leader. She ran her fingers back up the inside of his leg and took a firm grip of his crotch. "But he's certainly packing something."

More laughter rose between the trees.

"You can call yourself a lucky man. I think she likes you."

The female bandit took a step back, but not before one of her hands slipped along Raylan's waist and removed his pouch. She shook it and tossed it back to Jorak. She blew a kiss toward Raylan, then walked off and took her place amongst the others again.

"See? I told you we'd find something to share on you," said Jorak as another man tied Raylan's arms behind his back. "Search the others as well."

Raylan cursed internally. Without their money, he would not be able to buy Galirras any food if needed. He knew they could probably arrange things with the official outposts, and the dragon knew how to take care of himself, but it provided a certain safety to be able to decide at random where and when they purchased food for Galirras. Besides, sometimes Raylan just felt like spoiling him a bit.

In the meantime, he saw the others squirm uneasily as each of them was searched from head to toe. Raylan tried to twist his hands free, but found them too tightly bound. And even if he could free himself, he was not sure what to do. They were outnumbered two to one—at least—and none of his own had any weapons.

At that moment, a shiver ran through him as Galirras entered his mind. Instantly, a smile formed on his face. This changed everything.

Raylan stood up and took a deliberate step forward. Jorak looked at him in disbelief.

"What d'you think you're doing? Got a death wish?"

"Not at all, but I just remembered I didn't answer your question," said Raylan.

"My question?"

"You asked if there was anyone else. Out there. Well, you see, there is. But he's not one to just walk up to people. Nor does he carry any weapons—that you can remove, that is."

"What're you on about? Sit back down before I let Gilly gut you like a fish."

"No, see, I don't think you understand. It's not that he's afraid to meet new people. He just doesn't like to walk. He's more one to just, you know. Drop in."

With a deep thump, Galirras landed heavily on all fours. The campfire sent a puff of burning ash into the air. The dragon extended his wings as far as the clearing would let him and shot off a windblast at the nearest archers. They tumbled through the air and landed in the low ferns that made up the forest floor. Galirras sent a thunderous roar between the trees. He added a little bit extra to the waves of sound with his wind power, increasing its volume. It was enough to make a few of the bandits grab their ears in pain.

Shouts of terror rose from Jorak and his group. Men and women alike scrambled away through the trees, the bandit leader right behind them. He dropped his sword and Raylan's money pouch, chasing and screaming after his subordinates.

"Wait for me, you cowards, or I'll have all your hides, damn it!"

In no time at all, the strangers were gone from the clearing. Galirras fluttered his wings and folded them up. Peadar, who had not yet been tied up, jumped up to release the others.

"*Perfect timing, little one,*" said Raylan privately. He smiled.

"*Do you want me to chase them to the next valley?*"

"*Nah, it's not worth it.*"

"Alright, everyone. Let's pick up our things and go," said Richard as soon as Peadar freed him.

"Go?" said Raylan. "What about food and rest?"

"Food? Rest? Did you not just see that group of bandits nearly take all our stuff?" said Richard, perplexed.

"They're long gone now. I'm sure they learned their lesson—"

"Or they'll return with even bigger numbers," interrupted Richard. "I knew it was a mistake to stop early today. We'll ride through the night and rest in the morning. It's about time we picked up the pace, anyway."

Raylan heard one or two groans escape people's throats. He let out a sigh of his own.

"*Did you at least have a good hunt?*" he asked Galirras in his mind.

"It was most pleasant indeed," answered the dragon, eyes swirling excitedly at the memory.

CHAPTER EIGHTEEN

Ruins

HIGH ABOVE THEM, the sun burned unrelentingly. The horse let out short snorts. It had stopped foaming around the mouth days ago; it was simply too dehydrated to produce any saliva. This was the fifth day crossing the burning seas of sand. At first, Trista had tried to give the poor animal water from the bags they had found, but it quickly became clear that even if she gave it all at once it would not be enough for the suffering animal. So, with a heavy heart, she stopped.

The steed stumbled. Decan, who had been half asleep on its back, suddenly found himself face downward on the ground with a mouthful of sand. Freed from his weight, the horse regained its balance and kept going.

"Are you alright?" said Trista, rushing up to her brother. Thankfully, she had been the one carrying the baby.

"Yeah, I'm okay," said Decan, sounding surly.

They had ridden together on the first few nights, when it was cool enough for the animal to carry them all. But during the day they took turns, giving the person on horseback time to rest while the other led it by the reins, or later simply followed it as the horse found its own course. The trained animal had seemed to grasp their westerly direction and had simply continued on the path with minimal corrections, choosing the easiest routes around or across the dunes they encountered. It had allowed them to travel almost constantly, with minimal time spent sleeping. Once, they had come across another sandstorm, but it had only lasted half a morning before dissipating again. Trista did not know how many miles they had traveled, but she guessed they had crossed quite a distance. She just hoped they were not running around in circles as she tried to set their course using the sun.

Trista pulled Decan to his feet. Her skin was severe sunburned. They tried their best with the canvas and clothes from the wagon, but were simply unable to cover their skin the entire time. She drew in a sharp breath as Decan accidentally grabbed one of the blisters on her arm. He swiftly pulled back his hand, leaving sand stuck in the wound.

"Sorry."

Her lip cracked for what felt like the hundredth time as she tried to give her brother a reassuring smile.

"It's okay. I don't feel it much," she lied. "I'm more worried about Dalkeira. She's looking worse every day. Her scales have completely dulled. That can't just be the sand, like she says. She needs to drink."

Dalkeira had quickly recognized that she, like the horse, would not have enough to drink even if she took all of it—so she stopped drinking completely, ensuring Trista, Decan and the baby drank enough every day to keep going. Trista had tried to convince her otherwise, but the dragon had simply refused to listen. Trista could not figure out if Dalkeira was being stubborn, trying to prove something, or just worried she would lose her frail human companions and be stuck out here alone.

After they found the horse, Dalkeira took to the air a few times at night; the sun exhausted her, not to mention made her thirsty. During those first nights, when she still had the energy to fly, Dalkeira scouted their surroundings, only to find that the sand stretched on for miles in all directions.

Perhaps if a dragon flew from waterhole to waterhole it would have made good time crossing this unforgiving landscape. But following the siblings at such a slow pace used up too much of Dalkeira's energy, and by the time she realized her 'mistake' exhaustion had set in and it was too late. They were all in this together.

Dalkeira stopped taking to the air entirely, especially during the day. The dark blue color of her wings' surface quickly absorbed the heat of the sun, causing further dehydration and ultimately heatstroke. Walking was not much easier—and a great deal slower—but at least a fall on the ground would not result in her breaking her neck, which was a real danger when crashing from the sky. She tried to make the best of it, holding her wings slightly spread as she walked, allowing the flow of air to cool her as it passed over her chest and wings. Trista had draped a piece of lighter colored clothing across her dark blue back as well, though doubted if it did anything to help.

Further down the dune, the horse stumbled again and sank to the ground. Heavy, raspy wheezes rose from its throat as it lay exhausted in the sand. The steed made no attempt to get back to its feet. Its head swayed gently, its eyes unfocused.

"I think it's time," said Trista.

Dalkeira, walking some ways behind them and struggling with every step much like the horse, lifted her head to see what was going on.

"*It cannot carry you anymore?*" the dragon asked with an exhausted tone inside Trista's head.

"*No, I don't think so. It can't stand up anymore,*" Trista replied, her throat dry from sadness and thirst.

"*Then do it.*"

Trista handed the baby to Decan. She approached the fallen horse and sat beside its head, gently stroking the animal's neck and nose. The horse rolled onto its side, unable to keep itself upright any longer. Trista slipped around it and unfastened the saddle and bags, freeing up the animal's belly and allowing it to breathe more easily.

"Decan, do you want to say goodbye?"

Decan swallowed and nodded softly. He moved closer with uncertain steps and lay the baby carefully on the horse's belly. He put his own arms around it; resting on the steed's flank, his head rose and fell with its irregular breathing.

"Thank you," he whispered.

The baby made a soft noise, as if to thank the horse in her own way, after which Decan picked the child up again and moved away. Trista watched him go as he dragged the saddle bags after him. Farther down the dune, he sat using the canvas for shadow and checked the bags to see what there was left to eat. Not much remained after five days of travel, Trista knew. They still had about half their water, conserving it as much as possible. But both siblings were in a constant state of dizziness and thanked the goddess when the sun god finally left the sky to pursue the water goddess for her favors.

Trista softly stroked the horse's head, whispering soothing words to it.

"Thank you so much for taking us this far, my brave, brave animal. Thank you for your strength. Thank you for your loyalty to us strangers."

The horse attempted to whinny, its eyes wide as it tried to get up.

"Shh, shh. It's okay. You can rest now. Your job is done."

Carefully, Trista moved her right hand behind her back, grabbing the knife she had taken from the dead soldier's body. It was a lot sharper than her own hunting knife. Bigger, too. Slowly, she stroked the horse's face as she moved the knife under the exhausted animal's throat. She made sure the scared and confused animal did not see it, although she doubted if the horse was still clear enough in the head to recognize it.

"Shh. There you go. Just lay down your head and close your eyes. It'll be over soon, I promise."

A few days earlier, Dalkeira had brought up the topic of eating the horse. Trista had wanted to use the horse for transportation as long as possible, but it was like a walking buffet for the dragon, and as the horse's condition deteriorated, so too did Dalkeira's own. The dragon insisted the meat and especially the blood would help sustain her in their travels. Reluctantly, Trista had agreed to it, but only if the animal—or Dalkeira—could not go on anymore.

She knew Dalkeira had done her best to hold out as long as she could. But if the horse had not fallen by the end of the day, Trista would have taken its life herself to allow Dalkeira to feed. The dragon was beginning to look awfully skinny and dull.

Instead of Dalkeira killing the horse, Trista had decided to do it herself. For starters, she did not want Decan to be reminded of Rudley the goat more than necessary. Second, the horse had served them well, so she intended to make its end as painless and quick as possible. It did not deserve to suffer. Dalkeira did not yet have the size or the strength to take the steed's life swiftly enough. And if the horse hurt Dalkeira in a frightened spasm, Trista would never forgive herself.

Still, she dreaded the moment. She understood the stakes and necessity, but that did not make it feel right. With so much death around, Trista would rather sustain as much life as possible, but it was a truth of life one must eat in order to survive.

This conflict had been on her mind since she agreed to let Dalkeira feed on the horse. At first, it had made her angry, but her will to protect and take care of Dalkeira was stronger. The link often involuntarily shared their emotions and needs, which meant she had been fighting the increasing hunger and thirst oozing from the dragon these past few days—despite the small meals she was eating herself.

"Do you want me to do it?" said Dalkeira, feeling Trista's reluctance.

"No. I'll do it. It deserves a quick, clean kill, don't you think?"

"I can make it quick."

"When you're bigger, certainly. But clean? Not so much," Trista said in a jokey attempt to lighten the mood and make what she was about to do easier. It did not help.

She stroked the horse a few more times and lifted its head into her lap. Her fist tightened around the knife, knuckles whitening. Then in one fluid motion she cut the animal's throat, deep, like she had seen the clan people do when slaughtering a pig. As she severed its major arteries, hot blood rushed out instantly. Despite her mental preparation, the sensation of it flooding over her leg caught her off guard. She stared down, her eyes as wide as the horse's.

"I'm sorry. I'm sorry," she repeated over and over as she stroked the dying animal's mane and nose. It kicked its hindlegs back and forth in a desperate struggle to hold on to life. Then a final gurgle escaped the steed's throat before its muscles settled and went completely still. Trista let out a sob. Down the slope, the baby started crying in Decan's arms.

Trista felt sick to her stomach. She stood up to avoid what blood had not spilled onto her yet while Dalkeira moved in, trying not to get too much sand on her dinner. The dragon quickly started drinking the flowing blood, clearly not wanting to waste any of it.

Trista turned away and joined her little brother and the baby at the bottom of the dune.

"Has she eaten anything?" said Trista.

"Just two bites."

Trista looked at the child as they unwrapped and cleaned her as best as possible. The little girl had been losing weight ever since they found her at the wagon. The water was keeping her alive, but did nothing for nutrition. Without proper food, the little one would surely not last much longer. The knot in Trista's stomach tightened as her fingers traced the girl's tiny ribs.

Trista bit her cracked lip. The weight of her companions' lives rested on her shoulders, but she was helpless in providing them with what they needed. Silently, she wondered what else they would need to sacrifice to survive. She shuddered as a horrible thought crossed her mind.

Would I feed the baby to Dalkeira? Or Decan?

Thankfully, Dalkeira was too busy eating to pick up on the disturbing thought, and Trista quickly pushed the question out of her head.

"You alright?" said Decan.

Trista forced a smile, feeling a quick nip of pain as the skin of her lips split again.

"I'm fine. Just very tired."

She looked behind her to see Dalkeira feasting on the horse's carcass. Trista could feel the dragon gaining strength with every bite she took.

"I'd better see if there are any parts we can eat ourselves. And we should drink the blood; it will give us some much-needed liquid. And maybe we can dry some of the meat in the sun while we rest and wait for the night."

"You don't want to keep going?" said Decan.

"I don't think I can. My legs need rest. Besides, if I know Dalkeira at all, she'll probably fall asleep with a full stomach. We'll need to keep her in the shade. Perhaps you should get some sleep as well? We'll continue when the sun is lower and the temperature drops."

Trista forced herself to stand and walk over to Dalkeira, trying to breathe away the knot in her stomach and the dizziness in her head.

* * *

If the vultures in the sky could speak, their talk would surely be filled with the strange group crossing the sea of sand below. A woman, a boy and a baby—and one of the strangest creatures they had ever seen. It had the ability to fly, but seemed unwilling to do so. It looked blue, like the water that was always so hard to find, while the color of sand showed in spots on the bottom of those strange, featherless wings. It did not look like any bird they knew, but then again, they did not presume to know everything—nor did it matter. The only thing that mattered was when they stopped moving. When would one of them drop and not get up anymore?

As their eyes followed the weary wanderers, the vultures soared the thermals high above the ground, patiently waiting for their next meal. By the looks of it, they would not have to wait much longer.

* * *

Trista had been right about Dalkeira. After her meal, she quickly fell into a deep, exhausted slumber. Trista waited until the sun was low in the sky before waking her to continue their journey.

They had cut some raw meat from the horse, which they had then dried in the scorching sun as best they could. It did not taste great, but their hungry stomachs thankfully accepted it nonetheless. Trista and Decan even drank some of the blood, but Trista had quickly gotten nauseous.

Thanks to the horse's sacrifice, they had the strength to travel a few more miles. Dalkeira especially seemed to enjoy the boost in energy. Although her thirst was not completely quelled, the blood had provided her with much-needed fluid to counter her dehydration. She took to the air that evening, climbing as high as possible on one of the last remaining thermals of the day. But all she reported seeing was sand, as far as her eyes could see, and some strange black birds that effortlessly sailed on the wind.

They continued their way, covering as much distance as possible every day and night. Once, they found a few rocks which they used to create some shade with help of the canvas. Since the horse was now gone, they made the decision to avoid traveling during the hottest part of the day, using that time to rest beneath the canvas whenever possible. Walking during the night was easier and kept them warm as the temperature dropped to a near-freezing low.

As quickly as Dalkeira had recovered, she crashed again after only two days of walking. This time, dehydration set in much faster than before. Trista, Decan and the baby were not in a much better position. Their food was all but gone, and they only had a few sips remaining in their last water bag.

Trista focused on what little food they had left, rationing it as best she could. She carried a few empty water bags around her neck, tied together with strings of canvas, refusing to abandon them in case they ran into a waterhole. She flinched as the bags touched her exposed skin with every step she took. Her arms were numb and heavy from carrying the baby; her shoulders hurt from the makeshift sling in which the girl hung on her chest.

The sand crunched beneath her feet. She looked at them; strange, distant things. Her vision spun from dizziness. A new sound from behind made her look back.

"Dalkeira," she croaked.

The dragon had slumped onto her side and could not get up anymore. Trista and Decan made a futile attempt to get her back on her feet, but it was no use. The dragon was barely conscious.

"Let's roll her onto the canvas," suggested Decan.

It was the best idea given the circumstances. Trista knew she would not be able to carry the dragon, especially with the child slung around her shoulders as well.

Dalkeira's growth had slowed whilst in the desert, probably because of the lack of food and water, but she already surpassed Decan in length. Trista expected the dragon's weight to be too much, but when she and her brother grabbed hold of the canvas and started pulling, they were surprised at how light Dalkeira was. Yet even the lightest feather becomes a heavy burden under the worst of circumstances and after another two days and nights of walking, Trista had nearly reached her limit.

* * *

As far as Trista could tell, Dalkeira was only vaguely aware of the constant scraping across the ground. Her three pupils swirled whenever she was able to force her eyes open, the small, sparkling vortexes less bright than usual. At intervals, Dalkeira would gain a moment of clarity before slumping back into a near comatose state. All Trista and Decan could do now was try their best to safely drag the dragon across the dunes. They only covered a few miles per day now, every dune looking more impassable than the last.

The next time Dalkeira came round, it was night. She tried to lift her head, but only succeeded in turning it. She watched Decan pull with all his might, trying to get to the top of the next sandy hill.

Trista looked back as the whispered thoughts of the dragon seeped into her mind. *Why is he working so hard for me? He does not want me around... so why does he help her to the point of his own exhaustion?*

Trista looked at her brother as her winged companion's confused thoughts spiraled on and on. Whispers—like evil spirits—that the boy had no obligations toward the dragon, nor did he want her around, claiming his sister's attention. But there he was, helping Trista drag this dead dragon weight with them. *Her* weight. And with it, most certainly dooming themselves in the progress.

Forcing her gaze forward again, Trista tried her best to push the whispering thoughts aside, lest she succumb to their doubt and simply give up. But behind her, the dragon gathered all her energy, pushed off and unexpectedly rolled herself from the canvas.

Both siblings stumbled forward at the sudden absence of weight. Behind them, Dalkeira slid back down the slope before coming to a halt.

"What in the goddess' name are you doing?" Decan called, spitting out another mouthful of sand—a situation he was really started to dislike.

"*You go on without me,*" said Dalkeira in Trista's head. "*If you keep dragging me around, you will have no chance of making it out alive. Just leave me. I am as good as dead.*"

"What are you talking about? We're not going to abandon you here and leave you for the vultures," said Trista sternly.

Startled by the fall and Trista's loud voice, the baby started crying. Her voice did not seem to have much energy left either.

"Shh, shh. There, there. It's alright. It's okay. Dalkeira just isn't thinking clearly," said Trista, trying to calm her.

Decan walked back down with the canvas and spread it next to Dalkeira.

"Come on. On you go," he said.

"*No.*"

An answer the boy did not hear.

"What has gotten into you, Dalkeira?" said Trista.

"Fine. Be like that," said Decan. "But if you think we'll just leave you here, you're wrong."

He crouched beside her and pushed her onto the canvas, but Dalkeira rolled herself off the other side.

"You stubborn, ignorant, spoiled lizard! Do you think it's all about you in this world? That you get to decide how things go in life? Well, it's not!" Decan screamed.

Trista saw her brother's frustration grow, but this time she had not the energy nor the will to stop him from yelling at the dragon.

Decan crouched a second time, but instead of pushing her, he picked up Dalkeira's head and front leg. He moved under her and shifted her across his back. It was a strange sight: a small boy with a larger dragon slung on his back. As Decan began to move up the dune, Dalkeira's tail dragged behind them like a snake slithering across the sand.

"You have no idea how much you mean to my sister, do you? Always too busy thinking about yourself. Stilling your own hunger first, going to places where you want to go. And then, when we've given you all of it and things go bad, you just decide to give up. Well, I won't let you. You owe us, you owe Trista—and you owe *me*!" ranted Decan, as if the words powered his steps. "You owe me a goat!"

Trista snatched up the canvas and followed them. She was impressed by the amount of energy Decan still had, but expected it would not last long. She silently followed, waiting for the inevitable.

Decan's ranting lasted for several dunes before he quieted down. He needed every leftover piece of energy to make sure his feet kept moving. And they did.

Dalkeira was even more confused by the boy's gesture. Did he not hate her? Why would he go through all the trouble to save her if he wanted her gone?

I do not understand.

"*Because we're family now, and family sticks together,*" said Trista, who had picked up on the dragon's thoughts for once, instead of the other way around.

Against Trista's expectations, they were still walking by the time morning came around. Perhaps the dragon's stubbornness had rubbed off on Decan, because he refused to sit down and rest. Trista had to admit his walking speed had decreased dramatically, but nevertheless, he kept moving his feet one step after another. Sometime during the night, Dalkeira had slipped back into unconsciousness, reluctantly accepting the fact she had no control over the situation in spite of her own stubborn resolve.

* * *

"Decan," said Trista, finally breaking the silence of their difficult walk.

"Hmmm," grunted her little brother as he took another step.

"I just want to say that I'm proud of you. You're growing into quite the man. You know, I haven't been able to keep track of the days as much, but I think you turned fourteen a while ago."

Decan did not say anything for a while. He finally broke his silence as they reached the top of another dune.

"I would've been at sea with father. And you know, Triss, I'd give anything to be there right now, smelly fish and all."

"Me too."

She listened to Decan's heavy breathing. The sky slowly turned away from the dark of night as the unseen sun crawled toward the horizon. Then it happened. Decan's feet dragged just a little bit more than he expected. Out of balance, he slumped to his knees and struggled to keep Dalkeira on his back. The unconscious dragon slid off and started tumbling down the slope. Trista did not even have the strength to shout. Dalkeira rolled, slid and came to a halt halfway down the hill, sand covering her wing and tail.

"At least it wasn't the slope we just climbed," said Decan, panting. He took a moment before getting back to his feet.

Unexpectedly, a tremor shifted the land. It was not as strong as they had experienced back home, but they both recognized the feeling without question. The ground waved beneath them. Trista, looking around, saw the ripple carry along the landscape. In the distance, a small avalanche of sand slid down a dune in response.

"Do you hear that?" said Trista, staring at her brother, uncertain of what her ears told her.

Decan lifted his head. He clearly heard it too; the familiar sound of rushing water, which seemed so very conflicting with their current dry surroundings.

He gasped.

"The sand. Look at the sand."

At the foot of the dune, sand slowly started to move, picking up speed as it went. It gravitated toward the lowest point between two dunes.

Before Trista knew it, half the hill on which they stood started to slide down an unseen hole beneath the surface.

"It's a maelstrom of sand," called Trista, who had seen a similar thing happen off the coast during winter storms. "Dalkeira!"

The flow of sand now reached the spot where the dragon lay half buried. As more of the tiny grains started to slip away, Dalkeira slowly slid down with them.

Decan grunted as he pushed himself forward. He staggered down the hill and fell to his knees next to Dalkeira.

"Come on, you overgrown lizard. Wake up."

But as he tried to pull Dalkeira onto his back again, his own footing fell away, the sand shifting beneath him. He tried to claw his way up the dune, but merely succeeded in pushing more sand down toward the whirlpool. His own legs were already half buried.

Against her better judgment, Trista put the small child down on the sand and jumped down the side of the dune herself. The maelstrom was several yards wide now, pulling in more and more sand from its surroundings. The sound morphed into the noise of a thousand tiny insects scurrying away.

Both Decan and Dalkeira now sank toward the hole. If Trista moved any further she would just end up in the same position. Desperately trying to think of something to help, she saw Decan tiring from the struggle. The boy was exhausted.

"Grab hold," yelled Trista as she threw one end of the canvas to Decan.

Decan wrapped his hand around the fabric and pulled. Trista dug her heels in the sand. She forced all her remaining strength into her arms and followed her little brother's example. Briefly, it seemed to help; Decan pulled one of his buried legs free, but then Trista's own footing broke. Before she knew it, her feet sank away and she was on her back sliding after Decan and the dragon. The desert was intent on sucking them under.

Behind her, the cries of the forsaken child called for her. But Trista could not escape the flow of sand. She saw Decan desperately pull on the piece of cloth, Dalkeira sagging from his shoulders with every move he made. The dragon's tail was already swallowed up by the center of the maelstrom. Trista spread her arms and legs; anything to try and slow their descent.

"Triss, help!"

But the boy knew there was little his sister could do at this point.

Trista saw Decan's leg disappear into the maelstrom now. Dalkeira was already half submerged in the sand, though her long neck meant that Decan would be the one to go under first.

Trista screamed in frustration. She jumped forward with her knees on the canvas and grabbed Decan with both hands. She yanked on his arm and still they sank. With one hand behind his back to hold Dalkeira and his legs already gone, Decan had nothing left to give.

"Triss," was the only thing he had left to say.

His eyes were wide as the sand reached his shoulders.

"No!" Trista screamed, unwilling to let go. Then everything stopped.

It took a moment for Trista to notice. Apart from his arm still clutched in her hands, Decan was up to his neck in sand. Dalkeira's neck and head dangled to the side, sand crusted on the edge of the dragon's nostrils as her weary breath rasped in and out.

"It stopped?" said Decan warily.

"I think so," said Trista.

With caution, she slid closer. She forced her hands to let go of her brother, hesitating for a moment to make sure he would not disappear, then started to dig. First carefully with one hand, then two. She freed Decan's other arm as quickly as possible so he could help. It was not easy, but she used the canvas to prevent the loose sand from sliding back. After a while, Decan's chest was freed, allowing him to breathe more easily again.

From the angle of his body, Trista was glad to see her brother's legs were not as deep as she feared. Yet freeing him was anything but easy. She let out a breath of relief when she finally pulled him out of the sand. Together, they continued to dig out Dalkeira. With both their efforts, it was not long before she too was freed from the hungry desert.

A new cry made Trista look up the dune. The child had been quiet for so long, Trista shamefully realized she had forgotten about her. Three large vultures hopped around the wailing child, plucking at the baby's fabric.

"Get away. Go on, skid. Ha!" clamored the siblings together, as Trista crawled back toward the top.

The birds flew off under loud protest.

"Is she alright?" called Decan from below.

"Yes. I think so," said Trista, unwilling to tell him the child looked severely dehydrated.

"Good. Can you help me get Dalkeira up there?"

A short while later, all three collapsed next to the small infant bundle. They all lay flat on the sand, catching their breath.

All of Trista's muscles protested. She could not imagine how Decan must feel. And to make matters worse, Dalkeira remained unresponsive.

"Triss, is that a tower?" she heard Decan say out of the blue.

She opened her eyes, only to find herself facing the wrong way. Her head felt heavy; it took great effort to roll it to the other side.

"Tower? Where?" she asked. "You sure it's not another mirage?"

"There, down to your left. And isn't it still too early for a heat image?"

Trista convinced her eyes to refocus. Then she saw it: a tower, slumped, sticking out of the sand. She saw part of a wall, too, and now that she looked more closely it seemed a few of the dunes were actually roofs.

With protesting muscles, she sat up. "I—I can see it."

She rolled to her knees and strained to get back to her feet.

"Maybe we can make it there before it gets too warm," said Trista with a sparkle of new hope. "Let's go. I'll carry Dalkeira."

Decan merely nodded. Trista pulled him up. Their moment's rest proved enough for them to stand again, though Decan was swaying lightly back and forth.

"I can't make that…"

"Yes, you can. You can hold on to me, okay? Now come on, before our feet figure out what we're doing."

Trista pushed the child into Decan's arms and guided him in the right direction. Her will to survive kept her legs moving, fueled by her newfound hope and curiosity. But as they got closer, reality and disappointment settled in. When they neared the tower and walls, it became clear everything had been deserted a long time ago. Parts of the stone structures were broken off. Of the tower, only the highest was still sticking out of the sand.

"A small city. Let's find some shade and rest before we check things out. Maybe there's something useful," said Trista, refusing to listen to her own disappointment.

They managed to climb through a large V-shaped hole where part of the wall had corroded over time. The desert sand reached as high as the wall itself, burying most of the city's buildings well beneath the surface. They sat in the shadow of the tower, away from the burning sun. Trista put Dalkeira down as softly as possible. Decan slid down beside the dragon, baby in hand, unable to stand any longer. Trista followed his example.

When Trista opened her eyes again, part of the day had slipped by.

"I think we fell asleep," whispered Decan as he noticed his sister waking up.

Trista looked around. The shadow of the tower no longer covered her completely, making her feet uncomfortably warm.

"Only for a short while. The shadows haven't moved much." She looked at Decan and the small bundle stirring in his arms. "How's she doing?"

"She's still breathing. Besides that, I don't know."

Trista gave the baby a quick check, but did not take her from her brother's arms.

"Do—don't you think we should give her a name, or something?" said Decan.

"A name? I suppose you're right, but I haven't got the faintest clue what to call her."

Decan looked at the little girl's face as he held her, but offered no suggestions. "We'll think of something," he said.

Trista gave a small nod. She passed him the last of their rations.

"Eat and drink something, okay? Even if it's only a bite. I'll go and have a look around," said Trista.

"Be careful," said Decan.

She flashed him a small smile. Her little brother was a shadow of his former self. Cheeks hollow, dark shadows under his eyes. Trista wondered what she looked like herself. Probably not much better. Her arms and legs looked thin. She could easily count her ribs, and her clothes were stained from sweat, sand and blood.

She put her hand on Dalkeira's chest, which still slowly rose and fell. Dalkeira was almost gray instead of blue. The dragon's tongue hung partly out of her mouth, while the membrane of her wings felt thin and fragile. Trista clearly saw the veins running through them. Inspecting the webs between Dalkeira's claws, Trista noticed the nails were worn from walking through the sand.

Perhaps this is it. Perhaps this is where our journey ends, Trista thought tiredly. *No!*

She forced herself to get to her feet once again.

Must not give up. Must do… something. I promised Mother and Father. Goddess give me strength…

Using the wall for support, Trista looked for anything that could be of use to them.

If there was a city here, it must have meant people—and water.

She wandered around as the sun continued to climb. Turning a corner, she tried her luck with one of the metal-barred windows, but it would not budge. Continuing deeper into the complex, Trista passed through a low passage, which was in fact a high ceiling from back in the city's glory days. Trista wondered what had happened.

Did the sands simply swallow the city? Did the water run out? Were they attacked, conquered and abandoned? Where is everyone now? She would probably never know.

She climbed through an unbarred window. It had a high arch, but was not very wide. Inside, the room was pleasantly cool.

We can stay here for a while and rest, she thought.

There was not much to see on the walls. They were once colorful by the looks of it, but much of that had faded, their plaster peeled off throughout the years. Trista slid her hand along the rough wall as she moved across the room, until she tripped and fell. She saw a shiny edge sticking from the sand. It had been buried just below the surface. She dug around it with her hands and pulled out a platter of sorts. It had been polished to the point of near perfect reflection before the sands of time took their toll on it.

She used her shirt to clean the platter, restoring some of its shine in the process. Then she saw her reflection and froze. She did not recognize the woman staring back at her at all. Her face was even worse than Decan's, skin peeling off her cheeks and forehead. Her lips had lost nearly all their color and her gums looked like they were pulled back. Startled, she felt her teeth and could have sworn she made them move. Her hair looked terrible. It was dry, almost hay-like, and the only way she knew it was hers was the characteristic red color. Trista had never cared much for being pretty, but the image staring back at her was disturbing. None of the strength she brought forth to keep going—to push herself and her brother forward—was visible in that shiny platter.

She let it drop from her hands. If she had not been so dehydrated, her tears would have freely flowed. Now, barely one tear formed in her eye. She felt broken inside, exhausted, not just from walking, but from keeping it together. This time, it was not so easy to talk herself back on her feet. She pulled up her knees and let her emotions flow out, even if her tears would not.

* * *

In the meantime, Decan was somewhat recovered. After eating a few bites, he gave some water to the baby in his arms. Looking at the dragon, a mixture of worry and annoyance turmoiled inside. He was still angry at her for giving up. He did not want to admit it, but after venting all his frustrations, he felt a lot better. He had come to realize none of this was Dalkeira's fault, just like his sister said. Somehow, he had focused all his own anger and fear on the dragon, simply because she showed up at the same time everything started happening. He had been shocked—furious—about Rudley the goat, but Trista was right: the three of them were all they had. If they did not trust and take care of each other, they would never make it. So he wanted Dalkeira to survive as much as he wanted himself and his sister to live.

The baby in his arms made some protesting noises.

"And you too, of course."

Decan took the water bag and gave the baby another sip. Then he moved closer to Dalkeira. He tilted her head and let some water drip in her mouth. Her tongue made the slightest of movements. He shook the bag, judging the amount of water in there. There was not much anymore, but Dalkeira really needed some right now. Carefully, he poured more water in the dragon's mouth, and this time he saw her swallow.

* * *

Dalkeira slowly opened an eye, trying to focus on Decan's face.

Where am I? Are we still in the desert? She had trouble forming her thoughts. Trista was somewhere nearby, but her human companion was not happy. *Has something happened?*

Her senses were all garbled. Her eyes would not focus and the taste of warm water lingering in her mouth was barely noticeable. She concentrated on the only sense that seemed to be somewhat functioning. She smelled the sand; she would never forget that smell, ever again. She smelled something more solid, too. Dried clay, or some type of stone. It did not have the salt smell of the coastal cliffs, but more a sweet edge to it. But there was something else. Something just outside the range of her nose. She tried to lift her head, sniffing the air.

"Easy. Just stay still," said Decan.

Dalkeira was so tired she almost gave in to the simple suggestion without objection. But then her nose caught it again: a brief whiff, an odor floating through the air. It was very faint, but the urge it unleashed inside Dalkeira was strong. Once more, she tried to sit up.

"Don't move. Please, you need to rest," said Decan again.

It was no use talking to the boy; he could not hear her, and she did not feel as if she had enough energy to call out to Trista. The only thing she could do was look Decan straight in the eye and softly shake her head.

Decan let out a sigh.

"Fine. What is it, then?"

Carefully, the boy put the baby down in the shade, tucking the canvas around her to make sure she did not roll over. After that, he helped the dragon get to her feet.

Once upright, Dalkeira took another sniff of the air. Her mind was driven by blind instinct now—not active enough to register what she smelled, but pushing her to go find it nonetheless. She took another deep breath, and another, and suddenly her thoughts fired up. She knew this smell.

Water!

And not the stale water from the bag either. This was fresh, running water, she was sure of it. She sniffed again, this time moving her head to get a sense of direction. She flicked her tongue out, tasting the air, then slowly walked away from the tower's shade.

Behind her, Decan quickly checked the baby was okay before he followed her toward the center of what might have been a square. There, Dalkeira wobbled back and forth. She held her head high and low; swiveled it from left to right while breathing in deeply through her nose.

She was certain there was water, but she had trouble pinpointing *where*. It was not behind one of these walls, but it did not smell far off.

No, not far away, but blocked. Hidden, thought Dalkeira.

She crossed the open space near the tower again and suddenly stopped to sniff the ground.

Here!

Without hesitation, she started digging with her claws, moving sand and then gravel away. Instantly, the smell got stronger.

"Trista! Something is up with Dalkeira! I think she smells something!" shouted Decan behind her.

The spot where Dalkeira was digging grew larger and larger. The dragon pushed the sand away like an animal gone mad.

"What is it? What are you looking for?" Decan closed in to get a better look.

Dalkeira was now in full frenzy. Her entire body screamed for fluid. Her nose directed her downward, into the ground. Her claws dug deeper and deeper. She noticed the sand slipping away, like there was a hole beneath the surface, and refocused her efforts upon that exact spot.

"No! Stop," Decan called.

* * *

Decan saw the sand shift. But having missed the maelstrom that morning, Dalkeira paid no attention to it. Decan jumped forward to pull the dragon back, but it was too late. This was not a slow-streaming maelstrom; loud cracks and rumbling echoed hollowly beneath their feet. A pit roared into existence and before either of them could react the ground swallowed them whole... the desert finally got its meal.

CHAPTER NINETEEN

Scarred

CORZA? ARE YOU AWAKE, sweetie?”

The bed creaked as he rolled onto his other side. He flinched. Fresh cuts made his skin stick to his nightshirt, making his entire back burn. Old tears had dried on his cheeks. He hated the salty taste of them. He always tried to hold them in so as not to agitate his father any further. But the belt had torn into his skin right from the start, and the pain had become unbearable.

Soft footsteps on the hardwood floor approached his bed. Outside, the night bell rang. He pulled the blanket over his chin until only his eyes were visible. He was not in the mood to talk, not even with his mother. He stared out of the window; the dark palace was barely visible against the blackness of the mountain. Those who lived there seemed untouchable.

The mattress bobbed slightly as his mother sat down.

“Son, he doesn’t mean it. You know that, right? It’s just the drink in him. Your father has had a rough week, with losing the warehouse and the increased taxes and all.”

Corza squeezed his eyes shut to counter a new set of tears and pulled his cover higher. Taxes? That was the reason his back lay open?

His other scars had not even healed yet. Last time it was a spilled drink. Before that, a fight he picked with his older brother, who had his own dirty ways of torturing him thanks to the great role model their father was. Besides, was their family not one of the wealthiest in the city? He was certain his father would find a way to make up for his losses.

His mother’s hand slid under the blanket and scratched through his hair.

“You’re my special boy. You know that, don’t you?” said his mother, her hand continuing to stroke his hair. “You’re my strong boy. Stronger than you think.”

His mother slipped under the blanket with him. Her smell comforted him as she wiped away his tears.

"You're becoming so big already. Before long, the ladies of this city will stand in line for a chance to impress you."

"Girls don't like me much. They're mean. They say I look worse than the skeleton soldiers. Smell, too," said Corza softly.

"They're just jealous. You shouldn't allow them to hurt you like that, ever."

Corza instantly stopped moving. His heartbeat drummed in his ears.

Does she know?

"What's wrong? Is there anything you wish to tell me?" his mother asked lovingly.

Corza kept his gaze locked on the palace outside. He did not know how to explain it. He knew what he had done was wrong. His mother had explicitly told him not to. But it was just a kiss, and not a good one at that. It had been cut short, interrupted when the tip of his tongue almost got bitten off. It was not until he ran upstairs and Corza saw his brother enter the hallway—laughing—to give the girl a coin that he knew why.

"It's alright, my sweet boy. You don't have to tell me. Your brother already told me everything," flowed his mother's voice. "He saw you. You and that maid—Freya. And I don't blame you. It's more than normal for a boy your age to be curious. But you don't need them, Corza. These girls are only interested in your fortune, your power. The family name. She tries it with both your brothers and I wouldn't be surprised if she tried it with your father, too. But she's a hard worker and her tolerance for pain is quite high."

The night's shadows hid his mother's smile.

"But she doesn't see you as special. Not like I do."

His mother kissed his ear. Her hand trailed down his neck and arm and slipped inside his nightshirt to run along his chest. He felt nauseous, and not just from the pain. His entire body became rigid. He tried to fight it, but it was like his entire body was paralyzed—except down there.

"You don't need any of them, my sweet boy. They're all whores. Trying to screw their way to the top," whispered his mother. "You have me, don't you? You'll always be my special little boy."

"Mother, please, my back hurts."

"I'll be careful. Just lie back and try to relax. Let your mother take care of you the way you always like."

He turned his gaze back out the window to the dark palace. She had been like this ever since his eldest brother was forced into the army. He knew there was nothing he could say or do to stop her. Out there, in that mysterious place, the Stone King sat on his throne. Corza bet there was no one in the world who could hurt the Stone King, or make him do anything he did not want to.

The bed creaked from his mother's movement. Corza tried to ignore the agonizing stabs in his back. He hated his body for not listening to him; he hated his brother for setting him up; and he hated Freya for going along with it. But most of all, he hated not having any control over what happened to him. He just wished everyone would leave him alone.

A shudder ran through his mother's body, announcing the end of her special time. Corza bit his lip and fought back the tears. She sat back and slid to the edge of his bed.

"I love you so much, my handsome boy. It frightens me sometimes. The world out there is big, and not much of it is good. I think you father tries to toughen you up, but I just don't see it. You're such a soft boy. Kind. Gentle. I want to keep you like that… with me," said his mother, now with tears of her own filling her eyes. "Soon, they'll come for you. Perhaps it will be some girl; some woman. You'll think you're in love, but it will be nothing like we have. Or perhaps the army will claim you. They're talking about another law for households that have more than one boy. How are you going to survive in such an environment?"

A strange look came over his mother's face. She bent over and picked something up from the floor beside the bed.

"But fear not. I've found a way to keep you safe, my sweet, sweet Corza. The army and girls won't bother you after this. I just had to enjoy it one last time. I wish I didn't have to, but it's a necessary evil if we want to stay together, you and me. And you want that too, don't you?"

His mother did not expect an answer. She rarely did.

Nervously, Corza sat up straight. Something in the woman's hand shimmered in the moonlight.

"Wh—why did you bring those, mother?"

Without a word, his mother moved on top of him, this time with her full weight. He could not move even if he wanted to. With her back toward his face, she forced his legs open.

"Don't worry, I've spoken to the eunuchs at the eastern gate. They've assured me you'll still be able to live a rich life," said his mother as she opened the scissors. "But this way you won't have to worry about any of those nasty things out there. You can stay with me, my sweet, sweet boy. Forever."

"No, mother, wai—AAAAH!"

Corza shot upright, his shirt drenched in cold sweat. He grabbed the throbbing scar between his legs. The walls of his room spun. He threw back his blanket and rushed outside onto the balcony. He breathed in deeply. The fresh air helped, until he noticed his missing finger. The contents of his stomach rushed up through his throat and disappeared over the edge of the railing. Below him, the city sounds of Tal'Kabur clanged toward the sunrise, as if summoning a god. He rested his head on the balustrade for a moment and spat on the ground.

"Fucking whore," he hissed through his teeth.

But an icy calmness already flowed over him. His anger seeped away, letting the fear remain, even if he wished it not to. His fists clenched and hit the stone. Pain shot through his severed finger, which was still healing. He looked at it in disgust.

"Never again, Corza. Remember?" he said to himself. "You said *never again*. You go to the top, where none will dare touch you—ever."

He pushed himself away from the balustrade and went back inside. Opening a trunk in the corner, he filled the large wooden table along the wall with flasks and bottles. A metal ring stand was set over a stone bowl, into which Corza put a small porous stone. He opened one of the flasks and poured its liquid into the bowl. The strong scent of alcohol filled the room.

He looked at his hands; the trembling had stopped. He clenched his fist again. It felt very wrong to be so calm when so much was out of order with the world. He looked at the table; everything was ready. Now he only had to get the cream from the cellars.

With large strides, he exited his room and headed for the stairs. He was pleased to see his guards were alert and awake. It seemed the execution of those fools who let the twins in the other day provided the desired motivational effect. Descending the stairs, sounds of those waking up within the castle greeted him at every level. He passed the kitchen, getting brief surprised looks from the kitchen staff, but they knew better than to ask the high general about his business.

Eagerly, Corza arrived at his destination. In the far corner of a tiny dead-end corridor, he opened a door. Stepping inside, the sour smell of urine assaulted his nose. In the corner, a large cauldron hung above a fire, the yellow liquid inside it boiling and foaming. The smell was enough to make Corza gag, but it was what he needed, so he bore with it.

"Sir, I wasn't expecting you until tomorrow," said the man who stood stirring the gallons of urine. Strangely enough, the man did not seem bothered by the stench that oozed from everything within the room.

"Never mind that. Do you have some ready?" asked Corza impatiently.

"I just finished a fresh batch, sir. Please take it," said the man, pointing to a bowl next to the door.

Corza snatched the bowl from the table on his right and turned around to leave.

"Keep making more. I need to build up some reserves," he ordered, exiting the room without waiting for confirmation.

Carefully holding the bowl, Corza hurried back to his room. One of his guards opened the door for him, allowing him to put the bowl on the table. He walked back to close the door.

"Make certain none disturb me, not even a silent shadow," he said strongly, then slammed the door shut.

He hated this part. It was disgusting. His entire room would smell like weeks-old urine for days. But there was nothing to be done; this process required a certain delicacy he could not entrust to anyone else. Besides, those who helped might start asking questions—something he could never allow.

No one must ever know.

It took gallons of urine to skim enough foam from the cauldron. Soldier's urine, or that of a bull, were best, but any animal of the male variety could be used. The more dominant and aggressive, the better.

He returned to the table and scooped half of the cream into a large rounded flask. Using his spark stone on the bowl filled with alcohol, Corza brought a calm, blue flame into existence. He grabbed the cream-filled flask with metal pliers and softly swirled it through the flame.

It did not take long until the cream started to bubble. Corza poured in a clear liquid to smoothen the cream before bringing it back above the flame. The steps were repeated several times, until the slight yellow color of the cream was nearly white.

The product was one he stumbled across many years ago, when they were looking for ways to enhance their forces' fighting power. Their thorough research into aggression as one of the aspects of a soldier's capabilities had been a pet project of his, to reclaim that which he lost under the hand of his mother. That was, until he was 'politely' asked by Lord Rictor to focus on the ghol'ms.

Corza stared at the solution, judging its purity, and smiled.

See, mother? I have regained what you took from me.

The scar below his belly still throbbed after the nightmare.

Some, at least, he thought bitterly.

He put the flask on the metal stand and grabbed the final, secret ingredient. None of the other generals knew about it. In fact, Lord Rictor was not even aware that Corza had succeeded in making it work. As far as everyone else knew, those days of research had been a waste of time.

Corza took a larger bottle from his trunk. In it was a tiny kzaktor and some twigs to keep it fed.

"Come on, my friend. Time to go to work."

Corza's hands moved calmly and precisely. Grabbing the tiny animal with pliers, he agitated it just enough to catch a few drops of the acid it excreted. Gently, he put it back and made a mental note to give it some fresh leaves and branches later that day. Turning back, he diluted the acid a total of seven times. If the acid was too strong, it would ruin the batch. Too watered down and the reaction he was looking for would be insufficient. It was all very precise.

He held up the liquid against the light.

Perfect.

Painstakingly slowly, Corza dipped a small glass rod into the diluted kzaktor excrement, took it out and let it hover over the cream-filled flask. One drop was all he needed. Holding his breath, he watched the liquid gather at the bottom of the rod. A drop collected, grew heavy—and fell.

Pulling back the glass rod, Corza watched the drop hit the prepared cream. As soon as it landed, the crystallization set in. It spread rapidly across the surface of the cream, producing the sound of fast-freezing water. With a smile, the high general watched the milky-white crystals complete their transformation until none of the cream was left.

He delicately shook the flask, dislodging the crystals from the glass. With tweezers, Corza took a small piece of crystallized cream, put it in a tiny brown flask and added enough water to fill it up. Walking back out onto the balcony, he held his finger on the bottle and calmly shook it.

He held the bottle up against the light, observing the tiny pieces of crystal generating even smaller bubbles. Satisfied with the result, he took a relaxing breath. He put the cap on the bottle, sliding the tiny glass rod that was attached to the cap into the liquid. He pulled it out and held back his head. Hovering above his right eye, he let the drops fall—*one, two*—before moving to his left. *One, two.*

He closed the bottle as the effects of the dose surged through him. His heart rate increased, his pupils widened and his mouth went dry. A shudder ran through his body, acknowledging his fine work. The invisible blades of hatred and anger slipped back into his hands as the drug coursed through his body.

"Now, where were we? Oh, yes. That *fucking* whore."

His voice was sharp with fury. He used the newly created anger to push away his fears, to burn away the calmness his mother had forcefully bestowed upon him; that feeling of indifference that he loathed. Rage was the only thing strong enough to counter what was inside of him. It had become his tool to help him achieve his goals.

"Never again, mother," he spoke. Then he let out a wordless roar. Back inside, the door flew open.

"High General Setra! Are you alright, sir? Sir? Where are you?"

The soldiers rushed through the room as Corza walked back in from the balcony, his exterior calm, but fury raging inside him. He composed himself and noticed he was still wearing his nightshirt. No wonder the kitchen staff had looked at him strangely. He took the sweat-soaked shirt off and threw it in the corner. Moving over to the closet, he grabbed a fresh set of clothes, put them on and continued with his armor.

"Both of you, go and prep the young prince," he said, still fighting to keep his voice under control. He always needed a moment to reach a stable level of anger, but once there, it would no doubt carry him through the day.

"It's going to be a long day. I feel I need to take my mind off things."

"Trista! Something's up with Dalkeira! I think she smells something!"

Trista looked up at the window her little brother's voice had come through. Only now did she feel Dalkeira's excitement trickle into her mind. She wiped her tears and wondered what was going on. She forgot her exhaustion, even when her muscles were kind enough to remind her when she got to her feet and climbed out the window. She circled back the way she came. She heard Decan's voice, then suddenly a loud cracking sound rent the air. She rushed around the final corner—just in time to see Decan and Dalkeira disappear in a cloud of dust. Dalkeira attempted to fly, but she was too exhausted and out of balance.

Trista dropped the plate that was still in her hand and raced forward. She stopped just in time to prevent herself from going over the edge of the gaping hole in the ground. Forced to take a few steps back as the sand beneath her feet started to shift, she lay herself flat on her stomach to spread out her weight and peered into the dust-filled hole.

"Dalkeira? Decan? Are you alright?" she yelled.

She heard coughing from below as the dust slowly settled. Rays of sunlight broke through the haze in the hole. The scene beneath the surface slowly took

302

shape, including two shadows moving in the dust. The baby's crying filled the air now as the rumbling sound had finally died out.

"Decan? Are you okay? Where's the baby?"

"She is not here. She is still beneath the tower," said Dalkeira in her head as the sound of coughing continued, along with something that Trista thought resembled a dragon's sneeze.

Trista turned around and spotted the child at the base of the tower.

"What about Decan?" she said, swiftly walking over to comfort the crying girl.

"He is alright. Just caught a large breath of dust on the way down."

Baby in arm, Trista returned to the edge of the hole. She could clearly see the subterranean chamber now, an enormous pile of sand covering several large slabs of stone that lay broken on the floor. Dalkeira and Decan were at the base of it, dusting themselves off.

"The ceiling caved in," said Decan after finding his voice again. "But the sand broke our fall."

On the edge of the sunlight, something sparkled.

"What's that in the corner?" said Trista.

Dalkeira looked in the direction she pointed and trumpeted.

"I knew it! I knew there was water here!" cried the dragon inside Trista's mind.

Dalkeira darted forward and sniffed the water up close.

"Water? Are you sure?" asked Trista.

"It smells fresh, but where is it coming from?" said Dalkeira in answer to Trista's question.

"There must be an underground water source nearby," said Trista.

The dragon took a quick taste to confirm, then plunged her entire head into the water. As she drank, Trista saw the color of Dalkeira's scales darken, as if the water flowed directly into her skin. Decan wobbled over and washed the sand out of his mouth and eyes.

It was a small reservoir of sorts, surrounded by a foot-high stone wall. Behind it, the water was several feet deep and constantly replenished through a hole in the wall. A separate hole drained off the water if it got too high, preventing it from overflowing. Around the basin hung flaxen roots, leading to small patches of moss that had withered away a long time ago, deprived of sunlight.

Trista carefully looked around, making sure not to get too close to the edge of the hole. The rest of the room seemed very empty. Apart from a few stone benches and some pillars that held up the ceiling, she could not spot anything of interest from her point of view. Several of the pillars had crumbled, which would explain the collapse of the roof.

Seeing her little brother drinking freely made Trista painfully aware of her own thirst. She threw their water bags down.

"How about you fill those up for us?" Trista said to her brother.

Decan looked up apologetically.

"Sorry, Triss, let me get that for you."

Decan quickly returned with the filled water bags and climbed to the top of the pile of sand to throw them to her. The water bags slushed into the sand beside her. Trista quickly grabbed one of them and gulped down the cold liquid until she had to stop for air. Then she gave water in small amounts to the baby as well, allowing her to drink as much as she deemed safe. With this basin, they could make sure the baby had plenty of water. Dehydration would not be a problem anymore. Food, though…

Below, Dalkeira sniffed the dead roots, but turned up her nose.

"These do not smell like food."

"Decan, do you see any way out? It's too high to jump and I don't have a rope to pull you out."

"No, nothing," called Decan after checking around.

"I can search some more up here, but I haven't seen anything yet that might act as a ladder," said Trista.

Decan slid down the pile of sand again to take a few more sips of water, then started looking around more earnestly. It was not long before he disappeared from Trista's sight.

* * *

"There's a few doors here," Decan called out to Trista. "Two of them have crumbled, but two others lead further into the building. It's very dark, though."

Dalkeira got out of the water and walked back into the sunlight so she could examine the hole where Trista waited. Decan lingered around the doors, trying to see if he could spot anything in the pitch-black hallways.

"I can carry him out when I am a bit more rested," said Dalkeira.

"Are you sure you'll be able to carry such a load? I don't want you crashing back down and getting yourself hurt," said Trista.

"Of course I am sure," said Dalkeira, annoyed that Trista would doubt her. The dragon walked around the pile of sand. *"What is that boy doing? He should spend his time drinking instead of wandering around."*

Decan turned toward her.

"I can't see anything down there at all; it's way too dark. Doesn't look like a way out."

Dalkeira decided to have a look of her own. Her dragon eyes would surely be able to see better in the low light then any human could. She set off for the doors when a swift movement caught her eye.

"Decan, look out!" she bellowed.

Bronson lifted his heavy head. His left eye throbbed painfully. It was swollen beyond the point of opening. His shirt was gone, but he registered the afternoon breeze brush against his skin, which glistened with sweat and blood. Thankfully, it had not been too sunny today, but despite that he was parched. His last drink was hours ago. He still tasted the bitterness of the herbs that were in it.

His head spun. Since the twins showed up, High General Corza had doubled his efforts to torture him. Bronson was forced to swallow a herbal liquid every single day. "It's good for you," his captor said. But it clouded his mind; made it difficult to resist. During the torture, the same words were repeated over and over, until it was like they were carved on the inside of his skull.

Your life is over. You belong to me. You will serve Corza Setra in life and death. There is no other truth but the words I say.

Every time he repeated the words—sincerely—Corza gave a reward. A piece of food, some fresh air or a sip of water. He licked his dry lips at the thought of it. He even got to see his sister once. But if he refused or got it wrong, the outcome was less than pleasant.

Bronson fought hard to keep his sanity. In his rare moments of strength, he longed for death. He wished for nothing else. It was the only way out of this living hell. Against all hope, he waited for a mistake; for the general to accidentally kill him. But his torturer was much too skilled for that.

In his moments of weakness—when his reasoning seemed to slip away— Bronson believed the words with every fiber in his body. He truly wished to serve the general. He would thrash around in his straps, not to escape but in desperation that he could not help his master. He wished for this man's kindness. He desired to offer him his loyalty. Protect him. Help him achieve his goals.

Then, when his mind inched back from the abyss of insanity, shame fell over him. He loathed himself for being so weak and desperately tried to hold on to his anger, tried to resist. But it was a losing battle and he knew it. It did not help that while the herb mixture numbed his will, it heightened the sense of pain in his body at the same time. The slightest touch was like a burning coal pressed against his skin. It was excruciating, while the damage was kept at a minimum.

Bronson had managed to take advantage of it once. In his torture-driven-madness, he regained enough of his mind to push the general's buttons. The man had gotten so riled up, Bronson's punishment had been extreme. He passed out from the pain soon after, hoping to never wake up again. His mind was a cart, slipped away into the deep mines of nothingness.

Afterward, when he came to in his bed, he cried. It had not worked. The high general was gone—which meant Bronson would get time to recuperate before it all started again.

But today was different. There was something terrifying in the sessions this day, a relentless anger he had not seen in the general before. Bronson had passed out twice already, yet every time he came to, his demon was still there. His throat hurt, like he was swallowing knives. His voice was almost completely gone from all his screaming. He did not resist anymore; those days of stubbornness were long behind him now. He did what he was told, immediately, but still Corza grew angry at times. A misspoken word, a wrong tone or delay too long. Bronson could not help it—the herbs made it difficult to focus.

So his screams had filled today's morning until his voice finally gave out. It did not matter. Nothing he said had any effect. No promise; no declaration of devotion; no wish to serve or amount of crying made any difference. It was like the high general was not even listening to him anymore. Corza merely wanted to break him into a million pieces.

Bronson let his head drop, muttering some incomprehensible words.

"What was that?" asked Corza. He sat nearby, sipping a drink. "I can't hear you."

"Wa'er."

"War? Yes, you could say that we're at war. Although it is pretty one-sided, so perhaps it is a bit of an overstatement, don't you think?"

"Wa—ter," tried Bronson again.

"Oh! Water!" said Corza. "I misunderstood you there. You must learn to pronounce your words properly. Sorry, I don't have any water. All I have is this ale, which, by the way, is very well cooled. Do you want some of it?"

The high general came over and put the mug against the prince's split lips. Corza tipped the mug so fast half the ale missed Bronson's mouth and washed down the side. The brew stung the fresh cuts all over his chest. He tried to swallow as fast as possible, but could not prevent himself breaking out in coughing, spraying the ale all over the balcony.

"Now see what you've done," said Corza angrily. "Wasting perfectly good ale. You'll pay for that."

The general pulled out his Roc'turr.

Bronson did not react. He did not care anymore. There was no fear, no anger, no hope. His mind stood at the edge of the abyss.

Perhaps you should just fall.

The thought came out of nowhere, but they were his own words, spoken in his own voice.

You are weak. Nothing. You have no use for this body.

Beside him, Corza waited for a moment and lowered his dagger. The general pulled Bronson's head up by the hair.

"It seems there's not much left of you, Prince of Iron. But I'm not done with you yet. I will rebuild you. Make you whole again."

With unfocused eyes, Bronson stared beyond Corza. He saw himself stand on the edge of the balcony. He tried to laugh, but produced little more than a gurgle.

It's happened. I've gone mad. Delirious.

The image was him, but not like he was now; scarred, weak and beaten. It was him before. A man, proud to be a part of the Iron family, among the best fighters in the court. Fearless. His ghostly image turned around to face him. It looked tired. Bronson stared at himself, displayed in full armor, swords in hand. Blood ran down his face, wet his hair. The image's head hung low from exhaustion, just like his own on the rack. The man swayed lightly back and forth on his feet, but his eyes… his eyes remained strong. Determination resided in those eyes.

The battles must have been heavy and long, thought Bronson sadly as he continued to stare at his own ghost.

And they are not over yet.

The Prince of Iron was not sure if the words came from himself or from the image. The image disappeared as the general spun him backward into a horizontal position. Corza unstrapped the prince and brought him back up. The unexpected decrease in tension around his arms, legs and head, made Bronson slump to the ground before his muscles could react. There he lay, jerking and twitching. He forced himself to look up at the balustrade, expecting to see nothing but sky. Instead, the bloodied warrior image of himself stared down at him, demanding he get up.

His former self squatted down and extended a hand. It took all of Bronson's leftover willpower to make his body move. And every time he thought he could not and wished to give up, those piercing fighter's eyes told him otherwise. He pushed his knees under him. Leaned on his hands and pulled his head back to look up. The vague image of an offered hand hovered right in front of him.

Bronson groaned and stretched his arm. The weight of a mountain leaned on his hand as he brought it up. The prince reached for the balcony railing and pulled himself up with the greatest effort.

When Bronson stood on both feet and leaned heavily on the stone handrail, the high general slowly approached him, as if afraid to startle him.

"Even after all that, you still refuse to let go. I must say, it's almost admirable." Corza spoke gently. "But it's futile."

The general took the prince's chin and turned his face toward him.

"I can see it in your eyes, you know? You'd rather die—jump to your death instead of giving in. Just like that morning with those bitches. That iron will certainly is impressive. But you may not die. It is not your decision to make. Your life belongs to *me*."

Corza smiled.

"Believe me, I understand. It's only natural for your situation. That wish for things to end. However, I want you to understand: dead men have no value. And you still do, even if you can't yet see it. It's clear that at this point, you only think of yourself. But your life is so much more," whispered Corza. "Tell you what. Why don't I show you the value of your life? Allow me to give you purpose once more."

Corza brought his fingers to his lips and whistled. Across from them, the other tower's balcony door swung open. A guard urged two women outside. Bronson strained to lift his head. It had been days since Corza brought them out.

"Kayla? Mom?"

"Bronson! Oh, no, look what he has done to you," his mother cried.

"You monster! Why don't you let him go?" screamed his sister.

The high general briskly lifted his hand to indicate the women to be quiet. After being forced to listen and watch Bronson's torture, Kayla and their mother knew better than to defy Corza's gesture.

"I know you believe it is me you hate. That I cause all this pain and suffering. But you're wrong. That honor belongs to none other than the Stone King. I am merely a tool in his hands," said Corza. His disgust did not sound feigned. "He's the one you should focus on. *He* planned the attack on Tal'Kabur. *He* killed your father. And *he* ordered your torture. Even told me to include the whole family."

The sentence lingered in the air. Unsure whether the high general lied, Bronson merely stared at his sister, her image a blurry, blue shape.

"He's a terror that walks this earth. And he will not stop until he rules it all. Just look at his hand," Corza continued. "It's built from the very stones of the underworld. If you want to hate someone, hate him. Loathe him. And then help me kill him."

Bronson's head spun. He tried to think of the weeks of torture, but his mind refused, his memories shattered from the pain and herbal mixtures. Was the man with the black hand truly behind it all?

"Take a good long look. Your dear sister and mother are right there. They say twins always have a special bond; growing up together; being so close from the moment they are conceived. And the bond between a son and his mother— well, that's always *special*, right? In any case, you wouldn't want them to suffer. You care for them."

Corza reached out again. He grasped Bronson's chin and shook the prince's head.

"*Look*. Do you see them, Prince of Iron?" hissed Corza in Bronson's ear. "Do you see how young and untainted your sister is? Her whole life still in front of her. Just like yours. Hell, even your mother has a good few years before she starts to wither."

Bronson stared at the other balcony. His heart bled from sorrow and love. From the corner of his eye, he saw the warrior beside him sitting in silence. The ghostly figure stared with him at the queen and princess in bloodied determination; there was no way he would let the high general win. The warrior image grabbed Bronson by the neck and forced him to look down.

There lies the freedom we seek. The words rang inside Bronson's head. The Prince of Iron looked down into the chasm and back at the women again. Desperation filled Bronson's mind.

"Let it go. What use is dying?" said Corza. "Give your life to me and under my guidance we shall remove the Stone King from this world. Your family will be free again."

The small truths within the lies fell into place in Bronson's broken mind. Had those women not asked him if the high general planned to kill the king? If that was true, the rest must be as well. His iron will strained under the pressure of this flawed logic.

"In fact, your heart will beat for three," the general's voice carried on. "See, many of the men have always wanted to get their hands on something as pure as royalty, but I've kept them safe. Told Lord Rictor I needed them to get resistance information from you, and to help control the people. That is *their* value, and mine in turn. Because should I die, they will be robbed of my protection and surely follow me into the afterlife without delay."

The high general's face inched closer.

"And then there's you. Your life, which you believe has no value. But it has value to me. You will be my sword, my tool. But should you so carelessly choose to die without my consent, that value will be lost, and I see no other way than to make those fine ladies my very next project. With my plans ruined by your death, I would need the distraction, and I'm certain your mother and sister will keep my thoughts off things for a while. Just look at that perfect skin. It makes me ache to take them under my care."

The high general's words trailed off. He looked engulfed by his own imagination. Bronson smelled the ale on Corza's breath.

"I have an entire jar of kzaktors that I think would love to get a taste. You believe these weeks have been too much for you? With them, I will keep going for years! I'll break them down, until they do not recognize themselves anymore. Their screams will fill the night sky for months to come. I will take them with me wherever I go and let every soldier visit them at night. Or perhaps I'll just let them hold hands and drop one of them over the balcony to see how long they can hold on to each other. There are so many possibilities!

"But they can all be avoided by killing the Stone King. That's your value, and that's your purpose."

Both versions of Bronson—one real, one not—jerked their heads around and stared at Corza defiantly.

"There's that fighting spirit again. That proud 'will of iron'. You still think you're in control. You still think you have a choice," said Corza. "Fine. I'll give you a choice."

The general took something from the ground and put it on the stone railing. Squirming legs and a high-pitched screech greeted Bronson from inside. The pliers lay next to the jar.

"Take it out," commanded the high general.

Bronson stared at his tormentor in silence, unsure what to do.

"Suit yourself," shrugged Corza and gave a signal to the other balcony.

Immediately, the soldier grabbed both sister and mother by the neck and held them far across the handrail. His sister screamed in terror. The Queen of Iron struggled to get out of the soldier's grip while keeping hold of her daughter's arm.

Bronson quickly grabbed the jar and opened it. He reached inside with the pliers and took the kzaktor from it.

"Careful. Don't squish it," said Corza. "Now, listen carefully. I want you to nod if you understand. Your life belongs to me. You will work for me. Fight for me.

310

You won't stop breathing without my command; you won't stop living without my order. Your life belongs to *me*. Fail me, and your sister and mother won't even have time to grieve over your demise before I start my work with them."

Inside, Bronson's will tried to withstand the barrage of pain and doubt. This was it. *This* was the moment of triumph or utter despair. He felt it in his bones. With every word Corza laid on him, Bronson inched closer to the abyss in his mind. To compensate, he stepped away from the balcony's balustrade. The warrior image of himself stood and turned around to look at him. His self-image grabbed a new wound that appeared on its ghostly side. Blood seeped through the fingers, but the eyes… the eyes remained strong. Defiant. The personification of his will of iron.

The prince's own eyes could no longer hold back tears. They ran over his face as he silently wailed at the agony of his powerlessness. Then the high general spoke again.

"I will not torture you anymore, young prince. From now on, I will not touch you until it's your time to die. That is now all up to you. Your life means the lives of your mother and sister. Your pain will show me your value. That you're obedient. That you serve me. That your life belongs to *me*. You can make sure that nothing ever happens to them. Do you understand?" said the high general. "*Your* pain will keep them alive."

Tears kept flowing. His mother and sister watched from the other tower, longing to comfort him and take away his pain. Pain; it made Corza's threats only more real. Salty rivers flowed across Bronson's face and stung his wounds. He could do nothing other than nod his head in earnest.

"Then do it."

Bronson held out his hand. With his other, he dangled the tiny kzaktor above it. He lifted his head, diverting his eyes from what he was about to do. In front of him, the ghostly image shook its head. The warrior in Bronson thought about throwing it at Corza. Throw it and grab his dagger, but it would not make a difference. It would doom his sister and his mother. And in all honesty, he could barely stand, let alone throw the tiny creature with intent. This was the only way.

"That's it. Your pain should be visible. Wear it as armor." Corza's voice slithered into his ears. "You let that creature eat away the part that wants to hold on the most. Cut it off. Discard it. You'll feel better. You'll be without responsibilities. Free from fear of choosing wrongly. Your life will belong to me."

Inside him, Bronson's subconscious stared into the black abyss of insanity at his feet. The darkness pulled him in. His mind strained to the point where it was unable to bend any further.

Slowly, he lowered the kzaktor to his arm.

"That's it," said the general under his breath, his words filled with expectation.

"No, Bronson. What are you doing? You don't have to do that. Bronson! Stop!" screamed his sister across from him.

Her words made his fear drop away. His anger, his doubt. In that moment, he felt nothing but love. Love, and the desire to save his sister; to save his mother, even if that meant he had to condemn himself to a life of pain. In front of him, the wounded warrior with the defiant eyes swayed and stumbled a step back. Shock and disbelief showed on his face. Without another word, the ghostly image fell backward off the balcony and disappeared from sight.

Inside, the abyss swallowed Bronson whole. He broke into a thousand pieces and a thousand more. For it was his voice that screamed the call of defeat as the kzaktor dug itself into his arm.

The Prince of Iron collapsed to the ground, grasping his arm in agony, and entered a world of pain. Everything else was pushed back into the darkness. Love, happiness, independence—all disappeared into this black hole, where the pain enclosed it in a wall of armor.

Behind him, Corza pulled out his Roc'turr. The high general was grinning like a madman.

"Let those bitches try to take him from me now," he said in triumph to himself, before raising his voice for all to hear. "Let them know that I, Corza Setra, challenged the *will of iron* and won. I didn't bend it. I didn't reforge it. No; I *broke* it! *Nothing* is impossible for me. Never again!"

CHAPTER TWENTY

Sha'cara

DALKEIRA HAD NO idea how, but for the first time ever Decan actually heard her. She saw the boy startle at the sound of her voice. Behind him, an animal shot out from the dark hallway. It scurried low across the floor with its jaws wide open, closing in on Decan's leg.

It looked a lot like the small lizards Decan had tried to catch for her back on the island, but its build was much more muscular and its skin was covered in short, rugged feathers. Its length was impressive, easily reaching half the boy's height. It had a large, rigid tail and long powerful claws that seemed adjusted for digging or walking in loose sand. Its head was on a short, thick neck, the mouth showing a row of small but razor-sharp teeth as it tried to clamp down around Decan's calf.

Dalkeira's warning gave the boy just enough time to react. He sprang forward and the jaws of the feathered lizard snapped shut behind him. Tumbling forward into the sand, Decan turned around and scrambled back, away from the creature.

"What's going on?" yelled Trista from above.

"*We've got company,*" Dalkeira informed her.

The lizard did not seem inclined to give up. It took powerful steps through the sand after Decan, its flat, wide head swaying side to side as it walked closer. A forked tongue flicked in and out of its mouth.

Dalkeira jumped forward between the strange-looking lizard and its prey, letting out a hiss as she spread her wings to increase her size.

Even without her wings, Dalkeira was at least twice as big as the ground lizard, but where Dalkeira's build was lean and quite skinny, this animal easily outweighed her by half. The lizard, unimpressed by its winged cousin's flamboyant display of size, let out a hiss of its own and took a step sideways. Saliva spat from its mouth to accompany the threatening sound. On the lizard's back a row of spikes raised, showing a sail of skin with a deep-red frilled membrane.

Dalkeira was taken aback. This was the first time she had encountered an animal that did not turn tail and run right away. This was clearly a challenge. She circled the low-walking lizard as it followed her movements. She figured it would be best to go straight for the throat. The belly looked like another vulnerable spot, but the sail on its back would make it difficult to flip over.

"Decan, get back here," ordered Trista.

The boy needed no encouragement. He put his feet under him and ran toward the pile of sand and stone. Dalkeira made sure the lizard remained focused on her as he sprinted away. She used her agility to out-turn the lizard, waiting for the moment it would break eye contact as it tried to keep Decan in sight. As she got behind it, the lizard finally switched directions and turned the other way to meet her.

Dalkeira jumped forward. Using her claws, she pinned down the animal's closest feet to prevent it from lashing out at her. Her jaws struck the creature's neck as she bit with all her might into the tiny feathers behind the lizard's head. Drinking water had certainly been refreshing, but she still had not fully recovered her strength from the lack of food and rest. The lizard's skin was tough to break through and the muscles made it difficult to bite deep enough.

Dalkeira clenched her jaws together as hard as possible and shook her head. The lizard's flesh tore as she ripped a piece of skin from its neck. Bleeding heavily, the animal thrashed around, launching Dalkeira upward, but the damage had already been done. With a single bite Dalkeira had severed the main artery of the belly-crawling creature. Now she only needed to wait until it bled out.

The thrashing slowed and the lizard grew still. Dalkeira launched forward, driven by the scream of hunger inside her.

A fresh kill! Food!

She tore at the flesh around the wound. It was difficult to rip off, but she managed to swallow a few bites before hearing the lizard hiss again. Startled, she jumped back—only to see her kill lay motionless in the sand.

"Dalkeira, the door! There's more," called Decan from the other end of the room.

The dragon could now hear a multitude of hisses coming from the dark hallways. The sound flowed into the room like a river, bouncing off the walls. She stared at the doorways. Her eyes readjusted to the darkness just as two more lizards entered the room, both at least two feet bigger than the one dead in front of her. She gazed wistfully at her kill, quickly tore off another piece and took to the air. She flew straight for Decan, who was already climbing to the top of the sand mountain.

"*I am coming, Decan,*" said Dalkeira, but her voice did not seem to reach the boy anymore.

She tried to remember what she had done to let her voice reach him. It was not that she had focused on him, and she could not hear his thoughts. It was more like she had deliberately not focused on anything in particular; just sent her voice into her direct surroundings. She tried a second time.

"Decan, get ready. You grab me. My claws will cut you open if I catch you!"

"Be careful!" called Trista from above.

The boy looked straight at her as she approached. He had heard her. The look in his eyes still showed his confusion at hearing Dalkeira's voice for the first time, but he knew better than to stop and ponder on these events while giant lizards were trying to eat him.

Dalkeira reached the boy, slowing her approach as much as possible by beating her wings at an angle. She could not hang still in mid-air, but her approach was slow enough for Decan to make the jump. With arms spread wide, he locked them in an embrace around her waist.

Dalkeira gasped as the added weight knocked her out of balance. She quickly beat her wings to adjust to the new point of gravity, only barely able to stay in the air. She further increased her efforts to get out of the hole, but only managed to climb a few feet before her exhaustion caught up with her.

Both dragon and boy crashed down onto the pile of sand again. Dalkeira slid down the slope, trying to pull in her wings to prevent injury. At the top, Decan was able to keep himself from tumbling down and quickly scrambled to his feet.

"Triss, what do we do?"

"I'll look for something!" she called down before disappearing from sight.

Dalkeira rolled back to her feet and turned to face the oncoming lizards. The animals raced toward her, expecting the dragon to be vulnerable from the fall. Immediately, she jumped further back, trying to get a better position. Her reaction slowed the lizards' approach. With caution, they stalked closer to her. One snapped its jaws at the other as they argued over who would get the first bite of the unfamiliar intruder.

The pecking order established, a mass of feathers, claws and teeth rushed toward Dalkeira. She could do little but retreat to a safe distance every time the lizards got close. She needed to create an opening before she could even think about launching an attack. She repeatedly positioned herself so that one lizard was blocking the other, but the creatures simply clawed over one another to get to her.

In the meantime, she saw Decan looking for another way out of the room, but the distance to the collapsed ceiling made it impossible and the walls were much too smooth to climb. The dark hallways were definitely not an option either; who knew what else was out there? There was nothing else he could do but wait and see what Trista came up with from above.

With trembling hands, the boy picked up a large piece of stone and hurled it toward the closest of the two lizards. It hit the animal on the head, making it turn around with a hiss to look at this new attacker.

Right away, Dalkeira used the distraction to jump at the other lizard. Unfortunately, the starting angle had been wrong for a direct assault on its neck, so she clawed at its flank instead.

But as soon as Dalkeira leaped, the second lizard turned toward her again. It had deemed Decan too little a threat and refocused itself on the bigger and closer obstacle. Dalkeira shifted to dodge the incoming attack. The gaping jaws and sharp teeth missed her by an inch, but a claw tore through her skin on her lower back. She trumpeted at the unexpected jolt of pain.

She opened her wings again in the hope the sail membrane on the lizards' backs would raise up in response. It would give her a chance to stay more hidden from the furthest one. But neither animal reacted to her threat. They outnumbered her; they saw no need to bluff their way to victory when their jaws could do the talking for them.

She jumped up and flew away with the lizards in hot pursuit, their heads stretching upward, forked tongues eagerly following her around. With little room to maneuver, Dalkeira was forced to land close to the water she had so eagerly drunk from earlier. Then she noticed something peculiar: both animals avoided the sunlight, scurrying along the wall as they approached her.

Behind her, Dalkeira smelled the fresh water she had so longed for these past few days. Despite her drink, it had lost none of its appeal. She looked over her shoulder and saw an uncountable number of sparkles flowing around; inviting her. She mused about how easy it was to glide through the water, how its refreshing touch upon her scales would cool her wound. Almost easier than flying. The water would work with her, assist her, as if it was listening to her—and suddenly she had an idea. Although perhaps idea was too big a word for it. Feeling, urge, or gamble was more appropriate.

She flipped around and jumped into the water, marveling in the sensation as she submerged herself in the cold liquid. For an instant, the water bit the scratch on her back before it brought a cool, welcome relief. She raised herself to her feet. The water easily reached her chest, but with her long neck, Dalkeira had no trouble staying above the surface. The lizards, with their stumpy legs and short, thick necks, would have much more difficulty staying above water— or at least that was what Dalkeira hoped.

But the water did nothing to deter the lizards. They reached the side of the basin and threw themselves into the water, barely able to keep their noses above the surface. Their rigid tails offered little help to stay afloat, but in combination with their hind legs allowed them to rapidly swim toward the dragon.

For the third time, Dalkeira spread her wings, but this time not to bait her attackers. She felt larger, like the water surrounding her was actually a part of her. Like she could just reach out and—and—

Both lizards were upon her already and launched their attack.

Deep inside Dalkeira's mind, she rejected the events in front of her. The incoming attack was an insult to this marvelous connection she had with the water. She was queen of this domain; this was her place and those intruding should be banished. Inside her, something rushed forward out of the depths of her core and pushed. A small wave formed in front of her and moved away. It did not look very powerful, but it hit one of the lizards right in its widespread mouth. The animal panicked as the water forced its way down its throat. Having the advantage of movement for as long as they were in the water, Dalkeira jumped up and used her wings to dodge the other lizard's attack. The feathered creature had little choice but to let Dalkeira pass over its head. As its legs were too short to reach the basin's floor, it used its tail to launch itself out of the water in an attempt to snap at the dragon's legs, only to drop back in failure with a splash.

It turned around as quickly as possible, but Dalkeira had already pushed the other lizard underwater with her front claws. The animal thrashed below the surface under her weight. Unable to keep sufficient pressure on the panicked lizard, she thrust her head under and tore a piece of flesh from the muscular neck, just like she had done with the first one. The water ran red as blood flowed out of the lizard's wound.

Resurfacing, Dalkeira called out in triumph, but the other lizard cared little for its fellow hunter. Its eyes grew wide, the smell of blood sending it into a frenzy. It dashed forward, trying to take a bite out of Dalkeira's own neck.

The increased aggression triggered another defensive push deep inside the blue dragon. This time, a more direct stream of water hit the attacking lizard from the side. It was more powerful than the wave before, but

Dalkeira was disappointed to see her attacker barely flinched. She dodged its lunge in an eruption of water. She circled to the side, trying to rush it. With all her might, Dalkeira threw herself into her attacker's flank. For the third time, the water came to her aid. Together they hit the lizard with such force that it slammed into the nearest wall. Dazed by the impact, the lizard slid down and sank back into the water, showing its vulnerable belly. Dalkeira wasted no time and pounced forward. She ripped open the softer skin with her claws and killed it without hesitation.

High up on the sand hill, Decan stood with another stone in his hand. He cheered as Dalkeira finished off the last lizard, and slid down the sandy slope.

"How did you do that?" said Decan.

"Do what?" said Dalkeira.

She had difficulties coming to terms with what just happened herself. However, she had no intention of letting anyone else think she did not know precisely what was going on.

"There! You just did it again! You spoke, and I heard you!"

Dalkeira let out a sigh. From a distance the fight must have just looked like a lot of splashing in the water. It seemed Decan had not noticed anything special. That was good. It gave her some time to explore it herself.

"I guess you finally figured out how to listen," said the dragon with a scoff.

One by one, Dalkeira pulled the lizards out of the water. She was still hungry and had every intention of devouring as much as she could.

Trista's head popped over the edge.

"What's happening? Are you two alright?"

* * *

Trista dropped a long string of tied-together canvas into the hole.

"You go ahead and climb out. I want to get my fill first," said Dalkeira to the boy. In Trista's head she added, "*I can finally make myself heard.*"

A flow of complacent pride entered Trista's mind. Dalkeira was very pleased with herself; she had not only just killed three large attackers, but also figured out a way to communicate with lesser-linked humans. The past days of hardship were forgotten for the moment as she took another bite from the lizard carcass and swallowed it whole.

"*When you're done, can you carry some of that out of there?*" asked Trista politely.

But before Dalkeira could answer, a rumbling hiss rose from the darkness. Startled, Decan and Dalkeira looked at the dark doorways.

"There's more?" said Decan, frightened.

The sound of scuffling claws flowed from the dark underground corridor. It intensified, coming closer.

"That is not just one animal. It cannot be," said Dalkeira wearily, as the sound grew louder.

A flood of lizards burst out of the shadows and poured into the subterranean chamber. Some were as small as Decan's foot; others were closer in size to the three that lay dead on the ground. Dozens—hundreds of lizards came running through the entrance. The little ones used their tiny claws to climb along the walls and get up higher, while the bigger ones plowed through the sand. Some even dove into it, trying to bury themselves.

Decan was already moving again, up the pile of sand and rubble. There, he grabbed the improvised rope of canvas. He tried to climb up, but his arms were weak. He kicked his legs and tried to get his feet twisted around the improvised rope, but it was no use. He fell back, punched the sand in anger and started to cry.

Dalkeira, staring at the sheer number of lizards, cautiously stepped back into the relative safety of the sunlight.

"How can that many survive down here? There is water, but what do they eat?" said Dalkeira inside Trista's head in a misplaced moment of curiosity.

Trista stretched forward to look at the increasing number of lizards. The room flooded with the scraping sound of claws on stone and sand. Their hisses blended into a constant noise; it was almost like the breaking of waves on a beach.

"Something is strange," said Dalkeira. "They are not attacking us at all. They act... scared. Like they are running away from somethi—"

Her sentence was cut off when a massive lizard crashed into the room out of the dark. It slammed into the stone door frame, barely fitting through the entrance. A large piece of ancient stone hurled violently through the chamber and squashed one of the smaller lizards on the sand.

The enormous animal was at least twice the length of Dalkeira. Its thick, muscled body clearly outweighed her far beyond that. The smaller lizards shot away as the creature snapped its jaws at near impossible speed, grabbing one of the mid-sized lizards with its teeth. It shook it wildly, tearing it in half. The monster threw its head back and swallowed the first half before picking up the other out of the sand and gobbling that down as well.

"They eat their own! That is how they are able to survive," said Dalkeira inside Trista's head.

Dalkeira turned to Decan, who forgot his tears as he stared at the oversized lizard in complete shock. For all its size, it was still covered in a dense layer of feathers along its back, while the head, legs and belly showed the more traditional hard skin that Trista and Decan knew from the small island lizards back home.

"Boy, you have to try again! There is no way I can stop one so big. Get up on that rope!" said Dalkeira as she pushed Decan to his feet with her head.

"I'll pull you up. Just grab hold as hard as you can!" called Trista. "Twist it around your arm!"

Decan wrapped the makeshift rope around his hands and held on tight. Trista pulled with all her might, the canvas cutting into her skin. From a distance, the baby regarded Trista's efforts with little comprehension of the dangers that moved beneath them. Trista slung the rope over her shoulder to take the tension off her hands.

"It's working!" she heard Decan shout from inside the hole.

It was a bad choice to call out. The large lizard's head shot up and immediately took notice of the strange being dangling from the ceiling.

It is coming this way! said Dalkeira directly to Trista.

Trista's muscles were cramping in protest. She dug her heels in the sand and took another step. But she was already completely out of breath. The long walk through the desert had drained her too much.

No!

She shook her head and gritted her teeth. She had to do this. She had to save her little brother. She had *not* rescued him from the soldiers only to have him die in this goddess-forsaken place. She would *not* break her promise to their mother and father.

She breathed a few quick breaths and took another step—and fell on her back in the sand. One of the knots in the makeshift rope had come undone. She heard Decan yelp as he crashed back down hard and hit the pile of sand for the third time.

Dalkeira shot forward and grabbed the boy's shirt with her teeth to keep him from sliding down. The large lizard lurked at the edge of the light, its long tongue flashing in and out.

"Stay in the light. They do not like it," said Dalkeira.

The remark gave Trista an idea. She looked around for the metal plate she had been carrying. Spotting it, she quickly ran over and returned to the hole in the ground.

"Catch," yelled Trista, dropping the metal plate into Decan's hands. "Reflect the sunlight at it!"

Her little brother did as he was told and redirected the sunlight straight into the creature's eyes. It let out a hiss and violently thrashed around, trying to escape the bright light.

"Triss! I think we just made it angrier!" said Decan, sounding worried.

The giant lizard moved its head out of the beam of light and took a step forward into the normal sunlight. Decan aimed the mirrored light directly into its eyes again. Once more the lizard thrashed its head around, this time sticking it in the sand and throwing sand up into the air. The dust cloud lessened the effect of the beam, enough for the lizard to take another step forward.

"You stay away from him!" shouted Trista, throwing every rock she could find. It had no effect at all.

Trista was looking around for another rock to throw when a shadow fell beside her on the ground. Startled, she looked up to see a dark silhouette standing only a few feet away. A pair of strong eyes peered out at her from the folds of a blue-scarfed turban that covered most of the head. The stranger's clothes were clearly meant to defy the desert heat. Simple cloth pants and light leather shoes allowed easy movement on the hot sand. The torso had a plain leather breastplate which was barely visible beneath the loose cloth coat, which consisted of the same fabric as the pants. A band was tied around the waist, holding together the coat, the sides of which reached as far down as the knees.

Had the situation not been so dire, the difference between their outfits would have made Trista extremely self-conscious, having nothing but torn and dirty clothes wrapped around her own head and body. The stranger did not seem to notice, looking Trista straight in the eye. The desert traveler held two long spears tipped with long, sharp bones. A leather bag rested on his hip while a small curved dagger hung on the other side.

Trista reached for her own dagger. In the background, the baby let out a cry. Trista saw the stranger's eyes move from her weapon to the baby to the hole and back.

"Triss! Help!" called Decan.

Trista looked desperately back and forth between the unexpected stranger and the hole, and decided to take a chance.

"Look, my little brother is in trouble down there. I need to get him out, or he'll die! If there's anything you can do, please, please help us!"

The man looked at her in silence.

"Please. I don't know if you can understand me, but please help him!"

Slowly, the desert traveler moved to the edge of the hole and peered inside. There, the large lizard was getting close to the top. Decan had moved onto the other side of the pile, trying to stay out of view of the large predator. Dalkeira had jumped into the water, trying to distract the lizard, but it had clearly set its mind on Decan for its next meal.

Trista saw the eyes of the stranger grow wide and heard a gasp. Thrusting both spears into the ground, the stranger ran away from the hole, grabbing something from his back. A rope was thrown and tied around the nearest slab of stone that had fallen from the tower over time. The other end was rolled out, revealing a cleverly constructed rope ladder. With the end of the rope ladder in hand, the desert dweller leaped into the hole in one fluent motion. The rope snapped tight as the man's weight pulled the rope ladder down the hole.

The masked man landed right in front of Decan, then quickly opened his bag as the giant lizard moved in to attack. Quick hands produced two small leather pouches from the bag and threw them directly at the oncoming lizard. One disappeared into its mouth; the other hit the lizard on the head, where it erupted into a small cloud of red powder.

The lizard flinched as the powder surrounded its eyes and nose. The taste was clearly not very pleasant either, as it shook its head wildly back and forth. The large creature thrashed around so violently it rolled all the way down the slope again, where it hastily crawled into the water, submerging its head. Dalkeira jumped to the side to prevent herself from being squashed.

In the meantime, the stranger pulled Decan to his feet and urged him to climb the ladder. Trista helped Decan out of the collapsed chamber. Nimbly, the desert dweller quickly followed, pulling up the rope ladder as he did.

Trista was about to say thanks when Dalkeira burst out of the hole, wings beating furiously in order to gain enough height to escape the room now infested with lizards. The man grabbed a spear out of the sand and pointed it at Dalkeira, his feet shifting in order to make the first strike. The dragon let out a hiss in surprise.

"No, wait! Stop! She's with us. She's a friend," said Trista quickly, jumping in front of Dalkeira and holding up her hands toward the stranger.

Trista looked their savior in the eyes, urging him to put down the spear. The stranger's muscles visibly relaxed, but the spear remained in his hand. Trista turned to Dalkeira and ran her fingers over the arch of the dragon's eye.

"Are you okay?"

"*I am fine,*" said Dalkeira privately, clearly unwilling to give away her ability to communicate to the stranger just yet.

Trista looked at the gash on the dragon's back.

"It looks clean enough, but let me see if we can clean it out some more. Just to be safe."

"That won't be enough."

The voice was thick with an accent Trista had never heard before. A hard 'f' sound on the lips and deep, rounded pronunciation of the vowels—and surprisingly feminine. Trista looked up at the stranger, who, in response to Trista's surprised look, now removed the scarf from around her head. Without it, the eyes suddenly looked much more womanly, accentuated by the fine lines of her face. Despite those elegant lines, the stranger wore a stern look. Her hair was short, dark and spiked, apart from a longer lock of hair on the left side of her face. A string of colorful beads was braided into it. Her skin was a deep bronze, which Trista doubted was just from exposure to the sun. On the woman's face thin white lines had been drawn in wavy and circular patterns. Several went down the neck, disappearing beneath her clothing.

"You're a woman?" said Trista.

"So are you," said the stranger pragmatically, with a rolling 'r' that lay far back in the throat. "You'd better dress that wound with some fevergrass— baell'wek saliva is a source of infection. Even with such a scratch, it's best not to take any chances."

Trista stared at Dalkeira before turning back to the stranger again.

"I'm sorry, I don't know what fevergrass is."

"You don't? What are you doing in such a dangerous place without it? And why do you want to capture a baell'wek when you already own such a fine sha'crow?" asked the woman. "Does she not follow your commands well?"

"Sha'crow? Are you talking about Dalkeira? I don't own her. She's— we're—"

Trista was at a loss for words. She had no idea how to describe her connection with the dragon; how to say she would battle a thousand black ships if needed to free her; how she would cross the largest deserts to keep her safe, how—

"Family," said Dalkeira out loud.

The desert woman looked surprised.

"A sha'cara, then? And it speaks? With words?"

"I prefer *she,* and I do. My name is Dalkeira, and where we come from it is custom to formally introduce oneself when meeting someone new," said the dragon, repeating with attitude what Trista had once said to her during their travels.

The stranger looked Dalkeira directly in the eyes.

"My name is Aslara. I'm from the Minai tribe, and where I come from it is custom to thank the person who saves your life."

"I did not need any saving," said Dalkeira.

"Maybe not before, but you do now. That wound will call the fever upon you and you will die if not treated correctly. So here," said Aslara as she dropped a bundle of half-dried grass at Trista's feet. "Grind that between two rocks with a tiny amount of water and apply the paste to the wound. If she's careful and keeps it on there for at least a day, she should be fine."

"Thank you. My name is Trista, by the way."

"And I'm Decan. I did need saving, so thank you," said Decan, who had just gone to get the baby.

Aslara gave a short nod and brief smile.

"And who is this? How did she end up all the way out here in the Endless Sands?" asked Aslara, gesturing to the child.

"She hasn't got a name yet," said Decan.

"We found her just before we entered the desert. In the arms of her dead mother," said Trista.

"How long has it been? What do you feed her?" said Aslara as she unwrapped and examined the malnourished child.

The small baby had lost every ounce of fat she had. Her eyes had not opened much in the last few days, as she hung on to life mainly by just breathing. Trista had tried not to think about it too much, but she knew the child was withering away right in front of their eyes and there had been little they could do about it. It brought a lump to her throat.

"Chewed meat and water. It's all we have—or had."

Overwhelmed, Trista let her head hang and her tears flow. She was unable to hold it back any longer; that fear of inadequateness she tried to hide in front of Decan and Dalkeira. She had spent all her energy just to keep going, but it had not nearly felt enough. Her little brother silently approached her and put his arms around her. A moment later, the light touch of Dalkeira's head rested on her shoulder as well.

"You did great, sis. You brought us all the way here. We would never have made it this far without you," said Decan softly.

For a while, Trista could not move. As she cried, the strong hug from her two most precious things in the world slowly filled her with energy again. She finally looked up when the sound of rummaging reached her ears. She dried her tears.

"What are you doing?" she said to Aslara, who was going through one of the small travel bags around her waist.

"The child isn't beyond saving. I have some herbs and goat's milk with me that she can drink. Hopefully that and the water will be enough until we get back to the village," said Aslara.

"A village? Is it far?" asked Decan, clearly unsure how far his legs could carry him.

"A three-day walk on foot, but the Endless Sands will end before that. You should all rest and gain your strength. Eat and drink. We leave before the sun fully sets."

Decan groaned when he heard the distance. Three days—it might as well have been three months. Each step already needed every ounce of perseverance. Trista, too, doubted if she would be able to last that long.

"I'm sorry, but we don't have any food left," said Trista, unable to think past this first obstacle in her mind.

"Don't worry about that."

Their savior put her fingers to her lips and produced a long, high-pitched whistle. A moment later Trista heard fast-approaching hooves. An animal dashed round the corner at great speed.

It was not as mystical as a dragon, but it was unlike anything Trista had ever seen. It resembled a deer, an animal one of the merchants visiting their island had shown Trista a drawing of the previous summer. She remembered how majestic and proud it looked in the drawing—a characteristic this creature seemed to share.

But there were differences. This animal was more muscular than the lean body she had seen in the drawing. The chest and neck especially reminded her more of the mountain goats that roamed the island in groups. Its legs looked strong, despite the fact they were long and stretched, making the animal almost as high on its legs as a small horse. The flat, wide-spread hooves seemed to have little trouble walking across the loose sand, barely sinking into it with each step. It had two long, slightly curved, sturdy horns on the top of its head; in front of each, two smaller horns were present. The face had a beautiful pattern of stripes running across the nose.

The animal approached Aslara and slowed to a stop. It snorted briefly at the sight of Dalkeira, but gave no indication of fear. A simple harness sat around the animal's head, but there was no saddle present. Some bags and other items were tied to the side of the mount, who calmly stood waiting as Aslara greeted it with a few light scratches to the neck and behind the ears.

"Good girl."

The woman inspected the gear hanging from the animal.

"Ah, *there* you are."

She grabbed a smaller water bag from the creature's side. She opened it and sprinkled a few dried herbs into the bag before allowing the baby to slowly sip from the goat's milk mixture inside.

"Just as well. I don't think the milk would've stayed fresh for much longer," said Aslara. "What's the matter? You all look like you've never seen a desert tibu—"

She was confronted with three pairs of eyes staring back at her.

"You don't know what fevergrass is, you've never seen a desert tibu. Where did you all come from?"

It was hard for Trista to focus her thoughts; her head was still fuzzy from the heat and events.

"Beyond the sand. Beyond the water before that. The world has been falling apart around us. We had nowhere else to go," said Trista.

"Beyond the Endless Sands? Nothing comes from there. How long have you been walking?"

"Too long. I lost track. Nine, ten days?" said Trista.

"Ten days through the Endless Sands? On foot?" exclaimed Aslara in disbelief. "You're lucky to stay alive for that long without a pack animal."

The tall, confident woman carefully gave the baby back to Decan and passed him the milk bag as well. She gently scratched the desert tibu on its nose and grabbed the reins.

"I wouldn't dare travel this way alone," said Aslara as she brought her face to the tibu's cheek. "Come, follow me."

She led them through a number of passageways leading deeper into the city.

"Let's get you out of the sun. I'll see if I can fix something to eat for everyone."

Aslara made sure all of them were comfortable inside one of the buildings before she disappeared out of one of the windows again. The shade offered protection from the relentless sun; the small windows and high ceilings were clearly designed to keep the inside of a building as cool as possible.

Decan stared around them as he gently fed more milk to the child in his arms.

"I wonder what kind of people once lived here in such a place."

Trista did not react. She tried to get a feel for the events that had just happened, but now that the danger had passed, it was hard to concentrate on anything. Her head spun from exhaustion. Her body just wanted to sleep, drink and eat, preferably all at the same time. Instead, she forced herself to grind the stringy plants Aslara had tossed to her between two small stones she found, so she could apply the paste to Dalkeira's wound.

"We are just going to trust her?" said Dalkeira, as the blue dragon sniffed the crushed herbs. "What if they do more harm than good?"

Tired, Trista looked up at the dragon. Dalkeira looked healthier now. She had begun to recuperate after drinking the water and grabbing a few bites from the feathered lizards she killed. Right now, Dalkeira was the most alert of them all.

"Why not? She saved us, didn't she? Nobody forced her to do so," said Decan.

"Maybe she is just waiting for a better time, when I am not around," said Dalkeira. "Did you notice she constantly stares at your hair?"

Trista moved over to apply the paste.

"I hadn't," said Trista, too tired to argue.

"Why would she do that?" said the dragon. "I do not trust her at all."

"Perhaps my red hair is just as uncommon here as it was at home," said Trista. "Are you sure you're not just insulted she thought you were my pet?"

Dalkeira snorted.

"Do not be silly. I could not care less what she thinks. And anyone who believes they can keep me as a pet will have a very unpleasant surprise in their very near future."

Trista showed a tired smile.

"All done."

Dalkeira swung her head around and reviewed Trista's work. Apparently satisfied that at least the wound looked properly dressed, she rose to her feet.

"I will go and see what she is doing," said the dragon.

But before Dalkeira could exit the building, two feet landed softly in the sand as Aslara returned. She dropped two medium-sized baell'weks in the sand. Each had a puncture wound from a spear straight through the heart. Aslara put down a full water bag. She went back outside, but almost immediately returned, carrying a smaller package wrapped in leather and a crudely made stone bowl.

"One is for us to eat. The other is for your sha'cara," said Aslara, gesturing to the lizards in the sand.

She put the bowl firmly in the sand.

"You know how to use that knife?"

Aslara pointed at the knife Trista wore on her hip.

"Cut off the heads and make sure you do not cut yourself on their teeth. Gut and clean the one we'll eat."

The request brought back the unpleasant memory of killing the horse just a few days before. Reluctantly, Trista moved over to their intended dinner, while Aslara put a small piece of hard, brown material into the bowl.

"What about the skin?" said Trista.

"Pluck the feathers. The rest will burn off in the fire."

Trista was confused. There was no wood to make a fire with. She wondered how they were going to roast anything. Beside her, Aslara carefully poured some water in the stone bowl, leaving the tip of the brown material just above water. From a small bag on her side she produced a small white crystal, which she held in the sunlight shining through the small window.

"What are you doing?" asked Decan.

"You'll see," said Aslara.

She moved the crystal around until a dot of light focused on the tiny tip above the water. Within moments the tip of the brown material started to smoke. Aslara carefully blew on it. Suddenly, a tiny flame jumped into existence. Even stranger, the water burned as well.

"How is that possible?" said Decan.

"See this?" said Aslara, pointing at the clump of brown in the bowl. "The water soaks it up. It's not actually the water that burns, but the oil floating on top of the water."

Outside, the sun passed its highest point. Trista saw the heat radiate in front of the windows. She was happy to be eating in the comfort of real shade for the first time in weeks. The lizard tasted surprisingly good once Trista got over the smell of burned feathers. And while Dalkeira had first turned down the offered food, she knew better than to waste it in the current stream of events.

The dragon was now quietly snoring in a corner, though she never seemed to be sleeping very deeply; Trista noticed one of Dalkeira's eyes open every now and then.

"How were you able to get the water and food? Don't tell me you went back into that hole," said Trista as they neared the end of their meal.

"The baell'weks can be found throughout the entire ruined city. Many sleep for days on end, some even for a full moon cycle, only waking to eat. The tiny ones eat plants. There's a few water sources in the maze of rooms where sunlight reaches as well. It allows the crawling plant to grow in the waste of the lizards. But the population has become unbalanced," said Aslara. "The ground shakes, shifting the sand. The sunlight disappears, or the underground water. They're forced to move into one another's territory. The weak get eaten; the strong get bigger."

"Bigger than the one that almost got us?" said Decan.

"Sometimes. There's stories in our tribe of a baell'wek the size of five fully grown men—they call him 'Laeri Baell'wek', the Ancestor. Some say he's a deity, protector of them all, but the stories are as ancient as the creature. No one alive now has ever seen it."

"Thank the goddess," murmured Decan, relieved.

"Aslara, why are you doing this? Helping us?" asked Trista. She carefully gave the baby some more goat's milk, relieved to see the child took a liking to it right away. The tiny human ate much more from the milk than she ever did with the chewed meat.

"You looked like you were in trouble."

"But you know nothing about us."

"That should not prevent one from helping those in need of help," said Aslara.

"You're right. It's just that we haven't come across many people lately who did not mean us harm."

"Would you care to tell me what happened?" said Aslara.

Trista started talking; about the journey, and the sacrifices they had been forced to make. From the beginning—losing their parents, the soldiers and black ships—to the days at sea and how the goddess had guided them to the main continent. Aslara was visibly fascinated when Trista mentioned the ocean—water as far as the eye could see.

"And you can't drink any of it?" asked Aslara, surprised.

"No. There are fish in there you can eat, but the water will just make you thirstier."

"That makes it even more cruel than the Endless Sands."

Trista continued her story, telling Aslara about the bodies of those who had not made it. About the man who had sent them into the desert, and how they had encountered the child, alone in her dead mother's arms. The words flowed out of Trista's mouth like an unstoppable river. It felt good to finally talk about the horrible things they had encountered; to share them with this person she barely knew. Perhaps this way, she would be able to let go of some of the misery she had inside.

After the story, Aslara looked at Trista and the others, and smiled. It was a smile that gave Trista the feeling of being completely understood. No additional words were needed, nor could Trista utter them if she wished. She was overcome with exhaustion again. Reliving their journey had drained her of what little energy the food had given her.

"Well, Trista of the Waterclans, I'm happy my instincts were right. When I saw your reaction, it was sharp and fierce, but you never took the first step to attack. You were just being cautious," said Aslara with another smile. "Thulai helped as well. She has an excellent sense for spotting bad people and she wasn't bothered by you lot at all."

"Thulai? Who's that? Doesn't she want to come in and eat as well?" asked Decan, who had been exceptionally quiet during the story.

Aslara laughed.

"No. Her hooves aren't really made for window climbing, though mountains and deserts aren't a problem."

"Hooves? Oh!" exclaimed Decan, his face turning red as he realized Aslara had meant the desert tibu outside.

Trista looked up and met the Minai woman's eyes. They made her feel lighter, her energy somewhat rekindled. The corners of her mouth curled into a smile. Seeing Decan's reaction, she broke into a laugh.

Aslara smiled. "Good. It's good to hear you laugh."

Aslara climbed up into the window frame again. There, she turned to look back.

"And speaking of her, I'll need to tend to Thulai for a bit. I suggest you all get some sleep. We leave before sundown. I don't want to be caught here after dark."

The afternoon sun made Aslara's dark hair shine and her skin glow. Trista was struck by the strange beauty in front of her, one she had not seen—or noticed—in a long time. The desert woman was not just strong and lean; as Trista looked deeper, past the exterior, she saw an inner strength and confidence that naturally flowed from their new friend. The woman's certainty in being was enticing.

Trista's head lightly buzzed. Her fatigue caught up with her again, pushing away the spark of energy she had just felt. Her eyelids grew heavier with every passing moment.

"Why's that?" she said, rubbing one eye as she lay down.

"Because those bigger baell'weks that *do* wake from their slumber? They hunt at night."

CHAPTER TWENTY-ONE

Bitten

W*HAT DO YOU want me to say? I don't think we have any other options,"* said Trista.

They were walking through sand-covered alleyways and narrow streets at roof level of the old, crumbling buildings. Most signs of civilization had long been washed away by the waves of sand moving through the city over the decades. Just smoothened stone remained, defying the never-ending grind of tiny grains of sand.

Aslara had woken them a short while ago. The sun was barely visible above the highest walls that still stuck out of the sand; it was time to leave.

Without delay, Dalkeira started up another private conversation with Trista about her distrust of Aslara.

"Look, I know you have not met many people that weren't trying to kill us, but the world normally isn't like that. She's not one of those soldiers," added Trista.

"That might well be. And I agree if she wanted us dead she had every chance to try, or would simply have left us in the pit. But still, something is off. The way she looks at you, and me when she thinks I am sleeping. I cannot figure out what goes on behind those dark eyes. There is something she is not telling us."

Dalkeira snorted. She would be happy to leave all this sand behind soon, Trista knew. The rest and food had done all of them well, but even the dragon must feel her muscles ache from the long days filled with walking and their narrow escape the day before. Decan had offered to carry the baby girl for the first part, but Aslara said he and the child should sit on Thulai's back when they got out of the city. The strong desert tibu could have carried more of them had there not been any other luggage, but Aslara had no intention of going into the desert without provisions.

The words reminded Trista of their own inexperience with traveling. Now that she had a moment to recover and gain some energy from a good meal and available water, her thoughts were much clearer. In fact, she had not felt so clearheaded in a long time. There was indeed something about Aslara, but Trista did not sense it in a negative way. The woman's strength and direct way of approaching things left quite an impression on her.

Walking through the sunken city, Trista heard soft scratches and hisses coming from inside the buildings. From the corner of her eye, she noticed several lizards quickly shot away as their small group passed the final few yards to the outer wall. They cleared the outskirts of the city and walked out into the desert. The last rays of sunlight disappeared from the sky in front of them as the sun gave way to the moon. Behind them, the ruined city sprang alive with the ghostly hisses of hundreds of lizards emerging from underground. Chills ran down Trista's spine at the idea of being stuck there at night.

"I think she means well. She saved Decan and the child. And she has such a gentle creature with her. I mean, I've never seen an animal listen so well to a human. There's not a shred of fear in that animal toward her master, just complete trust. It's impressive," Trista continued.

She shocked herself by speaking her mind so bluntly. She had not intended to take a stab at Dalkeira like that. She had not expected to feel jealousy. But clearly she was sad, somewhere deep inside, that the bond between her and Dalkeira—although strong—was not on such a refined level.

"Let's keep our eyes and ears open for now and see if she can lead us out of the desert like she said," added Trista quickly in the hope that Dalkeira did not notice the previous remark.

The dragon gave no reply. Trista looked behind her and saw that Dalkeira had stopped. She was looking back toward the city.

"What is it?" asked Trista.

Dalkeira turned toward her and started moving again. She did the dragon's equivalent of shrugging her shoulders.

"It is nothing. I thought I saw something move along the city walls," said Dalkeira. *"But I guess it was nothing."*

Trista looked back, and indeed saw nothing except the tower and walls of a half-sunken city in the sand. Dalkeira took a few leaps and launched herself into the air. The push of air flowed past Trista as Dalkeira beat her wings to gain height.

"Where are you going?" called Trista after her.

"Like you said, to keep an eye on things—from above."

Trista sighed. She quickly picked up the pace to catch up to her other traveling companions. Their little group disappeared over the top of the dunes as the nightly survival of the baell'wek began. The sand at the base of the ancient wall softly vibrated before it slowly rose to form a large hump. It slid along the length of the wall, calmly scraping along the stones of the old city. A deep rumble came from underground, triggering an orchestra of hissing protests from the city's smaller nightly inhabitants.

Tears welled in Trista's eyes. Relief flowed over her like a mother's embrace, taking away any discomfort from her feet and muscles, if only for a moment. Their first night had gone by quickly as they followed Aslara through the desert. Decan and the child had mostly traveled on Thulai's back. It had been a silent trip; none of them saying much, preserving their energy for the journey. Trista felt the continuing tension of Dalkeira's distrust toward Aslara as the night went by. But when the first rays of sunlight announced the morning's break, Trista found herself reaching the top of a sand dune, together with Dalkeira, to be greeted by her brother's shouting.

"Triss, look. We made it! We really made it!"

And there it was. Completely unannounced, the desert ended. Trista took a deep breath as her eyes filled up from happiness. The doubt of the last few weeks slid from her heavy shoulders. She really thought they would not make it. That they would end up like the soldier and his horse, buried beneath the sand far away from the waters she loved. She looked at Aslara, who calmly kept walking. It seemed the goddess was still looking out for them, offering them guidance when they needed it most.

The landscape itself changed unusually abruptly. It was as if an invisible barrier held back the loose sand, as Trista saw a sharp line where the desert bordered on a dry-looking, but life-supporting, landscape. Low shrubbery could be seen here and there, thin little twigs with sharp thorns trying to protect the small, dry leaves between them from any passing herbivores. Their surroundings changed color, from the fine yellow-white of the sand dunes to a darker red earth crust that stretched for miles on end.

There were no hills once they left the desert dunes behind. And while, for the first part of the day, the red earth showed mostly empty—apart from those out-of-place-looking thorny plants here and there—the ground was littered with rocks, large and small. Walking became a lot less tiring with such a hard surface beneath their feet.

"Step on the rocks or go around, but don't put your foot over them to where you can't see," advised Aslara. "Snakes and other creatures might use them for shade and can strike at you if startled."

The scorching heat of the desert was replaced by a slightly more bearable dry hotness, but as the sun rose and their road continued, it became clear they still needed to find some shade and rest. Aslara pointed to a strange shape on the horizon.

"That's where we're going," she said.

Small patches of dry grass started to fill up the landscape. First around the edges of stones, then later larger patches firmly defending their place in the landscape all by themselves. Small trees greeted them here and there with minuscule, feather-like leaves. At dawn, Trista spotted some tiny animals. A desert mouse, small lizards and strange-looking beetles; even the occasional bird. Aslara speared a snake that slithered by. It was not big, but it was dinner nonetheless.

Dalkeira approached a small tree, barren of leaves, its branches twisting and turning. She sniffed at the strange waterdrop-shaped nests that hung from the branches.

"It is like an entire colony, but no one is home," remarked the dragon.

As their guide, Aslara displayed her knowledge of the land. They followed tracks of long-gone animals and dried up streams. They even passed several empty waterholes. All the while, Aslara kept them on track, even when their destination disappeared behind the increasingly taller withered shrubbery. When they finally arrived, the strange shape turned out to be a tree, though tree was too simple a word. The giant stood high above the plains, a rounded trunk with wide horizontal branches at the very top. The trunk looked like a puffer fish about to burst, it's bark smooth like oiled leather. Instead of branches, large, sharp thorns covered the trunk from the bottom up, some of which were so large one could easily use them to climb all the way to the top. Snaking down the tree were several dried-up vines that carried old, wrinkled, dark red fruits.

"We'll stop here for a while. We can eat and rest, and then continue when night sets in," said Aslara.

After Decan and the child had dismounted, Aslara relieved the desert tibu of her pack harness and reins. She let the animal wander off to find some dry shrubbery to eat.

"How's she doing?" Trista asked her little brother, pointing at the baby.

"Better. She slept most of the night. Just woke up again. Looks like she's hungry."

"I can take her for a while if you want to rest," said Trista.

Decan thankfully handed over the child and immediately lay his head down in the shade of the tree. Trista spent some time feeding the baby. They were back to chewing meat again for her, at least until they could reach the village Aslara spoke of. They still had plenty of water to drink, though Aslara urged them to ration wisely. Dalkeira had been offered a full bag of water, which seemed to be enough for her to keep going and counter the dangers of dehydration.

Trista saw Dalkeira sitting quietly on the edge of the shade. She seemed mesmerized by the large tree in front of her, softly swaying her head in and out the sun. Trista thought she heard the dragon hum a soft melody that trickled into her mind. When eventually the baby fell asleep again, Trista was about to mentally reach out to Dalkeira when Aslara joined her and offered her lunch.

"She's something else, your sha'cara," said Aslara, nodding toward the dragon.

Trista looked at the dark-eyed woman, unsure what the remark meant.

"Why do you say that?"

"She feels it. The life inside the Taori," answered Aslara.

"Taori? What life?" said Trista.

Aslara smiled gently.

"Taori is a guardian of life," she said, pointing at the tree. "Some call them the Thorned Pillars of Life. They're worshipped amongst my people as protectors of all that is born and dies."

That puzzled Trista. She regarded the dried-up tree in front of her.

"Pillar of Life? I don't understand. I don't mean to offend, but it doesn't even have any leaves to provide us with shade," said Trista. "All I see is a dried-up trunk and those shriveled-up red pods. How can you call that life?"

"There's more to it than you can see. Your sha'cara does. But perhaps I shouldn't be surprised, for I'm certain she's a true-to-life winged ancient."

Trista let the remark slide as she walked over to the tree to get a closer look. One of the vines hung in front of her all the way to the ground. Trista almost expected it to go straight into the ground, as if it was a long-stretched root from a plant up high. Some of the plants that grew on the cliffs at home had similar roots. They curled along the rocks, searching for small bits of earth to settle in.

Just above her hung a dark red pod. Now that Trista was closer, she saw it was not actually as hard as she thought it would be. She stood on her toes and carefully reached for it.

"More to it than you can see," she mumbled to herself.

She looked behind her as she stretched her arm upward.

"Does that mean you can eat these?" she asked.

"No! Stop," answered Aslara. "The blood fruits are forbidden. They poison those foolish enough to try them!"

"Blood fruit? That doesn't sound tasty at all," said Trista, quickly lowering her hand.

"It does not? It sounds like something that could taste like meat, or perhaps even like one of those larger fish," said Dalkeira's voice inside her mind.

Trista looked at the dragon, but apparently the remark had been thoughtlessly made, as Dalkeira continued observing the tree with great interest.

"It's like she sees the life flowing inside," said Aslara, who followed Trista's gaze. Seeing Trista's reaction, she pointed up to the sky. "Life that slowly feeds the area around it as the waters stay up there. Without the Taori, the desert would reclaim the red earth until nothing was left. Their legs stretch out many times beyond that of their own need.

"Legs? You mean the roots? In the ground?" Trista wondered.

Aslara gave a small nod.

"The reach of their legs allows the surrounding plants to use the Taori's water in times of drought."

"Rain! That's what you mean by 'life'," said Trista, finally understanding. "Of course. Water, the source of life. It's the touch of the goddess. But does it really rain here at all? I haven't seen a drop of water fall from the sky since we reached the coast."

"It will. The time is near. The Taori know it, and I think your sha'cara feels it, too."

"Okay, stop. *Why* do you insist on calling her sha'cara—or 'winged ancient', for that matter—when I told you her name is Dalkeira? It's very rude," said Trista.

Aslara laughed.

"I apologize. I don't mean to be rude. Sha'cara isn't her name. It's what she *is*. The one that guides you. She connects you to the realm of… this," she explained with a sweeping gesture. "Plants, sand, animals. Your companion as well as your counterpart. The First Mother was said to have met such a sha'cara. A special one; a winged ancient. They met under the Thorned Pillar of Life at a time when they were being chased and hunted. You should consider yourself very lucky to have received such a guide."

Trista looked at Dalkeira, who now lay curled up with head under wing . The smallest of tingles flowed inside her body and mind. It had been a while since she felt it. And now she did, the feeling was less strong than she remembered. Had she been too preoccupied with doubt and worries to let the presence of their bond come to the surface? Or was something else going on?

"I can see the bond you have, but I would ask if all is right. Even now, your face shows you're not sure. The journey? Has it sown doubt?" said Aslara, as if she had read Trista's mind.

"Doubt? She's never said anything about doubt," said Trista, troubled.

"Maybe it isn't her doubt."

Trista did not have an immediate answer. Aslara left her with her thoughts, using the remaining time they had to rest. Trista tried to get some sleep as well, but Aslara's words kept running in her head. The heat did little to help her fall asleep. She felt weak, sweaty and filthy. She wished she had been able to bathe in the ruined city's water basin, like Dalkeira had done. Feel the cool water on her skin, as if she was back in the ocean.

When she eventually fell asleep, Trista's old dreams returned. The heat transformed to fire, surrounding her without escape. She searched for a way out and remembered the water. She looked up into the sky, darkened by smoke, wishing, begging for the cold water to descend. But it did not come; not a drop. Dalkeira's voice never spoke. The fire crawled closer and closer until she started to feel her skin burning. Then the fire rushed toward her and engulfed her whole.

Startled, Trista opened her eyes, her skin wet from sweat. Seeing the strange tree towering over her, she lay back on the ground. Sighing heavily, she closed her eyes, trying to catch some more sleep, knowing full well it was not going to happen.

During the following days, Aslara continuously led them northwest. The dry vegetation increased, but rarely did it grow far above Trista's head. The sporadic trees all seemed wrinkled and knotted, the bare branches waving gently in the wind. They encountered five other Pillars of Life, each larger and older than the previous one. Aslara poured a little bit of water at the feet of each huge tree, mumbling a few gentle words. When Trista asked her what she was doing, their guide explained that she wished to ask for permission to cross the land, to express her intent to do no harm beyond the need to survive. It reminded Trista a lot of the way her own people were taught to live in unison with the ocean.

At the end of the second day, dark clouds formed on the horizon. With the flat landscape, they could see the clouds coming from miles away. The temperature lowered slightly at first as the sun disappeared behind the dark layer in the angry-looking sky. But it soon felt like the clouds pressed all the heat together, making the air hot and clammy.

Trista longed to feel the raindrops fall on her face, but as the world darkened, still no water came forth. Instead, lightning crackled amongst the clouds creating a complicated show of illumination, while loud bangs of thunder rumbled over their heads, as if some angry animal was growling at them from above.

Dalkeira was fascinated by the display of power. To her, the entire sky seemed to flow like the ocean, the constant movement of waves set ablaze by the sharp lines of lightning. It carried on through the evening without so much as a drop reaching the red earth. When it eventually cleared up, the stars had filled the sky and the baby was finally able to fall back asleep now that the thunder stopped.

Apart from when the storm passed over, Dalkeira spent most of her time in the air, only coming down to rest her wings and sleep, or enjoy a small meal and some water. It was clear the dragon did not approve much of their current company, but Trista could not figure out what Dalkeira found so unnerving about their guide. Aslara seemed calm and decisive in her ways. She had answered all questions Trista asked up till now and none of the answers had sounded suspicious or loaded with secrecy.

The village they were headed for was on the edge of a small mountain range they could now see in the distance. They would be able to rest there for as long as they liked and regain their strength. Aslara said they would be expected to earn their keep as soon as they were capable, just like everybody else, which to Trista seemed like a natural, and logical, thing to expect in such a difficult and harsh environment.

The desert tibu was rarely far from Aslara's side. The animal seemed to have plenty of stamina, able to survive on the barely edible vegetation that crossed their path. Trista had seen it use its horns to unearth the roots of small plants, though it usually ate the dry bark of twigs and yellow grass as a main source of food.

"It's remarkable how easily she returns to your side every time. Doesn't she ever wander off?" said Trista after the animal had rejoined them once again.

"She's a good friend. She wouldn't just leave us here."

"Is she yours? I mean, your sha'cara?" said Trista.

"No," Aslara answered with a smile. "She's a sha'crow. A helper or supporter."

"Sha'crow? You mentioned that before, when you first saw Dalkeira. What's the difference?"

"One can have many sha'crow. Our people learn to train them from a very young age. But you'll only have one sha'cara in your life. That sha'cara chooses you," Aslara explained calmly. "While it's true that some sha'crow offer themselves on special occasions, more often they're captured and trained."

"And these animals never leave? Escape?"

"Some do, but that's usually when the training is still underway. Some species more than others," said Aslara.

"Was that the reason you were at the ruined city? To capture one of those, uh, lizards?"

"Baell'wek. And sort of. Or at least I thought I was, until I saw you."

"What do you mean?" said Trista.

"I think I was meant to save you. Why? I'm not sure yet, but I hope things will become clear when we reach the village."

It was the first time Trista noticed Aslara did not give a straight answer.

"*I told you. She is hiding something,*" Dalkeira said later when Trista mentioned it to her.

"*Maybe,*" said Trista privately, right before Dalkeira took off again.

* * *

The extra flying was doing Dalkeira good. Her flying muscles were building up a lot quicker now, even with the limited amount of food she was getting. The downside was that she was still constantly hungry, but after surviving the desert she deemed it a minor inconvenience. She had become more practiced in finding the hot air streams going upward, allowing her to stay in flight longer without using too much energy. Her skill in turns and other aerial movements seemed to increase as well.

The small rudder wings near Dalkeira's shoulders were now actively involved with flying as well, allowing the dragon to make tiny adjustments while the larger wings remained motionless gliding through the air.

Dalkeira's bird's-eye view gave her excellent oversight of their surroundings. In the distance, she saw several of the Pillar of Life trees spread across the landscape. If she concentrated, she could even make out the roots breaking through the surface here and there. Some of them literally ran for miles in every direction, connecting with the roots of other trees far away.

She was still amazed every time they passed one of the large trees. Her eyes could not actually see the water inside them, but she sensed it, running in tiny streams in the trunk, down into the ground along the roots.

Below her, Trista and the others were crossing a dried-up riverbed and decided to follow it. The deep red groove ran across the land from the mountains in the northwest all the way toward them. The mountains, or rather mountain from the looks of it, reminded Dalkeira of the island's cliffs, its shape not running into a pointy tip, but more as if someone had pushed part of the land straight up, forming a raised plateau. She tried to spot the village at the base or on top of the strangely shaped mountain, but did not see anything of the kind.

The shrubbery on both sides of the riverbed was now higher than before, providing cover for any larger species that might come roaming the lands in search of water. But rarely did Dalkeira spot any large animals traveling the red earth beneath her; only smaller ones that could live off the morning dew that formed on the vegetation during the cold nights.

Once, she spotted a half-decayed carcass with a very long neck, too decomposed to eat. She had seen two striped donkeys off in the distance, but she lost track of them as their own little group moved in the other direction. Several times, Dalkeira was passed by birds in the air, large and small, none of which seemed bothered by the larger flying dragon. But that was about it. It was strange to see so few animals in comparison to the space available. The biggest groups she saw were only two or three animals strong, most of which had horns similar to the desert tibu, but more curved.

Those animals Dalkeira did see were either too large to kill, or too small to be bothered with. She would have liked to try and hunt one of those strange donkeys, but it would not be a quick hunt and she did not want to leave Trista alone with Aslara for too long just in case she was right about the strange desert woman. In the meantime, her hunger had slowly increased again since her last meal.

Then, as the group below her continued their path through the dry riverbed, Dalkeira's eyes caught a flash of brown and white. The movement amongst the high shrubbery piqued her interest by being just the right size to hunt. She banked toward the spot where she had seen something move, increasing her speed to get in front of Trista and the others down below. A tiny group of three animals carefully walked amongst the bushes, nibbling on the branches. They were like miniaturized versions of the desert tibu—perhaps a related species. Their bodies were much smaller, small enough to allow a quick and clean kill. And they only had one small set of horns on their head, which Dalkeira expected would pose little threat to her scales.

She turned her head to check on the siblings then decided to get herself a swift meal. She bent into a low dive. Almost instantly, one of the animals raised its head and let out a high-pitched call. Dalkeira opened her wings and leveled off, ready to throw her claws forward. By now the animals had broken out into a run amongst the shrubbery. Dalkeira quickly closed the gap between them with the speed of her dive, and threw out her hind legs to pounce on the nearest of the three runners. Had she been bigger, Dalkeira would simply have picked the animal up with her front legs, but for now she needed the power of her hind legs to take it down.

But just when Dalkeira thought she was successful, the small animal leaped straight into the air, dodging its attacker. All three animals started bouncing all over the place, changing directions so quickly Dalkeira's wide turns could not keep up. Their thin legs acted as springs, almost instantly launching into the air again as soon as their little hooves touched the ground. The dragon attempted several more times, but the animals' speed and agility made them impossible to catch.

After the fifth failed attempt, Dalkeira found herself on the ground, breathing heavily from the effort she had put in. As the last of the jumping animals disappeared into the shrubs, she looked up at the sun and reluctantly took back to the air. With every foot of altitude gained, her level of annoyance and frustration increased as well.

"Had any luck?"

It was Trista's voice in her head.

"I do not like this land very much. There is not enough water and the animals are not behaving as they should," said Dalkeira. *"I wish it would rain. I barely see a sparkle of water in the air."*

"Don't give up too fast. You haven't really hunted in a while. I'm sure you'll have more success next time."

Dalkeira rejoined the group on the ground and took up position beside Trista.

"I am tired. Are we getting close?"

"Aslara said it isn't much further. We're to visit one more of those life trees and spend the night there. She said the village is about half a day's travel from there on out."

Dalkeira did not mind visiting another of those trees. She felt relaxed when she was close to them. Her dreams were always pleasant when near them, as if the trees helped clear her mind. She dreamed of beautiful songs carried across the red plains.

When they arrived at the Pillar of Life, Aslara took her time to do her ritual of gratitude. Afterward, she made a small fire at a safe distance from the large tree. Instead of hunting, she dug up a tightly-tied package buried at the base of the tree. It was filled with thick roots and herbs and a pot containing a full water bag.

Aslara spent some time cutting the roots into smaller pieces and adding them to the water in the pot. As she cooked it over the fire, it became a strong-smelling soup to which Aslara patiently added the herbs, one after another.

Dalkeira retreated to a place close to the tree when it became clear no meat would be served today. Aslara had offered part of the soup to her, but the dragon had refused, doubting it would taste good. She lay quietly with her head under her wing, pretending to sleep while the others ate.

* * *

The soup had an excellent strong taste, slightly on the salty side. It was a welcome change in flavor after eating almost nothing but meat for weeks. The baby also seemed pleased with the taste, allowing Trista to get a good deal of water inside her as well. Trista was happy the little child had been able to withstand all the hardships they encountered. Tomorrow they would reach the village where she hoped the child would be safe.

"What will happen to her tomorrow?" asked Decan, who had been thinking along similar lines.

"I guess she will stay in the village."

"We're not going to take her with us when we leave? Or will we stay there as well?"

Decan had grown attached to the little dark girl, especially after all the times the small child had brightened their days—if only for a bit—with her giggles.

Trista knew how he felt. While they had only traveled together for a short time, to be responsible for something so innocent and helpless… it had made them care deeply for the child.

"I don't know. First, we need to rest. It does not look like there are any soldiers here or else Aslara would have mentioned them, so perhaps we should stay. But Dalkeira still wants to go further west. If we do, we've got no idea what we might run into on the road."

Decan looked at her with disappointment on his face.

"I understand how you feel, but we can't take her with us. She needs to be somewhere safe, don't you think? We need to think of what's best for her."

Decan thought about that for a moment and gave a reluctant nod.

When they had eaten and Decan was fast asleep together with the baby, Trista tried to gather her thoughts and think of the way forward.

If everything looks good, perhaps he should stay behind as well.

She watched her little brother sleep. She did not like the idea much, but it was probably the safest thing to do.

While Aslara quietly tended to the desert tibu, Dalkeira joined Trista, whose gaze was turned to the south. In the distance, another storm flashed and rumbled as large, dark clouds traveled the skies.

"Couldn't sleep yet?"

Dalkeira shook her head.

"I wish it would rain," Dalkeira said quietly, looking longingly at the distant clouds.

"Me too."

They sat in silence for a while, each lost in their own thoughts. When Trista looked to the side, she saw Dalkeira looking back at her.

"*What?*" asked Trista privately.

For a moment, it looked like Dalkeira was about to say something, but hesitated.

"*Nothing. Never mind,*" said the dragon, after which she got up and walked back to the tree to try and sleep again.

Trista watched the dragon, wondering what Dalkeira had wanted to say. A thin sliver of doubt trickled into her subconscious as the dragon lay back down. Trista could not help but wonder if Dalkeira was thinking about the connection between them. It felt off ever since they left the buried city. Perhaps even before that.

Her thoughts once again returned to her little brother. Perhaps they should both stay at the village if they were welcome… and let Dalkeira go on by herself. After all, the dragon would be able to travel much faster without them and follow her journey to the west. After some pondering, she gave up with a sigh. She would not be able to make such a choice quickly, or easily. She followed Dalkeira's example and lay back to get some much-needed sleep.

The next morning, Trista was woken by Aslara softly shaking her shoulder. Feeling reasonably rested, Trista rubbed her eyes, glad the recurring dream had not shown its face that night. Aslara said something to her, but her head was still groggy from sleep.

"What?" said Trista.

"Where's Decan?" asked Aslara again, more urgently. "I came back from a quick walk around and he was gone."

Instantly wide awake, Trista looked at the spot where Decan and the baby had been sleeping. Neither were there. She looked at Dalkeira and saw the baby lay peacefully sleeping beside her.

"Dalkeira! Wake up! Decan is gone!"

"*What? What is it?*" The dragon sounded sleepy.

"*Decan is missing. Do you know where he is?*" Trista asked, this time inside the dragon's head.

The dragon almost jumped up, noticing just in time the sleeping baby snuggled against her side. She looked up angrily.

"I do not know. She must have taken him while I was asleep," said Dalkeira, glaring at Aslara.

Trista stared at Aslara, who seemed as calm as ever, then back at the dragon.

"Don't be absurd. Why would she do that?"

"Well, she is not denying it, is she?" said Dalkeira, matching Trista's tone.

"I don't react to foolish accusations," said Aslara calmly.

"Look, I don't know what your problem is with Aslara, but you're not helping," said Trista angrily. She picked up the baby, the movement so sudden the child woke and started to cry.

"Why don't you do something useful? Take to the air and see if you can spot him!"

Frustration burned inside Trista. She did not understand why Dalkeira was being so problematic about Aslara when her brother was missing.

"What's going on? Why is the baby crying?"

Decan came running around the life tree with a dead hare in one hand and a spear in the other. Panting heavily, he looked at his sister, who stared at him in disbelief.

"Triss? What's the matter? Did something happen?" he said again.

"Where were you? Why did you leave the camp without telling anyone? I thought something had happened!"

The words burst out with such force that tears followed in their wake. Trista immediately regretted yelling at Dalkeira. She looked at the dragon, but Dalkeira wouldn't meet her eyes. The dragon was restlessly whipping her tail through the sand at the bottom of the Pillar of Life. The sand hissed behind her, but the sound was drowned out by the baby's screaming.

Trista reached out with her mind, only to encounter an unusual cold feeling as the dragon actively ignored her mental approach. Since she could think of no way to work things out with Dalkeira, Trista focused on reassuring the baby. She walked back and forth, softly rocking her. In the meantime, Decan look confused by his sister's outburst.

"I was only gone for a few moments," said Decan. "I saw this hare come by and wanted to catch it for Dalkeira. She didn't get to eat anything yesterday, you know."

Decan handed the spear back to Aslara.

"I hope you don't mind. I borrowed one of your spears. It's a bit dirty from poking it down the hole where the hare was hiding."

Decan's eyes held all the apologetic innocence of a child. Aslara examined the spear quietly.

"It seems undamaged, so no harm done. Nice catch as well," said Aslara as Decan turned around to give Dalkeira the hare.

"But Decan…"

The boy turned back.

"…don't take it again."

Aslara's face had taken on a peculiar hardness. Decan swallowed audibly and nodded.

As he dropped the hare in front of Dalkeira, Trista saw something move behind the dragon. A slender, black shape straightened up with a sharp hiss—this was not a happy snake.

The snake officially announced its presence with a vibrating rattle from its triple split tail. Immediately, Trista's little brother sprang into motion.

* * *

"A Black Rattler," warned Aslara.

"Dalkeira, look out," screamed Decan at the same time.

Decan pushed Dalkeira to the side as the dragon started to turn around toward the danger. Decan kicked up a cloud of sand and dirt to scare off the snake, but it only got more agitated.

"Decan, don't!" said Aslara, trying to get the boy to move back.

But it was too late. The black snake coiled then launched its attack at incredible speed. Four small, venomous teeth sank into Decan's lower leg with deadly precision. The boy screamed in pain, grasping his calf.

"No!" yelled Trista as the snake closed in for another attack.

CHAPTER TWENTY-TWO

Welcome

"No!"

Trista's voice rang through the air, spurring Dalkeira into action. The dragon shot forward and pinned the snake down. The venomous creature squirmed frantically as sharp dragon claws pushed it into the ground. It was at least five feet long and thick with muscle. The snake's body coiled around Dalkeira's legs, trying to fend off its attacker.

Before the rattler could turn around for a second bite, Dalkeira's head shot forward, snapping her jaws around its head. She shook the snake back and forth wildly, slamming it into the ground multiple times before she pinned it between her claws once more and ripped the head clean off.

She flung the snake's head away into the shrubbery and looked around. Satisfied the danger had passed, she leaped back to where Aslara and Trista were busy observing Decan's bite.

"This isn't good," said Aslara.

"Can we suck out the poison?" asked Trista worriedly.

"No, it will only damage the flesh more. We need to make a cut and let it bleed. It's already moving up his leg."

A small black line began to form just above the puncture wounds on Decan's leg. Dalkeira bent forward to see what they were doing, her eyes swirling with worry.

Before Trista could object, Aslara took out her knife and skillfully made two cuts along the bite. Blood swelled from the wound as she poured water on it to increase the flow. Alarmed that Decan showed no reaction to the cut, Trista put her hand on her little brother's cheek. The boy felt warm to the touch. His eyes half closed.

Aslara whistled Thulai closer. The desert tibu, who had been nibbling on some twigs further away, rushed toward them.

"He's in shock," said Aslara. "He needs to get to the village—now. The life listener might still be able to save him."

Aslara unloaded Thulai's entire pack and threw it at the base of the Pillar of Life. She grabbed Decan and hoisted him onto the desert tibu's back.

"I'll ride ahead. Leave everything and follow me toward that mountain," she said, pointing ahead. "You see where the dark shadowed rock is on the left? Head for that and I'll send someone from the village to meet you."

Aslara wasted no further time, jumping behind Decan on Thulai's back and nudging her sha'crow into a run. The animal sped off at incredible speed while Aslara held Decan as close and steady as possible. Trista saw her little brother's limp arms and head swaying back and forth as they disappeared from sight.

Dalkeira took to the air to follow them a while longer.

"They are indeed going straight for the mountain," said Dalkeira, as if she had doubted Aslara's intent. *"And with that speed they will be at the village in no time. Who knew that creature could run so fast?"*

With all the commotion, it appeared she had forgotten her anger toward Trista, at least for now. Trista herself was too busy to react, packing her belongings. She gathered Decan's things as well, constantly keeping a sharp eye on the baby in case any more uninvited guests decided to show up. Fortunately, with the little possessions they had, she quickly finished.

"Let's go!" she called, grabbing the baby and walking as quickly as possible. Above her, Dalkeira followed, flying in large circles as they slowly made their way toward the mountain.

Half the morning had passed before the argument with Dalkeira re-entered Trista's mind. She was so worried about Decan she had barely thought of anything other than her little brother. Fear gripped her throat again at the thought of losing him after coming all this way.

She looked up to where Dalkeira's dark blue silhouette circled overhead. Her wingspan was impressive, even at her moderate size. The dragon had stayed airborne all morning, apart from the occasional break to rest. Trista had assumed the dragon was keeping an eye on things from above, but now figured Dalkeira probably had little interest in talking to her after their fallout.

"I'm sorry I yelled this morning," Trista said in her mind.

She saw Dalkeira bank and go into a dive. Within an instant, the dragon landed next to her in a cloud of red dust. She looked at Trista, slightly tilting her head, her long neck stretched out toward her bonded human.

"As you should be," said Dalkeira. "It was uncalled for."

"I was afraid. About Decan. But you're right, that's not an excuse."

Trista did not know what else to say, but for now, it seemed enough. For some time, Dalkeira walked in silence with her and the baby, but it did not feel as forced anymore.

"Do you have any idea if we are getting close?" asked Dalkeira after a while.

The mountain had been creeping closer and closer as Trista tirelessly moved toward it, driven by her desire to get to Decan as fast as possible. Currently, the high, red mass of stone loomed over them as they tried to find their way through the high bushes and small, dried-up trees.

Trista sighed.

"I lost track of the rock formation Aslara pointed out some time ago. I think we must be getting close."

"Let me see if I can spot it again from the air," said Dalkeira. She took a few steps forward before pushing herself into the air with her wings.

As the dragon ascended, Trista made her way through a dense part of dry vegetation. She moved some shrubbery with her hand and stepped under the prickly branch to get past it, turning her back to protect the child in her arms from the long thorns.

"Yima kho lasjo."

Startled, Trista looked around, but the words had come out of nowhere.

The sound of scraping twigs made her spin around. Instinctively, she held the baby tight to her chest in case she needed to dodge.

A figure emerged from between the thorny bushes. Their outfit was strikingly similar to the one Aslara wore, the difference mostly being its color. Where Aslara's scarf turban had been blue, this person's attire was much more in tune with their surroundings: beige and red, to blend into the background when moving between the low and high bushes. The weapons were similar too, though more abundant. The long spear was easily identifiable as the same kind Aslara had carried.

Trista's muscles were ready to go. She shuffled backward, uncertain if she should leave. Something in the voice had made the unrecognizable words sound less than friendly. Her hand moved below the baby, her fingers slipping around her dagger. A dissatisfied murmur rose from the baby, who was still sleeping.

"I said, stop right there," said the same voice, now with words more familiar, thick with the same accent they had gotten used to from Aslara.

Trista was about to ask about their savior when a strange, growling chuckle announced the presence of a dog-like creature pushing its way through the bushes. A large torso, with an arching back sliding down to hind legs that were small in comparison to the long, heavy forelegs and paws. Its wide head was topped by large, narrow pointed ears. The pelt on its belly was short with black and brown stripes, while a spiky mane of thick, black hairs ran along the spine, stopping halfway down its back. A tail swept back and forth, its black tufted end just above the ground.

"Dalkeira, I've got company."

"Where are you? The plants are blocking my view," called Dalkeira's voice in her head, but Trista's focus was drawn toward the creature inching toward her, head held low, ears lying flat.

"You look uncommonly normal for a Karnis'h," said the voice. It was accompanied by a low growl from the bulky canine. Trista met the warrior's eyes.

Another woman.

"I mean no harm," Trista said slowly.

"Wise choice. The opposite would not go easy with my friends over there," said the woman.

Friends?

A second laughing growl introduced itself. A second creature's thick head pushed through the shrubbery on the right, its long, pointed ears flat against its head. It was only a few steps from where Trista stood.

Cautiously, Trista took a step back as the second animal moved clear of the bush, ignoring the plant's long thorns.

"Now, hold on. We're here to meet Asl—"

The sentence was cut short when Dalkeira crashed through the overhanging branches and twigs. She unfolded her wings after clearing the prickly canopy and threw her claws forward.

The dragon slammed into the closest of the two creatures. She rivaled them in size, but they still outweighed Dalkeira's slender build.

Despite the unannounced interruption, the animal was completely unfazed by the dragon's sudden appearance. The muscled animal adjusted its stance to intercept the incoming attack and, with a strong movement, threw Dalkeira past it onto the ground, reducing the results of Dalkeira's grand attack to a few minor scratches.

The dragon slammed heavily into the ground. Thankfully, she slid forward instead of rolling over her extended wings.

"Dalkeira, wait!" called Trista.

But the dragon was completely consumed by the moment. Enraged by her failed attack, she leaped back up and hissed at the two creatures that now circled her from a distance.

"You stay away from her," Dalkeira screeched.

Both creatures hesitated. Fighting another animal was one thing, but apparently they had never seen one that voiced commands like a human. The slight hesitation was quickly thrown aside at a whistle from the woman. With a chuckling growl, they moved in to attack.

Dalkeira readied herself for another jump, but had made the mistake of focusing completely on the four-legged threats. Unnoticed, the beige-dressed woman swiftly repositioned herself behind the dragon. A net sailed over Dalkeira's head and completely entangled her. Furiously, she fought against the instrument that limited her freedom, but the desert woman swiftly moved in, spear held high above her head ready to strike.

Trista's heart jumped with fright as the woman brought the weapon down. But instead of piercing the dragon, the spear was thrust into the ground with the greatest precision, pinning down both net and dragon.

Dalkeira roared. She bit at the rope, but could not easily get it between her teeth.

Before Trista had a chance to move, the desert woman pushed down the dragon's head and jabbed something behind one of her fins. Dalkeira reared up with a snarl, snapping her jaws at her attacker. Then her eyes rolled back into her head and her entire body went limp.

"What have you done? Leave her alone!" yelled Trista.

The baby in Trista's arms erupted in wails. The woman looked up in surprise.

"A child? Why would you bring a child to spy on us?"

"What? I am looking for Aslara. You're from her village, aren't you? We came with her!"

"Aslara? She's not supposed to be back for days. Have you done something to her? Stop lying, or I will set my friends on you," said the desert woman angrily.

"I'm not lying! We ran into her in the sunken city in the desert. She saved us. But my little brother was bitten by a snake near one of those big trees that way," said Trista, pointing to the southeast. "She took off on Thulai with my brother, telling me to follow as quickly as possible."

The woman rose to her feet, judging her from a distance. The lack of response made Trista's blood boil.

"You tell me what you've done to Dalkeira right now, or else I'll—I'll—" Trista took a step forward to get to the dragon's side.

Both creatures let out those strange growls and moved in ready to pounce, but the woman held up her hand, ordering them to stay put.

"Relax. Your friend's just sleeping. A simple dart dipped in a high concentrate of sleeping berries. If you behave, your creature has nothing to worry about. She'll wake up before the moon gets to its highest point," said the woman in a voice as unwavering as stone.

Carefully, Trista came closer, keeping an eye on the woman and her pets. She put her hand on Dalkeira's chest; it calmly rose and fell to her breathing. Trista looked up in anger.

"Midnight? I can't wait that long. You have to wake her up now! I need to get to the village and find my little brother."

"You must be mad with heat—or hunger, from the looks of it—if you think I'll just take you to the village because you say so," said the woman. "Even if you're not a spy or a scout, I don't know you. Your friends could be hiding somewhere, ready to follow us. There might be more of these flying lizards, waiting to kill everyone back home. I'm not taking any chances. Stick out your hands; you'll be bound and blindfolded before we go anywhere," said the woman. She took a step forward.

Trista stepped back, but instantly heard a chuckled growl behind her.

"You have got to be kidding," Trista cried. "Friends? Does it look like I'm traveling with company? Everyone is already at the village. I want to see my brother. Besides, how can I carry a baby with my hands bound and no way to see where I'm going?"

She had had about enough of all the obstacles on her road to get to Decan. Inside her was a typhoon of emotions. She was hungry, exhausted, hot, worried sick, angry and unable to pick any one of them to specifically focus on. Her thoughts were hazy at best as she sought solutions to the ever-growing problems presented to her.

"My, my. Someone has a temper, doesn't she? Fine, you can give the child to me."

"Not a chance."

"You know, I can easily let my striped friends here grab your legs and drag you there if you prefer."

Trista looked at the large creatures. One of them bared its teeth at her and let out that chuckling growl again. She pulled out her dagger, wishing she had kept the larger soldier's sword which now lay abandoned in the desert.

"They could try, but they won't get to me unharmed. Who knows; maybe I'll get lucky and stab one of their eyes out," said Trista, trying to maintain the calmness in her voice as she bluffed.

"I doubt it. You look like you're barely keeping it together as it is. It's a wonder you're able to hold that weapon—and the child—at all," said the woman, remaining unimpressed.

Trista knew she spoke the truth. She felt tired, all the way down to her bones. What little reserves she had built up were gone again. Her bluff had failed; the entire situation was headed in the wrong direction.

And if I'm dead, how can I help Dalkeira? Or see Decan again?

Trista sighed and sheathed the dagger again.

"Look, if you truly know Aslara, you must know she wouldn't invite just anyone to the village. We needed help and Aslara offered it, for which I'm eternally grateful to her. She said someone would be sent out to meet us, but we got lost getting closer to the mountain," said Trista. "I just want to know if my little brother is alright. Once he is, we'll continue our way west. We don't want any trouble."

The woman looked at her in silence for a long time. Both chuckling creatures remained perfectly still, waiting for her decision.

"You said it yourself. I'm no threat. I'm barely hanging on. I'm exhausted, too hot and thirsty. We lost our family and now the only one I have left, my little brother, is in real trouble. You have one of my dearest friends in this world captive. I promise you, I won't cause any problems," tried Trista again.

Strong eyes stared back at her, the same deep brown as Aslara's. Finally, the woman spoke.

"You're right. You don't look like much. You shouldn't be any trouble. Fine, you may come without bonds or blindfold. But know this: the moment you think about causing harm, or try anything funny like betraying my trust—the trust of the village—you'll have to answer to them," said the woman, gesturing at her two companions. "We will hunt you down before you can reach the first Taori."

Trista walked through the maze of shrubbery, the baby closely pressed against her. The netting that held the unconscious Dalkeira had been bound around the necks of the two striped creatures, which were now dragging her along through the dirt.

Trista had made a futile attempt to convince the woman to release Dalkeira, only to be met by silence. When she tried again, the woman had offered to place her and the baby in the netting as well. Trista had swallowed her words.

Both the large, striped creatures and the desert woman were walking slightly behind her. Trista felt the three pair of eyes burning into her back.

"What kind of animals are your sha'cara? What do you call them?" asked Trista, trying to build some trust between them.

"What do you know about sha'cara?"

"Nothing, apart from what Aslara explained to me. They're companions that share a strong bond with their humans, but I thought Aslara said you only have one sha'cara in your life. But you seem to have two. Unless they're sha'crows, like Thulai."

"You sure ask a lot of questions for someone in need of help," said the woman.

"Just trying to make conversation."

"Don't, and stop playing dumb. Everyone knows they're striped hyen'sta," snapped the woman. "Anyone can spot them on the plains from miles away if they care to look."

"We're not from around here. We came from beyond the Endless Sands," said Trista in an effort to be open about herself.

"Lies. No person crosses the Endless Sands. They all end up fleshless bones."

"Yeah, that's what I keep hearing, and yet here we are."

One of the striped hyen'stas let out a chuckle.

"Shut it and keep walking," commanded the woman.

Trista was unsure if she meant the hyen'sta or herself. She decided not to try her luck any further and focused on soothing the baby and making sure not to trip over the many twigs and roots.

The woman walked slowly, perhaps deliberately delaying their journey to the village. Trista fought the urge to break out into a run and find her little brother, but without knowing where to go it would be a waste of energy. So she forced herself to walk slowly and carefully while she tried to keep an eye on the two hyen'sta trailing behind her with Dalkeira in tow.

They closed in on the base of the mountain and spent some time moving along the foot of it. The sunlight dappled the red stone. Dry grass was scattered up the sides in irregular patches. The mountain rose up high, towering above them like a fierce guardian of the landscape.

Trista became aware of the sound of people. The murmur of voices, tapping and the laughter of children.

As she entered the village, Trista felt strangely uneasy. It had been a long time since she was surrounded by so many people. She saw children playing, chasing after one another, and animals that were a lot like the chickens back on the island. To see so much activity within these dried-up lands was surreal.

Pieces of conversations reached her ears, but none of the words made any sense. Men worked on a number of dwellings constructed from branches, mud and grass. Others prepped food; the smells made her mouth water.

The buzz of activity overwhelmed Trista; she had to use all her willpower not to slump to the floor and stay there. She tried her best to keep the image of Decan being rushed off by Aslara firmly in her mind, to force her feet forward. Her emotions had drained her as much as the walk itself. Her eyes had trouble focusing and her head started to spin.

Shouting from above drew her attention as she fought to keep her eyelids open. Wondering if she was already dreaming, she saw a lot of the huts were not on the ground, but built into the side of the mountain. She had not noticed them until the sound made her look up. A gathering of walkways snaked across the red stone wall, supported by long poles tied together. A combination of natural caves and manually cut rock seemed to act as basic housing.

The raised voice Trista heard belonged to an elderly woman, casually sitting twenty feet off the ground with her feet dangling over the edge. It seemed she had been weaving a basket from long grass when a few children raced past her, chasing a chicken that had fled up the walkway. The walkway shook so hard that the woman's basket and materials nearly tipped over the edge, resulting in the stream of angry words thrown after the kids. Still, she seemed more concerned about her things falling than herself dropping off.

Some of the women were wearing clothes of a similar style to Aslara and Trista's captor. Others had much simpler outfits. The men mostly worked shirtless, their different shades of skin glittering sweatily in the sun. It was the opposite for the children, who wore little more than long shirts and lacked any form of pants or footwear.

One of the older children ran further ahead into the village after seeing Trista's captor. The settlement stretched out into a narrowing canyon, shielded from most prying eyes. A moment later, Trista saw Aslara approach them with long strides.

"Aslara! Sa oled tagasi!" The woman pulled off her turban and scarf as she rushed past Trista to get to Aslara.

It was the first time Trista saw the face of her captor. She was the definition of stunning. Hazel-brown eyes and lightly-tanned skin. Fine cheekbones, with full lips that showed a dazzling smile. She was not at all what Trista had expected after hearing the strong words the female warrior had uttered. Long, straight, dark hair emerged from under the turban. It looped back through a metal ring, which kept it together, and dropped down behind the woman's neck.

Trista shifted her feet to keep standing upright. A haze of exhaustion slowly flowed over her.

Meeting halfway, the stunning Minai woman took Aslara's hands and rested their foreheads together. Now it was Aslara's turn to smile. The loving gesture brought a sparkle to her eyes.

"Ita blei sa tagasi juba, ma lanmou," said the woman.

"I am too," replied Aslara. "But please use the common tongue. We have g—"

Trista's captor bit her lip in a smile then brushed a quick kiss against Aslara's lips, whose smile in turn briefly flashed into a grin before she softly pushed the woman back.

"Shiri, you know I don't like you stealing kisses in front of everyone."

Shiri took a step back and looked playfully sad.

"I couldn't help myself. I'm just so happy you're back so soon," said Shiri with a smile.

"As I was saying, I see you've met our g—" started Aslara again, when her gaze fell on the wobbling Trista and motionless dragon in the net. "No, Shiri, what have you done?"

As Aslara rushed over to Trista, Shiri's expression darkened.

"Are you okay?" Aslara asked Trista.

"I found her wandering the shrubs. Her winged friend attacked us, so I took her down," said Shiri before Trista could answer.

"I'm fine," lied Trista, ignoring the other woman's interruption. "But I'm not so sure about Dalkeira."

Aslara pushed the two hyen'sta out of the way. Neither of them even uttered a rumble of disagreement as they let Aslara check on the dragon.

"Why did Dalkeira attack you? Did you even bother to introduce yourself first, Shiri?" said Aslara sternly.

"Look, I wasn't taking any chances. I thought she might be Karnis'h! And it's my duty to keep this village safe," Shiri said defensively.

"It's my duty too, but that doesn't mean we don't have to stop and think. You're always jumping to conclusions; and how could she be Karnis'h? Look at her. You're my Second. You should know better," Aslara reprimanded her, gesturing at a few of the nearby men to help carry Dalkeira to one of the huts.

Second?

"We'll move her out of the sun. She should be awake before morning," said Aslara to Trista.

"You're going to lock her up?" Trista managed to choke out.

"Not exactly, but I imagine she won't be in the best of moods when she wakes. And I don't want anyone near her until either you or I have spoken to her. I don't want anyone getting hurt," said Aslara. "Best to get her out of the netting while she sleeps as well, don't you think?"

"What about my brother?" mumbled Trista, almost too afraid to ask.

"Oh, of course. I'm sorry. He's holding on for now. Our life listener is doing the best she can, but it is still too early to tell. I'll bring you to him right away, but first let me take that little one off your hands."

Aslara carefully took the baby from Trista's cramped fingers. Trista's hands felt strangely empty and painful without her. Now that she was finally here, she did not feel like leaving the baby behind at all.

Am I really going to trust a group of strangers with this child?

Aslara called one of the women over.

"Yes, Akima Matri?"

As Aslara explained the situation, the woman's face broke out in a grand smile. The child changed hands again as the short, rounded woman skillfully took her in her arms, speaking soft words of comfort.

She shifted the baby to a more comfortable position and walked away. As she did, she bared her well-filled breast to see if the child wanted to latch on. The other children, who had stopped chasing the flightless birds to watch the event unfold, now rushed over to the plump woman to get a glimpse of the newly arrived child. It looked so natural, Trista's heart swelled with relief.

"Don't worry. She's one of our den mothers. The child is in great hands," said Aslara, who noticed Trista's gaze following the child.

Trista had no idea what a den mother was, but Aslara's reassurance was good enough for now.

"Come. Let me take you to Decan."

Instead of going further into the village, Aslara led Trista along the edge of the settlement. There on the outskirts was a hovel, larger than the others. Outside lay all kinds of herbs drying in the sun. There were little twig cages, mostly empty apart from a few that held a tiny bird or two. A small herd of goats wandered aimlessly around the hut. Here and there hung small bones tied on strings, gently rattling against each other in the wind. A thin trail of smoke curled out of the top of the roof.

356

Trista's tired mind jumped from one sight to another, trying to keep up with everything around her. A question floated up to the surface as she followed Aslara into the strange structure.

"You called her your Second," she remarked. "You're telling everyone what to do. And that woman, she called you… Akin Matri? Like it was a title. You're not just a member of this tribe, are you?"

Aslara smiled like a child caught with a secret.

"*Akima Matri*. It means leading mother. The Minai is my tribe to lead."

As she processed this new fact, Trista's eyes adjusted to the darker surroundings. The scent of herbs lay so thick in the warm air that she tasted it on her tongue. Her mouth burned from the exotic flavors invading her senses and her eyes stung from the smoky air. She rubbed her eyes and forced herself to look around. There, to the side, was Decan. Her knees almost gave out. Lying on a table covered with straw, her little brother lay frighteningly still.

I'm too late. He's dead, I'm certain of it.

She approached the table, using her hands to make her way through the low-hanging herbs and bones. Decan looked awfully pale in the dim light. Trista struggled for air. The dizziness in her head grew stronger. Her vision began to spin, deforming everything she saw.

She touched Decan's skin and felt it was unnaturally cold. Someone had removed his clothes. Lines of white were painted across his skin, from the feet all the way up to his heart. The cold touch of his skin brought back the image of her dead father and mother. Their lifeless bodies had also been unable to return the warmth of her touch.

Trista gasped for air. She could not breathe, like someone was choking her. Her mind gave up trying to make sense of it all. With no idea which way was up or down, the ground called her tired body toward it. Trying to keep hold of the table—and keep Decan in her sights—she slid to the floor as her exhausted body finally shut down. The world disappeared into the distance, its light moving away from her fast. From somewhere at the end of the dark tunnel in front of her eyes, Aslara's voice called her name as her head was caught by gentle hands before it hit the ground.

CHAPTER TWENTY-THREE

Slumber

DALKEIRA WOKE UP with a splitting headache. During their travels in the desert dehydration had often given her a nagging pain in her head, but this was something else. This felt like someone had driven an axe straight into her skull. She groaned and tried to move. As she slowly rose to her feet, recent events crept back into her mind.

Trista! Those creatures!

Bewildered, Dalkeira circled round to shake off the net, only to find out she was no longer tangled up in it. Her muscles were stiff and the left side of her body was sore. She roared, her voice rustling the leaves from which the roof was made.

"Where am I? What have you done to me? Where is Trista?"

She spread her wings and beat them to test their strength. The movement threw up a cloud of dust and knocked over a bowl of dried flowers on a table nearby.

"Oh dear, oh my, there's really no reason to make such a mess of things, you know. They're perfectly safe," said a soft voice from the corner.

It was immediately followed by a shrill call from the same direction. "Oh maai."

Dalkeira spun around and hissed. She lowered her stance, ready to pounce on anything that tried to surprise her. But nothing happened. A small figure simply stood there, waiting. Behind it, a large, black bird fluttered its wings and stared back at Dalkeira with dark, beady eyes.

It was not exactly what the dragon had expected. This was not the tall warrior who had bothered Trista and pinned her down. This frail specimen was small—very small, actually, barely half a head taller than Decan. The woman was old, too; face all wrinkled and missing a few teeth, her dark skin a strong contrast to her near-white hair.

If she wanted to, Dalkeira was sure she could snap her in two without any effort at all—and she was pretty sure she wanted to. She took a step forward, head low, wings half open, ready to clamp her jaws around the first body part that came close enough.

But the woman remained perfectly still. She let Dalkeira get as close as she wished. Then the dragon saw why. The woman could not see her. A blindfold of deep red cloth was tied around her head, covering her eyes. Dalkeira raised her head to face level and flicked out her tongue.

"You have one chance to tell me where Trista, Decan and the baby are. I suggest you use it."

She stared intensely at the blindfold as if her gaze could pierce into the silver-haired woman's eyes behind it.

Yet the old woman remained perfectly still, as though watching her. The dragon's anger slipped away. The woman had an alarmingly serene feel to her.

A small wrinkled hand slid over the bottom of Dalkeira's jaw. The touch was unexpected, but instead of lashing out, the dragon found her muscles relaxing from head to tail. A pleasant warmth flowed through her as the woman slid her hand along her neck.

"You must be thirsty, my child. Why not have a drink?"

Using all her willpower, Dalkeira shook her head and jumped backward.

"How did you do that? What kind of trickery is this?" exclaimed Dalkeira.

The woman took a step forward, raising both hands.

"It's alright. No one will hurt you here anymore. You're safe here. None of the Minai would ever hurt a winged ancient one."

"Stay away!" hissed Dalkeira, confused. "I alone will decide when I am safe! Now, take me to Trista!"

"Are you sure you don't want some water first, my child?" asked the woman calmly.

"Stop calling me your child, *old woman*! You cannot even see who is in front of you, let alone know who or what I am!"

"Oh dear, oh my. Yet, you're still throwing a fit, aren't you?"

"Oh maai," called the raven.

"I can see plenty clear," said the old woman. "I easily see your form doesn't hide the youth of your mind, even if you are one of the ancient winged sha'cara. But don't be offended, my child—when you become my age, everyone in the world seems a little young."

The woman let out a chuckle, but Dalkeira remained silent.

"Suit yourself, my child. Please, follow me. I'll take you to the red-haired woman."

The old woman walked over to a small door in the corner and opened it. The dragon was surprised to see she had no trouble moving around, despite the fact her eyes were covered. Dalkeira heard a quiet conversation outside, but it was too soft to hear the words. Following the woman, the raven disappeared through the door as well.

For a moment, Dalkeira stood alone in the silent room. Reluctantly, she walked over to the door and stepped outside.

The sky was filled with stars. The air had cooled again, as it often did during the night. Dalkeira was glad the sun was not there to greet her; perhaps she should have taken that drink after all.

The village unfolded between her and the mountain. Next to one of the huts, the dragon saw two familiar sets of ears and eyes stare back at her. Behind them, the beige desert woman stood silently with spear in hand.

"It's okay, Shiri. She's calmed down… somewhat. You can let Aslara know I'm taking her to my hut," said the elderly woman as she shuffled on.

"As you wish, Duvessa," replied Shiri, observing Dalkeira with a look of disdain.

Dalkeira was even less pleased to see the woman and her two pets and let out a low rumble in her throat. In response, a chuckled growl was thrown her way, one that was certainly meant to add insult to injury.

"Don't mind them. We're all friends here," said Duvessa as she led her away from the village.

"Friends? You could have fooled me. They threatened Trista, and *she* attacked me from behind," said Dalkeira. She followed Duvessa, constantly looking over her shoulder; none would get the jump on her again.

"Oh dear, oh my, that's all in the past now, my child. This way."

"Oh maai," said the raven from one of the roofs before it glided down and landed on the old woman's shoulder again.

Duvessa reached up, gave a small seed to the bird and scratched its head.

Dalkeira followed the strange duo to a large hut. She squeezed herself through the door, following the woman and raven inside. The air within tingled unpleasantly on her senses. Bunches of plants hung from the ceiling everywhere. To the side, a pot hung above the embers of an old fire.

In the middle of the room were Trista and Decan. The siblings lay still with their eyes closed, their skin gray with white lines drawn all over them.

"Don't worry, my child, they're still breathing," said Duvessa, who saw Dalkeira carefully sniffing the brother and sister.

"What have you done to them?" Dalkeira asked suspiciously.

"The boy has been put in a deep sleep to stop the venom from spreading. The girl was exhausted and the sun has put a spell on her. Her body needs rest; everything is out of balance."

One of the walls had a large root breaking through it, or rather, the wall seemed to have been built around the root. Judging from the size, it was part of a very large plant or tree.

"Oh dear, oh my, it's time for his next dose already," said the old woman, holding Decan's wrist lightly in her hands.

"Oh maai."

She put her other hand on the top of the boy's head and trailed her fingers down to his neck. Carefully, she lay Decan's hand back on his stomach and walked over to the large root in the wall.

Dalkeira inched closer to Decan's face, flicking her tongue nervously in the air. She saw the boy's chest rise and fall, then nothing for a long time, then finally rise and fall again. The old woman was telling the truth. She watched Duvessa take hold of the root and softly squeeze a milky-white liquid out of it into a bowl. Turning round, Dalkeira inspected the gray layers and white lines on Trista's skin. She flicked her tongue over it, sniffed it, but it did not seem like anything special. Somehow, the lines looked familiar, like rivers running over the body. Yet she could not place what was so familiar about them.

"What is this on their skin?"

"A special mixture of herbs, mud and lifesap. The sun has damaged their skin. It will need time to heal," said Duvessa. "It might do you some good as well, my child."

"I am fine," Dalkeira said stubbornly, who would have loved to receive a good scrubbing of her skin—and a drink.

Dalkeira smelled Trista's hair. She noticed Trista's eyes rapidly moving behind her closed eyelids. She flicked her tongue across Trista's forehead, which was feverishly warm. Moving to the far side of the table, Dalkeira slid her head along Trista's arm, letting it rest when she reached the hand. She regretted her fight with Trista. It did not feel good to have left things like that between them now they were unable to clear the air.

Anxiously, the dragon observed how the older woman mixed the white liquid with some herbs and poured it from the bowl into Decan's mouth. For a moment, Dalkeira thought she saw Trista move, but when she circled the table, Trista's eyes were closed.

Inspecting the root, Dalkeira sniffed the part the woman had squeezed.

"The juice you just gave him. It comes from one of those large, thorny trees?"

"Oh dear, oh my, the Taori indeed. I see you are as smart as you are curious, my child," said Duvessa with a smile.

"Oh maai!"

Dalkeira looked annoyed at the raven, who merely fluttered its feathers under her gaze.

"Both admirable attributes, yet one gets you in trouble while the other can get you out," continued the old woman. "It's good to train your head. You never know when you might need it."

Dalkeira observed and followed the woman for the rest of the night. When daybreak announced itself, Aslara came by to offer Dalkeira food and drink. The dragon could no longer resist the water offered, which was surprisingly cold, but still refused the food. She was not yet ready to accept Aslara's help so willingly again. She figured she would go out and hunt by herself later, then regretted her decision as it dawned on her that she would have to leave both siblings behind. There was no way she was going to let them out of her sight when they were like this.

Those first days in the village, Duvessa seemed to be constantly brewing herbs, making small potions from them. She put leaves in both Decan and Trista's cheeks, made them swallow the different liquids and once poked Trista's finger to check the color of the blood as it formed a drop on the skin.

On the second night, Decan's leg lost its fiery color around the bite. The old woman kept a close eye on the wound, but seemed satisfied with how it was healing.

Decan woke up some time before dawn. He was groggy and complained that his leg hurt, but he was glad to see Dalkeira waiting for him to explain everything that was going on.

While Dalkeira and Decan talked, it was clear Trista still had a long way to go. For the second time that day, the old woman washed off and reapplied the gray mixture to Trista's skin. Duvessa was drawing new patterns on her body when Trista opened her eyes.

"You're alright, my child. Sleep. You'll feel better in a day or two."

Hearing the remark, Dalkeira jumped up in the middle of one of Decan's sentences and hopped over to the table.

"Is she back? Is she awake?" Dalkeira said eagerly.

Trista fought to keep her eyes open, only to slip off into sleep again without a word.

The morning came around once more. Aslara dropped by to welcome Decan to the village. The boy, apparently judging Trista to be in good care with the older woman—and Dalkeira—keeping watch, eagerly accepted Aslara's invitation to meet the rest of the Minai people. He had been locked up long enough in the hovel and was clearly dying to stretch his legs, even if one still hurt when he walked on it.

Dalkeira wondered briefly if she should keep him close, but figured these people would not save him only to hurt him again.

Perhaps Aslara is not hiding anything after all, she thought as she watched Decan walk out the door.

Another day and night went by during which Dalkeira kept a close eye on Trista. The fever was still unwilling to break, but the life listener—as Decan had called Duvessa after he returned from Aslara's tour around the village— was away more often. Other things in the village required her attention. Besides, the important thing to do now was to keep Trista cool and make sure she got enough fluids. Thus, Duvessa only returned when it was time to give Trista her next drink, or apply some of the lifesap mixture. The life listener allowed Dalkeira to keep watch, which meant the dragon got some additional time alone—which was highly appreciated.

Decan spent the nights in the hut with her, but unlike Dalkeira he had no trouble finding his sleep—despite the fact his dreams remained restless with night terrors.

For the dragon, the call of sleep now continuously pulled on her, but she did not want to let Trista out of her sight. That woman and her two dogs were still out there. She would not risk it. She slept only small amounts; when Decan promised to keep watch, or when the warmth of the day made it impossible to stay awake, but she often stirred awake after a short time, asking if anything had happened.

While waiting for Trista to wake up, Dalkeira found herself with a lot of time on her wings. Her thoughts drifted, frequently circling back to the events in the desert and the sunken city. With nothing else to do, she pondered relentlessly as she paced around the room. She looked at Trista again. What if she did not wake up anymore? Dalkeira was not sure how that would make her feel. It would be much easier to go west without being bound to the ground by her traveling companions. Yet the idea of losing Trista wrung her chest into a painful knot.

Divided, she strolled over to one of the larger pots in the hut and looked at the water inside. Apart from here, she had not seen any water at all since they left the city in the desert. Yet here stood multiple pots, filled to the brim.

They must have a well nearby.

Staring at the water, Dalkeira thought of her fight with the feathered lizards and how the water had come to her aid. She dunked her nozzle in to quench her thirst. Strangely enough, her hunger had almost entirely disappeared; only her thirst remained. She stared into the pot again as her reflection reformed on the bobbing water's surface. The sparkles sluggishly flowed around. They were much less active than when she saw them in a freshwater spring, or the ocean itself. The water felt… tired. Amongst the sparkles, she saw the reflection of her own swirling vortexes look back at her.

The water surface grew still and waited, waited for Dalkeira to stir it alive. She lightly touched outward with her mind, but nothing happened. She tried again, this time concentrating harder, trying to recall the feeling she had when fighting those feathered crawlers in the sunken city. Staring intensely, she noticed the faintest increase in activity amongst the sparkles in the pot. A third effort commenced. This time, the water gave her the satisfaction of seeing the tiniest of ripples move across the surface. She let out a satisfied snort.

This should be interesting.

For the rest of the day, Dalkeira spent every bit of time she had alone in the hut refining her 'watertouch', as she had decided to call her unusual skill. The more she practiced, the lighter she felt, as if her body had been waiting to free itself from its physical confinements and touch the world beyond. Not to mention it tamed her nerves as a pleasant calmness flowed over her every time she shaped the water with her mind. Although it was not really her mind doing the work. It was her… intent. Her entire being stretching out, like moving an invisible muscle.

She only stopped when she heard Duvessa, Decan or anyone else approach the hut, and by the end of the second day she was pleased to see a fast-moving whirlpool form in the pot in front of her. With some more practice, she could stop and redirect it the other way without much effort. It was very satisfying—no, liberating. The more she practiced and grew in skill, the more convinced she was that it would not be so bad if she went and explored what lay to the west on her own.

On the third day of her self-imposed watertouch training, Dalkeira was focused on the pot when she heard Trista stir on the table. She walked over, thinking she was finally about to wake up, but the sounds were those of a nightmare.

Slightly disappointed, Dalkeira resumed her morning practice. As a challenge, she forced the now easily-created whirlpool upward out of the pot. Her claws scraped the ground as they involuntarily clenched in response to her focus. Her

364

head swayed back and forth as her eyes focused on the water. Slowly, the water began to rise, first inching closer to the edge of the pot, then higher. She forced the whirlpool into a more compact tornado, narrowing it, stretching it upward.

Unexpectedly, the door opened and Duvessa stepped inside. Dalkeira had been so consumed by her efforts that she had not noticed the life listener approaching the hut. Startled, her concentration was instantly gone. The small water tornado splattered to all sides, soaking everything around the pot, including Dalkeira herself.

"Oh dear, oh my, if you wanted to take a bath, you should have told me. There are better places to do that," Duvessa said with a smile that betrayed she might have seen more than she would admit.

"Oh maai," said the raven from the corner.

"Just thirsty," said Dalkeira, acting as normal as possible.

The interruption had replaced her feeling of bliss with plain dizziness, thrown from the heightened state of mind she had reached these last few days. Suddenly, Dalkeira felt very drained and *very* hungry. She looked longingly to the door and back to Trista. Her stomach rumbled loudly. Perhaps it was time to leave her side… for a bit.

"Looks like we got here just in time," said Decan, entering the hut with Aslara in tow.

"We've brought you something to eat," Aslara said as she held up two desert hares.

"No, thank you. I do not need your help," replied Dalkeira stubbornly. Her stomach growled.

"Your stomach disagrees. How do you expect to stand watch if you don't properly take care of yourself?" said Aslara. "You must be starving by now."

"Come on, Dalkeira, you've got to eat," added Decan, "I even helped chase them from their den so you could feast."

Dalkeira's stomach spoke again before the dragon could utter another protest. Decan grabbed both hares and offered them to her.

"We take care of each other, remember?" he said. "Eat."

Dalkeira could no longer fight the boy's logic with her own stubbornness and reluctantly gave in to her renewed hunger. She only needed a moment to rip the first hare in half and gobble it down. She took her time with the second hare while Decan and the two tribeswomen prepared and ate their own evening meal. All the while, Decan enthusiastically told stories about the village outside: the dwellings in the mountain, the amount of people and animals, and the strange language most of them spoke.

"The baby is doing well, too," said Decan, nearing the end of his tale. "The woman said she's gaining weight again and likes reacting to the other children."

Not long after that, Decan went to bed. Tired from the impressions of the day and his recent recovery, he quickly fell asleep. Shortly afterward, Duvessa made her excuses and left, leaving Dalkeira and Aslara alone in the company of Trista, who still lay silently slumbering in the depths of her mind.

Dalkeira continued to gnaw on one of the hare's legs, intent on ignoring Aslara. *What I would not give for a nice juicy fish right now,* the dragon thought idly. After a while, it was Aslara who finally broke the awkward silence.

"Has she said anything today?"

Dalkeira simply shook her head.

"Don't worry. She'll wake up soon enough," added Aslara.

"I know. And when she does, we will be on our way again. Decan, too."

"Are you sure that's your decision to make? Or wise, for that matter?" said Aslara. "You all look like you need to recover much of your strength. And you're welcome to stay. The rains are coming, and with them the times of plenty."

Dalkeira looked Aslara straight in the eyes.

"Stay? With that *woman* ready to attack me again?" said Dalkeira.

"Who? Shiri? She realizes she made a mistake. You have nothing to fear from her anymore."

"I am not so sure," Dalkeira spoke thoughtfully. "But you are not going to give up easily, are you?"

"What do you mean?" said Aslara.

"I mean you want something from her. From Trista."

Aslara let out a sigh.

"You really *are* headstrong, aren't you? Look, I know you don't trust me, winged ancient one, but I have no ill intent," said Aslara. "I just want to help."

"No, you do not," stated Dalkeira bluntly. "You might be *willing* to help us, but there is something you want in return. Trista might not see it, but I do. Ever since we left the island we have been chased, threatened, cheated and nearly killed by other people. People who were all looking for something they wanted, or thought they needed. I think it is human nature. You might not want to hurt her—you have convinced me of that at least—but you want something. I can sense it."

Dalkeira's head spun. Having been awake for almost two days straight, this was not the best time to have this conversation. During her watertouch training, her thoughts of leaving without the siblings seemed sound, but what would she expose Trista and Decan to if she abandoned them here?

Dalkeira shook her head. She would not allow Aslara to fill her mind with half-truths or faulty reasoning.

"Back in the sunken city you kept looking at Trista. Her hair in particular. And I have seen you look at me, while you thought I was sleeping. You introduce yourself as one of the tribe, but now that we are back here—wherever this is—Decan tells me you are their leader. What did he call it? Matri? If you hid that from us, it is likely there are other things that you are not telling us as well, and I want to know what they are," demanded the dragon.

Aslara looked at Dalkeira for a long time.

"Well, I'm pleased to see Duvessa was right about you. You're an excellent sha'cara for her. A great protector," said Aslara. "And I must admit there have been a few things on my mind, but you'll have to forgive me; this isn't the right time."

"Not the right time? The only time is now."

"But much is still uncertain," said Aslara, apologetic. "All I can say is that we *think* you and Trista are important to the tribe. Duvessa spoke of a lifevision. A prediction. A—a story of old. Many visions visit a life listener. Even as a child. When the moment draws nearer, they become more vibrant. Stronger. Until it overpowers all other visions for a while. Some visions are passed on from generations of life listeners before us."

"Vision? Story? That does not make sense. How could anyone know where we would go?"

"I'm sorry. I don't know. But the fact that Trista is accompanied by a winged ancient like yourself is already proof enough that you are both important."

"Wait—does that mean your tribe has encountered my species before? Are there any other dragons living nearby?" asked Dalkeira.

"The First Mother was known to be paired with a winged ancient. The tribe's history mentions a few others were as well, but these great sha'cara disappeared from our lands without a trace generations ago. The stories are few. Duvessa might have better answers; you'll have to ask her."

"What about what Duvessa saw? The story," said Dalkeira.

"All I know is what she told me. 'A wandering mother with hair of fire riding a raging, winged river.'"

"And you believe that is us?" said Dalkeira.

"Well, you're blue, you've got wings and I've never seen anyone with hair as red as fire apart from her. Not even in the other tribes," said Aslara, pointing to Trista on the table. "As leader, I need to take the words of guidance into account. So when you all crossed my path, it was clear to me I needed to bring you back here."

"To do what?" asked the dragon suspiciously.

"I wish I knew. But Duvessa is convinced it impacts all of us. The entire tribe's future hangs in the balance, and with it the Red Plains. Like I said, you'll need to talk to her about it if you want to know more. But first, you three need to regain your strength. That means eat, sleep and drink."

The tribe leader was not wrong there. Dalkeira was fighting to keep her multiple eyelids open, and they grew heavier with every passing moment. Sleep sounded wonderful right about now.

"So why did you not just tell us? Why the secrecy?" the dragon asked. Her jaw spread wide from a yawn she could not repress.

"You really can't see? It's not all about telling the truth. A leader learns it's just as important to pick the right time to share the knowledge she holds. Since I wasn't sure—and I'm still not—I wanted Duvessa's confirmation," said Aslara. "Besides, what would I say? 'Hi, we just met, but I think you have an important part in the future existence of our tribe. Please follow me to unknown events and possible danger'? Would you have believed me? Do you now?"

"Not really," Dalkeira said skeptically. "Though I suppose you *could* be right."

Her distrust was subsiding now she had a more complete picture. And with her hunger eased, sleep was the sole competitor for attention within the dragon's exhausted body.

"You should get some rest. We can speak more about this later, I promise," said Aslara as Dalkeira's head hung low. "Really, it will be alright. We'll get Trista back on her feet and then we can talk. Now rest. I will sit here and keep an eye on things."

Dalkeira still did not like it much. Here she was with her own road to the west to follow, stuck waiting for her bonded human. But she *was* tired. As tired as she was back in the desert when Decan carried her.

Family sticks together.

Unable to fight it any longer, she lay down near Trista's table, determined to get to the bottom of all this winged river nonsense… tomorrow.

* * *

Trista felt heavy and light at the same time. The world floated around her. As she blinked, her shady surroundings came into focus. She tried to move her head, but even that was too much effort. Her vision blurred, then refocused. Slowly, she recognized the still body of Decan lying beside her.

I'm on a table too? she thought, confused.

Something pressed against Trista's hand. It felt familiar, but she could not turn her head to see what it was.

A small silhouette appeared next to her brother and opened the boy's mouth. The shadow poured something between Decan's lips and disappeared again. Trista tried to follow the figure, tried to speak up, but slipped off again, back into the darkness once more.

The dark greeted her like an old friend; one she was reluctant to meet. She looked around. That other place had been much cooler. Here, the heat that had haunted them for weeks in the desert still clawed at her, harassing her to give up. The same heat that had destroyed her skin, and her hope.

Fire erupted around her. The laughter of black soldiers echoed in the empty space. The flames closed in, just like they had done before. She looked for a way out, but the fire did not want her to leave.

"Dalkeira! Where are you?"

Still no answer came. Trista sat on the ground, arms around her knees. She cried; cried for her parents, cried for her brother, for losing the most special thing in the world and for the inevitable to come. But the flames were unforgiving, inching closer, hungry for their prey, driven forward by the darkness behind them.

"Dalkeira? Anyone? Help me!"

A breeze swept past her face, cooling the tears on her cheeks. She looked up and saw nothing but flames moving in for the kill.

As if triggered by her stare, the fire rushed forward to consume her. Trista threw up her arms, knowing full well it would not stop the pain; then, unexpectedly, an immense gust of wind crashed into her. It hit her with such strength she had trouble staying upright. The turbulent force surrounded her with a thunderous roar. By the time it stopped, the flames were all but extinguished. Trista lifted her head once more to see who was there, but all she saw was darkness. From far away, a voice emerged from the nothingness.

"And who might you be?"

Trista blinked. She was back inside the hut. Branches of dried herbs swung gently above her in the lightest of breezes. It was darker than before; colder, too. The sound of a tiny night insect reached her ears from far away. Something cool touched on her skin and she tried to move her head, but her body was still too heavy to make even the slightest of movements. She turned her eyes as far to the side as possible and saw a small shriveled hand loosely drawing patterns on her skin. Her eyes traced the wrinkled skin up the wrist, arm and shoulder, following a path toward the face. It was a small woman, busily drawing lines along her skin. Deep creases of age ran around the woman's eyes. They were unusual eyes; eyes that despite their clouded appearance watched her closely. The face was surrounded by strands of silvery hair, complemented by a smile that was missing a few teeth. Trista tried to speak, but a warm touch on her shoulder stopped her.

"You're alright, my child. Sleep. You'll feel better in a day or two."

"Is she back? Is she awake?"

Dalkeira's familiar voice made Trista's heart jump with joy. She was still there. Her ocean beauty had not abandoned her after all. She tried to reach out with her mind, but exhaustion prevented it. Forced to give up her efforts, she drifted back to sleep.

Laughter woke Trista from the darkness. She blinked, trying to remember how long she had been lying there. The hut was much lighter now; sunlight fell in through the open door. She lifted her head, surprised that her body was finally obeying her commands again, and slowly sat up.

Her muscles were stiff and cold, like they had not been used in a long time. Trista surveyed her arms, legs and the rest of her near-naked body, following the lines trailing the curves of her muscles. They circled her belly and curled around her breasts, reaching all the way up to her neck.

Carefully, she slid off the table, making sure her legs would not give way before putting her full weight on them. She looked at the table next to her, but noticed with shock that it was empty.

"It's alright. He's fine," said Aslara's soft voice. "He's outside, probably playing with the other kids."

The dark-eyed woman sat in the corner of the room on a sawed-off tree stump, calmly watching her.

Blood rushed to Trista's cheeks at the naked state she was in. She looked around for her clothes and saw them lying nearby. Her legs wobbled as she tried to take a step. Realizing her intent, Aslara jumped up and handed her the clothes.

"You have nothing to be ashamed of," said Aslara, though she sounded apologetic.

After getting dressed, Trista tested her legs once more, this time feeling confident enough to let go of the table and take a few steps. Aslara approached her with a small bowl of water.

"Here, drink this. You look like you could use it."

Trista took the wooden bowl and slowly poured the cool water down her throat. She felt it slide all the way down into her stomach. Her eyes caught a familiar shine of color lying on the ground.

"She's been sitting here for three days straight. Refused to leave your side, not even for food. I finally convinced her to eat something this morning; she fell asleep almost immediately after it. Poor thing."

"Dalkeira listened to you?" Trista said in disbelief, trying to shake off her grogginess.

"Barely, and I must admit Decan helped. However, I am happy to say we've had a moment to talk."

Trista wondered what that meant, but for now she was just glad the dragon was alright. She put her hand on Dalkeira's muzzle. The dragon opened an eye and looked up at her.

"Good morning."

"*You are finally awake!*" said Dalkeira with a sigh of relief inside Trista's head. "*How are you feeling?*"

"I am, and I'm glad you're here. Go back to sleep. I won't go far. We'll talk later."

Dalkeira's head pressed against her hand. She recognized the feeling immediately from before.

"*No, I want to stay with you,*" said Dalkeira.

The dragon rose to her feet and shook her head before stretching her legs.

"*Did you not sleep well?*" asked Trista privately.

"*I did, actually. Just deep,*" Dalkeira's thoughts replied. "*I dreamed of the Taori… and a song. It was strangely soothing.*"

Trista smiled. She let her hand run along the back of Dalkeira's head before turning to Aslara.

"I want to see Decan. Can you take me to him?" said Trista.

Aslara took her arm and guided Trista toward the door. She had to shield her eyes against the sun as they emerged from the shadows. Dalkeira followed them out into the day.

Laughter greeted her again as Trista stepped carefully outside. As her eyes adjusted, she saw a group of children running after a ball made of grass. Multiple men and women observed the spectacle, laughing with the children who ran around, tripping over each other. The game looked like total chaos, but that did not seem to bother the players at all.

One of the boys had much lighter skin than the others, but was just as invested in the game as the rest. Seeing her brother run back and forth brought a smile to Trista's face and a tear to her eye. Decan seemed to limp a little on the leg that had been bitten, but besides that was full of energy.

"You can sit here," said Aslara, gesturing to a spot just outside the hut.

Aslara's voice made Decan look up from the game. The commotion quickly drew everyone's attention. The sound of the game died down as the villagers looked at the new arrivals. Dalkeira emerged from the hut and positioned herself next to Trista, clearly trying to look as majestic as possible. All conversation fell silent as people's eyes turned toward them.

"Triss! You're awake!"

The boy rushed over. Trista let Aslara's supporting arm fall and took her little brother in a full embrace, laughing in relief. It had been a while since she felt so happy. They had done it, all of them. They had survived one of the most inhospitable regions Trista had ever seen.

Aslara clapped. "Everyone, after a few days' delay I'm glad to officially introduce Trista of the waterclans. She and her family will be guests of the Minai for now. They don't speak our ancient sounds, so please show them our finest hospitality and have patience with your words, or use the common tongue," announced Aslara. She then repeated the words in her native language.

Decan broke off the hug and looked at his sister with a grin.

"How are you feeling?" asked Trista.

Decan spoke reassuringly. "I'm fine, really. The leg still hurts a bit, but Duvessa said it will get better over time as long as I keep it moving."

"Duvessa?" said Trista, confused.

"The old woman. They call her a life listener, Triss. She helped me. Gave me all kinds of drinks." Decan's words spilled out quickly; he was clearly hyperactive from the game. "Some were really disgusting, but Duvessa said I had to take them if I wanted to get better. She helped you too, you know."

Images of the wrinkled face and white eyes drifted back into her mind. She remembered Aslara had mentioned the name before, back at the Pillar of Life.

"Life listener?" said Trista, still trying to make sense of it all. "Why life listener?"

"I don't know," said Decan, shrugging. "I guess she listens to life?"

She must be some sort of a healer, thought Trista.

"She is, but not only that. I suspect she is much, much more," replied Dalkeira privately.

"Well, I'm glad you're alright, little brother," Trista said.

"What about you?" asked Decan. "You've been on that table longer than I have. Are you feeling okay?"

Trista ran her hand lovingly through Decan's hair.

"I'm fine. Don't worry about me. I'm still a bit tired, but what I really am is hungry."

Hearing the comment, Aslara signaled to one of the nearby men.

"Why don't you sit down here for a while. You can enjoy the game and get some solid food in your stomach," she said.

Trista gladly accepted. The game started back up and Decan hobbled back into the chaos again. For once, the temperature felt pleasantly warm as Trista sat in the shadow of the hut. Her muscles absorbed the warmth and melted into a state of relaxation, as if she had been frozen solid on the inside until now.

Observing the lines on her skin with renewed interest, she noticed that much of the damaged skin was already starting to heal. Flakes of skin dropped off her nose when Trista scratched it. The layer of gray mud also cracked and fell off in some places.

Dalkeira positioned herself beside Trista on the ground, putting her head on Trista's lap. Trista softly scratched the ridges of the dragon's head. Dalkeira relaxed under her touch.

"You're much bigger now than when you hatched," said Trista inside her head. *"Even with so little food. I wish I could get you more food."*

"Do not worry. I will get bigger still."

"I want to see that. I'm glad you're still here. I… I was afraid you had left us."

Dalkeira remained silent for a moment.

"Well, I am still here."

The dragon shifted her head slightly, as if to find the perfect spot to lie still.

"And perhaps it is best if we stay awhile," added Dalkeira after apparent consideration.

The suggestion felt strangely soothing to Trista. She was about to comment when one of the men returned to offer her some dried, sweet fruits in a woven grass bowl. Besides the fruit, there were slices of a baked, white root and some green leaves that looked suspiciously like seaweed. It struck her as odd to see seaweed so far from the ocean, but her stomach overruled her mind before the thought had fully formed.

There were twig-like things in the bowl as well, which had a salty and smoky taste. When she asked Aslara what they were, they turned out to be smoked lizard tails. Not that it mattered to Trista; she happily accepted everything and filled her stomach with whatever was offered. Between bites, she slipped Dalkeira whatever she wanted. It was clear the dragon needed it as much as she did.

The spectators fully invested themselves in the game again, their laughter returning soon after. More at ease—and with some food in her belly—Trista thankfully joined the others in following the playful match. Every now and then, she spoke with Aslara about the things she saw around her.

"I can't thank you enough," she said to the leading mother. As she spoke the words, Trista put her hand on Aslara's arm and squeezed it gently.

"Don't worry. I'm glad you pulled through. For now, take your time and regain your strength," Aslara said tenderly. She put her hand over Trista's to reinforce the words.

* * *

As they talked, no one noticed the figure in the back observing the new arrivals from a distance. Shiri's eyes narrowed as she watched Trista and Aslara. One of the hyen'sta let out a rumbling growl. The other chuckled softly.

"Razza, Shuka, come on. Let's go," Shiri said harshly to her sha'cara. "We need to train."

As both animals walked toward the base of the mountain, they each let out a soft whimper. It was clear there would be no rest for them today.

CHAPTER TWENTY-FOUR

Garden

WHY DID THEY ask us to come? I should be up in the sky, not digging around in the dirt."

Annoyed, Dalkeira scraped her claws on a rock to clean them and looked up. The blue sky was lined with white stripes, as if an enormous dragon had split open the cloud cover with its wing. The sparkling spectacle was like a special invitation.

"They didn't; I asked Aslara if we could come," said Trista. "I thought it would be nice for us to spend some time together with her and the other huntresses, but outsiders are not allowed to join the hunt. So she asked if we could dig up some roots."

Trista used her spear to chip away the hard, red earth before pulling out a round, white and slightly dry root.

"A dragon is not meant to dig," Dalkeira said stubbornly.

"You're in a mood, aren't you? This hunger is clearly doing you no good."

"If they let us hunt with them, maybe we would not have to want for meat so much," said Dalkeira. "All we get is plants and a lizard leg or tail if we're lucky."

Trista looked at the dragon, but decided to let it go.

"Where have you been going these last few days, anyway?" asked Trista, changing the subject. "I haven't seen you around much."

Waiting for Dalkeira to respond, Trista scratched the dried mixture of mud and herbs on her skin. It itched at times, a sign that her burns were nearly healed. But even with her skin much better, she had decided to follow Aslara's advice and continued applying the mixture to protect her skin from the scorching sun.

After her recovery it had not taken long before Trista noticed she and Decan were the only light-skinned people in the village. Many had skin as dark as the baby they found in the desert, although others of the tribe were also lighter toned, like Aslara.

None of the Minai were too bothered by the influence of the sun god, and even Decan had developed a deep tan over the last few weeks during their travels. It was only *her* skin that had trouble with that fireball high in the sky.

Trista had wanted to make a hat of dried grass—something every ocean fisher in the waterclan knew how to do. But she had not needed to; instead, some of the Minai women had offered her and Decan enough fresh clothes to dress themselves. She had accepted the gesture with tears in her eyes. After all, their clothes were in desperate need of replacement.

"No place, really," said Dalkeira, evasive.

Trista touched the soft, supple fabric of her new outfit with her fingertips. She felt like a new person when she emerged from one of the huts fully dressed. The clothes covered most of her skin while keeping her temperature down. In combination with the mud on her face and arms, she could now easily move around in the sun during the day. Still, she preferred mornings and evenings if she could time it.

"Do you like it here? In the village," said Trista hopeful.

Dalkeira looked at her and let out a sigh.

"It is fine. You and Decan needed the rest," she said without much conviction.

This time, Dalkeira changed the subject.

"Tell me again why they painted your face?" she asked, looking at the lines that marked Trista's face.

"Aslara said it's a blessing for those who travel."

"It looks silly."

"Well, I figured it couldn't do any harm. Besides, Aslara said it looked good on me," said Trista.

Staring down at the next root, she missed the look Dalkeira gave her, but the dragon's disapproval over the remark seeped into her.

"Look, I'm just trying to fit in a little, okay? Should you not do that, too? How are you getting along with the others?" said Trista. "Shiri and her *dogs* aren't still bothering you, are they?"

Trista had avoided Shiri ever since they arrived in the village. She figured if the huntress wanted to talk or even apologize, the Minai woman would come to her. Until then, it was probably best to stay out of her way.

"Hmph. I dare them to try again," snorted the dragon. "I am not some poor animal weakened by hunger and thirst anymore."

During their first few weeks of rest, the Minai's diet took some getting used to. The roots they were digging for were fine to eat—if a bit tasteless—but they were often complemented with small amounts of larvae, termites and other insects. It had taken Trista a few days before she tried them; the sensation of eating something that was still alive had not been appealing.

Unfortunately, real meat was scarce. Hunting parties often got back to the village empty-handed, and even Dalkeira had trouble finding lonely prey she could catch. Those animals in the immediate area were rarely seen and small in general. Besides, they were experts in avoiding predators. Only the most skilled huntresses were stealthy enough to occasionally come back with a successful kill, which was then prepared and shared with the entire tribe. Each tribe member shared equally, while most of the sha'cara provided for themselves. That was alright if you lived on plants, but it meant not much meat found its way to Dalkeira. The dragon's growth had slowed to a crawl and what she gained in length, she almost lost in width. She was not *losing* weight, but her build was becoming very stretched.

Nevertheless, Trista had never considered Dalkeira weak and was about to say so when the high-pitched calls of the huntresses carried through the air. They were followed by the sound of twigs snapping.

"*Something is coming this way. It sounds big,*" said Trista privately.

A tauroryx burst out of the shrubbery and ran straight at them. It was a small specimen, much smaller than its distant cousin, the desert tibu. You could see the resemblance, but the tauroryx's build was leaner and it had small, curly horns instead of the tibu's long triple ones. Its white feet were covered in red dirt from the chase. Seeing no other huntresses around, Trista jumped up, spear at the ready. She was just about to throw it when Dalkeira jumped in front of her, claws extended to grasp their intended dinner.

"Watch out!" said Trista, barely able to hold on to her weapon and prevent it from ending up in the back of Dalkeira's head.

Startled by Trista's sudden appearance, the tauroryx's reaction to the dragon was extremely quick. It changed directions and shot past the dragon's claws, knocking Trista off her feet. The beast quickly disappeared into the shrubbery behind them and sped off.

"Whatever did you do that for?" said Trista, annoyed.

"I believed you could not handle it alone. Besides, it is like I have told you before—I hunt better from the sky. Alone," said the dragon.

"But that's not what it's all about," spoke a stern voice behind them.

It was Aslara. She glanced around to assess the situation and extended a hand to get Trista back on her feet.

"It's already difficult enough finding prey during these times. It's important to work together. To be part of the tribe and face our challenges in unity," she said. "Even if that means simply digging up roots."

"That's what I was trying to explain to her," said Trista apologetically. She dusted herself off.

Shiri and two other huntresses emerged from the other side. Trista immediately noticed the disappointment in their eyes.

"I told you she would not have it in her," said Shiri.

Meanwhile, Dalkeira paced restlessly.

"You go and be part of the tribe. I have other things to do than listen to this woman's insults," she said.

The dragon turned around and launched into the air. The rush of wind ruffled Trista's hair. With a few strong beats of her wings Dalkeira set a course toward the village.

"What's gotten into her?" asked Aslara.

"Beats me. She's been acting strange the entire week."

"Well, you can figure it out when we get back. First things first, we need to catch some food," said Aslara. "Come on. I'll show you another place where you can dig while we scout for more prey."

The huntresses gathered their things and followed Aslara as she walked off again. They would have to travel far from the village today to find meat. Trista stared in the direction Dalkeira had gone. The cloudless blue sky stretched as far as her eyes could see.

And still not a drop of rain in sight, she thought with a sigh.

"Got it!"

Decan jumped up and down with joy. Trista watched her little brother do a small victory dance before he raced off to pick up his stones.

They had been in the Minai village now for three weeks, resting and regaining their strength. Trista was happy to see how quickly Decan had become friends with the other children in the village. He even started to pick up a few of their local words. Her little brother seemed more and more like a normal kid again with each day spent playing games, helping around the village, and sometimes getting up to no good.

"Did you see that, Triss?" said Decan, returning with a handful of large pebbles. "Here, I'll show you again."

Decan placed one of the stones in his slingshot. He quickly spun it a few times before expertly releasing the stone. It shot through the air at incredible speed, smashing into the woven basket the kids had dug up from somewhere in the village. The basket spun around on it axis. It wobbled, fully intent on falling off the rock it had been placed on, but changed its mind at the last moment and kept its place on top of the stone. The old basket was littered with holes from many pebble attacks.

"Well done! You're really good at this," Trista said to her little brother.

Proud, Decan prepared another stone, but just as he was about to release it they heard a heavy *thud* and saw the basket fly off the rock, out of sight.

"Hey! No fair," exclaimed Decan.

One of the girls had a large grin on her face. She stuck out her tongue, then she and the others started laughing. It was not long before Decan joined in their laugher as well.

"Seems like you have some competition," said Trista, who had to suppress a chuckle of her own. "Still, I'm surprised how quickly you picked this up. Are you sure you haven't done this before? At home?"

Decan shook his head.

"But, it is really simple. I can show you if you like," said Decan.

"No, thanks," said Trista, who remembered her first futile attempts a few days ago all too well. "I'll stick to my spears if you don't mind. What I wanted to ask you was whether you've seen Dalkeira? I can't find her and she's not reacting to my calls."

"Nope, sorry," said Decan. "Last time I saw her was this morning, after she got back from her hunt."

"Ah. Do you know if she caught anything?"

"Only a snake, she said. Then she left in the direction of Duvessa's hut. Maybe she's there?"

Again?

"Alright, thanks. I'll check."

The dragon had been spending more and more time with the old life listener these last two weeks. Trista had not spoken much with the old lady herself up till now. In fact, the woman had been mysteriously absent, apart from brief checkups to make sure Trista was healing properly. But for some reason, it seemed Dalkeira had taken a peculiar interest in the woman.

Trista tried not to let it bother her, but she was as if Dalkeira was moving further and further away from her—and just when she thought their relationship had been improving again.

She froze when a giant cat jumped directly in front of her. The animal's size easily rivaled Dalkeira's. Two enormous canine teeth ran down from the upper jaw. The creature's red-brown coat flowed over its lean, muscled build. It shifted its large paws on the sand, staring directly at her. Trista caught a glimpse of multiple retractable, razor-sharp claws, with a fifth—substantially larger—hanging on the side of each front leg.

High-pointed shoulder blades stuck out above its back, as if the bones had shot past their intended stopping point. Between the shoulders and along the spine were small, black, armored bands, all the way to the long, tufted tail. A hairy, brush-like comb ran across the top of its wide head, while the sides were significantly shorter—apart from one longer lock braided with colored beads.

"Demarus! Don't do that! You scared the crushing depth out of me."

The large re'lion tilted its head—its version of shrugging—and walked away.

"Wait," Trista called. "Do you know where Dalkeira is? I've been trying to find her everywhere."

The creature looked back, but did not make a sound.

"Look at me," said Trista to herself. "I'm so used to talking to an animal I already expect all of them to say something back."

Trista spread her hands out to act as wings, then hissed.

"Dalkeira? You know, with wings?"

Demarus sat down and looked at her with a blank stare. She sighed.

"Do you at least know where Aslara is? Perhaps she knows where Dalkeira is. Aslara?"

That name seemed to spur some action into the animal. The re'lion moved toward the village, looking back every now and then to make sure Trista was still following.

Trista had first met Aslara's sha'cara last week when they moved into one of the village huts to free up the life listener's place. It was nice to get out of Duvessa's hut. Trista certainly had not dared to complain, but it was great to get away from the thick smell of herbs and piles of bones lying around everywhere. Their current hut was a bit more crowded, with three other women and a man sleeping there last night, but the numbers changed every day. The people of the Minai did not have a standard place to sleep. When it was time to turn in, they just looked for an available place to lay down their heads.

During their introduction to Demarus, the large red cat had circled Dalkeira but never once made an aggressive impression. Dalkeira had taken an interest in observing the large predator. Sometimes she followed him in the air to observe him on his way or on a hunt. She was intrigued by the stealth Demarus was capable of. And while technically they could not communicate, both re'lion and dragon seemed quite content in each other's company. Unfortunately, the large predator did not seem too willing to help find the dragon right now.

Trista quickly followed the cat into the village. As she walked between the huts and hovels, Trista enjoyed the activity around her. She had not noticed it the first time, being half out of this world, but the village was constantly buzzing with people and animals. Children were learning to work with smaller animals. There were some cattle species and some thin mountain goats, who freely ran up the mountain side, every day. Thulai also had several companions of her species represented within the village. According to Aslara, not all were sha'cara, but many people enjoyed the company of animals next to their usefulness for things. The pelts or hides were used for creating hardened leather armor that was worn over the lighter clothing; milk was there to drink and make cheese from; meat and eggs to eat, and several of the Minai made use of an animal's strength to assist in the chores of everyday life.

Rounding a corner, Trista heard Aslara's voice. With an elegant leap, Demarus landed behind the leading mother and rubbed his head against Aslara's side to greet her.

"Hey, Dem. Had a good hunt?"

Aslara ran her hands firmly through the re'lion's mane.

"I see you bring company. Perfect timing," said the Minai leader as she saw Trista approach.

"Aslara… Lasjika," said Trista, noticing the den mother Aslara was speaking with. "How's the baby?"

The woman smiled and pulled back one of the layers of fabric in which the child was wrapped.

"She's fine, Trista of the waterclans. She drinks well… and eats some of the cooked… roots. When the times of… much are here, she will grow quickly," said the den mother.

Trista waited patiently for the woman to find her words; not all the Minai were fully adept in the Terran language.

"Are you sure she's not a burden? I still feel bad for handing her off like that," said Trista.

"Oh, don't worry, child. It is our way. You warrior types should not be weighed down by the burden of raising children. You can leave that to us, the den mothers. Besides, if I am not mistaken, she was never your responsibility to start with, right? She was lucky you came along when you did."

"That is kind of you to say, but I'm no warrior," said Trista apologetically.

"Nonsense. Of course you're a warrior. You fight for what you believe; you fight to stay alive. You've told me yourself. Truth given, you can use some training, but you're definitely a warrior," said Aslara. "Here, the den mothers take care of the tribe's children. From the moment they need milk to the day they're ready to stand alone and face what the Red Plains bring."

Over the weeks, Trista's admiration for Aslara had grown tremendously. It was inspiring to see such a strong woman in charge of so many moving parts of the tribe. The leading mother's interest and guidance had really helped Trista come to grips mentally while her body took the time to follow its own path back to health.

"Wait, so they don't live with their mother? Or father?" asked Trista.

"Some do. Some don't. The parents can see their offspring at any time, but they don't necessarily sleep, eat or live in the same place, no. Such is the way of the Minai; we all take care of each other. Just as it's common for our life listener to name a child that is born."

"Every child? Isn't that incredibly difficult to come up with?"

"It is not the listener's choice. It's the flows of life that... provide," said Lasjika.

"But it can indeed take many moons before a suitable name is finally found," said Aslara. "Not this time, though. I was just telling Lasjika here that we should go and look for you. Duvessa visited me late last night—she said a name has been given to the child."

"Oh really? What did she say?" said Trista, who had been trying to find a suitable name for the baby girl for weeks.

"Er'lun," said Aslara.

"It means lucky traveler," added the den mother.

"Er'lun?" Trista said it a few times, trying to get the pronunciation right. "That's a beautiful name. I think she'll be happy with it. Thank you again for taking her. I'm really glad she made it."

A tear welled in Trista's eye. At least this was one thing she had done right.

"Really not a problem, dear," said the den mother as she stood up. "I'd best be going to check on the other little ones."

Demarus rolled over at Aslara's feet, showing his belly to the leading mother. He yawned as Aslara indulged his obvious wish to be scratched. Trista observed the large canines and other sharp teeth before the re'lion's jaws closed again.

"You know, I'm surprised none of the Minai are afraid of Demarus walking around. Him being a predator... I mean, eating other animals and all. Does he always just come and go as he pleases? He totally snuck up on me earlier. Made my heart jump."

"During the drought, he's often gone for days on end to hunt for himself. He doesn't want to burden the tribe with his constant need for meat."

"But even the other animals seem unaffected by his presence when he returns," said Trista.

Aslara looked up as she continued to scratch Demarus' chest.

"It's really not that strange. The only predators here would be sha'cara, which have a deep understanding with their chosen humans. Other than that, predators aren't allowed to be kept; only those that eat plants."

"But what about Shiri's hyen'sta? Clearly they're both sha'cara since they're allowed in the tribe, but you said a person will only ever meet one sha'cara. How can she have two?"

"You're very observant, aren't you? I like that about you," Aslara said with a smile. "And you're right. She's a special case; Razza and Shuka are twins. Sha'crow come in pairs every now and then, but Shiri is the first time a sha'cara twin came forth in the history of the tribe. It's not always easy, but Shiri's strong-willed and Razza and Shuka respect that. She holds a position of great honor as my second in command, as well as our first huntress."

And your lover, thought Trista, immediately wondering why the thought had sprung to mind.

"What about those creatures in the sunken city? Didn't you say you were there to capture one of them?" said Trista.

"Not so much capture; more to scout and prepare. Assess the danger. There's never been a baell'wek sha'cara and several of the more daring huntresses had expressed the wish to try and find one. Duvessa asked me to go… but that's not important now. Truth is, a sha'cara would never eat one of their own," explained Aslara. "Still, accidents happen. They're animals, after all. Instinct is strong. But so are the ways of the Minai."

With a final pat on the re'lion's flank the leading mother rose back to her feet.

"Our ways are deeply rooted in the world of animals. Huntresses can search for years before they encounter their sha'cara, and some never do. We have the life listener to guide us, but that is no guarantee. If they are found and join us, sha'cara *are* Minai, just like the women and men here around us. And Minai protect each other. We don't hunt our own; we're not rotten in the head like the Karnis'h," said Aslara.

"The Karnis'h? I've heard that name before," said Trista. "Shiri called me that when she first saw me. Who are they?"

"They're the death and destruction that haunt our dreams," said Aslara. "They pick everything bare wherever they go. Grabbing the fruits of other people's labor. We never see them during the times of plenty, but when the rains stop and we are forced to travel north, they always find us. We move around in hopes of avoiding them. Traveling the plains, following the herds. The Taori guide us, and if we're careful we don't see them for many moons. But we're not always so lucky."

Aslara's voice turned so dark Trista was not sure if she wanted to ask the next question. She swallowed away the lump in her throat before she uttered the words.

"W—What happens when they find you?"

"Nothing good. Those they kill are pulled away into the night, never to be seen again. Food and animals are taken. Women and children disappear screaming into the dark. We used to be many more, but the Karnis'h are a never-ending plague. We have no idea where they come from. And if we take any of them out they always return with more, a relentless pack of animals that does not give up. It's slowly destroying our once-thriving tribe. And we're not the only ones."

Images of black soldiers flowed back into Trista's mind.

"Will they come here?" asked Trista.

"I dare not think about it. They've never come this far out. Their territory lies further north, so this place has stayed hidden. It's where we've been safe for many generations. But we're not taking any chances, even during the times of plenty. That's why Shiri and a few others are always patrolling out there—just in case," said Aslara.

"Don't the men protect you?" said Trista.

Aslara looked at her and suddenly broke out in laughter. It was pleasant laughter, clear and high, not meant to deride her in any way. It somehow made the serious leader Trista had gotten to know over the last few weeks look very girlish. Trista could not help but feel like an unknowing child. She sheepishly looked around to see what was so funny.

"What?"

"Haha! Sorry, it's been a long time since someone made me laugh like that," said Aslara, lightly touching Trista's arm. "Thank you for that. You really haven't noticed yet?"

"Noticed what?"

"It's us who protect them, not the other way around," said Aslara. "The men are builders. Workers, not fighters. They're not allowed to be fighters. We, the women, lead this tribe, like our mothers before us and their mothers before them."

Trista's cheeks reddened as she thought back on the last few weeks. As the images floated through her head, she tried to remember details of what she had seen. Things started to fall into place. Aslara being the head of the tribe. The den mothers taking care of all the kids, and the all-women hunting team she had joined. And then there were all the sha'cara Trista had been introduced to—all bonded to women.

None of the men had spoken to her unless absolutely necessary. Looking back now, she could not remember a single time one of the men had idly chatted with her, unless spoken to. All the men had been busy working on the huts or tending the goats up in the mountains, creating tools and hunting weapons or simply doing the cooking together with a few of the women. Trista had not seen one of them carry a spear, sword or knife.

"But why? Don't you need all the hands you can get to defend the tribe?" said Trista.

"No!" Aslara said fiercely with a shake of her head. "Fighting is like an addiction for men. Our foremothers taught us that. Any man who shows aggression is likely to fall prey to it again; searching for it, to see what he can defeat and conquer, including women. If we didn't need them for offspring, I wonder if we'd have any men here at all."

Trista must have looked bewildered, for Aslara let out a sigh.

"You really do come from a different world, don't you? Are you going to tell me the men there never fought? Or refused to take no for an answer?"

Trista thought about the boys who loved to challenge each other back on the island, to see who was strongest. It seemed so normal to her for boys to do so. She had even enjoyed it herself when they had challenged her. She had been in a few play fights when she was younger, but stopped when her breasts started to develop—not because they hurt, but because the boys started behaving strangely whenever she wanted to join in. She never experienced any trouble with intimidating company, though, and even then, she had excellent aim with her knees.

"I—I suppose you're right," said Trista, uncertain if she should go against the statement or not.

She tried to keep her mind open to all these new realities, but at moments like this it was abundantly clear there were big differences between the Minai and the waterclans. However, despite these differences she felt at ease here. Back home, she had always felt trapped in her role as a woman. Being forced to find a husband, start a family, be a good wife—it never felt like the path she was meant to walk. She looked at Aslara. Here was not only a beautiful, strong and decisive woman, but a great and well-respected leader of her people as well. She saw why Shiri was so impassioned by the leading mother. The combination was very attractive.

By the goddess, how her parents had tried to shape her into something they deemed suitable. Not once had they stopped to ask what *she* wanted to do; if she told them about it, it was easily dismissed.

The thought came as a shock. It was the first time in a while she thought of her parents. It felt wrong to be annoyed at them now they were dead. For a moment, a flare of guilt rushed through her.

No, she thought.

She had nothing to feel guilty about. She had kept her word. She had kept Decan safe, and so much more. This was not about her parents anymore. This was about her. Perhaps it was time to let go of home a little, and start her own path.

Mother, Father, I think we're at a good spot here. I think we'll be alright now.

"A man of the Minai is not allowed to raise his fists in anger. Ever," continued Aslara, unaware of Trista's wandering thoughts.

The remark brought Trista back to their conversation. She was not entirely sure how you could prevent anyone from getting angry occasionally. Still, getting angry and acting on it were two different things—such as when she had her own angry outburst at Dalkeira back at the Pillar of Life, the morning Decan got bitten.

"Oh, I almost forgot. I've been looking for Dalkeira all morning. Do you know where she is? She wouldn't have left the village without telling me, would she?" asked Trista.

"Have you looked in the caves? If not, they're probably still in there," said Aslara.

"They?"

"Duvessa is with her. I saw them go in this morning."

"Do you know what they're doing?"

"Didn't ask. I'm sure Duvessa has her reasons for bringing her to the watergardens."

"Watergardens? What watergardens?" said Trista, confused.

"You mean you haven't seen them yet? I asked Shiri to show you days ago."

Trista hesitated.

"I—I don't think she likes me very much. She wants nothing to do with me."

"Mother of all! That woman can be so stubborn sometimes!" said Aslara. "Alright, follow me and I'll show you the entrance. You'll understand when you see it. And tonight, I'll have a serious talk with Shiri."

"No! Please don't. She already doesn't like me as it is. I don't want to make it worse."

Aslara remained silent, glancing at her several times as they walked through the village.

"Really, it's nothing," said Trista again.

"Alright. If you think so. You're still a guest and I'll respect your wishes." said Aslara. "Just promise me you'll let me know when it becomes a problem."

Aslara halted. She pointed out the start of the caves.

"Here we are."

Demarus, who had followed them, immediately lay himself down at the leading mother's feet again. He seemed content with soaking up the sun and letting the rarity of his full stomach settle. The entrance in front of Trista did not seem very big. If Dalkeira had gone in there, it would have been a tight fit.

"Just follow the tunnel till the end. You should be able to spot them easily," said Aslara, pointing.

"You're not coming with me?"

"No, I need to check in on the new wall paths. The rains are upon us; we need everything checked before that."

Trista looked up toward the sky again. Nothing but blue.

"You know, I'm beginning to think it never rains here," she said over her shoulder as she headed for the entrance.

"It will come. Just wait and see," said Aslara with a smile. "Oh, and Trista? You don't have to only dig for roots. For variety, you can also help here in the watergardens."

"Thank you," Trista said, a little disappointed. She had hoped to join a hunt. "But I don't know if Dalkeira will want to."

"Well, see what you can do. I have another thing in mind, but I need to discuss this with Duvessa first. Perhaps she can have a word with the winged ancient as well."

The remark stung Trista's pride. She did not need anyone else to make Dalkeira understand.

"Oh, and I'd like you to start training with a few of the younger women here. I've seen you handle your short hunting spears quite well; it should form a great base to get some better weapon experience."

"You want me to learn how to fight?" Trista asked uncertainly.

"A warrior should always strive to improve one's skill."

"I told you, I'm no warrior," began Trista.

"And I told you, *nonsense*," said Aslara. "I have seen the inner strength you possess. You have the heart of a warrior. Not one that looks for a fight, but one that seeks to protect; to keep fighting for a belief. To live. You might not think of yourself as one yet, but you most certainly are. You would be an excellent leader too, I think. You led your own to safety when it was needed, which is not always easy."

At her feet, the big cat rolled over on his back and stretched his legs. His large paws stretched with them, revealing for a moment his sharp claws. Aslara rolled her eyes and chuckled. She knelt to give Demarus one final scratch.

"Come on, you lazy cat. You can sleep later."

Trista stepped into the gloomy tunnel as Aslara and Demarus walked the other way toward the walkways.

Am I really a warrior? A leader, even?

She had expected a network of smaller caves, much like her hideout cave back on the island, but she could not have been more wrong. A single, small tunnel led deeper into the mountain. The daylight from the entrance behind her faded, allowing the darkness to slowly move in. By the time the tunnel bent slightly to the right, she could barely see where she was going.

Unpleasant memories of the first night she encountered the soldiers bubbled to the surface of her mind. A mixture of fear and relief settled inside of Trista as her emotions about the soldiers, Decan and Dalkeira all flowed together. For a moment she hesitated, contemplating turning back, when a familiar tingle entered her mind.

Dalkeira.

Her thoughts reached out, but Dalkeira could not hear her yet. Trista quickly continued down the tunnel. As she turned the corner, red light announced the end of the rocky hallway. Relieved, she stepped out of the narrow passage, only to be welcomed by the largest underground expanse she had ever seen.

In the middle of the cave, a single beam of sunlight fell through a large hole in the side of the mountain. The stone dome showed constantly changing reflections that made the walls look alive and moving. The light show illuminated the entire dome's red stone walls, bathing the cavern in a warm glow.

Trista immediately recognized the patterns of light on the walls, confirmed by the sounds of slushing water. She surveyed the gigantic stone dome; the water body that stretched out in front of her covered more than two-thirds of the entire cave's floor. There were multiple layers of water, confined in small, natural terraces. Acting as a mirror, the water seemingly doubled the size of the cave, intensifying the massive feel of the chamber.

Trista had missed the presence of water; she felt it in every fiber of her body. The sound, the smell, the reflection of sunlight… Trista let it all soak in as she knelt near the water and let her hand run through it.

The cave was pleasantly cool in comparison to the temperature outside. Her eye caught a familiar color under the water's surface.

Water and food, they're both here.

She reached in and pulled a green leaf from the underground lake. She instantly recognized it as one of the main foods served every night. Together with the water, the Minai had all the essentials they needed to stay alive here, even if the rains made them wait. She saw some men and women wade through the low water, their pants rolled up above their knees. They were selectively picking green leaves by hand.

To her left a smaller water pool lay on an elevated platform. It was used to fill containers with drinking water. Trista noticed water slowly flowed over the edge into the lower basin that held the plants. The plant basin took about half of the total water space in the cavern, but all of it was quite shallow. From there, it flowed into another modest and slightly lower pool, where multiple children were helping a den mother wash clothes. A couple of smaller sha'cara lessened their thirst before following the watergarden's tunnel back out again. Birds simply flew in and out through the sky-hole. The last pool, which took up the other half of the water reservoir, seemed to be for bathing. The mornings Trista spent washing from a tiny bucket to save water suddenly seemed very unnecessary. It was the darkest of the four water bodies, so Trista figured it was the deepest as well. Around the shore, two of the smaller Minai children ran around, naked.

The sound of splashing water drew Trista's attention further down the bathing basin. She looked around the cave and noticed a small figure standing a ways off.

Duvessa. But where's Dalkeira?

Behind the old woman, a wall of red rock was pierced by a set of large roots. They were the same as those in the life listener's hut. The Pillar of Life roots had forced their way through the wall to get access to the underground water source.

It was a strange, unearthly scene in front of her. It looked like Duvessa stood on top of the water, in front of the roots. But as she moved closer, Trista saw that part of the reservoir was actually very shallow.

She carefully followed a rocky path that lay just beneath the surface of the underground lake. The water felt soothing to her feet. Skillfully, she kept her eyes moving to spot the darker parts of the water, which indicated the places where it ran deep. Small, cold waves slushed against her feet as she approached the old woman.

The life listener took no notice of her. Instead, she stared intensely at the water. There, in one of the deeper parts of the underground lake, moved a shadow. The wave that formed along the surface told Trista all she needed to know. It was Dalkeira who swam beneath the surface.

"If she wanted to take a bath, I could've helped—" began Trista, but Duvessa interrupted her.

"Shhh," said the old woman with a finger against her lips.

She waved Trista over and grabbed her hand in a warm, gentle but firm grip.

Trista's eyes followed the shadow shooting through the water. Dalkeira moved at incredible speed, much quicker than Trista remembered from their time at sea. Unexpectedly, the shadow stopped, as if something was in the way.

That's new.

A moment later, the water around the shadow started to churn and violently blow bubbles. Trista stepped forward to call out, but Duvessa's grip intensified, urging her to stay put.

"Just watch," said the life listener softly.

The water broke out in a wild display of bubbles and splashes. Trista unintentionally held her breath when a large eruption of water burst through the surface. Dalkeira launched herself upward, spinning. Three coiling streams of water followed her straight up into the air. They looked like water snakes trying to get at her tail.

A good distance above the water, the dragon forcefully spread her wings. For a moment, she hung dead still in the air as gravity tried to catch up with her. Waterdrops from Dalkeira's wings flew everywhere. Trista expected the water snakes to grab the dragon's feet, but instead they bent outward and continued to circle the dragon, forming a moving wall of water around her.

"Good, good! Now keep going. Try to bring them together," called the blindfolded woman, who listened intently to the rush of water.

Beating her wings, Dalkeira went into a dive, forcing the three streams of water to combine into one large, moving vortex. Both dragon and water hit the underground lake with force, the sound of impact bouncing round the cave. Diving in and out the water, the dragon seemed to bend the lake around her.

Trista could not believe her eyes. She knew Dalkeira had always been built for water as well as the air, but this was something new. The dragon shaped the water at her will. Trista knew of no other creature in the ocean that could do anything like it.

Dalkeira's shadow made a sharp turn toward them. It slowed and stopped right in front of them. The dragon climbed out of the lake onto a submerged, rocky plateau, panting.

"Well done, my child," said Duvessa.

Dalkeira shook herself to get rid of the water on her skin and wings. "That was quite good, was it not?" said the dragon, sounding pleased.

It was only then that Dalkeira noticed Trista standing there, eyes spread wide, mouth slightly open. The dragon froze mid-movement. She put down the leg she had lifted to inspect and sat down quietly.

"Trista. What are you doing here?" asked Dalkeira.

"What am *I* doing here? What are *you* doing here? That was amazing!" said Trista, unable to hide her enthusiasm.

All her annoyed feelings of that morning disappeared in the face of such a marvelous display of... of... Trista had no idea what to call it.

"How long—? When—? How did you—? Amazing!"

"You are not angry, then?" said Dalkeira, tilting her head.

"Angry? Why would I be angry about this?"

"Dalkeira was afraid that you would be angry because she didn't tell you right away," said Duvessa. "But don't be too harsh on her, my child. Part of it is my fault."

"You've both lost me," said Trista, confused. "How long has this been going on, then?"

"Since the sunken city in the Endless Sands," said Dalkeira, using the Minai term for the desert settlement. "I want to become stronger for our journey west."

"West? Why? I thought we were going to stay here."

"For a while, yes. But we need to go west," repeated Dalkeira.

"Why?" asked Trista. "Why do we need to follow this road into nowhere? It's nearly gotten us killed at least half a dozen times already. It's safe here. We can stay. Be happy."

"Happy? I will not be happy until I know what's out there calling me. I want to go."

"And what about what I want? What about Decan? What he needs?" said Trista forcefully. "I don't understand where all this is coming from. Did you not say you wanted to stay here? Why did you not just tell me?"

"I wanted to tell you, but it was never the right time. You were constantly occupied with Aslara, or focused on Decan, or the baby. And when we speak, you do nothing but yell at me," said Dalkeira defiantly.

Though Dalkeira's words sounded strong, her eyes swirled nervously. Bright green spots phased in and out of the deep blue colors of her eyes.

Trista's skin crawled in anger. Dalkeira's accusation immediately triggered the will to defend herself. Preoccupied with Aslara? Paying attention to

Decan? Yelling? It had been Dalkeira who had acted so rude to Aslara in the first place!

The image of the leading mother drifted into her head. Trista took a deep breath and forced herself to step back from the whole situation.

What would a leader do? How do I reach beneath the surface of anger to the ocean of reasoning?

"I—" started Trista.

She stopped and let out another deep breath.

"I appreciate your honesty. I'm sorry you felt that you could not come to me with this. You are one of the most important things in this world to me. You should be able to tell me anything, and I should be there for you when you need me."

The acknowledgment brought an unseen smile to Duvessa's face. In front of Trista, the dragon visibly relaxed but made no effort to continue their conversation.

"Perhaps it is best to call it a day, my child," suggested Duvessa to Dalkeira.

"Not yet, old woman," said Dalkeira as she turned around. "I still want to practice some more."

The dragon walked off toward the large tree roots nearby.

"What's she doing?" asked Trista.

"She feels connected to the flows of life that run through the Taori. It makes it easier for her to concentrate."

Dalkeira positioned herself between the roots, facing the water. Trista noticed there were strange patterns on the cave wall behind the dragon. It looked like the written script in the books of the merchants who visited the village. But there were two different forms. One was circular, large and flowing. The other patterns were much smaller, with sharp corners and lots of tiny stripes.

"What are those strange scribblings behind Dalkeira?" asked Trista, observing the dragon slowly wading into the water.

"Words of the first sha'cara. Honoring the Taori. Giving value to the balance of life," said Duvessa. "Our stories tell that the winged ancient called on her sisters and formed this cavern, this mountain, where first there was nothing. They moved the earth, brought the water; thus this sanctuary for the Minai came into this world. Their stories were made part of this place."

Dalkeira was chest-deep in water now. She lifted herself onto her hind legs a few times, as if to get the movement right.

"Stories? There's more?" asked Trista.

"Oh dear, oh my. Simply look around, my child, and you will spot them quite easily."

It was true. Now Trista knew what to look for she spotted several other places with similar symbols on the wall. Some were very hard to read because of the water's reflection. Others had not withstood the decay of time very well, but they were plentiful, and spread across the cave.

"And the smaller symbols?"

"Similar words in a language long dead."

Satisfied by the preparations, Dalkeira spread her wings and took a deep breath. Her chest swelled with air. For a moment, she looked like a statue; perfectly still, holding her breath as she concentrated.

Dalkeira stomped her front legs into the water as she made a powerful forward movement with her wings. She extended her neck, low over the water, and let out a roar that echoed across the surface. Moving away, the water pushed itself up into a wave three feet high. It rushed forward, pushed by an invisible force. It grew in size as Dalkeira directed more water into it. It swelled another foot just before it smashed into the wall at the other end of the lake. The thunderous noise of water subsided as the clear liquid slid from the red rock back into the lake again.

"But how? *How* is she doing this?" said Trista in disbelief. "You say the first sha'cara moved the earth. If that's true, and both are considered winged ancients, does that mean that every dragon can do something like this?"

"I don't know, my child. Before Dalkeira, I had never seen a winged ancient before. *She* calls it her watertouch; and that's what she does. She touches it, without ever reaching for it. She feels drawn to the water. Says she can see it, too. Not like we see it, but as if many tiny pieces of water make one whole."

"I remember she once told me something similar, many days ago. But I never expected her to be able to command water like this."

Trista turned back toward Dalkeira, who launched another wave. This time the dragon tried to divide her concentration between the wave and two spheres of water she pulled up from the lake. With a push of her mind, she launched the first sphere after the wave. The second sphere fell apart as she lost control of it, but the first one crashed into the back of the wave, disrupting the flow of it. It quickly dissipated before it could reach the other end of the dome.

"You know, my child, that was a very important first step you made back there," Duvessa said in a soft voice from behind Trista. "Perhaps there is still hope for you both."

"And why are you helping her?" asked Trista in a flat tone, suddenly feeling as though Duvessa tried to steal Dalkeira away.

"Because she asked me."

The life listener fell silent, as though waiting to see how the waterclan woman would respond. But Trista didn't speak, instead trying to figure out what she could have done differently.

"I can't hear her anymore, you know," said Trista after a moment. "I used to hear her all the time. So often that, sometimes, it was just too much with everything going on. But now I try to reach out and she's not there. She pulls away. She's gone, and I hate the silence of my own thoughts."

"Oh child, she's not gone. She's right there. Waiting for you to reach out once more—or perhaps waiting for you to listen more closely. You know she practically threatened to eat me if I did not help you and your brother? She's very strong-willed, that one."

"That she is."

Trista let out a chuckle, followed by a sigh.

"But how am I supposed to fix this? Where do I begin?"

"You're mistaken, my child. You've already begun. You just need a little help. Help that perhaps the ways of the Minai can offer," said the old woman. "Has Aslara mentioned the ba'roshia to you at all?"

"Ba'roshia? Not that I know of," said Trista. "What is it?"

"It is our ritual of bonding. At the end of the introduction period, sha'cara and Minai both enter the lifedream. They do so to experience each other's world. To receive better understanding of one another and to forge a bond that cannot easily be broken," explained Duvessa. "From what Dalkeira told me, the way you got to know her was not in very peaceful surroundings. It sounded… forced. Perhaps the ba'roshia can make amends and complete the process started during your introduction. It won't be easy, and there's danger involved. Some who enter the lifedream lose their way…"

Trista had no idea what ritual Duvessa was talking about, but she agreed that those first weeks had not been pleasant for any of them. Being constantly on the run, she had to divide her attention between the dragon and her brother. She did not know what kind of ritual this was, but if it meant she and Dalkeira could become close again, she was more than willing to try.

"Just tell me what to do."

CHAPTER TWENTY-FIVE

Assassin

SHE WANTS TO do what?"

Shiri pushed Aslara's hands away from her shoulders. Her eyes shot fire. The second-in-command disliked going out on long patrols more and more. Every time she returned, she was greeted with another story about Trista or Dalkeira. It was like Aslara's head was filled with nothing else but concern for the newcomers. What happened to the time her lover was concerned about her? Interested in her?

"Duvessa wants to make those two official Minai," Aslara repeated calmly. "I think it's a great idea. We can use the help during the big hunt."

"Why? She isn't even a good huntress," said Shiri, bewildered. "And why is Duvessa meddling in hunting matters anyway? My group has always done right by her guidance."

"She's not. Duvessa believes a ba'roshia is needed, and that's only allowed if you're part of the tribe."

"But she's not! She's just an outsider. And trouble if you ask me."

"How can you of all people even say that?" said the leading mother, indignantly. "You know it has been done plenty of times before. To replenish our bloodlines—and other reasons."

"Would men even be interested in someone like her?" said Shiri, ignoring the remark. "With her strange coloring, and skin that can't stand the sun. And what about her little brother? He's happily chatting to any girl like it's nothing. He might already be too old to change his ways."

"I'm sure he'll come around," said Aslara. "But that's not what this is really about, is it? Why don't you tell me what's really bothering you?"

"What's really bothering me? As if this isn't enough?" snapped Shiri. "Fine, I'll give you more. You're so focused on these outsiders you've forgotten what we've been trying to do. How we're trying to keep everyone safe."

"By hunting and killing the Karnis'h? I told you I would think about it; nothing more. If you want to spend your days trailing the Red Plains looking for them, I won't stop you. But don't fool yourself into thinking I'll approve a full-on attack. We haven't the numbers. These things can't be considered lightly."

"Really? Because it seems to me you're not considering it at all. They're getting closer every year. Tracking us, hunting us. All *you* do is spend time with Trista. I see how you look at her, all smitten by her unusual looks."

"Oh, stop it. I have no such interest in her. You're a beautiful and strong woman. I've challenged the laws of our tribe to be with you. Defied the advice of our life listener," said the leading mother. "How can you, of all women, be jealous? You have the honor of carrying the title of second-in-command *and* first huntress, a combination unheard of in our ancestral stories. I couldn't be more proud that you're my chosen. Now quit being stubborn. If you can't see you've got nothing to worry about, you need to let Duvessa check your eyes and head."

Aslara saw the skeptical look Shiri threw back at her.

"I just don't like how you look at her."

"And how's that?"

"I don't know. *Intrigued.* I'd prefer if you stayed away from her."

"I can't do that. They're new to the tribe; they need guidance, and that's my responsibility. Besides, I wouldn't be the only one in the company of different women… or men," added the leading mother.

"What do you mean?"

"Your late-night visits with some of the builders."

"You know about that?" said Shiri, taken aback.

"Of course. What kind of leading mother would I be if I didn't?"

Shiri turned away in shame, then turned back.

"Let me explain, and please don't be mad about it. I did it for us. For you. I thought it would make you happy to have a child of our own, to share in that miracle of life," said Shiri, moving closer. "I wanted to give that to you. To fill your heart with more love than you could imagine. Especially since you are unable—because of the title and all—"

The tribe's greatest honor was often considered a cruel destiny as well. The laws in place meant a leading mother was forbidden to have children, to prevent a leader from favoring their own flesh and blood. After the celebration of a newly appointed head of the tribe, there was a more saddening ceremony for a leading mother to undergo. A private ceremony between the leading mother and the life listener. It was not without risk, scarring internal organs with one of the strongest poisons on the plains. Infections were a serious danger. But, if all went well, the chosen mother-of-all no longer possessed the physical ability to carry a child inside her.

Aslara held up a hand.

"Do I look angry? It's alright. I accepted this part of my life a long time ago. And what you are doing is perfectly accepted among the tribe. I'm just surprised you have made the attempts to get with child, given your plans to flush out the Karnis'h. Apart from that, I don't blame you for anything. And I'll admit I've been interested in Trista from the start—but not for the reason you think."

Trista's name triggered instant revulsion in Shiri. She looked back in disgust and increased her distance again, folding her arms.

"This better be good."

"A while back, Duvessa had a lifevision. She's had troublesome visions before, but nothing like this. The Red Plains were swallowed by shadows. Vultures picked the bones of hundreds clean as the darkness engulfed all. Animals, humans—everything. All was lost until a woman with burning hair appeared out of nowhere. Being pushed forward by a wild river of water, she drove away the shadows allowing the sun to return."

"And you believe *she* is this woman who will push away the darkness? She doesn't even fight well! What if those men she always speaks about follow her here? What if she's the reason this darkness comes? Even if she intends no harm, she might doom us all," said Shiri. "I don't like it. *I* think we should send them off."

"I agree; she doesn't fight well," said Aslara. "That's why we're going to teach her. But I won't send her away because of your insecurities. She's done nothing wrong, and many of the tribe have already taken a liking to her. Shiri, I love you with all my heart, but my first responsibility is to the tribe. This is bigger than you alone. Now come to bed. Tomorrow, Trista will become one of us and we can drop this whole outsider nonsense completely."

* * *

The night had crawled by but offered little rest for Trista. Decan had tossed and turned restlessly, caught in one of his nightmares several times during his sleep. She spent some time singing soft lullabies for him, which seemed to calm him somewhat, even if he said during the day that he was too old for them. Her own nerves for the ceremony had been the other culprit for the wasted nighttime.

She yawned as she walked toward the watergardens. Duvessa shuffled ahead of her, the blind woman's fingers sliding lightly along the cold rock walls of the tunnel. Decan followed closely behind them.

"Are you listening to the rock?" asked Trista, who knew Duvessa did not really need the touch to find her way.

"Oh no, my child. I'm sure the mountains have stories to tell, but I can't hear their voices. I simply like to feel the surface, made smooth by the touch of hundreds of our foremothers."

The large dome came into view. Aslara had said the ceremony would be short and simple, but when Trista stepped inside the large complex, she saw the entire tribe there to bear witness. Women, children and men, but that was not all; the watergardens were filled with animals. Birds sat high on the edge of the stone roof's hole, the other animals mixed in between the humans. The gathering was an impressive—and intimidating—scene.

At the back, Shiri leaned against the wall, observing it all with a dissatisfied look on her face.

"Water is the giver of life and the cleanser of souls," began Duvessa, who led the ceremony.

A voice sprang to life. One of the tribeswomen let out a high-pitched, rolling call. It was immediately followed by three deep blows of a horn. Its vibrant sound set a rhythm which was adopted by the clear thumping of a drum. The woman continued to sing loud and proud in her ancestral tongue. Every few lines, she stopped, and a group of women and men sang back at her. The group's voices carried clear through the dome.

Fascinated, Dalkeira walked around the singers.

"*It is like they tell a story,*" the dragon said privately, so as not to interrupt those who sang. "*It is like the song I hear when I sleep, though that resembles more the sound of whales.*"

Dalkeira walked another circle around the group.

"*Do you think I could sing as well?*" wondered the dragon.

Trista watched her observe the way the women and men produced different sounds in their throats. Walking back, the dragon sat next to her and tried to reproduce the tones. The effect was less than melodious and Dalkeira quickly stopped.

"*I am certain I just need a little practice,*" she mentioned to Trista as lightly as possible, obviously trying to hide her embarrassment.

The drums slowly dropped away, as did the choir. Only the woman's voice remained, supported by the soft tones of the horn. Then even that stopped.

"Please step forward, my child," Duvessa invited Trista.

She offered Trista a wooden bowl. It contained sap from the Pillar of Life's roots.

Trista slowly took a sip from the sweet, cool liquid and handed it back. Aslara stepped forward and used a special mixture of red clay, water and herbs to draw a pattern on Trista's face. Behind them, Duvessa spoke words in the language of the song.

Finishing the final markings on Trista's face and neck, Aslara gently placed her hands under Trista's ears, along her jaw. Trista stared into the leading mother's eyes. Her face flushed as Aslara leaned in close. Was she going to kiss her? The thought made her heart race.

Trista closed her eyes in expectation, but instead felt the leading mother's lips press softly against her forehead. Trista opened her eyes, unsure whether she felt relieved or disappointed. She looked up at Aslara's smiling face. The leading mother took a step back and turned around.

"Today, we gather here in our ancestral hall—surrounded by the written word of our foremothers—to welcome new members to our tribe once more. From this day on, this woman will not merely be a guest; she will be one of us. No longer will she be 'Trista of the Waterclans', but Trista, huntress of the Minai! She brings with her a brother, Decan, and her sha'cara, Dalkeira; a winged ancient that has not been seen in generations. On this day, under her guidance, they join us as well," said Aslara loudly. "Welcome them, embrace them. Teach them our ways, so we may keep strong and pursue the balance of the flows together."

Together, the women in the tribe—except for Shiri—sent out a high, vibrating shout of official welcome. The men joined in with low whooping and stomping their feet on the ground, followed by any animal able to call out in its own way.

As the cheering carried on, Trista felt Dalkeira's curiosity and excitement rise.

"You deserve a bit more, I would think," said the dragon's voice inside Trista's mind.

Dalkeira waded into the underground lake and spread her wings. A fountain of water spouted upward, creating a thin mist that drifted toward the rays of sunlight falling through the hole. As the thin drops reached the sunlight, colors filled the air. The tribe's greeting intensified under the display of a beautiful rainbow.

In the back, Shiri silently observed the spectacle, seeing for the first time how Dalkeira performed her watertouch.

The tribe's enthusiastic greeting made Trista break out in a grateful smile. Close to her, Decan showed an equally wide grin. She wondered if they had reached a place where they could belong again. A place where nobody would chase them anymore; where they were safe.

Aslara turned back toward her and brought their heads together. For the briefest moment, their foreheads touched, a gesture Trista found more intimate than the kiss of a few moments ago.

"Welcome, Trista of the Minai," said the leading mother softly. "I expect great things of you."

After Aslara came Duvessa, who gave a similar greeting. One by one, every woman of the tribe approached her and put their forehead against hers. They spoke kind words of welcome or expressed their happiness to her. Most in the Terran language, some with native words. In those instances, Trista simply smiled and nodded.

Several of the women politely greeted Decan, but Trista noticed the gesture of acceptance of touching foreheads was only offered to her.

Is it because he is a child still? Or a boy?

The tribesmen and children trailed off, while most of the animals lingered, waiting for their Minai counterpart to exit the cave.

In the end, only Shiri remained with Razza and Shuka. Trista waited, wondering what the first huntress would do. The leading mother invited her partner forward, but Shiri scoffed and walked off, the two hyen'sta following her. Aslara let out a sigh.

"Oh dear, oh my, try not to worry, my child. She'll come around," said Duvessa to the leading mother. The raven repeated her words. "And now that we've gotten this out of the way, let's prepare for the ba'roshia," said the blind woman, grabbing Trista's arm. "Mind leading an old woman back to her home?"

Near the tunnel entrance, the young initiate and old life listener looked back at Dalkeira. The dragon was still playing around with waves. Setting them up, running them across one another to form a more complex pattern and then splitting them in two different fronts again.

"Are you coming, Wavebreaker?" called the blind woman. "You can continue practicing after the ritual."

The two different waves bent toward the center and crashed into each other, producing a large, foaming splash. Dalkeira trumpeted in triumph. She turned her neck around.

"I prefer 'ocean beauty' over that one," Dalkeira said in all earnest before she launched into the air and disappeared through the dome's hole.

"One thing is for certain, my child," said Duvessa as they made their way out through the tunnel. "She'll always be one for flattery."

Dalkeira was waiting at Duvessa's place. The old woman sent Trista to get two bowls from the large hut. Next to the hut stood a smaller version of

400

Duvessa's dwelling, solely built from large, dry leaves. It was just big enough to hold four people, or in this case, a woman and a growing dragon.

"I still do not understand why we have to do another ritual," said Dalkeira.

"Because you need it, my child. And Trista needs it as well. The ba'roshia will help strengthen that which has been lost—or are you saying you don't feel something missing?"

"I do," said Dalkeira reluctantly, wondering if it was for the best.

"A sha'cara without its bond is fated to lose its way without proper guidance, as is the human tied to it. You need each other for the things to come; the flows have shown it," said Duvessa. "And don't give me some excuse about it being better this way, because trust me, it's not."

Dalkeira looked at the old woman, wondering if she could have heard her thoughts, when Trista came back around the corner.

"Is this what you were looking for, Duvessa? More root juice?"

Trista handed the life listener two bowls filled with Taori sap.

"And a little bit extra," said Duvessa with a mysterious smile. "Now, in you go."

They were met with a blanket of warmth as Trista opened the flap to enter the hut.

"It's boiling hot in there."

Trista looked back at Duvessa, who simply smiled. Tired of waiting, Dalkeira crawled through the opening, keeping her wings carefully folded as tight as possible.

"I do not mind in the slightest," she said.

In the center was a small fire, or rather the remains of one. A pile of stones had been put around it which had clearly absorbed the heat. Duvessa expertly rekindled the flames as she gestured Trista and Dalkeira to take their place.

A bucket of water stood near the entrance. In it floated several herbs. The water had a heavy, moldy, flowery scent to it.

"Now, pay attention. You will be on your own in here. None can enter while you visit the lifedream. First, drink the lifesap. All of it."

Duvessa watched as Trista emptied her bowl and offered the other to Dalkeira. When both bowls were finished, she continued.

"Well done, my children. Now pour the water on the stones. Be careful not to put out the fire."

With a hiss, the hut filled with steam. Dalkeira shook her head as the strong smell of herbs penetrated her nose.

"Good, good. Now keep doing that every five breaths. Slow breaths. I'll be outside."

And with that, the life listener left them to their fate.

* * *

"Wait, what are we supposed to do?" said Trista.

"You'll see," came Duvessa's voice from beyond the thin, leaf-covered walls. "Just relax and keep doing what you're doing, my child."

Soft singing started outside the hut, accompanied by the soft sound of a drum. Trista did not know if it was the old woman herself who sang, but she heard at least two different voices.

"Well, I guess it's just you and me," said Trista, pouring another spoonful of water on the hot stones.

Dalkeira remained silent and put her head on her legs, trying to get as comfortable as possible. With every spoonful the air heated up further. The smoke from the fire blended together with the steam, forming a powerful-smelling mixture. It became difficult to see as Trista's eyes teared up from the stinging air.

"Are you alright?" asked Trista, hearing Dalkeira snort.

"I'm fine," said Dalkeira distantly. "The heat is actually quite pleasant. Very different from the dry heat outside."

Trista started to feel light in the head. The room was lightly spinning. The flames made shadows dance on the wall as Trista's vision blurred in and out of the light.

Dalkeira, who had been making water globes from the tiny drops floating in the air, let out a large yawn. Her sharp teeth sparkled in the light of the fire.

"Is that singing getting louder?" asked the dragon sleepily.

The sound did indeed seem to intensify, guided by a clear *tok* of wood hitting wood. Or perhaps it was their senses that were imagining things—at this point, Trista did not know anymore. She had trouble keeping her head up, like she was suddenly overcome with exhaustion again. With effort, she poured another spoonful. The fire sizzled like angry snakes. The shadows slithered across the wall. Big, black snakes with triple tails. Fear clawed inside her. She tried to move, but her limbs were like stone. Supporting herself as best she could, she lay down and ended up on Dalkeira's side. The familiar feel of the dragon's skin countered the fear and sparked a warm, blissful feeling inside Trista's mind. She wished she felt the dragon's warmth, but the hot air circling made it difficult to discern from her surroundings.

402

"I miss you. Where'd you go?" said Trista suddenly, as if she had only just noticed how far they had actually grown apart these last few weeks.

Water ran across her cheek and she realized it was a tear that ran from her eye. Dalkeira used her watertouch to softly brush it away.

"I am here. Still here. It was you who went—" was all the dragon said before they both drifted off into the lifedream.

The *Behemoth*'s anchor line swayed heavily with the movement of the waves. It was an impressive ship, and a design Bronson had never before seen in his life. Nearly four hundred feet in length, it featured not one but two massive hulls connected in the middle. Its deck could hold a small castle's courtyard, easily reaching a hundred and fifty feet in width. He was not surprised the ship was all the way out here. There was no way the harbor was deep enough for such a colossal boat.

Bronson grabbed the anchor line, taking a moment to rest. He stared back at the coast, where the high general's boat slowly made its way back to the harbor. He had acted as rower for High General Setra's late night meeting and slid off the boat on their way back. For once, the high general manned the oars himself to get back to shore.

Above Bronson, the moon hung low, hidden behind a blanket of clouds. The night was warm, but the water cool. He shivered. The darkness brought him comfort and much needed cover, but the water would eventually cool him too much if he stayed there too long.

The broken prince grabbed the chain firmly and locked his legs around it. His most recent cuts burned in the salty water, but at least his strength had returned thanks to the high general granting him rest. He quickly moved up the iron chain till he reached the ship's anchor hole. There, he flattened himself against the handrail and listened to the sounds of the massive ship. The footsteps of a guard, the creaking of wood, the closing of a door as the crew moved around. It would be a while before things quieted down. He installed himself in a corner and waited.

Bronson startled awake as the snap of an improperly tied sail roused him from his doze. He looked up; the moon was high, which meant it was time to move. He listened for any sounds nearby. Only a handful of guards were on deck; the rest of the ship and its crew slumbered. He looked back at

Tal'Kabur once more as he readjusted the mask across his mouth. The city's chimneys smoked uninterrupted. A new batch of worked Talkarian steel would be loaded onto the boats again in the morning, but for now the harbor and streets lay silent, awaiting daybreak.

Bronson rubbed his legs and took three short breaths to get the blood flowing again. He closed his eyes and hit the back of his head against the ship's wood. The pain helped him focus. Then he jumped over the rail onto the massive deck.

On board, Bronson found the deck loaded with supplies. He moved stealthily between the crates and tuns, passing a few of the guards unnoticed. He peered into a dark manhole, saw the coast was clear, and quickly went below decks. Circumnavigating the crew's quarters, he swiftly sneaked through the ship. He halted before a corner and carefully peeked around it. Two Darkened stood at the door. These disciplined soldiers would not dare sleep while on duty. Bronson inched back and counted the doors in his part of the corridor. The layout of his master's drawings had been spot on up till now. That meant the third door should be a small storage room, filled with trivial things.

He slipped into the room and wasted no time with his surroundings. He climbed out the viewing port and clung to the side. This was the tricky part. There was not much to hold on to as he traversed the ship's hull. He stretched his neck to look around a bulky overhang—and there it was. High General Setra had been right; the windows were always open on warm nights.

Opportunity.

Bronson stretched his leg, ducked under the overhang and crawled through the opening with less noise than a ship's rat. His bare feet landed on animal skin.

Even better, he thought as he pulled out both his knives. He preferred swords, but with the distance he had swum they had not been an option. The smaller blades would just have to do. He waited for his eyes to adjust; even with the clouded moon, the entire room lay shrouded in darkness. His fists clenched firmly around his weapons, ready to stab anything that jumped at him from the dark.

But nothing moved. The royal quarters were quiet—apart from a deep, serene breathing to his right. He looked around as the moon partly broke through the clouds. On the far wall were two sets of doors, probably leading back to the hallway. A heavy desk stood in the center, its wood skillfully decorated. Maps and writing materials lay spread out across its surface, accompanied by a small, stone oil lamp which had been turned off for the night. Bronson recognized Tal'Kabur and a large part of the mid-continent on the most detailed map that lay open. A large cross was drawn just south of Shid'el, the capital of their trade partner Aeterra—right in the center of the Crescent Moon Massif.

Leaving the desk, Bronson sneaked closer to the source of the breathing, alert for any unexpected sounds. He stared at the bed. His heart pounded in his throat. There he was—the object of his hatred. The reason his city suffered and his father was slain. Peacefully asleep under a blanket of the finest fabric; white hairs on the pillow.

Bronson gritted his teeth and twisted the knives in his hands.

Just a few more steps.

He moved with the sway of the *Behemoth*, but apparently the ship had no intention of letting its ruler be slaughtered. As Bronson put down his foot, the plank underneath creaked loudly. The broken prince stared at his foot, calling forth the names of the damned. When he looked up, the Stone King sat straight up in his bed.

"Who's there?"

Bronson launched forward, hacking down with both knives. The Stone King screamed as the blades dug into his chest. Like a madman, Bronson pulled back the blades and stabbed again and again. Hands clawed at his face, but he welcomed the pain. Pain meant obedience.

Holes appeared in the blanket and the bed darkened with blood. His victim weakened. Bronson had done it. He killed the tyrant that slew his father. He saved his mother and sister. Thoughts of triumph filled his head as the life fled from the Stone King's eyes.

But his triumph was short-lived. Bronson stared in horror at the man's arms. *Arms*—plural, not singular. His master had warned him of the stone arm and its inhuman power. This was not the tyrant.

Behind him, a door slammed open so hard it nearly flew off its hinges.

"Assassin," roared Lord Rictor.

The entire ship suddenly swayed as if in response to the Stone King's call. A low rumble traveled through the ship. Lord Rictor stormed toward the broken prince, who just stood there, aghast at his failure.

Your heart beats for three.

His master's words echoed in his mind. They were his wake-up call.

Lord Rictor's hands nearly wrapped around Bronson's throat as his body twisted away from the incoming attack. They tumbled over the bed, flew off the other side and slammed into the wall. Bronson was the first on his feet, jumping back as Lord Rictor swiped his arm across the floor.

The other door crashed open as the two Darkened from the hall rushed into the room. An axe hurled through the air. Bronson ducked and sprang back up to meet one of the Darkened swords. His hands blurred through the air as he circled both men. He grimaced as he stared into the skeleton face of the Darkened, but years of dual-wielding practice surfaced and he drove his knife up through the man's chin. Blood spewed from between the warrior's sewn-shut lips as he dropped to the floor in a puddle of blood.

Bronson rolled across the wooden desk to avoid the Stone King's next attack. He dropped to the ground as a sword slammed into the desk's edge. He kicked out and rammed his elbow into the Darkened's jaw, dislocating it. The skeleton-faced man twisted around, exposing his back. Bronson drove his blade low into the soldier's back, severing the spinal cord. Abandoning his knife, which was lodged between two of the Darkened's vertebra, the broken prince grasped the tiny oil lamp and threw it at Lord Rictor, who made his way around the desk for another attack. The tyrant brought up his stone arm as a shield. The lamp shattered, soaking the inhuman arm in oil. It did nothing to slow the man down. Bronson brought up his arms to shield his head from the incoming punch.

It felt like a minecart ran into him. His head slammed against the desk. Bronson stumbled back around its corner and tripped over the dead Darkened lying on the floor. But he was not the only one who ended up on the floor. In front of him, Lord Rictor's bare feet slipped in the newly-formed puddle of blood. Bronson quickly crawled away, searching for the knife he had dropped.

A small axe barely missed his foot as the Darkened, dragging his paralyzed legs across the floor, took a swing at him. The broken prince wrenched the weapon from his attacker's hand and brought it down hard upon the man's shaved head.

Shouts streamed in from the hallway. Bronson dragged himself back to his feet and saw the twins run through the door.

"Lord Rictor!" screamed one of them. Both women readied their weapons.

The Stone King did not react. He lunged at Bronson, intent on disposing of this insolent attempt on his life. The broken prince grabbed the only weapon within his reach. He pulled the sword from the desk's edge and slashed at the tyrant's face. It was an unbalanced slash; his teacher of old would roll over in his grave if he saw. But it stopped the Stone King's furious charge. Bronson's sword deflected off the stone arm, erupting in a fountain of sparks. The lamp oil was instantly set ablaze, engulfing the entire arm in flames.

Lord Rictor recoiled from the flames, trying to keep his arm away from his face. Bronson tried to get his bearings. He saw the window he came in through and decided to make a break for it. He was out before he knew it, greeted by the cool sea. Nobody had tried to stop him.

* * *

Inside, the twins pushed Lord Rictor to the ground and threw the blood-soaked blanket over his arm. A few of the Darkened put out the burning maps, set afire when the Stone King thrashed around.

With the flames extinguished, the furious ruler got back to his feet. He looked out the window and then at the burned maps on his desk.

"Do you want us to send out the boats, Lord Rictor?" asked Taimila.

One side of her hair was now significantly shorter, burned by the flames as she had pushed her leader down.

"Do not bother. He is long gone," said the Stone King. He twisted his head around and stared into empty space. "And where were you during all this? I could have died!"

"We came as soon as you called," Calissa said amiably.

But Lord Rictor did not hear her. Instead, he turned back toward the desk and brought down his stone fist.

"Useless!"

The dark wood split in two with a loud crack. Only then did he turn and look the twins in the eyes.

"Go ashore with a small force and rouse the city. Someone will pay for this. I do not care who."

Air rushed past Trista's face. She was falling, of that she was certain. Far below her, the ground stretched for miles in all directions. She tried to remember how she got there, but could only pull up a few hazy thoughts about the ceremony that morning. At least, she thought it was that morning.

The view was breathtaking, but the thunderous pounding of air rushing past her ears made it clear she was on her way down. Clouds quickly passed her as she tried to move her arms and legs. She felt strange; light and heavy at the same time, and as though she had no control over her limbs. Was she back on Duvessa's table?

While she tried to figure out what was wrong, the ground charged toward her. The mountains no longer looked like anthills, the trees were starting to show their shape more clearly and the small puddle below her was growing into a tremendous lake. If she did not do something soon, she would get firsthand experience of gravity showing who was in charge. And she was certain the solid rock was less forgiving than these clouds she kept passing. She tried to scream, but no voice found its way out of her throat, only a low rumble. Her throat; another thing that felt different somehow.

Trista forced herself to tilt her head and look at her body, half expecting to see ropes wrapped around it. The swivel of her head felt strange as she tried to look down. The perspective was off, like it was nowhere near her body. She looked at her hands—only to be greeted by blue webbed claws. She let out a cry, which emerged as another grunting rumble followed by a panicked trumpet sound. Amongst the alarm, something whipped behind her.

A tail! I have a tail?

The ground was now getting up close and personal. She instinctively looked away, shielding her body with her arms. She arched her back and felt the snap of wings—*her wings*—as they unfolded and caught the stream of air. Leaning back, her descent became less drastic. The airflow decreased as her wings carried her on the wind. Her stomach dropped as she started to rise again, at which point she finally dared to look around properly. She beat her wings to gain altitude again, allowing her heart to slowly find its normal rhythm—at least, until the moment she realized: she was flying.

CHAPTER TWENTY-SIX

Bonding

IT WAS NOT every day a member of the waterclans—or Minai, for that matter—found herself miles above the ground she normally walked on. Trista tried to make sense of it all while her dragon body banked left. She had encountered a hot rising air flow which she now idly followed like she had seen Dalkeira so often do during their journey. Still, she was surprised at how relaxing it felt.

Her muscles moved beneath her scaled skin. Everything felt like the first time—even blinking felt strange—but familiar at the same time. Was this really her, or was she just a passenger stuck inside Dalkeira's mind? She tried to call out, but received no answer.

Trista must have spent quite a while pondering her situation, because by the time she looked around again she had gained enough altitude to pass through numerous clouds. As she approached them, she marveled at the sight of thousands and thousands of shiny silver drops that sparkled in the light of the sun. The tiny specks twirled through the air, chasing each other around like little fish as she came close before flowing together again to form the image of a normal cloud as Trista moved farther away.

The world seemed strange and distant. She wondered if there were people living down on the ground. Decan? Aslara? It all seemed so small and insignificant. She was perfectly content with where she was. Just her and the infinite sky.

The former human in her felt the power in her muscles as she gained more control over them. The two smaller rudder wings above her main flight wings helped make tiny corrections during her maneuvers. She breathed in forcefully to enjoy this unknown freedom. Her chest instantly radiated a pleasant warmth. Her body became lighter and drifted upward.

Her other life felt even further away than the ground below. She tried to remember details of her time spent walking on it, but the images refused to form in her head. Perhaps she had always been here. Perhaps this was her life, and the other, the dream. Maybe she had always been a dragon.

A soft tone reached her ears, or rather touched her mind. The sound came from the west; first a single tone, then more. The melody was one of the most beautiful compositions Trista had ever heard. The low notes could shake a planet to the core even as the high notes lifted one's spirit up beyond the clouded skies. The complexity was beyond any human musical performance, consisting of sound and thought at the same time.

Below Trista were the Red Plains and Pillars of Life scattered along them. The roots spread out across the land, flowing the waters of life through their tremendous network. The entire network glowed a blueish-white color that resonated with the intensity of the song. The music had an incredible pull on her. Her entire being focused toward the west, far beyond the lands that stretched out before her. She began to fly toward it, uncertain if it was by choice or force.

Then a cracking sound intruded on her thoughts, drawing her attention away from the music.

What noise could reach all the way up here?

She looked around, but saw nothing. Another crack rolled through the sky. The song was now completely gone. She banked toward the east and gazed at the horizon below. Mountain tops and forests. Lakes and deserts. All the landscapes she knew existed surrounded her as she tried to pinpoint the cracking sound of—

Stone. It's stone I hear. Like a cliff that splits from a tremor.

A change in the light caught her eye. She adjusted her trajectory and kept her gaze firmly locked on the area where she had seen something move. At first, nothing happened; then suddenly the land fell into shadow. The cracking sound broke through the air once more, this time lingering much longer as the shadow crawled forward across the mountains and trees. Trista flew closer to inspect what was happening.

After some time gliding toward it, doubt entered her mind. Was she approaching it, or was the shadow moving toward her? The cracking intensified. She saw the darkness move across one lake, then another. It seemed to pick up speed along the way.

Finally, she was close enough to observe what was happening in full detail. The shadow was in fact the darkest rock Trista had ever seen. The cracking sound ran across the world as large rocks shot out of the ground, petrifying trees and flowers—even water—into a deep, black stone surface. Following the stone came the darkness; all light swallowed into a void of nothingness.

A pillar of black stone shot out of the ground at incredible speed, almost knocking her straight out of the sky. She beat her wings to get away from the barren, rocky wasteland forming below her. She saw deer flee the oncoming evil, only to be swallowed up by a chasm suddenly forming in the ground. Rabbits and fish turned to stone. Centuries-old trees toppled under the weight of petrification. It was like the entire landscape was burned by an unseen fire and left charred and deserted.

As she retreated to a safe distance, the rest of the world came back into view. The shadow expanded in all directions. She flew to the west, but it was not long until she saw the same darkness on the western horizon. It was quickly approaching from every direction. The world she knew was disappearing in front of her eyes.

Trista did not know why she had the urge to look down, but as soon as she did, she knew something was there, waiting. She folded her wings and bent into a dive. This was no uncontrolled drop, nor was there any fear of crashing into the ground. It was smooth and fast; natural. But no matter how fast she descended, the darkness closed in at equal speed. All around her, the black stone rushed across the land. As she fell below the highest mountain tops, she saw snow petrify into black stone as the shadow rushed down the mountainsides to gain on her.

Directly below her, Trista noticed a figure, frantically waving up toward her. She focused her eyes to make out who it was, drawing the image into full detail. Strangely enough, the desperate-looking gesture was not what shocked her. It was the fact that the figure who called out to her had long red hair and clear green eyes that stared straight at her as she dove from the sky. Trista stared straight into her own human face as she rushed toward the ground.

"TRISTAAAAAA."

The voice from below was her own, but she had not used it. It carried all the way to her bones. Her mind reached out. The world around her slowed. With her dragon eyes, she saw the human's mouth decelerate to a point where the lips barely moved. She knew she was still diving at an incredible speed, yet she barely moved forward. And all around them the darkness unrelentingly pushed forward, fighting against the decreased motion of time.

Trista gazed into those familiar green eyes like they were windows. Behind them she saw—or rather felt—bewilderment. But she knew... she felt, what precisely was there, behind those eyes and it only added to her confusion. Because the green eyes that stared up at her—no matter how familiar—were not her own.

Dalkeira!

Unable or unwilling to stop, Trista pushed her dragon body forward in that frozen moment of time. She tried to reach her friend before the gaining darkness swallowed her. Her scaled nose inched closer to the human hand that stretched toward her in panic. The black stone was now mere inches away from them. It rushed up Dalkeira's human-shaped legs, overtaking skin and clothes. Everything around them had turned to stone; even the sky began to darken.

Unable to move, Trista watched the human form in front of her start to petrify. She stretched her long, sleek neck even further, inching closer to the tip of the finger that awaited her touch.

Human eyes, driven by the dragon's emotion, stared frightened at a blue dragon shape that descended from the sky. It was like a painting, the scene frozen in time. How much time went by as the space between them decreased at a snail's pace? A day? A night? A lifetime? Trista could not tell.

Only part of the arm and face of Dalkeira's human form were still free of stone, but the dark growth did not stop there. Dalkeira screamed with her human voice, mouth stretched wide as her face hardened and her tongue was swallowed up by dark stone. Only the arm remained, then the hand.

She was so close; Trista smelled her own human scent. The black stone crackled along the wrist, then hand, then finger, until finally her scales made contact. The touch sent a rush of warmth into every fiber of her being. Dragon, human—perhaps she was both. Two minds bound as one, the world not complete when one was without the other.

The light of a star imploded where they touched. An eruption of the whitest light burst into existence, only to find itself immediately swallowed by the stone darkness that collapsed in onto them. In that moment of warmth, of complete understanding, their world departed into nothingness as a shrill, high-pitched ringing entered their minds and overruled all their senses.

"Am I dead?"

Trista stared into a void. She looked down and saw her own two feet. Normal, human feet. A small layer of water ran past her toes, but the color was too dark to see if she stood on solid ground or if the water's depth was infinite. Around her, the sound of drips echoed, but she dared not take one step for fear of affecting the reality in front of her. Perhaps she was indeed standing on water, on nothingness, held up only by the fact that she did not know she could fall.

"*Not unless I am dead as well.*"

"*Dalkeira! I can hear you again! Where are you?*"

"Right here," the dragon's voice said, right behind her.

Dalkeira emerged from the darkness as if stepping into a beam of light. Trista jumped at her and hugged the dragon around her neck.

"I'm so sorry about everything," said Trista.

Dalkeira bent her neck slightly to return Trista's hug.

"I just had the strangest dream," said Dalkeira. "I was… *you*."

"I think I had the same dream, but different," answered Trista. "I was flying. I was *you*, high up in the sky. It was like I was being drawn somewhere and everything else faded into the background."

"The song! You mean you heard it?" said Dalkeira excitedly.

"I had no idea it was so beautiful," said Trista. "Did you hear it as well?"

"No."

"What happened, then?"

"So much fear, doubt, hope, love—so much flows through you humans. I thought I knew from our connection, but I truly had no idea. The feelings were intense. And at first, I could not stand it," said Dalkeira, clearly still impressed. Suddenly, she brought her sparkling eye close to Trista, as if remembering something else. "Speaking of which, who walks and stands on just two legs to begin with? It feels so very unstable."

Stumped, Trista looked at her. The dragon shook her head.

"It was all very strange and unpleasant. After I finally figured out how to walk, I spent all my time searching for Decan and myself—I mean, my dragon form—which was confusing. I could think about nothing else. But soldiers were everywhere and there was nothing I could do to find you both; to protect you. I felt so helpless, but I never feel helpless!" said Dalkeira forcefully. "I saw how I, how *you*, lost everything. All the things you cared for. Family, friends, those who inspire…"

"Aslara," said Trista softly, picking up on the reference. "I wish I hadn't yelled at you that morning. When Decan got bitten by that snake."

"It was not that I was upset about you yelling," said Dalkeira. "I saw you were worried about Decan. But you choose that woman we barely knew over me. Trusted *her* over *me*. Though I cannot fault you for that now, as my reaction was not entirely based on logic."

"You were afraid of being left behind. Just like me," said Trista.

"That woman made such an impression on you. She still does. I felt you slipping away from me from the moment we met her at the sunken city."

"So in response, you pulled away too," said Trista, beginning to understand Dalkeira's reasoning. "Dalkeira, I'm so sorry I've given you any reason for doubt, but the truth is that for a long time I wasn't sure. You know; sure about if this was the life for me. Nobody prepared me for this. I mean, I always wanted to leave the island, but who could have imagined this? Fleeing for our lives, trying to take care of two precious things who needed me, as well as myself. Ever since you hatched, I wondered constantly which was the correct path to take."

Trista fell silent.

"It—it wore me down. I felt so tired. I could not abandon Decan and break the oath I made to my parents. But this odyssey to the west… it was constantly calling you, I *saw* that. *Felt* that. But what I didn't know was that it was in me as well. I didn't recognize it before, but now that I've heard the song so clearly, I know for certain I've felt it all along."

Trista put her head against the dragon's, like she had seen the Minai do so many times now.

"My dearest waterdancer, there's nothing to be afraid of. I'm sorry I have made you feel abandoned for so long. But know this: there's no way another person is going to get between us. You are my destiny and you are linked to my soul. I'm ashamed to say that for a long time I wondered if my life would not be easier without a dragon in it, but the truth is you add to my life in ways I had never noticed were missing. No, that's not true; I think I have always noticed, but I was never able to see it."

Dalkeira was quiet for some time.

"I believe I understand now, too," she said finally. "And I am sorry as well."

She let the words linger in the air as she enforced them with her thoughts inside Trista's mind.

"For I believed I could do better without you. That I did not need anyone in this world to survive. Yet it was I who was dragged through that endless, waterless landscape by the two of you. All the while I questioned myself how it had happened. How I could be weak, and you and Decan so strong. It is your love. The bond you have but none can see or feel. And I understand now that while we are connected, we are of two minds and two hearts. I did not in the beginning. Understand, I mean. But now I do. Now I see that in your heart there is no limit to what one can cherish; to the amount it can hold. Decan showed me this in the desert. He stopped fighting it first; stopped fighting for your attention and love, and accepted me. But I—I wanted to leave you both, stop being a burden. Or maybe I saw you as the burden."

"You were never a b—" began Trista before Dalkeira cut her off.

"I know, I know, and neither are you. Nor Decan. I see that now. Your little brother said it already then, in different words, with his own version of wisdom. And I realize now that your will to protect him does not diminish your attachment to me. Nor does your wish to learn from those you admire. For we are *family*, even if I am not related by blood."

Trista smiled as the last of her doubt vaporized like a puddle of water in the hot desert sun. Finally, she could again focus on the future instead of running away from the past. The warmth she had missed so much these past few weeks rushed back into her mind.

"This time it's my choice. *You* are my choice," said Trista. "I acknowledge you as the water of my life. Together, we'll protect those who are dear to us."

"And knock down those who stand in our way," said Dalkeira defiantly.

"I finally recognize you. See you with all that is. You are mine, and I am yours," said Trista.

For a split second, Trista wondered if this was what it was like to seal a waterbond with someone. Dalkeira's eyes swirled in pleasure as a soft hum rose from her throat, until suddenly the roar of flames erupted all around them.

"No! Not again!" said Trista.

She looked around helplessly as the flames closed in from all sides. Dalkeira stepped forward, shielding her from the closest inferno.

"You have nothing to fear here," said the dragon. "You are strong and kind, Trista of the waterclans. You will overcome many dangers. And for those you cannot overcome alone, I will be there. Just get behind me."

Trista wondered what Dalkeira was doing. Then she noticed the water on the floor begin to spin. While the flames drew closer, a spinning sphere of water surrounded them completely. Trista heard the sizzle of flames trying to reach them. The fire was nearly upon them, surrounding the entire liquid shield. Dalkeira braced herself.

"Hold on," she said.

With one big push, Dalkeira blasted the entire sphere of water outward, completely extinguishing the flames surrounding them.

"See? Nothing to worry about," said Dalkeira.

With the flames gone, the dark now simply filled up with steam. Trista saw the image of Dalkeira becoming blurry.

"The steam is getting thicker. I can hardly see you anymore," said Trista in a slight panic.

"Do not worry. I will be with you, even if you cannot see me," came Dalkeira's voice from the fog.

The hollow, empty world disappeared in a thick layer of steam. First, Dalkeira disappeared, then her own feet, hands, and the rest of her body. Everything faded away.

Slowly, Trista opened her eyes. She looked around, trying to focus. In front of her, Dalkeira yawned and opened one of her eyes. They were still in the hut. The fire in the middle had long gone out. The stones had lost all but the last of their warmth. Outside, Trista heard the voice of the life listener sing on undisturbed, though the accompanying beat had moved from wood to a rattle on a drum skin.

Trista stretched her arms above her head, letting her body know it was time to start moving again. She was a bit stiff, but felt wonderful—like a cloud she had not known was in her head had finally been lifted. She looked at Dalkeira.

"I'm glad that…" Trista tried to put her thoughts into words. When she could not, she just sent a mass of warm feelings to the dragon.

"*I'm just glad.*"

Dalkeira's eyes swirled as she accepted the flow of warmth from Trista. The dragon let out a rumble.

"*It is strange. I feel lighter, but I do not think I lost any weight or decreased in size,*" said Dalkeira. "*Perhaps it is my stomach that is empty. Can we go and eat?*"

Trista laughed heartily.

"I could use a bite as well. Maybe tomorrow we can find larger prey for you to eat. If you want to hunt with me, that is."

"It will be my pleasure. I will even allow the others to come with us," said Dalkeira semi-seriously. "If we cannot join them, we will let them join us."

"Duvessa, you can stop now. We're back."

Outside, the sound of the old woman's voice died off, but the strange drumming continued uninterrupted.

"Really, you can stop now, Duvessa," said Trista, making her way to the small door.

As the flap opened, a familiar smell drifted into the dragon's nose.

"Water. I smell water," said Dalkeira, now wide awake.

The dragon quickly followed her out of the hut, nearly bumping into her. Trista held her face up to the sky and laughed out loud. Rain poured down on her; it wet her skin and soaked her clothes. The sky was dark with clouds, but this time there was no lightning, no thunder. The heavens let their drops fall toward the red earth. It was a welcome worthy of the goddess. Dalkeira shot forward and spread her wings. She bounced around Trista like a young goat chasing a butterfly.

"Rain! Rain! Rain is finally here!" The words echoed so loudly in both their heads that Trista was uncertain if the thought was her own or not.

Behind them, Duvessa observed both dragon and woman with blindfolded eyes, and smiled.

"Oh dear, oh my, you brought the rains back with you it seems, Trista of the Minai. The times of plenty have finally arrived."

The next few days went by in a haze of hard work and sleep. Trista began her training with the long spears the Minai carried. It took up most of her time, and although she preferred her light fishing spears, she had to admit the large, strong spears of the tribe had an excellent feel to them. For now, Aslara made her carry one around with her.

"It needs to become one with you," she had said. "So carry it around everywhere, until it does not get stuck behind things anymore; until you can grab it with your eyes closed. Be *aware* of it. It will sharpen your mind and ready it for the first big hunt."

Trista wondered what the leading mother had meant by that, as she had joined them a few times already during hunts for food. Nonetheless, the tool— or weapon, depending on how one looked at it—slowly became a part of Trista's normal routine. She was happy to see she was not the only one in training. A handful of Minai girls were undergoing similar training efforts. Even though they were much younger, it reassured Trista that she was not singled out, though her inexperience often led her to stay and practice her forms long after the others had left.

The rest of her time was mostly spent with Dalkeira and Decan. In the evenings, she visited Aslara, or chatted with a few of the other women who spoke Terran. Life stories were told, or the day's training discussed. Everyone had their own advice to give—always with the best intentions, of course.

At first, her muscles objected to the sudden increase in activity. But after the fourth day, Trista noticed her body adjusting to the new rhythm. Back on the island, she had spent entire days on boats, diving, swimming or scavenging, so it was not like her body was not used to hard work. However, the months on the road and surviving the desert had certainly taken its toll; one that was now slowly undone as she built up her strength again.

The water level of the underground lake rose quickly as every day the rains poured in. The water was soon high enough to stream out of the tunnel the Minai used to access the watergardens, so preparations were made to guide the flow through the village. Trista also finally understood why many of the Minai slept on the side of the mountain instead of in the few huts located on the ground. With each rainfall, water rushed down the mountainside, forming fast-moving streams that snaked through the village. The high entrances of the doors stopped most of the water from coming in, but one hut had already been completely flooded when part of a weak wall was swept away. As a result, the mountainside huts now tended to get a bit crowded every night.

After their lifedream, Trista and Dalkeira had spent the night together watching the water stream into the cave. Trista was pleased to finally feel the water goddess' touch again. Dalkeira took the opportunity to impress Trista with her watertouch. Now they were reconnected on a deeper level, the dragon loved to show off her skill by splitting the curtain of water that fell in through the hole. She formed water bridges, and orbs which she then shot through the downpour. She even tried to create a vortex of water as it came from outside, though that still proved too great a challenge.

Each day, after the rain, the sun broke through and heated the underground lake. It was still cold, but warm enough for Trista to join Dalkeira from time to time. The cool water worked wonders for Trista's sore muscles after a long day of training.

"I feel like you're getting faster and faster in the water," said Trista in her mind. Dalkeira's shadow passed under her in the water; the water pulled on her legs as the dragon shot by.

"It feels much easier here than in the ocean," said Dalkeira as she popped her head above water. "This water feels lighter than the salt waters of the sea."

Dalkeira arced a stream of water over Trista's head. It seemed to Trista that the days after the ba'roshia had done them both good. Dalkeira especially seemed to be in a playful mood, which was not very common. She knew her dragon was a proud dragon, but in Trista's opinion that pride sometimes prevented Dalkeira from enjoying things to the fullest. She wondered why today was different.

"You really are something else, my little waterdancer," said Trista.

"Little? Are you sure about that? Could a little dragon do this?"

And with those words, Dalkeira disappeared underwater. Trista expected to feel the dragon shoot below her even faster, but instead Dalkeira's snout suddenly pushed against her legs and launch her out of the water. It was anything but elegant; Trista tumbled back down into the water with a large splash. She resurfaced, coughing heavily, and looked around, bewildered. For a moment, she wanted to yell at the dragon. How she could do something so unexpected? But she stopped herself as Dalkeira came closer. The dragon's eyes swirled with playful mischief.

"Well, that could have gone better," said Trista, laughing in between coughs. "How about you give me a bit of warning next time? Come on, let's try again."

This time, Trista made sure to keep her feet still as she saw Dalkeira's shadow rise up from the deep like some kind of sea monster. The thought gave Trista goosebumps. The power of the dragon's movements was very intimidating. It reminded her of dragging one of the large ocean fish into her boat. The muscled fish were often difficult to control, and you had to be quick to give a killing blow or you would run the risk of the fish injuring you as it tried to flop back into the water again. As Dalkeira grew larger, the power she possessed would be immense. Trista could not imagine anything in the world that might withstand it. Certainly not her. She had never been so glad Dalkeira was on her side.

Trista launched into the air, the goosebumps quickly replaced by an exhilarated feeling. With a somersault, she splashed nimbly back into the water.

Dalkeira dove deep and swam right up to Trista, who was holding her breath and enjoying the image of her sha'cara moving underwater.

"*Grab hold,*" said the dragon.

Trista let her hands slip along Dalkeira's skin to hook them around the shoulders, where Dalkeira's wings connected. As soon as Dalkeira felt Trista's grip, she shot forward through the lake. She pushed herself forward with tail and webbed claws, her speed so great Trista could barely hold on. They returned to the surface so Trista could draw another breath of air. Immediately after, Dalkeira went off into the deep. The movement was so fast Trista had to risk releasing one hand to pinch her nose and clear her ears.

"*Easy, easy. I'm slipping,*" said Trista in her mind.

Dalkeira slowed down, checking back to see how Trista was doing.

"*It's more difficult to turn my head underwater than in the air,*" remarked Dalkeira in her head. "*In the air, my wings keep me level so I can freely look around, but here, every time I look back, my body follows.*"

Trista also noticed the dragon tired more quickly than when she swam alone. Given how fast her own arms lost their strength with the intense grip she had to maintain, she suspected the additional drag from her holding on was the reason why.

She tried to keep up by swimming, but they were simply going too fast for her legs to be useful. And after an entire day of training, it was not long before her arms started to shout their aching complaints.

"Can you move with just your tail and front legs? I want to try something," said Trista when they resurfaced again.

This time, Dalkeira moved slower, letting her hind legs hang behind her. It took a moment for Trista to figure it out, but on the fifth attempt she was able to place her feet on the inner side of Dalkeira's hind leg. Now that her legs could bear the force of the movement, it was a lot less tiresome to hold on to the dragon's wing joint.

It took some time for Dalkeira to adjust to the new posture. The movement was not as powerful as swimming with all four legs and tail, but they still made good speed, especially after Dalkeira decreased the water's resistance with her watertouch.

As the light faded from the cave, both Trista and Dalkeira got more creative. They tried all sorts of acrobatics; Trista crawling and standing on Dalkeira's back; being launched into the air by the dragon's tail, then softening the landing with a pillar of water—Trista had never laughed so loud.

"Come on. We'd better get out of here," said Trista eventually. "The sun is long gone and I'm getting cold. Besides, tomorrow is the big day."

Dalkeira pulled Trista to the side of the lake, where they both climbed back onto solid ground. The dragon shook her skin and wings to get rid of the excess water.

"If I wasn't already wet, I would be now," teased Trista. "Let's go. I could use a fire and some food."

"I wonder if it will be another day of eating plants and bugs," said Dalkeira with a yawn.

The dragon did not care much for the plant diet, but it seemed she was too tired to let it bother her today.

Trista looked at her friend. Over the past few weeks, she had often worried about Dalkeira, and not just because of the deteriorating bond. The dragon had grown very skinny. She would easily win a competition between them in length, but it was her weight that concerned Trista.

Now that she was aware of it, Trista wondered if it was because of Dalkeira's watertouch. The techniques always called for a large amount of concentration; in addition to that, the dragon spent extended times in the water, constantly moving. There was no way the insects and plants could compensate for that amount of energy use. Thankfully, the dragon did not seem exhausted; merely tired from their afternoon. And though she was thin, her winged companion appeared to be all muscle with plenty of power.

Trista ran her hand across Dalkeira's skin, tracing the warm dragon scales.

"Maybe the huntresses got lucky and caught another hare or large bird," offered Trista in consolation. "They've been bringing back more and more each day. Decan said he was going to look too, but it is against the rules for him to carry a spear now. He was not very happy about that. In any case, Duvessa said it will all change soon, maybe even tomorrow. After all, these are the times of plenty."

CHAPTER TWENTY-SEVEN

Lights

TRISTA SAT BEHIND Aslara, Shiri and half a dozen other women from the tribe, calmly waiting. There was an intense silence in the life listener's hut where they gathered. With this many people, the room was crowded, the air thick from heat. Yet none dared move.

Dalkeira poked her head through the doorway.

"Does she know?" the dragon asked privately, surveying the room with her vortex eyes.

"I don't think so. She hasn't moved for some time."

At the front, Duvessa stood with her head leaning against the life roots, the tips of her fingers moving along the roots' surface. Her mouth softly muttered words Trista could not hear. In the corner, the black raven hopped nervously back and forth on a dried branch.

Trista had been pleasantly surprised when she was invited to join the huntress' gathering in the old woman's dwelling.

"Shiri does not seem happy you are here," said Dalkeira.

The Minai woman, who sat next to Aslara, threw a glance over her shoulder cold enough to chill the room.

"I know, but she made no objections this morning when Aslara said I could sit in."

"Perhaps she could not, since you are now an official member of the Minai."

"Maybe."

Movement at the front drew Trista's attention. Aslara rose to her feet to grab Duvessa's hand.

"And?" said Aslara.

The old woman smiled.

"They're here. They're following the rains. The times of plenty are drawing near," said the life listener with a smile. "A three-day journey to the northeast. The valleys there, past that region's Taori—that's where you'll find them."

It was all they required. Smiles broke out across the room as one of the huntresses stepped outside and called out the good news. The joyous cheers of the Minai rose up among the huts as the news spread through the village.

Those huntresses who had not fit inside the hut gathered to receive the blessed markings on their faces, after which the hunting party set out toward the northeast. Several sha'cara joined them, as well as a group of desert tibu that would carry their kills back to the village.

Duvessa's raven guided them for half a day before returning to the village, after which Dalkeira took over as their eyes in the sky. She flew together with one of the other sha'cara, a beautiful golden-feathered eagle. As first huntress, Shiri led the group in front, with both striped hyen'sta roaming ahead of her, following any scent trails they found.

Now the rains had arrived, the Red Plains completely transformed in a matter of days. Grass and other plants shot up out of nowhere. The low shrubbery sprung to life, sprouting new leaves on every branch, and within no time at all there was little left of the red earth as green took over the landscape. Water, collected in shallow pools, filled with activity as dried frog and fish eggs—buried beneath the earth—hatched and started entire new generations of life. The pools merged together to form larger lakes. Streams flowed together to form creeks and then rivers. Everywhere, the flows of life transformed the earth.

The further north they traveled, the more animals they encountered. Water birds of all sizes appeared to feast on the newly-arrived abundance of food, and to build their nests. They were joined by other species, like the large gray animals with their long legs, featherless heads and large, double-billed beaks. They chased down frogs and snakes as they emerged from the mud—and, according to Dalkeira, were quite tasty themselves.

But Trista was most impressed with the Pillars of Life. When they reached the first Taori, she saw it was completely transformed from the barren, white tree into a giant with thick, dark green leaves. Its canopy cast a shadow of a hundred feet across the land now that leaves crowded the branches. Among them ran the vines, now filled with large, flat leaves and colorful flowers that gave off a wonderful, sweet and seductive smell. And between those flowers and leaves hung the bloodfruit. They had become enormous. Most had doubled in size, absorbing the freshly fallen rain. They sat invitingly between the long thorns of the trunk. If Trista had not known any better, she might have tried one, if only to see what they tasted like.

"Most plants close their leaves during the day as the sun trails the sky, but not the Pillars of Life. Their leaves are thick and strong, able to withstand the strength of the sun while the rains are here. And it will rain every day now," said Aslara. "The animals that journeyed north during the drought are on their way back, following the rain clouds. These birds are just the start. We're hunting bigger prey, of which we'll see plenty very soon."

"*It is marvelous to see so much green. The island and desert were nothing like this,*" said Dalkeira from high above, where she was playing 'follow the leader' with the eagle. "*The sky is filled with sparkles. There is water everywhere. It rises up from the ground and comes together high above. It will not be long before a new cloud is born.*"

"*That's funny,*" remarked Trista. "*I never expected clouds to be made from water off the ground. It seems the goddess can touch the sky after all.*"

"*It happened at sea as well, perhaps even more so. I wish you could see it—it is unlike anything in this world,*" said Dalkeira.

"*I did. The lifedream, remember?*" said Trista.

She held up her hand to shield her eyes from the sun. She gazed up and saw Dalkeira's silhouette circle the sky. The dragon moved playfully through the air, her stomach temporarily filled with smaller snacks. As she followed Dalkeira's movements, the sunlight hit a certain angle, almost blinding her. But as the glare hit her eye, Trista swore she saw a column of sparkles floating toward the sky, with the dragon circling around it. Uncertain of what just happened, she shielded her eyes from the sun to get another look, but there was nothing there.

"Decan seemed alright with you leaving this morning," said Aslara, unaware of Trista's internal conversation.

The leading mother led Thulai by the reins, the animal calmly carrying their travel equipment.

"What? Oh, yeah. He and some of the children were going to help Lasjika get relocated today," said Trista. "He's adjusting. And I think he'll find his place soon. If only his nightmares would go away."

"They're getting no better?"

Trista shook her head.

"During our travels, he often slept restlessly, but since we stopped in the village things have only gotten worse. It's like events have caught up with him now we've stopped moving," she said. "During the day, you barely notice anything's wrong. He's his chatty old self. It's like he has two faces. His day face, which beams with happiness and playful curiosity; and his other, filled with terror and tears."

"When we get back, he should talk to Duvessa. Perhaps there's something she can do about it. She tends to be good at that stuff," said Aslara, before moving further along as someone called her name.

424

For three days straight they were constantly moving, only stopping for small breaks to eat or sleep. Trista thanked the goddess for the weeks of rest—and the training—as they had given back much of her strength and stamina. It had been a long time since she felt this good, even if the days of walking were long and tiresome.

It was late in the afternoon of the third day when the next Pillar of Life announced itself across the now grass-filled plain. Above her, Dalkeira, who was soaring the warm air currents with ease, trumpeted and flew ahead to check things out for their arrival. It would be their rest stop for the night.

"That's strange. I thought those mountain geese always flew north this time of year," Raylan heard Peadar remark.

"They do. They're late breeders" said Ca'lek. The dark-skinned scout looked up. "But I think that particular group has passed us four times already since this morning. See, the front and rear bird are both pure white—very uncommon in this species. Probably a family group, but it's like they've completely lost their way."

"Could they be on their way to the southern mountain point?" asked Raylan, exiting the stables after putting one of their horses away. He looked up to see what they were talking about.

"Not likely," replied Peadar. "My master always taught me northern mountain geese nest near the same rock formation where they're hatched. Like it's engraved into their heads."

All three men watched the arrow-shaped formation make its way south. The *River's Hill Inn*, their home for the night, offered a nice view of the valley below. Behind them ran the river they had followed since leaving Azurna. In front of them, the first of many fields of grain within the Crescent Moon Massif lay before them. Beyond it, the large mountain range dominated the horizon. It would not be long now, perhaps a few days, before they would spot Shid'el in the distance.

Despite a wet morning, it had been a beautiful afternoon. Small clouds drifted above the valley; their shadows crawling across the yellow landscape. Raylan had not minded the summer rain; it was even quite pleasant, not at all like the cold, chilling rains they had up north. Besides, he had a feeling the wet riding of the day had helped convince Richard to stop their convoy at the inn. Raylan more than welcomed the luxury of a normal bed after their constant travels these last few weeks. The group had not encountered any more problems since they scared off the bandits, and Richard had been pleased to see them make excellent time on their way to the capital.

Along the way, Richard had made it a point to stop and inform the villages about Azurna's difficult situation. According to him, it was an official request from Lord Algirio, but Raylan wondered more than once if it was not a form of guilt.

Now, the setting sun slowly colored the sky a deep orange. The first star would soon come out. Behind Raylan, Ca'lek stroked his horse's neck.

"Are you certain we can't keep going? She looks absolutely fine to me," said Ca'lek to Peadar. "The sooner we get there the better, no?"

"No, we can't," said their animal specialist. "These horses are near exhaustion. We've been riding almost three days straight since our last stop. They need rest. Were it not for the unfortunate lack of horses at this inn, we'd have swapped them out and kept going, but now I must insist on a night's rest. That way, we'll travel twice the distance tomorrow, rather than just continuing without any sleep."

A horse put its snout in Raylan's back. It smelled the hay inside the stables, and was eager to join the others for the night.

"Alright, alright, I'm coming," said Raylan to the animal. "Why don't you two go and eat supper? I'll finish up here and sit with Galirras for a while, have my supper after."

"You sure?" said Ca'lek.

"Yeah, go. Just save me some of that stew and a jug of ale," Raylan said with a laugh.

"Thanks, Raylan," said Peadar. He ran off.

"Guess the horses weren't the only ones hungry. I'll make sure he leaves some for you," added Ca'lek. He slapped Raylan's back before disappearing as well.

Raylan finished putting the horses away and headed for his friend, but not before he raised a bucket of fresh water from the inn's well.

"You fancy a bit of a scrubbing?" said Raylan in his mind to Galirras.

He hobbled with bucket in hand over the tiny path behind the inn, which led to a more isolated meadow. Normally, a few cows lazily grazed there, but tonight it functioned as a nicely sheltered nest for Galirras to sleep in.

The dragon raised his head sluggishly. He had been snoozing after a very satisfying meal. The innkeeper had sent one of the servant boys to go with Raylan and purchase a nice fat cow from a local farmer. There was still plenty of big game for the dragon to hunt, but for once Raylan did not feel like explaining—in detail—to the local population that Galirras really meant no harm; and, if the angry mob pressed on, that the dragon was officially under the king's protection. Of course, this was not entirely true, but it was close enough to the truth for Raylan to use it as a last resort to keep things calm and under control.

Who would have guessed a large flying dragon could cause so much panic in the hearts of the common folk? Perhaps that was why Raylan was in such a good mood. No angry or scared people meant that nobody had shown up to voice their complaints at him or the group.

Raylan allowed himself another smile. He *did* feel good; much better than he expected. Perhaps the distance they put between themselves and Azurna had helped. He even looked forward to seeing his home soon, despite the news he brought. Their traveling for the last few weeks, though at a high pace, had been pleasant; the weather was warm, the food plentiful, and he and Xi'Lao continued to improve their communication as they both struggled to come to terms with their own grief. The memory of his brother lingered in his thoughts. He pushed it away, not wanting to bring down his mood.

Thankfully, Galirras provided distraction. The dragon lay on his back as Raylan reached the meadow. One of his wings lay stretched across the ground.

"You may proceed," rumbled Galirras' voice.

"Well, aren't you a spoiled little dragon."

Galirras raised his head.

"Admit it. You enjoy it just as much as I do when my scales shine in the sunlight."

The dragon's eyes swirled playfully. Though the days on the road were long, the quiet time had done the dragon well. All his wounds had healed and he had little to complain about. They had spent time together in the air every single day, though Raylan spent the majority of the time riding his horse so as not to isolate himself from the group.

"What do you think will happen when we arrive at Shid'el?" asked Galirras after a while.

Raylan wiped sweat from his forehead. Tail, back and wings were done, which left the chest, claws, neck and head.

"I don't know. I guess once they see you they'll have no choice but to believe us. They'll probably order a war council. The first thing to do is send out scouts to find the Stone King's army. Once we know more precisely what their goal is, they can come up with a way to stop them. If we can stop them."

"Well, I will fight if we must. I would rather not see any more of our group hurt," said Galirras.

"Me neither, but you can scarcely take on that entire fleet by yourself, can you? There are just too many."

Raylan scrubbed strongly behind the spiked comb that ran across the back of the dragon's head. Galirras let out a sigh of enjoyment as he pressed into the sturdy brush.

"I'm worried the entire Aeterran force might not be enough to stop the likes of Corza and his men," continued Raylan.

"But we have come by so many people here already. Surely Aeterra has more people than we saw on those boats?" said Galirras. He rolled back onto his feet and lowered his head to give better access to Raylan.

"More? Perhaps, but not in one place. And it takes time to pull together such a large force, not to mention move them. And you're talking about farmers, shepherds, fishermen—men who work, not fight. These won't be trained men, even if some might have been drafted years ago. Even if we *could* rally every man and boy in the kingdom, get enough to outnumber our enemies two to one, *and* convince them to fight, it would still be difficult to take down such a large force. Every trained Doskovian soldier is worth at least five armed farmers in skill."

"So why do we not ask the emperor for help when we meet him?" said Galirras.

"That was my idea as well. I'm hoping Xi'Lao will be able to assist us with that, but first we must get there. Which means we have to go to Shid'el and convince the king and council that this is really happening, so they'll allow us to get help from the emperor while they prepare our own forces. It's a logistical nightmare."

"Assist with what?" asked Xi'Lao, emerging from the tiny path leading into the meadow.

"To ask your emperor for help in what is about to come," said Galirras, without much tact.

Xi'Lao was silent for a moment.

"I fear that might prove... difficult," said Xi'Lao, stretching out her sentence doubtfully.

"But it might be our only chance to gather an army large enough in time. We'll need those forces to join with Aeterra—and any other capable force we can find, for that matter," added Raylan, baffled. "Why wouldn't he help us?"

"The emperor," began Xi'Lao, searching for the right words. "He is not fond of working with other people. He believes those who are outside of Tiankong will corrupt our way of life. Perhaps if his son were to rule, things could be different. But that won't happen for many years; the emperor's bloodline is known for its vitality and long life."

"But we need equal numbers if we want to have any chance of defeating the Stone King," said Raylan.

"Not necessarily. Our history is filled with battles in which a smaller force was able to outwit and defeat a much larger enemy," said Xi'Lao, before adding, "But the number of men is not the biggest problem, is it? They do not have men alone; the ghol'ms are the real threat. If we do not come up with a way to take them out of the battle, it does not matter how many soldiers we can gather."

"You're right there. Galirras can't take them all down."

Raylan sat and let out a deep breath.

"You're done, little one."

The topic had left little of his good mood. The stars already lit up the sky, but at least it stayed pleasantly warm. Tomorrow, they were to ride out at first light again. They should probably head in and lay their heads to rest, but both he and Xi'Lao sat quietly against Galirras' flank. Raylan scratched the dragon's nose, deep in thought. His arm buzzed lightly along his scar. Ever since he saved Xi'Lao on the castle's plaza, his arm had felt… off. Not his own. The feeling was not always there, but sometimes he noticed a numbness from the elbow down, like the feeling one gets after sleeping on it wrongly. Tingling, yet numb.

After Azurna, whenever he was alone, Raylan had attempted to call forth his own power over the wind, without success. He tried again later with Galirras nearby, but still nothing had happened; just that unpleasant feeling. Like something gathered on the inside, but could not find its way out.

Raylan pinched the bridge of his nose. All these unanswered questions gave him a headache. He noticed Xi'Lao stared at him and met her gaze.

"What?" he asked tiredly.

Xi'Lao shook her head.

"Nothing. Your brother used to get the same expression when he tried to come up with solutions he could not see yet. I am certain if he were here, he would do everything he could to make it work."

"Well, I could certainly use the help."

"I have been thinking myself," said Xi'Lao, "about when we return to the Empire."

She looked at him.

"The dragon archives and the grand masters; they might have information that could help us fight the ghol'ms."

Raylan brightened.

"That's right," he said with a little more enthusiasm. "You told us about the grand masters being experts at using life energy, right? Do you really think they can help?"

"That is my hope. Or that there are scrolls in the dragon archives that hold information about moving stone," confirmed Xi'Lao. "It is just that…"

"Just what?"

Both Raylan and Galirras looked at her as she hesitated.

"No, never mind. We will figure it out when we get there."

After a short silence, Raylan was about to call it a night when without a sound the night sky flared up in color above them. Pink, green and blue; dozens of colors flowed across the stars.

"I have never seen the sky do that before," said Galirras, who was the first to notice.

Raylan looked up, wondering what his friend was talking about, and forgot all about his intention to return to the inn.

"The sky curtains?" Xi'Lao said in surprise. "But we are much too far south for them to paint the sky."

"Sky curtains? What are those?" said Raylan.

"And how does it do that?" asked Galirras.

The pink color of the sky reflected in the dragon's constantly moving vortex pupils before it slowly flowed into a dark green. It lifted Galirras' eyes to a whole new level of beauty.

"We used to see them at the monastery, up in the mountains. But only during the winter. My grandfather told me they were the trails of dragons, which tore open the night sky with their claws to reveal the hidden colors of the world. It was not until later that I read a very different explanation in a very old scroll."

"Which was?" said Raylan, wondering if the explanation would not spoil the unknown beauty above him.

"It was written that many of the empire's wisest men worked together with dragons to unravel the mysteries of that which surrounds us. They spoke about a world power and the sun's light in the sky. How the combination of the two could create the lights."

"World power?" said Galirras. "Like my wind power?"

"Not precisely. Remember I spoke about how everything holds its own life energy? Well, our world is no different. It has its own *chi*. Its own power, and it shows in different ways. There are places in the empire where you can make metal stick to metal. The scroll talks about this being the result of the world's life energy. But such concentrated spots are extremely rare. They believed this power was ever present, yet gathered more above the white caps of the north and less in the south."

"What does that have to do with these lights?" asked Raylan.

"The dragons said that, at times, this world power could become strong enough to rip apart the sun's light that touched the tiny pieces in the sky. You would not notice it during the day, but at night it provides amazing views," explained Xi'Lao. "They were convinced certain animals were able to see or feel such earthly forces and use them to find their way across the lands and oceans. Unfortunately, the scrolls never explained how the dragons knew all this."

"Hold on. At night, there's no sunlight at all. And how can it break the light? You can't touch light, can you? Wouldn't it just get dark?" questioned Raylan.

He thought about Ca'lek and Peadar's bird conversation earlier that evening.

"Ugh, my head's starting to hurt. I think I like your grandfather's explanation better," added Raylan.

"As do I," said Galirras. "It would be amazing if others were up there."

Raylan reached out with his mind as his hand stroked the dragon's neck.

"Still pretty to look at, though," said Raylan out loud.

"That it is," replied Galirras.

"That it is," echoed Xi'Lao.

The trio took their time to enjoy the show, until Raylan's stomach growled so loudly he could not ignore it any longer.

"I'll head in and see if there's any food left," he said. "You want to head back?"

"I will stay a while longer," answered Xi'Lao. "The lights remind me of home, in a good way. I am certain Galirras does not mind sharing his meadow with me for a while longer. Do you, Galirras?"

"It will be my pleasure," said the dragon politely.

"No problem. I'll come back and check in with you both before I go to bed. See you in a bit."

* * *

Galirras watched Raylan disappear into the shadows. Xi'Lao lay her head against his side and gazed back up at the painted sky. He moved his head close to her so she could scratch his favorite spot above his eye.

He enjoyed the time he spent with Xi'Lao. It always felt different, perhaps because she was the only woman in the group. Though she could fight like the best of them, she was certainly more refined in her ways. Polite in her conversation; thoughtful in her opinions.

Any peasant who approached the meadow and stumbled upon the unlikely duo would turn right around and go back the way they came, likely with a quick stop at the *River's Hill Inn* for a drink.

Both woman and dragon spent some time practicing Tiankonese—a request made by Galirras in preparation for his visit to the empire. After going back and forth a few times in the conversation, Galirras stretched his legs, fluttered one of his wings and settled back into a more comfortable position.

"I am glad both of you are getting along again. I did not like it when you were mad at each other," said Galirras.

Xi'Lao looked him in the eye.

"You have got it wrong, special one. I was never really mad at him."

"Why did you not talk to him, then?"

Xi'Lao looked back up at the illuminated sky; it changed from green into purple.

"I do not know. I felt sad. I still do. I think in a way Raylan reminds me of Gavin. Despite their differences, they are more alike than one might think. Before you hatched, it was clear that all Raylan wanted was to outdo his brother. But when you bonded with him, it… changed him. And I think the loss of his brother changed him even more."

Galirras stared at her, his nostrils slightly flaring.

"Not in a bad way, I think," apologized Xi'Lao, seeing Galirras look at her. "Not at all, even. He became more like Gavin. In the way he cares for things. In the way he leads, even if he does not see it himself. And it hurts. It hurts so much to see this person I loved in front of me, but not be there."

Tears ran from Xi'Lao's deep brown eyes down her cheeks. She laughed and wiped them away.

"I never thought to find such honor in a foreigner. So… selfless, and proud to keep others safe. Values that are among the highest one can have in life."

The dragon spent some time mulling over Xi'Lao's words. Keeping safe, protecting; he had never given it any thought as a choice. He looked back, but saw that Xi'Lao was lost in her own world of thought, staring at the colored sky.

"Can I ask you something?" he said after a while.

Xi'Lao rolled her head to the side and looked at Galirras' head as it bent back on his flexible neck.

"Do the archives mention anything about dragons walking in someone's dream?"

Xi'Lao thought for a moment.

"I do not believe so. Why do you ask? Did you and Raylan share a dream?"

"It was not Raylan. At least, I do not think it was. Whenever he dreams, it is more like thoughts that flow over the edge of a bucket."

"Someone else, then?" asked Xi'Lao.

"I am not sure," replied Galirras. "The memory of the dream is very vague. Perhaps it was my own."

"When did this happen?"

"Some days ago. I think there was a woman. She was very afraid. She was calling for someone."

Xi'Lao looked at him.

"I am sorry. I can offer little help. I do not remember anything about dream walking in the scrolls I studied. Could it perhaps have been something you ate? Was it that time you tried a few of those berries?"

"I do not believe so. But it certainly was a very peculiar happening. And warm."

"Warm?"

"Yes, I remember this distinct heat when I woke up, even though the morning was brisk and the fires extinguished," reminisced Galirras.

After a moment, he shook his head.

"It was probably nothing. But speaking about heat; are you not constantly warm?"

"Warm? How so?" asked Xi'Lao.

"I mean with your condition…"

*　*　*

Back at the inn, Raylan stashed away the bucket and brush. The smell of the stew was beckoning him when he noticed one of the horses had kicked over its water trough. He spent a moment fixing it, then renewed the animal's water. As he gave the thankful animal a pat on the neck, he remembered he had left his fur coat in the meadow. As worn as it was, he had better pick it up now or he would probably forget to do it later, and then it would be soaked with morning dew the next day. He really had come to dislike the smell of wet fur during their days riding in the northern rains of the Dark Continent.

He sighed and turned back toward the narrow path under the trees, his stomach urging his feet to pick up the pace. As he neared the end of the path, Galirras' and Xi'Lao's voices floated toward him.

"…and he does not need that kind of distraction."

He forced his feet to slow down and held still in the shadows. He heard Xi'Lao get to her feet.

"I think I will head inside as well. I am getting cold. Thank you for keeping me company. And Galirras? Can you promise me not to tell Raylan?"

Raylan noticed a hint of disagreement flowed from his winged friend.

"Please?" asked Xi'Lao.

"Promise," rumbled the dragon's voice.

Quickly, Raylan took a few steps back and started walking again as Xi'Lao ducked under the branches of the first tree.

"Oh, hey," said Raylan, noticing the slightest startle in Xi'Lao's posture. "Sorry, didn't mean to scare you. Just came to get my coat. You headed in already?"

"Yes, to get some extra sleep. Tomorrow is another early start."

"I know, but we're almost there. And then we can start planning our next move."

Xi'Lao gave a small nod and continued toward the inn. Raylan entered the meadow, where Galirras looked up at him.

"You are back already? How can you eat faster than I?"

"Forgot my coat," said Raylan with a smile. "You alright? You feel a little… agitated."

He kept the question vague on purpose. He did not want to put his friend on the spot and force him to confess a secret, and thus break his promise.

"I am… fine. Just pondering."

Raylan grabbed his coat and walked back.

"Alright. Well, let me know if you want someone to ponder with. I'd be happy to help."

A stream of gratitude filled his mind as he left to eat his meal and join the others in conversation.

* * *

Outside, Galirras returned to his skygazing. The colors flowed like an ocean. It was almost hypnotic.

It was not long before the dragon fell into a deep slumber, but not before he noticed an unusually bright star shine through even the sky's most radiant colors. A star that seemed to have a small tail.

During their overnight stay near the Pillar of Life, the huntresses sat together around the fire. Trista used times like these to get to know the other women better. Their stories about the hardships the tribe—and women—endured showed a remarkable inner strength in each and every one of them. The huntresses of the Minai were indeed to be admired.

Dalkeira, tired from traveling by wing all day, bid Trista goodnight before she retreated from the group and lay with her head tucked under her wing. The dragon quickly dozed off.

When Trista went to check up on her after a while, she saw the familiar twitch of muscle in the dragon's neck and wondered if Dalkeira was following the song in her dreams again.

"How are you holding up?"

Trista looked up to see Aslara standing next to her.

"I'm fine. Tired, but fine," said Trista. "All these stories… they're amazing. I— I mean, some are sad, of course, but they make me feel proud to be accepted by all of you. I can't deny that my origins will always lie with the waterclans, but I never expected to find anything that would feel like home so far from the ocean."

Trista looked up at the night sky, filled with stars. There were so many, one could almost mistake it for an ocean. It made her feel very much at peace.

"Tell me, Aslara," said Trista. "Why do some of you speak the same language as me and Decan, while others don't know a single word? Their speech is so different at times, even between the different women around the fire."

"The answer to that lies in our past. The Minai accepts those who come looking for a connection to the flows. Over time dozens, if not hundreds of new members were accepted from other tribes, each with their own habits and forms of speech. Some retain their old voice, passing it from mother to child; others let their mother tongue go in favor of a more shared form of words."

"And the language we share? Where did that come from?"

"It was a gift from the winged ancient to the First Mother. The First Mother passed it to the tribe, providing a central language none within the Minai could claim as their own," said Aslara. "Why? How did you come by these words?"

Trista thought for a moment.

"Terran is the largest represented language in the mid-continent. Sure, there are variat—"

The last word stuck in Trista's throat as the sky burst into color. Waves of green, red and purple flowed past the stars before they gave way to other complexities. The patterns appeared random, but trailed the entire sky like a curtain of colored mist; rivers flowing upside down.

Next to her, Aslara stood with her own mouth wide open. Around the fire, other huntresses jumped up and pointed to the sky.

"What is *that*?" said Trista.

"It's beautiful," spoke Aslara in awe.

From the fire rose the sound of excited murmurs.

"Akima Matri, are you seeing this? The flows of life are in the air," said an older huntress, clearly impressed by the spectacle. "It's a good sign for the hunt. Don't you agree?"

"I'm sure it is, Eyl'sa. The flows are lighting our way," replied the leading mother.

"Have you ever seen it before?" said Trista.

But Aslara shook her head.

"Never, not even in the stories of mothers before us."

To everyone's delight, the lights remained in the sky for the better part of the evening. They had a strange, exhilarating effect on the group. The tension of the first big hunt was completely gone. Even Shiri seemed reasonably chatty, even though Trista was part of the circle.

Halfway through the evening, Trista tried to wake Dalkeira, but the dragon was too tired to care about sparkling lights. Trista figured the dragon was quite used to seeing sparkles up high anyway, so decided to let her sleep. Instead, she accepted Aslara's invitation to rejoin her on a rock and enjoy the enchanting view.

By the time the moon climbed toward its highest point, the colored lights slowly dissipated again until just a sea of stars remained. Having watched the last part of the show together with Aslara, Trista thanked her for the company and decided it was high time to turn in. She went to find a spot to relieve herself first before joining Dalkeira to sleep.

Trista was circling the Pillar of Life in search of a more private place when a noise drew her attention. She spotted Shiri near the tree's trunk. For a moment, she hesitated, debating if it would be better to go the other way.

No. If I want to be a part of this tribe, I shouldn't avoid her. Perhaps it's time we talked things out.

"Shiri, is that you?" said Trista, walking over. "I thought perhaps we could talk. Clear the air under such a beautiful sky."

Trista's approach seemed to startle the first huntress. Strange, since Trista had not believed anyone—or anything, for that matter—could surprise Aslara's second-in-command. Right away, Razza and Shuka rose to their feet. They hung their heads low, bared their teeth and let out a pair of chuckling growls. Shiri looked over her shoulder, quickly stuffing something into her bag.

"What's that?" said Trista naively, alerted by Shiri's uncommon reaction.

But the second-in-command did not offer her a reply. She quickly walked off, whistling the hyen'sta to follow her.

"Get lost," she said sharply as she passed Trista.

Baffled, Trista watched Shiri until the desert woman was swallowed up by the surrounding shrubbery.

"Guess now was not a good time after all."

A few moments later, she returned and lay down next to Dalkeira. After such a long day of walking, she had expected sleep to find her with no trouble. Yet there she lay, considering the image of Shiri's hands and what she had held. Had she seen that shape and color correctly? Or had the moonlight played a trick on her?

Maybe I should tell Aslara.

But if she was wrong, it would only worsen things between her and Shiri. Her thoughts shifted as she stared up at the sky, where a bright star shimmered in the darkness. Trista had never seen such a strong light, not even during her nights in the coastal cavern. Her mind distracted, she finally drifted off to sleep before reaching a decision about Aslara's lover. In her dreams, Dalkeira's thoughts slowly seeped through.

"Tomorrow... tomorrow, the hunt truly begins."

CHAPTER TWENTY-EIGHT

Betrayal

*T*HE WALLS—*they are so high,"* said Galirras in amazement. *"It is like the forest with giant trees."*

"The mountain helps. And they're always expanding. Looks like they made some nice progress since we left to find you," replied Raylan. *"You can see all of the Crescent Moon Massif plains from that wall on the right."*

"And it never fell?" asked the dragon.

"Crumbled, but never fell. Shid'el is the oldest city in Aeterra. It's been around for centuries; started against the foot of the mountain and worked its way up. It's withstood dozens of wars. Some of them pretty bad, but it always offered hope. They don't call it the white beacon for nothing. Plus its elevated location provides an excellent defensive position."

Raylan looked at the city from his unusual point of view. It still bewildered him to look at things from dragonback. It provided a sense of overview that he did not get on the ground, like how the layout of the city looked like a tiny maze with its squirming streets and tiny people moving around.

I wonder if royalty always feels like this?

Beneath them, the city stretched along the south side of the mountain. Grassy slopes turned rugged and gray toward higher altitude, the white city a strong contrast against the darker background. Streets and houses decorated the mountain's foothills down toward the grain-filled plains, like an avalanche of buildings had slid down from the higher slopes. The working parts of the city lay close to the fields and river that flowed past from the mountains. The higher quarters held the upper class and cultural parts of the city. Mills were spread throughout, rising above the houses every so often like pillars with vertical mill blades spiraling from bottom to top. The mills used cloths hung in wooden frames that could be turned to catch more wind—or less, depending on the day. The mills of Shid'el were always turning, always grinding. Spinning towers always at work.

"That's the grain quarter down there, near the fields, bursting out of its walls. It's mostly newcomers who end up working the grain fields. They had a fire a few years back, nearly took down half the quarter," said Raylan, pointing downward. *"Flour and bread are the city's main exports. That and whatever is mined in the mountains. They say the fields of Shid'el feed half the kingdom. And every year the city grows bigger, stretching further out onto the plains."*

The dragon banked left. They started to rise as the large leathery wings caught a hot air spiral.

"They are nearly at the castle gates," remarked Galirras.

Raylan shielded his eyes against the sun and tried to spot the others down in the city. Richard had asked them to stay aloft until called upon, giving the group a chance to explain the winged guest they brought with them. They were quite high up, but Raylan was certain plenty of eyes had spotted them by now.

"Why don't we get a bit closer, then?"

Galirras beat his wings lazily every dozen heartbeats or so. He was not in a hurry to return to the ground. The afternoon sun was nice and warm, he was not really hungry, and the view was rather pleasant.

"That big building over there; that's the cathedral Peadar is always talking about," remarked Raylan, who noticed Galirras was taking his time. *"And there's the merchant quarter. And there, to your left, lies the guilds ward."*

He pointed out the complex layout on the higher plateau, where many of the city's bigger buildings lay.

"Is that where your father is?"

Raylan felt longing with a stab of pain. It was more than a year since he had seen his father, first because of his army duties, then the relic assignment. Their group left in the middle of the night when they set out to find Galirras' egg. Not many had been able to say goodbye to their families.

"Yeah, a little further off to the side. Near that lower slope. The street always gives a nice view of the city beneath it."

They neared the castle fortress, which towered above the rest of the city. Built on a smaller, elevated part of the mountain that reached out onto the plateau, the castle's white walls ran straight up from the terrain's edges. A long road with several guardhouses and towers wound round the back of the castle, where the main entry point lay. The last part of the road's approach lay over an arching bridge that covered several gaps in the mountain terrain.

The first courtyard behind the gate was large, surrounded by several defensive towers on one side and the main castle structure on the other. Several other inner wards lay beyond it, divided up by multiple walls. Once you passed through the castle's buildings and main keep and went out the back, you came upon the Doorstep of the Gods, as the royal plaza was called. It had no wall around it, not even a handrail. It overlooked the entire city and the mountain range that dominated the horizon.

The plan was to land on the plaza once Richard had explained the situation. It was an ideal spot for a dragon to come and go; spacious and high up. But for now they had to wait.

Below them, Raylan saw the group on horseback enter the first courtyard, where they were met by three figures descending from the guardhouse's steps.

"*Is that normal?*" asked Galirras, confused. "*I see men moving along the walls.*"

Raylan leaned to the side to look below them. Everyone was busy dismounting when soldiers rushed in from all sides and lowered their spears to the group.

"What's going on?" he mumbled, too softly for Galirras to hear.

A few of the tiny figures in the courtyard gestured wildly, most likely wondering the same thing. Some of their own group drew their swords and closed in together.

"*We have to do something,*" said Galirras nervously.

"*Let's get down there.*"

Raylan tightened his legs and moved his weight into the turn Galirras made. The wind rushed past him in their rapid descent. Galirras sheered above the walls of the castle and let out a roar.

Those on the walls looked up in fright, some immediately covering their ears. Galirras climbed into a right turn. He stretched his neck around.

"*They have archers on the walls. They are aiming their arrows at us.*"

"They're going to shoot us down? What's happening?" yelled Raylan, bewildered. "Don't let them hit you. But… please don't kill anyone either, okay?"

Galirras let out a windblast to blow a hole in the arrow salvo, then flew in low above the wall. The strong gust of his wings threw back a few of the men, while others ducked for cover.

"*They're surrounding Xi'Lao,*" said Raylan inside Galirras' head, quickly looking down at the courtyard as they passed. "*Only her.*"

"*What? Why? They cannot take Xi'Lao. She has done nothing wrong,*" said Galirras, the words betraying his growing anxiety.

All spears were now aimed at Xi'Lao, who stared at those around her. She had not even pulled any of her knives from her belt. Everywhere, Terran soldiers ran through the castle. Doors and hatches swung open as more and more of them poured onto the walls. Galirras was forced to increase their distance to prevent any stray arrows from hitting Raylan.

No longer at spears' end, Richard stood in front of the man in charge. Raylan saw him yell and wave his arms wildly at the guards surrounding Xi'Lao and toward the archers on the walls. Galirras continued to circle the castle in wide turns, until finally Richard seemed to convince the commander of the guard to lower their weapons.

Raylan saw Richard wave the signal to begin their approach. Yet the spears remained pointed at Xi'Lao while her hands were tied behind her back. He double-checked to see if the archers had lowered their bows. They had complied with their commander's order, though it was a little unnerving to see their arrows still nocked.

"*Should we go down there?*" asked Galirras.

Raylan hesitated.

"*I don't know. Richard thinks it's safe, it seems. Can you land in the courtyard?*"

"*That is not a problem,*" replied the dragon. "*But I will not quickly be able to take off again with those walls around me.*"

Galirras came in low, barely clearing the walls. Above the courtyard, he beat his wings in a long, turning motion to hover in one spot. His wind power provided additional lift, enough to keep himself in the air. The space was plenty big for a creature of Galirras' size to stand in, but with so many people around it was still a challenge to find a suitable spot to land. He took a moment to look around to avoid accidentally trampling anyone.

Raylan heard shouts all around him as the guards dashed for cover, either in fright or to clear a spot for them to land. Dust flew everywhere from the force of Galirras' wings. Somewhere in a corner, buckets and a few shovels tumbled over. Their own horses whinnied, uncomfortable even though Galirras had traveled with them for the past few weeks. The snap of beating, leathery wings echoed between the walls, while Raylan's own squad shielded their eyes from the fine debris and sand that was blown into the air.

With a thump, Galirras dropped the last few feet to the ground. In a flash, Raylan stood with both feet on the ground and made his way toward Richard and the commander in charge.

"What's going on? Why's Xi'Lao tied up? Who—"

A few soldiers rushed forward and raised their spears toward Galirras. The dragon raised his head to keep the points away from his eyes. Raylan grabbed the nearest weapon with both hands, swung it around and ripped it from the unprepared soldier's hands. The man ended up flat on his face from the unexpected move.

"Don't you dare point one of those things at him," said Raylan angrily. He threw the spear next to the soldier on the ground.

He turned to find half a dozen soldiers now pointing their weapons at him as well. Behind him, Galirras let out a threatening rumble and took a step forward. Immediately, the archers all around them on the wall drew their arrows and took aim.

"Enough! Let him through, and give the creature some distance," bellowed the guard's commander. "And you, hothead. You'd better control that beast of yours. Lieutenant Brand has assured me you can, or it will be a swift death for the both of you."

It was only now that Raylan recognized the one in command. A man with tanned, aged skin. A beard graced his jawline, black, rugged, scattered with the white hairs of wisdom. His short hair on top had an unusual parting where a scar ran from the hairline above his eye to the back.

"Commander Ymes? That you?"

"That's High Commander now, kid."

"High Commander? What happened to High Commander Klavvas?" interrupted Richard.

"Fever took him a few months ago. Damn shame as well, for such a man to die in his bed."

"What are you doing here?" asked Raylan.

"I'm here to lock up this lying young lady. Orders from the court. She's an impostor."

"What's he talking about, Richard?" said Raylan, astounded.

He moved closer to Xi'Lao.

"You're not just going to let this happen, are you? Xi, tell him he's mistaken!"

But the Tiankong woman only looked back at him in silence, her eyes two deep brown pools of mystery. No tears, no sparkle; nothing. It was like she was not even surprised. Uncertainty seeped through cracks of Raylan's confidence.

"No," he said abruptly, drawing his sword. "You're not taking her anywhere. Any one of you who dares touch her will meet the wrong end of my blade."

Instantly, his world burst into sparkles that flowed through the air around him. His hand tightened around the hilt of the sword. A throbbing sensation pulsed in his arm.

"Easy, kid. I have orders to follow, with or without you standing in the way," said the high commander. "All I know is the Thirty wants her captured, by request of the empire. Something about no official party ever being sent to Aeterra to request aid of any kind. If you've got a complaint, take it up with the council."

Baffled, Raylan looked between the commander and Xi'Lao.

"Lower your sword, Raylan. You're not helping," urged Richard. "We have no idea what's going on, so don't make it worse.

At the back, Galirras slowly lowered himself inch by inch, ready to pounce.

"No. They can't. It's got to be some kind of mistake," said Raylan. "She's been with us the entire time, Richard. She fought with us; guided us. Helped us! You must know she spoke the truth. Gavin would've wanted us to protect her. Wanted *me* to protect her."

"Gavin's not here. Your brother is *not here*. Remember, Raylan? I'm the one in command," said Richard, his voice turning cold with authority. "Now, lower your sword. That's an order. I'm not going to ask again."

Raylan shifted his feet, his eyes darting around the courtyard. About ten soldiers between him and Galirras. Could he make that? Without killing them? If he did, he would be branded a traitor. The king and council would surely hunt him down. Kill him. But with Galirras, they could go anywhere—if they could clear the walls filled with archers.

"Raylan, stop. Please. They are right, okay?"

Xi'Lao's words cut deeper than the sharpest sword. They were like ten pounds of steel thrown on his back. Baffled, he lowered his weapon and turned around.

"What? What do you mean, they're right?"

"I am so sorry. I wanted to tell you. I really did. I just did not know how. I so desperately wanted to clear my grandfather's name... so I made everything up."

Beaten without a clash of swords, Raylan stared at Xi'Lao in disbelief.

"No," he said. "You can't let them do this. You can't let them take you."

"I am truly sorry. Please forgive me."

"Last chance, kid," said High Commander Ymes. He gestured his guards to advance.

Raylan's hands trembled. His breath was short and shallow in his throat. Slowly, his fingers unwrapped from the hilt, one by one, until his sword clanged on the ground. A nearby soldier quickly jumped forward and kicked it away from him.

"But I—I thought we were beyond that. That there were no more secrets."

"I am sorry," Xi'Lao repeated, her head lowered in shame.

"Take her away," said the high commander. "The king and council will decide what to do with her next."

The guards led Xi'Lao away into the castle. Raylan stepped forward, his path blocked by two large, armored guards.

"Xi!"

Beside him, Richard approached High Commander Ymes once more.

"Sir, despite this unfortunate turn of events, we've got urgent matters to discuss. I need to convey our report to the Thirty immediately," he said.

"I'll send word of your arrival. They'll be interested to know the rumors were true. In the meantime, the beast stays put. The rest of you report in at the lower level barracks."

"I'd rather stay here with Galirras," Raylan said.

"Fine by me, *if* your commander agrees. But you'd better make yourself presentable before you even think of going before the Thirty," said the high commander.

"I'll see what I can find out about Xi'Lao," said Richard with a nod before he quickly followed the bearded man inside.

It was not long before the others reluctantly disappeared, none of them given a moment to discuss things amongst their group. Galirras and Raylan remained in the courtyard, surrounded by forty guards.

"Are you familiar with that man?" asked Galirras privately.

"He was in command of the new recruits' training camp. Taught all the greens how to properly hold a weapon."

"Why did he take Xi'Lao? Will she be alright?"

"I don't know, but I intend to find out," Raylan answered.

He sat down on the dragon's front leg and folded his arms. This was not the homecoming he had imagined. All around, soldiers looked warily at them, uncertain what to think of this unusual duo.

"And what about the child?" asked Galirras anxiously. Nervous flashes of orange showed in the dragon's eyes.

"Child? What child?" Raylan said out loud. He threw a confused look at Galirras.

"The one in her belly…"

Harwin squinted, waiting for his eyes to grow accustomed to the bright light that crept through the window. Outside, the call of a rooster announced a new day.

He heard the door of his chamber open and quickly closed his eyes again. Soft footsteps entered the room, and he peeked through the slits of his eyes with a smile on his face. He was still amazed that such a well-built woman had the skill to move around with less noise than a mouse. She was not fat, but well-rounded in the hips. A mature woman, and one Harwin enjoyed looking at. She placed a bowl of fresh water on the dresser and approached the bed.

"Good morning, Mister Harwin. Time to wash your wound a final time."

Her voice was pleasant to the ears, like sweet wine to the tongue, her tone betraying their comfort with each other.

Harwin pretended to wake as a gentle hand touched his shoulder. He sat up and let out a groan in earnest as his joints protested the increased activity.

"Good morning, Rose," he said with a smile.

Another sweet thing on her, that name.

"Your wound is looking well, all nice and closed. Are you ready to finally get out of here?" asked the woman.

"I can stay a while longer, if you want," he answered with a grin. "I know you'll miss our little morning routine after I'm gone."

Rose gave him a genuine smile.

"Oh, stop it. You're only moving to the other wing of the castle. It's not like you won't be able to come and visit if you wish," said Rose. "Lord Algirio wants to offer additional space to those families who need it most. The entire second level has been transformed into a mini version of the city."

She spent a moment washing him, paying extra attention to the stab wound on his belly.

"Is your mother liking her new place?" asked Harwin as Rose pulled a fresh shirt over his head.

"She does indeed. She wants to help rebuild, like everyone else, but says she'll only be in the way of the younger men doing all the heavy lifting. So she's helping out on the courtyard markets as much as possible."

After the devastation of Old Town and the harbor, the castle markets had shifted from showing the latest fashions and curiosities to providing things like food and basic necessities. Much had been lost in the tidal wave and people had salvaged what they could, but a lot was irreversibly damaged.

"It's good for her to keep busy," commented Harwin.

A smile from Rose acknowledged what he had not said about her father. "It is."

Harwin made to turn and get out of bed when Rose stopped him.

"I'm sorry. I really can't let you go with that state of facial hair. Signora Bonni would scold me for it," she said with a laugh. "Sit back while I get some scissors."

Harwin stroked his ragged goatee and pulled it into a point.

"It has been a while since I've seen a proper barber," he admitted.

A moment later, a few quick snips of the scissors addressed the problem, followed by the careful rasp of a razor blade.

"Eyes up here, Mister Harwin," said Rose sternly as she caught his gaze slipping down to her chest.

Harwin grinned.

"Apologies, ma'am. Just enjoying the natural beauty in the world."

A final snip of the scissors and quick scan around his face followed.

"All done."

Harwin finished dressing, observing his healed scar. It felt a bit tight, but the pain was no longer present. Behind him, Rose tidied up, her movements efficient and elegant.

"I'll be going, then," said Harwin. "Thank you for your expertise. It was a pleasure to be under your care."

He grabbed his sword and shield and headed out. He looked back over his shoulder one more time, thinking that perhaps it would not be such a bad time to settle after so long in the army.

"Mister Harwin?" said Rose as he opened the door.

He stopped and turned.

She smiled, her fingers fiddling with the hem of her apron in a very girlish way.

"If you ever feel like enjoying the natural beauty of this world some more, come look me up."

Harwin returned her smile.

"Thank you, ma'am," he said politely. "I might just do that very thing when I have the chance."

Harwin made his way to the second level plaza. He massaged his shoulder to get the blood flowing and rotated it to loosen the joint.

"Getting ready for another day of dragging stuff around?"

He looked up to see Brenton Baltor coming down the stairs.

"That, and these blasted beds are way too comfortable. They're making me feel lazy and old," Harwin said with a smile.

"Today was your last day in the healers' wing, right? You moving across the plaza?"

"Actually, I was thinking of crashing in the barracks. Leave the other housing to a family that truly needs it. The tent encampment is overflowing as it is," said Harwin. "Besides, now that I'm officially healed according to the experts, it's about time to continue on to Shid'el and join the others. Thought I'd put in another day or two of helping and rebuilding the city, as appreciation for the provided care, and then go."

He wanted to get out of bed and help with the cleanup days ago, but the healers had refused to let him go at first. He was about to discharge himself when Rose challenged him to a game of checkers—a game he often played with his fellow soldiers. But it was not until after she had completely devastated him that he found out she was the ruling champion of Azurna Castle. She had baited him into another seven days of bed rest.

Harwin looked at the Talkarian prince as they made their way through the corridors. Two swords hung from his belt. Since the attack on the harbor, the prince had not been seen without them.

"Will you be joining me in the city? We can grab a proper ale after. I heard they reopened *The Old Bull*."

"I'm afraid I can't. The *Twins* is scheduled to be back this afternoon with supplies from up north. I'm meeting my guards outside to go to the harbor early and make certain they're done with the temporary dock to receive them."

"Ah, so you'll be leaving soon?" said Harwin. "Back to the island, I mean."

"Indeed. I'm worried about everyone back home. I still haven't heard back from them. If Lord Algirio hadn't convinced me to send the *Twins* on a supply run north, I'd probably have left already."

"Prince Baltor, if you have a moment. There's an urgent message for you."

A messenger came running up behind them. Brenton took the message and broke the seal.

Speak of the devil, thought Harwin, but he swallowed his words just in time as he saw the expression on Brenton's face change.

"What's wrong?" he asked the prince.

"My father… he's dead," said Brenton in disbelief. "I need to speak to Lord Algirio immediately. They've taken over Tal'Kabur."

"What? The city?"

"No. Everything."

The Talkarian prince turned right, taking the corridor away from the plaza.

"Tell my escort the harbor visit must wait," he called back to the messenger as he increased his pace.

Harwin quickly followed the prince.

"If this is just reaching us now, the king and council need to be made aware of it, too," he said. Brenton looked at him questioningly. "I need all the information we can get, if you don't mind."

The Talkarian prince nodded as they jogged up the first stairs to the higher level. They entered the high plaza, where they were welcomed by the clang of alarm bells coming from the city.

"What's going on?" the Talkarian prince asked the nearest castle guard.

"The black sails, milord. They're back!"

Additional bells joined the call as Harwin ran to the rampart. He stared to the east, but saw nothing.

"Where are they? There's nothing off the coast."

"Not there," called the soldier, running off to man his post. "South. They're coming from the south!"

- To be continued -

PLEASE CONSIDER LEAVING a review and/or rating in the online store and on Goodreads if you enjoyed the story. There's no greater gift you can give to me as a writer and it really helps other people find their way to the world of Aeterra and the oncoming battles against the armies of the Stone King. Thank you for your support.

About the Author

AUTHOR A.J. NORFIELD lives with his loving family on land, but below sea level. He tries not to worry too much about climate change and the melting of the polar ice caps. His wife, and two little rascals, keep him engaged and grounded while he pursues goals of publishing a story that has been stuck in his head for years.

In his free time, if available at all, he enjoys a wide variety of gaming, reading, writing, drawing and socializing. As a longtime forest and mountain enthusiast, he often wonders about his flat surroundings and how to escape them. It was during these ponderings that his dragon-fantasy series, *The Stone War Chronicles,* grew wings and took flight.

His interest in dragon-fantasy novels has followed him ever since he was young enough to read. This interest—together with several broken nights thanks to his daughter's sleeping schedule—eventually lead to the hatching of *Windcatcher,* the first novel in his dragon-fantasy series.

Inspired by established names such as Anne McCaffrey, Terry Goodkind and Naomi Novik—to name only a few of many—he looks forward to carving his own path in the fantasy genre.

Follow *The Stone War Chronicles* online:
Website: http://www.ajnorfield.com
Facebook: http://www.facebook.com/ajnorfield
Twitter: @AJNorfield
Goodreads: AJNorfield
Bookbub: https://www.bookbub.com/profile/a-j-norfield

Be sure to follow A.J. Norfield on Bookbub and Amazon to stay informed on any upcoming releases!